DAUGHTERS

DAUGHTERS

Elizabeth Buchan

WINDSOR
PARAGON

First published 2012
by Michael Joseph
This Large Print edition published 2012
by AudioGO Ltd
by arrangement with
Penguin Books Ltd

Hardcover   ISBN: 978 1 4713 0885 7
Softcover   ISBN: 978 1 4713 0886 4

**British Library Cataloguing in Publication Data
available**

Printed and bound in Great Britain by
MPG Books Group Limited

For Belle, in gratitude

'She dreams of golden gardens . . . '

Wilfred Owen, 'The Kind Ghosts', 1918

FORTHCOMING MARRIAGES

Mr A. R. Havant and Miss E. Russell

The engagement is announced between Andrew, only son of Mr and Mrs Nigel Havant of Boynton, Hampshire, and Eve Russell, daughter of Mr William Russell of Hackney and the late Mrs Mary Russell.

Chapter One

Curious how much pleasure she took from saying, 'My daughter ... actually my *step*daughter ... is getting married.' It ran against the grain of her own experience but her pleasure was not to be underestimated ... that visceral need to see a child settled.

She had got used to answering questions such as 'What sort of wedding?' and 'Do you like him?' (To the latter she would reply, 'Yes, I do.')

Did she like Andrew? The little she knew of him, yes. She could list the pluses: affable, well mannered, liked a joke, normal. He was also—she was assured on all sides—brilliant at his banking job, and unusual because he was a man who took the long view. These were all excellent attributes to offer up in conversational exchanges.

As for the wedding, Eve had always been the sort of person who would want a traditional one. Everything about it would be bound to appeal to her love of beauty and social drama—the dress, the flowers, the ancient vows in church, the staging of dinner, and the dancing.

There were many such conversations. With the friends and neighbours who said, Of course you'll be doing this, that or the other. Or, That *is* the convention, you know. There were the sly, covert appeals for an invitation: 'I know we're not strictly connected but we'd love to be there.' And all the delicious, jokey chats with the girls.

'You're pleased, then?' Lara's friends would say, with varying expressions—some were envious at her

1

good fortune in having a child settled.

Yes.

Yet at night, in the half-wakings and drowsings, Lara sank through what seemed to her the layers in her mind . . . through the bitter-sweet, the dark, the half-forgotten and half-remembered. There, in her deepest imaginings, a bride glimmered. Sacrificial. Luminous.

When, on those white and violet nights, she finally fell asleep, it was to find herself in her own wedding dress, running towards a church with a long train hooked over one arm, a torn veil streaming out behind her.

Why was she was running? She never understood. Only that when she awoke from the exhausting, debilitating dream, her heart seemed to be shuddering with grief and longing. For the dead? For the past? For the shadowy image of the girl she no longer was?

One cold autumn evening Lara inserted Eve's engagement announcement in the bottom right-hand corner of the photo collage that hung in the kitchen. The photos reflected the two ages of the family: pre-divorce and post-divorce. Her favourite was one of Jasmine, Eve and baby Maudie in the pushchair, with herself and Bill standing behind. The girls were grubby—'I'm not in the mood for washing,' Eve had informed them. Lara liked this photograph in particular because it showed them real, solid, breathing . . . and happy.

Maudie's best friend was called Tess. Over the years Vicky, her mother, and Lara had become a team, welded together by school runs, sleepovers and dramas. (The ear-piercing drama had been a major one—'If you don't let me, Mum, I'll get my tongue done too.')

'How do you survive?' Vicky asked occasionally.

Usually Lara replied, 'I just do.' But survival had been more cunning than the lightly tossed-out reply suggested. Compared to the world's great wrongs, her position had not been dire, but it had taken all her energy to deal with it. She had learned to tackle each day, each minute even, with patience and no flights of imagination whatsoever.

The nights were different, of course.

'It's as if you're punishing yourself,' said Vicky.

'As it happens, I did go for a manicure,' said Lara. 'With a sadist.'

'Avoiding the issue,' said Vicky.

Lara stepped back, knocking a poinsettia with her elbow. It fell to the floor, the pot broke and earth scattered. Never mind. The floor needed a wipe and she had only ever tolerated the poinsettia, a present from a patient who ran a garden nursery. Its crimson foliage was so wilfully cheery.

'If you hate it, throw it out,' Jasmine urged her.

'I can't do that,' she said. 'I can't kill it.'

Now stalk and roots lay in a welter of the dry potting compost favoured by nurseries—the stuff that tried to look like proper soil but didn't. She swept up the mess, plus a posse of dead flies that had met their fate behind the pot, and dumped it outside in the garden—if you could dignify such a scrubby, neglected patch with that name.

The phone went and she picked it up. 'Bill.'

Her ex-husband didn't often phone. Fifteen years on from the divorce, their relationship wasn't easy but both he and she had learned to accommodate the fact that they had failed. What had happened had been, so to speak, placed inside a cabinet. The door had been shut and locked, thus hiding the grief and poison. But, it had got better. Of course it had.

'I thought you should know . . .' He paused, and her stomach did a small flip. He began again: 'How do I put this, Lara? I'm getting married too.'

Her eyes snapped shut—and the door to the cabinet swung open. 'I suppose I should be surprised.'

'I suppose.' Bill sounded put out.

'Only—and I'm quoting—because you're a useless husband.'

'Correction. I said I was *your* useless husband.'

He had always made her laugh, and she did so now. 'Oh, Bill.'

The tension dissipated a little.

On their respective phones, each waited for the other to resume.

Bill went first: 'I wanted to say . . . I wanted to say . . . This sounds ridiculous, but I hope this is all right . . .'

She caught her breath. She wasn't going to go back over that now. She had been Bill's wife. Then she wasn't. End of story. 'You'll be happy,' she said. 'I know you will.'

'Thank you.'

('Do you like your husband's new wife?' How would she reply to that one?)

'Why now, after all this time? You've been with Sarah ten years.'

'Things change. I've changed.' He added, unnecessarily, 'And so have you.'

She could still spot his evasions. A thought occurred to her: 'I take it you'll be getting married after Evie's wedding.'

'Possibly before.' He sounded cautious. 'There are reasons.'

'Oh? Obviously ...' She was tempted to say, *Obviously Sarah can't be pregnant* ... but it lacked grace. 'Won't you be taking some of the spotlight off Evie?'

'No.'

'I think she might feel a bit put out.'

'It's a wedding, not a coronation,' he said.

'But you know what store she sets by everything being perfect, and perfectly planned.'

'Too much fuss?'

'Only if you're a flinty killjoy. Anyway, you don't believe that.'

'Since I'm footing a large part of the bill, I might.' He cleared his throat. 'But you don't honestly think I'd do anything to overshadow Eve's wedding? Do you?'

'No.' Lara changed tack. 'Have you told the daughters yet?'

'Our girls?' The idea appeared to startle him. 'No, just you.'

She flashed back to the time when their instinctive response had been to turn to each other first. *Tell me, tell me everything.* 'That was nice, Bill, but shouldn't you?'

'I wanted to discuss a few things.'

That was unexpected. 'The girls ...' She groped for the appropriate words. 'The girls will be ...' She wasn't sure if 'pleased' would do. 'The girls will be intrigued and ... happy.'

So many dealings with Bill—tender, ecstatic, estranged, dark ... and bitter. From the moment she had clapped eyes on him in the Cornish café and the flare had gone up in her heart (her life had changed, *just like that*), to the naked moment when, pregnant with Louis, she had undressed and reached for her nightdress, only to sense Bill's gaze raking her body, and experienced a chill at what she had done.

Someone—Maudie? herself?—had left the sugar jar on the sideboard with a trail of silvery grains. The weekend's newspapers still colonized the table and a couple of supermarket coupons for reduced-price coffee and cereal had fallen to the floor by the sink. Phone tucked under her chin, Lara retrieved them. Tenpence off instant coffee. An introductory offer for a bathroom cleaner. She totted up the savings they represented.

'Don't be fooled, Lara,' Jasmine might say. *'What you save here in the supermarket is grabbed from you there.'*

'I like the illusion of saving.'

'That's why my business is growing.'

She smoothed them out on the table.

'Lara, will you come to the wedding?'

'No.' The word plummeted from her lips but she managed the gracious rider. 'Thank you.'

'Pity. I'd like you there.' He paused. 'I really would.'

She forced herself not to say, *And I would have liked you there while I brought your daughters up.* To say, or to imply, any such thing would be unfair.

The day she met Bill.

Flashback.

Blue sea, patchy Cornish sunlight. She has bleached salty hair, and sand from the morning's surfing caught between toes and buttocks ... She is post-finals, steeling herself to find a job and begin life. He trails into the café with a double buggy and she looks up from polishing the Gaggia, which has become her personal fiefdom. Faded cotton trousers. Mussed hair. A couple of tiny scratches on his chin. He catches her eye—and she sees anguish and fatigue in his. She steps towards him. He is taking a holiday with his tiny daughters to get over his wife's death and failing to cope. It's hard to look at someone you imagine to be so capable only to discover they're actually on the edge. One more push and he'd go over. Yet it's impossible to help him. You can't order grief to go away. 'It settles in,' he says. 'Like the weather.' She finds herself mourning his vanished future—or, at least, the one he wanted to share with the woman he loved. It makes her consider how greedy we are as a generation. We're used to death being confined to old age, we demand it so, and it shocks us rigid when someone young dies.

'Just talk to me,' he says, as he tries to give a bottle to the baby and a mug of milk to the toddler.

She drops down into the chair beside him to help. He is bereaved and stumbling, but grief makes him beautiful. The most potent of combinations. Death has touched him . . . and such a death with its terrible glamour . . . fascinates her.

Later, she wrote on a piece of paper and stuffed it into her wallet. 'Pity is like mercury. It's quicksilver, rising, pushing its way to the surface.'

Later still she wrote: 'I never knew what happiness was. Now I do.'

The day Bill left her.

Written in the household diary: 'He's gone. We failed.' Two short sentences. That was enough.

Now he asked, 'Is this to punish me?'

'I'm long past that.'

Was she? She hoped she was. 'You cannot imagine the depths of distaste I feel for the person I once loved ...' A statement often heard in her consulting room. Lara had never felt like that about Bill.

I'm grateful for that small concession, she frequently told herself. I am.

Bill did the throat-clearing that meant he had a tricky subject to tackle. 'There's something else I wanted to discuss. Could you come over? I think it would be easier face to face.'

She glanced at her diary. 'I could manage next week.'

'I was thinking tonight, Lara.'

The clock on the kitchen shelf said seven p.m. 'Bill, you are all right?' The inner anxiety meter clocked on. Illness, bankruptcy ...?

'Yes, but I do need to talk to you. Negotiate, really.'

'OK, but you must tell the girls your news.'

'Yes,' he said. 'I must.'

It didn't take long to snatch up her coat and let herself into the dark.

The cold had come early this year. Arctic winds had swept in and the going underfoot was treacherous. She planted her feet carefully, and thought out each movement. The cold crept up the sleeves of her coat and her nose watered. Yet she enjoyed those still, morbid evenings when the streetlights were filtered in an orange haze through icy air. 'I don't like spring,' she had confessed to Vicky.

'Why on earth not?' Vicky had wanted to know.

'It makes me ... sad.'

'Oh, that,' said Vicky. 'We're all sad most of

the time.'

Lara plodded on. Living in the city meant she was cut off from nature—a safety curtain stretched between her and the realities of weather. Anyway, unlike spring, with its unpredictable dewy growth and pale flowers, you knew exactly where you were with winter. Wintry landscapes. (Long lines of humans trudging through them like the remnants of Napoleon's army.) You needed resilience to survive winter.

Three minutes later, she had reached the end of the street and was ringing Bill's doorbell.

'Congratulations,' she said, to the figure holding open the door.

'Thank you.' Sarah kissed her. She was in her work clothes of black trousers and jacket and smelt of lavender soap and fabric conditioner. Not unpleasing. 'Bill's on the phone to Jasmine. I suppose I should offer you a drink.'

'You suppose right.'

Sarah marched her into the kitchen and she sank down into a chair and changed her mind. 'Sarah, do you think I could have a cup of tea instead?'

The radio—as frequently—was set to a classical-music station. A medley of waltzes was playing, which usually she would loathe. Yet for once they soothed Lara as she watched the unflappable Sarah move around the kitchen. When it came, the tea was strong. 'Thanks.'

Sarah devoted a lot of her energy to making people feel comfortable and usually succeeded.

It had been a long day and Bill's news took some absorbing. 'So why am I here?' She clocked the large sapphire on Sarah's finger and the worm of envy gave only a tiny wriggle. Lara was pleased

9

about that. Happiness was elusive and Bill and Sarah were due some.

Happy or not, Sarah was in a snappy mood. 'If you don't come to the wedding, Lara, it will look as though you bear me a grudge. Considering I didn't meet Bill until after Violet, and you and I get along fine, that can't be the case.'

'I don't want to upset you,' Lara said, 'but . . . let's just say it's better if I'm not there.' Sarah looked embattled and she added, 'No one thinks I bear you a grudge. That would be impossible.'

'The girls will be upset. Actually . . .' Sarah stared at her tea '. . . if you're talking of grudges, the boot should be on the other foot. *You* had his children. You and the sainted Mary.'

She sounded sad as she always did when the subject of children came up. 'I left it too late,' she had once confided to Lara. 'Then when I met Bill there wasn't any question . . .' No more needed to be said.

Lara was curious. 'Does Bill still think of Mary as sainted?'

Mary had died giving birth to Eve—a rotten, horrible, mean death, as deaths in childbirth always were. Naturally, everyone was inclined to canonize Mary, which was difficult for those who had stepped into her shoes. 'Saints do try the patience,' Lara had once pointed out to Bill, in the days when they still amused each other.

'Yes, he does.' Sarah waved the hand with the ring in Lara's direction. 'But you know.'

'I know.'

The clock on the wall ticked off the seconds. It was not an uncomfortable moment, exactly, but not a comfortable one either.

Then Sarah said, 'Don't worry, our wedding won't steal Eve's thunder. In fact, all this is really about her. Bill will tell you.'

'I did suggest Evie's nose might be put out of joint.'

Sarah stiffened. 'It won't do her any harm.' She fiddled with the ring. 'Eve can be . . . I sometimes think she speaks out of turn.'

'Don't.'

Don't criticize the daughters.

Sarah gave Lara one of her looks. 'She can be very keen to tell people what's what.'

Indignation spiked Lara's good intentions. 'If you mean she's courageous and honest, then I won't deny it.'

'You always defend her.' Sarah's voice dropped. 'Always. I find that strange . . . admirable . . . when she's not . . .'

'Stop right there, Sarah. She *is* my daughter.'

Thin, restless Eve, with her remarkable speaking eyes and her common sense, always braced against disaster.

'How can that be?'

She was tempted to say: *If you were a mother you would understand.*

Not on.

'Sorry.' Sarah gazed down at her tea—as if to extract the meaning of life from it. 'I've known Eve for ten years and I don't think she likes me very much.'

Lord, Lara thought. Are we beginning to talk honestly? 'Eve needs to be very sure about people.' Sarah looked sceptical. 'She does, Sarah. But once she's made up her mind, she's yours for life.'

'She's taking her time.' Sarah could be wry.

Fair enough.

Yet no criticism of her girls was allowed to pass. That was how it was with Lara, and anyone who knew her had to reckon with it. 'Eve's had to deal with the fact that her birth killed her mother, and then her parents separated.' Lara checked herself. 'Sarah, let's not get into this . . .' Regretting not the defence but its vehemence, she concentrated on the sparkly-pin order of Sarah's kitchen. *Calm down.* The jugs were arranged on the shelf in height order and the knives slotted into the knife block. In Sarah's domain, nothing was permitted to lie around.

Lara and Sarah exchanged a look. Talk honestly? Possible?

It had been years, yet neither woman was absolutely at ease with the other. The journey had got so far but no further. Sarah had a good job in local government where she managed a fair number of people, and Lara had her own skills, but all of this shrank in the face of the other woman. Their conversations tended to be muddled (and over-compensatory).

Why not? *Why not?* 'Sarah, do you feel guilty?'

'Goodness, Lara. What on earth . . .' Sarah flushed. 'I'm not in your consulting room.'

'Even so. You know you're blameless.'

If anyone was guilty, it was Lara. Guilt she knew about.

'Yes and no.' Sarah was nervy but, since the news had been announced, more confident. 'OK . . .' She was trying out the words for size. 'Lara, this seems to be a good moment to straighten a few things out that I need to know but Bill won't ever discuss.' One woman talking to another about a man. 'He loves his girls, and I never understood why he didn't take them with him.' She added hastily, 'Not Maudie, of course. But Jasmine and Eve.' Unnecessary for her to add: He's their father and you're not their real mother.

Flashback.

She tastes coffee and sea salt on her lips as she hurries from the afternoon shift at the café to Bill's rented holiday cottage and her second meeting with him.

He takes her by the hand and leads her upstairs to view his sleeping motherless daughters in their cots. 'You remember Jasmine?' He points to a wrapped-up package of silky hair and plump limbs. Then he points to the smaller one. 'And Eve?'

She's speechless. Patches of light filter through the thin holiday curtains on to the walls. There is a clutter of children's clothes. The sweet-acrid tang of nappy cream and urine. The pretty children laid out like votive offerings.

Bill says, 'Aren't they beautiful?'

'Yes.' As she speaks, she knows she has made a commitment . . .

She loved them. Then, now and for ever. Passionately. (Each bone outlined under their pearly skin. Each childish curl. Every stumbling word.)

'They had had enough to put up with already in their small lives. I couldn't let them go . . . I *loved* them, Sarah, as I love them now. They were mine.'

'And Bill's?'

'Bill's too. But Violet had a different take . . .'

'Oh, let's not forget Violet.' Sarah focused on a perfectly folded tea-towel hanging over a rail.

The subject of Lara and Bill was—of course—

still vexed, and Lara's heart gave its customary shuddery fragile thud. 'Violet was adamant she didn't want children. So it wouldn't have worked anyway. But if it had been you ...' For the thousandth time, Lara thought (selfishly), Thank goodness Bill met Violet first.

Sarah said, 'I would have taken them. I would have done anything ... I wouldn't have hesitated.'

Neither would I, thought Lara. *Neither did I.* 'Sarah, I wouldn't, *couldn't*, have let them go without a fight.'

Sarah—dear Sarah. Honest, long-suffering Sarah of the brown eyes and gentle expression.

'You think I don't understand because I'm childless.'

Lara did not reply.

'It's funny how the female body isn't always up to the job,' said Sarah, 'more often than you'd imagine. Otherwise I might not be sitting here. We assume it'll be straightforward, but it isn't.'

Now, *that* they both understood. Two ovaries, one uterus, one willing body, an array of hormones and conditioning devoted to making it work. In Sarah's case, it didn't. In hers, it did—*just*—and then ... it didn't.

'No,' she said and, even now, her voice sounded raw.

As raw and desperate as when she had screamed, 'No. It's not true.'

Chapter Two

Sarah grabbed her handbag, rummaged in it for her lipstick and applied it. 'Have you noticed that as we get older lipstick gets caught in the creases?'

The repair was a measure of her agitation. Normally Sarah wouldn't dream of doing such a thing in public.

'No,' Lara replied.

'You haven't done anything to your mouth, have you? Plumped it up? It looks very . . . big.'

'No, I haven't.'

'As a matter of interest, when I marry Bill does that connect us in any way? New wife/old wife sort of thing?'

'We're already connected.' There was a touch of wistfulness.

Sarah smiled. 'Being an only child, I like the idea of connections.' She continued, 'The girls *will* hate it if you're not at the wedding.' Again, she tried, 'If the past is still in the way, don't let it be.'

It had been cold for some time and Lara had developed a chilblain on her left index finger. It itched and burned. It was burning now with added intensity. 'I appreciate the invitation.'

'Lara . . . I hope you wish us well . . .'

Was Sarah pleased that Lara had dug her toes in? Did it imply she minded that Sarah had— finally—snapped up the prize, which was Bill? She proffered her olive branch. 'I do.'

'I wish you had someone too.'

So gently and sweetly spoken that Lara could not possibly take umbrage. Could not *possibly* say,

Don't go there. 'There are too many other things, Sarah. My life is full enough.' She could have added, *And I have been there.* Instead, she turned the subject. 'What are you going to wear?'

'Since you won't be there, it's hardly of interest ...' Shrugged. 'As you know, clothes aren't my thing.'

Flashback.

A girl hurrying up the church path in a white dress and overlong veil. The girl who imagines that taking on a man and two tiny stepdaughters will be easy simply because she wants to do it. No, longs to do it.

The wretched veil. She finds it impossible to control.

'But I will make an effort,' added Sarah.

Mobile in hand, Bill came into the kitchen. As tall as ever (of course), he was stockier than he used to be, but his hair was still Anglo-Saxon fair and (lucky him) his jawline almost as firm as it had been when she'd first met him. He had lines and shadows—not those of a man who had lived hard, but of a man who had grieved hard. Lately, he had mellowed and allowed himself to smile more.

'Lara, sorry to keep you.' He held up the phone. 'The girls are pleased.' He kissed her cheek. 'Actually, check that, I haven't managed to get hold of Maudie.'

The touch of his face against hers was like two templates fitting together after a long time. Bill's aftershave had never changed. Neither had the slight rasp of his five-o'clock-shadow cheek, a bodily quirk that Lara knew he hated.

She was conscious of Sarah's watchful gaze and disengaged herself. 'Congratulations to you both.'

There was a tiny pause. A shimmer of air—like the pulse before a storm.

Sarah rubbed her freshly slicked lips. 'Lara, my great-uncle died last month.'

'I'm sorry.'

'He was so old he said he wanted to die,' said Sarah. 'Apparently. I didn't know him, only of him. My mother used to mention him from time to time but not often. The two sides of the family didn't get on. So . . .' she glanced at Bill '. . . it's a bit of a shock . . .'

Bill caught up the slack. 'Gurley had no heirs and Sarah has inherited his house. Membury Manor.'

'Five bedrooms,' said Sarah. 'Not too big. Lovely gardens. We . . .' again the stabilizing glance at Bill '. . . went and had a look.' She seemed breathless with her own good fortune. 'We're going to live there. Let me show you.' She took a photograph from a shelf and laid it on the table. 'Look.'

Georgian. Beautiful.

Lara raised her eyes from the photograph and encountered Bill's. How was she going to take the news, they asked.

Sarah slipped a hand around Bill's waist. I understand, thought Lara—with a sudden and shocking jolt of jealousy. This is what she *can* give him. And will.

Bill said, 'The girls are grown-up now. They don't need me around in the same way.'

She heard herself saying, 'Maudie isn't quite. She still needs a bit of guidance.'

'She's eighteen. If anything, I'll be closer to the college there. You have to let go some time.'

She watched him dig his hands into his pockets. She watched Sarah tighten her grip around his torso. She felt her responses quicken and sharpen into defensiveness. 'But your jobs?' Bill worked in a quasi-government department that regulated food standards. He hated it. Always had done ... Once or twice, Lara had urged him to branch out. His reply was always the same: he must, he had explained, with that charming, patient smile of his, wait until the children were grown.

'I'm setting up a branch of the business in the local town. And Sarah is transferring.'

'Lara,' Sarah intervened, 'here's the tricky bit. We wanted to talk to you about financial arrangements. This is going to be expensive for us.'

'It needs doing up,' Bill offered quietly.

She saw what was coming. Guttering. Windows. Dry rot. 'Of course, a house like that will eat up money.'

'I can't continue with the same level of payments to you.' Bill was uneasy and on the back foot. 'I'm afraid we'll have to renegotiate.'

Sarah opened a drawer, produced a spreadsheet from a file and placed it in front of Lara. With immaculate presentation, it spelled out an altered future.

'I see.' Bill was proposing to reduce the monthly amount to the extent that it would affect her mortgage repayments.

She stared at them. Both of them imperfectly masked their concern.

'Bill, I'm not sure ... We agreed in court that you would support Maudie until she was launched.'

He pointed to a figure. 'That I will do.'

Sarah said, 'Apparently, the manor has a wonderful garden.'

Lara was ratcheting through the implications. 'Of

course you must do what's best. Can this wait until I make other arrangements? I don't . . . I don't want to lose the house.'

'We can't have that,' Bill agreed.

'But people do.'

Startled by Sarah's interjection, Lara looked up.

Bill turned on her. 'Sarah!'

Lara said, 'Shush, Bill, there's no need. Just let me think . . .'

To date, Sarah had taken pains to conceal her resentment at having to underwrite a previous wife (she should count herself lucky that Mary was dead). Yet alimony *was* the devil and, after a couple of seconds, Lara forgave her.

When she and Bill had divorced, the house in north London had been sold, the money divided and used to buy two very small terraced houses at opposite ends of the same street in the unsmart end of Hackney so that the children could ferry between them. 'Such an odd arrangement.' Neither her mother nor her father had approved and told her so.

But it had made sense for Bill's daughters, the little girls who were desolate at the fracture. 'Making the best of it is what matters,' she had informed her parents. 'I have to stay here and hold it together.' At least, she and Bill had managed to keep *that* promise (forget 'for better for worse'), at first, in the grudging spirit of bitter armistice, then, as the years passed, with increasing confidence.

Sarah said, 'Lara, please don't think we want to be unreasonable.'

She laid her hand on Sarah's arm. 'Of course not.'

God help me. How many nights had she lain

awake over the years straining to push all the pieces into the jigsaw?

Bill said gently, 'Lara?'

She wondered if he had dismissed from his memory their early days together. The tenderness, the gratitude, the perfect storms of love.

One day she might ask him.

One day, too, she must say to him, *We need to think about Louis. You did promise.*

She got to her feet. 'Bill, Sarah, I'm truly happy about your news but I need a bit of time to reorganize.'

'But Maudie is *grown-up*,' said Sarah, helplessly.

She knew from his expression that Bill was thinking, I must not be unfair—and the old, stubborn regret raised its head.

He said, 'We could always reschedule but . . .'

Sarah examined her nails—pearl pink and oval. Her pretty features, once so dewy and (as Lara acknowledged of her own) remaining so courtesy of age-defying moisturizer, reflected frustration. 'But I'm sure you'll see it's fair.'

Of course she didn't mean to but, at a stroke, Sarah threatened to undo the good work of ten years. Lara couldn't entertain that notion—not when they had got so far. She tweaked the edge of the cuff that poked out beneath the sleeve of Sarah's black jacket. 'You're losing a button.'

There was a bang on the front door. It opened, then closed with a snap.

'Dad?' Jasmine came into the kitchen and squared up to her father. 'When were you going to tell us, then?'

Bill ran his hand over his daughter's dark head. 'I've told you now.'

She was closely followed by Eve, who dropped bag, laptop case and packages on to the floor and tugged at Bill's sleeve. He turned to hug her.

'What took you so long, Dad?' Her big eyes shone.

'Actually, I'm a pretty fast worker,' said Bill.

She reached up and gave him a lingering kiss on the cheek. '*Actually*, it's Sarah who should be congratulated. Think of what she's had to put up with.'

Lara observed them fondly. 'You haven't heard the whole of it.'

It never took much to make Eve anxious. Her tone switched. 'Has something happened?'

Bill presented Eve with the photograph. 'Our new home. We hope.'

Eve's reaction was all that Bill might have hoped for. 'It's beautiful,' she breathed, in the way she did when she was talking about something she rated. 'Perfection.'

He touched her cheek. 'Here's the thing. I want this done and dusted and for us to be moved in by May so that . . .'

How slow she had been on the uptake. In a flash, Lara read the ulterior motives behind the projected move—among them, a father wishing to be equal to the occasion.

But Eve was quick to get it. 'You don't mean . . .?' Now she wore the glowing, happy look bestowed only on those she trusted and loved—otherwise reserved for antique furniture or a painting, objects of special desire.

Father of the bride . . .

'I do mean.' Bill sent Lara a wry look. *Do you really want to throw a spanner into the works?*

21

'I'm hoping you'll want to hold your wedding at Membury.'

*   *   *

Maudie, are you there?

However tired she was, Lara always made time for the weekly Facebook catch-up. Maudie was attending a sixth-form college in Winchester and living with Bill's sister, Lucy. 'I want to get out of London,' she had pleaded. 'Please let me.'

Lara had argued that Maudie was too young to leave home but Maudie had had her answer: 'I'll be with family, and since you have to work early in the morning and in the evenings, it makes sense.'

Lara repeated this to Jasmine, who laughed. 'Mum, Maudie just wants to leave home.'

Maudie had always been her own person. She had been born with a placard reading 'Do not mess with me.' It hadn't been easy, but when she announced that her best friend, Tess, was also going to the college, Lara had conceded defeat. Arrangements had been made. Maudie had packed her bags and spent her terms for the past eighteen months lodging with her aunt Lucy.

'Maudie . . .'

The things taught to you by having children . . . One, your body will never be the same again. Two, most parents are schizophrenic. Three, a sense of perspective is vital—this, courtesy of Jasmine, who had considered studying oceanography and marine biology. 'A humpback whale's pregnancy,' she had informed Lara, 'lasts twelve months and she gives birth to a calf between twelve and fourteen feet long.' (Nothing like a few facts to put childbirth in its place.) Jasmine had also told Lara, 'Orcas, the killer whales, maintain a strong relationship with their young throughout their lives.'

Fourth point: she was an orca mother.

'But, in the end,' said Jasmine, 'the orca mother can't keep up.'

'I can't bear it,' said Lara. 'That's awful.'

'No, it isn't,' said Jasmine. 'That's how it should be.'

Maudie ... so missed. So increasingly (she sensed) *gone*.

From her customary perch at the kitchen table, she could see, hanging companionably beside Eve's willow-pattern and Jasmine's black freebie from the local garage, Maudie's scarlet mug, and the half-empty box of her favourite cereal, which no one else would touch.

Those were Maudie's markers, which, in her absence, Lara cherished. She reached up and cradled the scarlet mug. A few self-indulgent tears threatened. Stupid, she knew.

Where was Maudie? Not geographically, but where in her journey? Which brought Lara to the fifth point: as Maudie's mother, and always wrong, she would probably be the last to know.

Lara typed:

Maudie? How did the week go? Not revising too late, I hope.

It was the sort of question she had posed over the years. First to Jasmine, then Eve. Now Maudie.

'*Listen* to you, Mum,' Jasmine would say. 'Stop *fussing*.'

And Lara would reply, 'If I was an orca you wouldn't think twice about answering my questions.'

No wonder, in her dream, Lara was always running.

The brides—those white-clad, luminous girls of which she had been one—had known nothing. Stories about them were legion in books, poems, fable. Some had been willing, some forced. Some had died of fright and violation. Some had lived half-lives of desperation and depression. Some had flowered, if only for a time. (Lara's story.) Others had lived unremarkably. And the ones who survived, happily or not, found themselves asking these questions of their children.

Lara needed to know if a daughter was eating and sleeping properly, wearing clean clothes, had enough money for the bus . . . and it was her business. Who else's would it be? It annoyed the children. It annoyed *her*. No one volunteers for eternal sentry duty, she had pointed out more than once. No one wishes to have their senses on permanent receive mode to reassure oneself that everyone is OK.

How do you feel about the news, Maudie?

She dropped her hands into her lap. Immediately Maudie came back:

What news?

Oh, Lord. Bill had forgotten to track her down.

Your father and Sarah are getting married in

24

the spring.

Lara pictured Maudie reading this, gazing intently at the screen through narrowed blue eyes. The shrug—used when she didn't want to anyone to know that she was hurt.

They're planning to move to the country. Fabulous house which S. has inherited. Your father wants Eve and Andrew to get married there. Andrew's parents want him to get married at their house. I think she should be married in London where she lives. Don't you? Watch this space.

Eve will do what Dad wants

came back the answer.

Maudie, Sarah wants me at the wedding but will you forgive me if I don't go? I'll try and explain to the others

. . . she was throwing sops, trusting that Maudie would feel that, on this point at least, she had been consulted first and was not the last to know . . .

but I wanted to explain to you before I talked to the others. I don't want to make a big thing of it but I would prefer not to be there.

I don't want to be there either. Dad won't mind whether I am or not. Nor will Sarah.

It's your father's wedding.

It's a formality,
the straightforward Maudie replied.

Only that.

*   *   *

In the early days after the separation, whenever Lara had met Violet—which she hated doing and avoided—she thought she spotted a gleam of amusement in Violet's eye. The notion that Bill and Violet joked privately about her was torment.

'Do you discuss me with Violet?' she had once asked Bill.

'Not really,' he answered. He had lied. 'Why would I do that?'

'I thought maybe ... I thought discussing me might bring you and Violet closer together.'

'There are other things to talk about.'

She had flushed.

Of course. Of course. And she was in danger of becoming obsessed with her situation. One of the paradoxes of divorce, she had concluded, with the strange, raw vision she had developed after it, was that it did not bring liberation—far from it: the inner world of regret and obsession became a prison.

As a child, she had watched her mother pin a paper pattern to dress material. Tongue poking between her lips, she had cut into the fabric and the edges had uncoiled like sleepy snakes, dropping to the floor. Eventually the match between pattern and material was achieved. 'As good as *Vogue*, lovey,' she had informed her round-eyed daughter.

But no lasting match had been achieved between

her and Bill.

Jasmine had been twelve. Eve nine. Maudie almost four.

The family had sat at the breakfast table. *Two years ago, a baby had been born and died. A son.*

Food had become a burden and Lara battled to eat. Life had become a burden. She poured a glass of juice for Maudie. Maudie ignored it. Jasmine pinched Eve, who cried. A pan of milk heating on the stove boiled over and filled the kitchen with the nose-pricking smell of burned lactose. Lara observed the pan and the milk and thought, It doesn't matter.

Eventually Bill heaved himself, slowly, heavily, to his feet and switched off the gas. Lara watched him, as tears seeped down her face. When he turned to face her, there were tears on his cheeks too and he was stiff with emotion.

Then he had told her.

He hated himself, he said, but he had to go. 'I no longer trust you.'

'How?' she spat at him. 'How could it be "for the best"?'

'Because we can't live like this.' He was white with the effort of explanation. 'You can't because it's destroying you. And I won't because it's destroying me.'

'Don't do this in front of the children, Bill.'

Three anxious faces were staring at him.

'What am I thinking?' He checked himself. 'Of course I shouldn't be saying this in front of them.' He clamped his lips together.

There hadn't been much time to think. Any time, actually. Jasmine and Eve were due on the school run, and Maudie was to be dropped at a child-minder's. She had got them ready. Coats on. Shoes fastened. A shadowy film of silent to-ing and fro-ing across a chaotic kitchen and hallway.

When the girls were gone, they faced each other across the littered breakfast table.

'Is there someone else, Bill?'

He sighed. 'There wasn't but ... It's more of a friendship. She ...'

'She what?'

'She's a comfort.'

'And I'm not?'

He turned away. 'Listen to us, Lara. *Listen.*'

She observed his back. What could she read into it? Nothing she wished to read, and she stood for a while in the kitchen, waiting to touch base with the normal sounds. But there was silence. Why didn't the boiler thump? The pipes rattle?

She went upstairs and shut herself into the bedroom. She needed to look at Bill's things. There were his shoes stuffed into the cupboard, the jackets (all similar) exuding whiffs of aftershave and sweat. There was his dressing-gown in blue paisley. Handsome.

She tried pretending that she hadn't heard what had been said. ('I'm selectively deaf,' her grandmother used to say. 'You'll find it a useful condition.')

At that time, her ambitions had centred on peaceful interiors that smelt of ironing and fresh bread. Of transporting children, of family outings, of visits to the cinema with popcorn, and Sunday roasts with properly crisped potatoes.

Now what?

Hours later she emerged to discover Bill sitting on the top stair. 'Shouldn't you have something to eat?' He touched the place where her hipbone jutted through her jeans.

Her head pounded. 'Why would you care?'

'I may be leaving you,' his voice drifted in from a long way away, 'but I'll make sure you're OK.'

She could see the scene clearly. To the onlooker, it was him and her having a—more or less—civilized conversation. But, at her hidden centre, she was molten with rage and pain. 'You're not taking the children,' she said, proud of keeping her voice steady. 'Don't think it.'

'You don't know what you're saying.'

'Yes, I do. *My* children . . . I won't lose my children.'

At that, he appeared uneasy. 'As it happens, Violet isn't . . . keen.'

She rallied her forces. 'Bill, you don't have to do this. You have a choice.'

He stared up at her. 'I don't think so.'

The look on his face reminded her so vividly of times past—times when it had been all right between them and they had been happy, more than happy—that her defences crumbled. She heard herself blurt, 'It would be easier if you were dead,' and had the satisfaction of seeing him pale.

It was true. If Bill had died she knew she would have coped better. The refuge and decorum of widowhood was so much easier an option than that of the abandoned wife.

'Stop it.'

'Why aren't you dead instead of Louis?' she blazed at him.

Uneasy and shocked, he followed her down the stairs into the kitchen. 'Lara . . . can I ring your mother?'

'Don't talk to me.'

Pain was a protean thing. The pain of childbirth, seemingly unbearable at its worst, was, Lara discovered, bearable because it was forgotten. The pain of a collapsed marriage? Different again.

The pain of bereavement? That was of another order.

The two together?

'At least, the agony cannot grow any more,' she wrote in the notebook, after Bill had left. 'It is just there, a poisoning thing, anchored and immutable, and I've got used to dealing with it. What I can't handle is waking up in the morning, all clean and washed with sleep and revelling in those seconds of unknowing, only for it to hit me . . .'

If Bill's going hurt, the struggle to subdue pride and rage and maintain a civilized face in front of the girls was almost worse. This would be a lifelong discipline—as tough as taking religious vows. She pictured herself as a figure in a classical painting kneeling in front of an infant Christ or a saint, promising silence and obedience, however hard. Lara's lawyer advised, 'You *have* to negotiate.' True, cutting herself off and sending violent messages via silence was more disturbing than being vocal, but, said the lawyer, it was not an option.

'Why did he go?' asked Lara's mother. (She was a persistent woman and wouldn't countenance Lara's attempts to fob her off.)

'I got pregnant with Maudie, then Louis, and that began a whole long story,' she said. 'You know the rest.' To counter the tragedy, a traumatized Bill had taken refuge with Violet. The Shrinking V., slim and gleaming with desire, raising her thin arms and crying for more of him to the exclusion of anyone else. Who could blame her? Who could blame him?

Thinking, Children's lunch, Lara had taken a knife out of the kitchen drawer and Bill had backed away. He looked at her with dawning incomprehension—her lovely husband, who couldn't cope with his grief and its repercussions any longer.

'Go to Violet.'

'Lara . . .'

She raised the knife. '*Go*.'

Chapter Three

A large white envelope fell on to the hall floor.

Lara was on her way out to work but she picked it up. 'Lara'—Sarah's handwriting.

Sarah never gave up.

Inside, there was a sheaf of paper and a note. 'Please take a look.'

The first document was a photocopy of an entry in *Country Houses and Their Importance*. 'Built *c*. 1751 by disciple of Robert Adam. Property of the Coates family until 1962. Thereafter property of Gurley Smith. The house, a small-scale commission, reflects early Adam characteristics and preoccupations and it is said that Adam himself insisted on designing fireplaces and pediments. The result is work that has a sense of overall unity, or flow.'

The second was from a garden gazetteer, dated the previous year. 'Once superb, Membury House gardens have fallen into neglect. However, if on Open Days visitors are prepared to look beyond the pedestrian planting and lazy maintenance, they can find the odd gem, including a fine example of a Roman myrtle tree, said to have been planted by Jane Austen's great-nephew.'

The third gave a short history of the Coates family, who had grown rich on the manufacture of imported cotton from the American colonies. Josiah Coates had had the foresight to back the new flyer-and-bobbin system for drawing cotton in the late 1750s and had never looked back. Eventually the family had died out, owing, the writer speculated, to a genetic problem that appeared to have invaded it. As a result, only one out of three children survived, the last dying in 1961.

Now Sarah took up the story, penning in her neat hand: 'My great-uncle Gurley bought it from the Coates executors and occupied it for over forty years. He never married.'

Finally, Lara picked up some printed pages, which had been torn out of a book—by the look and feel of them a cheap paperback. Again, Sarah's writing along the top margin: 'My mother told me that she was sure that the novelist, whose name was Matthew Banks, had modelled the house in the book on Membury and the village.'

Coat shrugged on, bag in hand, she stood in the hallway and began to read.

The writer was impassioned by his subject—and, possibly, a little overwrought:

Montford House was situated to the west of Middleford. Running between fields, which in summer were bright with poppies, corncockle, charlock and mayweed, the road through the centre of the village wound down towards the old London road and Alton, and took in the house on the left.

At ploughing time, the rooks rose above the ridge where the plough teams had danced on the turn of the land. On cold days, the ground rang with the sound of hoofs, and the air echoed with the swish of the muck-spreading teams as they moved in lines across the fields, and the cries of workers harvesting cabbages. At dusk, the teams plodded home to the rattle of chain and harness. In summer, the flies rose in clouds above the crops and the herb-rich meadows. Pigs rooted in grasslands, poultry foraged, and the streams feeding the watercress beds, for which the area was famed, ran cold and clear. The shimmering silence was broken only by the corn soughing, the crack of oak and elm, and the tin-can caw of the rooks. Sheep and cattle dotted the horizon like the colourful images from a medieval book of hours . . .

As she read on—and there were several more pages in kind—the tiny hallway appeared even more cramped than normal. Outside in the street, a siren sounded and the dustmen scraped bins along the pavements. Looking down, she noticed the feathers of dirt drawn on the tiles by the draught. Looking up, she saw the grime etched into the glass panels of the front door.

'Dirty, nasty place, the city,' her mother had said, when she arrived to help out after Bill had left. 'You can't stay here. You need to come back home to Cornwall. Live near us. *Please*. It's better for the children.' Her complexion had gleamed with fresh air, and the smugness of the committed country dweller. 'We can arrange things. Schools, friends . . .'

Lara had been standing in the centre of the room. It was strewn with children's stuff. She hadn't changed her jeans in weeks. Her hair draped lankly on her shoulders. The room needed painting and, because of the rain beating outside, it was dark. As she stood there, it seemed to her that the walls were closing in. They were both prison and security of sorts.

No.

'Lara,' her mother argued. 'Think of the children.'

At that, Lara turned on her. 'I think of *nothing* else.'

Here, hidden in the streets, she could wear blinkers, put her head down and look neither right nor left.

Over the years, she had become successful as a city dweller: grafted into its ways, its smells, its variety, its indifference. It suited her. She had grown to love the rough-and-tumble—and she had taught herself, above all, to be a creature of its streets and tumult.

Yes, the city was dirty and brutish, but the lobby who argued that it was only that did not know the half of it.

The final line of Sarah's note read: 'Please come and see Membury. I want you to *know* it as much as I will.'

*   *   *

34

Eve's email to Lara began:

Wedding Plans, Stage One

First Question: What kind of wedding?

Typical Eve. Clear and decided.

She continued:

Once we have the location, then we can set the date. We can't do anything without the location. Love Bridezilla

What kind of wedding? In Eve's case, it was a rhetorical question, and what Lara wanted for Eve was what Lara had wanted for herself—but better.

. . . the streams feeding the watercress beds, for which the area was famed, ran cold and clear. The shimmering silence was broken only by the corn soughing, the crack of oak and elm and the tin-can caw of the rooks . . .

How strange. Matthew Banks's description of the village had crawled inside her head and gone to sleep, waking every so often to nudge her. 'The shimmering silence . . . the crack of oak and elm . . .'

She found herself wanting to go there so she could see it for herself.

Bill was amenable and, after consulting him, Eve arranged for Andrew and Lara to travel down to Middleford the following Sunday.

It might be a Sunday morning, and freezing,

but it was astonishing how busy the station was. Cluttered with groups, luggage, vendors, the forecourt was an animated panorama of ants.

Punctual as ever, Eve was already there, waiting under the clock. Lara paused to take a good look. Black beret, short circular fifties jacket, jeans tucked into Spanish leather riding boots. Her restless gaze was everywhere as she talked into her phone.

Eve spotted her, terminated the call, snatched Lara's hand and held it to her cheek. 'Thank you for coming.'

She kissed her stepdaughter who smelt—slightly—of cigars, which would have horrified the fastidious Sara. 'Where's Andrew?'

'Buying papers. Everything OK at home?'

'Fine.' Lara dished out the cappuccinos she had bought at the kiosk. 'Here. I bet you haven't had breakfast.' Eve shook her head. 'I've got one for Andrew, too.'

He joined them at the ticket barrier. 'How early is this, Lara?' he asked, but kissed her with his usual grace. 'Fiancée and mother-in-law, I'm a lucky man.'

He meant it and didn't mean it. It was the kind of compliment he tossed out, oh, so charmingly. She held out the coffee. 'Starter fuel. Any good?'

'You know something?' he said. 'I think I want to marry you.'

Eve slipped her hand into Andrew's coat pocket. Beside him she looked small and fragile. 'Only a tiny point, but I got there first.'

Andrew shrugged. 'Sorry about that.' Above them the departures board flipped to reveal the platform. 'This is ridiculous,' he said. 'We should have taken the car. It's freezing and it might snow. Great.'

'Much quicker on the train,' said Eve, in her practical way. 'Carbon footprint.'

'Oh, God.' Andrew rolled his eyes. 'Not that.' He turned a straight face on Lara. '*Now* I humour her but . . . just give it few years.'

'No,' said Eve, quietly. 'You agree with me.'

'Do I?'

She looked up at him and said, 'You do.'

He rested his hands on her shoulders, turned her round and pushed her gently in the direction of the train. 'If you say so.'

On the journey down, Andrew and Eve sat opposite each other and didn't talk much for the hour or so it took. Andrew hunched back on the seat and closed his eyes, an unread newspaper on his lap. Lara squinted at the top story's headline, speculating on the date of the general election. This year, next year, some time, never, she thought. Eve opened her laptop (which never left her) and tapped away. The demands of the on-line high-fashion retailer for whom she worked never let up. Once, she lifted her eyes to Lara. 'I have a good feeling about Membury,' she said. 'Don't you?'

Mum, you won't leave me like my real mum did?

No, Evie, I won't.

A landscape of frost-embellished back gardens, washing lines and scrubby infill plantings of pines flew past. Clickety-clack went the train, and Lara computed the things that mattered to its rhythm. Eve and Andrew had somewhere to live. *Clickety-clack.* Andrew's parents had offered them a run-down cottage in the grounds of their larger house. They were handsome and capable. *Clickety-*

clack. Their future seemed straightforward. It seemed good. *Clickety-clack*. How different would things be, having a daughter married?

Clickety-clack.

Halfway down, flakes of snow drifted past the carriage window but didn't settle.

Every so often, Eve consulted her phone.

'Evie, darling, it's the weekend.'

She raised those remarkable eyes from the screen and sent Lara a funny little smile. 'Haven't you noticed that work is twenty-four/seven these days?'

Well, yes, she had.

Andrew said, 'Let me sleep, girls.'

So easy his manner.

From the station at Middleford, the taxi driver took them down a couple of lanes, and Andrew, who had woken up, said, 'Will this work?' The lane had narrowed. 'It's much easier access at my parents' house. People will get stuck down here.'

Eve looked alarmed. 'Don't.' She flashed him her special smile. 'Trust me.'

'I do. I do.' Now his phone went round and round between his fingers.

Lara looked out of the window at the undulating Hampshire countryside, the frost painting it with a Dickensian sparkle. Settled into it was a traditional-looking village, which, as the result of new builds on its flanks, showed signs of sprawl. It had a grey-stone church, far too substantial for the size of the village, which probably indicated that it had been built on the profits of the medieval wool industry.

'I'm so excited,' said Eve.

Lara hunched forward. A wedding here would

be picture postcard, no doubt of that. No city dirt and grime to soil the hem of a wedding dress—only soil and good, honest mud.

Andrew read her thoughts. 'It's certainly a good setting.'

'Begin as you mean to go on.' She smiled at him.

He did not return the smile but took her gloved hand, and patted it.

A house came into view.

The taxi turned into a drive and sped towards it. A grey sky bore down on them as they passed trees whose bare branches permitted the sunlight to freckle the frozen earth at their roots. Lurking around them were clumps of *Helleborus orientalis* and, flaunting pale green flowers against lingering snow, *Helleborus argutifolius*.

Winter's sleep.

Deep and cold.

She gazed. Beginning in her feet, a shudder went through her. Fragments of the old dream nagged at her. The ragged memories of a childhood spent in a garden rushed to the surface. It was as if the swaddling in which she had bound the remnants of her early self had loosened.

Why? What?

Enfolded over this garden—indefinable, but there—was the suggestion of many lives, the whisper of now-vanished presences who had walked its boundaries, loved it, and had been intimate with its corners and the long lie of the land. Lara closed her eyes. She, the city spirit, found herself, to her astonishment, envying those presences. They had known the smell of its wet earth after rain, the dry meadow scents of summer, and the rot of frost-nipped fruit in the autumn garden.

Will I ever be whole?

The question was posed by her inner voice. She and it were old acquaintances. Sensible, matter-of-fact, quiet, it had, over the years, asked many questions of Lara.

They drew up in front of the house.

Wrapped in a headscarf and a sheepskin coat, Sarah was waiting in her car parked in the drive. She had driven down the night before and had put herself up in the local B-and-B as the legal niceties were still in train. 'Terrible,' she said. 'Why don't people spend their money on proper beds instead of tassels on the curtains and knick-knacks in the bathroom?' She turned to Andrew. 'I know your parents would probably love the wedding at your home but Bill is so keen for his daughters to marry from . . . well, hopefully from Membury. Providing . . .'

There. The unvoiced ifs and buts.

Eve looked bewildered. 'Didn't Dad come with you?'

'He'll be here later.' Sarah tucked her hand under Eve's elbow. 'Shall we go and have a look? We can't go further into the house than the hall as the lawyers are being bossy, but I've got permission for us to go round the grounds. And I've discovered the perfect position for a marquee . . .'

I must pull my thoughts together, Lara told herself.

Ten seconds, and it was apparent to her that this house was the place where Eve would be married. It was beautiful and crumbling. Much of its charm lay in its decay—and in the fact that it had survived.

Ten seconds, and she *wanted* Eve to be married from here.

Clods of frozen earth clung to her shoes as she paced in Sarah's wake and breathed in the smell of a garden suspended and its woody undertone of leaf decay.

'Wonderful, *wonderful*,' Eve said. 'Mum . . . Look over here.'

Fretted and patchworked by old browns and new greens, with occasional splashes of winter colour—a clump of crocuses under a tree, the pale hopeful stars of the viburnum—the garden was patiently enduring its months of suffering in order to begin again.

She observed Eve's deepening commitment to the idea, could almost see the plans taking shape in her head while Sarah paraded this way and that and flirted with Andrew.

'And here,' said Sarah, padding ahead, in boots with thick rubber soles, 'is where I think the marquee should be.' They filed around a hedge and emerged in an area containing a sunken lawn edged by neglected flowerbeds. A myrtle tree stood in one corner and, flanked by statuary, a flight of steps led to a second expanse of lawn below and a small wild area in the distance.

Eve emitted a small sound of joy. Even as a tiny girl, she had loved flowers. (And her cardboard houses.) 'Look at this.' She nipped at the leaves of the box hedge edging one of the beds. 'Such colour. Even now. Velvet, yes?' She held out her hands. 'Smell, Mum. Divine, isn't it? So fresh.' Her gaze travelled around the sunken garden, a winter vista of cold-stiffened grey-greens and lichen-etched stone. She paced up and down. 'Where's my notebook?' She stripped off her gloves, wrote something down, blew on her fingers. 'Imagine it in summer.' Off came her beret. 'All scented and dreamy with warmth.' She came to a halt by Andrew, her frozen breath spiralling up into the air. 'What do you say?'

He took possession of the beret, 'Come here,' and settled it carefully back on her head. 'Let's discuss it later.'

'No—now, please.'

'Evie, *later*.' He tucked in a rogue strand. 'What about Lara?'

Eve appealed to her: 'Do you approve? You *must* approve.' The chill had whipped colour into her normally pale cheeks and her eyelashes into spikes. She looked young, pitiless and determined, and Lara's heart turned over.

'Evie, don't bully Lara.'

Eve frowned. 'I'm not.'

Andrew was checking the messages on his phone and Lara heard his sharp intake of breath. With heightened colour, he dropped it back into his overcoat pocket. 'Eve,' he said, 'I've been thinking. Let's not have a big, fussy wedding. I'm not sure I want it.'

'That can't be true,' she said, with a sound of distress, and backed away. 'Why didn't you say so before?'

'I should have done.'

The wind was freshening, buffeting their cheeks with its icy breath. Tactfully, Sarah moved away down the steps.

'Andrew. *Please*.'

His phone pinged. Then again. Lara saw that Andrew really wanted to look at those messages. Body language. 'Hey,' he said, his gaze sliding past Eve. 'I've got to take this call.' He moved away.

Lara watched him hunch over his phone by the myrtle, talking softly, rapidly. Eve flipped over the pages in her notebook. 'Evie,' she began, 'just one thing. We have to be careful about the expense of —'

'Don't worry,' she cut in. 'Dad said he'd got it under control. There's money.'

'Ah,' she said. Dry as a bone. 'There is, is there?'

'Problem, Mum?'

She looked into the oh-so-familiar face. There was nothing so strong, so *unfightable*, as what flowed between her and her daughters. If asked, she couldn't have described mother-love but she could have told you it felt deeper and wider than the universe. 'No problem, Evie.'

Andrew ceased talking. He gestured at them. 'Sorry.' His gaze did not quite meet either woman's. 'We were discussing? Lara, how would you feel about the set-up? Would it be difficult for you? I know that you and Bill and Sarah . . . but . . .?'

'That's very sweet and thoughtful of you,' she said. 'I appreciate it, but I'll be OK.'

'So?' Eve was impatient.

'I give in.' Andrew pulled up his collar against the wind and was, clearly, searching for his customary emollient self. 'If it pleases you, Evie.'

'It does! It does!'

'OK.' Andrew's gaze drifted past the group to a middle point in the distance. Then he waved at Sarah, who took it as a signal to rejoin them.

Eve was glowing. 'Let's set a date, then. Sarah, when do you think you and Dad will be sufficiently settled in?'

'Is there a pub anywhere?' asked Andrew. 'I could do with a drink.'

Sarah said, 'There are still things to be sorted.'

Behind Eve's back, Lara signalled to Sarah. *Say nothing.*

'But easily sorted?' Eve's breath puffed into the air. Little clouds of excitement.

Sarah looked at Lara. 'I think so.' She gave a cat-with-the-cream smile, and placed a chatelaine's hand under Lara's elbow. 'We can decide details later.'

* * *

Having chosen the incline on which to position it, Robert Adam's disciple had unleashed his master's taste for Palladian classical proportion but had deployed it to build a house on a human scale. The sort of house, Lara thought, which had nooks and crannies and places where the sun poured in through the windows.

Sarah glanced at her watch. 'Bill should be here any minute.' Eager to show off her new domain, she shepherded her caravan of the hopeful towards the house. 'Only a quick look.'

She was halfway up the steps when Lara called, 'Sarah, do you mind? I think I'll go back to the garden.'

Sarah swung round. The hand resting on the balustrade whitened.

'Sorry,' said Lara, and added silently, But I can't quite . . . you do understand? 'See you later.'

Once at a safe enough distance, she claimed a moment to steady herself. Breathe in the icy air. Her verdict on the house? Nice. *Stupid.* It was better than nice . . . much, much better. But it was Bill and Sarah's, not hers, to love . . .

Leaving a trail of frozen breath, she crossed the lawn, passing a copper beech whose branches swept grandly to the ground.

Unhappiness, fleeting or settled, is a condition of being alive, her sensible inner voice informed her. *Nothing to be done.*

Hands dug into her pockets, she turned a thoughtful 360 degrees. The garden was brittle—that was the word—and she understood how it felt. Everything was huddled in on itself, packed down under leaf mould, dry husks and stiffened earth.

There was one exception. In a frost pocket created by the wall, which ran from the house to the drive, a shrub poked its branches through a drift of ice. I don't care about the weather, it seemed to say. Balled yellow blooms were held aloft on naked branches, draping like twisted ribbons over its white ice-cradle. Drawing closer, she inhaled a light, delicate, joyous scent, which stopped her in her tracks.

Where next? By now she had reached a lawn that sloped down to the stream running through the bottom of the garden. Full-bellied with winter rain, it flowed sullenly past ice sheets as thin as gelatine leaves and over acid-green weed. The cold crept up through her feet, inching up her legs.

Nothing much moved: the frost held everything in its grip.

She couldn't, *mustn't*, love it here.

She sensed, rather than saw, Bill come up behind her.

'Not with the others?'

'As you see.'

'I spotted you as I came up the drive.' He added, 'You look lost.'

She stuffed her hands into her pockets. 'Sarah's very sweet and wants me to like the house. And I do.' Inside the pockets, her fingers balled into a fist. 'I do.' She paused. 'Sarah's very generous.'

'She is.' Bill squinted up to the terrace that ran along the house's southern aspect. Seeking Sarah out.

He moved along the bank. 'I'll show you round.'

She didn't like to mention that Sarah had already done so, but followed in his wake. He pointed up the bank to where it looped away and out of sight. 'That's the boundary.'

They reached a tiny landing stage by the stream, which, like the garden, was rotting and neglected. Once, children might have sat there and fished. She imagined the ripple of water, the flash of blue and silver scales, a child's excitement.

Bill placed an experimental foot on it.

'Careful.'

'Don't worry.' He pressed into the wood and little puffs of rot rose. 'It needs a lot of work.'

'I've got the message,' she said angrily.

'And what message would that be?'

'You need the money.'

He was the first to drop his gaze. 'Sorry. That was clumsy.' He piloted her away from the stream into a small paddock, scrubby and infested with thistles. 'I'm planning a vegetable garden near the house, and here, bees and massive compost heaps.'

With one ear she listened to him. Plans, schedules, cultivation techniques. 'There's so much to do, Lara.' This was an aspect of Bill she had not suspected. Despite the years they had been apart, the gap in her knowledge was hurtful.

The other ear listened to her own breathing . . .

soft, rapid breaths. And, then, the tap-tap sounds of the garden holding itself intact against the cold.

'I didn't know you had this side to you,' she admitted at last.

Bill stopped talking. 'No, you didn't.' He touched her arm with a finger. 'There were lots of things we didn't know about each other.'

'No,' he had said flatly, when she told him she wanted a second baby. 'Maudie is enough.'

It hadn't been easy having Maudie. The labour was long, Maudie the wrong way round (typical), and the delivery was nerve-shredding. None of that would have mattered—except that it had had an incalculable effect on Bill.

'I couldn't bear it,' he had said, when he visited her the following day, 'if what happened to Mary happened to you too.' He didn't add, *And it nearly did*. He didn't have to. 'I couldn't bear it, Lara.'

Battered and bruised, she had lain in bed looking up at him with a drip in her arm, sucking in the blood like a vampire, so eager was she to be up and to show how perfectly all right she was.

Lara remembered now when she had changed from being a trusting girl into something else. The exact moment. She had been in the supermarket, helping herself to a bag of potatoes—English Whites, the best for roasting. A light clicked on in her head. Blood mounted into her cheeks and her knees forgot their load-bearing duty. At one moment, she was a mass of uncertainty, at the next, fully resolved.

Now the wind whipped strands of her hair against her lips. 'We never sorted it, did we?'

'No. We didn't.'

'Bill, when Louis was born . . .' He held up a

hand as warning. *Don't.*

After Louis was born, Bill had held him until they had taken him away.

'Bill ... we always meant to do something in memory of Louis. *Something.* I rather like the idea of a seat in a park so people can sit on it in the sun ...'

'I can't talk about it, Lara. OK?'

'Even now?'

'Even now.'

Why, oh, why had she said anything? Why stir up the memories of how drained and dead, barely alive, she had been at that time? Bill too ... with his burdens of sorrow and fear. She knew then, as she knew now, that nothing else would ever be so cataclysmic. It was some knowledge to have on board before you were thirty, and its repercussions ran wide and deep.

She anchored her hair back with both hands and pushed the conversation on to the practical, the normal, the non-threatening. 'You'll be occupied with the house. It'll give you plenty to do. I'm glad you'll be busy.'

That amused him. 'I'd hoped to be slowing down.'

'No, you didn't.'

'You mean *you* wouldn't.'

'That's it,' she countered. The idea made her flinch. 'Think of the days when you were forced to stop work at sixty.' Her feet had made matching dark prints on the icy grass, companionable and humdrum. 'Nor should you. Anyway, Maudie and Jasmine have a way to go before they're settled. And there's the wedding.'

A rusting lawn roller had been abandoned by

the paddock gate, and Bill used it as a convenient mud scraper. 'You shouldn't take so much on your shoulders. The girls will cope.' He looked up towards the lawn where a figure was hurrying towards them. 'Sarah's coming.'

'I hope you'll be happy.'

'I think we will.' The roller emitted a thud as he banged his foot against it. 'I hope we've got it right this time.'

That hurt. She wanted to grab him and say, *We could have got it right*, but she wasn't quick enough.

'Hi,' said Sarah, out of breath. She glanced from Bill to Lara. In her haste, her coat had flapped open and mud speckled her skirt. 'I was expecting you inside, Bill. We were all expecting you. Eve is beside herself.'

'Darling,' he slipped an arm around her, 'sorry to keep you waiting. As usual, I took a detour.'

'Good thing I know you, then.' She was affectionate, possessive, in control.

'Through and through, sweetheart.'

He meant Lara never had.

Chapter Four

Recently the doctors' practice had expanded, which was not surprising as it served an area of high-density population. Two new full-time GPs had been taken on, which meant Lara had had to move out of the consulting room she job-shared with her fellow therapist, Robin Brett. Space was now at a premium and, eventually, they carved a new office out of a utility room that had been used to store lavatory paper and cleaning equipment. They furnished it with a couple of tables, plastic chairs and cheap carpet tiles.

The new domain was good. Old broom cupboard it might have been, but its latest incarnation as a consulting room represented years of her patient study and consolidation.

Lara got out the files for her morning clients and read through the first two sets of case notes.

Help me . . . heal me . . .

This was the cry of much of humanity, the seam of need that ran through the everyday.

'I'm training to be a counsellor,' Lara informed Bill, when Maudie was eight and he, she and the children had had time to adapt to their haphazard life. 'With special emphasis on . . .'

'On?'

'Bereavement.'

He had been astonished. Things were bad then. Rock bottom, in fact. Looking back, they were struggling to learn a new language and neither of them had mastered the vocabulary. Often they had got it wrong. The linguistic gap was evident when Bill had pointed out that Maudie was only eight and needed *looking after*.

She had exploded, 'She needs a father.'

'She's got one, Lara.' He had whirled around, faster than she had ever seen him move before. 'Don't you ever forget it.'

After qualifying, she had been fortunate to find a GP practice with an enlightened view on therapeutic services. She worked three days a week for them and another full day at a private clinic, which gave her a day's leeway to study and catch up. In theory, this left the evenings and weekends free to concentrate on the children. In practice, it took time to build up her list of clients, of whom a sizeable majority wanted to see her early in the morning or in the evening. The irony did not escape her either that, having been sad and blighted for so long, she was earning a living from other people's misery.

A stream of people washed in and out of her consulting room. *I hate myself/my partner/my children. My life has no meaning. I'm frightened.* There were some to whom life had been unbearably cruel. Others had painted themselves into psychological corners and, unwilling to take the first step out of them, thrived on being miserable and self-conscious. Then there were the plain bloody-minded—who frequently included teenagers. Each contributed a piece to the mosaic. Each provided a strange kind of antidote to her own predicament . . .

'Is it justifiable,' she asked her professional mentor, at one of their regular meetings, 'to use others for oneself . . . if only in a small way?'

'Physician heal thyself,' was the response.

If she had ever been tempted to write a blog, it would have been entitled: 'The Divorcee's Guide to Cheeseparing: how to keep sane with three children, a job with anti-social hours and an income that depends on the misery of others'.

As her practice grew, communicating with Bill became easier. Perhaps, in listening to others, she learned the missing vocabulary.

It had not always been so.

Flashback.

They talk more in court than outside it. Must improve, she thinks.

'My ex-husband is tucked up down the road,' this was the modern divorce, she plans to say in the blog she never writes, *'with Violet, his new partner. We have regular contact.'*

Each week, Lara asked him, 'What time do you want to pick them up?'

Each week Bill replied, 'Five thirty,' or 'After work.'

Had Shrinking V. still been around when Lara began work?

Chronology did a melting trick whenever she thought about that period of pain and readjustment and it was impossible to be precise about dates and events. It was the other stuff—the loss, the anger and a persistent sense that she was off-balance—that remained pin sharp. All that—loss of confidence, a fear she would go under, her terror of never being whole—plus the death of a childish faith, which had persisted for so long, that life always worked out for the best.

'Consider it this way,' said her professional mentor. 'You can face your patients knowing you are as exposed as they are. You can't tell them anything about yourself, but you will know their journey.'

Robin knocked and put his head around the door.

She smiled.

Case Notes
Brett (Lt Col.), Robin. 51. Retired. Technical Officer (TO) Royal Logistic Corp. Served: Northern Ireland, Yugoslavia, Kosovo, Iraq. Survived (just). Left arm rendered inoperable after IED exploded too close. Since leaving army,

lived in Syria, published well-received memoir. Three languages, including fluent Arabic. Now qualified counsellor, working primarily with teenage boys.

Robin and she had joined the practice at roughly the same time, and divided the job between them. (Naturally they had different mentors to supervise their progress as counsellors.)

'I promise not to tread on your toes,' he had said at their first meeting. 'First rule of operations.'

She laughed. 'So that's how it works.'

'Conflict is the way of the world. I try to avoid it.'

'Why did you choose to do this?' She gestured at the consulting room.

'I didn't. It chose me.' He levelled at Lara the look—grave with the hint of a smile—she had come to know well and distrust, for it gave nothing away. 'The same reason as you, I imagine.'

'Survival,' she replied, thinking: *Jasmine, Eve, Maudie.*

'Exactly. Having risked it many times, I value my life. Please can we make other people value theirs?'

They had talked over the areas they would cover between them. He had filled in Lara with some detail about himself but no more than was necessary: divorced, childless, etc. *I am*, he informed her, by censoring the detail, *a closed book.*

Robin was perfect with the boys, those restless, under-parented, disengaged, sometimes violent boys for whom life was a trudge, a blank, a disappointment. Lara had listened in on a couple of his sessions, during which quietness fell over even the most antagonistic and twitchy patient.

Over coffee, she also listened to his Tales From

the Frontline. Sometimes she pictured him and his men spread out across the ochre desert. There, they followed him over difficult terrain, positioning their boots in his footsteps, pleased to be able to place their faith in someone. At the same time, they knew that that faith would not protect them. But it was better than nothing.

He shut the door because Daniella was known to eavesdrop. 'I've had a journalist on the phone wanting to do a feature about our kind of work.'

She envisaged the article, complete with headline. 'No,' she said. 'Not.'

'I've told him to stuff it.'

'Politely?'

'Ish.'

'Fascinated to know what your "ish" is like.'

'It's a mystery, Lara. Let's say he got the message.'

Publicity was never worth it. Any publicity. It ripped up the privacy that was so essential to the relationships.

'Thank you.'

'Don't mention it.'

Sometimes, when they were talking, Robin looked at her in a certain way. It made her feel a little breathless, light-headed. ('Inconvenient and inappropriate', to quote the rule book. Never, ever sleep with your colleagues.)

'By the way, are you happy with the workload?'

He cradled his bad arm, then eased it back into a normal position. *Blackened flesh. Splintered bones.* 'Sure. But I can always take more on.'

'It's possible I might have to expand. Various reasons.'

He was quick. '*Have* to expand rather than *want*

to expand?'

'Some negotiations with my ex-husband. He's getting married again, and it looks as though I might have to make up a financial shortfall.'

'You could do,' he said. 'On the other hand, you don't have to be bullied either.' Again a quick rub of the arm—a dusting-off gesture. 'There's a danger that the most significant relationship in one's life turns out to be with one's ex, whether happy or unhappy. Unlike the marriage, they're there for life.'

'There's always a connection,' she said.

'You mean the memory of a connection.'

Point taken.

He looked at her. She looked at him.

*   *   *

Their respective lawyers had got together and the upshot was that Bill's solicitor phoned Lara early the following Tuesday morning. 'I'm told this is the best time to get hold of you.'

'And?'

'Mrs Russell,' he barely concealed his impatience, 'I don't suppose either side wants to prolong negotiations.'

The implication behind the smooth inflection was that she was tricky, and she wasn't having it. 'We've been through that stage,' she replied calmly. 'After I was left.'

The rebound took a couple of seconds. 'My client has honoured his side of the divorce agreement to the letter.' True. 'He now wishes to renegotiate the schedule. He will, of course, provide for Maudie as agreed until she leaves university. It's the other payments.'

He continued for some time in this vein, pointing out how punctilious her ex-husband had been and arguing that the proposed amendments to the settlement were fair. His smoothness irked her. Not good. Peering down the tunnel of the past, as she had done so many wearisome times, she couldn't resist challenging him: 'If it's a choice between keeping up mortgage payments and behaving well, guess what ranks lowest on the list?'

He had heard it before, but he didn't like it.

Once, before the divorce was done and dusted, she had spotted Violet and Bill emerging from a restaurant. Violet was in a pair of coupe cigarette trousers, as skinny as malinky, he in his best grey flannel suit. They looked so unencumbered, so pleased with life, so *at liberty*. It was cold and they were busy fastening their coats, adjusting bags and briefcases, neither of them having to think about buggies or bottles or keeping a child warm.

And she went home, where the noise of children hit the ears, the needs of children tugged the heart. Three small heads clustered around her, drawing her deep into the conspiracy of their love.

Would she have had it different?

Bill's solicitor was persistent: 'May I remind you that when the original agreement was drawn up you were not earning. I am informed that you have been doing so for some years now.'

Impossible to refute. 'I would have to renegotiate my mortgage. Failing that, I will have to make plans to expand my practice.'

He did not say, *But that is what most people do.* His silence said it.

Cue sleepless nights and several evenings in the consulting room spent configuring and reconfiguring the numbers.

Daniella spotted something was up and took to skewering Lara with her pale blue gaze. After a week of this, she slid into Lara's room with a cup of tea. 'Lara, you know if anything is ever wrong, I'm here for you.' She was always anxious to keep the practice humming and in shape. It was her job and job anxiety was a condition of the new era. She set the tea down carefully in front of Lara and steered a Bourbon biscuit into the saucer as bait. 'Girls all right?'

The biscuit was touching—she must have gone out specially to buy it. Clever Daniella. She was reminding Lara that everyone had to pull their weight. 'Ex-husband—you know how it is,' replied Lara, and felt guilty when Daniella gave her hand a pat in womanly sympathy and, satisfied, retreated.

Teacup in hand, Lara wandered over to Robin's desk. There was an assortment of books, papers and a festering coffee mug on the shelf above it. On the desk there were pens, papers, a bottle of a vicious-looking liquid bearing the label 'Baghdad Bolly', a striped lanyard, a snowstorm paperweight of New York at Christmas and a postcard of the Krak des Chevaliers castle in Syria.

She picked up the postcard. Krak des Chevaliers was one of the most ambitious Crusader castles ever built. Sand and isolation surrounded it, the hot wind played over it, faith and territorial ambition had built and now maintained it. Blood watered it. But the intriguing point about the impregnable

Krak des Chevaliers was that it had only fallen to the enemy by a ruse.

She imagined Sarah saying, *Lara hates to be dependent. She'll welcome the chance to be free of you, darling.*

Sarah was correct.

But Lara needs it. (Bill might have attempted to make a stand.)

Is it morally right that she still gets your money?

She scolded herself. Sarah was *not* like that.

Their—*his*—daughter still needed a home. So did she. The house suited them, had suited them all. The dimensions, which didn't quite square, the cracked slates on the roof (which must be replaced), the unsmart kitchen and the shabby stair runner . . . The house kept their history and safeguarded it.

The previous night she had cried in her sleep and woken with wet eyes.

She wanted Eve to embark on her new life in a good and positive way, with the wedding she wished for, without tensions, without the burden of her and Bill's history. This would be her way of telling Eve: I believe in this for you.

She replaced the postcard, picked out a book on Middle Eastern history from Robin's shelf and opened it. 'In robes of brilliant silk, superbly crafted armour, and their weapons inlaid with gold, the Mameluke Army who waited to fight the Ottomans in 1516 were the ultimate warriors . . .' she read.

Suddenly she was there on the battlefield, far from the room that smelt faintly of cleaning fluid, waiting in the sunlight to move forward on the word.

Other worlds.

On an impulse, she scribbled a note, 'Were they the ultimate warriors?' inserted it into the place in the book and left it on his desk.

'Another cup?' asked Daniella, rematerializing at the door.

Startled, Lara stared at her—plump, pale and bossy. Her mind cleared. It was obvious: she must extend her mortgage and expand her practice.

*　　*　　*

Supper, glass of wine, a large slice of peace and something mindless to watch on TV, in that order. Upstairs in her bedroom, Lara conducted a long phone call about a distressing case, then surged downstairs and into the kitchen where she caught Maudie in the act of shrugging on her jacket.

'Hi, Mum.' She slammed down the lid of her laptop and shoved it into her bag.

'Maudie, we agreed not Sunday evenings. You have to catch the early train to Winchester tomorrow.'

'*You* agreed.' Maudie zipped up the jacket. Below it her matchstick legs in black leggings stretched for a mile. 'It's my life.'

'Shall we talk about this?'

'No,' said Maudie, adding, 'Spare me the counselling.'

The on-duty mother. *Discuss.* 'Maudie, I've just been trying to rescue a child who has none of your options.'

'So?'

'Worth pondering?'

Maudie flicked at a pile of books. Clearly, their unresponsiveness annoyed her and she gave them

59

a determined shove. The stack smacked on to the floor. Not that it made much difference to the state of the kitchen, but the last few days had been harassing and Lara had had enough. 'Pick them up.'

Maudie's stubborn, troubled face and over-blackened eyelashes assailed Lara as she went about the task of retrieval.

'If you wish to break the agreement, that's fine. But you say you want to go to university more than anything else. To do this, you need to study and you need to rest.'

'I do. I do.' She whipped her rangy figure upright. 'But it's difficult. The others think it's stupid. There *are* other things, Mum.' Her mouth tightened.

Sensing confusion, Lara bit her tongue.

'Exams, exams, exams . . . I don't want to do them.'

This was an astonishing *volte face* for, up to that moment, Maudie had been fixed in her determination to dominate and triumph over the system.

Lara snapped on the kettle. 'OK. Mother-daughter summit.' She folded her arms across her stomach. 'I'm listening.'

Maudie folded herself on to the bench that served as seating for the table. Taking after Bill, she was the tallest of the daughters and practically filled the tiny kitchen. The stubborn, troubled expression cleared as she confessed, 'OK. I don't mean that about the exams. That's all fine. It's just I'm in a bit of a state.'

'Tell.'

Frisson of maternal anxiety. Maudie may have been heading for nineteen and inclined to moods but a gin-trap mind propelled her Nordic blonde five-foot-eleven frame. (Where had she sprung from? The goddess Freya or, failing that, Brünnhilde.)

'I've done something,' she said.

Lara steeled herself. Drugs? Pregnancy? Cheating?

'Alicia . . .'

Case Notes
Alicia Runyon, 26, Tutor in English (with special reference to Feminist Studies) at the Winchester Sixth Form College. Winner of Kathleen Snape Award for the best essay on feminism in literature. To quote: 'a work of the highest intellectual standard combined with the scholarly ideals'. On a couple of years' secondment from her native US . . . etc.

Lara waited.

Maudie's eyes reflected the colours of a deep and stormy fjord. 'Alicia says . . . I mean, Alicia is keen . . .' She leaped up from the bench.

Lara folded her arms and leaned back against the cooker.

Maudie took two paces to the right. Two paces to the left. 'OK,' she said. 'I've applied to Harvard.'

'*What?*' Lara reprised the last few weekends. Maudie's closed-down expression, plus the irritation (plenty of that). There had also been the quick-to-anger Maudie and the quick-to-despair Maudie. 'When did you decide this?'

Maudie shrugged.

'And without telling me. Or anyone?'

Maudie was flapping her wings. Hard.

'Yup.' She had calmed down. 'Alicia's explained everything. I take their, I mean the US, SAT exam and apply for funds. If successful, I go next year.' She stacked the last book on the pile. The confession appeared to have brought a new resolve. 'It's sorted, Mum.'

Lara said, 'What do *you* know about funding?'

Quick as a flash, Maudie said, 'If it was left to you and Dad, nothing.' She tugged at her hair. 'Why don't parents teach you useful things?'

'We had to have one flaw, surely.'

'No, but really,' she said.

'And you never thought to discuss it with me?'

'I discussed it with Alicia. We went over and over it. She told me about the financial things and she helped me with the forms. I've done spreadsheets. I'll have to work in the vacations. Of course. And live like a pauper—but, hey . . .'

Lara found herself tiptoeing through a maze. 'Spreadsheets? Oh, spreadsheets. Could I remind you a spreadsheet is not the real thing?'

'Stop it, Mum. You're not listening.'

Lara folded her arms more tightly. Snap, went the wire-cutter that Maudie was wielding. 'I'm your mother, Maudie. I had a right to know.'

'Of course,' agreed Maudie, in a kindly way, 'and I'm telling you now.'

Lara persisted, 'You should have told me earlier. I can see that Alicia is very useful, but she's not family.'

'Shall we just leave her out of it?'

'You brought her into it.' What was it she told her patients? Negotiate. Face up to the problem. 'Are you sure she's the right influence, Maudie? Should she be influencing you? Think about it.'

62

'Most friends do influence each other.'

'If she's that much older, it must be hard to contradict her.'

Maudie adopted the expression that meant she was trying, *she was really trying*, to be ultra-patient. 'Alicia and I understand each other very well, and it's not a question of who's older and who's junior. We're friends, that's all.' Leaning over, she dropped a kiss on Lara's cheek. 'Don't look so worried. I'm a big girl now.' She swung the strap of her bag on to her shoulder and picked up her phone. 'I must see to my own life. So . . .' Again, the kindly smile. 'I'm just going round to Tess for half an hour or so.'

'Why are you doing this, Maudie?'

Maudie had vanished.

The kitchen seemed empty. Cold. Maudie was going. Maudie was gone?

She rang Jasmine and told her of Maudie's plans. 'Jasmine, she's barely out of nappies.'

'Let me get this right. Maudie applied to Harvard and failed to mention it?'

'Yes.'

'Out of the mouths of babes and sucklings. Wait till I tell Eve.'

'I find it difficult to take in. It's awful, actually.'

'I sympathize. To have such a clever, determined daughter must be hell.'

That made her laugh.

Jasmine said, 'Did you know that Maudie means "battle maid"?'

'How on earth did you find that out?'

'I commissioned research on names. I store stuff like that in the office database. It's surprising how often it comes in useful.'

'And you and Eve?'

'Didn't have to research those. I'm a sickly-scented flower and Eve was the first woman.'

Again, Lara laughed.

Jasmine became serious. 'Maudie has to go, Mum. She was laying the ground when she decided to go to sixth-form college and leave Brightwells.'

'I can't help wishing to stave off the day.'

'I see. It's "Make me chaste, O Lord, but not yet."'

Afterwards the phone rang and rang in the silent kitchen. For once, Lara did not pick it up for she knew it was likely to be Jane Hatfielde, a private client who had taken to ringing in the early mornings and evenings. 'There are people who are quiet,' she had explained to a much younger Maudie when she began her work, 'but there are people who are noisy, and if they happen to be paying, they make themselves felt. It's what happens.'

Young as she was, Maudie had an innate sense of natural justice. 'But it shouldn't be the fussers who get all the attention.'

'That's how it is.'

'I'd fight them,' she said. 'But why do you have to work, Mum?'

'I have to earn money because we have to look after ourselves. When you're older, we'll think about your future. I don't want you to do—'

'Do what, Mum?'

'Do what I did.'

Flashback.

Kneeling down in front of the chest, she opens the bottom drawer. Inside, wrapped in tissue paper, is the white crocheted shawl. The paper is becoming brittle, but the wool is still pliant and downy as she ruffles it between her fingers. She remembers how transparent she had felt as she had stowed it away, so paper thin with grief that people might look through her. She remembers, too, how she wept and trembled, and how her mind refused to accept that Louis no longer existed. She remembers Bill saying, 'I will never forgive you,' and waking one night to find he was no longer in the bed with her. She remembers going into Maudie's room—still a baby, the only baby—and holding her.

Sitting down at the table, Lara dropped her head into her hands.

Maudie was cutting the umbilical cord.

This was how it felt to disengage.

Goodbye to supervising every breath a child took.

Goodbye to piecing together childish tales. The pick 'n' mix of woe and joy.

Goodbye to sticking plasters on grazed knees, fingers and toes.

Don't be stupid, she thought. All that had ceased some time ago.

It didn't seem like that. And the feelings of loss were as sharp as they had ever been.

Into her mind stole an image of the shrub in the garden at Membury that had had flowers like tumbling ribbons. She had looked it up. Witch hazel, *Hamamelis mollis*. A plant hunter's trophy smuggled back from China in the 1870s. Twigs had been packed, no doubt, in earth and dampened canvas and cherished on the voyage home. Or set in glass planters (to shield them from the salt) and tended on the long, rolling sea passage. It was known as the Epiphany Tree because it was supposed to be at its very best at the time when the Magi had found the Christ child—the one at

Membury had bloomed early—its yellow flowers symbolizing the gold they had brought, its scent (nature's way of attracting the few pollinators around at this time of year) the frankincense, and its bitter bark the myrrh (which belonged to death).

Her hands tightened over her head.

Chapter Five

The name on the phone fascia read 'Saunderson' and her pulse quickened with annoyance. She flicked it on. 'Jasmine here.'

The voice at the other end—loud, male and angry—blared into her ear. Rowan Saunderson was livid about the piece in the evening paper. 'How dare it suggest there's no difference between Vegetalès' new logo and, to quote, "any other common-or-garden one"?' He ran out of breath and was forced to a halt. 'The reason we hired the Branding Company was precisely to avoid this sort of situation. So get out there, earn your vast fee and sort it out.'

It was past nine o'clock. Jasmine was still in the office. Her head ached, her stomach rumbled. She anticipated a shower, the moment of stepping into it and the exquisite sensation of hot water pounding at her neck and shoulders.

But here was the thing. This situation was nothing new. Discomfort was axiomatic to her working life, and a daily discipline. Everyone she knew, and rated, endured the same. Rowan talked and talked, and she flicked up the Vegetalès account, rechecked the huge amount of money they owed the Branding Company and encouraged him to let it all out.

After a few more minutes of heavy-duty abuse, she realized she would have to deploy treachery. Not something she enjoyed. She cast her eye over the adjacent office. David, her assistant, had gone home and could not, therefore, be witness to his own crucifixion.

'As it was so early in the game, we allowed my assistant to brief the journalist. She assured him she was on side. Obviously, she changed her mind.' She gave Rowan a moment to absorb this. 'It does happen. But once we get going, and the creative team are still working on it, there will be dozens of favourable articles.'

'Pay a journalist to bad-mouth the opposition.'

'No.'

'Oh, for God's sake. Don't tell me it doesn't happen all the time.'

'It doesn't work, Rowan.'

'Take that idiot off my account, then. Results, Jasmine, results.'

As if she didn't know. 'Bad feedback is part of the story. We discussed it, if you remember. The creative team are working night and day on the package.'

That set him off again.

He really was very old-fashioned. 'Jasmine, are you listening?'

'Absolutely, Rowan.'

But she wasn't.

Over the years, she had developed skills. Top of the list was manipulating cranky men, 'The ones who are congenitally bad-tempered and demanding, plus the ones born with an assumption that the world is arranged to suit them,' she explained to Duncan, when he was wooing her.

'And women aren't like that?'

'Can't tell. Not enough of them around in top positions.'

'You are.'

She smiled at him over the table in the *luxe* restaurant to which he had taken her. 'It's a mystery how these people get up in the morning.'

He smiled, revealing beautiful teeth. 'I'll tell you how,' he said, 'when we're alone.'

Clever Jasmine, Duncan often said—because he was generous with praise and proud of her achievements. He had, like her, a quicksilver understanding of what it took to rise from a modest background into a pole position (in his case) at the bank. From time to time, they discussed meritocracy and questioned if they had benefited from it. Jasmine was inclined to a romantic view of how society helped those who wanted to make their way. Duncan was sceptical: 'It's probably every man and woman for themselves.'

She pulled her thoughts back into line. 'Rowan, please listen to me. It's important that no one suspects you're rattled. It's not good for the image. I'll phone the team later and see if we can do some damage limitation.'

On she talked, finessing Rowan Saunderson into acceptance, until he went away, leaving her with merciful silence and the slight hiss of her conscience over David. Quite soon, that subsided too.

She got up and went over to the film-editing unit, extracted a CD from the safe (nothing was kept on easily hackable computers) and snapped it into the machine. The image of Vegetalès' latest moisturizer, packed in eco-green and gold, accosted her on her screen, and beside it the flawless face of a top model. In the bottom left-hand corner, deftly tucked into the line of peripheral vision, was the logo. The ad moved on, executing a progression of shape-shifting illusions, all promising beauty that—the underlying message ran—could only be relished alongside social responsibility. 'Enhance your world,' invited the strapline.

Question: how could they persuade women to take Vegetalès' skin-care products to their hearts?

The obvious answer: by telling them to buy products that made them better-looking, and cared for the environment.

She knew, the team knew, everyone knew that creating demand did not work in a straightforward manner.

She had written the paper for a trade magazine.

Women buy into the illusion *with their eyes open*. They know that Model X or Y does not look like her image and, if she did, it would almost certainly not be due to the products. However, offer female focus groups the chance for a product to be sold them in a more honest manner, they decline it roundly. If they are asked whether being sold products by the thin and beautiful makes them feel miserable and inadequate, they agree, but not to a change in approach. The conclusion has to be that women do not wish to be reminded of the realities of the female face and body.

The ad ended and she saw her own reflection

in the computer screen. *Pale, raven-haired avatar.* She loved the images summoned by those words, envisaging herself floating through star-studded space . . .

Back at her desk, she speed-dialled. 'David, sorry about this but you're off Vegetalès. Don't ask.'

'You dropped me in it?' He wasn't pleased but, since she was his boss, he moderated his response.

'I did.'

'You owe me.'

'I do. Claim it one day.'

It was late but she spent a further fifteen minutes or so constructing the 'to-do' list. On inspection, it appeared sparse and she cast around to add to it. 'Ring *FT* and enquire who on diary, etc.' Irrational, she knew, and indicating anxiety, but this type of housekeeping steadied her.

Shut down computer. Wipe desk top with the cloth she kept in the drawer. Check cupboards shut. Adjust window blind. All ninety or so staff of the Branding Company had left.

Silence.

No one was talking to her. This was the moment when her chest loosened, and the tension that was frequently her companion through the day said, 'So long, see you tomorrow.'

So quiet she could hear her breath.

Office solitude was peerless. It made her feel lonely, deeply so, but it was soothing. She had earned it. My God, she had.

After a while, she pushed back the chair (Aeron, top of the range) and reached for her bag (a Birkin, donated by a client but accepted after the account was terminated. As if that made it better!) Catching up her jacket, she turned off the lights.

Duncan's flat was by the canal, a new-build shimmering with chrome, glass and boldness. A child-free destination dwelling for people with no ties, the childless affluent could perch here for a while, then move on. Yet all was not entirely well in this glossy and fashionable Eden: the fountains in the central square never functioned properly, the plants died, the bolder flourishes of the architecture often leaked or fell apart, and arguments raged between landlord, management company and occupiers.

She let herself into his flat. 'Hi.'

'Hi.' His voice was just audible over the rugby match on the television.

Duncan was in his usual unassuming armchair from his family home. He was surprisingly attached to it for (he maintained) his taste was modernist and untraditional. 'You can't take the suburbs out of the man,' she teased him—for he had grown up in one of the ugly, sprawling overspills of Greater London.

He had not bothered to change, and was still in his suit with the waistcoat unbuttoned and the jacket flung to one side. His sleek, dark otter head rested against the back of the chair. She squinted at him. More than one beer in, she guessed.

She dropped a kiss on the top of his head. He reached up and caught her hand. One, two ... She took a few seconds to assess whether he would pay her further attention or not. No. This was a match night. 'Food?' she asked.

He gestured to the kitchen. 'Picked something up from Castello's.'

Duncan's kitchen had been fully and lovingly stocked. Since he rarely cooked, and seldom ventured into it anyway, she found his delight in pots and pans rather touching, if mystifying. 'All hat and no cattle,' she had teased, when he had first brought her to the flat. Then she had surveyed (with astonishment) the stainless-steel cooker and full *batterie de cuisine*. He hadn't appreciated the tease (Duncan could take himself a little too seriously) and she had not been invited over again for some time. Even now when they spent the nights together it was, more often than not, at her flat.

'Why haven't you moved in with him?' asked her friends and Eve. This was touchy. She didn't want to say, 'We haven't discussed it,' because the next question would inevitably be 'Don't you want to?'

The fridge contained a lasagne, Dijon chicken, a bag of salad, a bottle of vodka, the disgusting remains of some blue cheese, half a tube of tomato paste and a large bottle of Gaviscon for his stomach. Which meal would take less time to cook? She consulted the instructions on the cartons of (supposedly) homemade food. Was there a disconnect here? Could it qualify as homemade if the person who had made it had no idea about the one who ate it?

She made her decision.

Forty-five minutes later, she set the Dijon chicken in front of Duncan. He perched on the bar stool and ate heartily. 'Good day?'

'One or two glitches.' She outlined the Rowan Saunderson conversation and, since she was a natural mimic, captured his tone, which made Duncan laugh.

Actually, the conversation she would have liked to hold was a different one.

Jane rang up today. She's four months pregnant.
Great.
Duncan . . . don't you think?

The chicken was tangy and creamy, which diverted her. Duncan poured more wine. 'I've got a big deal coming up in the spring. Twenty-four-hour shifts, I imagine. Awful.'

'You love it. You're the original adrenalin junkie.'

He grinned, but didn't deny it. They talked about the things that interested them. Work. Deals. A little bit of politics. That was what she liked in particular about their relationship. He never bored her.

She said. 'You won't miss the engagement party, will you?'

'Lordy, Miz Scarlett, I don't think I can stand another word about this wedding.' He raised his eyebrows quizzically. 'What's going to happen when it's over? What *will* we talk about?'

Tricky men. Tactic Number Forty-two. Jasmine looked out of the window on to the fountains that didn't work. 'On second thoughts, it might be easier if you don't come. Then I won't have to worry about you.'

'As if.'

As if. Duncan was one of Andrew's closest friends.

He finished his plateful and pushed it away. 'Apart from anything else, you want me there to make a point.'

She wasn't going to make it easy for him. 'A point?'

'The wedding point.'

'Oh, the wedding point. Why would I do that?

I know your view.' It ran along the lines: what difference does a piece of paper make?

'I stick by it.'

'Then the engagement party can't be a high priority. Even for Andrew's sake.'

His mouth twitched. 'Wrong. Affection and friendship have a higher priority than principle.' Her feelings must have registered, for he reached across and took her hand. 'Shall we stop?' She returned the pressure on her fingers, and he frowned. 'Andrew tells me the whole thing is hell.'

'Does he?'

'He reckons Eve's only doing it the way she is to please Lara. She wants the big shindig.'

'Then Andrew doesn't know Eve. Lara has nothing to do with it.'

'I think she has plenty to do with it.'

Along with the chicken, the sleepy atmosphere had vanished. The protective shield was raised—as it always was at the least hint of criticism of Lara. 'Lara has been very careful not to let on what she thinks or wants. She's good like that.'

'For someone so clever—' He stopped and started again. 'None of you can see the influence she has on you. It's extraordinary.'

Lara's face, with its anxious, maternal expression, flashed across Jasmine's mind, stirring up both tenderness and, if she was truthful, irritation. 'What can you see that we don't?'

He did not answer directly. '*Her* marriage wasn't much of a salvation. Shouldn't she be warning you not to make the same mistake?'

Trust Duncan.

'Your logic's muddled. It wasn't marriage that was at fault, but the relationship.'

'She over-mothers you.' Duncan smiled to take away the sting.

'Despite everything, my stepmother—our mother —held us together. That's *not* over-mothering.'

He grew serious. 'You girls always stick up for her.'

'Not always. We often hate her. She can be as irritating as you.'

'Child-speak for "We love her really."'

'Lara only wants what we want.' Jasmine got up, rinsed the plates, stacked them in the little-used dishwasher, then handed out a slice of melon.

'Don't be cross, Jas.'

Since she had her back to him she could hide her little smile. 'I'm not cross.'

'YES, YOU ARE. Cross Jas.'

They ate the melon in silence. Then she laughed and shoved a tea-towel at him. 'On your feet.'

That night, Duncan was both tender and a little rough. 'Isn't it enough?' he whispered into her ear.

'What?'

'This.'

Still later, he said. 'I love you, Jasmine.'

*   *   *

Lara had always pushed them, all three of them. 'You might meet someone, Jasmine/Evie/Maudie,' she tended to say, if an invitation was extended to one of them. 'Knowing people helps.'

'Helps with what?' Jasmine wanted to know.

'The job, influence, life ...' She made the annoying fluttery gesture with her hands—which was Lara's way of trying to hoodwink people into thinking she was less acute than she was. A totally unnecessary attempt at camouflage, both Jasmine and Eve agreed. It was as if Lara's generation was still in shock as to how successful their feminist achievements had been.

Would Lara be disappointed if she knew how little her maternal pushing and shoving had influenced Eve and herself (Jasmine couldn't vouch for Maudie)? What might cheer Lara was the reach of her subtler influence. The I-am-watching-over-you kind of love that *I will never give up on*. It had bathed them all, from head to foot, and sent them out into the world dressed in its garments.

When she was in the fifth form Jasmine had written an essay entitled 'The Maternal Instinct in Whales'. It was really about Lara.

With regard to the pilot whale, there is a marked bond between mother and offspring, and this is particularly observable when a calf dies. Researchers have encountered on several occasions a pilot whale carrying a dead calf. This is an emotional experience for everyone.

This is where the similarities between humans and the whale become so very apparent. For example, a pilot whale mother will never give up on her dead calf. She will carry the calf in her mouth or on her back for weeks at a time, refusing to give up. Female pilot whales never stop believing in their child's ability to pull through. They will push their dead calf to the surface for air in a desperate attempt to give them life.

During this time the pod around the mother and calf acts as a barrier to the outside world, and allows the mother to grieve. The male pilot whales will dive for food and the rest of the pod will form a strong group around the female and calf, supporting her in her grieving process every step of the way. The maternal instinct of a pilot whale and that of a human are almost identical.

The pod will offer support and sympathy to the female just as a human family might do. You can see in her eyes the pain and desperation she feels towards her dead calf as it slowly decomposes in front of her. She will fight to the last second to give her child life, pushing it to the surface for air until she realizes that there is no hope left . . .

Jasmine still had a copy of the essay. But she had never shown it to Lara.

No.

Early one Sunday evening, not long before Christmas, she and Duncan dropped in at the house. Lara was out and Maudie was squashed up at the kitchen table, surrounded by papers and the laptop. Jasmine assessed the posture. Slumped. Head in mittened hands.

'Oh dear,' said Duncan. 'You don't look happy.'

'Thought you'd be revising with Tess,' said Jasmine.

Maudie had, as yet, to let her sisters in on her Harvard plan, but Eve and Jasmine knew about it. Lara had informed them in the solemn voice she kept for secrets, and emphasized, 'Maudie doesn't want you to know about it yet.' Short, but pregnant, pause. 'She takes the SAT exam for Harvard entry soon after Christmas.'

Eve said, 'You shouldn't have told us, Mum. It's Maudie's secret.'

Lara stared hard at her. 'What does loyalty matter,' she flashed, 'when I need your help?'

Lara had already worked out a pretty stringent revision timetable for Maudie. Could they, she asked, help her to keep Maudie sane and operational?

Jasmine agreed that she could.

Maudie had been crying what appeared to be angry tears for she was also flushed and tight-lipped. She was dressed from top to toe in black, with black mittens and black boots, and green nails.

'What's with the Hecate outfit?' asked Jasmine.

'Go away.' Maudie stiffened. 'It's not funny.'

'No, it isn't. Sorry.' Jasmine positioned a kiss on Maudie's fair, tumbled head.

Duncan dropped down on to the bench (bought for next to nothing in the salvage yard). It had done sterling work as seating throughout the girls' childhood. 'Hey, tell.'

Maudie grabbed Duncan's hands and clung to them. 'I can't *do* this.' She virtually crumpled. 'It's all too much.'

'You mean the exams?'

Maudie nodded, and Duncan signalled, '*Help,*' to Jasmine. 'Maudie,' he said, 'if you panic, you'll be useless.'

Maudie snatched her hands back. 'Don't joke.'

'Look at me—*look* at me! Am I joking?' Again he turned to Jasmine. *Team work, please.*

She came to the rescue. 'Maudie, listen to me. Everyone panics from time to time. Duncan and I panic a lot. But it's something we've learned to manage. We have to. You have to.'

Maudie pulled the mittens further down over her hands. 'You don't understand.'

'I think I do.'

'No—you *don't* understand.'

Jasmine scavenged in the cupboard by the door. 'You need time off. Do you think Mum's got any wine?'

'Good idea,' said Duncan.

'She gets all funny when I have a drink.'

'Mum ain't here.'

Duncan examined the bottle Jasmine produced and got to his feet. 'Stay here, both of you. I'm going out to get something decent. This is rat poison.'

Typical Duncan. She felt the familiar soft helplessness. To be with him was to be enveloped in . . . not exactly goodness but in the certainty that he would never allow injustice and meanness to get in the way. And if that *was* goodness, it frequently made her laugh and feel better.

It was all the more perverse, therefore, that more than once in the dark reaches of the night, she had considered leaving him. In the dark, problems had a habit of twisting into quite different shapes. If you rated reason and rationality, which she did, then they suggested that it *was* best to leave someone whose opinions on the important things were so different from her own.

She hunkered down beside Maudie. 'Whatever you're feeling, we've probably experienced it too.'

Twisting the ends of her hair around her fingers, Maudie hooded the blue eyes. 'I've got to tell you something . . . difficult.'

The weeping? But until Maudie said something, she had to pretend ignorance of the Harvard plans. 'Drugs, Maudie? Pregnancy?'

Maudie sent her look of utter contempt. 'You sound like Mum.'

Do I? That was a little smack in the face.

'I always thought I wanted nothing more than to get to Oxford. Now . . .' Maudie shifted uneasily. 'Well . . .'

Jasmine peered at her. 'Yes. You can change your mind, Maudie. You know that? In fact, you should think new and bold. Don't let tradition box you in.'

'You really mean that?'

Her knees twinged. 'I do. It's important we think differently.'

'OK.' Pause. 'I've told Mum . . .' Maudie drew a resolute breath '. . . I'm going to try for Harvard.'

'An excellent idea.' Courtesy of Lara, Jasmine had had time to readjust the balance. Truth to tell, she had been surprised that her admiration for Maudie's ambitions had been tempered with a tiny bit of jealousy.

'You think so?' Maudie was touchingly pleased. 'Mum doesn't. She says she does but she doesn't.'

Jasmine opened her mouth to deliver the sisterly lecture about seizing the day, widening the horizons. Too late: Maudie's screen pinged. She lunged at the keyboard and tapped into it. Jasmine hoicked a foot on to the bench. 'Don't mind me.'

Simultaneously, Maudie's phone came to life and she flicked it on. 'Hey . . .'

It was Tess, of course, Maudie's better-than-any-sister friend. They were planning to go out. 'See you in ten,' she said.

'Off limits,' Jasmine reminded her. 'Sunday evening.'

'And who are you?' Maudie jumped up. '*Who* are you?'

Jasmine grinned. 'Just your sister.'

Later, in her flat—Duncan had gone back to his for an early night—ensconced in her narrow bedroom, Jasmine sat on her bed and contemplated the windowsill. It needed repainting, and there was a suspicious dark spot directly underneath it. Damp?

Should *she* go away too? Try something new? *Think differently?*

She thought of the pilot whale nosing her calf to the surface and her desperate attempts to convince herself that it lived.

No, she never could, or would, tell Lara about that image.

Yet it would not abandon her. In her sleep, she swam through green-blue astringent waters, cradling a baby to her chest. She knew it was dying and her sobs for help cascaded in bubbles to the surface.

In the morning the alarm woke her. Exhausted, she focused on the white wall. The room seemed to resemble a prison cell.

*   *   *

The run-up to Christmas was frantic and Jasmine was in the thick of it.

Two Mondays running, she flew to Frankfurt for the day to pitch for a bank's business. 'A big deal,' she told Duncan. 'A lot depends.'

It had gone well. The team had suggested to the bank's top people that their institution had been founded on the toil of the men and women who had worked in the forests and forges. This deep-root connection to the earth should not be forgotten. The logo and literature should subtly suggest the

81

connection, thereby emphasizing reliability and the best virtues. Yet if a successful rebranding was to be achieved, they must also encapsulate change and a bright, smart, adaptable future . . .

Branding speak.

The second time, snow had arrived, causing mayhem in the airports. Jasmine found herself overnighting in a hotel and having dinner with her chief executive, Jason, who fussed endlessly over the altered schedule. She texted Duncan about Jason and he replied, That's being sixty for you.

She rang to cancel her supper date with Eve, who sounded manic. 'A lot of work's come in,' she said. 'Just as I'd cleared the backlog. It's going to stack up for a couple of months at least.'

'I was hoping to get going on the wedding.'

'Evie, you got going on the wedding a hundred years ago.'

At her end of the phone, Eve hummed and hawed. 'You know me. Am I driving you crazy? I don't mean to, Jas.'

'Bridezilla,' she said fondly. 'How's Andrew?'

'OK.' Pause. 'Ish. He gets bored with all the arrangements. That's why I need you, Jas.'

Early the next morning, she flew back, went straight into the office and didn't get back to Duncan's flat until late in the evening. He was high on a long-running deal, which had finally slotted into place only that afternoon. Otherwise he would have been asleep.

It wasn't a good sign when Duncan couldn't sleep. There he was, all bright-eyed and hyper with adrenalin, plus a glass or two of the celebratory stuff. 'Nothing lost, though,' he said, when she narrated the story of the travel chaos.

They were lying together in bed. 'I missed my supper with Eve. She wanted to make some decisions and required my cool, wise judgement.'

'Cool, wise judgement? I don't think so.'

Her finger found the point where the skin stretched over his hip and pressed. He yelped.

There was silence, broken only by the occasional murmur.

Eventually, he said, 'Don't let Eve use you too much, Jas. You've got your own stuff to deal with.'

Jasmine raised herself on her elbow. Her hair brushed Duncan's shoulder. 'Meaning?'

'She's a bit needy over the wedding.' He wound a finger through her hair and tugged it.

'Of course she is. That's what weddings do.' She wished she hadn't said that. 'It's her big moment.'

'I never quite know what she's thinking. I know you do, but not many others do. She hides behind the efficiency and the smart exterior. But Andrew has years of wedded bliss to sort that out.'

She nearly said, so very nearly, *And us?*

He knew well enough what went on in her head, and she knew the furniture of his—and that was what she loved about them. Duncan pulled her down and kissed her. *He knew*. 'Love you.'

Her need to know, to resolve, welled like physical hunger.

'Duncan?'

'Don't start, Jas. Please.'

'OK.'

He was murmuring his usual lovely things and, languorous as a cat, she let them drift through her.

She closed her eyes. At times like this, her body burned with a sadness she could never put her finger on.

'Put your arms around me,' he asked. *'Please.'*

With a soft laugh, she obeyed. 'Idiot.'

Describe how she had first met him.

It had been at the IT conference. She was there to bone up on the latest technology and totally focused on her career. She was not looking for love. He was there for research prior to a merger. He had a girlfriend. He was epically busy. There he had been: sitting across the aisle, tapping into his phone. The cast of his head, the manner in which one leg was folded over the other, sent a dart into her stomach. She shivered, and the thought had winged into her head: This is the man I'm going to marry.

'Are you with me, Jas?' Duncan was growing sleepy. 'Talk to me.'

She shifted to free his trapped arm. 'I was remembering how Eve made me stop biting my nails when I was small.'

Duncan slid a hand into hers. 'I don't believe you.'

'Do I care? No. Anyway, I couldn't stop gnawing and my fingers often bled. One day Evie decided to do something. Every morning she coloured my fingers blue or red, with one of her pens.'

'What a pair you were.'

'Looking back, I can see we were unsettled by everything that was going on. Not that we knew precisely what it was. Children don't. We just sensed it.'

He kissed one of her fingers. 'So pretty now. Eve's tactics obviously worked. I must thank her.'

'Yes ... and no. The day my father left, Evie painted them yellow and I gave in to the temptation and bit them. We were having breakfast. Dad looked at me and swore. Mum cried. Maudie cried. Something had happened, and all Dad could say was "Go and wash your mouth." '

He was growing sleepier. 'What did go wrong between them?'

The whale nudging its baby to the surface.

'It was Louis.'

'You never told me what happened.'

'All I know is he was stillborn.'

'I can't imagine ...' His voice was careful, considerate.

Memories of childhood. *Loyalty* ... She and Eve, a band of two. Retreating into the cardboard houses and allowing no one else in. *Togetherness* ... They were bound together. *Secrets* ... A baby boy had died. Her father blamed her mother for something. Something that had broken them. She and Eve had never known what.

'It destroyed their marriage.'

She knew Duncan was thinking, Who needs marriage?

*   *   *

He woke with one of his stomachs. 'God, Jas,' he threw an arm across his middle, 'this one's bad.'

She knew it. Too many nerves expended on deals. Too much adrenalin. Too many nights working straight through. Too much coffee. The result was acute stomach pain, which only got better when he gave in and went to bed.

Would this bout be prolonged? Or a one-dayer?

He groaned.

She got out of bed, padded into the kitchen, made him some mint tea and spooned it into him.

Trial and error had revealed it was the best thing for temporary relief. The mug empty, she hoisted him upright, helped him into the bath and sponged him down with hot water.

Eyes shut, he slumped against the enamel. 'That's better,' he said.

Willing him to relax. Astonished, as always, that his beautiful body should be host to a weakness that, hard as he tried, he could not master ... The efforts he made to conceal it from his boss and colleagues ... Such an unglamorous thing to suffer from, he once confided to her. Yet she loved him the more for it—absurdly more.

While Duncan soaked, she changed the sheets and remade the bed. Then she picked up his phone and speed-dialled.

'Doreen. It's Jasmine. It's the usual, I'm afraid.'

Doreen clicked her tongue. 'There's the eleven-thirty meeting but I'll say...' She considered. 'I gave the stuck-in-airport reason last time. Don't worry, I'll think of something.'

'If you have to, admit he's ill.'

Doreen lowered her voice dramatically. 'Leave it with me.'

Female collusion. It was a strange society that did not allow its men or women to be ill in the workplace.

The phone dangled between her fingers. Once, she had let slip to Lara about these episodes and Lara had been amazed at the subterfuges she and Doreen cooked up. 'I thought it was only working mothers who had to do that sort of thing.'

She gathered up the discarded sheets and rolled them into a ball. Living with Duncan? She would iron them into crisp slabs and stow them in a cupboard with lavender bags. They would sleep together on them and dream lavender-scented dreams. How about buying petunias to plant in a window-box and, in due course, deadheading the ones that had faded to encourage more blooms? She imagined spats with him over his refusal to hang up his clothes and him berating her for having so many bottles in the bathroom.

Traditional dreams.

Duncan crept back into the room and slid into bed. Jasmine rearranged the pillows and tucked him up. He looked up at her. 'Jas?'

'Don't talk. Everything's under control. Doreen's doing her stuff. Just concentrate on getting better.'

He closed his eyes.

She moved around, quietly restoring order. Trousers into the cupboard, sweater into a drawer, socks out of sight in the laundry basket. It was amazing how the smallest adjustments could change the aspect of a room.

It was at these times that she was at her most powerful.

Helping the person you loved was a good thing. It was one of the finer things of which human beings were capable. 'Isn't that how you feel about Andrew?' she had asked Eve.

After a moment, Eve had replied, 'I suppose so.' Sensing this was not quite the response Jasmine had expected, Eve had added hastily, 'Yes, yes, it is.'

Duncan opened his eyes. He was trying to negotiate past his discomfort to tell her something. 'I forgot to say, Jas . . .'

'What?'

'Andrew's asked me to be best man.'

Chapter Six

Wedding Plans: Set date . . .

It had turned into a family joke. These days, Eve's emails were only about one subject. It summoned Jasmine to the reconvened wedding meeting with Maudie and their mother. Supper was on offer.

Lara had just returned from the station where she had gone to pick up Maudie. 'Ungrateful girl, she tells me no other mother bothers.'

'Well, don't, then. Maudie's got a pair of feet.'

'But,' said her mother, 'I *like* to bother whenever I can.'

'As if you don't have enough to do.'

Lara seemed pleased by Jasmine's concern. 'It pays off, Jassy. Sometimes Maudie doesn't say a word, and we toil back in silence. But when she does, I find out something—such as the upcoming college prom, which was complete news to me.'

Jasmine looked at Lara. 'Do you ever give up?'

Dropping the knife she was using to chop carrots, her mother put her arms around her. A warm, scented hug.

'*Of course* I never give up.' Lara returned to the carrots. 'About this prom in the summer. They want limos and all that kind of stuff. Can you believe? Vicky says she's going to stand by the entrance to the racecourse to talk Tess and Maudie's limo in like a war correspondent. Apparently the entrance they make is crucial. It has to be timed right.' She flapped her hands. 'That's only the start of it.' She reeled off a list—dresses, cars, hair, spray tans . . .

In the middle Eve walked in, lined up carrier bags on the kitchen table and kissed them both. 'Sis.' She laid a hand on Jasmine's shoulder. Jasmine reached up and circled her fingers around her sister's wrist, which felt alarmingly fragile.

'I've bought confetti, and some ribbon for us to look at.' Eve kissed Lara. 'You know, fun stuff.'

At that precise second, Eve was in a happy place: soft, settled, more . . . at peace with herself. Jasmine knew her sister. Yes, she did . . . and it wasn't always the case with Eve.

'Talking of Maudie,' said Lara. There was a pause, followed by a dramatic pronunciation: 'Harvard.'

'Yes,' they chorused.

'You know that if she went it would be the first week in September.'

Eve stiffened. '*No!* That's the week Andrew and I had settled on.'

'Oh.' Lara's expression darkened.

'We hadn't told anybody because we'd only just managed to sort it out.' Eve called up the stairs: 'Maudie—can you come?'

Maudie mooched into the kitchen, sat down on the bench and twined her spider legs around one another. There was biro ink on her fingers. 'What's up, guys?'

Eve said, 'You can't start Harvard in that week. If you go, that is.'

Maudie didn't hesitate. 'Why not?'

'That's the wedding week.'

'I'll miss the wedding, then.'

'Don't be silly, Maudie. You can't miss it.' Eve was pale.

'I can't miss the beginning of term.' Maudie was flushed.

'It's *my* wedding.'

'It's *my* university.' Pause. 'My *life.*'

'The wedding isn't important?'

'To you, yes.' Maudie climbed right back on to her high horse. 'Evie, of course it's important. But it's not the whole deal, is it? It's the marriage that's the deal, and I back you on that. But I can't miss the start of term.'

Eve's fingers shook as she picked up a mug from the table and placed it in the sink. 'I suppose I should expect that kind of behaviour from you.'

'Evie,' said Jasmine, with a degree of caution. 'There's no need—'

'Why not? Isn't it best to have it out?'

Jasmine peered at her sister. The happy softness had vanished from Eve, who looked tense and defensive. 'Because you might regret it.'

Eve let out an angry sigh. 'I thought *you* rated honesty. I do anyway . . . Maudie, I have to say I think it's extraordinary you're even thinking of not being at the wedding.'

Maudie chewed a cuticle. 'What's that meant to mean? You're not the only person in this family with important decisions.'

Lara intervened: 'Enough.'

Eve swallowed. 'Now we know.'

Maudie regarded them with stormy eyes.

Eve appealed to Lara: 'Mum, say something.'

Maudie said, 'I'm eighteen. I can make my own decisions.'

Lara rallied. 'Stop this. Both of you. Eve, are you sure there isn't an alternative?'

Eve looked at her. *Traitor.* She produced the

Notebook from her bag and flipped it open. A fragment of blue ribbon drifted to the floor. It was a mark of Eve's agitation that she didn't pick it up. Jasmine didn't need to look at the Notebook's contents: she had already been astonished by the *depth* of the detailed notes under the headings— 'Flowers', 'Bridesmaids' . . .

Eve scanned her notes. 'Have you any idea how complicated it was to settle on that date?' Her voice was pitched low.

Maudie waged war on a second cuticle. 'Of course.'

Lara stepped into the breach. 'Eve, since nothing's been set in stone, wouldn't it be better—'

Eve flinched, and cut in, 'I should have known.'

'Eve . . .' said Jasmine.

'I should have known,' Eve repeated. Her voice now rose. 'When it comes down to it.'

'Meaning?' asked their mother, quietly.

'Eve doesn't mean anything,' said Jasmine. 'She doesn't.'

'You'd better not,' said Lara.

Eve picked up the house phone, dialled and turned her back on Lara. 'Dad? We have a problem.'

Lara dropped her hands on to Maudie's. 'Something will be worked out.'

'I'd thought Eve would be more reasonable.'

Eve held out the phone to Lara and said in one of her icy voices: 'Speak to Dad.'

Reluctantly Lara took the phone.

Eve snatched up her mobile and pressed a button. 'Andrew, can you talk? We have a problem.'

Maudie was busy texting.

Lara spoke urgently, then said: 'I know you think that Eve and Maudie have to sort it out themselves but you must have a view.' She raised her eyes to the ceiling. 'I see.'

Jasmine said to her mother, 'Let me talk to him.' Lara handed over the phone. 'Dad, we need a Solomon.'

He sounded amused. 'Eve and Maudie *should* sort it out between them. But, if you want my opinion, it won't do Maudie any harm to be a couple of days late. *If* she goes.'

She should have known he would take Eve's side. 'I don't think that's right.' She was stepping on ice as thin as—oh, impossible to measure even under a microscope.

Eve now thrust her mobile at Lara. 'Andrew wants to talk to you. Can I have Dad back?' She retrieved the phone from Jasmine and hunched over it.

'Evie . . .'

Eve shrugged and turned away but not before Jasmine had caught the measure of her hurt and distress. How fragile yet obdurate her sister could be. Both qualities battled away in her thin frame and Jasmine shuddered at their confluence.

*   *   *

Jasmine's abiding memory . . . as she had told it to Duncan.

She was sitting at the top of the stairs in her pyjamas—grey ones with pink edging. She *loved* them. The stairs had smelt of new paint, which made her head swim. Eve was asleep in the room they shared further along the passage and Maudie was in her cot.

She was listening for her mother—who, she knew, was not her real mother but was her mother all the same.

In her line of sight under the window there was a blue and white pot of hyacinths. Before Christmas, she had helped her mother to plant them. Three bulbs. 'One for each of you.' Her mother had flicked Jasmine's nose with a finger, speckling her cheek with bulb fibre.

She could never tell her mother her secret. Her and Eve's secret.

They hated Maudie.

They had decided to hate her before she was born. When her father had said, 'You're going to have a baby brother or sister,' he had not seemed pleased and they had taken their cue from him. Then she had overheard him on the phone to Aunt Lucy, saying, 'This was not my idea.'

Her mother hadn't been herself when she'd told them she had a surprise for them. Half smiling, half crying, she had told them they were going to be so happy when the baby arrived. She grew very fat and, one day, she was taken away and Aunt Lucy came to look after them.

No one had actually been truthful and spelled out that a baby cried and smelt—which Maudie did. Worse, she took up all the adults' attention.

Her toes dug into the sisal matting. Pinpricks of cold climbed up her legs. The house creaked and groaned, and the smell of the hyacinths drifted past her nose. Save for the light cast by the lamp on the table in the hall, it was dark, and she shivered, half pleasurably, half fearfully. The house was a special place and she knew all the secret bits that even her mother didn't suspect. Like the den in the attic, which she and Eve crawled into when they wanted to vanish. When she grew up, she planned to live in the house, too, but she hadn't told anyone about that. Yet.

Since Maudie's arrival, their mother hadn't been the same. She was just as nice, of course, but they could tell she didn't seem to think about them in the same way.

Not so long ago, their mother had made them sit on either side of her. She had told them that yet another brother or sister was on the way. She had smiled a lot. 'How exciting for us.'

But the surprise had never arrived, and her mother hadn't smiled or laughed at all. Instead she'd cried. A lot.

She was crying now in the room opposite the bottom of the stairs, which was why Jasmine was keeping watch because she wasn't sure if she should go down the stairs to help her. Her father was angry. 'What sort of life do you think we have now?' he asked, in a very loud voice.

There was a long silence. Then her mother cried out, 'A punishing one.'

On her perch at the top of the stairs, twelve-year-old Jasmine breathed in the smell of hyacinth—thick and cloying—and felt the iron of adult knowledge creep into her soul.

*   *   *

'I refuse to take sides,' said Jasmine.

Eve replied, 'You're my sister, Jas. We come from the same DNA.' She touched Jasmine's cheek, but her tone was huffy. 'We're in this together?'

The date crisis had run its course, and turned full circle. June was out because the workmen would be at Membury well into July. Late July was out owing to the Havants' summer holiday, which had been booked at great expense for the second half of the month. August was a possibility although Eve was reluctant—'No one's around in August'—but, as it turned out, no catering company worth their salt was available earlier than the September date.

Everyone was sick to death of the subject.

Jasmine and Eve were on a bus that had elected to drive extremely slowly through Hackney. Crawl. Brake. Crawl. Their destination was an East End museum, which had mounted an exhibition of house interiors through the ages. Just up Eve's street. The outing and the bus ride had been her idea of a planned detox from family snarl-ups. 'I'm taking you, Eve, but on one condition. We don't mention the word "wedding". OK?'

Eve broke the pact. Straight away. 'It's not that I'm *angry*. No, I'm not.'

'Aren't you?'

'But I can't help feeling Mum's putting Maudie first.' This was uttered in a brisk, matter-of-fact manner.

Jasmine wasn't fooled. 'I know.'

'Do you?'

'You know I do.'

'Actually, I was looking forward to a summer wedding.' Eve glanced down at her handbag resting in her lap. 'Warm. Lots of flowers. I'm happier in the summer.'

'You can be perfectly happy in September. It's a known phenomenon. History is littered with happy September people. There's fruit, colour. It often has the best weather. And . . .' she whipped out the marshalling argument '. . . Dad and Sarah will have had longer to settle into the house.'

Round and round went Eve's phone between her fingers.

'Stop it, Evie.'

Eve smiled at her—a tight, determined smile.

They shared flesh and blood. All they had. (Odd how she never considered her father to be flesh and blood.) The spat over the wedding date had only emphasized their closeness.

Yes, yes, their upbringing had been the best possible, under the circumstances, but Jasmine reckoned she was the only one who *really* understood Eve.

'Do you ever feel that we don't belong anywhere?'

Eve's eyes widened and Jasmine knew her question had hit its target. Even so, Eve took her time. 'Yes.'

'Outsiders, that's us.'

'Yes.' Eve shifted.

'Do you talk to Andrew about it?'

'Do *you* talk to Duncan?'

'Not about that sort of thing,' said Jasmine. 'It's a bit ridiculous. It's not as though we were abandoned or anything.'

'It isn't ridiculous,' said Eve. 'It's something you have to get used to.' They looked at each other. 'It doesn't matter,' she said. 'All that matters is that we manage to live with it.'

It was not a subject they had discussed often and it wasn't easy. How could something seem so momentous yet so trivial? Jasmine always ended up asking herself.

The bus ground around a corner and she wriggled a finger into Eve's closed fist. 'Sorry about . . . you know.'

Just then Duncan rang. 'Jas? Just to say I got home OK and I feel like hell.'

She considered. 'Do I need to know this?'

'Reporting in.'

The previous night Duncan had been out on the town. He had rung late from a nightclub. Sloshed.

'Just checking,' he had said.

'What are you checking?'

'That you're not in a nightclub too. It's a naughty place, but I have to be here, I really, really do. For work.'

'Duncan. Will you do something for me? Go and put your head in a basin of cold water.'

In the background, she had heard a soft, sexy voice say, 'Duncan, come over here.'

'Hang on a minute,' said Duncan.

She had switched off her phone. It hadn't meant *anything*.

She trusted him.

At the exhibition, Eve darted between rooms that had been mocked up to show domestic interiors through the ages. 'Look at this, Jas.' She pointed to a fireplace surrounded by seventeenth-century Delph tiles. 'Exquisite.' She turned and gestured to a pair of elaborately carved chairs. 'Wouldn't give those house room . . . but I *love* that material.'

It was hideous and Jasmine's feet were hurting. Never wear high-heeled boots to exhibitions. But it was hard not to be affected by the charm of the museum—normally she didn't much care for them. She preferred to think about the future. Here, though, the layout was simple and straightforward, and so was the exhibition.' "The home," she read out from the pamphlet, '"has been a central preoccupation through the ages."'

'Do you remember the houses you made . . . out of boxes and crates. How we banned Maudie from coming in?'

'Of course.' Eve had been obsessed with houses and dens, tracing windows, doors and chimneys with black marker pen on cardboard boxes.

'The Palace Box, with the drawbridge.'

'Oh, the Palace Box.' Jasmine linked her arm through her sister's. The houses had been ramshackle indeed. Sometimes she wrote in emphatic capitals, 'Eve's House' above the doors— which ranged from tiny portals to serious entrances. Older and more competent, she honed her building skills, hacking away at the boxes with scissors (carefully blunted by Lara) to construct doorways and rooms. She devoted hours to painting roofs and doorknobs and—often—a window-box with bright red flowers.

Arm in arm, they progressed from the Jacobeans to the Georgians.

A blue and white pot of hyacinths had been set on a walnut table that formed part of the Georgian *mise en scène*. Blunt green spikes nosed through the bulb fibre and the outlines of the flower bells could be seen unfurling inside their green cradle. The notes supplied by the museum pasted on the wall above them read: 'An increasingly popular plant in the eighteenth century, hyacinths were probably brought to England in the 1560s and, like the tulip, their bulbs commanded considerable prices. A contemporary herbalist wrote: "The Perfumers use is very much, but it is no use in Physick. It often raises the Vapours in Women.""

I bet it did, Jasmine thought, and moved away. She had never lost her dislike of the hyacinth and its heavy, cloying scent.

Fixed to the wall were the curator's notes: 'During this period, the family still tended to be larger than those of today. As with earlier periods, anyone who lived under a family's roof thought of themselves as part of the household. If well to do, a "family" might include stepchildren, orphans, spinsters and widows as well as servants . . .'

'Over here, Jas,' said Eve, and beckoned. She was standing by a walnut-cased clock, dated 1783, into whose handsome Roman face was incorporated a date dial. 'There's one just like it at Andrew's parents'. One day, Andrew will inherit it. It has to be treated with extreme care.'

'Lovely.'

Shockingly, Eve seemed to crumple. 'What have I got myself into, Jas?'

'Wedding nerves?'

'Yes and no.'

Jasmine looked into her sister's troubled face and tried to work out what was going on. 'This isn't about the stupid tiff over the wedding date, is it?'

Eve gripped Jasmine's hand painfully hard. 'No. No.'

'Is it Andrew's parents?'

Eve shrugged. 'God, *no*.' She managed a funny little smile. 'I hate 'em, though.'

'Andrew, then? You need more time? You haven't known him that long.'

'A year. People have got married after twenty-four hours and made it work. Anyway, he's the one.'

She knew she should say, *If you have a moment's hesitation, call it off.* Instead she offered, 'Nerves and doubts are part of the package.' Pause. 'I imagine.'

Why wasn't she being straight with her sister? Was it because, in watching Eve get married, she would be indulging in vicarious and deeply unhealthy shtick? Or, even more labyrinthine, that deep down she did not want Eve to get married because it would point up Duncan's lack of desire to marry her? So she couldn't advise her sister to call it off because it would be for the wrong reasons?

This was exhausting.

'It's going to be such a change,' said Eve. 'I can't imagine it.'

'But you are sure about Andrew?'

'Yes . . . yes.'

'That's the main thing.'

Eve rattled on, 'Perhaps we should ditch the big wedding and have a small one in the summer. Then it would be over.' She bit her lip. 'September's that much longer to wait.'

Jasmine tried to shape the words *Don't marry unless you're sure*.

'Jas, you're the only one I can trust.'

Finally Jasmine's tongue obeyed her. 'You don't have to get married, Evie. Call it off.'

Jealousy was the fingernail screeching down the blackboard.

The sisters exchanged one of their honest, plumbing-to-the-depths looks. 'Not getting any younger, Jas.' Eve did not have to elaborate further.

Eve's 'Not getting any younger' also meant that

Jasmine was nearly thirty. Fact: incontrovertible, unavoidable.

'You can't marry him for that reason. Anyway, it doesn't matter these days, Evie. Nobody gets married till they're forty.'

'Don't be silly.'

Think slowing biological clock, the ineluctable drying up of tender young tissue, inner decay.

Eve added, 'I told you, Andrew's the one. Really, truly.' Her voice rang with feeling.

'Even so, Evie, don't do anything that's not right.'

'What would you do, Jas?'

If she was marrying Duncan? 'Evie, you can't marry Andrew because you're frightened of not finding someone else.'

'It's odd. One day I think being married to Andrew will mean feeling secure. The next day, I feel anything but.'

'This is ridiculous. Marry him if you want to, but don't if you have the least doubt. There are plenty of other options. Plenty of other men. Plenty of other things to do.' *Liar.*

As quickly as it had come, the storm was quelled. 'Sorry, Jas. Just thinking out loud. I'm fine now.'

Jasmine pointed to the clock. 'Do you see where the date hand has stopped?'

'No.'

'September the fourth.' She was trying to reassure her sister. 'September again. The best month.'

'Jas,' said Eve. 'Stop humouring me.'

On the way out through the Victorian section, Jasmine read the curator's notes. 'Here the notion of the tight family unit was beginning to make itself obvious. Privacy was at a premium and family loyalty narrowed . . .'

*   *   *

For dinner that evening, she and Duncan joined up with Eve and Andrew at the Thai Palace. They ordered bamboo fish, paper prawns, grilled duck curry, Phuket satay, and got stuck into the Tiger beer.

Duncan was still a touch off colour from his carousings and was happy to sit back, saying nothing much. He draped an arm around Jasmine's shoulders, and did his trick of twisting a lock of her hair around his fingers. Andrew told tales from the boardroom, and did a masterly job of explaining the feints and counter-feints from the latest take-over battle.

Andrew had a habit—as did Duncan—of dropping jargon into the conversation. The two men bandied it around with obvious relish. *Big babies*, Jasmine thought, with a rush of affection, and realized that Andrew's brand of charm—a lazy amusement with most things—had grown on her. All the same, she couldn't say that she *knew* him.

There was not a trace in Eve of her wobble at the museum. She ate and drank, made a couple of good jokes and, more than once, leaned over to kiss Andrew.

Feng shui raised its head.

'It's used to orient buildings in an auspicious manner to improve life with positive *qi* . . .'

As a prime advocate, it was the sort of information Eve had at her fingertips. She was about to continue, but Andrew interjected, 'Positive *qi*, my arse.' He helped himself to the duck curry. 'Positive *qi* dictates we can't have the kitchen in the obvious place.' One chopstick poised like a sword. 'The place where it would be most convenient. Otherwise the dark gods might have it in for us.' He shot a look at his fiancée. 'Apparently.'

Duncan had been playing Let Me Grope You under the table with Jasmine. She caught his hand, and he squeezed hers to indicate amusement. 'I take it you can't negotiate with positive *qi*?' he said.

Eve said, 'Anyone would think that Andrew and I had not spent hours talking about this and agreeing on it.'

Andrew put down the chopsticks. '*You* agreed.'

'I repeat,' a little smile played around Eve's lips, 'a *joint* decision.'

Duncan's hand slipped between Jasmine's thighs. She pulled at his fingers. *Stop it.* 'Evie showed me the plans. They look good.'

'Providing we can get past the *feng shui*.' Andrew cocked an eyebrow at Eve.

Eve said patiently, 'As I've explained to my husband-to-be, it's a way of looking at life and making it more harmonious.'

'Not with the kitchen in the wrong place it isn't.'

'Andrew,' said Eve. 'You agreed.'

At this point, Andrew laughed.

That was all right, then. The atmosphere lightened and Jasmine relaxed. Andrew had been leading them on. He had been teasing.

Eve sent her a look, and she returned it. *Secure?* Once upon a time, they had ruled their secret kingdom—a land of imps, hobgoblins and cardboard houses. It had been theirs, entirely theirs, tightly governed and patrolled. Not even the ghost of their mother had been welcome.

Chapter Seven

At college she had studied the Romantics—the black-clad, scowling, rackety, super-intense bunch of poets—and their assorted suffering women and children, whose role it was to cook and darn so that Byron, Shelley, Hoffman *et al* were free to be creative.

Such inequalities, Maudie thought, pounding the pavements on the daily jog, her speed intensifying commensurate to the anger she felt on behalf of the downtrodden Romantic women. (Indignation was an excellent spur to fitness.) How pleasing, then, how compensatory for the rotten treatment of their women it was that quite a few of the men had died unhappily. Still—and the irony did not escape her—she approved of their ideas. Those cosseted Romantics believed they could kill off the Age of Reason with its dull, dry beliefs and its 'rakes, whores, bawdy talk, powder and patches'. In return, they etherealized sex, turned it into an affair of the soul.

Blood thudded in her ears.

Nick had taken her on the bus and up into the woods. There he had spread his coat and laid her down on it. The air on her body had been cool but he had been warm and eager.

'Etherealized' sex? Looking back, the thing she had had with Nick had been anything but etherealized. But at the end of the summer of that first year, she had told him to go. 'I don't want to see you any more. Not in that way.'

'Yes, you do. You know you do.' He had hunched over. Angry. Frustrated. 'Why?'

'Because.'

Truthful answer: she wasn't sure. She just knew that Nick would get in the way of the other things in her head. Tess said what a brilliant couple they made—so tall and fit. *That* had been part of the trouble. In the end—and she didn't pretend it showed her in a good light—she couldn't bear the idea of being shoved into a box.

Sweat dripped down her neck. Alicia approved her decision to get rid of Nick (who still sent her the you-are-dead stare whenever they met in college). 'Leave yourself free,' she had advised. Maudie had paid attention. Instead she thought about the future, which seemed to involve a lot of practicalities, which Alicia was excellent at demystifying. Sometimes she missed Nick—the swaggering, solid-packed urgency of him. At the same time, she rejoiced in her power to send him away. Almost as much as she had thrilled to the subversion of applying to Harvard without consulting anyone.

Time was behaving in a way that was new to her—it was slipping by fast. Looking back, she couldn't believe how much she had done already. Applications forms had been filled in, funding arrangements researched (that had taken a lot of work and some tense conversations with her father), timetables rearranged, SAT requirements minutely studied . . . then the exam.

In all this activity and practical application, there had been absolutely no space for Nick.

Once, during a tutorial, Alicia and she had debated personal autonomy. 'I just had to make something of myself by myself,' said Alicia, with the drawl that so fascinated Maudie. 'So should you. Think big. Think wide.'

'I feel so angry, sometimes,' Maudie had confided in her. 'I don't know why. I'm angry with the stupidest things. The house. The street.'

'Here's your chance to get away from them,' said Alicia. 'What have I just said? Think *big*.'

Alicia's confident, knowing advice made sense to the Maudie who was so hungry to establish herself. Knowing she was bottom of the pecking order in her oddly configured family gave her an extra push. A willingness to be the iconoclast.

That made her think of Eve, and the wedding preparations that appeared to grow bigger and more complicated each day. They had turned into an epic theatre production and, IHO, just as tasteless, leaving the family gasping like goldfish that had jumped out of their bowl.

It was all so ridiculous. Moreover, Eve reminded her of the presents that were beginning to trickle into the house: listed, wrapped, delivered and utterly predictable.

Back at the house, the laundry basket was overflowing (most of the stuff Lara's). She eyed it, planned to ignore it, realized her mother wouldn't, which was unfair on her, and began to sort the stuff.

The SAT exam hadn't been so bad. Critical reading, maths, writing . . . She had sat down to the papers numb with fear. None of her friends were doing them, which made it a lonely business. 'So what?' said Alicia. 'That's half the attraction.'

True.

She had got through. At the finish, she had put down her pen with an extraordinary feeling of accomplishment. Later, she felt as though she had been lashed with hazel switches in a primitive ritual to mark a coming of age. At the weekend, when she had come home, everything was exactly as it always was. China neatly stacked. Cut-out supermarket coupons on the sideboard in the kitchen. A bag of half-price apples in the bowl on the table.

But they didn't matter any more.

If she had *anything* to do with it, Maudie was going to leave all those behind. 'I agree,' she had told Alicia. 'A life of one's own *is* what one should aspire to.'

That had been a few weeks ago . . . And now she was in a rush to get her financial application sorted, which had to be in—so said the sternly worded on-line information—by March.

Tea-towels, towels, sheets . . .

Blues into one pile. Whites into another. She dickered over a pink T-shirt.

Dirty laundry had such a characteristic smell. Slighty musty, with a hint of mud and rain and, in this feminine household, there was not so much sweat as a *pot-pourri* of creams and scents. Sports socks whose inner lining had gone fuzzy with wear. A pair of jeans that had to be turned inside out. 'Texas Stretch', read the label. (Could Texas stretch? It seemed big enough already.)

If sock-darning and laundry were a direct consequence of love (and its tragedies, such as were experienced by Mrs Shelley and her crowd) she was not going to be part of it. Best not, then, to get involved.

Nick had looked so hard into her eyes that she had

become breathless.

But Nick wouldn't get it.

She sat in front of the screen and worked.

Work was good. Work was reliable. She liked it and it interested her.

Mother and daughter had spent hours in collaboration on the upcoming A levels. With coloured pens, they had constructed mind maps— neural pathways traced in blue, purple, green and red—that had visualized and classified Maudie's knowledge of the French Revolution, European nationalism, Shakespeare's *Henry V* and Fitzgerald's *The Great Gatsby*, plus ecosystems and, finally, genetics, inheritance and variation.

'There's quite enough variation in this family,' Maudie had pointed out, as she and her mother had toiled over the latter. '*Too* much.'

Lara had laughed. It had been a nice, happy sound and, after a moment, Maudie had joined in.

Her mother now put her head around the door to check on her. Not unexpected. Living with her mother was to have a blanket wrapped around her—soft, warm and, from time to time, stifling.

She wasn't paying attention to the mind maps. She was occupied, instead, in twisting the tops off her set of painted Russian *matryoshka* dolls, which, years ago, their father had brought back from a trip.

Her mother advanced into the room. 'You look bothered. Want to talk to me? I'm sure we can sort out whatever it is.'

That was another reason to fly away. Her mother was always trying to make things all right while Maudie's instinct was to face life head on. Things were not always all right. Quite a lot of the time they were awful.

Maudie shrugged and disinterred the smallest doll from the belly of its 'mother'—a tiny faithful replica, down to the last detail on the gaudy apron.

'Maudie, shoot.'

'Mum, I've got A levels, remember.' Mind Maps To Go. 'And the prom. Thought I'd ask Jas to come and choose my dress with me.'

'What about Tess?'

'Mum, it has to be a secret.' She picked up the smallest doll and rubbed her cheek on its cool glossy curve.

Her mother tried again: 'How about hair? Have you discussed *that* with Tess?'

'Nope. She'd copy me.'

'But Tess is your best friend.'

'My very best friend. So?'

'Don't you trust her?'

Maudie opened her eyes wide and looked hard at her mother. 'What planet are you on?'

'Would you ask . . . Nick?'

Despite everything, she found herself biting her lip, which she knew imprinted a tiny white circle on it. 'You know I won't. Why ask?'

'Because I wonder,' said her mother, infuriatingly.

'Well, don't.'

Her mother sat down on the edge of the bed. 'Why the long face, then?'

'Don't know.' She fiddled around with the dolls. 'I don't know.'

'Second thoughts about anything? You're allowed second thoughts.'

'No. *No*.'

She picked up the big fat mama doll. She had the

odd notion that, in some way, it represented her. Twist off its top and a fresh version of herself would spring forth. Then she experienced a tiny shock. Had she already reached the age—at eighteen and a half, for God's sake—to think, *Time to remodel*?

Her mother's phone rang and she dug it out of the back pocket of her jeans. 'Robin.' To Maudie's astonishment a faint blush crept over mother's cheeks. The blush was new. Definitely.

'Yes,' she was saying. 'I wanted to talk over some plans. Would that suit? . . . Yes . . . OK.'

Conversation over, she turned and met Maudie's gaze full on. 'And?'

'Nothing,' said Maudie.

'That was just Robin.'

'Sure. Work conversation, then?' But her mother wasn't rising to the bait so she stuffed the dolls back into their nests. 'You don't mind if Jas comes with me to choose a dress, do you?' She squinted at the dolls. She had put the final one back together askew.

'No,' said Lara. Patently she did, but Maudie wasn't going to be nice on that one. 'Best Jas goes with you. But wouldn't Eve be better?'

The face and top of the big mama doll stared at Maudie from above its plump wooden backside. It was most peculiar.

'No,' said Maudie. 'I need someone who understands.'

*   *   *

Shadowed by Sarah, her father emerged from the house and planted himself four-square on the grey stone steps that mounted to the front door. Lara drove up and hauled on the brake.

Maudie leaned over and whispered in her ear. 'OK, Mum?'

Lara's hands remained on the wheel. 'I think so.'

'You don't have to stay,' said Maudie, and Jasmine echoed, 'You can drive straight home. We can catch a train.'

'I said I'd come, and I will,' said Lara.

Bill and Sarah had moved in, and they had invited the family down to see the place properly. Only Eve couldn't make it.

Maudie let her hand rest on her mother's shoulder. Lara said, 'I wanted to see the garden again.'

It was hardly rural tranquillity, which everyone always banged on about when they talked about the countryside. Apart from the posse of workmen in overalls and low-slung jeans, there were heavy tyre marks 118

on the grass flanking the drive, mud spray, a pile of industrial-sized paint tins, wood stacked under tarpaulins and paint-spattered gravel.

Actually, it didn't matter. Maudie observed the serene frontage, including the balustrade. Normally a house made no impact on her but this one was undeniably lovely.

'Beautiful,' murmured Jasmine.

Maudie had left her hair untied, and shook it back over her shoulders where it floated in a blonde cloud. 'House or the *Country Life* couple?'

She tucked her hand under her mother's elbow. Whatever else, and however she might criticize her mother, her duty was to defend Lara in public. Life was changing, as she explained to Alicia, but this was a role she had taken on and she would see it through.

Bill waited for them to climb the steps, then said, 'Welcome to Membury Manor.'

Sarah surged past him. 'Don't be pompous, Bill.' She was nervous and held out her hands in theatrical welcome. Actually, they were both nervous: Maudie sniffed tension. 'I've got coffee waiting.' She ushered the party through the front door. 'We're in the small sitting room.'

Maudie hissed into Jasmine's ear. 'The *small* sitting room?'

Whatever the room was, or was not, it was lovely. Jasmine was clearly enraptured and drifted around, exclaiming over this and that. Cube-shaped, with huge windows, it had elaborate plasterwork but everything cried out for repair. Even Maudie could see that. Hundreds and thousands of pounds' worth of work. Arranged in it was Bill and Sarah's sparse selection of London furniture, which included a sofa covered with raspberry striped silk and an antique mirror. Although they were elegant, the two pieces contributed to the rather forlorn effect.

'It'll be superb,' said Jasmine.

Sarah said, 'God knows when we can do it up. Everything else has gone on fundamentals like electrics and plumbing.'

There was a special, cosmically depressing kind of boredom attached to conversations about houses ... *Never* would Maudie talk about them in the hushed, reverent tones that her mother and even Jasmine were given to.

Jasmine and Lara sat on the raspberry stripes. Maudie took up sentry duty by the window from where she was able to watch her father covertly, a habit perfected over the years.

That was easy for he never really looked at her.

Whenever she considered her father, she thought of a big man—however not?—but a big man inside whom lurked a chastened spirit. Someone who expected the worst and who was wary of his youngest daughter. Did she mind?

Yes. No. Yes.

But, her mother might be surprised to know, he kept tabs on his ex-wife. Not obviously—but not lovingly either. It was as if . . . and Maudie warmed to her burgeoning analysis . . . her father feared her mother.

Often, far more often than she wished, Maudie reprised the childhood visits to the house-at-the-end-of-the-street occupied by him and, first, Violet, then Sarah. Uneasy, often tearful, visits during which tentative roots were put down, tentative rapprochements established, only to be ripped up because neither father nor daughters could settle to the spadework that would make the relationships flourish.

He was asking, 'Maudie, how's the revision going?'

'For the A levels, OK. Ish. Got the mocks at the end of term. But, I've done the SAT exam.'

'You've done the SAT exam?' Her father's brows snapped together. 'Why didn't you tell me?'

Sarah said, 'Bill . . . don't.'

'You could have asked,' said Maudie.

Her mother and father looked at each other. Oddly united?

Sarah coughed.

'I think we'd better have a discussion,' said her father at last. 'To keep me in the picture.'

More than anything I want to get away from

England.

Sarah was wearing a pressed pair of light blue jeans, and a soft red sweater. Her nails, clipped and buffed, were painted shell pink and her hair gleamed frosted blonde. Her mother and Jasmine were also in jeans—blue-black ones (Jasmine's extra skinny), and both wore little black jackets. As for herself, she was in black leggings, a loose black jumper and lace-up biker boots. All three outfits were replicated in their thousands on any London street, but in the rural setting they had a startling effect. They were crows dropping in on a colony of blue tits.

Sarah poured coffee.

It tasted dreadful because it had been stewing in a Thermos—typical of the efficient Sarah. Maudie managed a mouthful and thought longingly of the tough, toxic espresso from the Italian down the street.

A framed photograph had been placed on the table beside the window. It showed Sarah and Bill on holiday in a hot-looking seaside venue. Maudie picked it up. 'Where's this?'

'Corfu,' said Sarah.

'Scene of your great triumph, Mum,' said Maudie. 'When you hired a speedboat and *drove* it.'

'I remember,' said Sarah. 'It was a very, very expensive thing to do. I was quite shocked.' She was only half joking.

'Are you implying that Mum was extravagant?' asked Maudie.

'Maudie,' interjected her mother.

'It was wonderful,' she pressed on. 'The *best* thing. It was the first time we'd been on holiday for years and we didn't stop laughing for the whole of it.'

A boatload of shrieking sisters, fierce sun, the friendly slap of water. Looking shell-shocked, her hair bundled up into a baseball cap, their mother had been clamped to the wheel. 'Am I going to make this, girls?'

None of them had had the least idea how little Lara knew about driving a boat, but she had said, 'We have to do something that takes us out of ourselves. Something bold and unusual so we can talk about it for ever.'

There *had* been the very interesting moment when Lara underestimated the width of the harbourage, an even trickier one when she misjudged the speed at which one should take a choppy sea, but they *had* talked about it for years. Still did, and the allusions to it were threaded on the string of their family mythology, like beads.

Captain, is that a wall?

How long is a foot, Captain?

Sarah put down her coffee cup. 'How about the guided tour?'

'I want to talk to Lara,' said Bill. 'We'll join you later.'

'Mum?' Maudie lifted an eyebrow. 'OK?'

Sarah said, 'Of course, she's *OK*. Your father isn't going to eat her.'

Five bedrooms, two reception rooms, one kitchen, one larder . . . Later, Sarah led them out of the french windows on to a patio of grey flagstones peppered with white and yellow lichen. It had been an expert channelling . . . 'Don't you think this room will be lovely? I've got my eye on a wallpaper based on an old Chinese print. If wishes were horses . . . but one day we'll get it done. We'll have to win the lottery. It'll take time. Lots of time, actually' (slightly nervous laugh) . . . through a house whose insides were being dismembered in the worst areas and where the dust lay in heaps from forays into piping, wiring and floorboard replacement, and from the hunting down of dry rot, mould and exhausted materials.

It was a relief to be outside.

A brick wall enclosed a generous garden. The brick was old, weathered and pleasing. There was talk that Jane Austen had once driven by on the way to visit her brother in Kent. Sarah pointed out a gate, 'which Jane Austen may have passed', with a possessive gesture.

Maudie said, 'But it hasn't been proved, has it?'

Sarah's mouth tightened.

More obvious work had gone on in the garden than in the house. Even she could see that.

'Your father has been labouring night and day. Can't keep him out of the garden,' said Sarah.

'Really?' said Jasmine.

'We've ordered masses of plants—lavender, catmint and more box—ready for the wedding,' reported Sarah, happily.

Jasmine touched Sarah's arm. 'You're very kind. I'm sure Eve's thrilled.'

'I wonder where your father is.' A hint of anxiety.

Aha, thought Maudie.

'He can't be far away,' said Jasmine.

That depended on what you meant by 'far'. 'Far' meaning stuff that did not involve Sarah. Maudie would have thought Sarah—safe in her house and new status—wouldn't mind that her parents were talking, almost certainly about Maudie. But houses and status were no protection against feelings.

In the vegetable patch outside the kitchen—the *potager*, as Sarah called it—they noted dutifully the caged raspberry canes, the chard and onions, which had been bullied into neat rows. Sarah treated Jasmine to a short lecture on growing vegetables.

That was too much. Maudie detached herself and set off across the lawn towards the paddock she had spotted beyond the stream. It was here she came upon her parents.

They faced each other across the beehive. Even from a distance, she spotted the tension crackling between them.

Actually, this was how she always thought of her parents: at odds with each other, even though things were better between them now. If questioned—and nobody ever did question her—she would have had to confess that it stank—but, hey.

'You should have told me, Lara.'

'Did you ever ask Maudie what she was up to?'

The exchange veered towards shrill. Quick as a flash, the terrors that had bedevilled her childhood raised their heads. Maudie breathed in. Slow, slow. Going away, she told herself, would help to wipe her mind clean of childhood baggage.

'*Stop* it, you two,' she called.

Her father turned his handsome head towards her. With a tiny chill of exclusion, she recognized a change in him. She had got her father wrong. How healthy he looked. How contented. The chastened inner man had taken himself off. In his place was a man who fitted his setting. He was thriving here. It suited him.

That hurt.

'Maudie,' said her mother, clocking her. 'Talk to your father about your plans. He wants to be kept in the picture.'

'Wants!' said Bill. 'I need to know. You're my daughter.'

Only when it suits you, she was tempted to say.

Lara was pale and agitated. There and then, Maudie renewed her vow to defend her.

A snippet of sun struggled for attention through the clouds. Lara lifted her face and sniffed. 'It *smells* as if spring is coming.' She folded her arms across her stomach. 'I'm going to look round the garden. You two sort this out.'

She sent them a tight little smile and picked her way across the paddock. Maudie watched her hunker down to examine the blooms under the tree.

'Crocuses.' Her father followed Maudie's line of gaze. 'We've discovered hundreds of them. They throw up a blue and white blanket. Sarah plans to plant many more.'

Her mother straightened up and drifted over to a couple of shrubs by the wall. Even at a distance she had a dreamy look about her—absorbed, detached.

Maudie pointed to the beehive. 'And this?'

'A long-held ambition.'

It was the first Maudie had heard of it.

'The bees are getting to know me,' he added, 'and I them. It's taken a few weeks but we understand each other now.'

She thought, Better than he understands us. Her father knew what his daughters looked like, how they spoke, what they did, but he knew zilch of what went on in their heads. He had not the foggiest about (1) her teenage love for the Kaiser Chiefs, (2) her ridiculous stab at trying to save money in a high-interest account, which turned out not to be much at all (3) her plans, *because he had never asked.*

Bill said, 'You blow smoke into beehives to subdue the bees before opening them. No one really knows why this works, but the theory is that the bees, thinking there might be a forest fire, take on honey in case they need to evacuate the hive, thereby becoming heavier, slow and docile.' He raised an eyebrow. 'You should open the hive as little as possible. Disturbing the bees makes them more inclined to bugger off. But it's a good idea to have a look every week, to check for signs of swarming because there are too many queen cells, too many drones, overcrowding, not enough stores. Then you can take appropriate action. Also you must watch for signs of varroa mite.'

Yup, her father knew his bees better than he knew her or the others.

'What happens if they swarm?' she asked.

'They won't if you manage them properly.' Comfortably into his stride, he gestured at the paddock, scrubby grass, thistles, rusting roller and all. 'The key is good management.'

Her mother paced alongside the stream. As she passed under a tree massed with pale pink blossoms, the wind shook the branches and rained petals over the blonde head and black jacket. In a dim, groping way, Maudie had always understood that her pretty, striving mother was unhappy. Now, she understood better what it felt like.

'Maudie,' said her father, 'can we cease hostilities?'

She returned her gaze to her father. 'Why did you leave Mum?' she hissed. 'Why?'

'Is that your business?' he replied, after a moment. The usual evasion.

'Maybe,' she said. 'But it's important, don't you think?'

* * *

Sarah had made sandwiches and laid them out on a table in the dining room. It was desperately in need of paint. Flakes curled off the cornices, two of the sash windows were crooked and the carpet was, frankly, disgusting. At least, the room overlooked the lawn, and a bowl of massed white narcissi, almost past their best, had been placed by the window.

'Jasmine, I made egg for you and, Lara, I know you like tuna.' In her customary hospitable way, she moved around the room pouring water, doling out paper napkins, fetching extra mayonnaise from the kitchen across the corridor.

Finally she sat down beside Maudie. 'Reading anything interesting at the moment?'

'I'm researching Eliza Hamilton.'

Sarah looked a tiny bit panicked. 'Should I know her?'

'She wrote *The Cottagers of Glenburnie*. *Very* famous.' Maudie ground the words out.

'Ah,' said Sarah.

'It has a handicapped housekeeping heroine and is stuffed with fascinating detail of nineteenth-century Scottish domestic life. The heroine is crippled from an accident and hot on personal cleanliness. In it, she battles with hairs in her food, bugs in her bed and trying to find water to wash in. Clean underwear was almost unheard of—can you imagine?'

They all stared down at their sandwiches.

'Spare us, Maudie,' said her father. He meant: *Please behave and don't the rock the boat of my nice new life.*

'I was just getting started . . .'

'I'll make coffee,' said Sarah. Lara offered to help. The two women left the room and could be heard chatting in the kitchen.

Bill addressed his daughters. His splayed fingers on the table left foggy imprints. 'Sarah and I want you to think of Membury as a home.'

Jasmine gave a tiny sigh. 'Dad, I think Mum's worried about money.'

Bill twirled his water glass. 'I'd like to point out that I've treated your mother as fairly as possible.'

Neither daughter commented.

His gaze moved from one to the other. 'I know you blame me. I just wish to say in my defence that there are two sides to a coin.'

'Not to a child,' intervened Jasmine, unexpectedly, and Maudie applauded silently.

Bill turned the water glass round and round, like the magician's lamp, only there wasn't any magic. 'I can't—don't—expect you to understand.'

'No,' said Maudie. 'Children don't understand being left.'

Silence. A pregnant one.

Bill now pushed the glass to and fro, leaving a smudged water mark on the table surface. Maudie was tempted to lean over and wipe it dry with her napkin. But, she didn't. She was never going to help him with so much as a swish of a napkin. Never. Ever.

She recollected the times when she had

considered running down the street. *Dad*, she had planned to say, *please come. We need you.*

Bill regarded his daughters. A nerve twitched at his temple. Did she catch a trace of regret, longing even, in the blue gaze?

* * *

That night, back with her mother in the London house, Maudie couldn't settle.

She recollected her father, or she thought she did, sitting at the end of her bed reading her a story: *Each Peach Pear Plum* . . . The room was filled with light and she lay spellbound.

She remembered the silence that dropped over the house the day he went, except for her mother's frantic sobs. And the Scottish neighbour who had come in, scooped up Jasmine and Eve—'a lovely pair of jessies'—and taken them away for the night, which Maudie had hated.

After that, there were no more stories at bedtime and the bedroom became a dark place where she huddled up and tried to work out what to do. As the youngest, nobody told her anything, but she knew she must try hard not to be a nuisance. *You're helping me by being a good girl*, said her mother but, however hard she tried, Lara still wept bitter tears.

Looking back, the sisters agreed they had all felt cold and hungry. Not physically, but inside. Between the waking moments of her current dreams, Maudie questioned if that was how all rootless people felt—if deep cold and hunger was a condition of displacement and loss.

Chapter Eight

Maudie banged her hand on the alarm clock to shut it up. Then she lay on her back, legs straight, and ran her hands lightly up her body. All there.

What would it be like to wake up and find that a fundamental part of you was missing? An arm, a leg, part of your mind. All of your mind. Soldiers at war faced the prospect every day and she owed it to them to spend a few seconds empathizing. It was so little, yet it was something.

Another day.

Nick.

She was not going to think about him. She sat up and clasped her hands around her legs. Then, because anxiety was a road companion, these days, she bent over and pressed her forehead to her knees. *Did I do OK in the SAT exam?*

All too evidently, her mother was taking a shower. The house was badly insulated. 'Don't ever stay with us,' she'd advised Alicia, when they had talked about her home. 'Intimacy's forced upon you. You can hear everything.'

Today?

After lunch, it was back to college for an afternoon class and the long haul. Before that, she was meeting Jasmine, who had taken the morning off to go shopping with her for the prom dress.

She got up, dressed, applied a lot of mascara, ate a piece of toast, packed up her rucksack and said goodbye to her mother for the week.

Deciding to leave school had been painless. Dealing with the consequences of finding her feet at college and in her aunt's home had been harder. The translocation had taught her that being on the move was not as easy as she had supposed. She had always been contemptuous of people who stayed put. Almost two years on, she conceded they might have a point, but to pay too much attention to her discovery would be to deter her.

On the way to the bus stop, she looked in on Donwell House, a centre for the homeless. The sights that occasionally greeted her there were sometimes frightening but she made herself do it. 'We have to do something,' she told her friends. It sounded good.

'Hi.' She poked her head around the community-room door. A waft of strong disinfectant hit her nostrils. In a corner, a couple of plastic chairs had been subjected to assault and battery and were upended.

'Hi there.' By now, Kath-on-Reception knew Maudie, but whether or not Kath-on-Reception rated her, she wasn't sure.

Maudie produced a hemp (no plastic for her) bag containing sponge cakes, chocolate digestives and a big box of dog biscuits. 'Any use?'

Kath stowed them in the box by her feet. 'Very welcome.' She didn't look at Maudie. 'One of them died last night,' she said flatly.

'I'm sorry.'

'Died of the cider that's never seen the apple,' said Kath. 'Are you going to sign the petition?' She thrust a clipboard under Maudie's nose. 'To try to make the government see that white super-strength ciders are killing people.'

'Of course.' Her hand trembled a little as she did so. With its complement of the suffering,

Donwell House made her uneasy and sad, which was precisely why she forced herself to return on a regular basis to donate or to perform small tasks, like washing-up or sweeping.

A picture, bright and peaceful, flicked across her mind of the campus at Harvard, with herself walking serenely towards the library. She had no idea if it was accurate but she could almost smell the shrubs flanking the path, hear the subdued hum of the air-conditioning inside the buildings, feel the edges of the books between her fingers, and taste easy-over eggs and hominy grits.

Jasmine was already waiting outside Selfridges and pushed her through the door. 'I haven't got long.'

Inside, wall-to-wall consumerism hit them. This, in turn, made her think of the homeless centre and, in the same heartbeat, she felt a frisson of guilt that she was here rather than there.

Jasmine forged a path towards the escalator. 'We'll work our way around the first floor.' She rolled her eyes. 'Evie should be here. She's so much better at this sort of thing.'

If Jasmine expected Maudie to give her a soft-soap reply, she wasn't going to get it. 'Evie wouldn't be interested.'

'Why do you say that?'

'She's made it plain that I'm a nuisance.'

Jasmine gave her a full-on look. 'You mean we think Mum prefers you because we're only stepdaughters? Maudie, that's too easy.'

'Is it?' said Maudie.

'Yes, it is.'

Maudie's pale, glossed lips twitched into a half-smile.

There began a slow, painful progress from concession to concession. *What kind of dress do you want? I'll know it when I see it. Colour? Not sure. Green—no, maybe black . . . no. Midnight blue?*

Two hours or so later, she paraded in front of a wrung-out Jasmine in a microscopic silver shift, plus a black pair of lace treggings. She raised a radiant face to her sister. 'They're brilliant. Thanks for being so patient.'

The outfit was packed up and Jasmine paid for it. 'But you mustn't pay,' Maudie protested.

'Just for the record, it's what sisters do.' Jasmine hooked the carrier bag over Maudie's arm. 'Have we sorted things, Maudie?'

She wanted to say, 'Not really,' because she had clocked it would never be sorted, and because she was beginning to see that the world never operated on complete transparency. 'Sure.'

Jasmine persisted, 'If you stir the pot between sisters and half-sisters or imply favouritism, you'll cause damage. OK? So leave it.'

Maudie poked a finger into the tissue-wrapped contents of the carrier bag. 'Sorry.'

On the train down to Winchester, she rang her mother. 'I love the dress, Mum.' She glanced at the carrier bag on the luggage rack. 'Jas was brilliant. She even picked a corsage for my wrist.'

'Oh,' said Lara.

Maudie knew that her mother would have loved to be there with them, happily enduring hours of boredom. Straightening seams, assessing hemlines, smoothing hair. Cluck. Cluck. Her mother would have said (as Jasmine had), 'Isn't black a bit old for you?' and 'That skirt's too short.' ('Did I *really* say those things?' Jasmine had asked Maudie, with some bemusement over their sandwich lunch.)

'Have a good week,' said her mother. 'Make sure you get a good night's sleep. I'll meet you as usual on Friday.'

Cluck.

'Don't do that, Mum.'

'Don't you want me to?'

'No,' she said. 'Big girl now, Mum.'

*   *   *

As it turned out, her mother was working on Friday evening—'an emergency'. Instead, she took Maudie out to lunch on Saturday at the National Portrait Gallery. Maudie was planning to do some research there on Tudor iconography, with special reference to Henry VIII and his wives.

Her mother was late, and while she was waiting, Maudie amused herself by reading the appeal literature. A portrait of Anne Boleyn required extensive restoration. Could the public help? She pushed some change into Donations.

'Poor Anne Boleyn.' She kissed an out-of-breath Lara when she appeared. 'Not only beheaded, but disintegrating.'

'Royal brides.' Lara kissed her back. 'Tricky. Let's have a look at you.' Lara made what she fondly imagined was an unobtrusive check-up. *Child's waistline? Not too thin. Hair? Groomed. Shoes? Surreptitious glance at wallet in bag to see if there was any money in it.*

Maudie did a bit of assessing of her own. Check: Lara's white shirt and black pencil skirt (a shade too tight), and the handbag, once smartish now used to death. Actually, more often than not, her

127

mother annoyed her by just being her. But having analysed this feeling (even Lara's outfits exerted a curious capacity to irritate), she realized it wasn't personal. It was the flicker of precognition. She was afraid that one day she would turn into Lara.

As they made their way to the restaurant, Maudie said, 'Isn't it time *you* found someone else, Mum?'

For once, Lara did not say, 'None of your business,' or try to dismiss the question. 'I've thought about it but I've been busy.' She smiled. 'I wanted to be sure I had the energy to look after you all properly. And . . .'

Good heavens. With a tiny thrill, Maudie grasped that she had been invited to converse on an adult plane. This was the moment when she leaped from one ice floe to another, from regarding her mother as a mother (irritating and fussy but her one true refuge) to seeing her as a woman, way, way out of touch but pretty good all the same.

'And?'

'I've felt . . . well, that that part of my life was over.' Her mother's hand touched her chest. 'Sort of frozen.'

All those years of her mother darting around, always busy, always tired . . . Maudie had observed without understanding and criticized without knowledge. But you had to do that before you grew into sense, didn't you? Yes. 'Mum, we're grown-up. You'll have to start thinking about your life after we've gone.'

'I know. Evie's wedding . . .' Her mother's grey eyes looked bleak. 'A milestone for everyone.'

'Think about it, Mum.'

'I'm used to just me, Maudie. It's a habit of

128

mind. And it's a great deal simpler. No negotiations necessary.'

'Easy-option position? Or what you truly want?'

'Good question,' said her mother. 'I'll reflect on it.'

'Mum, you *have* to be honest with yourself.'

'Now, where have I heard that before?' Lara reached for Maudie's hand and held it fleetingly to her cheek.

Maudie was enjoying herself. The boredom of being a child was slipping into the past and the future was interesting. They settled at the table in the restaurant with a view down to the Houses of Parliament and she said, 'If I want to be honest, I think weddings are hell and getting married should be conducted in a cupboard. Or in private. If you must marry.'

Lara was in the act of flapping open her napkin and looked alarmed. 'Maudie, don't go off on one. I need your backing.' She picked up the menu. 'I especially don't need any feuds. OK?'

'I know. Jasmine's already had a go at me.' Maudie leaned over the table. 'But for the record, on the possible date clash, *did* you feel it was a choice between stepdaughter and daughter?'

Don't go there, said Jasmine.

'Yes, no. Whatever, it was an impossible choice.'

'I bet Eve thinks you don't love her.'

'Possibly.'

Wasn't it better to get at the truth? To have things out? To relish currents of clean air? 'I think the worst of her. Actually.'

'Don't. Eve's your sister.'

'She's my half-sister, Mum. It's different.'

'No, *no*—it's not,' said Lara.

But Maudie knew, and her mother knew, that there was a difference. Deep down. Bone deep. The trick, as Maudie now realized, was not to get into a situation where it became obvious.

They ate their lunch and enjoyed one of the most expensive vistas in the world.

'Why are we here, Mum?'

'Thought we'd splash out. Just this once.'

Ah, the years of *not* splashing out. Hand-me-downs of every description—only lucky Jasmine had had new stuff, if there was any. Years of hearty soups, meat on Wednesdays and at weekends, and patrolling the supermarket's 'Reduced' section.

'I'm *really* suspicious,' she said.

'Just enjoy,' said Lara. 'Actually, I wanted to talk about the future. I'm going to have to work a little harder. Expand the practice.'

Maudie laid down her fork. 'Dad's pulling the plug? Not content with buggering off . . .'

Lara looked serious. 'Maudie, you must get this into your head. Your father is a kind and honourable man. It takes two, as you will know, and he is not only to blame.'

Maudie recollected the ramshackle house and the girls who swirled through it. Her mother had done her best, more than her best . . . but something had always been missing. She now understood. They had been searching—all of them—for the figure who wasn't there. Yet at the same time he *had* been there. Just down the road.

She was drunk on her own boldness. 'So, what did go wrong?'

The question obviously stung and, for a second or two, her mother seemed speechless with embarrassment and distress. 'There are some things ...' she said. She glanced at her water glass. 'What I will say is that I made a mistake, Maudie. A big one. Your father and I disagreed on something fundamental. I did something stupid. I broke the trust.'

'An affair?'

'I'm not going into the details.'

'Did you and Dad discuss whatever it was? Really discuss it.'

Her mother looked this way and that. 'It was difficult ... neither of us was very good at being open with the other.'

'Shouldn't you have been?' She was careering down her new flight path, grown and liberated. 'On something so important? Surely you owed it to us.'

'Stop,' said Lara.

'I've never been able to work out why it was that on one day Dad was reading me stories and the next he was gone.'

'Sorry,' said Lara.

She had dreamed of him, muddled dreams of him appearing on the doorstep and she, Maudie, being the first to fling open the door and hug him. Or she secretly phoning her father and negotiating his return. Later (she planned) he would tell her beaming mother, *Maudie did it.*

'I thought that ... I thought with Eve getting married, it might help to know ... to understand ... Was it Louis?'

Careless, heedless Maudie.

'Maudie, some things are private.' Pause. 'And painful.' Longer pause. 'You must understand that things don't always fall into place, however much you want them to. It doesn't work like that.'

All the same, affected as she was by her mother's distress, Maudie was thinking: It only doesn't work like that if you didn't *really* want it to work like that.

'Was it to do with the baby . . . with Louis?'

'Yes.' The pallor she knew so well had drained her mother's lips, and a tiny twitch of nerve at her temple betrayed . . . what? Suffering? Agitation?

Her mother's expression warned Maudie: trespass no further. Even she could see that. She snatched her mother's hand. 'Sorry, sorry.'

Lara's eyes were pools of unhappiness. 'Maudie, at eighteen it's difficult for you to understand. Why should you? Grief grows into you. Dry rot. Veins in the cheese. Ivy on a wall. Describe it how you wish. Every day is a bad day. But you do learn to cope.' She looked out over the roofs towards the Houses of Parliament, as if seeking validation from their neo-Gothic certainties. 'I'm not going to discuss it further.'

'OK.' Maudie was both frightened and exhilarated that she had gone too far.

Her mother pulled herself together. 'I want to talk about you. It's simple, really. You must be clever about what may lie ahead in your life, and be ready. Not to sound melodramatic, but I want you to be better prepared than I was.'

Maudie dived in: 'Harvard, then.'

Now her mother sought refuge in the distant pinnacles of Westminster Abbey. 'I asked for that.'

'Don't you want me to go?'

'Difficult to answer.'

A spot of salad dressing had spattered Lara's sleeve and Maudie reached over to dab it with her napkin.

'I'll have to change it before this afternoon,' said

her mother. 'Can't see patients like that.'

Maudie rested her chin on her hands and squinted at her mother ... *squinted back into the past*.

It had been May. A long time ago. Warm and breezy. Loaded with drinks and biscuits, Lara was taking the family to the park. Maudie must have been eight, and was battling to keep up with her sisters. Arms linked, Jasmine and Eve walked briskly ahead.

Maudie had a snivel. Every so often her mother made her stop to wipe her nose. She was cross and jealous. 'Why won't they wait for me?'

'Because.'

At the entrance to the park, an ice-cream van was advertising cones with a chocolate Flake. Maudie went into melt-down.

'No,' said Lara. 'No ice-cream.'

'Why?' wailed Maudie.

Again the wielded hankie. 'Ice-cream costs money.'

'You're mean. Mean.'

Her mother's hair was flopping over her face. It looked stupid, and her feet in gym shoes looked stupid too.

'For the record, Maudie, I hate you too.' Her mother shook with anger. 'And it's about time you learned about "No" or you won't get on in life.' Lara had picked up the bag. 'You have to be ready to deal with it.' Her mouth had worked in the way it did when she was upset.

A long time ago.

On the way out of the gallery, they stopped to look at poor desiccated Anne Boleyn. A group of students was clustered around the painting and a guide was at full pelt.

Anne's dark, knowing eyes challenged Maudie from the canvas. 'Please note the elaborate dress. This was inthe style of French Court fashion, something of which she was proud. And, by all the contemporary accounts,she was considered sophisticated and elegant. In the bottom left-hand corner, there is a sprig of rosemary.' The guide fixed on Lara and Maudie, the interlopers at the back. 'This is intriguing, for it was added later. As many of you will know, rosemary is for remembrance. In France, which Anne so loved, it was the custom to put a branch of it in the hands of the dead, and there are some stories of coffins being opened and the rosemary discovered to have grown over the corpse. Here, it is more associated with weddings and a sprig used to be tied to the arms of the bridesmaids and groomsmen. Traditionally, a bride also wore a garland of it to symbolize the loving memories she carried to her new home of the old one. The poet Robert Herrick wrote: "Grow for two ends—it matters not at all/ Be't for bridall, or my buriall."'

Wed or dead, rosemary, the portmanteau herb, did for both.

Was it of her remembrance—the slow beats of grief and regret in her king's breast—that pretty, witty Anne had thought as she was led out to die?

The guide paused. 'Whoever added this to the painting was probably aware of both uses for the plant. He or she is saying, "If no one else does *we* remember you."'

Chapter Nine

Round about lunchtime, Robin came into their consulting room.

Recently he had cut his hair shorter, which made him look younger. 'I know,' he said, as her gaze lingered on the white stripe at his neck a second too long. 'The schoolboy cut.'

Was she blushing? 'It's good.' Conscious that her own hair was tied back with an elastic band, and her skirt was longer than she liked, she slotted her knees further under the desk.

'Disturbing you?' She shook her head and watched him move, quietly and economically, around the office, stacking and filing reports and clearing the desk. Did the habits of a soldier die hard, or was he naturally tidy? She couldn't decide. In contrast, her desk was a minefield of biros, tissues, books and paper-clips. One day, she would clear it. She would.

'How did the visit to the house go?' he asked.

'Fine.' She was cautious. 'The house is lovely, so is the garden. Neglected, though, but there's a witch hazel, and a myrtle tree that was, apparently, planted by a connection of Jane Austen.'

'And?'

'First time I went it was a frozen landscape. Second time, there were crocuses and blossom. Sleeping Beauty had been kissed awake.' Her gaze drifted to the window. 'Funny. I found myself in love with it.'

'Is that so odd?'

'City girl, me.'

'Do you know the old Arab tradition? When Adam and Eve were turfed out of Eden, Adam took with him a grain of wheat, a date stone and a sprig of myrtle.'

She liked the image.

Clutching the remnants of his short stay in Paradise, stepping into the darkness where, save the slither of the serpent, the slightest noise was unknown? He and Eve both hugging their tainted knowledge?

'And did the angels look after them?'

'Must have done.' He swung a satchel made of the softest leather on to the desk.

Good leather was irresistible. Think of butter and cashmere, of luxury's seductive whisper. She regarded the satchel covetously. 'Who've you got?'

'Wesley-from-Chelsea. Who is in big trouble and neglected. Father's never there. He phones in from China occasionally but lives in one flat, the mother occupies another, and Wesley's in his own place between the two. What option does Wesley have except to be angry? Or to play two sides to the middle?'

'Making any progress?'

'I march him into the park and make him puff. Sit him on a bench and discuss whatever we've agreed is the day's issue. Then I march him back and we try to talk it through.'

As always, the idea of a distressed child caught her by the throat—it was so life-threatening, so deeply wrong. She busied herself with adjusting the venetian blind, which did hopeless service concealing how dirty the window was. Send memo—no, *talk* to Daniella about it. Actual speech achieved better results.

Robin propped himself against his desk. 'But if I drop Wesley stories of boil-in-a-bag meals, plus firing and manoeuvres late at night in a dark wood, a few descriptions of rain and mud, a screaming sergeant, I get through to him, even if it's only for a couple of minutes.'

Lara winced, and he said, 'The Wesleys bother you, don't they?'

With Robin there was no need to be evasive, or dishonest, partly because their association was a professional one but also because he had only to level his sharp, ambiguous gaze on her for it to seem stupid to duck the truth. Their conversations were often short, their meetings infrequent, but they ran through her life like a seam of sanity. So, she said, 'They do.'

'Me too.'

His answer hinted at disturbance. 'Do you think about the war much?' she asked.

'I think about all wars.'

Lara put her scattered biros into a jar. 'I mean the one you were in.'

'Did you know your grandparents?'

Startled, she looked up. 'Yes.'

'Did they ever talk about the war?'

'No, they didn't like to.'

'That's it,' he said. 'One doesn't.'

She felt reproved. 'Shouldn't we ask? I should have asked my grandparents and I'm ashamed I didn't. We accept that men are sent away with guns. They're told to use them. They do, and they come back unable to reconcile themselves with what they saw and did. Shouldn't we question the silence?'

'But, more often than not, they *are* reconciled to

what they do. They . . . I . . . become addicted to it.'

She shook herself mentally. She hadn't been thinking *clearly* enough. What was more, so ran her logic, if violence becomes addictive so, too, can sadness and guilt. With *those* she was intimate.

'OK. You want to know what it's like out there?' He was tracing patterns with his finger on the desk. 'Acute relief mixed with guilt at being alive. Envy for the buggers who made it home with not too debilitating a wound. Rage at the stupidity of it. Then . . . then that creeping devil which tells you, *You're enjoying this.*'

A tale told with a soldier's brevity.

'And did it affect you? Unacceptably?'

'There are things.'

'What things?'

'One day something happens. A trigger sets off a pattern of post-traumatic stress. You've probably read about it.'

She felt her way. 'I have.'

He stared at Lara. Long. Reflective. 'Let's say I dealt with it by going away and trying hard to think about anything but . . .' He dropped his gaze. 'You can't empty the mind.'

Two per cent of the men serving in Iraq and Afghanistan came back with mental problems. She had read the statistic recently. It probably hid a lot of others.

This was a man whose shame or disturbance had driven him away, and she wished she could peel off the layers and understand better. 'You went to Syria?'

He suspended the pattern-drawing. 'To the basalt towns, the red dawns and the nothingness . . .

'I pass by these walls, the walls of Layla,
And I kiss this wall and that wall.
It's not Love of the house that has taken my
   heart
But of the One who dwells in those houses . . .'

'And?'
'It's the story of Layla and Majnun by an early poet. They were star-crossed lovers and forbidden to marry. He went mad from love. Traditionally, the poets call it "virgin" love for it was never consummated.' He touched his injured arm. 'I read a lot of the poetry there. If you're going to have a breakdown, it's as good a place as any.'
'Did you . . . break down?'
Robin began to pack papers into the bag. 'I was looking for a place of safety. All soldiers do. Anyone does, who's had that kind of experience. But I was . . . am a different person.' He zipped up the bag. 'But my time for running amok has gone, thank God.'
Anyone does, who's had that kind of experience . . .
Suddenly she had to ask him, 'Did you, do you, feel whole again?'
The atmosphere in the room was electric—a crackling static of unanswered questions.
'Do *you* feel whole, Lara?'
The old question, which she considered so quietly and matter-of-factly. So often. She took her time. 'Yes . . . No. No. But I will be one day. When Bill went . . .' She stopped. 'These things take years.'
'Has Bill really left you? I'm not sure Carey's left me . . . or me her.' He allowed a pause to elapse. 'For that matter.'

'Yes, oh, yes, he's left me. And I've left him.' Again the sharp, ambiguous scrutiny. 'I can see you don't think I have, but I've worked at it.' She smiled. 'That's what I tell my patients to do. To deserve better of themselves.'

'People don't leave us, Lara.' He turned away and the strip of white flesh at his neckline glowed whiter. 'Do they?'

'No.'

'You know—and I know—that we encounter their non-leaving every day in our work, whether they're alive or dead. In Wesley's case, it's complicated because he's haunted by the parents he should have, and his own are still alive. The big question is: how do you live with your ghosts? The Chinese have one answer. They think every family has its complement of troublesome, antsy ghosts and they appease them from the word go. In the old days, the women used to cry in the streets calling the spirits of their dead and dying babies.'

'Don't,' she said quietly. 'I live with one. You can't control them, however hard you call out to them.'

Flashback.

She kneels down in her London garden. The noises and smells are very evident here. There are no skylarks swooping over a crop. No peaceful vista of flowers and shrubs. Only scrubby London earth and the lingering traces of urban fox. She runs her hands over her shaky thighs, jelly stomach, uselessly full breasts, and aches to feel her baby's body against her own empty one.

She folds her arms, and the quiet, sensible inner voice explains that unhappiness and grief must be endured—especially if the unhappiness and grief are her own fault.

The city noises grind on and, for once, she longs for silence, broken only by a whirr of wings and the sound of leaves. She longs for the tang of damp, sane, clean earth and the touch of the sun on her back. She longs for grief to climb to its zenith and to begin the journey back to earth.

But she doesn't deserve any of those kindnesses.

'Lara ... I'm sorry.' Robin's hand on her shoulder, his breath just hitting her cheek. 'You should have stopped me.'

Head bent, she searched for her voice. 'I'm fine. It was a long time ago.'

He took his hand away.

Confession was never easy for Lara. But she thought of the things she had smothered, which had turned black and festered. 'I did something to Bill I shouldn't have done. It seemed so simple at the time. I thought it was a solution. I thought I could get away with it, but I didn't. Guilt is a funny thing. It has periods of dormancy, then wakes up and the struggle to deal with it begins all over again.' Her fingers took on a life of their own and twisted together. 'I didn't get away with what I did, in the cruellest way possible. Of course, rationally, I didn't . . . I don't believe Fate was getting back at me. But a little bit of me does.'

He didn't ask her for explanation—for which she was grateful. Thus, she offered a partial one in return. 'It wasn't the obvious. It wasn't infidelity.'

'Infidelity may be obvious,' he said. 'But never easy.'

Lara caught an echo of what had gone on between him and Carey. *He away. She alone and angry.* She looked up at him. 'It's much better now.'

But he didn't look as though he believed her, which was not surprising for, in some respects, she did not believe herself. To bridge the slightly awkward silence that had fallen, she said, 'I *love* the bag. Can I touch it? I have a thing about leather. Can't resist. Ask the bank manager.'

He held it out to her, and it *was* butter in her hands. He watched her run a finger along a seam and said, 'I could take you to where I bought it.' She raised a questioning eyebrow and he added, 'Damascus.'

'Why not?' She spoke lightly, as if the idea might actually be a possibility and handed him the bag.

'Will you think about it?'

Instinctively she folded her hands across her stomach. 'Yes, I will. Thank you.'

He smiled. 'Other worlds, Lara.' He picked up the bag. 'They help . . . for me anyway. But don't leave it too long for the Krak des Chevaliers. Things change. One thing I've learned, the bits of the world you imagine are available are, suddenly, no longer.'

'Sorry about the questions,' she said. 'I didn't mean to pry.'

He zipped up the bag. 'It's not the questions. It's the having to take account of oneself that's harsh. But . . .' he gestured, and she was drawn into the circle of just him and her, 'you and I know it's the only thing.'

*   *   *

Bill and Sarah got married quietly on a Friday afternoon of spring sunshine and soaking showers.

Lara spent the day going over her business

142

plan and seeing patients—she had a particularly distressing case of depression that demanded her utmost care and skill. Once, she looked up to hope that Sarah's finery did not get wet. Other than that, to her satisfaction, she felt nothing much.

Later that evening, Maudie arrived home from the wedding. 'It was OK,' Maudie admitted, when Lara pressed her. 'Bit . . .'

'A bit . . .?'

'Stuffy.' Maudie glanced at her phone. 'I took a pic.' She flicked it on to the screen—and there were Bill and Sarah at the restaurant table, surrounded by wine glasses, both exhibiting a bad case of camera red-eye and, in Bill's case, a surprising suggestion of a double chin.

'Don't send them that one,' Lara advised.

'Why not? It's what they looked like,' said merciless Maudie, shaking her hair free.

Jasmine rang to give her report. 'Dad seemed happy and Sarah kept flashing her hand around. Food wasn't that good. And,' she sounded amused, 'guess who was there? Shrinking V., looking a bit raddled. I thought that might interest you. The raddled bit, I mean.'

Did it? She wasn't sure.

She finished talking to Jasmine, and the phone immediately rang again. It was Eve's turn. All three girls. Any dark doubts she occasionally entertained about her role in their lives disappeared. She pictured the three of them, sitting at the table as they had done when they were small—baby birds— and smiled with pleasure.

'The flowers were OK, mostly pale blue, which I didn't like that much. Sarah wore a nice coat and hat but her lipstick was the wrong colour.'

Eve was seldom malicious and her opinions were occasionally funny, or stringent, but usually straight. Sometimes Lara shuddered for Eve. Not everyone wished to benefit from the straight opinion.

'I took notes.' Knowing Eve, she had probably made sketches as well. 'I'll email them. The white wine was first class. I've alerted Andrew to track it down.'

'OK. Any gossip?'

'Sarah gave a speech along the lines of how one had to wait for the best things in life. Dad turned a bit pale at that one.'

'Was he happy?'

'I think so. He laughed a lot.'

At her end, Eve was shuffling paper. 'Mum, it was nice. I hope my wedding is as nice.'

Flashback.

She is waiting for him when Bill wheels the girls into the café in Marazion where she is working the afternoon shift.

Such a nice café, the Dog Fish: fresh paint and fresh fishy smells. Outside on the beach, summer light bounces off the sea—with its turquoises, greys and foamy whites—and the sands.

She is wearing a see-through linen shirt bought on Skopelos, tiny shorts and gladiator sandals with thongs twisted up to her knees. Stomach as flat as a surfboard.

Bill hands her three-month-old Eve while he wrestles with two-year-old Jasmine. Eve is sopping wet. The sensation on her bare thighs is unpleasant and it's too cold to be wearing tiny shorts. Gooseflesh runs up and down her limbs, like electric shocks, but she does her best. She offers to change the nappy and, afterwards, bends over to kiss Eve, quite forgetting she has slathered her mouth in lip gloss, which leaves a sticky blob on the baby's cheek. Grains of sands stick to it. She seizes a paper napkin and dabs them away, which makes Eve cry.

Bill has fled to Penzance. Running away, he says, from his grieving in-laws and trying to get a handle on caring for two tiny girls. Both objectives are over-ambitious (his words). Yet she understands the intentions behind them. He isn't a man to take to child-care, plus he's shocked, exhausted, incapable of rational thought, and angry about everything, both large and small. Some of his anger focuses on the gladiator sandals.

'It's Penzance not Delphi,' he snaps.

'What's it to you?'

'Sorry.'

'Don't worry,' she replies, as an extraordinary sensation flowers in her chest. Love? Sexual frenzy? 'I understand.'

'What?'

'I know you're angry because you're sad ...' Bill holds on to Jasmine and raises his eyes to the Cornish heavens. 'I know the sandals represent what you've lost. Freedom and youth ...' Throwing herself into the drama of loss, she continues in this vein, laying bare Bill's psychic landscape with all the authority of a girl who has known him for just a couple of afternoons.

She thinks he hears her out from pure astonishment.

On her lap Eve wriggles. She adjusts the baby's hat as if her future life depends on it.

Which it does.

Those were the memories that flowed through her mind: a warm, happy, unthreatening stream. Like the one of Bill driving her away from their wedding, and the shape of his hands on the wheel. Those hands with their surprisingly slender fingers had seemed beautiful and reliable. How she had loved them.

It was the other memories that wielded a whiplash—memories that were hard and savage.

She shook them out of her head.

Take stock.

She searched in the fridge. No milk. Lara snatched up her purse—leather, battered, darkened by countless handlings, bulky because she had been to the bank—and hastened to the corner shop. There, she queued to pay.

Robin was right. Bill had not left her. Nor she him.

On the way out she stopped to examine the bunches of flowers jammed into tin holders on a stand. Of late she had become more conscious of flowers. Their colours and structure had become points of interest. They repaid her study. How come the stamen was so shaped? What dictated the shape of the rose petal, the showy hollyhock and the lavender's spike?

This lot were the day's remnants and had a worn-out, hopeless look about them. Anemones, roses (clearly forced), ranunculus in pretty shades of pink, all drooping tiredly. They needed care and nurture. Lara hefted her purse from hand to hand. Yes? No? On impulse, she bought the lot.

It was a long time since she had done something so extravagant.

Back home, she arranged them in vases and hummed a snatch from a song.

In their flat pumps, her feet felt lighter, her skin smoother, and her hair brushed pleasurably on the

146

exposed skin at her neck. Her body was picking itself up, was instructing her to think of life, think of sex, think of the things that quickened the flesh and made one laugh.

*   *   *

A couple of days later, the postman delivered a package. It contained one bag of white and silver dragées, two types of confetti (delphinium and rose), three sample menus, and four lengths of ribbon that spanned the white spectrum. (All it needed was five gold rings and they'd have a Christmas carol.)

Lara seized the phone. 'Evie. A package of stuff has been delivered. Think it should have gone to you. I'll hang on to it until I see you.'

'I've been meaning to talk to you,' said Eve. 'Sorry. Sweet Mum, do you mind? My flat is way too small to store stuff and the cottage is completely dismembered.'

Lara didn't have to assess how small her own house was. 'Just where do you imagine I'm going to put everything?'

'Pretty please,' said the practical Eve. 'I'll keep it in my old room, and I'll get everything out as soon as possible. Promise.'

She couldn't resist: 'Your father now has plenty of room.'

'I know. I know. I just felt ... what did I feel?' For once, Eve was less than straightforward. 'Well, Sarah isn't you, is she? And you're you.'

Pretty please, Mum.

'OK,' she said.

Checking out the rest of the post, she discovered

a postcard. The same one of the Krak des Chevaliers castle she had seen on Robin's desk. 'Please come,' he wrote. 'It's a very good place to forget. Or, at least, to remember about other things that matter.'

The day was punishingly busy and she forgot about the postcard, arrived home late in the evening to discover Eve and Maudie at opposite ends of the kitchen table.

Hair anchored on top of her head with a biro, Maudie tapped into her laptop. Eve had samples of wedding stationery arranged in a fan in front of her. She lifted her eyes briefly from the task in hand. 'Hi. Cream or high white laid?'

'A glass of wine, actually.'

To Lara's astonishment, Maudie leaped to her feet and fetched her one.

Eve was wearing her black coupe cigarette trousers and a sweater with tiny satin bows at the elbows. The effect was chic, Left Bank and carefully composed. Lara sipped her wine. 'You have such a good eye, Eve.'

'Goes with the job,' said Eve. 'Might look effortless but I'm paddling hard under the water.' For a second or two, she looked bleak. Then she smiled. 'Don't look like *that*, Mum.'

Lara considered putting the cottage pie waiting in the fridge into the oven. But the energy wasn't there. Instead, she watched Eve and Maudie.

Eve was dark. Maudie was fair. Eve didn't care much for literature, preferring walking, dancing, ashtanga yoga and extreme therapies involving oils that cost a fortune. She was such a busy person. Even sitting down, she gave the impression of supercharged energy. Maudie liked running, puzzles (the more intricate the better), word games, encryption, etymology, psychological thrillers and garage music.

Eve squinted thoughtfully at the high white laid. 'Think that's the one.' She pushed it over to Lara. 'Agree?'

Elegant and suitable. 'Yes. How's the website going, Eve?'

Eve slotted the paper into the Notebook. 'Going nowhere but they still pay me.'

'Job hunting?'

'I should be, but the wedding's sucking up every second.' She eyed the wine bottle. 'Shall I have a glass? It's fattening.'

'For goodness' sake,' said Maudie. '*Have* one.'

'Can't think of anything but the wedding. The to-do lists.' Eve gave in and helped herself to some wine.

Click-click, went Maudie's fingers. 'Brides are supposed to be radiant, soft, tremulous.'

Eve swivelled around. 'And what's that meant to mean?'

'It's all so businesslike. I thought you'd be madly loved up with Andrew but it's all about which one of the many million varieties of confetti you should choose and if you're going to send save-the-date cards.'

Eve said stiffly, 'You don't know what you're talking about.' There was a tiny pause. 'Andrew and I are fine.'

'Did I say you weren't?'

'Stop it, the pair of you,' said Lara. Goaded, she heaved herself to her feet and stuck the pie into the oven.

But Maudie was on a winning streak. 'Aren't you

tempted to whisk into the nearest register office and get it over and done with?'

Eve threw her look: *Are you mad?* Her small, manicured hands shuffled the remaining stationery samples into a pile, which she slipped inside a plastic folder.

'The happy bride,' said Maudie.

'Such a myth, happy brides.' Eve gave a discernible gasp, then clasped the manicured hands to her cheeks. 'God, I don't know what's got into me.'

* * *

Over breakfast, Lara gave Maudie a talking-to. 'It's important that you sisters keep on good terms. You never know when you might need each other.'

Maudie wrinkled her nose. 'I can't see that happening. But, hey . . .'

'It might come as a shock but it's a difficult time for Eve. Being a bride is not easy. I'm not sure she gets on with Andrew's parents. There's all that business with the cottage, and I know they're disappointed that Andrew isn't getting married from their house. It all makes for tensions.'

Maudie sent her one of her looks. 'I'm not sure she's gets on with her bridegroom.'

'Maudie, that's plain malicious.'

'And if it's true?'

Curiosity triumphed over prudence. 'OK, what makes you think that?'

'Have you ever heard either of them say, "Go away, everyone, we want to be with each other"?'

'What a ridiculous thing to say.'

'Is it?'

150

Maudie's mouth clamped. This was surprising for she could chase a subject to death. Pointing to Robin's postcard, which had been propped up by the jams on the sideboard, she said, 'You should go.'

'Why?'

'Because you're worth it?' Maudie could be good at a sarcasm. 'Why do you think you should go?'

What would it be like ... a Mediterranean spring? A shudder of the cedars in the breeze, an explosion of jasmine, the butterfly released for a few days of life to glide on scented air.

'It's a thought.'

'Which means you're not going to think about it.' Maudie retreated to a document on her phone.

'Anything interesting?'

'An essay. *"Pride and Prejudice* as a Revenge Novel"*. Alicia's. She got a prize for it.'

'Ah.'

Lara focused on Maudie's bent head. The moment at which she'd realized she irritated her children had been one of the more profound epiphanies and jolts—among many— of motherhood. Perfectly normal, of course. Grandmothers, mothers, daughters connected to each other in a long, peevish line down the generations—each woman in turn thinking, *If I am clever and sensitive, I can avoid this happening to me.*

She propped her chin in her hand. 'Do you remember when you ran away to your father?'

'Yes,' said Maudie. 'What a mistake *that* was.'

Flashback.

'Bill, have you got Maudie?'

'I have.'

'For God's sake, I didn't know where she was.

Send her home.'

'Actually, Lara, she says she wants to live with me and I think it's a good idea.'

'It's the worst idea ever.'

'She says you hate her. She also says she hates you.'

'He didn't want me, did he? Couldn't cope with his own daughter.'

She went a little cold. 'It obviously still rankles.'

'Why wouldn't it?'

Lara's phone rang but she made no move to answer it. With an exclamation Maudie picked it up. 'Lara's phone ... Who? Oh, *Robin*, of course ...' With an infuriating expression, she pushed it across to Lara.

'Hi.'

'For your information, there's a flight to Damascus after Easter and I'm on it. I thought you might like to come too, see the city, take a trip to Krak des Chevaliers and—top, top option—I'll take you to the market for a bag.' Pause. 'It's a no-brainer, Lara.'

Maudie was eavesdropping unashamedly.

This was the first time in years that she had been propositioned. At least, she assumed it was a proposition. But it was hard to tell.

'Robin, I can't leave Maudie at the moment.'

'Yes, you can,' said Maudie, in a voice penetrating enough for Robin to hear. 'I can stay with Aunt Lucy.'

'You could if you wanted. Work can be sorted and the wedding isn't till September.'

She tried to organize her thoughts. 'Sorting the wedding feels like a campaign.'

'It's always amuses me how people think they know what a campaign is. They should come along on one some time.'

It was uttered lightly enough but it was a small rebuff.

'I shall have to be careful with my language.'

'Sorry. Didn't mean it like that.'

'Yes, you did.'

There was a frisson. A cool one.

'Do it,' said Maudie, extra loudly.

'Yes? No?'

She felt a clutch of panic.

Will it always be like this? This was the question she had asked the woman—the woman with an empty, grieving body—who had stumbled outside the house she used to share with Bill. The early-morning light streamed over London and she had stretched out her arms ... to encounter nothing.

'For God's sake ...' Maudie's voice was a whiplash.

Lara said, 'Hold on, Robin.' She covered up the phone. 'Maudie, Robin is a *colleague.*'

'Don't link your past experiences to present ones. Think of them as entirely separate,' she counselled her patients. 'Just because you've failed in the past it doesn't mean to have to fail again, and now.'

'Robin, thank you but no,' she said.

Chapter Ten

Eve's email:

Andrew's parents, Dorothea and Nigel Havant, would never be close friends. First off, Dorothea had the tact of a rhino. 'Andrew tells me you worked when the children were young.' For her own reasons, Dorothea was determined to make the point within minutes of meeting Lara. 'Andrew and Isobel always had me around. We thought it best. It's so important for a growing child.'

Second, and this was the gigantic elephant in the room, Lara was pretty sure they didn't care for Eve. It wasn't anything she could put her finger on, just an instinct. Possibly, this was because Eve didn't much like Nigel and Dorothea. Eve pointed out, 'I haven't had time to get used to them,' adding, in a slightly desperate way, 'but I will.'

Still, they put on a good show. As Nigel confided, 'We like to do things properly.' The consequence was that a hundred and fifty guests were ushered into a pillared room in the—slightly stuffy—Kensington hotel. The choice of venue had been the Havants', and theirs the starring roles in the receiving line.

'A receiving line,' said Maudie. 'Now I've heard everything.'

Bill was in his place beside Eve. She looked wonderful and was wearing her mother's diamond earrings, virtually Mary's only legacy, which her daughters took turns to wear.

'You ought to be in the line too,' Bill had suggested to Lara, in a kindly, even-handed way.

'Best not,' she informed. 'The politics are too complicated.' Also, she didn't wish to hurt Sarah or make her feel uncomfortable.

Instead, dressed in a Prada (bargain of the year) skirt and a short-sleeved black cashmere sweater, both of which she had swooped down on in a 'Second Hand Rose', she took up a pole position by an ivy-decked pillar to observe. She ticked off relations: middle-aged, old and older (the women tended to wear frocks with belts). Friends: young and very young. They were all clever-clever, sharp and making their way, and the girls tended to wear nothing much below the crotch. But, she thought, they looked as smart and confident as the younger generation should look.

Pretty soon Jasmine, in a short, tight Roland Mouret-inspired dress and pointed elastic half-boots, joined Lara and kissed her warmly. Lara pointed to the receiving line. 'Enjoy.'

Dorothea alternated her greetings between a practised 'Lovely to meet you,' and 'So wonderful you could come.' In her mid-calf russet dress and string of pearls (so modest and yellow they could only have been real), she made no concessions to the anti-ageing lobby.

'I rather admire her refusal to gussy herself up,' Lara whispered to Jasmine.

Jasmine wrinkled her nose. 'Yes and no.'

Every so often, Dorothea turned to her son and observed him with pride and an avid loving possessiveness that Lara understood perfectly.

Watching a child on show and willing onlookers to bow down in the face of their beauty and superiority was one of the (many) facets of a parent's vicarious and (precarious) existence.

The noise level climbed. Lara and Jasmine caught admiring comments about the décor and flowers. Eve had pinned down the florist, ordered bunches of cow parsley and asked her to mix into it dusty pink roses. Cow parsley, according to Eve, was known as the flower that 'breaks your mother's heart'. Not, she assured Lara, with a glimmer of a smile, that that was the reason she had chosen it. Lara couldn't resist asking about the *feng shui*. 'Don't be silly, Mum.' Eve embarked on a short lecture. Excitement circled her like a halo and, to Lara's fond, fascinated eye, she appeared to shimmer. 'Since I have no control over the room, true *feng shui* is not possible. OK?'

Whatever, thought Lara, surveying the precise positioning of the vases and the pretty lights. The effect was magical.

The happy couple stood tightly together. Every so often, Andrew put an arm around Eve or said something into her ear. Once, Eve leaned against him in a soppy way that gladdened Lara's heart. Where was Maudie? 'You must be thrilled about Andrew,' was a frequent comment to which she almost grew sick of responding.

'Lara.' Bill materialized at her elbow. Clamped to his arm was Sarah, looking very attractive in lilac linen with gold bangles.

Jasmine said at once, 'Lovely dress, Sarah.'

Bill drew Lara aside—and they regarded each other from across a great divide. He was looking well, with a fresh, vigorous tinge to his complexion.

'I wanted to say thank you.' He was referring to the new financial arrangement, which had now been formalized with the lawyers and signed off. 'We appreciate it.'

Their final sundering had taken years. Now it had happened, she felt maddening and contrary pangs of withdrawal. Did he? 'It was time to be financially independent of each other, wasn't it?'

For a moment, they hovered on the brink of saying something.

He lowered his chin in the way that had so often made her angry—but which, once, she had also loved to distraction. 'It's been a long time, Lara. I am sure we could have managed better but we've made it.'

'Certainly.' She smiled. 'Let's not go there.'

'No, let's not.' But he didn't sound absolutely certain—which was new.

They exchanged a look. They did, and didn't, want to venture further into that dark, sad place. It was too great a risk.

She steered them on to safer ground. 'How are things shaping at Membury?'

A gleam lit up in Bill. 'Hedges. They occupy me day and night. I'm trying to sort them out using, of all things, a billhook I found in the shed.'

She envisaged him using the ancient curved blade, stooping over to layer the roots and branches. Each hedge had different shapes and needs. Without being told, she knew Bill would be intent on finding them. He would make it his business.

'I like the outfit,' he said. 'Looks expensive.'

The old defensive reflex kicked in. 'What do you mean by that?'

There was a burst of laughter from a group standing close to them. 'For God's sake,' said a male voice.

For a second or two, their accord was in danger of disintegrating. Then Lara forced a smile to her lips and said lightly and wryly, 'If you mean I've been extravagant, let me assure you—'

'No,' he said, retrieving the situation. 'No, I didn't mean that. I meant—'

She took pity and rescued him. 'I know what you meant.' She thought of the second-hand shop with its discarded clothes on wire hangers.

Sarah caught her eye. 'You will come down to Membury again, won't you, Lara?' Her blonde features reflected nothing but concern. Lara leaned over and kissed her cheek. Because Sarah believed in things turning out for the best, sometimes they did.

'You're a very good person. I'll see you later.'

With Tess in tow, Maudie had now arrived, in a black linen shift Lara hadn't seen before and her hair drawn high on to her head in a tumbling ponytail. Black didn't suit her, and Lara was sorry because she had wanted to show off her daughter.

If Maudie's dress let her down, her manners (or was it conscience?) did not. She buttonholed Eve and exclaimed over her outfit—which, being Japanese, designer and incredibly chic, was everything of which Lara approved.

'Glad you like it,' she heard Eve say.

She and Jasmine went over to join them—only to collide with a pretty, frail-looking girl in a bright blue dress, who pushed past without regard. So hard and fast was the girl's flight that she clipped the edge of the table. The glasses arranged on it wobbled, and a jug of cow parsley and roses fell over on the starched tablecloth.

Dusty pink roses scattered on to the floor and disappeared underfoot. Cow parsley lay on soaked linen. Eve gave a small, startled cry and swivelled around. On seeing the girl, on seeing what had happened, she gave a second cry: slightly wild, slightly shocked. Lara's senses snapped into alert.

'Sorry, sorry,' said the girl. 'I'm so stupid.'

'Don't worry.' Eve was barely audible. She groped on the floor for a rose.

Andrew was immediately by her side. 'It's fine,' he said, and pulled her upright. '*Nothing* to get in a state about. OK, Eve?' He held on to her tightly.

Too tightly, thought Lara.

'My lovely roses,' Eve said, as if they mattered more than anything.

The girl in the blue dress vanished.

Andrew released Eve, grabbed a passing waiter and snaffled another drink.

Eve thrust the flowers at Lara. 'Take them away. Bin them.'

Lara was alarmed by Eve's expression. 'I'll deal with them.'

'Just do it, Mum. Please.'

She turned away and Lara found herself cradling wet stems and crushed blossoms. Someone had bothered to strip the roses of their thorns, and the scars appeared very white on the green-brown woody stem. She touched one. She knew about scars.

Eventually, in the corridor, she found a bin, stuffed the flowers into it and returned to the room, which was now a heaving, buzzing mass. Movement was restricted. 'Good,' reported Jasmine, in Lara's ear, casting her expert eye around. 'All good. Trust me, when you get this level of noise, it's going well.'

Holding a fresh glass of champagne, Lara edged through the guests and managed to corner the Havants. 'A great success,' she told them.

Dorothea's lipstick had worn off, her nose positively ached for a dab of foundation, and she was in tell-like-it-is mode. 'Eve did it all.'

Lara picked up the undercurrent.

'Dot,' said Nigel.

Lara thought rapidly. 'Oh dear, are you feeling excluded too?' She did the ridiculous thing of trying to clink glasses with Dorothea. 'I'll join the club. Eve and Andrew seem to have it all in hand. There's nothing for me to do.'

Dorothea shrugged. 'I've been given my orders. I expect you have too. I'm to research hotels for the guests overnighting after the wedding . . .'

'Probably quite easy on the Internet?'

With enormous triumph, Dorothea said, 'We don't have a computer.'

Round One to her.

'Best to talk to Eve, then,' Lara said. 'I'm sure it's very simple to deal with.' Dorothea looked doubtful. 'Eve is very clear-headed—if there's a problem, she'll sort it out.'

Dorothea fingered the yellowing pearls. 'She's very . . . decided, isn't she?' Nigel cast a wild glance in Dorothea's direction but his wife ignored him. 'Of course, given the circumstances, you will see things more clearly.'

The bad press endured by stepmothers never ceased to amaze her (blame Snow White). If Lara had got this right, Dorothea was assuming that she, Lara, would be more inclined to agree with a criticism, however oblique, of a stepchild as opposed to a child. 'Eve is organized and efficient and I admire her for it. I also love her more than I can say.'

Round Two to Lara.

'I don't think you understand.' Dorothea lowered her voice. 'I'm not used to being told what to do.'

Of course not. A lifetime of bossing was conveyed by that last sentence.

'Neither am I,' Lara said, sharpish. 'But it's their wedding.'

Dorothea tried one last tack. 'Imagine ordering cow parsley from *France* . . . but Eve wouldn't listen to me.'

The maternal claws unsheathed. 'Dorothea, this is not the moment. Why don't you talk to her and sort things out?'

'Good plan,' said Nigel, who had been listening in cowed silence.

'I'll see you later at dinner.'

They moved off. At that moment, Eve swung round to Bill and said something to him. He replied. She looked up at him, smiling and—Lara could tell—a little anxious. He bent over and cupped Eve's face with his hand. The likeness between them was peas-in-a-pod unmistakable—a likeness she could not possibly share. The light caught the diamonds in Eve's ears. Mary's earrings.

Mary, Mary, why did you have to die? You should be here. Time was, her feelings about Mary had been mixed—not particularly commendable. But at this moment she felt outraged on her behalf. Mary *couldn't* see her daughters. There was a membrane between her and them, between her dead state and their living radiance.

That made her think about change. For that was coming too.

Fact. In marrying Andrew, Eve would be quitting the closed, intimate circle of the oddly shaped family, which, against the odds, Lara had held together. Think years of sticky furniture and disgusting spaghetti hoops, of fighting knotted hair, of scooping up endless pairs of knickers, of straining in the dark to hear puffy little breaths, of lying awake with the cares of the world heavy on her shoulders, thinking, *This is it?*

She drank some of the champagne. Eve looked up, spotted her. After a moment, she raised her hand and wiggled her fingers. An old private signal.

That helped. Lara acknowledged the gesture and applied for reinforcement to the glass.

Ghettoed in a corner, Tess and Maudie were deep in conversation. At Lara's approach, the conversation guillotine whooshed down and the two girls, silenced, turned bland countenances in her direction. Tess was sporting a nose-ring, a fake tattoo on her arm and scarlet streaks in her hair.

'Sorry to interrupt.'

'We were just talking about Thailand,' said Tess. 'Backpacking ...' She shrugged. 'Do you think Vicky will let me go?' She always called her mother by her Christian name, which Maudie admired hugely.

'I don't see why not.'

A glance around the heaving room revealed that the older generation was beginning to drift away, leaving the achingly cool and young settled in for the duration.

The champagne was working. For an hour or so, Lara counted herself among the achingly cool and young. And why not? It wasn't often she was given the chance to spy (legitimately) on her daughters' lives. Nosiness was sweet indeed and her insides fizzed with elation. Who was Jasmine talking to? What was Eve saying? Once they had become adults, the daughters had whisked themselves out of Lara's life. Of course they had—and she had no *right* to know what was going on.

(If you believe *that*, said her still, quiet voice.)

She buttonholed a passing waiter for a champagne refill. Raising the glass, she focused on Andrew. Beside him Duncan told a long, elaborate joke. Andrew was listening and not listening. His gaze had veered past his friend's shoulder and fixed on the girl in the blue dress.

The fizz and elation evaporated.

What had Maudie said?

Have you ever heard either of them say, 'Go away, everyone, we want to be with each other'?

Making a deliberate effort, Lara turned away to seek out Eve. Surrounded by her friends, an aura— mysterious, enviable—of the spoken-for played around her, and she was enjoying the attention. Smoothing down the Prada skirt, Lara went to join her.

*   *   *

Soon after Maudie arrived at the party, her father detached himself from Sarah and buttonholed her. 'You haven't been to see me for ages.'

Do not blurt out: *as if you cared*. No. Instead, politely: 'You never invited me.'

'You have a permanent invitation.'

'I'll bear it in mind,' she said, and was rewarded

with his hurt expression.

She softened. 'How are the bees?'

'Not easy.' It was obvious that her father hated admitting his lack of competence—and she tucked the reminder away. 'Minds of their own.' He hesitated. 'Actually, they did swarm.'

She couldn't help saying, 'Perhaps they don't like Membury. Perhaps they think it's pretentious and prefer the cottage down the road.'

His eyes narrowed. 'Perhaps they do.' He stuffed a hand into his pocket. 'Maudie, don't spoil the party. OK? There's no need.'

True.

'We did get on better once.'

That was true, too.

'Don't be silly, Dad.'

There was a ripple of laughter from the group gathered around Eve. Her father and she looked across at them.

'Did you like Membury?' he asked. 'There're places I'd love to show you. I'll order the bees to behave.' He hesitated. 'You could bring your mother when it's warmer. She liked the garden. I could tell.'

Maudie said politely, 'I hope you and Sarah enjoy living in your beautiful house and garden.'

'Please don't be angry, Maudie.'

'I'm not angry.'

'You are. And I know why. A whole history ...' Suddenly out of his depth, he stumbled and collected himself. 'I'm sorry about the way things turned out. But we are where we are, and Evie's engagement party is the place to keep the lid on it.'

'I'm not angry, just resigned.'

Her father was superlative at keeping a lid on

things. Piling up layer upon layer of the unspoken and ignored. She gave vent to an irritated sigh.

He raised an eyebrow. 'Normally, you're more vocal.'

Jasmine and Eve always said what they'd missed was their father reading bedtime stories to them. All Maudie could recollect with any precision (apart from the running-away episode) was the big, bluff father who liked nothing so much as a good tease.

'Where did you come from, Maudie?' Her father thought it hilarious to pretend she was adopted. 'The Russells don't mind aliens.' The confident, strident fun poked at her made her want to turn herself inside out. 'Tell me, do they have tea on Planet Maudie?'

It was typical of him to be so flat-footed. To get things so wrong.

'Abandonment has a long tail,' she remarked. He peered at her from over his glass, and she knew he was willing her to say things were all right when they weren't. 'How do you expect I'd feel? How any of us would feel?'

In honour of Eve, he was wearing a suit. Dark grey, smart. Sarah had ironed his shirt to icy perfection. The effect was to make him look like a banker, which, of course, he wasn't and never had been. 'Maudie, I really wish you'd talked to me before you applied to Harvard. I could have helped. Advised.'

'But that was the point,' she said stubbornly. 'I wanted to do it on my own.'

'But you know nothing about it.'

Didn't she? Alicia had told her tales of weathered buildings, clipped lawns, the deep-coloured fall . . . and the icy breath of winter that blew away the old notions of how to do things. 'I know enough.'

He looked down into his glass. 'This isn't the place to go into detail but what you do affects my position. You do realize that? You're the priority, of course, but didn't you think I needed to know?' There was a tiny pause. 'Cause and effect.'

She sent him a long look. 'I know about cause and effect.'

'Well, then.'

Now she looked anywhere but at him. 'I don't want anything from you.' Low-lying resentment, undercut with a kind of desperation, welled in her. 'I can manage without.'

'Maudie, how much do you know about it? Truthfully. You understand that I'll have to declare my financial position.'

'I'll get a loan,' she said. 'You stick to your ... plans.'

He gave up. 'To be continued,' he said ruefully. He was heading for Sarah when a thought struck. 'By the way, if you reach the interviews, remember to look the interviewer straight in the eyes.'

'Good God, Dad, that must be the first time you've ever given me any advice.'

'Which suggests it's well-meant and thoughtful.'

He had turned away but she caught his arm. 'You said bring Mum to Membury,' she said. 'Why would she want to come? Why would she want to see you? Is it because you want to flaunt the house in her face—which I think is pretty low? Have you ever thought about her life since you walked out on it? She works night and day and frets about us. It's about time she had a life and found someone else. Let her go.'

He glanced down at his shoes—black, highly polished. 'Oh, Maudie,' he said. 'Never mind.'

This was useless. She pulled at the neckline of her black shift. 'Sarah's waiting for you,' she said.

He stepped away. 'I'll see you at the dinner.'

A mirror ran along the side of one wall in the large room, and Maudie happened to catch sight of herself pinioned among the bright-coloured, oscillating mass—taller than most and, compared to Eve and Andrew's well-heeled, fashionable friends, awkwardly dressed. No doubt about it, she stuck out to her disadvantage in this smart, assured crowd. There was so much money here, so much chit-chat, so much grooming, so much taking-for-granted that food would be in their mouths and houses would be warm.

She edged her way over to Tess. She was talking to Jasmine and her streaked head was nodding. Sweet Tess, she must tell her not to nod like that.

That brought her up short.

She and Tess were about to change.

The Never Never Land of teenage contempt, slackness, rage and excess would soon have gone for ever. Worse, she, Maudie, would have to modify her splenetic reflections and become *reasonable*. Oh, God. At this party to celebrate yet another rite of passage, she understood far more precisely than ever before that she would miss her state of teenage anarchy.

Chapter Eleven

Duncan and Andrew had met at university and were friends. Very good friends. Together, they had shouldered epic drinking sessions, and set about careers that would earn them a great deal of money. They were quite open about the latter. 'It's a tough world,' said Duncan, who was used to skimping and his parents' money worries. 'Eat or be eaten.'

Andrew was less up-front about what he believed in or how he viewed his work—partly, Jasmine had concluded, because he had better-off parents than most on whom to fall back, and partly because he was more reticent. Or elusive.

'Do you talk to each other?' she asked Duncan.

'Are you having me on, Miz Scarlett?'

'No, I mean *really* talk to him? Do you share the really private thoughts?'

Duncan considered. 'Yes . . . I suppose we do. As much as I'm into that sort of thing.'

'You talk to me. A bit.'

'That's different.'

She kissed him.

Eve painted Andrew as a big softie and a kind person. Jasmine couldn't quite see this but was prepared to take her sister's word for it.

'What attracted you to him in the first place?' she had asked.

Evie had licked her lips. 'He's romantic. Very. A red-rose-on-the-birthday sort of person.'

Jasmine had blinked. 'You're not taken in by that sort of thing, normally, Evie. You always said you didn't do such stuff.'

A light had crept into her big eyes. 'Did I? How . . . short-sighted.' She gave a little sigh. 'It's really very nice, Jas. *Lovely*, in fact.' Ducking her head, she searched for something in her handbag. 'Andrew always has something interesting to say. He has views on what's going on. It's like having a hotline into what makes the world tick. He's logical as well as romantic. I like that.'

'Whose idea was it to get married?'

She had flushed painfully. 'Mine, really. I had to persuade him a bit—well, introduce the idea . . . But once I had . . .'

'Yes?'

'He said he thought it was an excellent plan for the future.'

'That doesn't sound romantic.'

Eve had laughed. A happy, light-hearted sound. 'Depends how you say it. And where.'

The party continued. Duncan tucked his hand under Jasmine's arm. They were talking with friends of Andrew's, Nell and Michael, and the simplicity and affection of his gesture gave her untold pleasure.

A waiter offered them a plate of beef and horseradish canapés and Duncan removed his hand.

She missed it.

Out of the corner of her eye, she observed Eve snatch up a glass of champagne and gulp a large mouthful. Nerves, she thought, for Eve never drank much. The engagement ring flashed in the lights. An ugly twinge of jealousy shot through her, which she wrestled with.

'Jas,' said Nell, 'please tell me where you got the dress. Otherwise I'm going to rip it off you.'

It was short, tight, black and suited her. The jealousy—thank God—vanished. She told Nell where she had bought it and a debate ensued on hot dresses, hot shoes and hot bags.

Nell's jacket didn't quite fit across the shoulders, and she kept tugging at it. 'You always look so great,' she said eventually, her tone combining admiration and pique.

Jasmine caught another flash of light from Eve's ring. Sometimes she was ashamed at how fragile the constructs were to which she clung—the people, habits and places of refuge. Was everyone similar? A falling-out with a friend, a failed work project, a reminder that Duncan had not asked her to marry him . . . Those happenstances had the power to destabilize her, however hard she fought against it.

Wasn't it enough that Duncan loved her? Reason said yes. Duncan argued: why cross the *t*s and dot the *i*s when there was no good reason to do so? Marriage was a state-and-Church sponsored piece of paper. This was the rational approach—'The only approach,' he insisted, deploying the logic he admired. On the necessity of being rational, she and he agreed. But nothing—neither rationality nor logic—could explain away, or neutralize, the breathless feeling that, from time to time, swept over her, or a bone-deep desire that lodged in her pelvis to be married, settled and to bear children.

Michael was asking about work, and she was replying. 'Brands are built on what people are saying about you, not what you say about yourself.'

A bored Nell drifted off, but Michael plied her with questions. 'If a brand works, and this is what we work towards, then people who use it adopt it. You come to feel that a brand of mayonnaise or face cream is yours. Job done.'

'Like "my M&S"?'

Duncan grabbed more of the passing canapés, and demolished them with his customary gusto and—this was the best description she could muster—the *gleaming* energy that had acted like a magnet on her. 'Got it in one,' he said. 'Like "my Nell" or "my Jasmine".'

Or *my Duncan*?

He grinned at Michael, who grinned back. Boys. *Mano a mano.*

'Idiots,' she said fondly. 'I'll see you later, I want to say hello to my father.'

Bill was talking to Dorothea, and Jasmine hovered by them while plans were formulated for the Havants to visit Membury Manor. Eventually Bill turned to her. 'Hello, Jassy.' He kissed her in the way he always did. Affectionate but brisk. 'All well?'

She knew perfectly well that, if he was fond of her, he wasn't very interested in her life and there was no point in going into detail. 'Fine.'

'Any big projects on?'

She smiled up at him. 'One or two, Dad. Nothing that's up your street.'

'I'm not that old, Jas.'

Look, Dad, she wanted to say to him, I want to know why I'm the one you favour least. She imagined his surprise, followed by the stag-at-bay look that always crossed his face if something *emotional* was being discussed. I understand, she might continue, that Evie and I are the children of the woman who *left* you, even if involuntarily. I have an idea of the pain you must have felt. I understand that you might associate me and Evie, especially

Evie, with that pain. But . . . Here she would force him to look into her eyes. With Evie it works differently, doesn't it? Perhaps because she was the direct cause of Mary's death you feel protective and determined to shield her from any guilt. I admire that. Perhaps it's much simpler. I know you love me, but I don't think you *like* me very much.

By this time, he would be well and truly panicked.

He was waiting for her to say something. Her lips twitched. She would let him off the soul searching. But something else Maudie had said floated into her mind. 'It doesn't matter two hoots about Dad. We're fine as we are. Just fine.'

Duncan was talking to Andrew. A circle of girls from Andrew's office surrounded them. Smart, pretty, glossy girls, who were no one's fools. As she watched, Duncan looked up and looked for her. His eyes widened in their private signal.

Take them away. Bin them.

She recollected Eve's expression as she had gathered up the cow parsley and roses and thrust them at Lara, and the warm, happy feelings engendered by the private exchange with her lover faded.

*   *   *

Some time later, Maudie elbowed her way, more or less politely, through the thinning crush and headed for the Ladies.

There, head bowed, she rinsed her face over and over and scrubbed at her lips. The china basin was bland, neutral, useful, and she gazed at it to reassure herself that some things were honest and

172

predictable. Eventually, when she raised her head, it was to witness Jasmine manhandling Eve into a cubicle.

'Eve OK?' She eased herself upright.

'Not sure,' said Jasmine. 'She felt a bit faint.'

An ashen-faced Eve emerged, made for the basin and hung over it. She turned a clammy face towards her sisters. 'I only had a couple of glasses.'

'Has anything happened?' asked Jasmine.

Eve retched. 'No . . .' She bent forward and her chin dropped on to her chest. 'And, before you ask, I haven't taken anything either.'

'You're not upset? Has somebody said something? Is it the mother-in-law from hell?' asked Jasmine.

Eve laid the back of her hand over her mouth. 'For God's sake, don't let Dorothea see me. The joy it would give her.'

Jasmine snatched up a hand towel, dampened it and dabbed Eve's forehead. 'Nerves. Too little sleep. Do you think you should go home?'

Eve closed her eyes for a second. 'Don't get water on my dress.'

'She can't go home,' said Maudie, flatly. 'The dinner.'

'I could explain to Andrew that Evie isn't feeling so good.'

'Don't do that,' said Eve. 'I'll be fine.' She attempted a smile. 'Start as you mean to go on.'

'Why don't I tell Mum, though?'

'No,' said Eve, dabbing at her mouth. 'She'll only flap.'

Jasmine signalled with raised eyebrows to Maudie. *Do you know what's up?*

Eve leaned forward to examine her face in

the mirror. 'Mustn't let Andrew see me like this, either.'

'Where is he?' Maudie said.

Eve licked a finger and smoothed an eyebrow. 'Don't know. Somewhere.'

She was preoccupied and agitated. Maudie touched her arm. 'Hey . . . what is it?'

Eve lowered her eyes. 'Brides . . . you know?'

'No, I don't know,' said Maudie. 'How could I?' She would never have imagined that Eve might be the *very* nervous type.

She watched Eve pull herself together, assembling the gloss and the smile. She brushed her hair and ran a lipstick over her lips. For a few seconds she stood still, drawing deep on herself. 'OK, sisters, let's go.'

Much, much later, when Maudie had had more than enough, the party was in its death throes. Surreptitiously, she checked the time. Only three hours or so longer and she would be free. She retraced her route to the cloakroom where the coats had been handed in and got lost.

A member of staff directed her down the corridor and to turn left. Treading along the red carpet—why was red so beloved of hotels?—she did indeed turn left and was faced with a couple of doors. The first turned out to be a disguised phone booth. The second led into a small lobby with yet more doors opening off it. Ever more impatient, she poked her head around the nearest.

It opened into a semi-dark room designated for smaller functions but, on the evidence, not recently. The air was stale, chairs stacked up against the wall and the table was shrouded under a protective cover.

In the ten seconds or so that she hovered in the doorway before backing out noiselessly, the details flashed over Maudie's mind's eye. The red carpet (again). The lingering, unpleasant smell of food and wine. The tomb-like table.

In addition, there was the couple, kissing passionately in the cold, stale dark. He was pressed up hard and greedily against her while she sprawled against the vertical wall, her blue dress hitched up over her thighs where his hand rested.

In the quiet, the rustle of their clothing, her small moan and his impatience sounded abnormally loud.

Stupid, she thought. *Get a room. Get a life.*

And went away.

* * *

After the dinner at Sackville's, when the goodbyes were being said, Jasmine held Eve close and kissed her, whispering into her ear, 'Something's wrong, Eve.'

The customarily cool Eve clung to her for a moment. 'Nothing that can't be put right,' she whispered back.

'Is everything OK with Andrew? Have you quarrelled?'

'Not here, Jas.'

Trailed by Maudie, a flushed and exhausted-looking Lara swept out of the dining area into the restaurant lobby. She put her arms around Jasmine and Eve and gathered them close. 'It was all perfect, wasn't it?' She was close to tears. 'Couldn't have gone better. Evie, you're a genius. How *did* you manage all the organization?' For a few seconds longer, they were held in her urgent, loving embrace. Then she released them and shrugged into her coat, which was being offered by a hovering cloakroom attendant. 'Next stop the wedding,' she said gaily.

Jasmine closed her eyes. If she ever found her world difficult and, sometimes, precarious, there was always Lara. *Always.*

Placing her hands on Eve's shoulders, Lara planted a kiss on her forehead. 'Eve, you're going to be so happy, and all of us are so happy for you, too. This is the beginning of your big adventure, and we're so happy we're all with you.'

Her eyes huge, Eve stood stiff and straight. Then she made a strange gesture with her hands. Warding off the evil eye? The enemy? 'Wish me luck.'

Jasmine found herself unable to reply. What a strange thing life was. It flowed unstoppably, and humans persisted in trying to shape it with such make-do-and-mend moments as a wedding or a funeral—which was so foolish and absurd. And necessary.

'It's wonderful,' said Maudie, more or less convincingly.

Lara's delight acted on them like a tonic. With fuss and chatter, the family swirled around the bride-to-be and eventually dispersed.

In the taxi with Duncan, Jasmine sat up straight, as wired as if she had taken Dexedrine or several espressos. 'Did you enjoy it?' she asked him.

He was drunk and sleepy. 'Very much.'

'Eve practically threw up in the Ladies.'

'Tut,' he said, twining a lock of her hair around his fingers. 'Drink or nerves.'

'Evie's usually pretty good at keeping calm.'

'That's brides for you. Shouldn't do it.' In the dim light of the taxi's interior, he examined the hair trapped in his fingers. 'Met a chap from New York. Interesting, he was.' He nuzzled her neck. 'I could eat you.'

She allowed him to slip his arm around her and to draw her in close to him. 'My Jasmine,' he breathed into her ear. 'Beautiful Jas. You smell like heaven.' She put a hand on his thigh and he covered it with his. 'Do you remember Rome? Our first weekend?'

He had undressed her in the hotel room, which was shrouded in thick dark green curtains, off the Via Giulia, poured brandy into a couple of tumblers and announced, 'We've got all day.'

It had been nice. Actually, much, much better than nice.

He looked up at her through half-closed lids. 'Since we didn't get to see much of Rome, I thought we'd revisit.' He walked his fingers up her thigh. 'See some things this time.'

How long was it now? Three years, but Duncan and she still did not live together. She tallied up their arrangement. She spent at least two nights a week in her flat, warming up pea and ham soup and pressing her office clothes. Very often she was out on business entertainment. Very often he was out doing deals.

The taxi slowed, and she squinted at the big catalpa tree growing through the pavement; it added much-needed grace to the cityscape. In every love affair, the partners absorbed a bit of their other half—which should make her easier-going and more humorous. *Very* necessary, she acknowledged. *You must lighten up, my Jas.* Would

177

he ever understand that life was a serious business? You only had one, it was fleeting and, therefore, should be explored with diligence and effort.

Should she move on?

Night thoughts were so lurid, and night decisions tended to be extreme.

She turned her head to look at him. He was gazing at her through the alcohol. Lust (good) was mixed with greedy anticipation (fine). But she couldn't imagine that she was the main focus of Duncan's thoughts. Not in the way he was in hers. Now, or in the future.

'What's the matter, Jas? Rome not an option?'

'Yes, it is. It's very much an option.'

Actually, she couldn't wait. To walk down the Capitoline Hill was to walk in Caesar's footsteps. To watch the feral cats stalking around Torre Argentina was to witness a sight as old as the city. And to stand inside St Peter's with Duncan, as she had done once with Lara, in front of Michangelo's *Pietà* was to be in the presence of emotion and artistry beyond anything she had ever seen before or since.

She captured his hand and pressed down on the pulse at the wrist. So soft, so precarious.

'I love you, Jas,' said Duncan.

'And I love you, you stubborn person.'

'Hey . . .' His lips pressed the spot at the base of her throat—and she caught her breath in a sudden rush of tenderness.

'Hey,' she echoed.

'My beauty, my lover, my friend . . . Jas.'

'Yes.' For a moment, she was supremely happy. Then she recollected he was extremely drunk. 'All that.'

She leaned forwards, tapped on the partition and instructed the driver to drop her at her road.

'Hey, what are you doing?'

'Going home.'

He struggled upright. 'That's not in the script.'

She kissed him on the lips. 'You're too drunk and I'd like some peace.'

He bit into her top lip—and desire danced through the taxi. 'Witch. Don't go. Please. Put the broomstick away.'

She laughed. 'You'll just have to manage.' With some difficulty, because of her short, tight skirt, she got out of the cab and instructed the driver to take Duncan home.

Shivering, she watched it disappear.

Chapter Twelve

As the spring advanced, Lara's plans to expand the practice pushed ahead. There were problems and there were moments of clarity. Nothing new.

First, she suggested to Robin that they go into partnership and he asked for time to consider the proposal. He sent an email:

Dear Lara, I nearly wrote Dear Sweet Lara, but this is business. I have thought hard about the idea and I'm going to say no to the partnership. But I'm here if you ever need back-up . . .

She wrote back:

What you mean is you don't like to be tied down?

The reply to that was

What do you think . . . ?

At that, she executed one of those (retrospectively) blush-making manoeuvres and whipped on to the Internet for a little light research. Then:

'A mind strange and dark, full of depressions and exultations'. Would that be you?

Have you just pinched that from the potted *Lawrence of Arabia?*

Now, why would I do that?

(She had.)

Because . . .

Do you really not wish to be tied down?

Ask me another time.

OK.

P.S. It's not so much depressions and exultations, although they are there. It's the photo in your head which you can't control

he wrote.

Flashback.
Holding Louis.
For the first and last time.

When they next met, Robin bought her a bunch of pink and black tulips and laid them in her lap. 'Homage to a May queen,' he said.

She laughed. 'That's a first. But thank you.'

'I've just been in the country and the bluebells are out,' he said. 'They look wonderful under silver birches.'

To her surprise, his words pressed a switch and she could picture the scene. Spikes of sunlight shooting between white and silver trunks on to the mass of blue below . . .

She cupped the head of the blackest black tulip in her palm.

'The swallows have arrived, too. But not the swifts yet. It's always a race for them to get here before they drop from exhaustion.'

Water from the tulips seeped on to her lap. 'How do the birds know where to go?'

He shrugged. 'GPS?'

She laughed.

Then Lara expressed her regret at his decision.

He replied, 'You'll probably thank me in the end. But use me. Ruthlessly. I have a couple of suggestions. People you might like to consider as partners.'

She took him at his word.

Together they roughed out a timetable for (a) recruitment, (b) finding an office to lease, (c) the launch of the practice in the autumn after the wedding.

She took on extra patients, one of whom was Kirsty, a middle-aged woman, still pretty but overweight. 'I *need* to lose weight,' she told Lara. 'I work in a world where it matters.'

'So why don't you?' asked Lara. 'What are the reasons?'

'That's the thing. I don't understand. I want to lose weight more than anything in the world, but I can't seem to make myself do it.' Kirsty's eyes filled and Lara pushed the box of tissues across the table towards her. 'One minute you're the bride—a *microscopically* thin bride—the next you're secretly buying industrial-sized bras on the Internet and you're an object of revulsion, even to yourself.'

As the plans began to shape up—plans that included an additional practitioner to help with the financial and administrative load—Lara grew increasingly optimistic. 'The practice recognizes,' she wrote in her preliminary draft of the literature, 'that a fulfilling life is not one of unalloyed happiness. No amount of wisdom can give us that. But if you are comfortable with yourself, you can help yourself to the world's possibilities. We will work with our patients to help them to live serenely with themselves.'

As she explained to Kirsty, 'You devised a strategy as a child to combat your fear and loneliness. This was eating and it was a good strategy because it helped you at that point. I have to persuade you that, now happy and successful in your life, you no longer need that strategy. I'm going to help you to abandon it because it's now impeding you, not helping.'

Kirsty would take time to absorb that one. She could tell.

One day, after she and Robin had collaborated in a long session and were packing up for the evening, she asked, 'How is Wesley-in-Chelsea?'

He winced. 'Think of your worst problem and double it. His parents are now divorcing and his mother is off to the Bahamas. The only thing that can be said is that it's not a shock for him.'

'Does it work like that?'

He considered. 'Was it a shock when Bill left?'

She wasn't prepared for the question. 'Actually . . .' Grief that went on and on. Recriminations. The loss of trust. 'Actually, it had an inevitability.'

'Same here.'

'You mean you and Carey?'

'A long time ago and far away.'

Up went her eyebrows. 'Nice phrase.'

'Pinched from Ursula Le Guin. It's impossible for two people to develop a friendship, which is what's required, after raging lust's died down, if one of them is hunting bandits, a.k.a. peacekeeping, in the Middle East, and the other one . . . well, the other one is diverted.'

Infidelity?

'Raging lust? What's that?'

Up went his eyebrows. 'Did I mention it?'

'Must have misheard.'

Pity mixed with laughter was a useless combo (Maudie's word). It took away one's capacity to think.

'It's just as frightening for those left behind at home,' he said. 'Waiting for the knock on the door. Not daring to look at the news. But it's also frightening because the person who comes back isn't the same. They can't be. Ever.'

She had a vision of a tall blonde keeping vigil in

grim army quarters.

'Carey was very angry with me in the end. I kept promising to come back home and try to to live a normal life. And I didn't keep the promise. I couldn't keep away from the action. Then I was wounded. It was a mess all round.'

'I think I know and I'm sorry.'

'Thank you.' He checked his watch. 'I've got to go.'

'See you.'

Thirty seconds later he was back. 'I forgot. That battle in 1516 you asked about, the Mamelukes versus the Ottomans. The Mamelukes lost. They were old-fashioned hand-to-hand combat soldiers. The Ottomans had got hold of gunpowder. That's how the world changes.'

Five minutes later, as she was locking up the office, a message came through on her phone: Drink Friday evening? R.

Thus, she found herself plaiting her way through a late-evening drift of tourists and commuters on London's South Bank. She was more or less on time. The day had gone well. It was much warmer than it had been. Here and there, tucked into odd patchy corners under concrete buildings, rogue daffodils drooped exhausted but the tulips still bloomed.

It was odd how one could 'possess' parts of the city—the places to which one gravitated. Hers was the strip of Embankment that ran from Vauxhall, past the SOE memorial and St Thomas's Hospital, snaking under the graffiti-adorned underpass and streaking east towards Shakespeare's Globe. Perhaps she had lived there in a previous life—a grubbing mudlark on the shoreline, a doxy working the streets, a toff in search of stimulation, or her ancestors had done—and memories of its sights and sounds were buried in her genetic subconscious. Whatever: she felt she *knew* the slap of the river on the starlings, its dark, powerful undertows and the life that spilled over from the streets to the shoreline.

Water and its secrets.

Looking down into it, she fancied the ghosts of ... mudlarks, costermongers, ferrymen, merchants, the dung collectors, the suicides ripping past in the tide.

And of her own past.

Flashback.

Bill asks: 'How many children do you need, Lara?'

'I just long to have another baby, Bill. I can't help it.'

And, for once, Bill confesses openly to an emotion: 'Don't you understand, Lara, I'm frightened? It's tempting Fate ...'

'I understand.'

'Do you?'

'But do you understand me?'

'I do and I don't.'

But it's impossible for him to share the all-encompassing, ravening ache usurping her body.

Yet they can, and do, share the loss.

Oh, yes.

After Bill had left, she had thought of herself as an empty shell, shunted by the wind and slapped by the water.

Empty.

The wind from the river picked up, bringing with it the smells of the rank, exposed mud.

As was her habit, she slowed down under the

arch where the second-hand books fanned out like conquered dominoes on trestles. Novels, some hideously bad, obscure volumes of poetry, out-of-date manuals were marshalled in rows. The operation pretended it wasn't out-and-out commercial but it was. She liked that.

With a finger, she traced the books running in a spine along one of the trestles.

Grandmother's Secrets: her green guide to health. So, Grandmother, what do you have to say? *Soupe au pistou* and *pesto* soothe the digestion. In a troubled age, ran the foreword, digestions were awash with acid. This was a condition of contemporary life: heartburn and nerves.

She progressed to the classics. *Jane Eyre* (very tatty), *Pride and Prejudice* (almost new), *Wives and Daughters* (untouched). She applied the marriage litmus game that she and the girls had played over the years. Two out of three novels she had lighted on (admittedly nineteenth-century ones) ended at the altar. Because the author had died, the third was unfinished although it was obvious that the hero and heroine were heading in that direction.

Smiling to herself, she looked up ... *Wives and Daughters* slipped out of her grasp back on to the trestle.

The soft notes of a boat's engine came and went. Lounging against the balustrade was a couple. She—young, incredibly slender, glowing. He— tall, clean-featured, graceful, his arm around her shoulders.

Abruptly, Lara turned away. Then turned back— to face whatever she had to face. She picked up the book and replaced it in its slot. *No, she wasn't going to be sick.* She recognized the girl. Of course she did. At the party she had worn the blue dress and knocked over the flowers. She also recognized him—*of course she did*—and the manner in which he was holding the girl. It was not friendship. Neither was it friendship when he bent over to say something into her ear.

Andrew.

A jumble of booksellers, tourists, hawkers and commuters separated them on the walkway but, inevitably, their gazes locked.

A pulse beat at the back of her knee and a second deep in her pelvis. Warnings of danger.

She walked towards them. Frowning, Andrew disengaged himself from the girl, but by the time Lara reached him, he had mastered himself and the frown was replaced with his customary smooth good manners. 'Hello, Lara. Did you ever meet Fern, an old friend?'

'Of course. At the party.'

Reliant as ever on his charm.

On closer inspection, Fern was even more faun-like than Lara recollected, with huge kohl-rimmed eyes. At Lara's approach, she shrank back.

'Fern, you must remember Eve's stepmother.'

Fern gasped, and her eyes turned into rock pools of distress and embarrassment. 'Of course. So nice to see you again.' She turned to Andrew. 'Andrew, I have to go.'

The words sounded as insubstantial as her frame. 'Don't,' he said. 'There's no need.'

But Fern was determined, and was gone, melting into the human river that ran alongside the watery one.

She faced him. 'Andrew?'

'Lara?'

'Is it what it looked like?'

'Lara, if you don't mind I don't have to answer that.'

'I think you do.'

There was a touch of anger. 'No, I don't.'

'Forgive me, but you're marrying Eve.'

'So?' He held her gaze, steady under pressure. He knew how to do that—years of practice at work. 'It *isn't* your business and Eve and I understand each other very well.'

He was so plausible and she wanted badly to believe him.

'I promise you,' he added, more gently. As if that solved the problem.

She raised her face to his. 'What you do does not concern me except when it involves Eve. She's my *daughter*.'

He thought for a minute. 'Lara, you can't interfere.'

'I *know* Eve.'

To her surprise and indignation, he took her hand. 'Perhaps you don't.'

Before leaving for work, the doorbell had rung and the postman delivered two Hungarian goose-down pillows, one traditional American quilt and a large red-leather photograph album.

She snatched her hand away. 'You must know that under her practicality, her smart exterior, lie all sorts of terrors, not least of being abandoned or betrayed.'

'I do.' He shifted his feet. 'Funnily enough, Eve and I do know each quite well.'

'*Why then?* Isn't she enough?'

The thin little girl striving to hide her panic: 'You

won't die, will you?' The thin little girl who had stood by the back door in the dead of winter when skin puckered with cold and holly crackled, looking up into the sky: 'Is my real mother up there?'

'Eve would never do it to you.'

'I'm not going to answer that.'

She breathed in dank whiffs and the tourist smells of hot dogs and candy floss.

'Lara,' he began again, 'this will change things.' Andrew was persuasive, assured—the man who achieved the big City deals. 'I mean between us. We'll no longer deal with each other in the same way. I'm sorry about it, but I understand it. Completely. But I must ask you not to interfere.'

'Sounds like a bad script,' she said, wondering if she should call him the names surging through her head. 'And you're right, things will change between us. I'll have to think about this.' For the first time, a flicker of concern briefly crossed his features. 'If you *had* to be with the girl, why weren't you discreet?'

He looked at her with a bleakness that shocked her. 'You of all people know—the therapist or whatever—sometimes things just don't tally up. Sometimes you're overtaken . . .'

Was she missing something? Did the sexual narratives of her children run to footnotes and addenda?

Tell Eve? Keep quiet?

Andrew laid a hand on the balustrade. 'Not everything is straightforward. I wish . . . I wish it was.'

Grab a pair of scissors and rip away his platitudes? The savagery of her response jolted Lara. 'Promise me you'll never hurt her.'

His gaze slotted past her to the river. 'Why would I do that?'

'What I'm asking? Of course, you'll hurt her. We always hurt people, even when we love them to distraction. We hurt the people we live with and love but usually, *hopefully*, without intention. What I should be asking is, are you *serious* about Eve's well-being? If so, what are you doing?'

He didn't answer.

Enough, she thought, and turned to go. 'I don't know what to say to you any more, or how I'll deal with you either.'

'Nor I you,' he said. 'But we'll have to try.'

As walked off, he called after her, 'Lara.'

Reluctantly, she halted. 'What?'

'*Are* you going to tell Eve?'

'I'll leave you to worry about that,' she said.

*   *   *

She met Robin at the designated bar. He noted at once that something was wrong. 'You OK?'

'I think so.'

'You don't look it, Lara. Can we dispense with the polite bit? Life is short.' He made her sit down at an empty table. 'I'm going to buy you a glass of the lightest and fruitiest wine I can lay my hands on.'

He headed for the bar. She lectured herself on maternal ethics. (1) Do not pry into your children's lives, particularly not their sex lives. (2) Remember, their sex lives are infinitely more exciting and ambitious than their parents'. (3) She knew nothing.

She knew nothing. Except . . . she knew something

of betrayal. She had sampled humiliation and lived with the kind of regret that, after a while, became a prison. In her work she had confronted deceptions, become intimate with the stratagems to which people could resort, the things they hid and pretended did not exist.

'The wine's gorgeous,' she told Robin, after downing a mouthful.

It worked chemically, and raised her spirits, plus Robin's shirt was a shade of blue she loved— Wedgwood with a touch of Greek summer sky.

'Does my shirt please you, Lara? It's got all your attention.' His eyes danced. 'Should I be jealous of it?'

Her smile felt stiff. 'It does please me. It reminds me of sailing over the Aegean. The sort of day when the islands come at you out of the heat mist and it's blue and hot and you think, I *am* in the land of the gods.' Alcohol skittered through her system. 'The children have never got over the day I hired the speedboat in Skopelos. It took years off their lives. But the sky was the colour of your shirt.'

'That's better.' He balanced a bowl of crisps on his good hand. 'These are apparently hand-cut by a virgin, or some such. Very special. Eat up because I diagnose low blood sugar.' He watched her bite into one. After a minute, he said, 'I'm good at listening.'

'As if you need to say that.'

'Even so . . .'

She raised her eyes to his. 'It would help. But it's confidential.'

'As if *you* need to say that.'

She struggled to release the words and he took her hand. 'Go on.'

Her hand lay in his. Flesh on flesh. Touch on

touch. How long since someone had comforted her in that way?

She imagined Eve walking along the Embankment with the sun pointing fingers of light along her path. *I'm looking forward to my new life, Mum. Apart from Dorothea, that is*. She imagined her swinging her arms, enjoying the simple sensations of air and exercise, tugging up the sleeves of her jacket. She imagined Eve slithering to a halt, her hand flying up to her mouth and her gasp of distress.

Lara described what she had witnessed. Robin listened, refilled their glasses and asked questions.

'I have to decide what to do.'

'Yes.' He considered. 'It's a pity you saw them, Lara. It might have been unfinished business. It might have been a goodbye. But, of course, once seen, it's no longer innocent and impossible not to pass judgement.'

'Innocent . . . I don't think so.'

He struck his finger once against the glass. It rang and she quashed it with her finger. 'A sailor will die.'

'It's possible that Eve knows about it. Those arrangements exist. But a relationship founded on a lie, or a deception, is not going to thrive. My strategy would be to tackle Andrew again, and to point this out. He'll tell you to get lost but . . .'

She noted his use of the word 'strategy'—military vernacular suggesting a clean, authoritative approach, a corrective for worry and confusion.

'Not talk to Eve? But I must . . .'

'You'll have to make up your mind, certainly.'

'I'll have to. I'm her mother. It's funny . . .' She searched for the vocabulary that would best describe the situation. 'You imagine that the mothering bit might come to an end when they leave home. All the protecting and fussing, I mean. But it doesn't.'

'Of course, and I know nothing about that. But my instinct ...' Lara clasped her hands together while she listened '... my instinct tells me you should spare Eve unnecessary distress until you're clearer in your mind as to what's going on. It may be nothing and *you* weren't meant to see it.'

'But I did.' Lara discovered that her fingers were now tightly clenched. Making an effort, she said, 'I'm sorry.' She fixed on the blue shirt and concentrated on steady breathing.

Robin observed her agitation. 'It's OK. This is very difficult for you.'

'Sorry,' she repeated. She released her fingers and the blood coursed through them. 'I know this isn't the same as facing a bomb. I know it's not the same as inching towards an IED in the searing heat with nothing between you and eternity except a pair of pliers.'

'Did I ever tell you about the real bastard one at the bridge where the main charge was tucked up under the crossbeam and impossible to reach? It's a good story.'

She grinned wanly. 'Be my guest.'

'But why don't we talk about castles and camels? There's so much more to say.'

'Of course.' She blinked. 'But I can't come ... I'm sorry about that too.'

'Even so,' he said gently.

They talked about Syria. She asked questions and Robin outlined his itinerary. Damascus, Krak des Chevaliers ... He told her a little about the landscape, about the country's swirling history of Ottomans, Mamelukes, Bedouins and what they meant to him. He also reiterated that, in his opinion, trouble might be brewing there now. The Middle East was changing. Fascinated, she watched and listened and wanted to respond . . . yet something ugly was in the way.

No fool, he got the message. 'Lara, this isn't working.'

'I don't mean to be rude.'

'You're not.' He looked round for the waiter. 'Do you want to talk it over further?'

'Yes and no. All I can think about is Eve—I can't bear this.'

'Of course, and you must consider what's best for her.' Flipping open his wallet. 'You don't need me to tell you that, always with these things, you have to be careful you're not really thinking about yourself.'

'I know.'

'*You* can't bear the betrayal? Wouldn't be such an odd thing, would it?'

She fell silent.

'Eve and Andrew and the others, they're young, Lara. They'll cope. That's what they do. There are a lot of rights and wrongs, but they have to decide which is which.'

Upset was making her stupid and clumsy. 'Is that what you tell your patients? That sexual betrayal could be OK?'

'For God's sake, *no.*'

The words whipped from him and her eyes flew to his.

'No,' he repeated, more moderately, and laid the wallet on the table between them. 'But as counsellors we acknowledge each case is different, yes? Humans are wildly different in their responses, yes?'

She bit her lip. 'Agreed.'

'What you and I might feel about or, rather, consider betrayal is not necessarily what others feel or consider.'

'Clearly Andrew doesn't,' she said.

Truth was often contrary and private, and she knew little of Andrew and Eve's relationship, only what they chose to show her.

'All I'm saying is, go carefully.' He pulled a note out of the wallet.

She reached for her purse. 'Please.'

Robin shook his head. 'My evening.'

'Thank you.' She folded her hand across her bag. The strap felt comfortingly familiar and she ran it through her fingers. 'You know, a family wedding magnifies everything, including the dramas. Everyone wants there to be hope and anticipation, fuss and frills.' She shrugged. 'Flowers and excitement. All that.'

As they strolled back along the Embankment to Waterloo, she continued, 'What I mean is, weddings trick us into believing something extraordinary is taking place.'

'In a way, it is.'

A rabble of commuters, walkers, performers still inhabited the area. London's lights were switching on. On the London Eye, the blue pinpoints acted as beacons.

'You've been kind, Robin.'

'Have I?'

'It's a case of "physician heal thyself" and you counsel well.'

'Work in progress,' he admitted. 'Learned between ops. The boys often needed to iron out the snarls in their heads. Combat doesn't end in sword-into-ploughshare stuff. It's a high-adrenalin switchback with the add-on of bullets. It's riding tailgate in the Ranger with a dirty great weapon in one hand and thinking you're God. It's coming home and knowing you're not. It's being alone with unpleasant things. Knowing, too, that you don't fit in any more with normal life. It's counting the days back, not forward, to the time when you were running with your mates down Bomber Alley.'

'Why did you join up?'

'I had a wicked youth and it was one way of sorting me out.'

'Did it?'

'Yes and no.' Robin dodged the outstretched sword of a living statue of Julius Caesar at the bottom of Hungerford Bridge. They stopped to look at it/him.

'How Caesar has fallen . . .' Robin threw a coin into his begging bowl.

'Shush. You might upset him and put him off conquering.'

A little further on, Robin said, 'I'm not sure if you're ever rehabilitated, Lara. One is unfinished business for ever.'

She thought back to their previous conversation. *The flashbacks*. 'A realist and stoic, then.'

'Yes.'

A final snake-trail of commuters was making its way across the bridge and towards the station, and Robin looked up as one of them clattered down the steps. 'Tim!'

Impatient, annoyed, the man halted with a

neat movement. 'What?' Then broke into a smile. 'Robin!' The two men clasped hands and shook. 'For God's sake.' He shook his head. 'I thought you'd gone out east somewhere.'

He was thin, almost gaunt, clean-shaven and neatly dressed in neutral clothes, with a pair of boots similar to the ones Robin favoured.

'You never could keep up,' Robin responded.

She was interested to see that Robin made an inventory of Tim's face. Nose in one piece. *Check*. Eyes intact. *Check*. Just like I do with the daughters, she thought. Front line, parenthood, they had things in common.

'Tim, meet Lara Russell. Lara, this is Tim West, companion in arms and the man to be with in trouble. We haven't seen each other for some time.'

'That's obvious,' she said, with a smile. And it was. The two men were sizing each other up with the fervour of people who knew a lot about each other, enough to trust them. 'Why don't I leave you both to it?'

However, Tim West couldn't stop. 'I'll ring you, Robin,' he said. 'OK? I promised Daisy I'd be home. This time at least.' He shrugged. 'What can you do?' With that, he hurried off trainwards but, just before he vanished, he turned and raised a hand to Robin.

He gave a faint sigh. 'Bad days. But glory days too.'

'You worked together?'

'Black ops. Don't ask.'

Something didn't quite add up. 'You're friends?'

'Yes,' he said simply. 'Very good ones.'

'Then why don't you see more of each other?'

'It's tangled.'

She could see him unravelling the contradictions.

'When you return from the front line, with or without injury, you realize that you have to relearn life. Nothing new, it's the warrior's fate. It's written about a lot. To do so, you must shuffle off what got you through out there. Tim and I understand that we shouldn't see too much of each other. He has a wife.' Robin's laugh was edged with . . . not bitterness, but blackness. 'Daisy reckons that the army's plundered their fair share of Tim. She's right. Carey thought that too.' She caught echoes of resentment. 'But she's also wrong.'

'I think I understand. A little, perhaps.'

He squinted down at her. 'It would be nice if you did. Even in a small way. Fighting is muddled, surreal, breaks the spirit, breaks the body and takes you to the edge of madness. Your mind runs round in circles. Yet here we are.'

She murmured, 'But you wouldn't have missed it.'

Beside her, he gave a nod of assent—a gesture of surrender and rebellion.

The colour of the sky had deepened into sunset—a lemony pink, tangerine and cassis. She pointed. 'Aren't they the colours of the Middle East?'

She had hit a nerve. He turned to her and she read in his face a longing and need as deep as the impending night.

An image from a dream flashed through her, of running barefoot through, of all places, the garden at Membury. Sharp, tussocky blades of grass had cut her flesh and her breath thudded in her chest.

It vanished.

Their faces and bodies were close. Something

was stirring—lust, curiosity, emotions that were powerful, raw, difficult. She wanted to will herself back into the thick of passion, glorious, messy emotion and frantic physical sensation.

Yet she held herself rigid.

I can't.

Robin stepped back. 'I'll see you, Lara.'

Chapter Thirteen

Wedding Plans: bridesmaids. Meet me: Janson's Health Spa, Friday 6 p.m. Cost: on me

'The bridesmaid question . . .' Eve met them in the lobby at Janson's. 'I thought we could sort it without Mum.' She surveyed her sisters. 'That's why I didn't ask her.'

Eve was looking particularly pretty in genius-cut jeans and a tiny jacket. Jasmine had come straight from work and had the dead look of someone at the end of the day. Maudie had just tumbled off the train. She was having trouble with a contact lens and her left eye wept.

Jasmine and she regarded their sparkling, energetic sister with some acidity.

'Why didn't you want Mum?' Maudie demanded. 'She'll have views.'

'Of course she has views. We all have views. Hers usually suck, but she's entitled to them, considering how she's putting herself out for you.'

As one, her sisters turned to look at her. Maudie *never* stuck up for their mother.

'I know she is,' said Eve, in a low voice. 'But she gets so involved . . . and then it's difficult to sort things out.'

Maudie changed her opinion. Eve was right. Fresh air and clear decision-making were needed in the endless wedding discussions. Particularly since she, Maudie, had other things to think about. Big things. Wonderful, scary things.

Jasmine peered at her. 'Looking pleased with yourself, Maudie.'

'And why not?'

'No reason,' said Jasmine. 'You just do.'

Hitherto foreign to her, financial matters were becoming a source of interest. She asked, 'Who's paying for the wedding?'

Eve fiddled with the strap of her bag. 'Andrew's parents have contributed. Dad is obviously paying the lion's share.'

'And Mum?' asked Maudie.

'She's paying for some things.' Eve shepherded them towards the receptionist, who sat behind an arrangement of spiky succulents clearly imported from outer space. 'Don't look like that, Maudie. She wanted to.'

Maudie sent an unsisterly look in Eve's direction.

The receptionist—immaculate, dewy and clad in white from head to foot—checked them in. It was, Maudie thought, like being attended by an airbrushed Disney angel. The progression from changing room (stocked with expensive creams and soaps smelling of stephanotis) to shower room (just as expensively set up) made her feel queasy. The on-show luxury was over the top. She wasn't used to it. None of them were used to luxury: it wasn't part of their lives.

They reassembled in the steam room, wrapped in identical white towels and turbans.

'Bridesmaids.' Eve plunged back into the subject. Eve, the terrier.

Half a dozen other women, sleek and cellulite-free, were arrayed in various poses on the tiled platforms. Maudie glared at them. *My body is a temple.* Yeah. Janson's might be a place of worship, but it was also a den of tyranny where the perfect female body reigned. No one with the slightest muffin top, the suggestion of a varicose vein, a hint of down on the lip would dare venture into it.

Eve settled herself on a platform. 'Please pay attention.'

'Oh, God,' said Maudie.

One of the women uncoiled herself like a spring and stalked towards the door.

The temperature rose.

A catwalk of ghastly dresses dotted though Maudie's mind. Only too vividly. Green meringue? Blue meringue? No, worse, far worse. Pink meringue dress. The sweat beginning to slide down her exposed flesh was only half in response to the punishing temperature.

Eve's face gleamed like a china doll's. 'The thing is, I take it you're both happy to be bridesmaids? If you aren't, Andrew's nieces would be fine.'

The get-out clause. 'The thing is—' Maudie began.

Eve interrupted: 'Just so you know, Andrew's fine about you being bridesmaids.'

It was an odd thing to say. Or was it? Whatever, Maudie didn't like the sound of Andrew's permission being sought.

If possible, Maudie's boredom with the wedding

—the blood-sucking jamboree—intensified. She lay flat on the tiles and plotted the Great Escape. From her prone position she said, 'Don't rely on me.'

Jasmine tucked an escapee strand of hair under the turban. 'Do you know why we have bridesmaids?'

'No, but you're going to tell us,' murmured Maudie.

'They were decoys for the devil, who had wicked designs on the bride. In the old days, they wore the same dress as she did to dupe him.'

'You'll keep me safe, then?' asked Eve. 'Won't you?'

Maudie sat upright.

'Of course, darling,' said Jasmine. Impassioned and quite determined.

Maudie caught Jasmine's eye. What *was* Jasmine trying to convey? A question mark, a worry? She couldn't work it out.

Back into battle. 'Eve … I'm trying to tell you I've got the interview for Harvard.'

'*What?*'

'That's great, Maudie,' Jasmine said.

Yet another of the sleek women sashayed out of the room, and three more drifted in. They were talking loudly and the steam room began to feel crowded.

'But that means …' Eve put two and two together.

'Eve …' Maudie was aware she was failing to tackle the subject head on. 'I'm far too big to be a bridesmaid, anyway.' She spread out her hands. 'Look at me. *Huge.* And you're so delicate.'

'Don't do yourself down,' said Jasmine, and then proceeded to put her own self down. 'Eve, I'm too old to be a bridesmaid.'

'Well, matron-of-honour, then,' said Eve.

They were flushed from the heat. Even so, a wave of additional colour swept over Jasmine's features. Maudie slipped her arm around the slender, slippery shoulders. 'And a beautiful one.' Eve had been tactless. Even an idiot could work out that Jasmine was touchy about being the unmarried older sister.

'Matron-of-honour is good.' Jasmine being Heroic. She was brilliant at Heroic.

The war heroine . . . Jasmine, codenamed Violette, slipping under cover into occupied territory, the Sten tucked under her arm . . .

Later, they sat on loungers by a turquoise pool, flanked by tropical plants. High above, suspended from the ceiling, there was a cage of parakeets, and the atmosphere was the hot, saturated one of the tropics. Jasmine's phone beeped. 'Sorry, have to answer this. Client.' Talking into it, she got up and moved away.

Eve was silent. The towelling turban stretched her face. Scrubbed of makeup, she was vulnerable. 'Do I get the feeling no one wants to be my bridesmaid?' she asked Maudie.

Maudie shrugged. 'Eve, if . . . if I get a place . . . look, it's not of my choosing.'

Eve sent Maudie a long, cool look. 'My God,' she said. 'You really would miss my wedding.'

'I've thought and thought,' said Maudie. *Those who dare win.* Even so, her stomach heaved. 'I know it's your big day, of course it is, and I'll be desperate about missing it. But isn't the marriage what's important? And I plan to be around for a lot of that.'

Eve stared at her. 'You've said that before.'

'So I have.' Maudie fiddled with her towelling turban. 'If there's a choice to be made, and I don't want to make a choice, but if I have to, I feel it should be to the advantage of my life. Just like you're making your choice.' She added, 'I *know* it sounds dreadful.'

'You're right,' said Eve, and the hand resting on her knee trembled. 'It sounds *dreadful* because I thought the whole point of a wedding was that everyone was there to participate in it. You make an effort.'

Jasmine sauntered back, dropped on to her lounger and closed her eyes. 'I could stay here for ever.' Then she murmured, 'I *am* staying here for ever.'

'Maudie's just told me that if she gets a place at Harvard she's finally decided that she won't be here for the wedding.'

Jasmine opened her eyes wide. 'Maudie, is that true?' She sat up and slipped into the eldest-sister straitjacket. 'Have you thought out all the implications?' She didn't appear to be hostile. In fact, the reverse.

'What else can I do?'

'I can think of an alternative.' The comment slid sarcastically off Eve's tongue.

I'm less brave than I thought. Maudie swallowed. The fissures in the family rock ran down the years. Eve walled up in her cardboard-box houses: 'Maudie Keep Out.' Eve and Jasmine's togetherness. It was never mentioned but she knew that those two felt differently about her. She had envied her stepsisters. They had an aura of tragedy—*lost their mother, poor darlings. Tinies.*

They had confidence. They had purpose. They had togetherness. Doused in untouchable suffering, they were special.

But . . .

Observing Eve's obvious hurt was difficult. But (she prayed) Harvard beckoned (and pink meringue repelled). What price one's own desires against another whom—shameful confession—she did not love as much as some she could name? Quickly, so as not to weaken, she said, 'Please, please, forgive me, Eve. It might not happen but I had to say something.'

'Actually,' Jasmine (war heroine) stepped into the breach, 'I'd love to be a bridesmaid.'

'Thank you,' said Eve. '*Thank* you.'

Faced with the fallout from her own self-interest, Maudie was brought up short by the steely power and purity of its opposite. *Lesson to be learned, Maudie.*

'I'm going for a swim.' Eve swung her legs off the lounger and moved to one end of the pool, poised herself on the edge and dived in. Her immersion seemed, to Maudie, designed to shut them out.

Jasmine appeared riveted by the spectacle. After a moment, Maudie asked, 'Are you worried about Eve?'

Jasmine didn't look at her. 'I don't know,' she answered.

'A feeling or a fact?'

'Sort of the former.'

'You think too much.'

Jasmine turned a fierce face on her. 'And you don't think at all.'

The too-sweet smell of stephanotis soap was setting Maudie's teeth on edge. 'Jas?' She picked up her towel. 'I'm sorry. Truly.' Jasmine was now watching Eve arrow through the water, and she struggled to make amends. 'We could always earmark a dress and buy it at the last minute.'

'Maybe. Suggest it to Eve.'

Maudie pleated the end of the towel between her fingers. At times like this she minded acutely that she had no proper sibling. If only . . . If only what? Occasionally she permitted herself to imagine how she and Louis might have got on. Maybe they would have gone go-karting together. Slashed their thumbs with a penknife and mingled their blood. Louis wouldn't have wanted her to be his bridesmaid. She knew that for sure.

'I'm only thinking of *you*,' Alicia had said when, the previous week, Maudie had had a wobble over Harvard and the wedding. 'You don't want to begin at a disadvantage.'

To think she might never have met Alicia—after all, it was only an accident that her aunt lived near the sixth-form college. Choosing a friend gave one an autonomy that was impossible for a child, and she was taken aback by how much pleasure she derived from this (slightly unlikely) alliance. It was a revelation to have one's future ambitions considered, and reflected on, in such an intense, focused way. In a crazily composed family such as hers, the individual drowned.

'Never have children,' she had advised Alicia, who had laughed.

A dripping Eve returned to the lounger and resettled herself, and they switched to discussing practicalities. The water slapped the sides of the stylish pool and the parakeets screeched, and Maudie broached the idea of having a dress in reserve. The swim had restored Eve's equilibrium, and she agreed. They thrashed out an *entente*. Jasmine would be chief bridesmaid, Andrew's two little nieces would be flower-girls and Maudie would step in as the second bridesmaid, if and when.

Eve snapped into Notebook mode. 'Funnily enough, you both suit the same colours.' She tapped a biro against her teeth. 'I was thinking dusky pink.'

Maudie groaned.

Jasmine had attached two tokens to her phone, and they emitted tiny clinks as she checked for messages. 'Let's take a day off and mount a dawn raid on the shops.'

'I've already had a look around.' Eve imparted the information as if she had been engaged on a mission of the utmost mystery and importance.

Maudie prayed hard: *Please, please, may I get to Harvard*.

*   *   *

'I fear Evie wants me to wear pink,' Jasmine told Duncan.

'You fear?'

'I do.'

For once they were at his flat for the evening and she had rustled up an omelette for supper.

He appraised her gravely. 'Yup. You look a pink sort of person. She's got it right.'

She dipped her finger into her glass and flicked water at him. 'You cannot imagine how I hate the thought.'

'Let me see. I cannot imagine how you hate

the thought.' He chewed and swallowed. 'Do you know? I can imagine. Mainly because in the next few painful months you will tell me over and over again.'

'Am I that predictable, Duncan?'

'Yup.'

'So, do you know what I'm thinking a lot of the time?' To her surprise, the idea was troubling. The no-place-to-hide sort of troubling.

He looked up sharply, and the tease vanished. 'Don't look so appalled. I thought that was what lovers aspired to.'

She put down her fork and pushed her plate aside. 'They do and they don't.'

Duncan did the same. 'That's odd,' he said. 'I really want to know what goes on in your head and it matters to me what you're feeling.'

She hastened to say, 'Me, too.'

He stared at her. Then his face cleared. 'That's OK, then.' He got up and came round the table to kiss her. 'You had me worried for a moment.'

She had herself worried. She had always told herself that her love for Duncan was complete, all-embracing, sealed. But sometimes, just sometimes, she realized that wasn't the case at all.

Chapter Fourteen

Eve's email:

Flowers and Guest List

Sarah pestered them to come down to Membury to discuss the wedding. 'She says it's important to take decisions *in situ*, and there's a wedding trade fair in the nearby town if we want to drop in on it. I think we have to go,' Lara explained, when she phoned Jasmine.

Jasmine was mired in a huge new project so hush-hush that it was referred to by the code-name 'Merlin'. It demanded every ounce of her energy and resources. She protested that she hadn't time.

'Hey,' said Duncan, to her enormous surprise. 'Not true, babe.' He insisted they took a Saturday off. 'I want to see the famed Membury,' he said. 'After all, if I'm to transfix the guests as best man, I'd like to see where I'm to do it.'

Bless. Duncan had decided she needed a day off. It was a happy thought and she guarded it carefully.

Here they were, then—Lara, Eve, Maudie, herself and Duncan—eating lunch at Membury.

The kitchen faced north. It was gloomy and smelt of damp, past lives and past meals. It needed fresh paint, a new cooker—actually, a complete overhaul. It wasn't going to get it. Bill had made clear that the budget for refurbishment was on hold. What is it that drives people to take on projects they know they can't manage? Jasmine wondered. Pride? Myopia? Still, if scaling the huge mountain of

Membury pleased her father, so be it.

As always, Sarah had done her best. Duncan appreciated the beautifully cooked roast chicken, with red peppers stewed in balsamic vinegar, and asked for a second helping. 'Sarah, you should be a TV cook.' Jasmine wasn't sure if Sarah considered this to be a compliment. But it was plain that she was charmed by his manners and sweetness. Duncan then interrogated Bill, politely but inexorably, on his plans for the garden. Jasmine eavesdropped with awe on his expert filleting of her normally uncommunicative father.

'Do you have oil seed rape round here?' Duncan was asking. 'I've read it acts like a magnet for bees. They ignore the apple blossom and race to the big smell.'

Duncan knew nothing, zilch, about bees.

The two men occupied, Sarah was at liberty to pursue her objectives.

She launched in: 'Eve, about the flowers. I'd like to do them.' She offered the salt to Lara, who shook her head. 'I've got plenty of ideas. Church, marquee, bouquet. I feel I've got my feet under the table in the village so I can get the flower rota on to it.'

Eve was about to have a fit. Jasmine stared hard at her plate.

'How do you feel about ivy twined around columns?' Sarah batted on. 'And for the tables? Ice-cream cartons are useful, the square ones. If you paint them gold or silver, they'll do as centrepieces. They'd look good with carnations and a nice evergreen sprig of something.'

'Sarah,' said Eve, 'I had other—'

'Evie,' said Jasmine, 'you eat masses of

ice-cream. You could start collecting now.'

She did everything possible to avoid Lara's eye.

Sarah turned on her. 'Are you poking fun at me?'

'No, Sarah.' But she had been.

'Carnations,' repeated Sarah. 'Long-lasting.'

Sarah had no idea what was going on in Eve's head. Or what the Notebook revealed. Why should she?

But Jasmine knew. Eve had been thinking chocolate cosmos, hydrangeas, peony roses, mint, marjoram and rosemary. A glorious clutter of English country flowers, rustic *and* contemporary— that had been Eve in full flow to Jasmine. Jasmine stole a peep at Sarah, who was not looking her normal kindly self. From her practical standpoint, Sarah wouldn't comprehend the depth of Eve's yearning romanticism. Or that her vision for her wedding was, like all great visions, complete and non-negotiable.

'Sarah . . .' Eve trod carefully '. . . you're so sweet to be so concerned . . .'

Her mother was quiet, Jasmine noticed. She was eating little and slowly, chewing each mouthful as if it was an effort. It occurred to her that Lara had lost weight. 'OK, Mum?'

Lara laid down her knife and fork, leaving half her food untouched. 'Sorry, Sarah. It was good, though.'

Jasmine fixed on the flower arrangement by the sink. Pale blue irises and florid yellow gerberas had been crammed into a variegated vase. The assembly (dire) contributed nothing to Sarah's case.

'Sarah, I've got the flowers organized,' began Eve.

The normally soft and conciliatory Sarah

211

had morphed into an opponent of steel. 'If you don't like carnations think about orchids.' She slotted chicken and potato on to her fork. 'Green cymbidiums are excellent. And canna lilies come in such strong, dark colours, these days, and their structure holds. We're going to have a shot at growing them, aren't we, Bill?'

Bill hesitated—and Jasmine's lip twitched. She knew he knew he had a tricky situation on his hands and she recognized his detached, sitting-on-the-fence expression. It used to madden her.

'Sarah,' he said, 'haven't we enough to worry about with getting the house and garden ready?'

Sarah ploughed on: 'Sunflowers will be cheap. I've checked.'

A strangled gasp escaped Eve. 'Sarah, I've already agreed with a florist. We've begun work on the concept.'

Sarah was puzzled. 'Concept?' Long pause. 'I had no idea. I thought one could use what was in season and plentiful. But I could do a *concept* for nothing. Isn't it very much the same as a simple flower arrangement?' Having thrashed through this verbal maze, she turned to Bill. 'Do you mind paying for a concept?'

'Dad and I have talked about the budget,' said Eve.

'You never mentioned it, Bill.' Sarah began to clear the plates in an offended way and Jasmine leaped up to help her.

She followed Sarah into the larder, which opened off the kitchen. 'Sorry about that, Sarah, but Eve is very particular.'

'Your father should rein her in,' said Sarah, crossly. Unlike her. 'She can't have everything.

I mean . . .' she gestured to the scummy wooden shelving and the tiny window, whose mesh needed replacing '. . . we don't.'

'Jas,' her father had once confided in a rare instance, 'people can muck things up badly, and there's no way back. So, you must be careful. I wasn't. I thought I could manage the situation with you girls, provided Lara and I were civilized.' The conversation had gone no further, but he had made a glancing allusion to it later. 'Even with the best intentions, it doesn't necessarily pan out.'

'Dad should have talked to you,' she said.

Sarah picked up a bowl of trifle with unnecessary force.

Back in the kitchen Lara took the bull by the horns. 'Why don't we discuss the guest list?'

'Ah, yes.' Sarah placed the trifle, which was stiff with cream, on the table and spooned it into bowls.

'Only a tiny bit, please,' Lara said.

'Minute for me,' said Eve. 'Here are the numbers. We divided the list into quarters. Andrew and I take half, Andrew's parents have a quarter and you and Mum have a quarter between you.'

'Oh,' said Sarah. 'That suggests we can only invite about ten people. I was hoping my brother and his family, and the Kirbys—'

'But they have nothing to do with us,' said Eve.

'But they are to do with me and, now, your father.'

'Oh, God,' said Eve.

'Bill, what do you say?'

Eve cut him off. 'Sarah, please don't ask people who don't know us. I know I'm plotting a big splashy wedding but it is *our* day.'

What was happening? Jasmine shot a look at

Lara. Sarah was the soul of moderation and tact but both had deserted her.

'You're the central attraction, of course, Eve,' Sarah said. 'But, in my opinion, ownership of a wedding goes wider. Particularly . . .' she glanced around her appalled audience '. . . since it's being held here.' She placed a particularly large helping of trifle in front of Eve. 'Don't you think?'

*   *   *

In the car on the way to the wedding fair in the nearby town, Eve, Jasmine and Duncan discussed the metamorphosis of the gentle Sarah.

'Frankenstein or what?' Glad to be shot of the politics and tensions, Duncan drove at a smartish pace. 'Here be monsters.' He poked Jasmine's thigh. 'That's a warning. Weddings change people.'

'You know something?' said a fired-up Eve in the back. 'You're right.' After a minute, she said, 'Could you slow down a bit, please? All that trifle's made me feel sick.'

They were still laughing as they paid the entrance fee to the wedding fair. Within minutes of entering, amusement turned to . . . not distaste but close.

'We're in the wrong clothes,' said Jasmine.

'Yup,' said Eve.

Attendees were predominantly female, decked out in checked two-piece suits with fringed hems and gold chains. They were mostly over forty. A few brides tried on dresses in inadequately curtained-off booths—some of which were replicas of medieval jousting tents—while the loudspeaker played Mendelssohn's Wedding March over and over.

What? Jasmine thought.

There wasn't a fresh flower to be seen or a bridegroom, but there were plenty of raised voices, with pink plastic, rampant consumerism and one-upmanship.

She watched Duncan pale. 'You've brought me to a horror movie.' He grabbed Jasmine's hand. 'Let's go.'

A girl modelling a wedding dress stalked past. Her face and shoulders were bright orange and the dress was skin tight.

Although she agreed with him in principle, Jasmine said, 'People have to earn a living.'

'I'm not wasting one more second of my life on this.' With that, he retreated to the car.

Eve and Jasmine wandered up and down the aisles.

'There's nothing here,' said Jasmine.

Eve swallowed. 'If I ever turn into one of those,' she pointed to a bride having a stand-up row in a fake medieval booth with her mother, 'you're to shoot me.'

*　　　*　　　*

At Membury, Lara helped Sarah with the washing-up. This was accomplished mostly in silence.

When the last plate and glass had been put away, she said, 'Sarah can we clear the air?' Sarah turned her back. 'About the flowers.'

Sarah fiddled with a saucepan. 'It's fine,' she said, meaning the opposite. 'I've got the message.'

'Shall we talk about it?'

'No.'

'Right,' said Lara. 'I'll go outside for a bit.'

She fetched her jacket and let herself out of the back door. The kitchen garden was in the rudimentary renovation phase. A row of onions had been set, while spinach and carrot shoots pushed through the earth. A sieve overflowing with pebbles and stones had been abandoned on the path, a garden fork beside it.

Hand on hip, she surveyed the husbandry. These were things, basic, honest things, on which she would like to fix, garden business and routine, not the terrible anxiety that was plaguing her.

She made for the sunken garden, the planned site for the marquee. To do so, she had to cross the lawn in front of the house. A figure stood at the french windows leading on to the terrace. Bill. She quickened her pace and went around the yew hedge. The sun played on her face and, after the city, the air was sweet and felt . . . She searched for the word. It felt *expectant*.

What was it about Membury that had so crept under her skin?

A couple of days ago, Robin had left a postcard on her desk of a myrtle tree blooming in Damascus: 'Further to the Membury myrtle. You might like to know that a sprig of it was traditionally tucked into a bride's bouquet and it has a long association with the goddess of love. Venus is said to have worn a garland of it (and not much else) when she rose from the sea . . .'

She had rung him up. 'You're being very sweet.'

'Is that what you call it?'

'Trying to divert me?'

'Possibly. Or part of a campaign that I was so rude to you about . . .'

216

The pulses sprang into action. A Mexican wave of them.

'I've said no,' she murmured, with real regret.

'Skirmishes are all part of a campaign. There can be one. There can be many. I leave the thought with you.'

In the sunken garden, she paused and looked up to where the myrtle grew.

Its DNA issued from the heat and dust of the east, which Robin understood. The person who had planted it had also understood its lineage, and its needs, and placed it prudently in a sheltered spot near the wall—but it looked as though it had battled hard to survive the winter. It was alive, but she knew that it yearned to be sending its roots down into Mediterranean terrain. 'But you made it through,' she informed it.

'Lara?'

'Go away, Bill,' she said, as he came up behind her. 'I don't want witnesses to my madness.'

'You haven't lost the habit of talking to yourself.'

'No, and I don't suppose I ever will.' She didn't want to look at him. 'I saw you watching me from the window.'

'I want to talk to you.'

The old tensions rose to the surface. 'Is something the matter?' Reluctantly, she turned. 'If it's Sarah, I'll get Eve to repair relations.'

He had changed into a shabby pair of cords and a jacket with torn sleeves, clothes he wore as easily and comfortably as a second skin. 'I wanted to talk about Maudie.'

'You could have rung.'

'I could have done.' Someone—Bill?—had been digging the flowerbeds. A pot full of stones stood on the path. Bill bent down, hoicked up another from the freshly dug earth and tossed it in with the rest. 'I know I've said this before but we must make more of an effort to talk about Maudie. I would have liked *some* say in her decisions.'

'You and me both,' she flashed back. 'Have you noticed? Maudie is now a law unto herself. Have *you* talked to her?'

He scuffed a shoe along the flagstone. 'Not really.'

'You're her father.'

He raised his eyes. 'Walk with me, Lara. I think it'll be easier.'

Her gaze drifted over the garden. Underneath its bones life was in full throttle. She could almost hear its pulses, the beat of its growth—the basic, honest things. 'Actually, I need to talk to you too . . . I must talk to you.'

They trod down the steps, walked across the lawn towards the area where the grass grew thick and tangled, and Lara said, 'You underestimate Maudie.'

Bill inspected a mole heap—a brown upheaval amid the wet green stalks. 'I used to stamp on these as a child. I wouldn't do that now.'

'Good.'

'As I grow older, I find it impossible to kill anything.'

She looked around. Garden. Sky rippled with cloud. New foliage. 'How can one think otherwise? Especially here.' The tips of her shoes were coated with mud. 'Membury is special.'

With sudden passion and eagerness: 'You see it?'

Like old times. All those occasions when Bill and she had sat at a table with the children, both of

218

them working frantically to feed one or another, or to mop up. There had been a togetherness in their actions, a sense of shared purpose. Sometimes he would glance at her lovingly. At others he would smile or make a joke.

'I do. Rather, I *feel* it.'

They studied the mole heap.

'Bill, will you make an effort with Maudie? Don't be like . . .'

'Like?'

'I was going to say like us.'

Point taken?

'I plan to.' His eyes met hers. His were rueful. 'But I'd like to know what you think about it all.'

'I accept Maudie's decisions.' *Be truthful.* 'I think.' They moved on from the mole heap towards the stream. It was—more or less—a companionable progress.

House, garden, sky and trees . . . There was unity in what she was seeing and, suddenly, she realized that an important element was missing.

'Time for us to sort things out, too, Bill?'

He had shoved his hands into his pockets. 'Is that possible?'

'Why so sceptical?' Her gaze rested on the spread of vivid green grass under the copper beech. 'With Evie . . . with Evie getting married, it's a good moment.'

Bill's lips tightened and he glanced at the house where Sarah was, no doubt, brooding miserably on what had happened over lunch.

She touched his sleeve. 'Bill?'

He wheeled around. 'It's all been said and done.'

The rapidity of his attack told her that he thought about it still.

Flashback

'Please, Lara,' he says. 'No children when we marry. It's a big thing to ask you, and I understand if you can't accept it.' She recollects his frightening grief for Mary, so intense still at this point. 'I can't go through that again. I . . . I can't fight it.'

'But that is such a big promise,' she says.

He smoothes back the hair from her face. The beloved face, as he often called it. 'Yes, it is. That's why it has to be clear now.'

She loves him too much to accuse him of being frightened of life. Or, rather, now that she is with him, there is no need to do so. She understands his fear, and agrees to the bargain. After all, having children killed Mary.

She marries him.

How ignorant she proves to be. Deeply ignorant of the longing that almost overnight takes root—a wordless song, a drumbeat in her blood.

Somehow, she persuades Bill to have what turns out to be Maudie and, despite the trauma of her arrival, Bill survives the episode, loves and wants his third daughter.

This is Lara's mistake. When she is up and about again, cooking, cleaning, mothering, she is clutching new-found knowledge delightedly to herself: the bad luck has moved on and found somewhere else to roost.

'Isn't Maudie enough? Aren't we enough, Lara?' he blazes at her, when she tells him Louis is on the way.

Bill now repeated, 'It's been said and done, Lara.'

They were standing very close—as close as in the early days when his proximity had set her senses dancing—and a little of the remembered electricity

220

crackled between them.

'We never really understood each other's point of view.' After all these years, the confession was a relief. 'I can finally admit it, Bill. But I was desperate . . . *desperate.*'

She felt him distance himself.

There were all sorts of things that might be said.

Such as: 'It was complicated. Louis died, or rather he never lived. You went . . . and we ended up hating each other. I don't know how the bad feelings could have been avoided.' She would fight the urge to fold her arms across her chest and defend herself from the arrows of hurt, betrayal and bereavement raining down on her. She could also say: 'Bill, you didn't have to leave me. You could have stayed and we could have dealt with the situation.'

He could reply: 'I felt you'd made it impossible.'

'But we should have tried, Bill.'

'Lara, I *did* try.'

The truth was, they had never talked properly about their situation. She had been too wrapped up in guilt and grief, Bill too angry.

He paced about under the beech, this way and that. Even now she felt his anguish. Finally, he swung round. 'Can *you* understand what it's like to be responsible for a dead wife and a dead son?'

'*Louis,*' she said angrily. 'That's his name.'

'Mary and Louis.'

'But it was my body and Mary's that failed, Bill, not yours.'

There had been the stupid tape of womb music she had planned to play to Louis. The thud of her system and his heartbeat, the only companions he ever knew. There had been the equally stupid furry blackbird, which, when squeezed, replicated its song. There was the tiny Babygro in blue and white stripes, with 'Ahoy There' stamped on the chest.

Lara closed her eyes. *Think sane, sensible, garden things.* She bent down and placed a finger under the spiky petals of a daisy. It felt as light as a baby's breath on her flesh. '*I* couldn't carry Louis to term.'

'There were too many coincidences.' His voice sounded a long way above her.

She addressed the daisy. (So ordinary. So beautifully structured.) 'You must forget all that, Bill.' She straightened up. 'Really. It's time.'

'OK. OK.'

They were now filing alongside the stream—and she knew, absolutely knew, that Sarah was watching them from the house. She took a deep breath and asked him about his long-term plans for the garden. He replied with a description of restructuring and planting, which she only half grasped—for the wedding he would do this and that; afterwards he planned big relocations—but it was good to hear his voice rise with anticipation and pleasure.

When they reaching the landing-stage, he halted. 'You said you wanted to talk to me about something.'

Actually, she had wanted to discuss Andrew and Eve, to ask his opinion about what she had seen. *As Eve's father, what would you do?* But she *had* to ask something else first. Now. The rest could come later. 'I read a book the other day about old houses and their gardens. Apparently, there was a tradition of planting a guardian tree in the north corner of the garden. It was supposed to protect the house from harm, and ward off the cold. I thought . . .' she placed a hand on his arm '. . . you . . . we could do something similar for Louis.'

He took time to answer. 'I'll think about it.' He sounded clipped and upset and she knew he wanted the conversation to finish. She couldn't blame him.

'Promise.'

'I promise.'

She brushed wet fingers down her coat. There was one more thing to get off her chest and then it would be done. 'I hated you for leaving me, Bill.' Her fingers tingled against the material. 'But I hated you more for not dealing with his death. And myself. There. I've told you.'

She tried always to avoid replaying the images of Louis's birth. When she did, it was to reprise Bill blundering away, out of the ward, down the corridor, leaving her marooned in silence. She had concentrated on the jug of water by the bed, the mound her legs made under the sheets, the picture hanging on the wall of lush purple moorland— anything—so that she didn't give in to the scream of despair and guilt.

She added, 'But I understand better now.'

'Can we stop this?' he said.

'Go and find Sarah.' She smiled politely at him. 'After the battle of the flowers, she'll need reassuring.'

She was heading back along the stream when he called something after her. She couldn't make out the words and didn't turn.

Her feet and ankles were damp and muddy but she didn't care. In the water, the weed was sucked this way and that. She thought: Not only does an unhealed wound sap strength, it poisons too.

She and Bill had been poisoned.

Her foot slipped on a branch lying across the

path. She stumbled. Fox fire darted up her leg and the impact shifted the branch aside, revealing ants tracing rapid geometric patterns. Rubbing her ankle, she stooped to observe them. Clever creatures. The mêlée was purposeful. They knew where they were going. A few seized pieces of food (almost bigger than they were) in their mandibles and dragged them away to a place of safety. The rest quick-marched in a column into the grass.

Regroup and save. Not a bad principle.

Carefully, Lara eased the branch back into place. If hers had been a place of dissonance—and its echoes were still audible—she could ensure that the ants kept their home.

Chapter Fifteen

The night before the Harvard interview, Maudie caught the train to London, then made her way down a street lined with expensive but uninspiring hotels and met her father in the Plantagenet Bar at the Sussex. On the journey up, a railway vista— cuttings, back gardens, sidings and suburban stations—had slipped past and she had watched it with some irritation. She didn't want to see her father.

She spotted him at once in a chair by the window. He got up and kissed her. 'What will you drink?'

'Orange juice. I need to sleep well.'

He ordered it, and pushed a bowl of upmarket nuts towards her.

'Is this advice for tomorrow?' She grimaced.

'More advice?'

'Yes and no. I thought I should touch base.'

The bar was non-flashy. Comfortable chairs scattered around the room. Polished glass tables. 'Are you enjoying Membury?'

His eyes lit up. 'Very much.'

'But the important thing is that you and Sarah are happy.'

His face softened. 'Yes, that. It *is* important.'

She forgave him a lot for that answer.

'Did you always know that Sarah was going to inherit?'

He hunted down a cashew in the bowl. 'No. Crucially, before you jump to any conclusions, neither did Sarah.'

'Would I jump to conclusions?' She was beginning to enjoy herself.

'Knowing you . . .'

'But you don't know me.'

He shrugged. 'You ran away to me, Maudie.'

'That was *years* ago.'

'I took it . . . wrongly, perhaps . . . After the initial shock I was pleased you'd come to me.'

It wasn't that she had hated her mother. It was more irritation that had screwed up into such a pitch that she couldn't stand one more day of *Is that essay done? Why didn't you eat your supper? Do you ever brush your hair?* But, just as much, she couldn't take any longer the noise and crowdedness of home: the constant attrition on the ears, the lack of space, even the crumbs on the kitchen floor. She longed for peace, for clean white rooms and to be autonomous, which made her different from her half-sisters. She wanted a room to herself and the peace to read all the books she wanted.

Packing her rucksack, sneaking out of the house when she knew her father would be back from work, running down the road as fast as the rucksack would allow, knowing perfectly well that her mother would be frantic when she discovered she was missing. Her father opening his front door—at that stage he was between Violet and Sarah. *His face.* The terrible realization that she had made a mistake, but refusing to acknowledge it. 'You will take me in,' she had insisted. 'I won't live with *her* . . .'

'If I remember, you called your mother quite a few names.'

She raised an eyebrow. 'Oh?

'Uncaring. Selfish. There were others. You also said she hated you and loved the others.'

Maudie peered at her father. 'And you've come all the way up to London to tell me that? It wasn't exactly true, you know. I played you off against each other. That's what teenagers do. If they spot a weak link they throw dynamite at it. If they're given a chance to cause trouble, they take it.'

Hindsight was ever golden.

Memories of that episode ('aberration' would be a better word) were uneasy. All the to-ing and fro-ing and emotional upheaval that had gone on as her parents negotiated what to do next. She had been stubborn, hysterical, obdurate. 'I want to live with Dad,' she had repeated, over and over again, because she felt she could not back down, and watched, aghast, as her mother dropped her head into her hands and cried.

It was as if a tempest had struck the household, catching up Lara's heartbreak in its path. Jasmine and Eve refused to talk to her. With every day that passed, Maudie's apprehensions deepened as she contemplated the consequences of her action.

Such a mistake. The most basic mechanics of living eluded her father, who showed no interest in learning. No food in the house, no clean sheets, no Cif cream for the bath or sink. Worse, she hadn't known she cared about these things until she didn't have them. Her vision of a cool, white, ordered world vanished in a tumble of dirty laundry on the floor and hairs blocking the plughole. *And* it transpired that her father did not understand her any more than anyone else did. Hardly surprising: she didn't understand herself.

'Can't you be nice to Mum?' her ten-year-old self asked him, as he tried to throw together a supper of scrambled eggs and fried tomatoes.

'I am nice to her.' He beat the eggs with a fork. 'Do I put milk in this?' He answered his question by pouring in a quarter of the bottle. The result was a greyish-yellow liquid.

'Jas and Eve said you left Mum in the bedroom all by herself, crying.'

'My God,' Bill said. 'I have the worst press in the world.' He caught her by the shoulders. 'Listen to me. I may be faithless, but I'm not heartless. Nor am I criminal. I made sure your mother was looked after. Now I make sure that I know as much about you all as I can get out of Mum.' He pressed his forehead against hers. 'I may not live with you but I need to know about you. Your lessons, your friends, the whys and wherefores . . .'

She stared up into his handsome face. For the first time, she experienced doubt and worry about someone whom hitherto she had trusted and certainly not questioned. 'But you left Mummy and us alone.'

He set a plate of scrambled eggs and caramelized tomatoes in front of her. 'Time you shut up, Maudie. You aren't old enough to understand.'

Eventually she had repacked her rucksack and returned to her mother and sisters. The sensation of clean sheets on her bed had been exquisite. And the cramped, noisy house? So comforting, so her home.

Bill had failed to connect with his daughter, but neither had she connected with him. The sisters questioned her closely: 'What sort of things does he do?'; 'Does he talk about us?'; 'Did he let you do anything you wanted?'

To the latter she replied, mendaciously, 'He did.' To their first question she said, 'Lots of things.' But the truth was that she didn't really know.

Because she was clever, it was easy—ridiculously so—to bait him from a distance. 'Don't let Dad know,' she would instruct her sisters, about whatever was currently being decided or when there was some ongoing problem. 'Or, if you do, *don't* tell him why.'

'Don't tell Dad,' she instructed her mother, after her GCSE results came through, all top grade.

'Why on earth not?' Lara's eyebrows shot up. 'He'll be so proud.'

'*Don't* tell him, Mum.'

Lara was ironing sheets with a rolling, swooping movement, designed to get it over and done with as soon as possible. 'He'll have to know sooner or later. And I would have thought you'd want to tell him.'

'No. Not.'

'But why not?'

'Because it will thwart him.'

Her mother set the iron down with a thump. It hissed in protest. 'My God,' she said. 'The Stasi should take lessons from you, darling.'

Bill sipped some whisky and rolled it around his mouth. She knew he knew that she knew he was watching her—a situation that was cubed by the reflections in a long mirror by the bar. 'I want to be sure you're making the right choices, Maudie.'

She noticed that he had had his front tooth recapped (Sarah?). 'I wouldn't be doing it if I didn't think so.'

'You sound so old,' he said.

'I am.' (She wasn't *so* sure about that.) The ice cubes clinked in her glass. 'If you're asking have I gone into the detail, worked out the finances, et cetera, I have.' She raised balled fists. 'Try me.'

Her father sighed. 'Is it so odd that I'm concerned?'

Her answer was swift. 'Frankly, yes.'

He winced. 'One day, God willing, you'll know about being a parent . . .'

Maudie slitted her eyes and her father's figure diminished satisfactorily. After the running-away episode, he had seemed different to her. No longer was he the person for whom she yearned, to whom she turned. He still loomed large—but she viewed him through a haze of disappointment. Later, she even began to think of him as menacing, a malign presence hunched over her thoughts and ambitions.

Placing her glass on the table with a thump, she asked, 'Did you, do you, ever have nightmares about leaving a young mother with three of your children?'

'The prisoner in the dock braced himself for

questions, cross-examination and damnation,' he said lightly. 'Since you ask, yes. It wasn't straightforward. There were things. Private things.'

'Will I never get to the truth?' she cried.

Her father was silent.

She thought of her mother. For years so stick thin she had been almost transparent. Hair badly chopped. Her habit of saying, 'I'm fine, don't worry,' when, clearly, she wasn't. Her occasional collapse into real illness. At those times, help had to be conjured out of nowhere. Aunts and friends were summoned, and the sisters knew they were in for a period when *Mum can't be pestered.*

She hated seeing her mother at bay. When illness hit Lara, it always seemed so *grave.* Older and wiser, she came to understand that Lara's collapses were an attempt to escape her lot. (For a few hours, at least.) Yellow and silent, she lay beached on the pillows with a range of medicaments lined up like tubular bells on the bedside table. *Nerves*, said her grandmother when she was alive. *Stress*, said the doctor.

Lara was obdurate and interfering, which, Maudie finally concluded, was vital to her survival. Older and wiser now, she understood that her mother was far too nosy and far too loving of her daughters to allow herself to go under. She admired that.

'Of course there were private things, Dad. There *always* are,' she said coldly. 'Like you sleeping with Violet. But I still think you shouldn't have left her.'

Then he said something that took the wind out of her sails. 'I'm not going to give up on you, Maudie.'

She got to her feet. 'I have to have an early night.'

He said quietly, 'I'm just telling you again that I'll help you in every way I can. Financially it won't be that much, as you know.'

'I expect not,' she said politely. 'What with the stately home and everything.'

'Maudie,' he caught her arm, 'let there be peace.'

She looked down at him. 'I'm going away, Dad, because I want to get away from everything that's happened. Don't you see?'

'But peace can break out?'

The appeal was not quite on target ... not judged finely enough.

'Wish me luck, Dad.'

The following day, as she was ushered into the interview room where three people waited to talk to her, she felt a strong flash of anger. Meeting her father had shaken her, and she had had a bad night.

I want this, she thought. *More than anything.*

One of the figures sitting behind the long table— groomed, middle-aged, grave—got to his feet and held out a hand. 'We've been looking forward to meeting you, Miss Russell.'

*   *   *

It didn't take long.

Normal Saturday breakfast at home. Check. One bowl of cereal, crackling after she had poured in milk. Check. One extra-strong cup of coffee. A mind only half operational. Check, check.

Running a hand through her hair, her fingers snagged in the strands. A line of gooseflesh erupted on the strip of skin between her pyjama bottoms and the grey marl T-shirt she wore on top.

For once, her mother was quiet. She was staring

into her coffee and attempting to eat a piece of fruit when both of them knew, she really wanted to eat toast and butter.

The radio was on, purveying political and financial news, none of which was reassuring.

The letter flap rattled, followed by a cascade of paper falling to the floor.

'You or me?' her mother asked.

'You,' said Maudie.

'No, you, Maudie.'

Maudie shuffled to the front door, scooped up a clutch of letters, handed them to her mother and returned to her wrestling match with the cereal.

Lara sorted. Bills in one pile. Junk mail in the other.

'Maudie . . .' She was holding out a letter. 'For you.'

The house noises suddenly took on extra resonance. The fridge and the boiler clucked like hens. She was sure she could hear something scuttling in the skirting. The tap dripped stones.

'Oh.'

'Open it, Maudie.'

She had anticipated this moment so often, steeling herself against its impact. Imagining the champagne effect of the best news, the brutal disappointment of the worst. But, she had lectured herself, she would take what came with the cool certainty and grace of the integrated adult.

'I can't open it, Mum. Please.' Her voice had lost its lower register.

Lara slit the envelope with her unused knife.

Maudie watched a parade of expressions flit across her mother's features. 'Oh, Maudie.'

Doubt. Sadness. Regret.

Pride.

'Maudie, you've done it. You clever, clever girl. You've done it.'

'Can you say that again, Mum?'

Her mother read out the acceptance ... pleased to offer ... satisfactory SAT results ... subject to A levels ... financial arrangements ... replies by 1 May. She laid the letter on the table, smoothed it and handed it over.

Maudie observed it from a great height.

Her mother jumped up, extracted a bottle of wine from the cupboard and slid it on to the worktop. 'For tonight.' Then she brushed her hand over her hair. 'Such good news.' She crossed to Maudie and put her arms around her. For a moment, she didn't say anything. Then she did. 'But you'll be leaving.'

Her mother felt as soft and yielding as ever. 'Yes.' The word emerged less steady than Maudie had counted on. 'Yes, I will. They're going to send information about freshmen's week ...'

'Oh, Maudie ...' Her mother was stroking her cheek. 'Freshmen's week, sophomores ... we'll have to get used to the terms. A new vocabulary.'

Her mother released her, and hunkered down to search for a casserole in the cupboard.

'I would have been going somewhere, Mum.' Maudie read and reread the letter—just in case the words fell on to the floor and vanished. 'I know it's going to change everything. I'll find it hard. I know I will. But you'll have the wedding.'

'Yes,' said her mother. 'There's the wedding.'

Chapter Sixteen

Eve's email:

THE DRESS!!! Now we have date, church and Membury on board, we start the fun bit. MEET ME . . .

The dressmaker's *atelier* was in Peckham, hidden in a network of streets, and it was taking all Jasmine's ingenuity to find it. 'But it's worth it,' Eve promised her. 'Talk on the grapevine is all about Ivanka. One day she'll be global and I'll be able to say she made my wedding dress.'

Only for Eve would Jasmine do this. It was a long way and she became impatient. Apart from anything else, it gave her time to reflect, and reflecting led her into dangerous waters.

From the bus, she looked down into the window of the house they were lumbering past. Inside, a woman picked up toys from the floor. The scene was so ordinary that instead of battling with a jealous thought, *I don't want to see Eve's wedding dress*, she concentrated on that instead.

Ringing the bell to the studio, she was admitted by an assistant, a neat, slender girl. Pin-cushion tied to a wrist with elastic. Hair in a high, old-fashioned bun. Pencil skirt. She led Jasmine into a large loft area where the light filtered softly through muslin and gauze.

'Please,' she pointed to rows of slippers in varying sizes waiting by the wall, 'we ask you to take your shoes off.'

Divided into a workshop, which had been curtained off, and a fitting room, Ivanka's *atelier* sold dreamy, unabashed femininity. Creamy walls. Fresh muslin at the windows. A faint suggestion of flower scents. A bowl of ruffled roses.

At one end, rolls of material had been swathed in protective cloth and stacked under the headings 'Duchess', 'Zibeline', 'Faille', 'Georgette', 'Marocain'.

Jasmine imagined the first explorers who had found the Silk Route, and borne these exotically named fabrics home. *Look*, they had cried to hungry merchants, as they unrolled bundles from their protective calico, *such beauty, such workmanship* . . .

'Please.' The assistant touched Jasmine's arm. 'Would you mind taking off your shoes?' She proffered a pair of slippers. 'I'll take you to the fitting room.' She swept aside a curtain and ushered Jasmine in.

Here, the space was arranged to convey intimacy. At one end, there was a rack of dresses in every shade of white, and a long mirror, at the other a shoe rack, with several pairs of bridal shoes, four white chairs, and a table on which were arranged water and glasses, pins, scissors and a tape measure. 'I'm afraid I can't offer you anything to drink but water,' explained the assistant. 'We daren't take any risk with the expensive fabrics.'

Apart from the dresses, there was nothing overtly expensive in the *atelier*. The *backdrop* had been fashioned from cheap, basic materials, but very cleverly. As usual, Eve had got it right, she thought. Her antennae picked up the underground murmurs as automatically as Jasmine picked up her morning cappuccino, and the results were always good. Just like her real mother. 'Your mother possessed taste and discernment.' That much Jasmine *had* got out of her father, who was not given to dropping details unless pushed. The snippet pleased her. She liked to think of 'taste and discernment' being handed from a mother to the outstretched hands of her daughters. A game of Pass the Parcel with useful DNA as the prize.

Not that she liked thinking about her mother— it made her uneasy and full of regret. Death was unfair and left gaps. She wanted to know what Mary had looked like. Yes, she had photographs, but photographs couldn't convey the movement of a person, the alterations of expression, the nuances of hair and skin, habits and gestures. Would Mary have slipped her arms around Eve and herself and said, 'My lovely girls,' as Lara sometimes did?

As so often, when she *did* permit herself to think of her mother, Jasmine found herself focusing on the moment when Mary, battered and exhausted, had given up the struggle. Mary would not have known but she had bequeathed to Jasmine a great psycho drama to revisit: she imagined panicking midwives, the doctor hastily summoned, her father crying, 'No, *no!*' and the wail of a newborn baby impacting dimly on the nothingness creeping through Mary's played-out, haemorrhaging body. Of only one thing she was sure. Even while her mother fought the nothingness, she would have called out for her children.

'Jas ...' Eve wiggled her fingers at her sister. She had been deep in conversation with a smart, white-faced girl, with shoulder-skimming black hair cut sharp as a knife and violet eye shadow. 'This is the brilliant, wonderful Ivanka.'

Hellos were exchanged, and she wondered if she detected just a hint of defensiveness in brilliant, wonderful Ivanka. 'It's always difficult when the relations turn up, I imagine,' she said.

The defensiveness vanished. 'They're ... supportive,' Ivanka grinned wryly, 'but I am used to it.' Her English was thickly accented.

For 'supportive', Jasmine read 'critical'. 'Have you been working here long?'

Again the defensiveness: 'I'm not an illegal.'

Jasmine blushed. 'I was interested.'

'Excuse me, then. I am getting used to the British who say one thing but think another. I think you call it politeness.'

'Right,' said Jasmine.

Ivanka spread three sketches on the table. 'Last time we talked, you preferred this one and the toile has been made up.' She gestured to Eve. 'Undress, please.' Turning to Jasmine: 'This is only the beginning of the process.'

The grave assistant spread a drugget over the polished wood floor in front of the long mirror.

Eve took off her sweater and jeans. Her back was white and tautly gleaming, her legs toned and smooth. How thin she was, these days, thought Jasmine. Too thin—seemingly consumed by her own energy.

Ivanka pointed to the shoes. 'Please find a pair,' she said to Eve. 'We can't try on anything without shoes. I imagine you will choose a pair with heels.' She disappeared behind the curtain.

Eve picked up satin pumps and slipped them on.

Ivanka reappeared with the toile cradled like a sleeping form in her arms.

At her command, Eve stepped into the skirt and the bodice was eased over her arms, then pinned into place. Ivanka arranged the folds of the skirt and train. 'A toile is not the real thing,' she explained to Jasmine. 'Depending on the material, the finished dress will fall differently.' She smiled.

The not-dress was sleeveless, boat-necked and fell in folds from a belted waistline to which an artificial flower had been pinned. It was fashionable—very—and unyielding in its retro-chic.

'Plain,' said Ivanka, narrowing the violet-embossed eyes. 'Veeery plain.' The 'very' crackled with Ukrainian emphasis. 'Plain is class.'

Eve stared at her reflection. It was as if, Jasmine thought, she was encountering herself for the first time. Picking up the skirt, she swayed from left to right and pointed a toe. 'For a woman this is the dress between baptism and burial,' she remarked dreamily. 'But the toile is a ghost dress. The negative behind the photograph.'

'*Don't*, Evie.'

Ivanka laid a hand on Eve's shoulder. 'Please be still.' She ran her hand down Eve's back and made a sweep across the shoulders.

'Do you like it, Jasmine?'

'We discussed making it in zibeline in order to get the structure.' Ivanka produced a marker pen. 'Or faille might do.'

'What do *you* think, Jas?'

Eve sounded uncertain, which was unlike her.

'If it was me . . .'

Ivanka drew a black line across the waist. 'It's important to get the balance right.'

Jasmine said, 'Would something softer, more flowing . . .? If it *was* me . . .'

Ivanka's pen halted.

'But it isn't you,' said Eve. 'That's why I need to know.'

The bell to the studio rang and a slippered Lara appeared. 'Sorry, so sorry. Couldn't quite fathom the instructions.' She took in the figure clad in the toile. 'Oh.' Her eyes filled with tears and she put her arms around Eve.

So like her.

After a moment, Lara stood back. 'Have I missed the decisions?'

'No,' said Eve. 'I waited.'

Ivanka flipped open the laptop on her desk. 'Now,' she said. 'We will do it virtually.'

The three of them gathered around. Touching buttons here and there, Ivanka manipulated a photograph of Eve on the screen and superimposed the dress made in different materials, and with modifications, over her image.

In the toile, the real Eve shivered as she watched the parade.

The conversation lasted a long time—oyster, chalk, satin, taffeta, chiffon. Jasmine's attention drifted. It was extraordinary, fascinating, the lengths to which men and women went to make their lives palatable, the milestones they inserted into them and what they considered important. She was as guilty as any, devoting time and organization to negotiating around the flatline of the everyday.

Again, Lara hugged Eve, an anxious, protective gesture.

Veils, petticoats, shoes . . .

She caught Lara's eyes. Lurking in them Jasmine saw an emotion she couldn't place and, in response, a tiny anxious flame lit in her. Lara was worried.

Why?

Among the rack of ruffled dresses, there was a plain sheath with long sleeves. She pointed to it. 'Did you try that one, Eve?'

She pictured herself in it. Tall, slender, with piled-up hair.

She hated feeling jealous, hated its condition of helplessness and obsession, the prison of self, all phrases Lara would use. Sibling rivalry was the subject of psychological study (and sit-com jokes) and Lara knew all about that too. She would probably explain to Jasmine that the feelings of displacement she had undoubtedly experienced when Eve was born had been intensified when Jasmine made the connection between Eve's appearance and her mother's disappearance.

All the same.

Imagine . . . *air cooling her skin as she shrugged out of her clothes. Her reflection in the mirror as she waited for a toile to be lifted into place over her head.*

She forced her thoughts into another channel. What mattered was Duncan, not a dress or a wedding. What mattered was how she tackled life—with reason and rationality, strength and confidence. The contemporary female.

Lara made Eve turn around slowly. 'Darling,' she said. 'Darling Eve. I wonder.'

Eve turned a questioning countenance on her, and Lara frowned. Again Jasmine felt the beat of her stepmother's anxiety.

'Eve,' said Lara, 'before you make up your mind . . . I'm wondering if you've considered a softer style, something a little more romantic?'

Ivanka tapped the pen against her teeth. *Click.*

'Why?' asked a flushed Eve. 'Don't you

think . . .?'

Jasmine went to Lara's aid. 'Evie, you know I was thinking the same.'

'But I love this.' Eve repeated the swaying movement. 'It's how I saw myself.'

Ivanka selected one of the abandoned sketches. 'See?' she said. 'Juliet, before the tragedy. Long fluid lines. High waist. Beautifully draped.'

Lara exclaimed, 'That's it! That's lovely. That's how I . . .' She corrected herself. 'But, of course, you could only wear this dress once. Whereas the other . . .'

'I have an idea,' said Ivanka, and issued an order through the curtain. The assistant appeared with a second toile, this time made up in muslin. She waited with a patient smile while Ivanka denuded Eve of the first.

'This was made for a customer last year,' Ivanka explained, and helped Eve into it.

It dropped into place. The black dressmaker's marks on it were—clearly—the imprint of another woman.

'Did she wear the dress?' asked Jasmine.

'Shoes, shoes.' Lara seemed distracted. 'You'll have to take care choosing the right shoes for a dress like this.'

'A little shaping in the bodice.' Ivanka patrolled around Eve.

'Did she wear the dress?' repeated Jasmine.

Ivanka lifted her gaze. 'The other bride . . . In the end she didn't use it.' She gestured to the assistant. 'The wedding didn't happen.'

The assistant dropped to her knees to pin up the trailing hem.

Eve had become a still white statue.

'Do you like this better?' asked Ivanka. 'I would make changes so it is yours.'

Eve turned sideways to assess her profile, and the toile flowed with her. 'Which material?'

'There's chiffon, georgette, marocain . . . They're good for draping.'

What kind of veil?

Which flowers?

'Wait,' said Ivanka. She whipped down a length of veiling from the rack and threw it over Eve's head. Its hem drifted to the floor. 'There.'

Suddenly, her sister was a phantom, summoned from the shadowy habitats of dreams and fantasies.

Lara went very pale, and Eve swayed.

Jasmine asked sharply, 'Are you all right, Eve?'

Eve turned her head, and the train undulated. 'Yes, I am.'

Marker in hand, Ivanka circled the shrouded figure. 'Here,' she said, lifted the veiling and drew a small circle on Eve's left breast. 'That's where we embroider the rose on the under-dress. Every dress we create has a hidden rose. It's part of the dress.'

What sort of rose? White, red . . . the colours of death and love? A rose with a thorn?

'Oh,' said Lara, faintly.

Eve peered at herself in the mirror. Then she lifted her hand and the veiling drifted around her. She cast a look at the discarded toile. 'Which?'

The nervy, steely irony of Eve's first choice—a throwback to the sharp lines and tough charm of the sixties—or the nostalgia and contrasting delicate charm of the second?

It didn't matter, thought Jasmine. There were no rules.

Lara said, 'Don't let us influence you, Eve.'

Eve slipped off the shoes. 'The Juliet dress,' she said.

'*Don't* call it that,' said Lara, sharply. She sat down on one of the chairs and rubbed her ankle. 'It's *your* dress.'

There was a short silence.

Lara snatched Eve's hand and held it to her cheek. 'You've been very clever. And it's all good.'

Eve smiled enigmatically. 'By that, do you mean I've been clever enough to find a partner with an income and, conveniently, a house?' She was only half joking.

'No,' said Lara.

Ivanka snapped the laptop shut. 'Are we agreed?'

Lara appeared to come to a decision. 'Eve, why don't we think about it for a day?'

'Why?'

'Please.'

'OK,' said Eve, but she was puzzled.

*   *   *

The postman delivered a copper pan (28cms), a chef's stainless-steel pan (24cms), a gingham tablecloth, a rose damask tablecloth (137 x 183cms), plus a set of table mats adorned with tasteful scenes from Ancient Rome.

When she returned from work, Lara bore them upstairs where they joined the growing pile. Hand on hip, she regarded them with dread and apprehension.

Back in the kitchen, she took a packet of steak out of the fridge, ready to make a stew to freeze for the weekend. As she chopped and fried the onion, she listened to the radio commentary on the general election. Very soon, a buttery-oniony smell filled the air. She added a sprinkling of thyme, sherry, tomato paste and—the *coup*—a couple of anchovies, to transform a watery liquid into a thick, velvety sauce.

Maudie sidled into the kitchen and dumped her book bag on the table. She sniffed. 'Is that stew? Oh, Mum, it'll have gravy.'

'You can pick the bits out.' Under the cover of cooking, Lara assessed her. 'You'll have to learn to like gravy.'

'No, I won't.'

'Think hominy grits and gravy in the States?'

Maudie's face lit briefly with yearning and excitement. 'Unfair, Mum.'

Maudie was impatient, snippy, tired. Blue was smudged under the mascaraed eyes, and the strands of hair at the nape of her neck, usually so shiny, appeared lacklustre.

Lara softened. 'You OK?' she asked. Maudie wound a lock of hair around her finger and tucked it into the barrette anchoring the rest. 'Did you sleep?'

'Sure.'

Mental note. Buy vitamin supplements, fish oil and Horlicks. Insist that Maudie had an eye and tooth check (teeth always went under stress).

'OK,' she said, and checked the time. 'Eve will be dropping in.'

'Oh, Lord.' A mixture of exasperation and impatience. 'I'm not sure I can stand it at the moment.'

Lara said, 'Come here,' and caught Maudie round the waist. 'Just so you're straight on the subject, Eve cares for you. Very much.' She peered into Maudie's face. 'You care for her a lot too. Don't you?'

'Stupid question, Mum.' All the same, Maudie was sceptical. 'But we're different.' When Lara released her, she resumed tackling her hair. 'Why wouldn't we be?'

Shortly afterwards, Eve arrived and took charge of the presents, writing notes and stowing them carefully. She had already spring-cleaned the wardrobe—'That's where moths lay their eggs, Mum'—and vacuumed every corner of the room. 'I have to get it sorted for Andrew, otherwise he mixes things up.'

'Isn't it going to be awful always having to negotiate over everything?' asked Maudie. 'Togetherness and all that . . .'

'I don't know,' said Eve. 'Haven't done it yet.'

With some awe, they watched her stack boxes, sort out pieces of china and grade the linen. A tea-strainer was logged in under the returns section of the list, and the most hideous vase in the world stowed carefully with the china.

'Who's given you *that*?' asked Maudie, in shocked tones.

Eve replied seriously, 'Carla and Charlie Kirkwood. It's very generous of them.' She added, 'People *are* generous.'

'Are they?' Maudie was frankly derisive. 'IMO, the vase should be a social outcast.'

Eve sent her a look dating from childhood. The one that said, *You are an irritating child and in my way*. She placed her hands on her hips. 'And?' She was cross. 'Since when did you have any taste?'

'How dare you?'

'Very easily,' said Eve.

'Shut up.'

The vase gibe had driven deep. 'It's always the same, Maudie. You always have a go. Whatever have I done to you?'

'Quite a lot, actually.'

Lara observed them both: the concept of non-dualism (Buddhist, she recollected) preached that there is no hard line between pleasure and pain. 'Stop it, you two,' she said. '*Now.*'

Eve returned to her lists and Maudie retired to the kitchen. Peace broke out in the bedroom.

'How's Andrew?'

'He's fine, I think. Haven't seen him for a couple of days.'

'Are the building works going OK?'

'Yes. But you should see the garden. Builder's yard. It'll take work to restore it. But it's tiny, as you know, and I shall love doing it.'

An image rose of the garden at Membury as Lara had first seen it—in its frozen suspension. 'You and your father both.'

Eve shuffled and reshuffled the haul. Clink went one plate against another. Paper rustled. Her biro moved across the Notebook. Her question, when she posed it, was uncharacteristically tentative: 'Do you think Dad was happy with either you or my mother?'

It shocked Lara. 'I'm sure he was with your mother. As for him and me, that's complicated. But it's a question I've asked myself many times. But, there were things . . . that are private to a marriage. You'll have private things, too. We were happy at the beginning . . . very . . . and I'm sure your father would say the same.'

'What you mean is . . . my mother didn't live long enough for him to become disillusioned with her.'

She should have been quicker on the uptake. Too late, she said, 'He *was* happy with your mother.' She peered at Eve. 'It's true.'

Eve's uncharacteristic introspective mood persisted. 'Is it odd that so many of us have issued from Dad's discomfort?'

'You were wanted,' Lara interjected. '*All* of you. We wouldn't swap one hair of your heads.'

'But he didn't want Maudie or Louis,' said Eve.

'It wasn't straightforward, Evie.'

Eve looked at Lara as if to say, *You're forgetting I'm an adult.* 'Dad went, and you couldn't rely on him.' She smoothed a page in the Notebook. 'I don't like to think about that.'

The sour smell of London earth—marked by the piss and dung of urban foxes and cats. Her grief as she knelt down in the garden. 'He could say the same about me.'

'I doubt it.'

Lara ran her hands through her hair. *The land of lost content.* 'You wouldn't know, Eve.'

Eve sorted and stacked. Full of foreboding, Lara watched. 'Does Andrew let you get on with decisions about the cottage?'

Eve checked some sheets. 'Thread count good . . . Funnily enough, Andrew has strong views. He's into cooking and interior decoration.'

That surprised her. 'You so often think you know someone, but you don't. I don't know Andrew and you're marrying him.'

Eve turned her head away.

'Still, a domesticated Andrew is good for when you have a family.'

'A family?' Eve sounded surprised.

'You *are* thinking of having a family?'

'I suppose we are.' Eve fiddled with the sheets. 'Of *course.*'

Should she speak?

Yes? No?

On her way downstairs, Lara stopped to wipe the window by the stairs. It was streaked with dirt, and the flowers she had placed under it had died. She bore them away. The actions were calming . . . but not entirely.

Packing a lunchbox for Maudie, she failed to find the ham she had bought for the sandwiches and dropped the banana.

'What's up with you?' asked Maudie. 'All fingers and thumbs.'

Lara kissed her goodbye. Maudie kissed her back. 'I can't believe college and all that will soon be at an end, Mum.'

'Make the most of it.'

To her surprise, Maudie held her tight. 'I will.'

Lara waited. Upstairs, Eve was finishing. Patting, filing, sorting.

Lara sneezed, a sign of tension. The kitchen felt hot and she pushed open the window. She sneezed a second time, so violently her body recoiled from the shock. She sat down on the bench. *I must get something more comfortable to sit on in the kitchen.*

Yes? No?

Got up again. For a moment, she was powerless to move. Eve's tapping footsteps were on the stairs.

Coming down.

Eve appeared in the kitchen and headed for the kettle. 'Evie,' Lara managed to say. 'I want to talk to you.'

'OK, OK ...' Light and carefree, the words danced. 'Before you say anything, I want to show you this.' She dived into her bag on the table and got out a tissue-wrapped object. 'About the dress ...' Eve whipped round. 'Look ...'

Nestling in the tissue was a Cinderella slipper, as slim and confected as the fairy tale.

Lara summoned courage. 'Is everything OK between you and Andrew? We haven't seen him for a while.'

'Is that what you want to discuss?' Eve looked astonished.

'Sort of.'

Eve thrust the shoe at her. 'Do you like it?'

Elegant, with a minute heel and satin ribbons to tie around the ankle, the shoe told Lara that Eve had definitely decided on the Juliet dress. 'Evie, it's lovely.'

The hand that was holding it out to her trembled a little. 'Mum, what do you mean you haven't seen Andrew?'

'I just wondered. Have you talked to him properly lately? Do you know what he's thinking? Is he happy with all the arrangements?' Lara cleared her throat, which felt constricted. 'It's important to keep in touch. *Properly* in touch.'

Eve's expression remained pinned in place. But ... oh, those years of knowing Eve's every mood. Lara sensed she flinched. 'Andrew knows what I feel, and I know what he feels.'

Lara captured the shoe and twined her fingers in the ribbon. 'But when did you last have a proper, serious conversation?'

A pair of big, cool-looking eyes trained on her. 'Why should I answer that, Mum?'

'You might have last-minute doubts.'

'No,' she said flatly.

'Sure?'

'Why on earth are you doing this?'

'Because I love you.'

Eve blinked. 'I know you do. But . . .' She retrieved the shoe from Lara. 'But sometimes it's as well to let things alone.'

'Ah.'

Inserting the shoe into its tissue, Eve wrapped it up.

Lara searched for her courage. 'Evie, don't repeat my mistakes. Don't get married without knowing each other properly.'

That girl in the overlong veil.

Eve's hand was arrested in the act of replacing the shoe box in the carrier bag. 'Whoa. What are you trying to tell me? That *I*'m making a mistake? Or that *you* made a mistake?'

'I did make a mistake but—'

'It isn't the same.' Eve's lips tightened. 'Don't push yours on to me.'

'Unfair, Eve.'

Eve dashed a hand across a cheek. 'Why are you doing this, Mum? What are you trying to achieve? Put me off getting married? Don't you like Andrew? If so, why didn't you say so before and I could have kept him out of your way? *I* could have kept out of your way.'

Lara grabbed the bag containing the shoes from Eve, replaced it on the table and took both Eve's hands in hers. The pressure that had been building in her released as she told Eve what she knew. 'Listen to me, Eve. I found out something. Quite by mistake. I wasn't looking. About a girl called Fern and Andrew.'

Red . . . white . . . The colours slapped into Eve's cheeks. 'That's gossip. Gossip. Why repeat it to me?'

'It wasn't gossip, Eve. I saw them.'

'What a thing to say to me.' Cool and contemptuous.

'It's the truth.'

Eve's nails dug into Lara's palms. 'And couldn't you have minded your own business?'

Lara clung tightly to her. 'As I told you, I love you. I'm your mother and I need to make sure that you're all right.'

Eve looked down at their entwined hands. She said, in a cool, distant voice, 'Take your hands off me, Lara.'

*　　　*　　　*

A lot later, as the evening sun slanted over the streets, long after a white, wordless Eve had packed up her stuff and left the house without saying goodbye, Lara let herself out into the scrubby, untended back garden.

She stretched out a hand. It was shaking.

However hollow her victory, it had been better to say something than nothing. Silence was conspiracy. That much she had learned in her work. Silence allowed children to be beaten, abused, neglected.

And deceived.

She knew, also . . . she *knew* . . . that this was the beginning of the long farewell to her daughters. They were leaving. There was nothing that could be done. There was almost nothing to say for this was the way life went. In the end, as they moved inexorably on, away and out of sight, they would be hidden from her.

Her heart contracted with the pain and inevitability of it.

Chapter Seventeen

Eve's emails increased in urgency by the week. Marquee ... flooring ... china ... glassware ... umbrellas.

Umbrellas? 'For the guests between the church and the garden if it should be raining,' explained Eve, patiently.

Lara marvelled at the depth and reach of her capacity to plan.

Bill sent Lara an email detailing the wedding costs to which she had agreed. She totted them up, entered the total into her on-line spreadsheet and swallowed. He had added, in a PS:

> The bees are at full throttle, and as I write, I'm spying on a thrush banging a snail on a stone and the dragonflies are swarming by the stream. Did you know dragonflies have almost 360° vision?

She wrote back to agree to it all.

How well she and Bill communicated by email— clearly their new vocabulary.

Maudie was deep in her exams. There were many phone calls, once a bout of tears, then a hysterically cheerful thirty-second or so report on a history paper. In yet another phone call, Lucy,

Bill's sister, reported that all seemed to be well. 'It's extraordinary, Lara. Maudie's up early, is back at the house on time, and does masses of revision.'

Sleepwise, exams were always a tough period—for Lara. Forget the girls.

'It's ridiculous,' she told Robin, when they met at the practice. 'After three daughters, it doesn't get easier.'

Robin made a noncommittal answer, which was unlike him.

'You OK?' she asked. He admitted to bad nights too.

She laid a hand on his arm, and looked into his face. 'I see nightmares. You're coming for a walk.'

The consulting rooms had been dim, as usual, and, in the daylight outside, their eyes watered.

'Have I got mascara running down my cheeks?'

'No. Even if you had, it wouldn't matter.'

She hid behind her sunglasses and they strolled over to the pond, which was shared by virulently green algae and ducks.

Robin pointed to a mother duck leading a flotilla of young into the rushes growing at the water's edge. 'That's you.'

She laughed, and they walked on. Eventually, she asked, 'Are you angry about something, Robin?'

People were pushing past them, and the sun made Lara sneeze. They regarded each other. Minus sunglasses, Robin narrowed his eyes against the glare and slipped his good arm around her shoulders. 'Survivor's guilt,' he said lightly. 'Think nothing of it.'

His arm was warm and heavy. Without thinking, she reached up and brushed his mouth with hers.

'Does that come under the heading of "soldiers'

comforts"?'

'It might.'

'Are you allowed just one ration?'

She stared up at him, and surrendered to the huge surprise of a body, so long inactive in this respect, suddenly making demands. 'Only if your name is Oliver Twist.'

This time he kissed her and made a more thorough job of it than Lara had. Her surprise gave way to the unmistakable, and very straightforward, feelings of desire, which she had feared were extinct. They weren't.

'Lara . . .'

'Yes.'

'Come to Damascus.' He licked his finger and held it up to the breeze. 'I postponed my trip and I'm thinking of going now. It's not too late to change your mind. Perhaps it's not the best time because it'll be hot, but it is changing, and who knows what may happen?' He paused. 'Seize the day, Lara?'

*   *   *

As agreed, Robin was waiting by the vodka bar in the terminal. It was eight thirty in the morning and, seeing was believing, it was already doing a roaring trade. He was wearing a shirt, trousers that aped combats, and a pair of serviceable lace-up boots. A small rucksack waited at his feet.

He kissed her lightly on the lips. 'Vodka?'

'*No.*' It was a second or two before she clocked the tease.

'You look very nice,' he said.

'So do you.'

There was a short, awkward pause. Lara pretended to adjust the strap of her shoulder bag. A couple of maps stuck out of the back pocket of his trousers and the cuff of his left sleeve had been buttoned down while the right was rolled up to reveal a muscular arm.

He hitched a strap of the rucksack over one shoulder. 'You can get drunk on the plane if you want. There probably won't be too much alcohol where we're going.'

The departures board indicated that the flight to Damascus would board shortly. 'Shall we go?'

'Sure.' But he stayed put. 'Just to warn you, I can't help too much with the carrying of stuff.' He gestured to her hand luggage.

'I didn't expect it. I know the arm's bad.'

'OK, sorted.'

On board, she peered out of the window as the luggage trains plied to and fro. 'You have to go, Mum,' Maudie had advised, in an adult way, 'and no second thoughts.' She added the rider that took Lara's breath temporarily away: 'Time you had a love affair.'

'It's not a love affair, Maudie.'

'Whatever, Mum.'

Jasmine had been wistful. 'Enjoy.'

Eve had not responded to the messages Lara had left for her.

Bill sprang a surprise. He rang up. 'Who's this man you're going off with?'

'What sort of question is that?'

'What it sounds like.'

'Why are you interested in what I do? It's Robin Brett, and I've known him a long time.'

'You'll be safe, then?'

'Of course I'll be *safe*.'

In the plane, she read the pages she had printed out from the Internet on Syrian flora and fauna—tamarisk, scrub oak, Aleppo pine.

'OK?' he asked.

'OK.'

Other than that, they didn't talk much. They read their papers, poked at the dismal airline meal and, after a while, Lara dozed.

You were born, grew up and expected life to run along a pattern. But it didn't and it hadn't. Here she was, on a plane at the start of a new route in her life ... and she had not expected it at all. Fit the pattern to the material, her mother had said.

How?

She woke. A map unfolded in front of him, Robin was watching her. She pushed back her hair. 'Hope I wasn't talking in my sleep.'

'No, only snoring.'

'You don't mean it?' She was beginning to feel more relaxed with him—and less astonished that she had agreed to the trip.

'No,' he concurred, and grinned. He pointed to the map. 'We'll get a taxi to the hotel in the old city, settle in, then go up to Jebel Qassioun and look down on the city as we eat.'

On the way from the airport, he explained, 'There's been a programme to restore the old quarter and the *riad* hotels. It might be a bit noisy, but I thought you'd like it best.'

Lara sat quietly in the taxi, which rattled. After a moment, she leaned over and wound the window down to allow in spicy scents and the smell of jasmine.

It was hot.

It was strange.

London grew faint. The notion of her family grew faint.

Hotel Talisman was in the north part of the Old City. It dated back three hundred or so years, had recently been refurbished and boasted three courtyards. In her room, she unpacked rapidly and haphazardly. It was important not to miss the tick of a single second. Every so often she gravitated to the balcony. There, she simply stood and looked. Already it had done her good.

Twenty minutes later, having changed into linen trousers and jacket, she waited by the fountain in a courtyard. Absorbed in the play of light on the water, she had almost forgotten she was waiting for Robin when he appeared.

'Sorry,' he said. 'I had to make some calls.'

She wondered what sort of calls, then decided they didn't interest her. A bubble seemed to have taken residence in her chest. 'No talking about our real lives, OK?'

He nodded. 'Done.' He shepherded her out into the street. 'The obvious sights. The Street Called Straight. St Paul's Gate. John the Baptist's tomb. But, first, we have a date.'

To walk in the Old City was akin to sliding into a lazy stream. If the noise was constant, nobody hurried. Leisurely. Leisurely. There were tourists aplenty. This was, she perceived, a greatly cosmopolitan city sheltering many races into which they merged easily.

Robin was tour guide and she was grateful.

They passed stalls selling leather goods, brass bowls, coloured glass and cheap Chinese watches. Lara learned on the spot not to make eye contact with any of the vendors and, whatever she might have thought, her skills at evading pests were rusty. In fact, nil. But she didn't care. It was like . . . It was like the moment when, after so many years of parenting (i.e., bent double with bags and shopping), she stepped out unencumbered and stood upright.

Other worlds. Content and excited, she hailed them silently.

'There's one of the gates.' They had stopped at a street intersection. Robin pointed up to the north wall. 'Bab Al-Faradis. It means "Paradise". The Romans called it Mercury Gate. Damascus is much the same shape as the early Hellenic and Roman city. The names were simply adapted.'

'To think . . .' she placed her feet carefully on the stones '. . . I might be walking where a disciple or an emperor walked.'

'To think, Lara.'

'Don't mock.'

'I'm not.'

'The footprint of the city is the same, you say.'

'The very same.'

'OK. We're treading through the deep litter of history and, in doing so, connecting with the past. But because nothing much has changed, it's also the present.'

'I think many people . . . how shall I put this? . . . have said something similar.'

'Many?' She was rueful. 'Thank you for pointing it out.'

'Actually, Lara, I'm not laughing at you.' Small pause. 'I promise. Making that connection is important.'

'Then we're in agreement.'

'We are.'

He told her about the Crusaders, and the long interregnum before the Ottomans conquered, and the fight the Arabs had subsequently had on their hands to secure their traditional lands. At last he said, 'I'm overdoing it, I think.'

'I'm listening to every word, Robin.'

Actually, she was looking. His eyes shone with passion, and the impassioned were always fatally attractive.

'I know I'm talking too much.'

She couldn't resist. 'Only a little.'

They halted at the entrance to a pedestrian underpass. 'Down the steps,' he ordered, 'then up the escalator.'

'And?'

'Prepare to be amazed.'

The escalator rose. She stepped off it and stopped dead. Coming up behind her, Robin narrowly avoided a collision. 'You're right,' she said, without turning her head. 'I am amazed.'

Colour. Confusion. People. Noise.

They stepped under the high corrugated roof and into the souk. 'Look up,' instructed Robin. 'The holes in the roof are bullet holes from the 1925 uprising against the French mandate.' Later, when they had pushed further into the interior, he added, 'This is built on the original Roman axis and processional way, which led to the temple of Jupiter. But now it leads to the Great Umayyad Mosque.'

The scents of an unknown place—spicy, perfumed, interesting. 'I love it.'

'Normally I would counsel you not to buy anything on your first visit. But we haven't that much time and we know what we want.'

She thought of home, the dim shops and draughty shopping arcades with their garnish of litter, the stained pavements and, to her surprise, felt a faint distaste. Here, she wanted to surrender to the noisy, good-tempered crowd. Here, she was dazzled by the stuffed eagles, water-sellers and scarves in rainbow colours, and wanted to be one of the many drifting this way and that.

Robin stopped in front of a booth. Hanging around the doorway there were leather bags of every shape and description.

'Wait.' He disappeared inside and returned to say, 'You don't mind?'

She smiled at him. 'How could I?'

A few minutes later, he beckoned to her. Space limited and at a premium, the shop was cluttered, very warm, and coffee had just been brewed. On the counter several bags had been laid out. Robin introduced her to the vendor. 'Abdullah is expecting you to take your pick.'

She knew the leather would be as soft as cashmere. And so it proved. Discussing the merits of each bag and making her choice was pleasurable and lengthy. So, too, was the bargaining over the price.

'I nearly lost face,' he said, as they emerged. 'If you had insisted on paying, I don't know how my reputation would have survived.'

'Please let me pay you, Robin.'

He came to a halt. 'You don't understand, Lara. I'm giving you the bag.'

There was a pause while they digested the moment.

'Thank you,' she said eventually. 'Thank you.'

Back outside the Souk Al-Hamadiye, she watched him flag down a yellow taxi and negotiate the fare. Fatigue had settled behind her eyes, but pleasantly so. As they drove slowly along the road, she was hit by a wave of warm, petrol-laden air ... and relaxed.

Soon, they were driving through an urban sprawl—piles of concrete, unfinished buildings—towards the rocky outcrop of Jebel Qassioun where they were to have dinner.

Robin sat back against the seat. 'It wasn't so long ago you could ride a horse into Damascus from Qassioun and pass through gardens and orchards full of roses, citrus trees and jasmine,' he said. 'The travellers who wrote about it always commented on the beauty of the ride. Damascus was known as the Jasmine City.'

Lara closed her eyes. She, too, could have been picking her way over the stones on her horse, bathed in warmth and flower scents, the sun on her back, jogging peaceably as she rode past the ancient orchards and gardens.

'What are you thinking?' he asked.

She told him and he smiled and took her hand. 'That's good. Dream away, Lara.'

Over dinner, they discussed the trip to the Krak des Chevaliers. 'Initially, I thought we might hire a car but ...' He glanced down at his left arm. 'Probably not a good idea. The roads can be mad and congested and you need your wits about you. So, we'll go white-van transport, which means there'll probably be other tourists as well. But don't worry, you don't have to talk to them.'

'What a strange picture you have of me,' said Lara, thoughtfully. 'I don't mind talking to other people.'

'I thought you might be tired. That's all.'

It had grown dark, and the city lights were spattered across the horizon. One light in particular caught her eye. It had an unblinking and beautiful radiance. A mosque? A palace? Fixed on it, Lara experienced a freshness and intensity of response, the like of which she could only remember from childhood.

A few days ago, Bill had written something equivalent in an email: 'Whenever I look at the garden at Membury, it is to look at it for the first time.'

She shared that sense of discovery. It was what she felt here.

'Lara,' Robin said eventually, 'nothing is set in stone. Nothing is expected of you.'

She smiled and held out her glass for a refill. 'That's a good place to be.'

'We're tired,' he said.

She nodded.

When she finally got to bed, it was to fall dreamlessly asleep, only to be woken by a knock on the door. This turned out to be a fully dressed and freshly shaved Robin.

'Oh, my God. Time?'

'Eight thirty. I let you sleep.' He looked at his watch. 'But we're due to set off in an hour.'

Old grey T-shirt, mussed hair and the toothpaste yards away in the bathroom.

'You look nice,' he said. 'Warm.'

She blushed. 'Give me half an hour.'

'I'll get some pomegranate juice sent up.'

'Rocket fuel would be better.'

Mist wreathed over the citadel as they approached. Looming through it were the castle ramparts, more massive than she had imagined.

'It's usually best to approach Krak from the west.' Robin paused to listen to the driver. 'But I think he's in a hurry. You can either close your eyes as we go through Al-Husn or just accept it. The village used to be inside the walls but, during their mandate, the French forced it to move downhill which accounts for the sprawl.'

The van eased through the centre of Al-Husn and up towards the castle, stopping only for the driver to conduct altercations with people who had parked their cars with the purpose of causing maximum blockage.

By the time they were deposited at the bridge that had replaced the original drawbridge, the sun had ripped the mist to shreds.

'There's no need to hurry.' Robin shielded his eyes. 'Welcome to the stronghold of the Knights Hospitallers.'

Above them, the buildings squatted monumentally. Faith. Arrogance. Power. All were invested in the stones.

'The castle was never taken.' He bought the tickets at the booth and handed her one. 'In all its long history. Except at the end.'

'I read that. It was a trick.' Lara followed him through a long, vaulted passage into the inner *enceinte*. 'It had to be a trick. With walls *this* thick, surely no one could take it in the conventional way.' They emerged in bright sunlight into the area between the ramparts and the inner keep.

'"But in 1271 the Mamelukes laid siege,"' she read from her guidebook.

'You sound about seven,' he said, amused.

'Some of us,' she said, 'need to catch up. Do not mock.'

Robin jabbed a finger towards the ramparts. 'At that point there weren't many Crusaders left to man the garrison. It was going downhill. A letter arrived from the Crusader chief in the Lebanon informing the commander that there were no reinforcements and instructing him to surrender. It was a forgery.'

The towers shimmered in the sun, turning the stone ramparts to grey silk. Up here, there was not much in the way of vegetation. Nothing distracted the eye from the business of defence and no one could move without being tracked.

'Totally totalitarian and grimly efficient,' Lara commented.

'But what a construction.'

'It is,' she said, 'but it's the belief in what they were doing that's the fascinating bit. OK, they had will-power and these defences ... but what mattered was their belief that they would conquer here. Surely, unless that was intact, nothing was going to work.'

They were mounting the ramp to the inner castle through the main gateway, which opened into the inner keep, an area with several staircases leading to terraces. Robin pointed out the places where boiling oil could be hurled down on invaders. Nasty. (Dead efficient.)

Lara walked over to inspect a colonnaded room opposite. She consulted her guide. This was the main meeting room, used when the citadel housed its full complement of two thousand or so

Crusaders and their horses.

Robin said in her ear, 'They discovered three tombs in this bit. Skeletons, swords and shields. The whole deal.'

An arcaded loggia ran alongside the meeting room. It reminded her of the cloister she had once seen in southern France. Perhaps that was its point. A little bit of home. Perhaps these iron knights had suffered homesickness and permitted themselves a glancing reminder in stone of what they had left behind. Perhaps they hadn't been so sure of everything after all. She pointed to an inscription on a stone lintel. 'And?'

'I think it says something about enjoying grace, wisdom and beauty but to beware of pride.'

'Good principle,' she said lightly.

How had this place worked? Answer: assemble the monastic ideals of self-restraint, obedience and celibacy, and fuse them with aggressive military discipline. The result? One of the most formidable fighting machines ever known.

Robin was checking an inscription. As a soldier, those criteria had been his, too. Thank God he had come home. Droves of Knights Hospitallers had died in battle in a place that was not their home or, crippled by wounds and disease, had been forced to remain here until they did.

Watching him, her thoughts went this way and that.

Turning to look down over the plain, she tried to empathize with the imperatives that had kept the garrison intact and operational. She failed. The sun beat on her shoulders, and the stones had a harsh gleam. This was an alien place.

Afterwards they wandered at will around the

castle's huge circumference. The air was fresh. Wild flowers bloomed in yellow, orange and blue and the sun beat on her back as she bent down to examine a speedwell growing on the sward.

She turned to Robin. 'Thank you,' she said. 'Thank you so much for bringing me here.'

For dinner Robin took her to Leila's, a restaurant in the Old City. 'This is the best roof terrace in town but because it's so near to the mosque there's no alcohol. Do you mind?'

More or less as he spoke, the floodlights were switched on and the shape of the mosque emerged out of the darkness. Lara stared at it.

'Do I mind?' She gestured to it. 'What do you think?'

They ate *mezze* and lamb kebabs, accompanied by flat Arab bread and tomato sauce. Afterwards, a dish of plain fruit—grapes, cherries and oranges—was brought to the table.

Lara couldn't stop smiling. Her body had developed an ache—a good, happy ache.

Robin selected a handful of cherries and put them on her plate. 'When did you decide to train?'

'I thought we weren't going to talk about our lives.'

He ignored her. 'When did you?'

She bit into a cherry, black-fleshed and sour-sweet, then another. 'Bill had left. By and large, there wasn't enough money and I had agreed to look after the three girls. But ...' she put the stones on to the rim of the plate ' ... tinker, tailor ... I needed to do something about myself too.' She added a third cherry stone.

He leaned over and flicked it into the line-up. 'Don't forget the soldier.'

'Oh, the soldier. Him.'

'Unless you prefer the sailor?'

She bit into a fourth cherry and added the stone to the rest. 'Let me see. A sailor? Perhaps I do.'

He raised his eyes from contemplation of the cherry stones to hers. 'Three girls. A lot.'

'I had to keep them. It was mad. But I wanted to shield them, and I thought Jasmine and Eve's lives couldn't be shaken up again. Anyway, Violet—the woman Bill went off with—made it clear that children were not part of the package.'

Robin chose his words with care. She liked that more and more about him.

'Carey wanted children but I wasn't around. The marriage finished, so when I came home I thought I needed to make up for my lack of children by trying to work with them.'

There was silence.

'And you, Lara?'

As ever, confession did not flow smoothly from her. 'I needed to work. I needed to stop thinking. But I also needed to make sense of what had happened. It was one way. I had to make my world less narrow. I had to climb out of the box and do something. I didn't want what had happened to me and Bill to be the only thing I thought about.'

He nodded. 'And did you make sense of what had happened?'

'Work in progress. And you?'

'It helped me deal with the fallout ... the demons ... and the worry that I wasn't up to life any more.'

After dinner, he took her to a typical coffee-house. Its walls were faced with striped marble to which had been fixed a large plasma television screen. Upstairs, where they sat side by side on a bench, an uneven wooden casement window opened on to the street. Opposite, underneath a street light, a plaque had been screwed into the wall that read, 'Classical Route'.

She drank her coffee. 'Robin, in the end, I tackled Eve about Andrew and the girl. I'm frightened I've done damage.'

Someone in the house opposite turned on music, which poured wildly and sweetly into the street.

'You might have done.'

There was an ashtray on the marble-topped table and it was at moments like this that she wished she smoked. 'Any mother would have done it.' She twisted the coffee cup around and around. 'But, equally, I torture myself that she didn't have to know ...' The cup stilled. 'Andrew made it clear that I didn't understand the situation and maybe he was right.'

'Lara, look at me.' She obeyed. 'Don't.'

'I *will* have done damage, even if it was the right thing for the right reasons.'

Robin folded his hands around his coffee. 'I'm not going to tell you it doesn't matter, or that I approve of what Andrew has done ... but in our work we encourage people to take responsibility for their lives. Don't we?' He leaned towards her. 'That's what you were doing.'

Don't interfere. She had ignored the quiet inner voice.

'Andrew ran a risk,' he continued. 'Usually it's only a question of time before something like that gets back. You saw him, told Eve, and she has the chance to think it through and make a decision before the wedding. Not after.'

She sighed. 'No fairy tale for Eve, then.' The smell of jasmine was almost overpowering. 'You so want them for the people you love. Even when you know so well . . . We hang on to our illusions, even at the worst of times.'

'Precisely at the worst of times.' His smile was tender. 'It's normal.'

After a moment, she smiled back at him.

A little later, he said, 'You know your funny little gesture? When you fold your arms so defensively? I haven't seen you do it here. I claim the credit.'

It was ridiculous how happy she felt.

Silently, he asked the question. Silently, she answered it.

In her hotel room, Lara sluiced her face in water and immersed her body. That was what the knights would have done before the great battles around the citadel on the hill.

Afterwards she brushed her hair until it hung silkily down and trimmed her thumbnail, which she had snagged on the bed covering. She assessed the results in the mirror. The figure that looked back at her was familiar and unfamiliar.

Once, on a short trip to Rome with Jasmine, they had devoted an unconscionable time queuing to see Michelangelo's *Pietà* in St Peter's. To her, it had been of the utmost importance to see it. '*Should* you see it?' Jasmine, ever mindful of Lara's feelings, had asked. Rightly so. For the pain on viewing the marble mother holding her precious burden in her lap had rooted her to the spot. *This is my dead son*. Into Mary's face was carved the suffering of every mother, including hers.

How obstinate she had been about her own well-being. Refusing to understand. Refusing to forgive. Refusing to heal herself.

Now it was different.

'Worth waiting for?' she asked the reflection in the mirror.

She let herself out of the room.

There was no answer to her knock on his door. She tapped a second time, and was rewarded with a muffled 'Come in.'

Hands clasped between his knees and head bent, Robin was sitting on the bed. He was still dressed. At her entrance, he lifted a chalk-white face. 'I'm sorry, Lara. It turns out that I'm no company.'

'What's happened?'

There was sweat on his upper lip. 'It gets me like this sometimes. It'll take a few hours and then I'll be fine.'

'The flashback?'

'They come out of the blue.'

'Do you want me to go?'

He closed his eyes. 'No, I don't. But I can't bear it if you pity me.'

She sat down beside him. 'Nothing wrong with pity. I could have done with it myself many times.'

'I'll order some.'

'I'll stay, then.'

He nodded.

Concerned by how white and clammy he was, she poured water from the bottle on the tray. 'Do you need anything else?'

He dropped his head into his hands. 'A reconstituted memory.'

'I'll try to arrange it.'

'Please.'

'Tell me.' She touched his shoulder. 'Tell me.' Quietly, she took off his shoes and eased him back on to the pillows, then climbed in beside him. 'Hold on to me,' she instructed.

His bag was on the luggage rack. His passport and wallet were neatly placed on the table. His boots were aligned side by side under the chair. The window was open. The city's night hum was a settled *legato*.

But the scent of jasmine floating in from the garden under the window was almost unbearable.

She took his hand in hers.

'It's like a record stuck in a groove. It plays over and over. It's the syndrome. Some people go mad with it.'

She plaited her fingers with his.

'There was Jack,' he told her, 'who had his leg blown off by a mine. He was the fastest runner I've ever known. They found his foot ten metres down the road. Then there was Rab. He lost his head. Literally. He'd only got married a month before. And you know what all this did to us? It made us hungry for revenge, and out we would go and try to hammer other human beings into the little bits they'd turned our mates into. But that wasn't it. I could cope with all that. It was the little boy who got in the way of the crossfire.' He was silent. 'He was somebody's son. He could have been my son.'

She released his hands, slid her arms around him and drew him close. *Go on.*

'But you never again see such colour as with death and fighting,' he said. 'Or feel so alive.'

'Go on.'

'The price of survival is the disbelief that I'm alive, and an inability to process the memories. And, on top of all that, there's still the hunger to . . . have it all back.'

She stroked his hair, conscious of every movement, every sensation. The gestures felt as new to her as if she was performing them for the first time. It wasn't exactly love . . . but a tuning in as closely as was possible to someone else. Behind her eyelids there was a light and, for that moment, her body and spirit were balanced in a perfect equilibrium and purpose.

'Hold on to me,' she repeated, and curved her arms the better to clasp him to her.

There was more. A lot more. As the night slipped away, Lara held Robin until, eventually, they slept.

Chapter Eighteen

Maudie was in the exam room. Her pen scratched over the paper, which was blotted with moisture. It wasn't so much hot in the room as saturated with the candidates' nerves and sweat.

She glanced at the clock.

Maudie's mantra (adopted by hundreds): Divide your time equally. Do not overrun the allocation but move on to the next question. Say what you're going to say. Say it. Say what you've said. The headache that had been threatening for the last week sat triumphantly above her left temple.

Yet she found it exhilarating to rise above her discomfort. It was a testing point where a good mind slotted into play. So, if the thud above her temple was making her sluggish, she would fight it with logic, reason and knowledge.

This was her final paper. English. Shakespeare. The questions were difficult. 'How far, and in what ways, do you see politics as a central concern in *Antony and Cleopatra*?' The public versus the private? How far should they interface? Increasingly, she was conscious of her ignorance, and it would not be unreasonable to demand of the examiner how eighteen-year-olds were qualified to judge? She didn't doubt that her life had been easy up to this point. Now it would grow more difficult. The idea that she was at an end, and at a beginning, prompted her to write feverishly.

The cheap paper under her fingers was both slinky and rough. Across the room, Tess coughed. Their private signal. Three places behind her was Nick and, every so often, she felt his gaze on her back.

The clock crept onwards.

At the finish, she slumped back in the chair. Exhausted. There followed the minutes of nothing as the papers were collected. She turned her head. Nick was looking directly at her. She knew what he was telling her, and it wasn't so very unwelcome.

The invigilators were taking their time. Maudie closed her eyes. She wanted to experience the moment of freedom. Intense. Velvet. Reverberant.

An emptied, drifting mind.

Yet Nick's scrutiny got in the way, and she tugged at the hair at the nape of her neck.

It was making her think of sex. Up in the woods with Nick. Those afternoons. Hazy. Dozy. Intense.

A couple kissing passionately in the cold, stale dark. He was pressed up hard and greedily against her. She, sprawled against the vertical wall, her blue dress hitched up over her thighs where his hand rested.

Oh. My. God. Maudie's eyes flew open and she took a huge, shuddering breath.

How stupid she had been. How unseeing.

The significance of what had been swimming at the back of her subconscious came into focus. *Andrew?* It had been Andrew with his hand up another woman's dress.

To her surprise, her first thought was to talk to her mother. But Lara was away. Then, as rapidly, she concluded it was the *last* thing she would do. Today was the day that put down the formal marker between her adolescence and the rest of her life, so why go backwards?

They filed out of the exam hall—Maudie's new knowledge tucked under her heart like a canker. Nick found his way to bump against her. 'OK?' he asked.

Flashing him a smile. (She couldn't help it.) 'OK. You?'

'It's nearly over. One more.'

'I'm done.'

Under the cover of the exiting bodies, he found her hand. She allowed it to rest in his. He muttered, 'Come over to mine, Maudie.'

There had been so much stuff between them. Then no stuff. Plus she wasn't going to be here for much longer. She had got rid of him for reasons that were no longer clear to her. At the time, she had thought she understood them. Not now.

She missed him. 'OK.'

Nick lived at the smarter end of the city, the house big and semi-detached. 'It's ridiculous, really,' his mother's painted lips had let drop, in the days when Maudie had visited it regularly, 'to have such a large house with only the three of us living in it now.' Nick's father had long ago struck out for pastures new.

Yacketty-yack, went Mrs Yates on seeing Maudie, her brittle body betraying a lifetime not only of trying not to eat but of trying not to think about food.

She led Maudie into what she always referred to as the 'the family room', which was pretty big too. Confected by an expert, the décor was a symphony of neutrals, so much so that the room almost disappeared. Everything was eye-wateringly expensive—curtains, upholstery, lighting—and appeared not so much untouched and unused as cryogenically preserved.

Flanked by a laptop, and copies of *Now* and *Loaded*, Nick's sister, Charis, sat at a circular inlaid table by the window.

'Here's Maudie,' said her mother, in a bright, ingratiating voice. 'You remember Maudie?'

Charis looked up briefly from the laptop. 'Hi.'

Blonde-highlighted hair scraped back from her face. Heavily made-up eyes ringed with exhaustion. On her right hand black nails. On the left pale green. Maudie rather approved.

She and Nick exchanged a look. Charis was the thorn in the family's flesh. Charis didn't care about anything much, and was consistent in expressing this position. She had, Nick explained on the way over, failed most of her GCSEs the previous year. She was supposed to be working for the resits, but Charis wasn't interested.

Mrs Yates muttered that she had an urgent meeting and left, shutting the door behind her, leaving them entombed in taupe.

'Have a good shop, then,' cried Charis, after her. She addressed the magazine. 'What meeting?'

'How's it going?' Maudie asked.

Charis gave Maudie the once-over. 'OK.' She shoved a magazine under Maudie's nose. 'Cool?' A Goth fingernail tapped the photo of a bikini-clad celebrity blonde along whose bare shoulder ran the legend 'die young and beautiful'.

Maudie gazed into a parallel world—a strange, ungrateful, dangerous place that didn't consider life a gift. 'Cool,' she echoed. 'But I'd rather be alive.'

The faint gleam of curiosity was blotted out of Charis's expression, and she took back the magazine. 'Sure.' She splayed her nails on the table surface.

Nick said, 'Come upstairs.'

Maudie took a deep breath.

'Another meeting,' said Charis.

Nothing had changed much. The same posters were tacked up on the wall. The guitar sat in one corner. The room was more or less clean and the computer was on. Maudie sat on Nick's bed and watched him take off his checked shirt. She reached over and held it between her fingers, relishing its thick, felty texture, gained from too many washes.

When he had undressed, he knelt down beside Maudie and eased off her T-shirt and jeans. 'I'm glad you're here,' he said.

The air played over her naked torso. 'Thought you were angry with me.'

'I was. I am.'

She put her arms around him and drew him close. Now it had happened, she was pleased. She remembered his smell and the way his hair grew at the nape of his neck. She loved his neck especially. For all his strength, he had a gentle, slightly hesitant way about him and she liked that too.

'Nick?'

'Shut up,' he said. 'You always talk too much.'

Maudie grinned. 'The old complaints are best.'

Halfway through she surfaced, and her thoughts took a wayward turn. She remembered Andrew and the girl. It seemed to her that knowing about it was infecting her like a disease. The images were spreading through her mind, tainting the things that had nothing to do with them. She shut her eyes and concentrated on Nick's beautiful body—the things he was doing, the things he was saying. Yet the more she tried, the more she failed.

A fingernail scratching a blackboard.

Afterwards, their bodies glossy with effort, they lay side by side on the bed. Nick's fingers twined idly in and out of Maudie's. 'Nice.'

Maudie focused on the poster of Radiohead. It had a grainy quality that made her think of old movies. 'It was.' She turned towards him—and had the oddest sensation that she was drowning. 'Sorry . . . about everything. I'm sorry.'

He grunted. 'Let's not go into that. You're here. I'm here.'

She smiled and traced a pattern on his shoulder. 'Come to the prom with me?'

'I might.'

*   *   *

'Jassy!' Maudie said urgently. 'Can we meet?'

'Of course.' She cast an eye over the calendar on her computer. 'This must mean you've finished. Congratulations. How do you feel?'

'Fine.'

A sixth sense informed Jasmine that this was not entirely the case, so when she met Maudie off the evening train from Winchester, she wasn't surprised to find her pale and preoccupied.

Over *pasta puttanesca* and wine, Jasmine deliberately talked about other things. 'I'm thinking of dragging Duncan on a whale-watching trip.'

'Where?'

'West coast of America. A couple of grey whales were spotted in San Diego bay recently. They've probably been left behind on the annual migration, perhaps because they're too old or ill.' She cupped her chin in her hands, and let her gaze rove slowly over her younger sister. 'OK. There's something the matter.'

'I slept with Nick.'

'So? Presumably you wanted to or you wouldn't have done it.' She peered at Maudie. 'Don't tell me, you *didn't* want to?'

'Sure. It was post exam.' She smiled a little. 'I did want to.'

Jasmine recognized the smile. It was one of dreamy recollection. 'So what's up?'

Maudie lifted her eyes from her plate. 'Can I trust you? I mean, *really* trust you?'

'If you couldn't I wouldn't be here. I put off a date . . . with my boss. There's a big project on. So big we have a code-name that changes every month—I can never remember it. I was supposed to be talking it over with him.'

Maudie's eyes turned stormy. 'I can't understand how a computer or a bank or whatever is worth all that trouble or money.'

'Grow up, Maudie. You can trust me. And?'

Maudie twirled the pasta around her fork. 'Jas, the engagement party. I just realized I saw something and I don't know what to do.'

Jasmine poured more wine. 'It's going to be a long evening. And, since I've probably sacrificed my career, I'm having more too.' She kept her eyes fixed on Maudie. 'Something that involves Mum? Robin? Harvard?'

'No,' Maudie said. 'It's Eve.'

'Evie?'

'Your favourite sister.'

Jasmine raised an eyebrow. 'Hey. It's me, not some cheap movie.'

'OK. OK.' Maudie licked her lips and began to speak.

Jasmine listened. Then she asked questions. *Give me the details.* Some things slotted into place. Eve's behaviour at the party. Her anxiety. Oh, Evie, she thought, and the seeds of deep outrage began to germinate.

'Are you quite, quite sure?' she demanded

'How can I be? It was dark.' Maudie fiddled about with the remnants of the pasta. 'Not one hundred and ten per cent—but pretty sure, now I've thought about it.'

. . . Eve saying in her happy voice: 'Jas, I *think* Andrew likes me.' The long discussions between the sisters as to exactly how much Andrew liked Eve. The way she lit up when Andrew was around. 'He's a big baby in some ways, Jas. In others, not. I haven't worked him out.' Then Eve saying in a peculiar, solemn voice: 'Jasmine, Andrew's asked me to marry him.' And of her asking Eve: 'Are you sure. Sure-sure?' . . .

'Why didn't you think about it earlier?'

'That's the point,' said Maudie. 'I didn't think anything of it. People have it off in all sorts of places.'

'So they do,' said Jasmine.

'It's strange,' said Maudie, 'but I feel like I've been corrupted.' She fiddled with the napkin. 'I wish I didn't know.' She thought for a second or two. 'It's horrible.'

'It might be, Maudie. Who knows?' Jasmine appraised her sister and struggled to master her growing fury. 'I thought fidelity was less of an issue with you and your friends.'

Maudie stared at her. *You are a fool.* 'Don't pretend you're a Victorian,' she said. 'My friends are one thing. But Eve's getting married.'

Oh, Evie, she thought. What can I do for you?

'Maudie, you're shocked.'

'I am,' said Maudie. 'And I'm shocked I'm shocked.'

The restaurant was filling up and the waiter moved from table to table lighting the candles, creating a string of radiance.

'The question is,' said Maudie, refusing a dessert, 'what do I do?'

It was a good question and Jasmine was not prepared to answer it there and then. 'Nothing,' she said, and repeated, more urgently, '*Nothing.* Leave it to me.'

'Are you sure about that? I'd much rather ...' Maudie looked lighter, less burdened. 'I'm not the right person. You are.'

*   *   *

Back in her flat, Jasmine flung her bag on to the floor and headed for the kitchen and the kettle. Her hand shook as she searched the cupboard for the most soothing herbal tea.

Eve.

For once, she was relieved not to be with Duncan. She would have been angry with him. *At* him. At *men*. At the whole damn thing.

She poured water on to the teabag. How dare Andrew help himself to her sister's life, only to use it wantonly, so carelessly? How dare he make it impossible to trust in him for Eve and her future?

Angry? My God, she was angry.

She drank two mugs of camomile tea, read up for the next day's meeting, sorted out the laundry and stuck her head into the cupboard under the sink. One of the troubles with living in two places was that she never managed to get ahead of herself on the shopping. Rubber gloves, wire-wool, water softener . . . She jotted in her electronic notebook.

There was a message on her phone—Eve:

Hey. Timetable: Wedding 4.00 p.m.
Champagne reception 5.15. Dinner 7.30.
Dancing. Hotels are booked.

She did not reply.

A second message pinged into her phone. Again from Eve.

Thought you might want to see this.

It was the latest report on Japanese whaling activities. She skimmed through it and burned additionally with indignation and renewed energy to *do* something.

For a long time she sat with her head in her hands. Through her laced fingers nosed the grey shape of the hunted whale, icy water cradling its flight. So mysterious. So terrifying. So other. And, yet, in its solemnity, its hot mammalian blood and its suffering, it was not.

She phoned Eve. 'Shall we meet up?'

'Oh, good,' came the reply. 'Come down to Membury on Saturday. I need to sort out some stuff.'

* * *

Duncan drove her down.

Jasmine was mainly silent as they travelled at speed along the motorway and filtered off at the turning for the village. The may trees had long since reached the end of the flowering season and stained pink and white petals heaped at the edges of the roads and blew around as they passed.

Normally she would have enjoyed the sight.

What do I do?

They turned into the drive. 'Have you spoken to Andrew lately?' She placed her hand on Duncan's knee.

'Not really. A couple of drinks with the lads, that's all.'

He was distracted—and she knew his mind would be on the upcoming megadeal, which was going to take up the next few weeks. 'He's happy with everything? The marriage? Eve?'

Duncan halted the car and pulled on the brake. 'I have no idea of his innermost thoughts but, at a rough guess, yes to all.' He frowned. 'These are not, I take it, random questions.' He put his hand under her chin and turned her face to his. 'So what's the current bee in the bonnet?'

'It's awkward, Duncan.' A moment's

realignment—then the decision not to speak. 'Look, it's nothing.' She placed her hand on the door handle.

He reached over and pulled her hand away. 'Stop it,' he said. 'You know it's not a good idea to set off a hare unless you want it chased.'

'I agree.' Jasmine swung her legs out of the door and reached into the back for her bag. 'And I'm not setting off the hare. OK?'

Duncan also got out of the car and shut the door with a snap. 'For God's sake.' He came round and stood over her. 'Don't play games.'

'End of conversation,' she said.

He was on the point of losing his temper. 'Something's got into you, Jas, in the last few days. I don't know what it is. I don't bloody care. But, if you ask me a leading question, you should expect me to want to know why.'

She knew perfectly well that her anger with Andrew was making her act stupidly and unfairly but she could not, as yet, master it.

Up on the terrace, Eve waved to them.

'Coming,' she called to her sister.

She abandoned Duncan by the car.

Wearing a hat and an enormous pair of sunglasses, Eve was sitting in the sun on the terrace, Notebook and coffee parked in front of her. She poured Jasmine some and passed it over. 'Sarah's in the garden. She'll be coming back in a minute. God knows where Dad is.'

Jasmine wrinkled her nose at the coffee.

'Jas, you've got to help me. We're at war over the guest list and I've got to get these invites out. Sarah's still upset about the whole thing.' Under the huge sunglasses, Eve's face was small and strained.

'I can't have Sarah's relations. I just can't. It's not what I planned, and I'd planned so carefully.'

'You OK, Eve?'

Eve shuffled stuff from the Notebook. 'Never better.'

Jasmine assessed her sister. All was not quite well—and her anxiety mounted. 'And the dress?'

'Going ahead.' Eve flicked through her phone's image bank. 'There. The Juliet dress. And don't give me any stuff about tragedy.'

Jasmine peered at it. It was undeniably beautiful, a dreamy, billowing fantasy. 'The rose,' she asked. 'Has Ivanka sewn it in?'

'She does that at the last minute, when she's sure the wedding is going ahead.'

'Sensible girl.'

Everywhere the garden revealed signs of work. The drive was freshly gravelled, the bed under the terrace dug and mulched and the lawn had been mown. The sun was now high in the sky, revealing a spectrum of colours so vivid and fresh that she caught her breath. On the wall of the house behind them, the climbing rose was throwing off buds of deep red.

Jasmine abandoned the coffee. 'The flowers?'

'I won.'

'Eve,' she said, picking her way with care, 'would it have been better to let Sarah have her head? Do people look at the flowers as much as the dress?'

Eve whipped off her glasses. 'Jas, you have no taste.'

'Harsh.'

Eve's lips twitched. 'Don't go there.'

'Even so . . .' She tallied the countless negotiations in the office when strategic withdrawal resulted in victory.

'But you're probably right,' Eve conceded. 'On the other hand, it's our wedding and Andrew's very particular. I'm discovering weddings are peculiar. Everyone wants a piece of them and they don't seem to care about the feelings of the bride.'

At the mention of Andrew, Jasmine felt uneasy. 'Heard from Mum?'

'I've heard nothing from Lara.'

'She had a good time in Syria. She sounded odd, but happy enough. I didn't ask for any details, but I got a load of stuff about Crusader castles—' Jasmine stopped. 'Since when have you called her Lara?'

Eve shrugged. 'It's about time, isn't it?'

Out of the corner of her eye, Jasmine caught sight of Duncan and Andrew crossing the lawn, deep in conversation. As she watched, they crossed into the shadow thrown by the beech where the lawn was patched with worm casts.

'Eve, there *is* something wrong.'

'No,' she repeated. '*No.*'

'Are you having second thoughts?'

Eve looked directly at her. 'No. Absolutely *not.* Everything is fine. I know I'm fussing about guest lists and things, but that's all show. You know me. I have to have everything perfect. But I'm happy. Happy, happy.'

Jasmine thought of the jealousy she struggled so hard to neutralize. She remembered, too, when Eve had told her she was marrying Andrew—*Jas, you will never, ever guess . . .* and her solemn expression.

The two sisters exchanged a look.

Was she really going to say, *Eve, I think you should know . . .?*

She thought of the exact moment she had first caught sight of Duncan. *That's it.* The beat of her blood as the thought formed. She had believed that nothing was going to stop what was going to happen. She had looked at him and known his secrets; the incidental pieces of information, his name, where he lived, were unimportant. If she had been told he had another woman, that wouldn't have made any difference either.

Chapter Nineteen

It was dawn on Prom Day.

Lara was awake, reliving the moment in Damascus when she had woken to find Robin beside her and experienced both yearning and joy.

It hadn't lasted, of course, and the moment had gone. Bright, hard sunlight had streamed into the bedroom across two people who were not going to find it easy to begin again.

For the time remaining in Damascus, Robin and she had retreated into politeness and were very careful with each other. They agreed that they had enjoyed their walk to The Street Called Straight, their visit to the old merchant warehouses, the khans, and their lunch, eaten on a terrace with orange and lemon trees. But on the flight home he had taken her hand and held it. 'Thank you, Lara.'

Something of the extraordinary intimacy of the night returned—and left her feeling bereft. She went home with a strange feeling that areas in her heart were physically raw.

But, soon, that faded too. Facing her was a

backlog of her existing clients, questions from the lawyers over partnership details, negotiating the new lease on consulting rooms, and hammering out the rules and conditions of the practice with the new therapists, Pauline and Ralph.

But at night ... when else? ... she was at the mercy of elements beyond her control and she thought of Robin with longing. A part of her was so grateful that she had been given another chance to feel passionately, to feel greedy for sensation and possession. Another part of her shrank away from it. The idea of going through it all again appalled her.

Then the new day would arrive and, once again, she forgot.

Now, she prayed. *Please ... Please ...* What exactly was she asking? Lara shaped her thoughts for the events of the day. Please let Maudie be happy tonight.

Maudie slept late and she permitted it. A rainwashed afternoon (much glumness) gave way to a milky lit evening. 'Oh, God, my shoes,' wailed the Nordic ice-maiden Maudie, as white and nervous as Lara had ever seen her. She fed her cups of tea, helped her wash her hair and talked gently to her.

Did she remember, she asked Maudie, when Jasmine had left school more than a decade ago and there was hardly any fuss? Hair tied back, tie loosened, Jasmine had walked out of Brightwells Comprehensive, climbed into the car and said, 'Let's go.' She had never once looked back at the buildings. Surprisingly, the matter-of-fact Eve had been more emotional and insisted that her friends came round to the house for pizza and chips. They had filled the house with the noise of starlings on the wing.

Maudie quietened. 'Mum, stop fussing. I'm fine.'

Lara slipped an arm around the thin waist. 'Hey,' she said. 'Shall we practise you walking on those ridiculous heels?'

At five o'clock Maudie ran the bath and lay in it surrounded by candles and listening to whale music lent to her by Jasmine. Lara stuck her head around the door. The whale music had reached a groaning passage. 'OK?'

Maudie dropped a copy of Doris Kearns Goodwin's *Team of Rivals* on the chair beside the bath and turned a face streaked with moisture towards her. 'The dress . . .'

'What about it?'

'Tess doesn't like it.'

The previous evening, there had been a grand showing and the two girls had conferred for hours.

'What did she say?'

'She didn't *say* anything.'

No comment *was* bad. 'It could be that she was jealous.'

'Not Tess.'

'Does it matter if she doesn't like it?'

The question was so beyond contempt that Maudie didn't bother to answer. Lara backed away and, with half an ear on Maudie's movements upstairs, made some phone calls.

From upstairs came a thump and she went upstairs to assess current progress. Maudie was having a fit over her hair, which had frizzed in the bath. Lara assessed it, fetched the tongs and set to work. It was a soothing enough task, and she had always liked the smell of hot tongs.

Maudie having expressed satisfaction, Lara returned downstairs and picked up the phone, which had been ringing. There was a message on the answer phone from Robin to say he was going away and would be in touch.

A little chilled, she replaced the receiver.

Then she remembered something Robin had said: 'I'm not going to foist my demons on you, Lara.'

And she had said: 'Isn't that for me to decide?' And, because she understood only too well that opportunities quickly melted away, she went on the attack and texted to his mobile: 'Please, don't run away.'

At six o'clock, Maudie appeared in the kitchen, one eye made up in smoky greys and greens, the other bare. She held up her mobile. 'Disaster,' she announced, in tragic tones. 'The limo has broken down and they can't supply another.'

Lara stared at her daughter.

'Mum?' Maudie shivered. She gazed beseechingly at Lara. She knew what was being asked.

'OK,' she said. 'I'll drive you all down.'

So it was that Lara found herself hovering alongside Vicky by the entrance to the clubhouse at Walmer Park racecourse outside Winchester. From this vantage point, they observed a progression of Lincolns and Chryslers deposit their passengers. An Indian boy arrived in a gaily decorated *tuk-tuk*. A girl rode up on her horse with—presumably—her adoring father driving the horsebox behind her. Yet another arrived on stilts.

The girls were in dresses the colours of sweets. Tangerine, turquoise, plum and liquorice black. Behind them trailed their reluctant and self-conscious Prince Charmings. Raw haircuts, hired dinner jackets, new shoes. One or two had bottles stuffed obviously into their jackets.

Without so much as a glance, they flocked past Lara and Vicky.

She caught Vicky's eye. 'Invisible.'

'Invisible.'

A pair of olive trees in tubs flanked the entrance (décor surely far too exotic for this staid English venue?) and the door was decked out with fairy lights. Beyond the reception area was the dance hall into which the guests were drifting.

Tess disappeared into the Ladies. Maudie paced up and down outside—a tall, nervy figure, who, despite the tuition, was not quite steady on her heels. 'This is so stupid and demeaning,' she had said before leaving home. 'Why am I doing it?' The silver in the dress caught the evening sun and, for a second, her tall figure blazed with a halo.

Lara thought Maudie looked as beautiful as it was possible to be and marvelled that, somehow, she and Bill had managed to produce her. Who else could match her wayward, independent, stubborn Maudie? She visualized her sailing into her future in a haze of silver light—successful, loved, wanted.

The door to the Ladies opened and out glided Tess in cherry red satin and green peep-toe shoes, her hair an almost convincingly natural blonde waterfall. Maudie whispered into Tess's ear, swayed slightly, righted herself and the pair moved towards the dance hall.

A sobbing girl shot out, her white dress shockingly splattered with red wine. Handkerchief in hand, her escort panted after her. But the girl

290

slammed into the Ladies.

'Fuck!' said the boy.

Vicky was dressed in a tight skirt and clinging, sleeveless sweater, which did not flatter her arms. She grabbed Lara's hand. 'My God, this is costing. Have you totted it all up?'

Lara tore her eyes away from Maudie's receding form. 'No. I thought best not to yet.'

Vicky gazed fondly after her daughter. 'It's known as Losing Virginity Night. You did make sure Maudie was OK?'

Lara was at her most wry. 'I think that's irrelevant by now.'

'Mind you,' Vicky checked herself. 'It took Tess three hours to do her hair, I don't imagine she'll want to mess it up.'

A posse of four girls and their swains pushed past them. The girls were brighter than birds of paradise, their necklines low, their skirts short.

Vicky said, 'Isn't it awful to be that age?' She rubbed her plump arms. 'The agonies.' Lara looked at her with sharpened interest. 'None of us have it easy,' continued Vicky. 'One day, I'll tell you about it. Shall we go and have dinner?'

Vicky was in top, gossipy form, and they enjoyed their pizza. Afterwards, they looked in on the clubhouse to check that everything was OK before they went home.

Inside the hall, it was crowded, dim and noisy. The beat of the music was almost an assault. The strobe picked out jerky, writhing figures, and Lara assumed Maudie and Nick were down there among the seething throng.

Leaving Vicky in conversation with another friend, Lara headed into the garden. With just a couple of flowerbeds and a hornbeam hedge, it wasn't much of one. Plenty of couples were there, too, some off their heads.

The night air was balmy on the skin. In the distance, she could just make out the racecourse and figures were running up and down the aisles in the stands. Behind the hedge, more couples were feasting on each other.

Perhaps it was summer's lease. Perhaps it was the sex going on around her or the changes ahead, but every detail pressed into her memory.

It made her think of Robin.

Then, from behind the hedge, she overheard a stroppy-sounding Maudie say, 'Nick, don't.'

'You don't have to go,' said Nick.

'I don't have to, but I want to.'

'What about us?'

'There isn't us, Nick. Not really.'

'Maudie, look at me. Now say that again.'

'Don't.'

'It's Alicia, isn't it? What's she got on you?' His voice had turned mean and ugly. 'She's persuaded you all men are awful, or some such crap.'

'Nick!' Maudie was beginning to lose her temper, too. 'Don't hassle me.'

'Don't I count?'

'Yes, you do. Yes, you do, Nick. Here, now, this evening. Please, don't make it more difficult.'

There was a long silence. Then Nick repeated his question: 'Don't I count?'

'No,' said Maudie. 'Yes . . .'

Lara turned on her heel and made for the clubhouse where Vicky found her. 'What on earth's the matter?'

She explained and Vicky laughed. 'Poor Nick.

292

Poor Maudie. I'm never sure if it's better to learn sooner or later how one's body and heart get one into terrible trouble.'

Vicky was spot on. Maudie was less hurt than confused—while Lara was less confused than hurt. Irony? As a professional, she dealt most days with the fallout from love turning sour, or love merely bumping along. She of all people knew you had to be strong and tough to deal with its pleasures and pains; sorrow was part of its essential nature. Those who negotiated through the squalls deserved applause.

Back at home in the small hours, the mothers having ensured that the girls and any of their London-based friends knew where to catch the hastily commissioned mini-van back to London, she was woken by noises in the garden. She slipped downstairs and opened the front door to discover Maudie bent double being violently sick.

The worst scenarios flashed through her mind. 'Have you taken anything, Maudie?' She shook her. 'Have you?'

'No.'

'Drink?'

Maudie raised a pair of streaming eyes to her mother. 'Shut up, Mum.'

'I warned you,' Lara said, as she led her indoors.

Maudie threw her a look of utter hostility.

Lara ran a bath and helped Maudie into it. Her daughter sat quietly while she sponged her with warm water, then dried her and got her into bed. White and exhausted, she lay back on the pillows and closed her eyes.

'Did you enjoy any of it?'

'No,' she said flatly.

Duncan was sitting on the edge of the bed in Jasmine's flat. It was mid-afternoon on Sunday and they had just made love unsatisfactorily. Jasmine was preoccupied and Duncan was tired.

He persisted: 'What's the matter?'

She thought of the conversation with Maudie. *Say nothing?* She twitched the sheets over her bare breasts. This was a new burden: to remain silent or not? Did silence constitute a moral stance or an evasion? 'Duncan, *have* you talked to Andrew recently?'

He shrugged. 'You keep on asking me that. We've probably said hello.'

'No, *properly.*'

Duncan got up and pulled on his jeans. 'Jas, are you about to embark on a meaningful conversation?'

Her sense of humour made a brief appearance. 'You're spared. It's not about us.'

'Lord, for your small mercies, thank you.'

She regarded him speculatively. Reason, honesty, openness. These had to be at the heart of any relationship and were supposed to drive the affairs of the world. She hauled herself out of the bed. 'Andrew was seen with another woman.'

He came round to her side of the bed and grabbed Jasmine by the shoulders. 'And *who* told you that?'

'Doesn't matter who told me.' She searched his face and discovered unwelcome information. 'You do know.'

His hands fell away. 'I never said that.'

'But you suspect.' It wasn't a question.

'It's none of our business.'

'Yes, it is.'

'No!' He spat out the word. 'It isn't. What Andrew does is his business.'

She wasn't sure she had heard correctly. Dumping her underclothes in the laundry basket, she got out a fresh set. 'Duncan, he's about to marry my sister.'

'And?'

'Apart from anything else, I feel so angry with him. I trusted him.'

'Isn't that for Eve? Not you?'

She pulled on her T-shirt. 'It's OK, then, to be cavorting with a girl from the office.'

'Don't be stupid.'

'You seem to suggest—'

'*I* seem to suggest!' Duncan fastened his belt. 'Am I hearing right?' He glared at her and got no response. 'You know what? It's what I think. I don't know what Andrew is doing, or not doing, and I'm not going to ask. He's free to do as he wishes.'

'Hang on. So you don't think something's wrong if Andrew's seeing someone else?'

'I didn't say that.'

'My God.' She sat down on the edge of the rumpled bed. 'How stupid I've been.'

Duncan tied up his shoes with savage little jerks. 'You always have to make such a production of everything, Jas.'

'So . . .' she chose the words carefully '. . . if I was seeing someone else you wouldn't necessarily mind because I'm free to do as I wish?' He paled a trifle and straightened up. 'Or you might be seeing someone else as well as this.' She gestured to the bed. 'Is that so? Be honest.'

How would it work? Phone calls. Meeting on a street corner or in a café in a strange part of town. The careful exchange of rules. *This doesn't mean anything*. Hotel rooms with tiny soap tablets and notices saying that the towels wouldn't be changed every day. The aftermath. Walking separately out into the street and thinking, That's that. Then going home to sit opposite Duncan at the kitchen and sharing a meal. 'Tell me about your day,' he might say. And, with another man's touch still fresh on her skin, she would tell him.

The idea was repellent ... Intriguing? Disturbing?

'So I can't trust you?' she said. 'Or, rather, we should have discussed this before.'

He grew ever paler and rubbed his stomach. That meant she had got to him. 'Now, you're being ridiculous. And insulting.'

'No. I'm trying to get at the truth. About what you think and believe. And what I think.'

Again, he touched his stomach. This time she was not going to fetch his stuff from the bathroom cabinet.

'How have we got here? Why are we discussing us when we were discussing Andrew?'

'The two are related. That's why. Either you know something. Or you approve of what Andrew might be doing. I can't tell. You won't be honest.'

At that, he turned on her. 'You're driving me mad, Jas.'

This was the Duncan who could tip into a rage—the side of him that didn't often surface. When it did, she usually managed to calm him. But not tonight. His angry eyes and white lips left her cold

296

and distant. 'I think you'd better go,' she said.

'You don't mean it?'

A mass of things slotted into place. Implacable and logical. 'I do.'

Hostile and disbelieving, he stared at her. 'You're being idiotic.'

'Go,' she said.

He shrugged and walked out of the room.

'And don't come back,' she called after him.

What had she said? *What had she said?*

She listened to the click of the front door. To her surprise, she was extraordinarily calm—exhilarated, even.

She straightened up the bedroom and settled down to work. One, it was the week when the code-name for the big project switched (again) and the transition required her attention. Two, they were pitching for yet another bank, plus a big travel company and the company in San Diego . . . Before signing off, she switched into her emails. There was one from Eve that started: 'Timings. Final Dress Fitting. Rehearsal'.

The information seemed to come from a very long way away. And she regarded it with the detachment of someone who was quite removed.

Question: was she angry only for Eve . . . or was she also angry with Duncan? And were the two different things impossibly mixed up?

Later she pulled the ironing board out from its hiding place behind a curtain and embarked on the waiting pile. The iron emitted its characteristic syrupy hisses. The clothes smelt of steam and detergent. She concentrated on those things.

As she was putting everything away, her phone rang. 'Maudie!'

'I'm outside. Can I come in?' Maudie shouted.

She arrived with hair tangled and damp from an evening downpour that had come out of nowhere. Her eyes were huge and her lips bloodless.

'What's the matter?'

'Can I talk to you?'

'Come.' She led Maudie into the kitchen. 'Drink?'

'Something soft.'

Juice carton in hand, Jasmine assessed Maudie's state. 'You had a big night, I take it? Did it go well?'

Maudie didn't answer. Her hand shook as she accepted the glass. Jasmine thought, She *has* taken something. Ecstasy, coke, weed? 'Hey, what is it?'

Maudie bowed her head over the glass. After a few seconds, she muttered, 'It's bad, Jas.'

It *is* drugs, she thought, and switched on the kettle for herself.

Maudie remained hunched over the table. 'I know I shouldn't mind. I know I shouldn't care a toss.' She looked up at Jasmine. 'It's so crass and awful, I almost can't tell you.'

'But you wanted to, otherwise you wouldn't be here. Also, I'm pretty unshockable.'

Maudie's smeared mascara left small black spiders under her eyes. 'Nick and me . . . you know.' She made a wobbly but explicit gesture with her fingers.

'You and Nick.' Jasmine dunked a camomile teabag into the boiling water. 'What's so terrible about that?'

Maudie went quite still. 'Someone took a photo while we were at it. In the garden.'

'Not brilliant, but—'

298

'It was Tess. My best friend, Tess.' She enunciated the name as if it burned her mouth. 'She thought it was a big joke. She thought I would think it was funny. She sent the photo to everyone in the class.' Maudie's eyes were the stormiest Jasmine had ever seen. 'She's sorry, of course, really sorry, but that isn't . . . I just can't believe she would think like that.'

'Well, that's one friend who won't be visiting you at Harvard.'

Maudie said, through gritted teeth, 'How *could* she? We were . . . you know?'

'Sweetie, I'm good without the details.'

'The whole class . . . the whole frigging world will pore over it.' She grimaced. 'Slapper, slut, you name it.'

Jasmine sat down opposite Maudie. 'Actually, is it very bad?'

Suddenly Maudie grinned. 'If you call me with my prom dress up around my waist bad, then yes.'

'So this thing with Nick goes on.'

'That's the strange thing, Jas. I thought it had finished. I'd absolutely decided. I told him to go and then . . .' Maudie shrugged. She raised her eyes to her sister. 'It's funny, isn't it? In the end, I've found it hard. I mean, I thought I had it all worked out. I thought I had everything straight in my mind. But I'm not sure I have.'

'The photo,' said Jasmine.

'Gross,' said Maudie, pitifully.

Gross, Jasmine thought, with a shudder of extreme empathy. 'OK, they've seen you *in flagrante*. Look on the bright side, it was only bits of you. Apart from loyalty, delicacy and privacy issues, it won't matter in the long run unless you decide to be a film star or a politician. Tess might have to rethink a bit, though.'

Maudie's fists clenched. 'How could she?'

Jasmine kept up the bracing approach. 'I bet everyone else is doing the same, and quite a few of them have been papped. Yes? They've all seen worse?'

There was a case for a moral pep talk—treat your body and your emotions responsibly, don't make yourself cheap—and there was a case for shutting down that line. 'Bet the others were envious. Gorgeous you. Gorgeous him.' Maudie didn't reply but she was listening. 'Put it down to experience and, by the way, how many of the class are you going to keep up with? The ones you do will be your real friends. To them, it won't matter.'

Maudie's eyes were dark with distress. 'I can't bear that they saw something so . . . private.'

'Maudie, you idiot. If you really felt that, you shouldn't have done it in the garden. What were you thinking?' Oh, Lord, she was beginning to sound like Lara. 'Yes, people will talk till such time as *they* do something stupid. Then they'll only be thinking about themselves. Trust me. People are mostly interested in themselves. The trick is to disguise it, but some people can't and some people don't, and at least you know where you are with them. That photo will not be important in the long run.'

Maudie considered. 'Thanks, Jas.'

'You look half starved. Would you like something?'

Maudie nodded. 'Haven't eaten all day.'

Keeping a weather eye on the thin, hunched, angry figure, she made them a sandwich. 'Eat,' she said at last, putting it in front of Maudie.

Maudie ate a mouthful. 'Jassy, you know what we talked about before—what I saw in the hotel. I've been thinking. We should tell Eve.'

This business with Andrew was everywhere, stealing through the family ether. 'I'm thinking it over,' she answered. 'But, whatever, I don't think you should be involved. OK? All you need do is to keep silent.'

'It's changed things, hasn't it?'

'If it's true, yes.'

'Even if it isn't,' said Maudie. 'We feel differently.' Jasmine nodded. 'Does Eve know?' she pressed on. 'Does she suspect? Even a tiny bit?'

'I don't know.' Jasmine hesitated.

'What do you think about Andrew?'

I want to kill him for Eve . . . for destroying our illusions. She chose to show moderation. 'Let's not say anything for the moment,' she said. 'It could get out of hand.'

'The stupid thing is,' Maudie sounded bewildered, 'it's made me feel I should be here for the wedding. I know Eve and I don't get on that well but it would be like abandoning her.'

'That's ridiculous, Maudie.'

Maudie ate another mouthful. 'I know. But there it is.'

Chapter Twenty

Eve's email:

Final, final guest list. Meet Sunday. Membury.

The message was bald, with no greeting and no signature.

Apart from the rehearsal nearer the date, it would be one of their last meetings at Membury. Lara could only feel relief. The whole thing—the wedding, the emotions, the politics—was becoming alarming. Everyone involved was on an ice rink struggling to keep themselves upright.

On their way down, she and Maudie drove past swathes of Queen Anne's lace clumped in the hedges. The sight never failed to lift her spirits. In the fields there were ox-eye daisies and poppies. It seemed so fresh and vivid and, if she permitted herself to be fanciful, expectant.

Stowed in the car boot were thirty square glass vases. Eve had bought them from Covent Garden Flower Market for Lara to transport down. 'I got up at dawn,' she had said coldly, when she handed them over to Lara. Intended as centrepieces for the dining tables in the marquee, apparently no other design would do. They chimed with Eve's colour scheme—the concept—and were to be filled with the white and green hydrangeas which had been promoted over the chocolate cosmos of Eve's original vision.

Maudie was quiet.

'What are you thinking about?' She knew her daughter. 'Are you worried about America?'

'Yes and no.'

'We must go through the checklist.' What would the house be like when Maudie went? Sound like? Feel like? 'It's only a few weeks. Clothes. All the paperwork. Et cetera.'

Maudie twisted a lock of hair between her fingers. 'Mum, what if I stayed for the wedding?'

Astonished, she took her eyes off the road. 'Maudie, I don't know what to say. Would it be wise to miss freshmen's week?'

'Um,' she said. 'Tell me if I'm wrong but I thought you wanted me to stay.'

'That was then.'

Lara had made the wrong response (more than likely) or Maudie had had second thoughts about the conversation: 'Actually, Mum, drop it. OK?'

At Membury—so scented, so awakened, so foamy with colour—a stony-faced Eve, who had come down earlier, offered Lara the barest of greetings. In virtual silence, they unloaded the vases and stowed them in the outhouse by the garage.

'What's up with the bride?' hissed Maudie.

'Don't know,' Lara lied.

'Yes, you do.' Maudie seemed uncharacteristically agitated.

'Listen,' Lara threaded her fingers through Maudie's hair and tugged gently, 'the run-up to a wedding is never comfortable. Things get said, tempers are short. There are misunderstandings.'

Maudie flashed back, 'Nothing out of the ordinary, then.'

Lara laughed.

Maudie permitted Lara to pat her hair back into place. 'So you think everything's OK with Eve?'

After a tiny pause, Lara said, 'Yes,' with all the conviction she could muster, and went to find Bill.

Looking tanned and comfortable in shorts and a T-shirt, he was working on a flowerbed in the sunken lawn. At her approach he straightened up. 'You look well,' she told him.

'I am,' he replied. 'Particularly as I plan to stay here while you lot thrash everything out.'

'I hope Sarah's not still angry.'

'You'll have to ask her.' He leaned on the garden fork. 'How was your Syrian trip?'

She shaded her eyes. 'Loved it.'

'Thought you might.'

He bent over to shave off a sliver of box with the pruning shears. 'Is Robin a serious thing?'

Even a short while ago he wouldn't have asked, and she wouldn't have answered. 'I don't know. Yet.'

He didn't pursue the subject.

'It's lovely here, Bill.' Having long since shed its blossoms, the witch hazel had retreated into being an ordinary shrub shrouded in its niche by the wall. A bee the size of a small aircraft was foraging in a clump of wild borage, its flowers an intense blue. The myrtle tree was coming into flower. She thought she could smell jasmine.

He straightened up. 'Pass me the trug, will you?' He rubbed at a swollen red patch on his forearm.

She did so. 'Is your arm OK?'

'Bee sting.'

She thought of a broken, grieving Bill, of cradling Louis while her heart disintegrated.

I told you.

You wouldn't listen.

She shoved her hands into her pockets.

Each of the plants growing here had survived winter, flouting death, botanical mistakes and reproductive sins. They were worth thinking about. Each petal of the rose that strained at the calyx, each spike of lavender, every spicy leaf of rosemary had triumphed over its earlier extinction.

'It's lovely,' she repeated.

'I know.'

'Bill, we have to talk about Maudie. She's doing a back flip and offering to stay for the wedding. I don't think it's sensible. What do you think?'

Bill gave his slow smile. 'I haven't heard you ask my opinion for years.'

She laughed. 'I am now.'

Bill held out a pair of filthy hands. 'I agree with you, it's probably not a good thing. I'll talk to her.'

'Go carefully.'

'As carefully as you, Lara.'

She pursued her lips. 'OK. Tell me I've made a pig's ear.'

'You've made a pig's ear,' he repeated, teasing and affectionate. 'Which god ordained that the modern nuptial should be so complicated?'

'I thought you were all for it.'

'I am. But I feel rather chastened by it all.'

Again she laughed. 'So do I.'

He rubbed the thumb of one hand over the forefinger of the other—a habit she used to know well. 'Since, in the teeth of sense and financial prudence, we're giving Eve this wedding, do you want to come and see the exact site of the marquee?'

Later, Lara perched on the terrace on a garden chair, its rush pattern impressing imprints on to her thighs. She caught sight of her ex-husband trundling a wheelbarrow heaped with compost between flowerbeds. He seemed happy. No, he *was* happy.

On the table between them was a stack of invitations wrapped in virgin tissue paper.

Eve was at her briskest. Avoiding Lara's eye, she handed out lists of names and addresses to her mother and Sarah. 'Have I missed anyone?'

Unlike Bill, Sarah was not happy. She placed her list on the table. 'I have to say something. I know I should brush it under the carpet, but I can't. I feel I haven't been treated fairly.'

Eve flushed. 'Sarah, I'm so sorry, but the numbers are tight. I'd hoped I'd explained.'

With some dignity, Sarah said, 'This is my house and I think I should be able to invite my brother and his wife.'

Admirable Sarah. 'Eve,' said Lara. 'Let's reconsider.'

Eve paid Lara no attention. 'Sarah, we agreed.'

Sarah said, 'Yes, but ... how *do* I fit into all this? I have a right to ask.' Her normally equable expression had been replaced by an angry one. 'We've had this discussion before. But a wedding belongs to the whole unit because it affects the whole unit.'

'While we're on the subject of the whole unit ...' Maudie hooked her leg over the arm of the chair and let her foot dangle. A thumb moved at the speed of light over her phone.

'Maudie,' said Eve. 'Can't you stop that?'

'No, I can't.'

'Can't, shan't and won't,' said Lara. 'Thought you'd both grown up.'

Maudie abandoned the texting. 'You're right.' She un-hooked her leg and knelt down, mock fashion, in front of her sister. 'Eve, I've been thinking ... I've been thinking hard. Please may I be your bridesmaid after all?'

'Don't tease,' said Eve, slipping an invitation into an envelope and writing 'Mr and Mrs C. Spall' on it. 'There's no need either to make it sound like martyrdom.'

'I mean it.' Maudie clambered back to her feet.

Sarah said, 'We've haven't finished our discussion.'

'You're quite right,' said Lara, her attention fixed on Maudie. 'Maudie, that would mean you missing almost the whole of freshmen's week. Not a good idea.'

Eve went very still.

Maudie addressed Eve from her great height. 'Eve, I know you've been put out and I'm sorry. But I can be here. I don't have to go.'

'Of course I want you at my wedding.'

'Maudie,' said Lara, desperately.

Here Sarah intervened: 'Maudie, have you thought this through?'

Lara turned to Eve. 'I don't know what to say but ...' It was as if all the years of her intimacy with her stepdaughter had never taken place—it was as if she was talking to a stranger.

Eve said coldly, 'Lara, I'm sure you'll do what's best for Maudie.'

*　　　*　　　*

Buoyed up by sacrifice—something she was not in the habit of practising—Maudie loped over the lawn towards her father. She could never resist the sound of pigeons in the trees and stopped to listen.

Nick.

Looking up into the branches, she experienced the slight nausea she felt whenever she thought of the prom night. Drink, music, their quarrel, the intense sensations of sex as they made it up, night air on her shamelessly bare skin. The photo.

Nick had been so stupid, so angry, and then so wild—and she had loved every minute of it. 'It's Alicia who's pushing you to do this,' he said. 'Why can't you be ordinary? Why do you let her organize your life?'

'Nobody pushes me,' she said, a finger pressing into his smooth chest. 'So take that back.'

She thought of the hours Alicia had spent outlining the possibilities for her life, coaching her, giving her courage. The born teacher and mentor. One day, maybe, following Alicia's example, Maudie might do the same for someone else. Whatever, she was pretty sure Alicia would not approve of her missing freshmen's week—*Sentimentality is weakness, Maudie.*

The pigeons' call was soft and glottal.

Nobody pushes me. Maudie stuffed the phone into her jeans pocket. Yet, to be honest, everyone was pushed about by someone. It was one of the things she had learned—and, funnily enough, it included Alicia, who had only the best of intentions.

She looked back over her shoulder at the trio of Eve, Sarah and her mother on the terrace—and was surprised by a surge of solidarity with Eve. At the same time, she *was* anxious to leave. The lure of the university campus was as strong as ever. Still, there were questions. *I'm running away? No, I'm merely running.* But could she thrive in a strange place, with strange people, and negotiate the subtleties of strangers?

'It'll be a place where everyone speaks the same language but probably doesn't understand anyone else,' she had said to Alicia.

'You think that, do you?' said Alicia. 'You can tell me when you get there if it's true.'

She pulled her phone out of her pocket to check it. Nothing. She stuffed it back. She didn't *need* to look at her phone.

Harvard: the pros and cons occupied many of her waking moments.

And so did Nick.

At the thought of him, she caught her breath.

As she approached, her father looked up. 'Dad, I've been told to tell you that lunch is nearly ready.'

He looked wary. 'Is it the Third World War up there?'

She stuck her hands into her pockets. 'Yes and no. Sarah feels left out.'

'I know she does.'

'Are you going to do anything? Or just . . .'

He would know what she was about to say. *Or just ignore it as always.*

'I trust your mother to sort it out. She has a better knack.' He hefted compost on to the flowerbed and forked it over. 'How are things?'

'Great.'

'Done all the paperwork and stuff? Did you get the letter I sent you about the finances?'

'Sure. Thank you.'

'You're going to have to find work in the holidays.'

'I didn't expect anything else. Anyway, I'd insist on it.'

The fork emitted little scraping sounds as he spread the compost this way and that. 'About freshmen's week . . .'

'I know what you're going to say.'

'In that case, you'll appreciate the wisdom of the argument.' A claggy, fibrous root had stuck to the tine of the fork and he tugged it off. 'Why the change of heart, by the way?'

Maudie examined her boot. Leather (cracked) and in need of polishing. 'I thought Eve needed all the support she could get.'

Her father stuck the fork into the remaining compost. 'Would there be any special reason for this unusual display of sisterly love?'

'No.' Maudie couldn't quite look him in the eye.

'Sure?'

After all, she reasoned, he had sugared off with another woman and it could be argued that he and Andrew were all of a piece. Why should she trust him to do the right thing by Eve? 'Quite sure,' she said.

They walked back to the house together. 'About the advice I didn't need to give you because you know it anyway,' said her father. 'Please believe I don't have any axe to grind. I really think it would be for the best.'

She fingered the phone in her pocket. 'That's nice,' she said cautiously.

She had placed her foot on the first of the stone steps when he stopped her. 'Maudie, you will keep in touch?'

'I don't know.'

'I am your father.'

'Yes,' she agreed, but something red hot and vindictive swept over her. 'I always wanted a *father.*' He looked as though she had hit him. 'But I'm grateful for all your help over Harvard.'

'Maudie . . .'

She moved further up the steps.

'How can I persuade you that both your mother and I did our best in difficult circumstances?'

Maudie looked down at his upturned face. 'But you *did* leave.'

'Yes,' he conceded. 'I did.'

'I would never leave my children. *Never*. And for Shrinking V. . . .'

'For God's sake,' he said angrily. 'Have you *no* understanding at all?'

But she wasn't listening as she ran up the steps and into the house.

After a strained lunch eaten mainly in silence, Eve said, 'I need to check the vases before I go. Will you help me, Maudie?'

Anything to avoid Sarah's terrible coffee. Maudie leaped to her feet. 'Sure.'

Despite the sunshine, the outhouse was cold and smelt of mould. There were bits of old furniture—a chest of drawers and a couple of chairs without seats—plus plastic sacks stuffed with stuff. Together they shunted the boxes containing the vases on to a bench under the window.

'I wonder what this outhouse was for.' Maudie divided up the boxes between them. 'I think I can smell whitewash and lime.'

Eve shrugged. 'Probably used by a gardener in the days when you had gardeners.' She began to inspect each vase in the boxes carefully. Maudie followed suit.

'Maudie?' Eve spoke in a low, urgent tone. 'I think we should have a talk.'

Maudie smiled. 'Not you too.'

Eve caught her arm. 'You don't know what I'm

going to say.'

'No, I don't.'

Eve returned to the task in hand. She lifted out a vase and held it up to the light. 'I think you must miss the wedding and go.'

'Eve!'

'I think the wedding's sorted some issues out and that's not a bad thing. You and I have had our differences and I'm sorry about that. But I've thought about it. I don't *want* you not to be at the wedding, but I think it's necessary for you to go. If you miss all the bonding and stuff, you'll be at a disadvantage.' She licked her finger and rubbed at a smudge on the glass and confessed, with some difficulty, 'I know what it's like to be different.'

Maudie was conscious of the breath going in and out of her lungs. She longed for one of Nick's brilliant vodka-and-limes. (Not a good sign.)

'When you're different, you're different, and for a long time, and I wouldn't like that to happen to you.'

'What do you mean "for a long time"?'

'OK.' Eve slotted the final vase of the first box back into place. 'Do you remember when Jas and I were at Brightwells? In the early days, I mean.'

'Not really.'

Yes, she did. Maudie sitting at the top of the stairs while her mother rushed about below with packed lunches and coats. Jasmine and Eve in stiff shiny blue skirts and white blouses. The way their shoes creaked. The bulging book bags. The sense of drama and urgency.

She remembered, too, her mother waiting for their return. Sometimes one or other of them would be crying or sullen. Sometimes one or other refused to eat the tea their mother had prepared. Sometimes both were too tired to talk.

'What about it?' she asked.

'When Jas first went, then me later,' said Eve, 'nobody wanted to be friends. They were *interested* in us but it was because our mother had died. Nobody knew how to treat us. They talked about us but didn't invite us over or anything like that. Worse, the teachers sometimes favoured us because they thought we needed extra attention. Later on it didn't matter, of course. But it made a huge difference in that first year. Ask Jas, she'll tell you.'

'You're giving me permission to go?'

Eve dived into her pocket, produced Sellotape and secured the box. 'The bridesmaid's dress is cancelled.' She shot Maudie a sly look. 'The pink meringue.'

'Eve . . .'

'It's all right, I know you called it that.' Eve continued. 'I've thought it through. I'll Skype you before I go to the church so you can see me. That means you'll have to get up early.'

'Oh, Evie.' Maudie found herself weeping. 'Of *course* I can get up.'

'Stupid.' Eve dabbed at Maudie's eyes with a tissue. Her touch was careful, even tender. 'Then that's that.'

'OK,' said Maudie. She replaced the lid of a box she had finished checking and held out her hand for the Sellotape. 'Evie, what can I say?'

'Don't say anything.' Eve stacked a box. 'It's nothing. *Nothing.*'

This was the Eve she knew. Unsentimental, fierce, terrified of giving way.

For a minute or so, there was nothing to be heard but the zip of the Sellotape as they stuck down the last boxes.

Eventually Maudie said, 'I hope you'll be happy.'

Eve had her back to her, stowing the boxes against the wall. Her movements were deft, decided, efficient. 'Is there any reason why I shouldn't be?'

'Well . . .' said Maudie. How stupid she sounded. 'It's like this . . .'

Eve turned around. An eyebrow flew up. 'It's like what?'

They exchanged a look. Was Eve sending her a message? *Keep quiet.*

'Nothing,' said Maudie, finally. 'Not worth talking about.'

Eve gave a tight little smile. 'Let's go in, then.'

* * *

Out on the terrace, Lara and Sarah finished writing the invitations. The bright sun bleached out the ink on the lists, and the pages became criss-crossed with amendments.

Sarah was pretty silent, and the corners of her mouth had gone down. Lara said, 'Sarah, I'm sorry about the battle over guests.'

'It's been an eye-opener.' Her tongue flickered over her lips.

'Please bear with Evie.' Lara wrote 'check Taylors' address' and 'Robin?' in her diary. 'I'm sure we can sort out the numbers.'

'Maybe,' said Sarah, with the same tight expression. 'But it was the attitude. The damage had been done.' She dropped her voice. 'As I say, it's been a revelation.'

'Anything in particular?'

Sarah looked up at her house. 'To think . . .' she began. Then: 'Forget it!'

'Let's not forget it.' Lara licked the final envelope and dropped it on the top of the pile. 'Please . . .'

Holding a mug of tea, Bill stepped out on to the terrace through the french windows. 'Have I missed the worst?' He looked from his ex-wife to his current one. 'What's up?'

Lara got to her feet and went to stand beside him. 'Let's have it out. Sarah feels we're taking advantage of her generosity and usurping her house.'

'I had no idea,' Sarah was now standing on the other side of him, 'that your family would be so overwhelming, Bill. I wish I hadn't offered the house.'

Bill didn't like that. 'I thought it was a joint decision?'

'Sort of,' said Sarah. 'But you couldn't have held the wedding here if I'd disagreed. Could you?'

'Well, no.'

'As I see it, it's a question of whether I'm part of this family, or not.'

'Lara,' said Bill, 'I insist that Eve invites Sarah's brother.'

The tight, tense expression on Sarah's face relaxed a trifle. 'Thank you, Bill.'

'I agree,' said Lara. 'You must tell Eve, and I will too.'

She and Bill exchanged a look—the complicity of parents acting in tandem.

'It's not been a good day.' Bill took Sarah's hand,

and the tiny flicker of jealousy on her face died away. 'Maudie and I have had words.'

'Shall I disappear?' said Sarah, looking weary again. 'Is this another Russell-family thing?'

Lara said, 'Don't, Sarah. We're all in this. What's Maudie going on about?'

Bill drew himself up to his full height. 'It's the old flashpoint. It was me leaving you.'

'Oh.' Lara sat down again. 'OK,' she said. 'I'd better tell Maudie the whys and wherefores about what happened and she can make up her own mind.'

Sarah's colour returned to normal. 'Lara, I'm not so sure that's a good idea.' She dropped down into the chair beside Lara and leaned forward earnestly. 'We do have a right to a private life that the children shouldn't know about.'

She was right. But. 'But, in this case . . . it was mainly my fault.'

'Possibly.' Sarah shot Bill a look.

Bill leaned over the back of the third chair. He looked immeasurably sad. 'Maudie's hostility is hard but that's no reason, Lara.'

Lara looked down at her hands folded in her lap. Their stillness belied the churning of her emotions. 'I think I owe it to everyone.'

'Well, that's a first,' said Bill to Lara.

It was an old, old joke. It meant things were better. Much, much better.

Sarah turned to Lara. 'Will *you* talk to Maudie?' Her customary gentle concern was back.

Lara reached over and touched her arm. 'I will.'

Chapter Twenty-one

'Eve had already cancelled the bridesmaid's dress,' Maudie informed Lara, as they started to drive back to London.

Lara was fussing with the wheel as she manoeuvred around a parked van in the village. The strain was making the tendons stand out on her neck. 'Had she?'

'She told me that Jas and she were treated in a funny way at school.'

'That's true.' Her mother looked neither right nor left. 'It was very difficult for them. It wasn't that the other children were unkind, but they marked them out. Particularly after your father left. I had many an anxious conversation with the teachers.'

Maudie said, 'You gave up quite a lot of your life for us.'

Lara turned her head to Maudie and smiled. 'But I wanted to. What else should I have done?'

'You don't regret it?'

They had turned out of the village on to the main road before Lara replied. 'Maudie, I've made many mistakes . . .'

Ever curious, Maudie asked, 'What mistakes?'

Her mother's lips tightened. 'Sometimes I felt unworthy of you all. And not up to the job.' She grinned. 'Sometimes, mind you. Not all the time.'

Maudie sat back in the seat. Now that the pink meringue was out of the picture, she felt an unaccountable loss. That puzzled her—her interest in such things was minimal. Even more complicated, it was followed by regret and a touch of envy that she would not be at Membury for her sister's wedding.

Then there was Nick. *Why can't you be ordinary?*

She recollected with a voluptuous pleasure the salty taste of his sweat. The feel of his skin. His cry. The way he had murmured into her neck when they lay together afterwards.

The way he had taken her hand and held it to his heart.

Closing her eyes, she concentrated on the important things. Absorbing a new country, new politics, a new culture. She imagined waking in her university lodging surrounded by books, the high, vivid colours of the American fall, learning to cope with the mysteries of student life, the Phi Gamma Delta idiom (was that the right way of naming it?). She braced herself as to what it would feel like to be a long way from home.

'You asleep, Maudie?'

'No.'

'Soon be there.' Her mother stepped on the accelerator. 'If you're worried at all—I mean, about coping—we can talk it through.' The hands on the wheel tightened. 'You can talk about anything. I'm listening.'

Was her mother trying to prove something? Struggling to throw a hoop over the right peg?

Skin taut around the knuckles, set of the mouth both determined and tremulous, hair as untidy as her own ... Lara was the only mother she was going to have.

'Mum, I've had it up to here with Dad,' she confessed.

'And we must talk about that. But later.'

Maudie continued, 'But I wanted to tell you that

318

you've done a good job.'

Her mother turned her head sharply. 'What job?'

'Bringing me up. I know you worry yourself sick about us all, but I'm fine, you know. You've told me what's what, and I've taken it on board.' She stared ahead. 'You did a good job as my mother.'

Lara gave a muffled gasp. A tear slipped down her cheek. 'Oh, Maudie.'

'Don't say it isn't true.'

Her mother glanced at her as if she was about to contradict her. But she thought better of it.

'Thought you should know,' said Maudie.

*   *   *

Jasmine was on a plane to San Diego (named after St Didacus, population approaching 1.5 million).

As was her custom, as soon as she boarded she flipped her watch to west-coast time and settled down to sleep for the first five hours. Then she roused herself (which she always did, however lousy she felt), ate the breakfast rolls she had brought on board, and began a day's work.

It was one way of dealing with jet-lag.

Travelling with her was her boss, Jason. Over the years, they had been frequent travelling companions and, after they had sorted out any misunderstandings (Jason had once turned up at her hotel bedroom only to be smartly dismissed), they'd got along fine.

They landed in mid-afternoon. It was a hot, blue-skied day and her spirits lifted through the fog of fatigue. (Clearly, her routine hadn't worked so well, this time around.)

Their hotel was comfortable and had a first-class

restaurant on the fourth floor. Jason (naturally) insisted they ate there. This they did the following evening after a hard day's work, putting the final touches in place for the pitch, and after Jasmine had phoned the company to check the timetable still held.

'There's an uneasy feel.' Jasmine speared a piece of chicken flambéed in brandy on her fork. 'Everyone's jumpy.'

Jason nodded sagely and necked some of the very fine Californian Chablis.

In her bedroom, the maid had turned down the sheets and left a chocolate on the pillow. On the desk by the window there was writing paper, brochures advertising the city's delights and a pledge by the management to be as eco-friendly as possible.

The drapes at the window were thick and muffled the street noises as she lay trying to sleep. She thought about Duncan. His habit of lying back on the pillows, his hands behind his head. The line of hair running down his abdomen, silky and soft. His way of reaching for her just as she was falling asleep. All that . . . and his refusal to front up to the question of Andrew. What did that evasion mean? Possibly nothing. But possibly a lot.

She was still furious with Duncan. But she was also furious with Andrew, and the two were in danger of becoming muddled. Whatever, she had to admit that the image she had cherished of Duncan and carried with her had changed. How to describe it? She felt as if she had *lost* the urgent necessity to love him and to keep him.

The idea felt cold and strange.

The following morning there were two messages

from Duncan.

She ignored them.

On her way to the meeting, Duncan called. He launched in: 'When you come home we have to talk.'

We have to talk. She almost giggled. It was the phrase most men ran a mile to avoid. She hunched a shoulder to keep the phone in place and got into the taxi. 'I think we do.'

'I left messages.'

'And?'

'I didn't want you to think that out of sight was out of mind.' He said it so sweetly that her heart jumped. 'And I miss you. And could you come home soon?'

At the pitch she found herself talking to a roomful of executives exuding a peachy, healthy glow—the by-product of fresh orange juice and multi-vitamins. 'If you're asking, "Why the Branding Company?" we answer that we are a multi-national company ranging over the cyberborders ...' And as she talked, she felt her powers surge to full throttle. The audience was attentive, and she ratcheted up her presentation yet another notch.

After her slot, Jason took them through the process of gestation. He told them that, as a fibre-optic company, they were responsible for bringing the world closer. Literally, they pulled borders together, advanced understanding and had become a necessity. From the early fibre-optic cables laid under the sea to the current state-of-the-art lines, those who worked with them had shaped the new worlds. With fibre-optics, people could see—they were the all-seeing eye of myth and legend . . .

He stepped aside. Flashed up on the screen was the logo of a stylized eye. 'This eye is the eternal eye.' Jasmine took up the slack—the routine was well rehearsed. 'You will see it in Ancient Egyptian tombs and the CCTV camera in our streets. It is old, it is new. It is timeless . . .'

There was a lot more.

'I think we're in with a chance,' said Jason later, in the waterside café over a salad and fruit juice. 'I've had a call.'

She glanced at her watch. Eight hours before the flight home. 'Can we debrief later? I'm about to go. A dive, a shortish one. Are you OK to abandon?'

He shuddered faintly. 'I'll take the ferry over to the island. I shall think of you as I sit on the beach.'

On application to the diving-expedition company, Jasmine had been offered the choice of diving in Wreck Alley or La Jolla Cove. Wreck Alley was named because of the ships sunk there to attract marine life but she had plumped for La Jolla Cove with its reef caves and kelp forests.

* * *

They were a full complement in the boat that headed for the cove. Jasmine strapped on her diving watch and adjusted her flippers. The instructor briefed them carefully, issued them with a number and a buddy, then said, 'As you know, it's not the season for grey whales. But there are sharks.' He paused for extra emphasis. 'And you guys all know that it's forbidden to touch the reef. OK.'

The sea enfolded her like a silken skin.

Down she went, her dive buddy just behind her.

It was a moment of release, so profound, so intense that it was impossible to describe.

A previous wind had stirred up the water and the disturbed sand still drifted over the kelp, rock and reef. A sea garden. The water was blue, light-filled, but hazy. She gave the thumbs-up to her buddy. They had been warned that, in some places, the bottom dropped from twenty feet to over a thousand and they steered away from it.

First off, she spotted a grouper in his hide. Then a couple of But rays, and a single Butterfly ray. The Butterfly ray was motionless on the ocean bed; only its eye twitched. Her buddy took a photo and, disturbed by this, it shot off in a cloud of sand.

A small shark glided into view. They watched it approach them head on. Suddenly it veered off and disappeared into the deeper waters.

Below her in that dreamy, rippling sea garden the kelp streamed like a bride's veil in the wind, its shapes and form eternal and unheeding.

Her body was weightless, sexless . . . The relief of being so was overwhelming. There were no feminine demands here, no biological yearnings. Just existence.

Jasmine swam on through a blue, dappled world where image didn't matter.

*　　　*　　　*

Time had slipped into fast forward. She wasn't sure how.

Then again she had been frantically busy. Arranging the move into the new consulting rooms. New patients to process. Others to reassure. Last-minute wedding arrangements.

Maudie would be off in forty-eight hours.

Lara rattled around the kitchen, stowing stuff in the cupboards. She was hasty and clumsy and a saucepan fell on to the floor.

Every so often, she glanced at her mobile phone. No messages.

In the last few weeks, this had become a habit.

On the way out to work, she couldn't make up her mind which jacket to wear. The black or the green? Did she care? Posing in front of the mirror, she found the image it reflected unsatisfactory. She pushed back her hair. Why was she looking like *that*?

She shoved her phone deep into her bag.

On the bus, she read her newspaper.

The phone appeared to burn in her bag. She ignored it.

Instead, she concentrated on the serialized extracts from the diary of a soldier currently fighting in Iraq.

12 May. Today I shot two men. The strange thing was I couldn't make the connection between pulling the trigger and the body which fell to the ground a second later.

4 Sept. I had no idea what heat on a long-term basis does to you. The lads talk about fried organs. But it's more the sensation of organs dissolving, dripping into each other. At the same time, the iron band around the head is pulled tighter.

17 Oct. Back home. R&R. Hated it. Checked out news website every two minutes. *Why wasn't I there?* Hated green fields and rain. Hated being cool again. Knew I didn't belong.

Robin.

She stared out of the bus window but her head was filled with images and memories of Robin. She hadn't planned it, *the invasion and occupation*, but it had happened.

He should have contacted her.

She wanted to ring him up and say, *You idiot. I don't care how broken you are.*

Plumper than ever, Kirsty was waiting for her at the consulting room. 'I don't understand,' she plunged straight in to her old lament. 'More than anything, I want to be thin, but I can't do it. It's like—like the bars of chocolate lie in wait for me. Ambush me.'

Lara opened the file. 'You know what I'm going to say.'

'Yeah, right.' Kirsty had it off pat. 'You can help me by showing me what's going on in my stupid brain, but the only person who can help me is me.'

More than chocolate bars had ambushed Robin—any soldier who was in the field. Thoughtfully, she regarded Kirsty and strove not to let her impatience—unusual for her—register in her expression.

'Because I can't have them, I think about them all the time.' Kirsty grabbed the edge of the desk. 'Fantasize.'

Yes, she understood.

Above all, she wanted to fold Robin into her arms—as she had done that scented Damascene night and for him to whisper into her ear the things that belonged between them.

'Lara,' asked Kirsty, sharply, 'are you with me?'

As she explained to some of her more sensitive

325

patients, empathizing with others, or feeling deeply for them, was often inconvenient. (But never wasted.)

Later she found herself trying to explain it to Maudie too.

'I don't understand,' Maudie was saying. 'I was so sure.'

They were going over her luggage in her bedroom, which was so small it could barely accommodate the bed and a chair, let alone the two of them. In summer it was often hot and airless but in winter it was freezing—not that Maudie had seemed to mind.

Maudie was checking through her books and Lara was checking Maudie's underwear and sweaters. She let them slide through her fingers. These would lie close to her daughter's skin. Keep her warm. Protect her.

'Does Nick feel the same way about you?'

'I think so.' She slid down to the floor and sat with her back propped up by the bed. 'I don't have to do this. I can cancel.'

'You can see each other in the vacations.'

'Mum, you're supposed to be the clear-sighted one. Once I go, it will change. You move on. Even if we could afford the flights.'

Lara took up position beside Maudie and clasped her hand. She turned it over and traced the heart line with a finger. 'Have you talked to Tess about it?'

Maudie looked up into her face. 'Nope.'

'And I note you didn't arrange a final girls' night out with her.'

'Nope.'

'That's odd,' she said. 'I thought you'd be

inseparable to the end. Tess has been part of your life.'

Maudie's fist clenched. 'Things change.' Pause. 'Told you.'

Finger by finger, Lara unwrapped the clenched fist. 'What will I do without you? There'll be a big Maudie-shaped space in this house. I won't know how to fill it. But you must go.'

Maudie chose not to understand. 'The house is stuffed.'

True: top, bottom, eaves, with Eve's presents and Maudie's luggage. But the day approached when none of it would be there any longer.

'Evie was very nice about the wedding. In the end.' Maudie shifted about on the floor. 'She's even said she'll come and see me off.'

The floor was hard and the carpet (which urgently needed renewing) strewn with fluff and bits of paper but Lara joined her. 'I want to talk to you, Maudie.'

'I know the facts of life, Mum. But ta for the thought.'

'Your father.'

Maudie frowned and turned her head away.

'The time has come to explain what happened.'

'*What?*'

'Listen to me.'

'I don't want to talk about Dad.' Maudie sounded strained, almost tearful. 'One day, perhaps.' She scrambled back to her feet and leaned on the windowsill. 'You and I did all right. That's enough, isn't it?'

From her seat on the floor, Lara was not to be deflected. 'I want you to think about something. Your father lost Mary in a terrible way.'

'Just the two of us, Mum.'

It had been traumatic, he confessed to Lara, all those years ago. The baby had got stuck. Then Mary's heartbeat dropped. They operated . . . and, afterwards, Mary haemorrhaged. And that was it . . .

'Mary's death had a terrible effect on him. You probably can't understand that, but you must try. As a result, he didn't want me to have babies. He didn't want the risk.'

'So I wasn't wanted.' Maudie spoke flatly, bitterly.

'You're not listening, Maudie.' Lara hauled herself up onto the edge of bed. She smoothed the sheet. 'Mary died having a baby and he was there . . . It wasn't that he didn't want children, he just didn't want to face the risk. Once you arrived he was besotted. What neither of us had reckoned on was that I would have a difficult time, too. I ended up having transfusions. It was unlucky and coincidental, but your father found it almost impossible to deal with.'

Bill holding a tiny Maudie.

'Isn't she enough, Lara?'

'Fear is a powerful thing but I didn't quite understand that then. I do now. I couldn't accept what he wanted. I was desperate for more children and . . .' she looked up at Maudie '. . . I got pregnant without his agreement.'

Easy. Far easier than arriving at the decision to deceive. Take one bottle of wine. One balmy evening. One still-slim girl hungry for more children and a man who loved her.

Easy.

Maudie moved restlessly. 'So?'

'You know what happened.'

'Louis,' Maudie said. She let out her breath with a soft hiss. 'So that's . . .'

Wrapped in a soft white shawl. Washed. His tiny hands curled like limpets. Dark hair.

'That was the beginning of the end.'

'All that . . . sadness . . .' said Maudie, and the fjord eyes were dark with the unwelcome revelation. 'But he shouldn't have left you for *that* . . . What sort of man is he?'

Lara joined Maudie at the window. She discovered that her hands were shaking and her legs had emptied of their stuffing. 'You're too young to understand, Maudie. In one sense, you're right. But when you lose trust in someone . . . it taints everything, even the smallest actions. Your father lost trust in me. He was frightened, profoundly so. So was I. Then we had to face the worst . . . and . . . it was my fault. And the worst destroyed . . . us.' She was trying hard to bring her hands under control. A cool, critical Maudie observed her struggle. 'Remember that.'

'*Why* have you never told me?'

'I couldn't.'

'Of course you could. Didn't I need to know?'

Lara caressed Maudie's cheek. 'It was private.'

'No, it wasn't because it affected us.' Her eyelids dropped. 'It affected the whole family.'

'Each time I talk about Louis, and people are kind about it, I feel I'm using their sympathy to smooth away the fact of his death. And it can't be smoothed away. I don't want it smoothed away.'

'No.' Maudie fell silent. 'No.' She hunched over the windowsill. 'I still think Dad's a monster.'

'No, he isn't,' she said. 'But I'm telling you this so you can think it over. I was wrong in what I did. But it happens to people and they do irrational things. Stupid things, too. When you're up against it, you don't know the lengths to which you might go. Bear that in mind.'

Maudie shrugged.

The hard-won confession was over and done with, and Lara's head and heart felt lighter for it. 'But you know something, Maudie? The wedding has made things easier. Because of it, your father and I have had to speak to each other regularly. It's . . .' she retreated to the bed and picked up a pile of T-shirts '. . . it's been a good thing. You must say goodbye to him.'

'I don't think so.'

'You must.'

Maudie did something she rarely did. She began to cry.

* * *

The day before Maudie's departure, Lara paid a visit to the new consulting rooms. The workmen had just finished the painting and it was possible to step from one light, airy room into a second light, airy room. She checked the plans for the furniture— desks and (important this) comfortable chairs— and ran an inventory of the cellophane-wrapped deliveries. Whoa, she thought, for the fumes of new paint and new carpet were so strong that she felt a little high on them.

Disregarding the plastic wrapping, she tried out a chair. ' "Everyone needs to accept what they are, and to live without fear and without the oppressions of guilt and lack of self esteem . . ." ' she quoted aloud from a well-known expert.

Kirsty rang. 'I've slipped,' she wailed. 'Two glasses of wine and a bar of chocolate.'

This society was crazy. Somehow wine and chocolate had turned into sins as shocking as apostasy in previous eras. 'What are you going to do about it?' Lara asked.

'Starve myself.' Kirsty was desperate.

'Make sure you turn up for your appointment,' she said.

She cast around the spanking new consulting room. Would spanking newness help Pauline, Ralph and herself to help others make sense of their lives? (It had better. The bills were large enough.)

And, then, seriously . . .

Her newspaper lay on the floor. 'IED blew off my interpreter's legs,' ran the headline.

She groped for antidotes to such troubling facts. And there it was . . . Into her uneasy thoughts dropped an image of the garden at Membury. There, the tussocky grass grew unimpeded, the bees worked, the myrtle struggled to survive, the stream flowed and, in the places where she had walked, poppies and ox-eye daisies bloomed. Memories, delicate and powerful, on which to draw. Memories that would nourish and sustain her.

The plastic covering on the chair imprinted red patches on her legs, like jellyfish stings. She reached into her bag, found the phone and dialled. It clicked to answerphone. 'Robin. I hope you're OK. I just want you to know . . .' She paused. 'I want you to know that I'm using the bag all the time.' She snapped off the connection, only to redial. 'Please get in touch.'

On the way home, she stopped at the pillar-box

to post a stack of wedding invitations, including one to Robin.

*   *   *

On the day of her departure, Maudie got up, washed and dressed. All normal. She stripped her bed and took the sheets downstairs, put them into the washing-machine and switched it on.

Her mother was standing by the window. She looked pale and tired. 'What about some porridge?' she asked. 'It'll keep you going.'

'That would be nice,' said Maudie.

Afterwards she threw away her old toothbrush, bagged up the sweaters she was leaving behind against moths and threw away a couple of used-up mascaras.

Not normal.

Later, at the airport, her gaze flittered from one thing to another—like a maddened fly. The check-in desk. The automatic ticket machines. The coffee bars. The two stuffed suitcases waiting to be checked in. A hammer knocking in the region of her heart added to a sense of unreality. *She was going away.*

Her mother slipped her arm through hers and spoke softly. As usual, she was concentrating on practical things—insurance, medical certificates, bank orders. Maudie listened carefully to the cadences of the well-known voice, committing it to memory, but took in nothing of what her mother was actually talking about.

Impossible to concentrate.

Huge piles of luggage. A man balancing three cups of coffee. A girl with dyed blonde hair.

332

Jasmine and Eve turned up. Jasmine kissed Lara—but Eve didn't, which seemed odd. Her family watched while she checked in two suitcases and a rucksack, so stuffed with books that Maudie found it difficult to lift.

'Promise me,' said Lara, 'that you won't attempt to carry it. Promise me that'll you get a taxi from the airport.'

Maudie had a sensation of swimming through deep, hazy water. 'Don't fuss.' She wanted to get the goodbyes over and done with—which, since everyone had made the effort to turn up, was difficult. Having packed the rucksack awkwardly, she made a great play of rearranging the stuff.

Something was missing. She couldn't put her finger on it. Or, rather, she could but didn't wish to spell it out.

Eve's embrace was careful and affectionate. 'I've got something for you, Eve.' Maudie delved into her bag and produced a small package wrapped in tissue paper.

'Maudie? Can I?'

Maudie nodded and Eve unpeeled the tissue to reveal the garter Maudie had made—a length of lace threaded with a blue ribbon. 'Something old, something new, something borrowed, something blue,' said Maudie. 'This hits the new and blue.'

Eve raised a glowing face. 'You made it for me? You *made* it?'

'I thought we could all wear it,' said Maudie, awkwardly. 'In our turn.' She grinned. 'Not that I plan to get married.'

Eyes welling, Eve wrapped the tissue around the garter. 'It's beyond price, Maudie. Do you know that?'

'Oh, Evie,' said Maudie.

Jasmine surged forward. 'Maudie, be a good girl. You'll love it over there. Don't forget us.'

Her mother echoed, 'Don't forget us.'

It was time to go through to Departures. Maudie picked up her bag. Saying goodbye was hurting far more than she had imagined it would and she was far more frightened than she had thought she would be. She wanted this bit to be over. She wanted to be far away. She wanted to leapfrog over this year of her life and land experienced and settled in.

Once there, she would cut her hair. Why hadn't she done it before she left? Why wasn't she leaving shorn to symbolize the pilgrimage she was making?

She shouldered her bag and stuck her boarding pass into her pocket.

'Give me another kiss,' her mother begged.

'You can come and visit me,' Maudie muttered, into her ear.

She raised her eyes from her mother's shoulder. They widened.

No? Yes. Her father *was* weaving his way at speed through the passengers towards them.

Remember what her mother had told her. This was the man who had been frightened and racked. Just as . . . just as . . . she was. The point of connection flared like bright phosphorus in her mind, and burned away the old grievances.

At the sight of him, she realized how much she had wanted him to come.

Dodging the obstacles, he reached the group. Tall, weathered, slightly shabby, these days, dressed in his garden jacket, he *seemed* safe, solid, father-like . . . and Maudie longed for him to be so.

Yes, she did. She did. Eve and Jasmine grinned like Cheshire cats. Lara stepped aside.

'I didn't expect you,' said Maudie.

'You didn't think I'd let you go without saying goodbye?'

'I did.'

Her father frowned. 'But I'm here.' He drew Maudie to him and gave her an unpractised hug. 'Goodbye and good luck.'

Maudie buried her face in his shoulder and inhaled the aftershave, a whiff of bonfire smoke, and a suggestion of an aromatic plant. She felt it was a place where she was protected, a place she had missed for most of her life. 'Goodbye, Dad.'

Chapter Twenty-two

A week to go.

According to the timetable, Eve was due for a last fitting at Ivanka's workshop.

Lara checked the final-countdown list.

She had tried hard to arrange a meeting, but Eve was having none of it. Except for the barest of communications, she refused to talk to Lara. In one email she wrote: 'You've said enough. Don't make it worse.' Neither had Lara been invited to the fitting.

For a long time, she lay awake. Questioning. Andrew? Eve? What more could she do to protect Eve?

Had she protected Eve—or merely exposed her to pain? How thin the line ran between morality, practicality and the deceptions necessary for survival.

Sleep when it came was fitful, and she fell into the dream where she was running down the path clutching her torn veil. This time she knew it was imperative to save Louis. But how and where would she find him? Panicked, she attempted to run faster, but her feet were too heavy. The veil whipped across her face and crept into her nose and mouth. Its lace patterns imprinted themselves on her tongue. She knew she was suffocating and she knew she must find Louis—but she also knew she was doomed not to.

She woke exhausted, but resolved on what to do. Against every precept of her professional life, she cancelled her two morning appointments and took a taxi to the *atelier*.

The neat, grave assistant with the pincushion on her wrist ushered her into the fitting room. Today there were white roses in a vase on the table, and a new sofa upholstered in white and pink. Jasmine's bridesmaid's dress, a scaled-down version of Eve's dress with ribbon lacing through the sleeves was hanging on the rack, alongside the pretty frilly frocks for Andrew's nieces, the flower-girls.

Pinned to the notice-board beside them was a full-page newspaper article about a wedding featuring one of Ivanka's dresses.

The dress was beautiful—which was not surprising. But it wasn't the main focus of interest in the article. In it, the entire wedding party had been assembled in their wedding outfits for a group shot that was headed 'A Family Wedding'. Arrows zoned in with chatty captions. 'Bride, groom, bridesmaids'. That was simple enough. The rest was not. 'Bride's stepmother', 'groom's step-sister', 'step-grandmother', 'bride's mother's third husband'. It was, Lara perceived, a clever, funny deconstruction of the complicated lines of the modern family.

'What are you doing here, Lara?'

Eve entered the room, so thin these days she was almost noiseless. She had changed into her bridal underwear—beautiful, lacy, boned and expensive. A wrapper was draped over her shoulders.

Lara made no attempt to kiss Eve. 'I thought you might need a second opinion.'

Eve opened her eyes wide. 'Did you?'

'I did.' Lara took a seat on the spindly sofa.

'I haven't forgiven you, Lara.'

She winced. 'I know.'

'I could ask you to leave,' Eve said calmly, but Lara noticed she was shredding a tissue. 'OK, stay . . .'

Lara was forced to strain to hear what she said. 'But if you utter *one* word about Andrew.' At that moment, Ivanka and the assistant backed into the room carrying the dress and, without a beat, Eve continued, in a perfectly normal tone, 'You've just missed Jasmine's fitting and the flower-girls'. It's a pity.' The shredded pieces of tissue had formed a ball she placed carefully on the table. 'Such a pity.'

'The smaller one is trouble,' said Ivanka. 'Big trouble.'

'Tell me about it,' said Eve. 'Her mother will be keeping watch.'

She shrugged off the wrapper.

Ivanka in her black T-shirt and tight trousers, her violet eye makeup as pronounced as ever, made an incongruous contrast with the light, white room and spumy foam of the dress she was hanging up on the peg. 'Now,' she said, and signalled to the assistant.

Both of them donned white gloves and, in unison, flexed their fingers.

Lara suppressed a smile. Maudie would have so enjoyed this little scene, a vaudeville act—and the pain-which-was-not-a-physical-pain that nagged under her ribs whenever she thought of Maudie returned and settled in.

Maudie had gone. There had been only the briefest of phone calls. 'Hi, Mum. It's all good.'

And when she had repeatedly asked, 'Do you need anything?' she was told, 'No, Mum. *Nothing.*'

She wished Maudie had wanted something. Then she could have bought it, wrapped the parcel with care, queued at the post office and sent it off—a tangible reaching-out.

The under-dress took a little time to ease into place. Totally absorbed in the process, Eve was the most patient of statues while it was done. After that came the dress itself. She held out her arms and Ivanka and the assistant eased the long tight sleeves over them.

'There,' said Ivanka.

Eve tilted her head and let out an audible sigh.

The assistant dropped to her knees and crawled around the hem.

'What do you think?' asked Ivanka. She picked up part of the train to test how it draped. The assistant whipped out a needle and thread and sewed a minute adjustment.

'The veil,' said Ivanka. 'It's important to try now.' The assistant got to her feet and disappeared into the workshop.

'The neckline,' said Ivanka, and busied herself with yet more adjustments. 'But you haven't said anything, Eve.'

Eve's eyes were huge. 'Thank you,' she said. 'It's all that I could want.'

Ivanka took a step back and made a long, thorough appraisal. 'It needs just a tweak under the arm. I'll fetch my pins.' She pinched a narrow space between finger and thumb.

The room was empty, except for Lara and Eve.

'What do you think?' asked Eve, in a neutral voice.

'It's wonderful,' she replied. 'Like a dream.'

The dream.

How would she interpret it?

The bitter-sweet, the fearful, the half-forgotten and the half-remembered anchored, glimmering, in her deepest imagining, a bride's image (hers, but timeless). White, sacrificial and luminous.

As she got up from the sofa, the pink and white stripes danced in front of her eyes. 'Evie?'

Eve swirled around. The train rippled like water and a section of the hem was caught by her handbag on the floor. Lara dropped to her knees and detached it.

'Evie darling . . .'

Eve replied, from above her, '*Don't* say anything, Lara.' She bent her head—the perfect image of the totem bride. 'I know what I'm doing. I'm not blown off course by stupid tales. OK?'

Ivanka returned with the pins. 'I do one more check.'

Later, when every single wrinkle had been ironed out, tested, adjusted, Eve got dressed. She and Ivanka discussed transport and delivery. Eve had arranged for her friend Julia to pick up the dresses and transport them to Membury on the Friday.

Lara had been made deliberately superfluous.

The assistant began the long, meticulous process of packing the dress into its calico bag. Lara watched. Eventually Eve picked up her bag. 'Goodbye, Lara,' she said coolly. 'I expect you have to get back to work.'

The door to this part of Lara's life shut with a click.

*   *   *

Jasmine sat cross-legged on the bed in her flat—her career-girl's cramped flat.

It was late. She had changed into her sleeping gear but she was still working on her laptop. Jason wanted the detailed report (which was running two weeks behind) on the San Diego trip. Every so often when she needed a break, she flipped on to the Internet to watch a programme detailing a scientific study of krill in the sea off Chile. Krill were a hugely important part of the eco-system—the blue whale, humpbacks and minkes fed off them. Their smallness was out of proportion to their importance and, because she was serious about the subject, she drew a diagram to trace the seven degrees of separation between the krill and its predators.

Reluctantly, she abandoned the cool, grey-blue vistas beamed up by the cameras. 'The All-Seeing Eye ...' she typed, but her heart was with the scientists tracing the trajectory of the krill's short, but remarkable, life.

Luckily (for how long?), krill had escaped farming and fishing. They contained too much fluoride, and when they died, a fast-working enzyme ate up their body tissue.

'The All-Seeing Eye . . .'

Krill laid up to ten thousand eggs in one go.

This time she flipped into her on-line diary. Anything free in late autumn? She isolated a two-week period to return to the west coast to dive. Two weeks without Duncan.

She was composing an email to the relevant company when she heard a key turn in the front door.

Duncan.

'Jas!'

She put the laptop to one side and climbed off the bed. 'Was I expecting you? Why didn't you ring?'

'Have you been answering my calls lately? No, you haven't. Have we spent any significant time together lately? No. Have we resolved our quarrel over Andrew? No. So, even you'll see that the negatives are totting up and I wanted to talk to you about them.'

She stood with one bare foot curled around the other and leaned on the door frame. 'That's no reason to come busting in.'

'That's every reason to come busting in, and what were you doing that's more important than sorting things?'

'Booking a holiday without you.'

The information didn't thrill him. 'If that's what you want.'

She looked down at her feet, sporting bright red nail polish. 'I do.'

He dumped his briefcase on the floor. 'You can have as many holidays as you wish by yourself but we still have to negotiate first.'

Jasmine found her dressing-gown, wrapped it around herself and pushed Duncan out of the bedroom. She stuck her hands on her hips. 'And?'

'As I said, we have to talk.'

Jasmine burst out laughing. 'And as *I* said, I *never* thought I'd hear you say that.'

He stood slap-bang in the centre of the living space, which was so small he dominated it. The neon frontage of the café opposite reflected blue and yellow light and shed an unflattering glow over him. 'There's no point in not being honest. I know you're angry about this girl and Andrew, and how it reflects on my attitude.'

'So you do know about her?'

He gestured with both hands. 'I don't *know* anything for sure.'

'Are you certain about that? Because if you do, I have to say something.'

He moved restlessly. 'Whatever. But that's not the point, Jassy. *We* are the point.'

She couldn't disagree.

'Have you talked to Andrew? Have you asked him if he's having an affair?'

'No.'

'Shouldn't you have done?'

'Why haven't you?'

'Because if I did it would drive a wedge between me and him, his future sister-in-law. Although I'm tempted. My God, I'm tempted to tell him exactly . . . But you can have that conversation.'

'Are you being deliberately stupid? If Andrew tells me he's having it off with someone, he knows perfectly well that I'll tell you, so your relationship with Eve would be compromised either way. Have you talked to Lara?'

'God, no. Think of the fallout.'

Duncan tried another tack. 'It's none of our business, Jasmine.'

'But we're all connected,' she pointed out. 'All of us. We don't live in a private bubble and what we do affects others. And Eve is my sister.'

'But you're not her keeper, Jas.'

'I'm bound to her. I have to protect her.'

'So why haven't you tackled her?'

'If I'm to ruin her life I need to know if it's true or not.'

He nodded. 'But that's not your deep-down objection,' he said shrewdly. 'Is it?'

There was no point in evasion. Honesty involved sacrifice and pain so she went into battle. 'Given your attitude, how can I believe in you?'

'You know you can.'

'I never worried when you rang up sloshed from nightclubs or went on your trips. I enjoyed the trust between us. I *relished* it because it suggested we were grown-ups. I had no reason not to trust you . . . except for an occasional blip. And I think you felt the same. But not any more.'

'Jasmine.' He ran his fingers though his hair. Nervous. Unsure. So unlike him. 'I could kill Andrew.'

'That's not the point. The point is, what are you doing about the situation? And the point is . . . given all this, given everything . . . I can't see a basis any more for you and me. Not a good one, anyway. What Andrew has done, or not, is one thing. What it's done to us is another.'

Disbelieving, she listened to the words that issued from her mouth. Clearly, they had been massing—a silent, stealthy secret army in her mind.

The dressing-gown belt had worked loose and she tugged it so tight it pinched her flesh. 'I feel differently about us. Something's been killed off.'

Duncan had gone very pale, and then he was angry. He stuck his hands in his pockets. Took them out again. 'Only if you want it to be.'

'It's time I faced up to it,' said Jasmine. 'I should have done much earlier. Andrew's done me a favour.'

Duncan emitted an impatient sound.

'I know that sounds melodramatic.'

'You're right. It *is* melodramatic, and rather adolescent, Jas. I'm not Andrew and you're mixing the two of us up. People have sex in the wrong places with the wrong people all the time. If we brought all of them to account, the world would stop.'

The blood rushed into her cheeks. 'Don't patronize me, Duncan.'

He moved towards her. 'Jas, I came here to ask you to move in with me permanently. It's my fault for not sorting this out earlier. I'm willing to change. I love you and need you, and I think you feel the same.'

Every inch of her quivered with shock. Life loved ironies, and it was expert at heaping grief upon insult.

He rounded it up. 'It's obviously too late.'

It *was* too late to retrieve the precious happy feeling between them. Only too clearly she envisaged the future tipsy phone calls from nightclubs, but in that future they would leave her with a sick, uneasy feeling and a question mark. The transparency between them had been muddied and she had no idea what secrets and lies were hidden in its murk.

'I hadn't faced up to it,' she said. 'Now I have. I feel nothing but disappointment.' She shrugged. 'After all this time.'

'Jas? Is that really what you're saying?'

Her craving to be with him, and to carry his children, rose up one last time—and she ignored it.

'Yes.'

So it ended. Not with a bang but with a whisper.

Chapter Twenty-three

Eve's email:

> Rehearsal, day before wedding. Please could everyone involved be in the church by 4 p.m. PS Just think—no more bossy emails . . .

Lara scrutinized the street map on-line and printed out a copy.

She ran through the list. Dress, shoes, first aid, sewing kit . . .

It was very warm: an Indian summer had arrived, and the city street was airless. As she ferried her luggage in and out of the house, the sun beat on her bare skin and the plastic bag protecting her wedding outfit wilted.

By mid-morning the car was loaded and she had checked the overnight bookings in the two hotels, as she had been asked. Eve and Jasmine were staying at Membury and she had a room at the White Boar.

The to-ing and fro-ing over the arrangements had been considerable and Lara was trying not to mind that she had been relegated to the hotel. Eve had sent yet another email: 'Lara, if you could keep an eye on the guests who are staying at the Boar I would be grateful.' There was no affectionate sign-off.

This was in contrast to the email from Maudie:

Darling Mum, I am in heaven. That's not to say it's been easy and I don't get homesick as I do. But I'm beginning to settle, and to get used to my surroundings, which are BEAUTIFUL. My corridor has some great people—bar a couple of exceptions who are rude about the British taking up spaces in their university. Freshmen's week was excruciating and I nearly ducked out of some of the stuff, but forced myself to go in the end. Alicia sent me some good tips. She'll be coming out later. Hope to see her.

You know something? I feel I understand better about things. About Dad and stuff.

I miss YOU.

Added in tiny, tiny type: 'I miss Nick.'

The print-out of the map was on the passenger seat as she drove through London. Instead of taking the obvious direct route, she branched off towards the river.

Halfway, she found a parking place, cut the engine and sat there for quite some time.

Her heart thudded.

'You are empowered to change things … not much, but an inch,' she told her patients. 'You just have to take the first step.'

She started the engine and listened intently to it. Her hands resting on the wheel were a little shaky.

Robin's flat turned out to be in a mansion block and there was nothing to distinguish it from any other in the city. It was built of durable brick, had some mildly interesting decorative features and an old-fashioned lift with a clanking gate, which she took to the second floor. She rang the doorbell and waited—not really expecting it to be answered.

But it was. By Robin. He looked thin, but suntanned and fit.

'I didn't think you were back,' she said. 'But I thought I'd try.'

'Yesterday evening.' He rubbed his chin. He stared at her, as if he was making up his mind, and a quiver of doubt went through Lara. 'Haven't shaved, but pleased to see you.'

She had anticipated this moment in so many ways that the bland 'pleased to see you' was disappointing. But she stood her ground. 'You haven't been in touch.'

'I should have been.'

She tried to smile. 'Since you didn't I've done it for you.' She was aware of the storm finally breaking in her—the one she had avoided for good reason. 'I've been worried, Robin. About many things. You. Me.'

'There was no need.'

'Yes, there was.'

'Hey …' He stepped forward. 'You look … lovely.'

'I will ask you to keep repeating that.'

347

'Will you come in?' He gestured to the interior.

Lara hesitated. 'I'm on my way to the wedding.'

'Shouldn't you be rushing around doing things?'

'I should, but for two things. I've been sidelined—stepmothers you know—and the fall-out with Eve.'

'Eve hasn't forgiven you?'

'No. Not surprising. I should have consulted you before I did it.' She flashed him a wry smile. 'On the other hand, whatever I said was going to come out badly.' She stepped into the flat. 'You haven't replied to the invitation.'

He pointed to a stack of post. 'Forgive me? I haven't worked my way through that yet.'

'I thought as much,' she said. 'Army training wouldn't allow you not to answer one way or another if you'd received it. So I kept a place, just in case.'

He grinned. 'I might not be able to come.'

'That's fine. Just say.'

'I haven't got the outfit.'

'Does that matter?'

They exchanged a look and she felt better. 'No,' he replied.

'Well, then. Come in whatever you want.'

'Do *you* want me to come?'

'Why do you think I'm here?' She paused. 'Could I have a glass of water?'

While he fetched it, she looked around. His flat was, as she might have imagined, austere: the furniture was nondescript; everything was clean and had its place. But it was fusty and unused. Unloved. She went over to the window and folded her arms. Outside, the London traffic roared.

She heard him put the glass on the table and

walk over to her. He placed his hands on her shoulders, turned her around, and unpeeled her arms from the defensive position. He seemed to radiate sympathy, which soothed her immediate fears, so much so that she was frightened she might break down.

'What matters,' he said, 'is that you're here.'

'Does it?'

'It does.' He touched the bare skin at her wrist where her pulse beat. 'I'm sorry about Eve. Quite a decision to have made and I know you're frightened she might not forgive you.'

She could have done without the ambiguity when she craved to be told that everything would be all right. 'Have you come back for good, Robin? Or will you be going away again?'

'I'm back.'

'Why did you go away? There was no need.'

He held her gaze, conveying meanings she did not, as yet, know or understand. That lay in the future? She hoped so.

'I hate being at the mercy of myself . . . I couldn't bear it that you saw me in that state. At least, then . . .' His smile conveyed regret. 'Couldn't have been worse, could it? There I was, about to seduce you, and what happens?'

She laughed. 'Start as you mean to go on.'

'A man's pride?'

'And a woman's,' she added tartly. 'Are you feeling better?'

The bald prim words did not match the intensity behind the question or the apprehension with which she awaited his answer.

'Much.' He seemed pretty sure. 'And you?'

'After the wedding I'll feel much better.'

'No,' he said. 'You know what I mean.'

She did: had her ghosts been laid, and her wounds healed?

* * *

Jasmine calculated that, if she was clever, she could avoid Duncan at the dinner. And at the wedding? They would have to perform with each other but they were adults. They would cope.

There was no point in telling Eve about the situation yet . . . no point in tarnishing her pleasure. Or in telling anyone. She had kept it to herself— and was sure that Duncan would do the same until after the wedding.

The funny thing was, she wasn't missing him as much as she had imagined. If anything, a small, inner coal of excitement at her freedom had been lit and was gradually accumulating heat. Far from mourning, her main reaction was *I've had a lucky escape*.

She rang up her landlord and gave three months' notice, then instructed an agent to find her a flat that was closer to her office. She had no doubt that this was the moment to take decisions and strike out along a different road.

Banking on keeping busy, she worked late and with feverish application, shifting between projects, pitches and long meetings. The upshot? She was exhausted—just as she wished it. After work she carried out small tasks in a meticulous fashion: trips to the hairdresser, the beautician.

In the early days of work, on leaving the office, she sometimes glanced up at the building. It appeared to be sheathed in gold, a place of promise and opportunity, where she had only to stretch out a hand to grasp its rewards. When, at last, she left for the wedding, it was bathed in light, still as golden, still as promising.

The night before she left for Membury, she packed with the utmost care. After she had finished, she went around the flat, removed every photograph of Duncan she possessed and shovelled them into a plastic bag.

Eve rang. 'I'm in the street,' she said. 'Do you want to go for a coffee? My last as a single woman.'

Still clutching the bag, Jasmine clattered down the steps. 'Why are you here?'

'Why indeed?' said Eve. 'I just wanted to hear your voice, Jas. Just wanted to see you.'

Us two.

Jasmine tucked the bag under her arm. 'Do you want me to tell you a story about a beautiful girl who met a handsome banker?'

Eve laughed. 'I never want to organize anything ever again.'

'I'll remind you of that.'

For a moment, she was silhouetted against the darkening sky.

Thin and, oh, so fragile.

'Evie, I love you,' said Jasmine.

'*Do* you? Promise me you always will.'

'You don't need to ask,' said Jasmine.

'Me, too. Always, Jas. *Always.*'

The traffic roared past. 'Shall we have that coffee?'

They progressed up the street. The bride was restless and nervy. Hardly surprising. 'What have you got here?' She snatched at the bag.

'Don't,' said Jasmine. 'Boring.'

'OK,' said Eve. 'What's the mystery?'

'The mystery is why you're here and not resting,' said Jasmine. 'But let's go.'

'So what *is* in there?'

'Boring,' said Jasmine.

As they passed the litter bin outside the takeaway, she dropped the bag into it.

It was a rational thing to do.

* * *

Andrew insisted on driving Eve and Jasmine to Membury. 'There's not much else for me to do,' he pointed out, 'and it means I can escape from my mother, who's driving me nuts.'

He and Eve chatted together in the front. Once, he directed a question to Jasmine in the back: 'Nervous?'

Her reply was cool and unfriendly. 'No. You?'

'Yes. Frankly.'

Jasmine observed the back of Andrew's head. Like many bridegrooms, he'd had a haircut that was just a bit too fierce and didn't suit him. He didn't look like a man who would deceive his bride-to-be, but he probably was and she would have to deal with it.

'Have you been in touch with Mum?' she asked Eve.

'Only briefly.'

They arrived mid-morning at the house. The drive was packed with catering and florist vans. Down in the sunken garden, the marquee was up, and burly men, with leather tool belts strung across their middles, were testing guy ropes and pillars.

They trooped over to inspect it. A pair of clipped

bay trees flanked the entrance, and several more had been positioned inside.

Surrounded by pails of flowers—foamy hydrangeas and lilies, pots of vivid green baby's breath and peony roses in blush pink and cream— was Sarah. Clearly harassed. Water slopped over the wooden floor. 'I need a table.' She was too preoccupied to greet them properly. 'Can you get me one, Andrew?'

The bride swept into action. Lists in hand, she moved around the tent checking the (elegant) striped lining, the positioning of the windows, the arrangement of tables, and the florists, who were working on the pillars. Jasmine noticed they kept their distance from Sarah.

'God knows where your father is.' Sarah buttonholed Jasmine: 'Could you fetch the vases for the table centres?' She stuck her head towards Jasmine. 'My hands are wet. Can you brush back my hair? It's in my eyes.' Without taking a breath, she pelted on: 'I *have* to get started. They're in the kitchen.'

By the time, Jasmine had ferried the vases to the marquee, the electricians had fixed up the chandeliers and the 'stars' that would shine in the ceiling, and had run fairy lights through the bay trees. A start had been made in laying the black and white carpet tiles over the flooring and creating the dance floor and the aisles between the tables. Sarah pounced on the vases and issued many orders to Mrs Baker from the village who had been employed to help.

Mrs Baker—sturdy and aproned—looked bewildered and Jasmine offered to show her the kitchen. 'Are you the bride?' she asked Jasmine.

'No,' replied Jasmine. 'I'm the eldest sister.'

Mrs Baker thought about this and said kindly, 'Well, never mind, dear. Next time.'

'Right,' said Jasmine, and fled into the garden.

As she ran down the steps, tortoiseshell butterflies clung to the spikes of late-blooming lavender and, in the place where the wild flowers grew, dozens more glided through the sunshine.

From her own reading, she knew the spectacle was deceptive. Autumn was coming and provision for it was being made out of sight. Where the butterflies danced seemingly without heed, the bees were laying in stores in the hive, working on the nectar at night to turn it into honey and foraging hard through the day.

Her father emerged around the side of the house. He was in protective clothes and obviously hive-bound. Sprinting up to him, she called, 'Dad!'

He waited by the kitchen door. 'Hello, Bridesmaid.'

'You look to be the only calm person on the planet.'

He laughed and gestured at the kitchen where several figures whisked to and fro. 'Despite appearances, Sarah's enjoying herself. She wouldn't admit it, but she's in her element.'

His skin was clear, and he looked relaxed, content. 'You're very happy with Sarah,' she said.

'I am, Jasmine.'

Did he murmur 'at last'? Or perhaps he'd thought it. Whatever. On Lara's behalf, she experienced another kind of jealousy. A fierce, protective regret for the happiness he had not had with her.

'Coming with me? I'm going to tell the bees

about the wedding tomorrow. Can't take any chances. Hang on. I'll fetch you some gear.'

She hadn't fully registered the sea-change in her father until now. The father who, during their fractured childhood, had stuck to the downbeat and practical, had turned into a man who considered it perfectly natural to tell the bees of family events. 'I didn't know you were a closet romantic.'

'Whatever that means. Nor did I.'

They walked companionably over the lawn—no longer damp underfoot after the brief hot spell. The path, too, had dried, and dust puffed up as they walked along it.

'Since we're here for a wedding, can I ask something, Dad?'

'Ask.'

'Are you and Mum ever going to be reconciled properly? Isn't this the moment?'

'That's a facer, Jas,' he said. 'I'm not sure I can answer it. You can't just decide to be reconciled.'

'I disagree.'

'You don't know enough yet, Jas.'

But I do.

'Has Lara ever discussed it with you?' She shook her head. 'Perhaps I should tell you what happened.'

He wasn't happy talking about it to her. His voice deepened and the hesitations grew more marked. It was a story about trust that had gone wrong—and she listened with some despair for its constituents chimed with her story.

My story.

The ultimate goal in the branding game. My mayonnaise. My face cream. My failed love affair.

'It wasn't Lara's fault that I was in the state I was in.'

'Which was?'

'Utter terror. A conviction that I had been marked by Fate, or God, or whoever. Bad luck does accrue around some. It's a force field.' Even now, his pain was evident. 'I think I was too tired to fight it.'

She wondered if he was now finding it easier to talk to her because she was the child he knew least well.

'I couldn't find a way to forgive Lara.'

'Mum was so young when you married her,' she pointed out. 'How could she have known how deep your terror was? How could she have understood? No one could have foreseen the coincidence. Anyway, she paid for it.'

'Yes, she did.' He stepped into the paddock. 'We all did. There are not many days when I don't remember Louis . . . just for a second or two.'

'I used to think your children didn't matter to you very much.'

Her father pointed to a chestnut tree in the field across the road. 'We might have played conkers. We might have gone to matches . . .'

He didn't mention his daughters. He certainly didn't try to reassure her. But that, she now realized, was OK.

They would never be very close. But close enough. That was plain to see. Despite their shared blood and bone, the chemistry between them lacked an essential ingredient. Not so with Eve.

Yet in the space between the beginning of the story and its end something had changed. She understood him better and the knowledge altered the way she would think about the past.

After all, she and he did own something in common, which was a relative ease in their dealings. A comfortable not-too-high-expectation relationship. Which was good enough.

He brushed some earth off his fingers.

Yes, it was good enough.

'You reckon the bees will be angry if you don't give them news flashes?' They were approaching the hive—Jasmine lagging a few feet behind her father.

Bill wielded the smoke can. 'If you listen, the hive has its own music.' He stooped to examine the entrance. 'The nectar is drying up, which means they get irritable. Bored and restless bees spell trouble. And . . .' He picked up the body of a dead bee by the entrance and held it up. In the golden September sun, its tiny form seemed shockingly vulnerable. 'See? Its wings have been torn off by the female workers. It had become superfluous.'

As it was September, the angle of the sun dipped lower. In the hedge surrounding the field, full-bellied hips ripened. Translucent clusters of berries glowed Schiaparelli pink and scarlet. Swallows gathered on the telegraph wires across the road.

Soon it would be autumn, and then the slog of winter.

Bill brushed more dead drones on to the ground and glanced up at Jasmine. 'A lot of water's gone under the bridge . . . That's one of the things one has to accept.'

She bit her lip.

The next moment he surprised her. Gesturing to the marquee, he said, 'By the way, Jas, I'm sure your turn will be next.' He took her hand. 'I suspect you might be feeling not so much sore as a little relegated. Please don't. Your time will come.'

The well-meant words had punctuated her careful calm and the fiction of not mourning Duncan that she had invested in. Of course she mourned him. *Fool*. With tears sliding down her cheeks, she found herself running along the bank of the stream in the direction of the rotting landing-stage. Here, she slipped down on to the bank. The level of the stream had dropped, and on the cracked mud opposite there was a dried-up entrance to a den. Water vole?

Fool.

Relegated she was not.

Sad, angry, disappointed, at the end of one phase, and at the beginning of life without Duncan—those things she was.

Chapter Twenty-four

The White Boar Hotel ('approx. five miles from Middleford', ran Eve's notes) had been commandeered by the Russell family and friends. It had passed Eve's inspection and ticked the right boxes: décor, service, location. Rightly so, Lara thought, inspecting the vast, comfortable bed and marble bathroom. She hung up her wedding outfit in a wardrobe that was equipped for every contingency with an iron, shoe-cleaning kit, anti-moth sachets and trouser press.

However, the prospect from the large window was of a clipped, repressed garden. No one, she thought, gains nourishment from such a constipated design, and sat on her resentment that she was not at Membury.

She was conscious of the minutes passing. After much debate, the timetable for tomorrow had been set out with military precision: wedding 4.30; reception 5.45; dinner 7.30; dancing 9 p.m. onwards.

It was about the only aspect of the wedding that was clear.

* * *

Up at Membury, all was movement, a swirling, slightly panicky but choreographed flow of people between the house and the marquee. Lara let herself in by the kitchen door to discover the kitchen was a wasteland of dirty china, saucepans and abandoned dusters. She found an apron and set about restoring some order.

'Thank God for you,' said Sarah, from the doorway. 'Hello, Lara. Have you seen Mrs Baker? I've had a row with her but I need her back.'

Lara sloshed hot water into a glass. 'No. What about?'

Sarah rolled her eyes. 'The hydrangeas, for God's sake.'

'Oh.' Lara nodded sagely. 'I see.'

'You are a darling,' said Sarah, and disappeared again. She reappeared with a pile of towels. 'You couldn't take these upstairs, could you? The flower-girls' room.'

Lara wiped her hands. 'I'm here to be ordered around.'

'You're a double darling.' Sarah blew her a kiss.

When she had taken possession of the house, Sarah had made it clear she and Bill had enough money only to redecorate the ground floor. The bedrooms would have to wait. And here, upstairs, the unfussy bachelor past of Sarah's great-uncle Gurley was still evident in the dull paintwork, worn carpets and warped casement windows. If the house could be said to possess a personality, this part of it was resigned, patient and utilitarian.

The door to the master bedroom was open. A moth to the flame, she was drawn towards it. A large bed was covered with a blue and white striped quilt and the curtains were made of the same material. Bill had chucked a sweater—the grey one she had noticed he favoured—on to the bed. A pair of his shoes roosted in the corner, and Sarah's necklaces were draped from a hanger hooked to the mirror. It was a peaceful scene with none of the turbulence of the days when Bill had shared with Lara.

Part of what she saw—the Bill part—was intimately familiar.

Someone once said that remembered electricity was the worst sort—all the shock and no light. They were right.

She backed away.

In the flower-girls' room the dresses, which were encased in plastic bags, hung in descending size order from the dado rail. Underneath them were ranged their sandals, in boxes. On the bed, ribbon sashes in creamy white had been laid out under tissue paper.

Lara remained motionless.

Life was suspended here. It waited to be called from the wings and to step on to the stage. Then the dresses would take their shape and the shoes would be filled.

'Lara.' Andrew put his head around the door.

She started.

'I saw you go upstairs. I'd like to talk to you.'

No customary kiss, and his usual affable expression had vanished. Instead, he looked as she imagined he might do during a big deal—unyielding. 'I feel we should sort things out between us.'

She glanced out into the passageway. Walls had ears. 'That's interesting. This is the eve of your wedding and you want to discuss our relationship.'

He kept his cool—as she would have expected. 'It's important.' He moved into the room and began to inspect the dresses hanging like so many portraits from their rail. 'Eve has impeccable taste. It's one of the things I admire in her.'

Lara recollected the old wives' tale. 'You aren't supposed to see these before the wedding.'

'We can do without the old superstitions.'

'But not the old virtues.' The words had flashed out before she could consider them.

'Lara, Eve told me about your conversation with her.' He winced. 'It did a lot of damage.'

'Without doubt,' she said. 'But so did you.'

'Perhaps.' Andrew leaned on the windowsill. 'Lara, I'd like us to reach an understanding.'

A consulting room, such as hers, was an arena rife with deceptions and counter-feints. Many times clients faced her and declared they wanted to talk about apples. And they talked about apples up to a point, but they knew, and so did she, they wanted to talk about pears.

She would push Andrew to talk about pears.

'Andrew, why don't we tackle the real issue? Fern. Tell me about Fern.'

'No.'

'Fine.' Lara made for the door.

He longed to talk, of that she was pretty certain. Most people wanted to master their significant experiences. With some people it took time and many forms. Dreams, nightmares, long conversations. Therapy.

'OK.' He had made a decision. 'Fern and I did have an affair, some time back. It wasn't important.'

That was a wriggle statement, of a kind Lara was quite used to. '"It wasn't important" has a habit of becoming the opposite.'

Andrew returned to his inspection of the dresses. But it was obvious he wasn't really seeing them. 'At the time, it was quite intense. Then we broke up and I met Eve.' She noted the body language: stiff shoulders and over-emphatic gestures. 'It was finished. Then we bumped into each other again.'

Pretty girl in the office. Perhaps Andrew had been her boss. Trysts in corridors. Text messages ... Lots of them, filling the spaces in the day. Incendiary looks in a meeting. The hotel room—almost certainly a cheap one—irradiated with incandescent feelings. Very powerful and potent, the office thing. What a mix of emotions it yielded—yearnings, apprehensions, the battle between what was right and the lust. Then the moment when he says, 'It's over,' and she fights back: 'You can't do that.'

Lara had listened to the scenario many, many times. It was a simple one but its outcome was not always predictable. That was one of its problems.

Andrew was wearing a shabby T-shirt and jeans

—not the sort of thing she had imagined he would wear. They chimed with his expression of sadness and regret, which she recognized only too well. But, above all, he looked baffled. He could not understand why he had allowed his careful plans to be undermined, or why he had allowed himself to become deflected. She felt a sliver of sympathy.

'OK,' she said. 'This is hard because you can't resolve these feelings in the way you resolve your work problems. They're not tidy and they won't be put into neat boxes.'

He shrugged.

'Andrew, what are you doing marrying Eve?'

Bending down, he picked up the tiniest sandal from its box and held it out. 'If the shoe fits. Eve and I fit.'

'Have you discussed Fern with Eve?'

'We've talked.'

'Did you tell her the truth?'

Stonewall. 'We talked.'

Anxiety made her extra sharp. 'Andrew, I've no idea what was said, nor should I. Strange bargains are struck between people, and are successful. But the bargain has to be what suits Eve and you.'

'You know Eve. Would she be marrying me if she had any worries? She accepts that Fern is in my past.' The tissue paper rustled as he replaced the sandal in its box. 'Have you considered, Lara? Eve's got what she wanted. A house, me, a life together.' He glanced away. 'She told me that was what she wanted.'

She noted the order. 'But she wouldn't want Fern.'

No answer.

A suspicion crept into her mind. 'You haven't

told her the whole truth, have you?' Andrew was silent. 'How can you say you love her?'

'By sparing her,' he said. 'From me.'

Lara raised an eyebrow.

'Of course, I care about Eve,' Andrew said. '*Very* much.'

The manner in which the words dropped stiffly, almost formally, told Lara everything.

'Poor Andrew,' Lara said, as the pieces of the jigsaw fell into place. 'You fell in love with Fern. You didn't expect to, but you did.'

Could Andrew explain to himself the fears and electric hopes? The exhilaration and the excitement? The moments of ecstasy ... pin sharp for being stolen? Probably not.

(She couldn't.)

'Why didn't you choose Fern? If you love her, you should have done. Would that not have been more honest?'

'Stop it, Lara.'

The atmosphere in the bedroom had become stifling and hostile. Various expressions chased over his features. Then, suddenly, Andrew's guard dropped.

'I can't deny I loved Fern ... love her, since we're being honest ...' He spoke passionately, poignantly, in a way he never talked about Eve. 'But I don't agree with you. Eve and I suit each other better. In the long term.'

Lara glanced out of the window. The figures of the caterers and florists were moving like ants in a steady stream between the parked vans and the marquee.

He pointed to the ants. 'You see? It's all been set in train.' He fell silent. Then he added, 'Eve and

I understand the form. Lots of people wouldn't, perhaps, but we do.'

'You can't hold to it very hard if you've been seeing Fern.' He shrugged and looked away, but not before she had glimpsed agony and regret. 'Does anyone else know about Fern?' she asked.

'No.'

She didn't believe him. 'For Eve's sake, you must see to it that people don't talk.' She grabbed his arm. 'You *owe* her that.' She added harshly: 'The form, Andrew.'

He threw Lara a glance of dislike.

She didn't blame him. 'I'm sorry ... It didn't work out the way you thought. But if you *have* chosen this way, which you seem to have done, you'll have to stick to it.'

He squeezed his eyes shut. 'It hurts Lara. It *hurts.*'

On the sunken lawn below the marquee the fireworks supervisor tried out a catherine wheel. Andrew and Lara watched as the sparks spluttered and faded.

'Andrew, you will be there tomorrow?'

*   *   *

At dinner at the White Boar (7.30 p.m., as per Eve's instructions), the guests divided up into camps. The bride's at the White Boar and the groom's at the Turnpike at the other end of town.

Afterwards Lara drove Eve and Jasmine back to Membury. The two girls chatted softly, with Jasmine occasionally asking her a question, but otherwise Lara kept silent. The day had been warm and dry, and a few streaks of late-summer lightning twitched across the sky.

At the steps to the front door, she kissed them goodnight. Eve unyielding and unfriendly. Jasmine holding her close. 'Wish you were staying up here with us.'

'So do I. But Sarah and your father have quite enough on their plates.'

Jasmine clattered up the steps with Eve following.

'Eve,' Lara begged. 'Don't be like this.'

'Like what exactly, Lara? Like a bride who has been told by her mother—*step*mother actually, the one person she thought she could trust—that her groom is playing away?'

'You've sorted things out with Andrew?'

Fitfully illuminated by the light over the door, Eve's expression was unreadable. 'Take a guess, Lara.' She turned and ran up behind Jasmine.

'I'm going down to look at the marquee,' Lara called, before the front door shut. 'Tell Sarah and your father I'm not a burglar.'

Shaken and sad, she wandered through the darkening garden. She smelt tobacco—probably one of the caterers smoking a cigarette—and could hear the murmur of voices outside the marquee. Another streak of lightning against the dark curtain of the sky. Down by the stream a fox barked, sharp and feral, followed by the splash of an animal into the water.

A sufficiency of work, family and peace was all that was needed to live life—and to live it properly. And yet when she was in a night garden such as this one, her senses quickened and demanded more. Anyone's would.

As she turned the corner into the sunken garden,

she gave a cry of surprise. The marquee appeared like a great white illuminated ship floating above it.

Inside, a couple of the florists were putting the final touches to the columns—waterfalls of orange blossom and the creamiest, most ruffled of roses. One of the caterers, who had an apron wrapped around her middle, was adjusting the position of the tables with the help of a diagram. 'Katie,' she called, as she juggled the last one. 'Katie!' Levering herself upright, she rubbed swollen fingers.

'Long day,' said Lara.

'Long day,' she agreed.

'Can I help?'

The woman gave a tired smile. 'All done, thank you.'

The lights from the marquee streamed out over the garden and lit mysterious paths into the garden's dark heart. Lara hovered at the entrance. Having warmed the earth, the day's sun drew out a medley of scents—dust, a hint of rose, the spices of lavender and box. It was an extraordinarily rich mix of texture and sensation, a swoony, dreaming softness, she thought, in which to drown.

'Katie,' called the caterer. *'Katie!'*

There was the sound of running feet and a white shape glimmered through the darkness. A figure skittered into a beam of light. It was wearing a white dress, and a torn white veil drifted out behind it.

Lara's heart somersaulted.

She hurried down the steps in pursuit. As puzzling and elusive as her dream, the white figure flitted this way and that. Lara ran after it, her feet stirring up eddies of dust. Sharp and offensive, ever stronger, the fox's odour sifted through the warm air. Lightning snapped in the sky overhead. Ever faster, the girl in white ran past the wild-flower area towards the clump of beeches . . .

Without question, she followed, drawn by a compulsion, astonished and a little frightened.

What phantoms were hissing to the surface? What manifestation of her secret life? What grief (and, sometimes, near madness) had Lara kept captive in her inner life, and struggled to hide?

The ease with which she was moving through the dark was astounding—it was as if she had followed this path many times. Beyond the wild-flower patch and the beeches, Lara could see the shimmer of the stream.

Breathing was beginning to hurt.

'Katie! I'm going home now,' echoed the impatient call from the marquee.

Ahead of Lara, the white vision slowed abruptly, swayed and appeared to fall to the ground.

Within seconds, Lara had caught up.

She discovered a little girl, who looked much smaller than the apparition she had chased. Nine? Perhaps ten? She was wearing a grubby white cotton frock, which was too long for her, and a veil attached to her hair with a pink plastic slide. Close up, it was a cheap and tacky thing sold in toy shops.

She had fallen over and her knee was bleeding. 'Ouch.' She tugged the veil off her head and dabbed at the wound with it. Crimson seeped on to the white and flowered, like spots of birth blood on hospital sheets.

The phantoms.

The ones that wouldn't leave her alone.

Flashback.

She lies in the bed in the hospital ward and watches

sunlight inch its way across the windowsill. My baby will be born soon. There is a flurry, and urgent voices issuing orders, faces she doesn't recognize materializing in and out of her vision, the cold, swimming sensation as the drugs kick in. Red blood pooling into the white hospital sheet. Soon she is floating above the bed. Don't go, commands the voice in her head. Stay. Later, the feel of Louis's skin against hers. Skin-to-skin was what the midwives had advised before the birth. But now they say, Let us wrap him first. She is hysterical, demanding that they place his still, damp, cooling little body against hers.

A strange sound?

Bill weeping.

Lara managed, 'Are you all right? Who are you?'

'I'm Katie,' the child replied. 'I'm the bride.'

Lara said, '*Of course* you are. I hope I didn't frighten you. I didn't know who you were.'

Katie threw her a child's look: patronizing and long-suffering. 'No.'

'There you are, Katie!' Her mother, who had been calling for her, hurried into view. 'Now, what have you been and done? I told you not to wear that here.' She bundled up the veil and put it into her bag. 'We're late. Katie loves dressing up,' she explained to Lara. 'I couldn't get a babysitter.'

She grabbed her daughter and they hurried towards the cars parked in the drive.

Lara was shaking. The bride, the baby that never lived . . . They had harried and haunted her.

It was time for them to stop and she must send them away.

She drifted towards the stream and watched the moonlight spread and contract over its moving surface. Dew was forming on the grass. Behind her, the light from the marquee streamed across a black lawn that was fretted here and there with reflections from the gathering moisture.

The old sensations—despair, rawness, disbelief. What did she teach her patients? Events that happen beyond your control are beyond your control. Deal with them. That was the clue to survival.

There was a touch on her arm. 'Lara?'

'Bill,' she responded, half sobbing.

'Hey, what is it?' The dark made him appear bulkier than he was. 'Did I frighten you?'

'I think I'm haunted,' she said. 'But I'm going now. I'll get out of your hair.'

He leaned forward and his breath touched her cheek. 'You haunt me, Lara. In so many ways. You shouldn't but you do.'

She was appalled, embarrassed.

Sweet memory.

Inadmissible memory.

'Eve said you were in the garden. She said you wanted to do something.'

'I should have asked you. But I wanted to cut a sprig of myrtle to put in her bouquet. It's traditional, you know. But I got waylaid ...' she managed a wry smile '... by a bride.'

He was puzzled. She explained and he laughed. 'We could pick the myrtle in the morning. It would be better then anyway. Fresher, sweeter.'

'We?'

'We.' He put a finger under her chin and forced her to look up at him. 'That's what I wanted to say and it would seem to be the moment. I wanted to put what we could to rest ... and since it's Eve's wedding, I wanted to thank you. For looking after

Eve and Jasmine. Bringing them up. I never got to tell you how much I appreciated it. I should have done and I'm very conscious of that. I also wanted to say ... I'm sorry.' He dropped his hand and shoved it into his pocket. 'I'm sorry about a lot of things.'

A breeze shivered through the warm air. She glanced up at the sky. *No rain, please.*

He was puzzled by her silence. 'What do you say, Lara?'

'Go on.'

'When grit gets in, it rubs and rubs until there's nothing left. I haven't been the best at forgetting, but so much is in the past. Let's keep it there.'

They turned and fell into step as they walked up towards the drive.

'I always blamed you for making me leave,' he said.

'Nothing could have been further from what I wanted.'

'My thoughts were skewed at the time. I couldn't reason any more. I know you didn't make me leave, and I don't ever think that now.'

They had, she thought, found the easy vocabulary. At last. All the familiar phrases they used to exchange, the jokes, were still there, waiting for recall. They had built the edifice of the marriage and allowed the earthquake to topple it. 'The thing is,' she said, 'it was both of us. *Neither* of us could deal with Louis so the marriage couldn't survive.'

'I'm sorry,' he said again.

She looked at him—the big, kindly, stricken man whom she had once loved and who had once loved her. That would never return and the memory of their mistakes was still there. Of course. But they had lost their sting.

They had reached her car. He opened the door and waited for her to get in. 'We can pick a sprig of myrtle for Eve's bouquet. Right?'

'Right.'

Chapter Twenty-five

The alarm sounded and Jasmine woke. She rolled over and pressed her face into the pillow.

Eve was getting married today.

Her next thought was for Duncan—and she wished it wasn't. He would be at the Turnpike, with Andrew and his family.

They had not seen each other. They had not spoken since his phone call a week ago.

'Jas, don't hang up. *Listen* to me.'

'It's over.'

'You're being ridiculous.' Cross and slightly menacing (which he could be).

'Give me one reason why it's ridiculous to expect to continue a relationship with someone I can't trust . . .'

'But you can . . .'

She pressed her face deeper into the pillow. *Confession.* As the weeks had gone on, it had become harder. Was this a usual pattern? Did the mind ever stop? If only it would. She might go mad with thinking, with *if only*, with the emptiness, the futility, the starting-all-over-again.

For God's sake, it wasn't as though she had had to fight a war.

Someone knocked at the door. Eve stuck her

head around it. 'Do you mind?' Paler than she should be. Or perhaps that was how brides *should* look on their wedding day. This bride was dressed in jeans and damp plimsolls that shed flecks of grass as she walked across the carpet.

'Oh, God,' said Eve, noting her debris trail, and pulled off the plimsolls. She scrubbed at a green patch on the carpet. 'You're very beige,' she told it. 'You could do with gingering up.'

Jasmine grinned, and pulled herself upright. 'Hey. You're supposed to be in bed being pampered.'

'Couldn't. I've had breakfast.' She went over to the window.

'Weather?'

'Beautiful. As I ordered. I saw a dragon-fly on the stream.'

A dragon-fly, Jasmine thought. *Good image.*

Eve said softly, 'Andrew left a pair of earrings on my breakfast tray, which was lovely of him.' She plumped down on the bed. 'So, here we are.'

They exchanged a look.

'So here we are,' Jasmine agreed. 'Happy?'

'Of course.' After a second, she added, '*Very.*'

'Did you see Andrew last night?'

'Very briefly.'

'Eve, you *do* love him?'

She flicked a look at Jasmine: *No further.* 'Oh, yes.' She got up and retrieved Jasmine's dressing-gown from the floor and draped it around her sister's shoulders. 'You'll get cold.' Then: 'Actually, I do feel a bit odd.'

Jasmine leaped out of bed and drew Eve close. She smelt of grass and country things. But she felt fragile and underweight. 'You have been eating?'

373

'Sure. All brides lose weight.'

'You'll have to fatten up on honeymoon.'

Eve's fingers crept into hers. *We two*. Tied together by their genes and by a death. 'Are you thinking about our real mother?' Jasmine asked.

Eve's hand felt lighter than a bird's claw in hers. 'Trying not to.'

'Same here. I sense she's trying to make her presence felt.' She splayed Eve's fingers and inspected her nail polish. Pinky, translucent, as delicate as mother-of-pearl. 'I can't help thinking— no, *feeling*—she's outraged that she never got the chance to bring us up, and never had the chance to interfere.'

Eve gave a sketchy grin. 'You're well informed. Does our mother speak from the ether?'

'Don't joke.'

'Might have to, Jas. Otherwise I might weep.'

Jasmine grabbed Eve. 'Don't do that. Brides can't have blotchy faces.' She searched Eve's face. 'You are *all right*?'

Eve put on the face she adopted when her back was against the wall. 'Nerves. Don't look like that, Jas. I'm bound to feel a bit shaky.'

Jasmine returned to the subject of their mother. 'I can't help also feeling that, if she's grateful to Lara for bringing us up, she's angry with her for being alive.'

'She shouldn't be,' said Eve. 'Lara did her ... best.' In a rare gesture, she rested her head on Jasmine's shoulder. 'Ever thought of being a psychic?'

'I wouldn't have blamed Lara if she hadn't loved us, but she did.'

Eve didn't reply to that. Instead she said,

'Remember the cardboard houses?'

'Of course.'

Eve and Jasmen's Haus. Top Secret.

'I never allowed Maudie inside.'

'You've probably marked her for life.'

*　　　*　　　*

A light buffet lunch had been laid out in the dining room at the White Boar and the wedding party were drifting in and out in various stages of dress. There was cold salmon, salads, plus a good selection of cheeses, to which Bill was helping himself with enthusiasm.

The party included Bill, Sarah, Jasmine and the bride, who had come down from the house, his sisters Frances (the excitable aunt) and Lucy (the calm aunt) and their respective husbands, Richard and Brad, plus a scattering of cousins.

A pale Eve was pushing a tiny amount of rice salad around her plate.

Bill stuck a huge chunk of cheese on a piece of bread. 'No one told me how nerve-racking it is to be the father of the bride.'

He didn't look at all nerve-racked.

Lucy broke off her conversation with Sarah. 'You'd better get used to it, Bill. You have more than one to walk down the aisle.'

Lara shot a look at Jasmine, who appeared to be fixated on a pot of lilies in the corner of the room.

Ferrying plates, pouring drinks, dispensing water and coffee, the staff came and went.

Brad was already sporting a glazed look. How was he going to get through the day? And Richard—browbeaten and depressed—shovelled pills from his pocket. 'To support the liver and kidneys,' he explained.

Jasmine murmured to Lara, 'At this rate, we'll have to book him into the Priory by the end of lunch.'

'Pills are his reason for living,' she whispered back. 'Think of the Cruel Existence with Frances.'

Lunch over, Lara went up to her room. It was far too warm. Pushing up the window, she spotted a spider's web slotted into the space between the sill and the brick return. 'Summer must be dying if you're here,' she told it. Then, gazing at the hexagonals and spirals deep in the web, she added, 'You're a marvel.'

It was a day tipped with gold. The coinage of early autumn.

A knock on the door. The corsage was delivered: ivory roses, with cream dendrobium orchids and ivy—all of Eve's choosing.

From room service she ordered mint tea to sweeten her system. (And to remind her of Damascus?)

Hat. Bag. Shoes.

She bathed and dried herself, then drew on her expensive sheer tights—and laddered them. Cursing, she got out the back-up pair and put them on.

She tackled her makeup. The woman in the mirror looked anxious, and she did her best with foundation and eye shadow to smooth her anxiety into an expression suitable for the (step)mother-of-the-bride.

Much thought had been expended on her outfit. It had boiled down to either a peacock-blue silk dress and jacket or an edgier dress in olive jersey. It was a source of exasperation that the old-fashioned colours—bright pinks, oranges and blues—from the fifties suited her better than anything. Vivid peacock added sheen to her looks but the olive made her feel subtler, foxier, more up-to-date. It had also been less expensive. She went for it.

Quite soon she was ready. Catching up her hat and bag, she gave herself a critical appraisal in the long mirror and left the room.

Up at Membury, she searched for Bill. 'God knows where he is,' said a harassed Sarah. 'Please don't distract him. I'm going to have trouble enough getting him ready on time.' She looked up from the list she was checking. 'Someone's got stuck at the station. I'm trying to find a free taxi and I need to change. Was it important?'

Well, yes and no.

Balancing carefully on her high heels, Lara made her way to the sunken garden. A constant stream of cooks and waiting staff shot up and down the drive at high speed and criss-crossed the garden. She spotted the woman from yesterday. 'How's Katie?'

'With her father. Long may she stay there.'

On reaching the myrtle, she looked round for Bill, failed to sight him. As she wielded the secateurs she had borrowed from the gardener's shed, a delicious green scent was released.

She laid the sprigs by the front door and went upstairs. She would have liked to cut the myrtle with him, but the agreement, the accord, had been the important thing.

Eve's bedroom was chaotic. The bed was heaped with clothes and boxes wept tissue paper. Towels nested on the floor.

Eve was having her hair done in front of the

377

mirror by Angie, her *über*-smart hairdresser, who had driven down from London. At Lara's entrance, Eve looked round. 'There you are.'

'Hi, Lara.' Jasmine had taken up sentry duty by the window. 'Goodness,' she said. 'Is that the Clarks? They're early. What are they doing up here instead of at the church?' She paused. 'She's wearing a terrible outfit and he looks a bit sloshed.'

'Oh, my God,' said Eve. 'It's really happening.'

'Just keep still,' said Angie, sticking in a hairpin. She bent down and switched on a pair of hair tongs.

The two little flower-girls raced up and down the corridor outside the bedroom. Their mother could be heard saying, 'Calm down, the pair of you.'

'Should I go and help?' Lara pointed at the door.

'No, their mum says to leave well alone. She'll cope.'

'How did the rehearsal go?' Lara broke the cool silence that had fallen.

'Bit nervy,' said Eve. 'Andrew didn't turn up until the last minute. Duncan had a bit of a problem hunting him down.'

Jasmine kept her back to them. 'You can rely on Duncan,' she said.

Dressed in her creamy white ruffled dress and satin sash, Daisy, the youngest flower-girl, burst into the room. She looked like an angel but she certainly wasn't one.

'Why did you choose sandals?' asked Lara.

'Thrift,' said Eve. 'They can wear them afterwards. Contrary to appearances, Dad and I have tried to keep expenses to a minimum.'

Lara noted the emphasis on 'Dad and I'.

'Nearly ready,' said Angie, approvingly, as she made the final adjustments to Eve's hair.

Daisy spotted the tongs and dived towards them. Lara executed a lightning manoeuvre, retrieved them —and burned a finger. 'Ouch.'

Daisy's mother appeared in the doorway. 'Is she being a nuisance? She is. I'll take her away.'

Daisy disappeared.

'There,' said Angie. Eve stood up. Her hair was caught back, and streamed from a knot on the top of her head.

'Lovely,' said Jasmine.

'Beautiful,' said Lara.

Jasmine took Eve's place in front of the mirror and Angie set to work. Eve removed her dressing-gown, revealing her lace underwear. With an effort, she said, 'Can you help me, Lara?'

She was thin, so thin. One push, one gust of wind, and Eve would be gone. 'You must eat up on honeymoon,' Lara admonished her, and cupped Eve's cheek. 'Promise.'

'That's what I said too,' said Jasmine.

Eve stared at her with big cool eyes. 'I will.'

'Evie?'

'Lara?'

There was no yielding in Eve's tone. *You've made your bed* ... she was saying. Lara removed her hand.

Sliding the under-dress off its hanger, she eased it over Eve's head and laced her into it. Eve waited patiently while Lara made the adjustments. As promised, a rose had been embroidered on to the bodice, a tiny, raised furled bud and thorn. Eve touched it gently. 'So lovely.'

Angie was manipulating handfuls of Jasmine's hair and pulling it back in a similar fashion to Eve's. 'Now the dress,' commanded Jasmine from her perch.

Lara eased it out of the protective calico cover in which it hung limp and lifeless.

'So exciting,' said Jasmine.

Angie suspended her labours to watch.

A doll-like Eve submitted to Lara's ministrations as the dress was eased into place.

A transformation took place. As they watched, the limp material came alive, flowing down and out behind Eve, turning into a thing of beauty and subtlety. All three women were transfixed. Eve had become . . . what? A magical creature. The bride of Lara's dreams. A girl at a crossroads.

'Shoes?' Lara hunted among the tissue paper and boxes on the bed. Eve lifted her dress, held out a foot.

Her hair done, Jasmine rose and vacated the position in front of the mirror. 'Angie will put the veil in place.' Her voice cracked. 'Oh, Evie . . . you are lovely.'

*   *   *

'Come on, come on . . .' Maudie dialled up Skype with a slightly shaky hand.

America was hot, she had learned, but absolutely freezing inside the highly air-conditioned buildings. As a result, she spent her new life peeling sweaters off and on, and she was freezing now. But, so far, that was the only thing of which she could possibly complain. Otherwise she had found the place where she belonged.

Everything was on such a generous scale here. The college meals. The weather. The freshmen events. In contrast, her life in the UK (as she now viewed it) had been a cramped waiting room in which she had been trapped for too long. Nick didn't agree:

That sort of rubbish so is not cool or interesting. I'll prove it to you when I come over.

Since he didn't have a penny, his coming over would not be any time soon. Whether she was relieved or sad, she could not decide.

Predictably, Alicia was thrilled:

I knew you would flourish. Everyone needs to get out of their box, and you're so smart. Remind me to put you in touch with Jackie. She's my next project. Clever just like you. She could go far.

Slight flash of jealousy. She, Maudie, was one in a long line of students whom Alicia would nurture. That was what teachers did.

She checked her watch. On time to the second.

And, to the second, the connection was made and there was Jasmine in her dress—a replica of Eve's but shorter, and in dusky, tea-rose pink.

'Jas, you look wonderful. Where are you?'

'Can't you see the stripes? In the sitting room. We reckoned it would be easier for Evie to talk to you in here.'

'I miss you.'

Jasmine's beautifully made-up lips parted in a sweet smile. 'We miss you too. You look so glossy and happy ... and American. It's all going fine. Eve's on her way. Lara's helping her down the stairs.'

'How is she?'

'Unnervingly calm and thin.'

Maudie fingered the sleeve of the sweater she had draped round her shoulders. 'Did you ever talk to her about what I saw?'

The face on the screen remained pretty bland. 'Not really, Maudie. I thought it best not to.'

Skype deceived one into thinking an exchange was more intimate than it was. Maudie couldn't assess from Jasmine's slightly blurred expression whether she was telling the truth or not.

'And Duncan?'

Jasmine frowned. 'Actually, that's finished. I told him to go. But no one knows. OK? Not a word.'

'Don't be silly. You two are welded at the hip.'

'Can't talk about it,' said Jasmine. 'I'll ruin my makeup. Anyway, here's Eve.' She blew Maudie a kiss. 'We'll talk soon. Think of us.'

'Jas!' she called. Jasmine's face reappeared. 'The dress. It's a really nice pink.'

Think of us.

Jasmine was replaced by Eve—who had turned into a bride. *The totem. The symbol.* She must research it some time. *The meaning and significance of the bride figure.* It would be a good route into a study of feminist literature, which she and Alicia had been discussing on email.

'Hello, Maudie. Here I am. Almost at the church. It's been quite a journey, hasn't it?'

'Good luck!' she cried.

As so often—actually, she thought, always— with these occasions, the conversation verged on the banal. Maudie longed to ask the important questions. *Are you happy? Are you sure?* But, almost for the first time in her life, she found that the straightforward questions were too difficult to articulate and her tongue was curbed. She struggled with disappointment as they exchanged information about the weather, airports and departure times.

'You look so beautiful,' she said at last, resorting to the tried and tested.

Eve glanced down at the dress, and the hand wearing her engagement ring smoothed a length of veil falling over a shoulder. 'Thank you.' She looked directly into the screen and her eyes seemed enormous. 'Thank you for calling.'

Maudie was surprised by the lump in her throat.

Almost as an afterthought, Eve said, 'I'm wearing the garter, Maudie.'

After the contact was severed, Maudie sat quietly for a few minutes, assaulted by acute homesickness. She should have been with her sisters. She *should* have been with her family at such an important moment. What on earth was she doing in the US? Of course, the grass was always greener on the other side of the fence but her regret felt deep and genuine. A sob rose into her throat. She sat and contemplated what she was missing and how, once again, she had managed to put herself in the position of the outsider.

Was that going to be the way her life ran? For a few more minutes, she contemplated her existence as the outsider, never quite belonging, never fully fitting in. It was a pleasurably painful examination—and the tragedy of it all was immensely appealing.

A text flipped into her phone: 'Coffee? Like NOW, Lindy.'

Home? Here? The future? Her thumb swung

into action. 'With you in 10.'

She shut down the laptop, let herself out of the room, and ran down the stairs. Already the memory of her sisters was fading. (In fact, deep down, she was growing to believe more and more that to put yourself through a wedding was incredibly old-fashioned politically and culturally, especially for a woman.) Anyway, regrets were wasteful. This led her logically to the notion that one day she would be dead, and the idea that she would no longer be out in the world enjoying it outraged her.

By the time she hastened out into the hot sunshine, all thoughts of her sisters had vanished.

For a second or two, she stood still to inhale the air of the Land of Opportunity, before loping in the direction of the coffee shop.

Of course she was happy here. Happier than she had ever been.

* * *

Two wedding cars drew up in the drive.

Time to go.

Outside, the flower-girls were being given a last-minute tutorial in their duties by their mother, aided by Bill. Holding a basket, he marched up and down. 'How's this, girls?' and reduced them to giggles. Nobody held out much hope that it would work.

Lara picked up her hat—wide-brimmed, with a single rose as decoration—and sat down to put it on in front of the mirror. Then she snatched up her bag and went downstairs.

Eve was standing in the hallway watching the departures.

'Is Sarah ready?' Lara asked. She and Sarah were in the second car.

'She's outside.'

'Right.'

'You'd better go,' said Eve.

'Good luck.'

'Thank you, Lara.'

This was not how it was meant to be.

'Eve,' she said desperately, 'please don't. Not on your wedding day.'

Eve lifted the dress carefully as she turned to Lara. 'I can't forget what you did,' she said. 'I can't. It's made me feel quite differently about you. I'm sorry, but it's true. If you loved me, like you always said you did, and I believed you, you wouldn't have done something so cruel . . .'

Lara's mouth was dry and her stomach churned. 'Eve, whatever I do is to protect you. Always, always. You can't possibly think that I would do anything willingly to hurt you.'

'I'm marrying Andrew, and you tried to drive a wedge between us . . . I'll never understand why you did it.'

'But you will,' Lara cried. 'If you ever have children.'

Eve shrugged, and the veil undulated down her back. 'Sometimes it's best to leave things alone.' She sent Lara a hard little smile. 'It's the therapist, isn't it, Lara? They can never let well alone.'

Lara bowed her head. 'If that's what you want to believe.'

It was too late to repair the breach. Any minutenow, Eve would go to her wedding, carrying her angry thoughts of Lara. Patients often questioned: *Why me?* Or *Why has my family been singled out?* And Lara would spend time convincing them that their particular sorrows/mishaps/sins were pretty much the same as everyone else's. (It was the old mantra: how they dealt with them would single them out.) Now, she had been reminded at first-hand.

Bill loped up the steps and stuck his head through the front door. 'Lara, Sarah's waiting for you in the car.'

Lara said, 'I'm not going to leave you on this note.'

'I'll see you in the church, Lara.'

'Is this how we're going to say goodbye on your wedding day?'

'Yes,' she replied, in a low, obdurate voice.

'Eve, where's your bouquet?'

Eve pointed to the long box on the table. Lara drew out the bridal bouquet—white peonies and roses with just a hint of blush pink. Its beauty, a tremulous, perishable beauty, was unquestionable.

The myrtle cuttings were by the door where she had left them. Very carefully, she inserted a sprig between a peony and a rose.

'What are you doing?' asked Eve, sharply.

Lara explained.

'No,' she cried. 'I don't want you meddling.' She snatched up the bouquet. The cool, determined bride had been replaced by an angry, spitting girl. 'Take it back, Lara.' The myrtle was pinched between finger and thumb. 'Take it back.'

Eve's anger told Lara everything. The nerves. The fears. The gamble she was taking. 'Evie, Evie, listen to me. Are you sure about this?'

The blazing, spitting bride shook like an aspen leaf. 'Oh, Lara, you're such a fool. I love Andrew.

More than I can say. OK?'

'Then it is OK.' Eve clasped the bouquet tighter. 'Careful with the flowers.'

'Go away.' At that, Eve's finger caught on a tip of florists' wire holding a peony in place.

The sprig of myrtle fell to the floor.

A tiny scarlet flower bloomed on the hem of the dress.

'No,' Eve cried. *'No!'*

The red and the white. Milk and blood. The colour of light and purity, and of the virgin's sacrifice. The colour of death.

Eve said, 'Quick—*do* something.' She sucked frantically at her finger.

Lara did nothing. 'Leave it, Eve,' she instructed. 'No one will see it. If you touch it, it will make it worse.'

'I can't be married with blood on my dress.'

'Look at me, Eve. Look at me.' Eve turned her face slowly to Lara's. 'Don't touch it,' Lara repeated. 'Believe me. No one will see it.'

'Mum!' she cried. 'Help me! Help me get through!'

*   *   *

In the car, Lara sat beside Sarah and pleated the folds of her skirt. The undertow of maternal anxiety rose in overwhelming waves to the surface. 'I hope Eve will be OK.'

'She'll be fine.' Handsome in brown silk, which suited her colouring, Sarah was matter-of-fact.

Lara wiggled a toe inside her shoe, feeling the glide of her expensive tights. 'The business of the parent is to be better and wiser than the child,' she told Sarah, 'but it's a close-run thing.'

'Let's give thanks that we've got to this point,' said Sarah.

Lara began to feel sick and leaned forward to open the window. 'Do you mind?'

'Go ahead.'

The car swept onwards along a road dappled by sun. 'I thought there would be a storm last night.'

'Bill said the same when he came in.' Sarah opened and shut her handbag. Then she opened it again, took out a lipstick, looked at it and dropped it back into the bag. 'Did you talk to Bill last night?'

'I did. Do you mind?'

'Me? No, of course not.'

But Sarah did, and Lara hastened to explain: 'We were sorting things out. Things that should have been sorted out long ago.'

'Bill is very fond of you.'

'But he loves you, Sarah. Really he does. He's happy these days and because he's happy we've sorted things out. You don't really worry, do you?'

'A little,' she confessed. 'You did have a lot together.'

'But so do you.'

More vulnerable than she would ever let on, Sarah settled her handbag in her lap. 'Lara, you look amazing. Hat perfect.'

'And *you*'re perfect, Sarah.'

The car slowed, and stopped in front of the church.

Chapter Twenty-six

Guests milled in the bright sunshine outside the church door as Sarah and Lara walked up the path.

Immediately there was a touch on her arm. 'You look beautiful,' said Robin, emerging from a cluster.

She turned round. 'You're here. That's wonderful.'

He leaned forward and planted a light kiss on her mouth. 'I was hoping you'd say that.'

It was a private moment, with one of the deep, penetrating, wordless exchanges that lovers, or potential lovers, enjoy. It's a promise. It's a manifesto. She closed her eyes. Then, opened them smartish so that she didn't miss a second—not one second—of him.

He was in a suit with a silk tie. 'You scrub up nicely,' she said.

He was looking down at her with some concern. 'You look worn out.'

'It's that bad?'

'Let me see ...' He ticked off on his fingers. 'One beautiful big mouth. One rather pretty chin. Lovely hair. Big hat. Terrible, I'd say.'

'The hat? Am I a meringue?'

He laughed. 'Yes. What did you expect?'

It was so silly, inconsequential ... yet she experienced a profound, almost life-changing, relief. Robin was there. He saw her for what she was ... worn out and in a big hat. But he didn't care. Because he, too, had been worn out and found wanting. Maybe he would put up with her bad singing voice, too, and all the rest of the baggage.

She introduced Robin to Sarah, who brightened considerably when she worked out how he stood in relation to Lara.

How sorry Lara was that Sarah had had to put up with the ex-wife's spectre hanging over her relationship with Bill all these years ... and how generous Sarah had been about it.

Robin parodied himself: 'OK, you two. Are the nerves under control? I'm good at steadying. Part of the training. Off to battle. No problem. Don't know the plan? Here's the manual. No idea? Make it up.'

In a bright green dress, Margaret Ellis walked up the path and headed in Lara's direction. A couple of children played among the graves where the long grass feathered around the lichened headstones. The flower arch above the church door was getting a beating from the sun. A couple of cars had parked badly in the lane, causing confusion with oncoming traffic. A trio of girls—very short skirts, low necklines and long, glossy hair with feather fascinators—walked up to the entrance. 'Are we late?' asked one.

Robin placed a hand on Lara's waist—at the point where the curve met the hip—and pressed down very lightly. It sent a frisson through her body. It was a first step. It was the promise.

He removed his hand. 'I shall be watching your hat.' He stepped into the church.

It was almost full. She walked down the aisle behind Sarah, accompanied by rustles as the already seated congregation clocked who they were. A royal progress.

The flowers—Eve's hard-won flowers—were

overwhelming. Waterfalls of lilies, roses, peonies and gypsophila shrouded every nook and cranny, and posies had been hung at the end of each pew.

'Are you sure you won't be overdoing it, Eve?' she had asked several times.

But no. As clever Eve had foreseen, the effect was beautiful.

She paused to exchange a word with Nigel and Dorothea. ('Dorothea's hat was small, neat and uninspiring,' she would write to Maudie, 'but smartish blue dress. She and Nigel weren't exactly *friendly*, but OKish. Slightly *de haut en bas . . .*')

Once settled in her pew at the front, Lara turned round. Almost there. Just one or two to go, by the look of things. She checked her watch. Five minutes or so until the best man and groom appeared.

Was she really sitting in this pew, in a wedding hat, waiting for Eve to be married? What an unexpected journey it had been . . . from the girl who had served fish and chips and bad coffee in a Cornish café to now.

Her skirt had a tendency to ride up her thigh and she pulled it down.

Guests were chatting. A few sat silently, staring ahead. Weddings had a habit of reprising one's own marital situation—as she well knew. How many of them sitting there were questioning the whole damn charade or telling themselves *If only I'd known*?

But she, smugly for those few minutes, felt very happy. So happy that she swivelled round to look at Robin. He was sitting quietly in his pew. He caught her gaze and held it.

She turned back. The idea of happiness was

frequently deceptive, its radiance short-lived. But she had learned that it had to be taken up. It had to be snatched out of the jaws of misery.

The flowers smelt heavenly. The choir was in place. The order of service sheet was plain and elegant. She glanced down at her hands. All that was evident of her nerves was a quiver in a little finger. That she could deal with.

Where was the groom?

Unable to resist, she took another look at Robin ... froze, swung round and stared fixedly at the altar. What *had* she seen? Answer: Fern. Stepping into the church with her hair swept up and a hat angled coquettishly over one eye—very Veronica Lake—she had looked neither right nor left as she slipped into a seat opposite the church entrance. Slight as she appeared, her expression was that of a woman who would not forgo her moment.

Had Andrew invited her? Or had she gatecrashed?

Sarah said in her ear, 'The bridegroom's cutting it fine.'

Lara's attention switched from Fern. She glanced at her watch. Something was wrong.

She rose to her feet. 'I just want a word with Robin.' To avoid walking back down the aisle, she skirted down the chancel. His radar locked on her, and she beckoned him outside.

He walked out into the porch. 'What's up?'

She whispered, 'Could you phone Duncan and find out what's happening? Here's the number. I'm going to call Bill and tell him to delay his and Eve's arrival for a few minutes.'

Outside, there was the bridal huddle—the vicar, Jasmine, the flower-girls and their (now exhausted) mother.

She flashed the huddle a hostess smile, 'Just checking,' and speed-dialled Bill. Out of the corner of her eye, she watched Robin talking into his phone. No answer from Bill.

She dropped her phone into her bag. 'And?' she mouthed at Robin.

'Duncan's trying to find him,' he said.

Too late: the bridal car rolled up to the church gate and halted. At the best of times, the hat was a liability. Lara whipped it off, fled down the path and reached the car as Bill emerged from it.

'Andrew hasn't arrived,' she informed him, in a low, urgent voice. 'Go round the block. Turn your phone on.'

'Haven't got it,' he said, shielding Eve from Lara.

'OK. Another five minutes.' He bent over and said to the still, white figure, 'Evie, Andrew's been held up. Shall we go and have a pint?'

Eyes huge, very pale under the veil, Eve replied, 'Don't, Dad.'

Lara bent over and said lovingly, 'Evie, it'll be fine.'

Eve gave her a terrified look, which almost broke her heart.

'Evie,' she repeated. 'It's fine.'

Mobile to ear, Robin paced up and down by the yew hedge. 'Can't reach anyone yet, Lara.'

The bridal car eased out of sight as a second car drove up at full pelt, disgorging Duncan. He ran up the path.

Lara went cold, then hot.

Jasmine had obviously taken in the situation. 'Duncan,' she called, and hastened towards him with Lara close behind her. 'What's going on?'

'It's all right,' he said. 'He's on his way. He was stuck in traffic.'

'But why wasn't he with you?' asked Jasmine, going red then white.

'Because . . .' Duncan's lips tightened. 'Because . . .'

Robin came up. 'Do you need anything done?'

'Take Lara back inside,' said Duncan. 'I'll mastermind the rest.'

'Good idea,' said Robin. 'I'll brief the vicar.'

'How could Andrew be so cruel? So stupid?' cried Lara, driven beyond endurance. 'Do you realize that girl is in there?'

There was a tiny shocked silence, Jasmine, Duncan, Robin and she, all acknowledging that they had colluded . . . in what? Each of them, she thought, would draw their own conclusions. It was a moment of utmost clarity, sharpness and tension. Then it passed.

'The traffic *is* terrible,' said Duncan.

'Yes, of course,' said Jasmine. 'Are you sure he's on his way now?'

'Absolutely.' Duncan looked shattered, with great circles under his eyes. 'I've just talked to him. He was . . . diverted. But it's all fine now.'

Robin came back to them, and placed his hand under Lara's elbow. It was confident, intimate gesture. Not so much you-are-mine but we-are-each-other's. Observing it, Jasmine's eyes widened.

Robin said, 'Lara, I think we should go back inside. Everything's fine now.'

No one was to contradict the fiction. Nor would she wish it. Already everyone was rewriting the history of the moment to suit themselves. 'Everything's fine,' she agreed.

How typical of Lara, Jasmine thought, watching her stop in the church porch to put on her hat. She always wanted to shield them.

Eve must be feeling terrible, frightened, even. So thinking, her anger mounted against Andrew. Against men. No, not men. Against the thoughtless and the selfish.

What had Duncan been thinking of, letting Andrew off the rein on his wedding day? A crisis, she sensed, had taken place but, since she and Duncan were not talking, she was never going to know what it was. Still, she had an idea of what might have happened. And she wondered how much of the smoothing over (if it *had* happened) had been due to Duncan.

Duncan was talking to the vicar, and she permitted herself a quick look. Mistake. She could not take her eyes off him. It was no use denying it.

A taxi drew up and disgorged Andrew—wildly handsome in his wedding outfit—and Duncan hurried down the path to greet him.

Her hand, holding the bouquet ever tighter, was damp with apprehension.

'Sorry, sorry,' Andrew apologized to the vicar. 'The traffic.'

He looked resolved she thought, but haunted.

The vicar wasn't pleased, but he had seen it all before.

The two men swept past her into the church.

Duncan didn't look at her once ... To her shame, this made her hot with anger.

Stop it, Jasmine. She adjusted her dress. She

adjusted her spirit and expectations. Of necessity, all three had to be uncrushed and looking good.

For the second time, the wedding car made its approach up to the church and stopped. Eve emerged, and a lump flew into Jasmine's throat. The bride, the lovely bride: shrouded in her veil and the dress that flowed so subtly, she seemed unearthly.

At the doorway to the church, Eve stooped to say something to the flower-girls, then leaned over to kiss Jasmine's cheek. 'Hey,' she said softly. Tears started into Jasmine's eyes.

No, she thought. *Mascara.*

The bride stepped forward and the curious, avid gazes of the guests locked on the figure poised in the door—a wraith from another dimension. One that evoked such deep desires and hope. Then, with a shock, Jasmine saw who was sitting directly in view of the bridal party. Eve would have seen Fern too. *That* was why Fern had positioned herself there.

Nothing to be done but go on.

She stepped into place behind her sister.

At the altar, Eve turned to give Jasmine her bouquet. As she did so, her gaze flickered down the aisle to where Fern sat. It lingered for a good ten seconds. Unmistakable. Then, turning to Andrew, she very deliberately laid her hand on his.

That gesture told Jasmine everything. Eve *knew*. Of course she knew. Her clever, striving sister had calculated that, if Fern was sitting miserably in a pew, it was she who was standing at the altar. Andrew was hers, and she had claimed him. That touch on her bridegroom's hand was her validation and act of possession.

In the vestry after the service, Eve and Andrew signed the register. In his first act as a husband, Andrew folded back Eve's veil to allow it to flow unimpeded down her back, and Jasmine prinked the hem of the dress.

The organist was working himself up for the Wedding March. Lara had tears on her cheeks. Dorothea was talking to Bill. When Jasmine handed Eve the bouquet, Eve placed her lips against her sister's ear: 'Get rid of her, Jas. Tell her to go from me.'

The procession re-formed, ready to return down the aisle. Duncan held out his arm to Jasmine. 'There's nothing for it, Jas, you'll have to take it.'

She ignored him. Instead, she said, 'Tell her to leave.'

'Who?'

'You know who I mean.'

The vicar tapped his finger against his lips.

The Wedding March sounded. Very loud and lovely.

*   *   *

The dinner and speeches were over and it had grown dark.

Duncan's had been short and very funny. 'Ladies and gentlemen,' he said. 'I want you to know that a lot of the things you have heard today about Andrew are not true.' He paused. 'Andrew is not a fluent Italian speaker. Never has been. Never will be, I suspect. But for the purposes of wooing Eve he turned into Dante. This was because he is a man of strategy and does his homework. He sent me on a mission to find out about Eve, and I duly reported back that she was passionate about Italy and the opera. He began to pepper his conversation with *"allora"* and *"andiamo"*. Unfortunately … I had reported back on the wrong girl …'

Much laughter.

The lights in the marquee glowed and the candles threw their radiant glow. It stole over the tables, over the flowers, the glass dishes heaped with silver dragées and the leftover food on the plates.

Jasmine watched Eve. Smiling, confident, in charge, being led to the dance floor by Andrew and taken into his arms.

Eve had made her bed and was going to lie on it. And very good she would be at it too.

What now?

Back to work. Do better. Tell Jason that the Branding Company needed to expand in the Asian market and why didn't they do something about it? Earn more money. Spend those two weeks on the dive. Think about whales. Dream about whales. *Do* something about whales.

'You're coming with me,' said Duncan. He had snuck up behind her and laid his hand flat against her scapula, as if to leave an imprint through the dusky pink dress.

'No.'

'Yes, you are.'

'I'll make a scene.'

'No, you won't.'

He took her hand and led her out of the marquee. Lamps had been lit by the entrance, and a row of them flanked the route down to the drive to guide guests to and from it. A few of the older ones were already drifting towards their cars.

'I can't hear myself *think* with that noise,' she overheard one elderly woman say to another. 'They must all go deaf.'

'Where are you taking me?' she demanded of Duncan.

'To the stream.'

'My dress.' She hoicked it up over her arm.

'Never mind the dress.'

'Typical,' she said.

'OK. If it's like that.' Duncan turned round and swept Jasmine up into his arms and strode across the lawn, bearing his pink burden.

For a second or two, she resisted. It was mad. It was romantic. It was ridiculous. But, unexpectedly, a light had burst into her life and she surrendered to it.

Down by the stream, moonlight spilled over the bank and the water shushed quietly over the hidden weed. Panting a little, he set her down. 'Couldn't do that for too far,' he observed.

'I'm not that heavy.'

'May I point out that it wasn't you who's just carried you for miles.'

The beauty of the night scene, the music in the background, the warm air . . . the sense she had of life hidden in the water, in the plants and the undergrowth was intoxicating.

'Listen,' she said. 'Not the music. The other things.'

'I can't hear anything.'

'Precisely. But it's there, the hidden bit of the garden.'

'When you've finished . . .'

The material at her wrist slid silkily over her skin, and the hem rippled around her ankles.

It was unlikely she would wear a dress like this ever again. But never again would she stand in a warm, moonlit garden and feel quite the same excruciating pain-pleasure of loving someone as she did Duncan.

'How did you get rid of Fern?' she asked.

'I called a taxi and put her into it. I told her if she didn't go I'd have to summon Security.'

'Security?'

'Well, it worked.'

'Poor girl.' She had probably been desperate to get one last sighting, Jasmine thought. Maybe she had reckoned that, on seeing her, Andrew would abandon his bride and they would steal off together through the golden day. Maybe Fern had had to experience the pain of watching Andrew marry someone else to finish it.

One of those scenarios? Some of them? All of them? Human motives were so layered and complicated, and she could not begin to fathom her own.

Duncan cleared his throat. 'Jasmine, can we begin again?'

As quickly as it had arrived, the light was doused. She was behaving like a teenager after too much to drink. She was being *deeply* stupid. Seduced by the gesture. (A lovely gesture, though.)

'I know what you're thinking,' he said.

'Do you?'

'You're thinking, He's a man made of sand.' He shoved his hands into his pockets. 'I want to persuade you that you're wrong.' His shoes making a soft shuffle in the grass, he marched up and down the bank. 'I knew about Fern. Or, rather, I suspected. Eventually I asked Andrew what was going on. He told me the thing with Fern had taken him by storm. He was completely bewildered. He begged me to help him deal with it and get him through to the wedding. The poor bugger was doubly poleaxed because he's so used to planning things down to the last detail, and this was a detail he hadn't predicted. He didn't ever not want to marry Eve.'

She listened with bowed head. 'Not good enough. *Not.*'

'Things aren't always black and white.'

She turned on him. 'That was the cruellest of things. Of all people, Eve needs stability and fidelity, not just sexual but the total package . . . It's a result of . . . you know, our background.'

'Oh, yes, I do. I'm never allowed to forget it. But, Jas, you aren't the only children who've had a hole rammed into their lives. The world is stuffed with them, and far worse stories.'

She watched him tramp up and down. Up and down. His form was silhouetted in the moonlight.

He stopped and swung round to face her. 'Here's the thing. I'll give you those things, Jasmine. I *gave* you those things but you didn't see it like that.'

Her heart performed a peculiar manoeuvre— as if it made to leap out of her chest, then scuttled back into position.

'I want you back. I can't live with you but I certainly can't live without you, and I don't see why the situation with Eve and Andrew should dictate what happens to us.'

'It was other things, too,' she said.

'I know, and I've thought about it. First off, trust. You could trust me again. That's a fact.'

Could she? Why was he answering the questions

for her? He sounded so confident, so up himself, and she stifled a weary giggle. Wasn't that just like him? Him and Andrew. Lords of the universe, both (with feet of clay).

However, that did not stop her loving him. (She would never love Andrew in a sisterly way now.) That fact was unassailable and non-negotiable. The question was: would Duncan be in her life or not?

He took both her hands in his and kissed each in turn. 'Here's how I see it.'

His lips fell on her starved flesh and she was amazed by the power and velocity of her physical reaction. It was as if she had been hit with a mallet. A hundred thousand stars orbited around her head.

'Marry me, Jasmine.'

'*What?*'

'You heard.'

'Marry you? But you don't believe in it.'

He sighed heavily. 'For you, I do.' He pulled her to him and tipped back her head. 'For you, Jasmine, but ...'

She murmured, 'There's always a "but" ...'

'But I refuse to go through this pantomime.' He gestured to the marquee. 'If you want to marry me, if you say yes, we'll sneak off to a register office, just you and me.'

His hands snaked up into her hair and tugged none-too-gently at it in the old way. She stared up into his face, searching. He kissed her.

Chapter Twenty-seven

It was another of those golden days.

The air was filled with seeds on the wing—dandelion, sycamore, thistle—jostling for a place and a future in next year's cycle. Landing here, there, everywhere.

Bill was dressed in his usual shabby trousers and grey sweater, which, because it was warm, he peeled off and tied around his waist. On the terrace, Sarah was giving Robin coffee. ('You're a brave man,' Lara had teased. 'Sarah's coffee . . .')

Up to the right, the area where the marquee had been was almost healed of the scars left by its occupation. In the beds, the summer blooms of roses and lavender had been replaced by dahlias—'Rip City', 'Chat Noir'—the deep reds and crimsons that Bill loved.

The sun was lower, forcing her to shield her eyes.

She thought of the shades of those who had lived there, and known the place as well as they knew their own hands and, because they had loved it, had left their stamp in the contour of the land.

She remembered, too, Robin coming to find her by the stream as the last wedding guests had stumbled and rolled out of the marquee. Dawn was breaking and, breathless with exhaustion but happy, she had taken off her shoes and was walking through the damp, whippy grass.

Suddenly he had come up behind her. 'Lara?'

She'd turned . . . and the beat of the garden's other life had never been louder. 'Robin.'

He hadn't said any more. He didn't need to.

Bill came to a halt by the patch where the wild flowers grew. 'What do you think?' It was a vantage spot. It was sheltered. It needed a tree.

Her gaze swept over the lawn, down the stream and up to the house. 'You'll be able to see it from the house.'

'That's what I reckoned,' he said.

'Well, then.' She smiled encouragement.

He handed Lara a spade and picked up a shovel—they had been leaning ready for use against the wall. 'Sure?'

'Sure.'

The spade's handle was encrusted with soil, which smeared over her hands. She didn't care.

By the time they had dug a hole approximately three foot square, she was panting.

'OK.' Bill abandoned the shovel. He bent over and clipped the string that was holding sacking in place around the root bole of the sapling lying on the grass. 'Can you give me a hand?'

Together they lifted it into place and, taking extreme care, spread out the roots before partially filling in the hole. 'Hang on.' Bill drove in a stake and tied the sapling to it.

In a few minutes the task was completed.

It hadn't taken long. Yet it had taken years.

They stepped back to survey their handiwork.

'I think the cherry was the best choice,' he said. 'Definitely.'

They had talked *acer*, *prunus*, olive even, batting the subject this way and that until they had reached agreement.

'As long as you ordered the white one.'

'I did.'

Then they were silent.

Eventually, Bill said, 'Louis's tree.'

She glanced at him. 'Thank you.'

He shook his head and she knew he was finding it difficult to speak. As she was.

For a second or two, Lara had to fight for calm. She thought of the shades who had lived there and felt the rawness of pure jealousy. *They had lived.* Louis had not. But, at least, some aspect of him would be at Membury, floating in the sunshine like the wind-borne seeds, growing alongside the rosemary and the myrtle, blossoming as the tree flourished. She would think of him at those times. And when the wind blew and the cold came, which they would, she would think of him then, too.

The tiny boy who had never lived.

Acknowledgements

I consulted many books in the writing of this one, chief among them the inspirational works of Dorothy Rowe. I hope that she does not mind that I borrowed some of her wisdom for my character, Lara.

Many thanks are due. To Garry Scobie for his (hilarious) information on school proms. To Lisa Comfort (www.sewoverit.com) for her vital input on making a wedding dress. To Camilla Grey, who introduced me to the world of branding and took infinite trouble. Any mistakes are mine. To the kind, patient friends who held my hand. They know who they are. To my dazzling publisher, Louise Moore, to Alice Shepherd, Jo Wickham, Claire Purcell and the rest of the five-star editorial, publicity, sales and marketing teams at Penguin. To Hazel Orme, for her never-failing tact and expertise. To my agent Mark Lucas, a huge ongoing thank-you, which is also due to Benjamin, Adam and Eleanor: the home team.

rest home for old gentlemen, I'd scare the living shits out of you lot. If this was the *Express*, and not just a load of old toilet-paper, I'd have fired you and your snotty little friends as soon as I set eyes on you.'

'I'll go and do the captions,' said Lovebold, edging towards the door.

' "String Symphony"! God give me strength!'

'You tell me what you want, Reg, and I'll do it.'

Mounce swung round in his chair indignantly.

'Oh, thanks!' he said. 'I'm not your wet nurse, you know. I'm not your private arse-wiper. Try and use a bit of initiative, sonny! You wouldn't have lasted a week on the old *West Midlands Post*. You know what I did once on the *Post*?'

'You mean when you tried to get through a police cordon by saying ... ?'

'I mean when I practically breezed through a police cordon by saying I was the Home Office pathologist! Know how I got my job on this paper?'

'You just walked in off the street ...'

'I just walked in off the street and told them to give it to me! Still, I'm wasting my breath telling all this to a pinhead like you.'

Mounce had re-immersed himself in the agency pictures. Very quickly Lovebold faded through the door and closed it behind him.

'Lovebold!' shouted Mounce. 'Come back here, Lovebold!'

Lovebold came back into the room, sighing noiselessly.

'Lend me a fiver, will you?' said Mounce.

Lovebold sighed again.

'Can't, I'm afraid, Reg,' he said.

'Come on!'

'I haven't got a fiver on me, Reg,' said Lovebold, pulling a single pound-note out of his back-pocket and showing Mounce the empty lining. Mounce took the pound.

'Don't give me this crap,' he said. 'Show me what you've got in your other pockets.'

'Oh, come on now, Reg. Be reasonable.'

'Let's see what you've got in your jacket pockets, for a start.'

'All right,' said Lovebold wearily. He took a small, tightly-folded bundle of notes out of his breast pocket, and counted off four.

'You can't fool Uncle Reggy,' said Mounce.

Lovebold fetched an expenses chit, while the matter was still fresh in Mounce's mind, and wrote down at random on it two nights' expenses in Wolverhampton, with lunches and entertainment for contacts, adding up to £6 8s 4d. He gave it to Mounce to sign. Mounce folded his hands and closed his eyes.

'For what we are about to receive,' he said, 'may the Lord make us truly thankful.'

A bluff, friendly, man-to-man relationship with your staff, he reflected as he scribbled his signature; that was the way to do it. A bit of bluster – one's staff respected it. A little turning of the old blind eye – they loved you for it. And if they ever took it into their heads to let you down you could always get them the boot for fiddling their exes.

Towards lunchtime the sky grew lighter again, and when old Eddy Moulton woke up just before one o'clock he had the impression that it was the following day. The days went very fast when you were old, he reflected. He began to copy out a piece of political intelligence about the intentions of Lord Derby.

It was the noise of Dyson coming in that had woken him.

'Did somebody manage to get some copy out of Morley?' asked Dyson. He sounded very cheerful. His arrival seemed to bring the bustle of the outside world into the room.

'Promised for tomorrow,' said somebody, looking up from a book he was reading for review. 'How did your thing go?'

'Oh, marvellously! I adore broadcasting; I really feel in my element. Do you know, Bob, I'm always sorry to get to the end of the script. I'd like to go on all day.'

He hung up his coat, and rubbed his hands together vigorously, full of smiles.

'I feel completely recharged, Bob,' he said. 'A tremendous sense of psychic energy. This afternoon I'm going to have a blitz on crosswords.'

He sat down at his desk, and began to stack papers together, and shuffle the stacks into a different order.

'As a matter of fact, Bob,' he said, 'I'm getting quite a following in West Africa. The producer had a letter this week from some girl in Conakry, of all places, asking for my photograph. Of course, I shan't send her one.'

'Why not?'

'Do you think I ought to, Bob? Perhaps I should. You think I should, do you?'

'I don't see why not.'

'Well, you know, it seems a bit film-starrish. I don't know whether I've got time to mess about sending pictures of myself out.'

Bob yawned.

'How about some lunch?' he said.

'All right. I mean, it's not as if I had a publicity manager. I am rather pushed. But you think I should?'

'Sure. Where shall we go? The Gates?'

'If we must, I suppose. Perhaps it would be rather mean to disappoint her. Eddy, we're going to the Gates. Will you keep an eye on things?'

One by one and two by two the sober, responsible men emerged from the main door again to go out for lunch. The Foreign Editor, the Literary Editor, the Diplomatic Correspondent, and the Rugby Football Correspondent made up a party to share a taxi to the Garrick. Mr Dancer, the Chief Sub-Editor, went to a workmen's café in Whitefriars Street. The senior advertising men, swishing rolled umbrellas, strolled grandly off to sip hock at El Vino's. The Editor shuffled out, unnoticed by anyone, and caught a number fifteen bus to the Athenaeum.

At the Gates of Jerusalem, just round the corner from Hand and Ball Court, Bob and Dyson found Bill Waddy, the News Editor, with Mike Sparrow, Ralph Absalom, Ted Hurwitz, and Andy Royle. It was that sort of set which went there. Gareth Holmroyd, the Assistant Industrial Editor, was buying stout for Lucy from the Library and Pat Selig, the woman's page sub. Round the far side of the bar Mounce was talking to a girl with brown eyes and straight blonde hair. He raised his glass to Bob and Dyson, and winked. It was the sort of pub where you'd expect to find the Waddy-Absalom-Hurwitz set, and Gareth Holmroyd, and Mounce leaning over some rather plain girl.

Bill Waddy was telling a story.

'Anyway,' he said, 'I said to this bloke in the colonel's pips, "Where the blazes are we . . . ?" John, Bob, what are you drinking?'

'No, no,' said Dyson. 'Let me get these.'

'No, no, I'm in the chair.'

'No, no, I insist.'

'No, no, certainly not. Mrs Dunfee !'

Mrs Dunfee, busy pouring more vodka for Mounce's girl, gave no acknowledgment.

'Anyway,' said Bill Waddy, 'so I said to this chap, who let me say was in the uniform of a full colonel, "Where the dickens are we . . . ?" '

'Yes?' said Mrs Dunfee.

'Oh . . . two more bitters, please, Mrs Dunfee. Pints?'

'Half for me, please, Bill,' said Dyson.

'Half for me, too,' said Bob.

'Two halves, Mrs Dunfee. Anyway, so I said – this bloke was in the uniform of a full colonel, I should point out . . .'

'Two-and-twopence,' said Mrs Dunfee.

'I said to him . . . I've only got a pound note, I'm afraid, Mrs Dunfee . . . I said to him . . .'

'You've got the twopence.'

'So I have. Anyway, so I said to him . . .'

'Thanks, Bill,' said Dyson, picking up his beer. 'Cheers.'

'Cheers,' said Bill Waddy.

'Cheers,' said Bob.

'Cheers,' said Bill Waddy. 'Anyway, so I said to this bloke . . .'

'Where was all this, Bill?' asked Dyson.

'Well, that's just what I asked this laddie in the colonel's uniform.'

'Oh, I'm sorry, Bill.'

'I said, "Where the hell are we, Colonel?" And *he* said, "I haven't the faintest idea!"'

'Fantastic,' said Dyson. 'Bob, can I get you a sandwich?'

Bob and Dyson drifted over to the sandwich counter.

'Perhaps I could ask Mounce to get one of his people to take some pictures of me,' said Dyson, gazing absently across the bar at Mounce.

'He's such a tit,' said Bob.

'Bob, why don't you do some broadcasting? We could easily fix something up for you at Bush House.'

'I don't think I'd like it, thanks, John.'

'You'd love it. I get a terrific kick out of feeling I'm known in parts of West Africa. I'll tell you something I've never told anyone, Bob : I'd like to be one of those terrible people you see airing their views about life on television.'

'So you keep saying, John. I think it's a horrible idea.'

'But think of it in practical terms, Bob! A hundred guineas an appearance and no script to write!'

'Even so.'

Dyson looked at Bob admiringly.

'There's a saintly streak in you, Bob,' he said, 'which I've noticed before. And of course you write like an angel. Another half?'

By half past two most of the sober, responsible men had returned to Hand and Ball Court, walking a little more slowly now as the day began to tell upon them. By three o'clock a certain amount of writing was being done. Bob was writing a book review for the *New Statesman*; Dyson a radio-script on oil prospecting for the schools' programmes. Locked away in his office on the fourth floor, the Editor was also writing. The room was chaotic. The raised surfaces were all covered with wrinkled page proofs and sheaves of yellowing galleys; the floor with stacks of books, and with old framed photographs which had fallen off the walls. They were of former editors, and ranked groups of schoolboys, dons, and officers. On a table in the corner stood a number of silver cups won by various athletics and boxing teams got up among the paper's staff; the Editor's raincoat and hat had been thrown down on top of them. The desk had disappeared beneath papers a long time ago. The Editor had abandoned it, and moved to a table against the wall, where he was typing very rapidly with two fingers on a small old-fashioned portable.

Mr Dancer, *he wrote.* PRIVATE AND CONFIDENTIAL.

I have been giving further thought to the eternal problem of how we may best *put the skids under* our friend Mounce. As I have stressed before, I have no experience of summoning employees to my office and telling them that they are fired, and after long and careful consideration I must tell you that I see no prospect of finding the courage to start – particularly not with Mounce, whom I find very frightening indeed. Besides, it would be against the whole spirit of this office, where we have always laid great stress upon security of employment. But in the case of Mounce, who has turned out to be our greatest mistake since Pavey-Smith (do you remember Pavey-Smith? He got the canteen manageress with child, obtained a refrigerator by fraud, charged dinner for eight at the Savoy to the paper, and then – mercifully – absconded with three months salary in advance), I believe we should be justified in adopting *guerrilla tactics.* This is to say, I think we might try *persecuting* him, within the limits imposed by our consciences and by ordinary discretion, in the hope that he will spontaneously resign, and disappear from our lives, taking with him what, if we are careful, need be only a comparatively small amount of the firm's money. As to *how* we should persecute him, I must confess that I have no idea. I am sure you will be able to think of something suitable; the world has come very low if a Chief Sub-Editor cannot think of discreet ways of making a man's life a burden to him. I have great faith in your abilities in this direction, and I shall give you full backing in any scheme, provided that it does not involve (a) my coming face to face with Mounce, (b) physical violence, (c) putting ourselves in any morally false position, or (d) giving any appearance thereof. I await your thoughts on the matter with impatience.

The Editor folded the letter up, crammed it into a small brown envelope on which he wrote 'B. D. Dancer Esqre' and pushed it through a sort of serving hatch to his secretary in the outer office. During office hours the passing of notes through this hatch was his only form of communication with the world.

'I always feel so sleepy in the middle of the afternoon,' said Dyson in the middle of the afternoon, yawning, and leaning back in his chair with his hands linked behind his head. 'I must cut out this beer for lunch. My system can't take it, at my age.'

'Neither can mine, at my age,' said Bob, yawning also.

'How old are you exactly, Bob, as a matter of interest?'

'Twenty-nine.'

'My God, you're young! My *God*, you're young! Do you know how old I am, Bob? Have a guess.'

'Thirty-seven.'

'I suppose I've told you, have I?'

'Yes.'

Dyson rocked his chair back on its rear legs and gazed at the ceiling for a long while, yawning from time to time.

'Do you keep a stock of photographs of yourself, Bob?' he asked at last. 'To send out to producers and editors and so on?'

'No. I don't do much freelance work, John.'

Dyson pursed his lips and shook his head slowly.

'When you get to my age, Bob,' he said, 'with a wife and children, and a mortgage, you'll be working all the hours God made. Saturdays and Sundays. Morning, noon, and night. I can scarcely lift my eyes from my desk from one day's end to the next. I honestly sometimes wonder how long I can stand the pace. A journalist's finished at forty, of course.'

He went on staring at the ceiling, occasionally blinking thoughtfully, and yawning, and sometimes opening his eyes very wide, as if to exercise the skin around them. Bob brooded over his book review. 'Mr Berringer knows his New York,' he wrote. A wave of honesty passed over him, and he altered it to 'Mr Berringer appears to know his New York.' The wave of honesty was succeeded by a wave of professionalism, and he altered it back to 'Mr Berringer knows his New York.' He put a toffee into his mouth.

'You'll rot your teeth sucking those things all the time,' said Dyson, without taking his eyes off the ceiling, hearing the familiar rustle of Cellophane and the faint slopping of salivaed membranes. Bob did not reply. Old Eddy Moulton smacked his lips too in his sleep.

'God, I was going to have a blitz on the crosswords this afternoon,' said Dyson.

He yawned twice in succession.

'God, I can scarcely keep my eyes open,' he said.

At five o'clock Dyson got restless. He jumped up and began walking up and down the room. The whole building was at last fully alive. The sub-editors' room was full. The copytakers' typewriters were clattering. The leader-writers were writing leaders. There were queues at the tea-trolleys.

Dyson went out and bought the evening papers.

'I feel I must know what's going on in the world,' he said, perching himself on the corner of his desk to study them. 'Don't you feel that, Bob?'

'No.'

'I read all the papers every morning. I'd feel a definite sense of anxiety if I missed a single one of them. You don't read any of them, do you, Bob?'

'I read the cricket scores.'

'You're a shit, Bob. I don't know how you can bear to work in newspapers. Of course, you write like an angel.'

He fell silent, reading.

'Listen to this,' he said suddenly. ' "Darkness at Noon for Londoners. Freak weather conditions brought darkness to Central London streets this morning. Lights went on in shops and offices all over the City and West End, as the sky grew black. By mid-morning it looked as if night had fallen." '

He looked up at Bob expectantly.

'I know,' said Bob. 'I looked out of the window.'

Dyson started to read the paper again, grinning.

'You're a real shit, Bob, aren't you?' he said admiringly.

Just after eight o'clock the glass in all the windows started to vibrate. Here and there light shades and other thin metal fixtures burred faintly, or ticked, or rattled. In Dyson's department, deserted, and lit only by the yellow sodium light coming in through the windows from the street-lamps in Hand and Ball Court, a ruler sticking out over the edge of old Eddy Moulton's desk moved itself slowly sideways until it overbalanced and fell on the floor.

The great presses in the basement were running for the first edition.

Two

When Dyson had read the boys a story and kissed them good night, he settled himself in an armchair in the living-room to wait for dinner, and gazed up at a section of plaster which had broken away in the corner of the room and peeled back a large triangle of wallpaper. He had painted the wall only a month or two before, which made its decay particularly irritating.

'God strikes again,' he said bitterly.

'What?' said his wife, coming to the door in apron and rubber gloves, holding a mixing bowl.

'Jannie, you didn't pick at it or pull at it in any way, did you?'

'Pick at it or pull at it? How could I possibly pick at it or pull at it? I can't even reach it to stick it back.'

She disappeared back into the kitchen.

He wanted to say, you might have been trying to get cobwebs down with a broom, but he knew she wouldn't be able to hear in the kitchen. God, it irritated him when Jannie asked a question, and then walked out of earshot before he could reply! It was one of her most infuriating habits . . .

She was back in the doorway again.

'If you want to know,' she said, 'it's the damp getting in through that bald patch under the children's window where the stucco's come off. The plaster's sodden.'

Dyson sat back in his chair and drummed his fingers gloomily on the arm. God had his eye on the house, there was no doubt about it. Slowly but surely he was gathering it to his bosom. He was coming in through the walls as rain, up from the ground as rising damp, down through the chimney as birds, and moving in mysterious ways throughout the fabric as dry rot, green mould, mice and earwigs. Dyson won brief tactical advantages with Polyfilla and emulsion paint, only to find that God had accomplished some vast strategic infiltration behind his back. The sad truth, Dyson realized, was that it was an unfair fight. If God had been prepared to start square, and spend most of his time and energy, like Dyson, on keeping up the crossword stock and explaining the rudiments of British political life to Africans, Dyson could have given him a real run for his money.

The Dysons had bought an old house deliberately, when Jannie was carrying their second child, after long and shrewd reflection. They did not want to live in the suburbs, in an ugly suburban house with uncongenial suburban neighbours, miles from town. They decided to find a cheap Georgian or Regency house in some down-at-heel district near the centre. However depressed the district, if it was Georgian or Regency, and reasonably central, it would soon be colonized by the middle-classes. In this way they would secure an attractive and potentially fashionable house in the heart of London, at a price they could afford; be given credit by their friends for going to live among the working classes; acquire very shortly congenial middle-class neighbours of a similarly adventurous and intellectual outlook to themselves; and see their investment undergo a satisfactory and reassuring rise in value in the process.

In the early years of their marriage, while they had still been content to live in a rented flat, they had often noticed the sort of place they now had in mind. Driving about London they had passed innumerable Georgian and Regency terraces which needed only a lick of pastel-shaded paint to make them habitable. But now that they were actually looking for them a curious thing became apparent. The houses had vanished. It was like trying to return to a place one remembered from one's childhood; the innumerable terraces could not be found – the appearance of the world had subtly altered. There were Georgian and Regency houses, certainly, but they were occupied by the rich already. There was no shortage of slums; but they were not Georgian or Regency slums, and in any case the prices already seemed to have gone up beyond what they could afford in anticipation of the middle-class invasion, improbable as that Armageddon seemed in those flowerless grey streets where abandoned motor cars squatted on flat tyres, bleeding their rusty insides and torn upholstery into the gutter around them. The houses they had seen belonged not to the real world at all, but to the world one glimpses out of the corner of one's eye, which vanishes when one turns to look.

Little by little they made concessions to themselves, swinging from each last concession to reach the next. They decided that they were prepared to settle for an Early Victorian house, provided it were central. Then they agreed that they were prepared to go a little way out, provided they could find an Early Victorian house. Like Tarzan swinging himself from branch to branch through the jungle, Dyson and his wife swung themselves farther and farther out from the centre of London, and farther and farther on through the nineteenth century, until they arrived at the year 1887, and number 43 Spadina Road, s.w.23. There the descending curve of demand at last met the unyielding base-line of supply. Looked at in one way, what they had acquired was an ugly suburban house with uncongenial neighbours, miles from town, which had cost all the money they could raise by mortgage, plus all the savings and borrowings they had intended to use for modernization and repair. But they didn't look at it in that way. And in any case, the uncongenial neighbours would soon be driven out by the great influx of congenial architects, journalists, civil servants, and university lecturers who would come flooding in to follow the Dysons' example, and who would float the whole district off the bottom and up to the £2,500 a year mark.

But the middle classes did not come to Spadina Road, s.w.23. Number 41, the house next door to the Dysons', continued to be occupied by Mr Cox, who was a lorry-driver, and by Mr Cox's wife and three children, his sister and brother-in-law and their three children, another sister who was a bit soft in the head, and Mrs Cox senior. Number 45, on the other side, went not up but down. It was owned by two elderly sisters. One of them died, the other was put in the asylum, and the house was bought by a West Indian landlord who broke it up into flats. Dyson was entirely in favour of both the working classes and West Indians. All the same, the particular West Indians and members of the working class living next door to him seemed to be very hard to get to know. And he couldn't help feeling that the refusal of the middle classes to follow his example and move to Spadina Road was a reflection on his judgment. He invited friends and colleagues out at the weekends to see for themselves the delights of the district. They agreed that s.w.23 had a village-like atmosphere and a distinct character of its own. They agreed that if you cut through the back-streets to the Tube, and the District Line was running normally, you could be in Fleet Street in under the hour. They agreed that Ecosse St George was a wonderful West Indian name, and that Ecosse St George and his wife Princess were wonderful characters to have for neighbours. But they did not move to Spadina Road.

A man described as a surveyor moved into number 84, it was true. The Dysons invited him to dinner as soon as they heard, and told him all he needed to know about the district – where the only good butcher was, what to do about the little boys who came in at night and shat in one's basement area. But it became apparent that whatever it was the man surveyed, he surveyed most of it through the bottom of a glass. He was on his way down in the world, like Spadina Road itself. He did not paint his house a pastel colour, and after a couple of evenings of watching his eyes become more and more like unfocused brown poached eggs, Dyson began to feel that the tone of the street had been higher without him. There was no doubt about it; God was leaning on Spadina Road, s.w.23.

'Incidentally,' said Jannie, reappearing in the doorway, 'they've been throwing stuff over the wall again.'

Dyson jumped to his feet, the adrenalin instantly flushing into his bloodstream.

'Which of them was it?' he demanded excitedly.

'I didn't see them – I just found it there.'

'You didn't touch it?'

'No.'

'You left it exactly as it was?'

'Yes, of course.'

'When I go out there now I'll find it *exactly* as it landed?'

'Yes, yes, yes. It's just beyond the second apple-tree.'

Dyson rushed out into the garden, without stopping to find a torch. It was a long, thin garden, set with blighted, infertile fruit trees which cowered between the yellow brick walls like sick dogs in an exercise yard. Dyson stumbled over loose bricks in the rank grass. There was a vague, yellowy urban nightglow in the air, and Dyson found what he was looking for at once. He got down on his hands and knees to examine it more closely, scarcely aware of the wetness of the grass. Old tin cans – twenty or thirty of them. Old Long Life beer cans. Dyson clenched his fists, and snarled aloud with rage. Not loudly, but definitely aloud.

He wouldn't have it. God knows he was kicked around by everyone, but he wasn't going to have his own garden treated as a tip. Positive action was going to have to be taken. But against whom? That was the question. Was the stuff coming from the Coxes' side or the West Indians'? The garden was so narrow it was impossible to tell.

He didn't think it was the West Indians. He didn't know, of course. But he didn't want to be the sort of man who went round believing that his West Indian neighbours were throwing old beer cans into his garden. That wasn't the sort of person he was at all. If by some chance it *was* the West Indians, then tact was called for. A friendly word of advice, no more – and he didn't want to raise the matter with them at all unless he was absolutely sure.

But if it was the Coxes . . . ! Well, by God, he wasn't putting up with this sort of nonsense from the Coxes! He'd asked Cox about it point blank, and Cox had denied it. But that proved nothing. If it was the Coxes he would get an injunction. He would damned well go round and post a load of rubbish through their letter-box.

He examined the position of the cans carefully. They were slightly nearer the West Indian wall, but that proved nothing in itself. They were quite widely scattered. Now that was interesting. They would scarcely have been thrown over one by one; someone must have brought them out of the house in a box, and shot them over in one load. Since they were now scattered it argued a long trajectory. And as Dyson peered at them in the faint jaundiced light it seemed to him that they were to some extent radiating out from an epicentre on the Coxes' side. They were! They had hit the ground on the Coxes' side first – he could see some sort of darker mark in the grass! – and bounced towards the West Indian side, scattering as they went!

In an excess of justified rage, now that he could permit himself some really justified rage, Dyson scooped up as many of the cans as he could and flung them back over the Coxes' wall. Some of them rang out against stones or bricks as they landed. The noise made Dyson hesitate. He had flung enough back to teach the Coxes a lesson, he decided; he would put the rest in the dustbin. He bent down to gather them up. But at that moment he thought he heard the Coxes' back door open. He decided that it would be better to collect up the rest of the cans in the daylight, when he could see what he was doing, and he straightened up and walked briskly back to the house. In his haste he missed his footing on the second of the wooden steps up to the kitchen door, and trod on the first with unnatural heaviness. It collapsed beneath his foot, with a scrunch of considerable self-satisfaction, as if God had been waiting for that little opportunity for some time.

Bob crept upstairs and let himself into his flat as quietly as he could, in the hope that Mrs Mounce wouldn't hear that he had come in. She didn't always hear; it was worth a try. The flat was dark and cold. He took off his shoes and walked softly about in his overcoat, turning on the Anglepoise light over the desk, and various lamps made out of old brandy bottles. He found a cold, dusty shilling behind the jar of multicoloured spills on the mantelpiece, and lit the gas-fire. Then he drew the curtains, and put a long-playing record of someone's dreaming strings on the gramophone, with the volume turned down very low. He looked round the room. It honestly didn't look too bad.

What did he have in stock to go with the chops for dinner? Still in his overcoat and socks, he went across and opened the kitchenette up to look. His gaze wandered vaguely along the shelf. The shelf was lined with old newspaper, and the sight of the newspaper, still greyly excited about the daily trivia of six months before, made him feel suddenly dismal. My God, he thought, I must find another flat, I really must. He lit a cigarette, and got down the tin of brown sugar. He drifted across to the mirror over the bookcase and looked at his reflection, holding the cigarette in his left hand, and eating a spoonful of sugar with his right.

He looked a bit tired, he thought. Been getting a little too much sleep recently, perhaps. Coming home and watching the television, instead of refreshing mind and spirit at the cinema. He was also getting a little paunchy, a little soft around the face. He ate another spoonful of sugar, and smiled experimentally. He had rather prominent eyelids, which came down when he smiled and made him look even sleepier than usual.

It was terrible to be getting paunchy at twenty-nine. He had been young all his life, and now suddenly youth seemed to be leaking out of him. He ate another spoonful of sugar. He'd have to go swimming at the St Bride's Institute in the lunch-hour occasionally with Ralph Absalom and that crowd. A few lengths a week – soon get the weight down. But my God, he thought, to find the fabric was beginning to need attention already, with another forty or so years still to go!

There was a soft scratching at the door. Mrs Mounce *had* heard him come in. He ate some more sugar, and looked at himself sombrely in the mirror.

'Bob?' said Mrs Mounce quietly.

Bob sighed.

'Bob?' said Mrs Mounce, rather anxiously.

He went across and opened the door.

'Hello,' he said, with polite surprise.

'Bob, darling,' said Mrs Mounce, holding a cigarette in her specially sophisticated way, with the whole flat of the hand upraised beside the face, as if for a one-handed salaam. 'Am I disturbing?'

Her bright little brown eyes looked past him into the room to see if he had a visitor.

'Come in,' said Bob.

'I really just looked in to see if you could possibly spare me some matches, darling,' she said, gliding across to the armchair and immediately curling herself up in it with her legs beneath her. She was wearing trousers, noted Bob, with relief. Mrs Mounce's knees and thighs were beginning to exercise a definite hold over him.

'I wouldn't say no to a drink, sweetest,' she said.

'There's nothing to drink,' said Bob. 'You can have a spoonful of sugar, if you like.'

'*Sweetest!*' she protested.

Bob pulled the chair away from the desk and sat down on it back to front, like a cautious lion-tamer. He nibbled another half spoonful of sugar.

'Reg working late?' he said.

'He's away overnight on a business trip.'

'Oh.'

'Did I hear a naughty note in your voice, darling?'

'No.'

'Because I shall have my door bolted and barred, sweetest, never you fear. I'll tell you that now.'

'Oh, yes?'

'I know you men.'

She laughed, and blew out smoke knowingly. Bob licked a few loose grains of sugar off the back of the spoon.

'There's not much you can teach me about men, darling,' she said.

'No?' said Bob absently. He was wondering exactly how old she was. About forty, he would have supposed, but in rather better working order than he was himself. She was slight and spry, with beady brown eyes. She had sharply pointed breasts, or at any rate a sharply pointed brassière, and a sharply pointed nose, around which the rest of her face gathered itself expectantly, the upper lip lifting to reveal two sharp upper incisors like a beaver's. She smoked almost continuously, the right hand poised in its salaam, the left hand brought across the body to support the right elbow.

'I've had such an awful day, darling,' she said.

'Really?' said Bob. The room was getting quite warm. He took off his overcoat and hung it up behind the door, then lay down on the bed, which served as a divan, with his cigarette and his tin of sugar.

'Don't you want to hear about my awful day?' she asked.

'Yes, yes,' said Bob. 'Tell me about your awful day.'

'Try and look interested, darling.'

'I am looking interested.'

'There's no earthly reason why you should have to listen to my troubles, of course, if you don't want to.'

'I do.'

She thought.

'Well, we've got the builders upstairs doing one or two tiny things which I should have thought could have been finished in a week, and they've been up there *seven* weeks now, and still not a *sign*! Dotty's been peering out of her door all day, as if it was *my* fault! As if I wanted them hanging around for two months—as if *I* asked them to hammer on the pipes ... !'

Bob let it wash over him, murmuring sympathetically from time to time, and spooning individual grains of sugar out of the tin to crunch. Mrs Mounce always had the builders in, and Dotty was always peering out of her door, a single, doubtful eye at the crack, because she owned the house, and no doubt wanted to keep some faint track on what was happening to it. Dotty's real name was Avdotya, Mrs Avdotya Stypulkowski, but people didn't want to make fools of themselves by going round calling someone Avdotya, and anyway she was rather dotty—rather old and rather Polish, and not entirely able to understand what was going on around her. Certainly she couldn't understand what was happening to her house.

The house was divided into seven furnished flats – one in the basement, and two on each of the other three floors. Mrs Stypulkowski lived in one of the ground-floor flats herself, and Bob in one of the pair on the first floor. The Mounces had first come to the house at Bob's suggestion, when Reg arrived from the provinces to become Pictures Editor. The ground-floor flat next to Dotty's was empty; they had moved in gratefully. Then gradually they had begun to colonize the house. First of all they had annexed the flat on the first floor, next to Bob's. Then they had taken over each of the top-floor flats in turn. How they had got rid of the previous tenants Bob did not know, nor what arrangements they had come to with Dotty about the rent. Were they really paying her the full rent for all four flats? Or had Mrs Mounce talked her into accepting a wholesale price? It was Mrs Mounce who was the driving force behind this expansionism. Her husband was scarcely ever there; more and more often he was away for odd nights and whole weekends, on freelance jobs, perhaps to pay the extra rent. What did she want with the four flats? She didn't sublet them. She never had friends to stay. She had no children – she told Bob once that she was unable to conceive. She went up and down the common stairs all day with a bunch of Yale keys, letting herself in and out of her colonies. Dotty stood with her door on the ground floor open a crack, watching her silently. A regular force of builders lived in the house almost permanently, moving slowly from flat to flat. They seemed to specialize in hardboard work. They installed hardboard partitions, covered up mantelpieces with hardboard panels, constructed hardboard kitchen units. They turned one of the second-floor flats into a den for Mr Mounce, by installing a hardboard hi-fi unit, and a suite of hardboard desks. They converted the first-floor flat next to Bob's into a hardboard bar, with concealed lighting behind hardboard pelmets. On Sunday mornings when Mr Mounce was at home Bob would sometimes be invited into the bar for a drink. Reg would stand behind the counter and dispense vodkas, then lean over it like a philosophical barman and talk about what a lot of crap it was that people talked these days, while Bob and Mrs Mounce perched up on cocktail stools, their knees tangling and untangling a foot or two in front of Reg's nose, and all around them Mrs Stypulkowski's original furnishings mouldered on unchanged. Occasionally the Mounces gave Saturday-night parties, to which they invited a number of other couples rather like themselves – large, melancholic men with small, bright wives – who all got drunk very quickly. The small, bright wives shrieked with laughter and showed their suspenders. The large, melancholic men leaned heavily on the small, bright wives and felt their bottoms. Bob, who was always invited, usually left at about this point, conscious that it was not suitable entertainment for the young. Once when he got back to his flat he found that he had left the door open and that a large, melancholic man and a small, bright wife were lying on his bed. He apologized for intruding, and went out for a walk while they finished. In the hall he found Dotty peering through the crack of her door. Silently, accusingly, the single troubled eye followed him down the stairs. 'I'm sorry,' said Bob helplessly to the eye. It was he who had brought the Mounces into the house. One day, he knew, the white-faced wholesale butcher in the basement would be edged out. Sooner or later he would leave himself. After that it would not be long before the hardboard men moved into Dotty's flat, to turn it into a sewing-room or a rumpus-room, and Dotty found herself out on the pavement with her three cats, her silver crucifix, her late husband's sword and medals, the active sympathy of the Polish Ex-Combatants' Association, and no house.

Bob became aware that a question had been asked. He took the sugar-spoon out of his mouth.

'I beg your pardon?' he said.

'I said, have you eaten, darling?' said Mrs Mounce.

'No.'

'*Sweetest!* You must be *starving*!'

She jumped out of her armchair and snaked across to

the kitchenette, rolling her bottom importantly.

'What are you going to do?' asked Bob anxiously.

'I'm going to cook your supper, pet.'

Bob sat up quickly on the edge of the bed.

'I don't know about that,' he said.

'Just put your feet up, darling, and tell me what there is.'

'Well, look, I don't know about this.'

She came twinkling across, seized his legs, and put them back on the bed. She leant over him threateningly, and Bob lay back, frightened of putting his eye out on her nose or one of her breasts. Also, he was painfully hungry.

'There's a couple of pork chops in my overcoat pocket,' he said, 'and you'll find a tin of peas or a tin of sweet corn next to the saucepans.'

He gazed at the ceiling. Mrs Mounce turned the television on, and the booming of impartial expert voices filled the room, drowning the dreaming strings on the gramophone. Through the noise Bob heard her singing as she worked – the first few lines of 'Jealousy', over and over again. The old grease in the bottom of the grill-pan melted, and released its familiar aroma. From time to time she emerged from the kitchenette, and glided about the room, her cigarette still up by her right ear, a fish slice in her left hand, her bottom catching the light inordinately.

'Oh God,' said Bob gloomily. There was a stack of *Vogue* and *Queen* magazines on the bedside table. He picked one of them up, and began to study the advertisements for underclothing and support garments. The women in the photographs all appeared to combine education and breeding with stunted pelvic development. Their eyes were soft and remote with the contemplation of spiritual things, and they seemed unaware of Bob's sleepy libidinous eyes following them as they wandered through the long summer grass in nothing but their matching sky-blue underwear, or magnolia pink roll-on and crossed arms. They didn't have bottoms. Well, all right, they had bottoms, but bottoms with sunken cheeks and spiritual expressions. A woman like that to grill his pork chops, thought Bob, and he would be reasonably content.

Dyson and his wife drank half a pint of bottled beer each with dinner, as they usually did. 'Our only luxury,' said Dyson, 'our one self-indulgence.' The warm pool of light shining down on the table enclosed them both against the darkness. They sat for a long time over their coffee, leaning their elbows on the table comfortably, gazing at the cheese, or at the dark green casserole which had contained the stew, or at each other, saying little.

'Gawain walked into a tree on the way home from school,' said Jannie, cutting another sliver of cheese to nibble. 'He said sorry to it.'

Dyson polished an apple on his sleeve, thinking about Gawain.

'I think half this dreaminess of his is just a performance, you know,' he said. 'He's playing up to us.'

'I think that's nonsense.'

'Well, he always tells us about these incidents, doesn't he? He thinks he's a clown.'

'He tells us just to reassure himself that we don't mind.'

'But we do mind.'

'But we don't let him see that we mind.'

Dyson put the first apple back in the bowl, and began to polish another one. Ah, Gawain, Gawain! He was a thin, fragile child, who often walked about as if in a trance, his mouth slightly open, his eyes gazing into the distance, unaware of voices calling him or objects in his path. He seemed to get on all right in the Infants' School, but Dyson was afraid he would start to be teased when he moved up into the Junior School the following year. Dyson blamed himself for calling the boy Gawain. It was scarcely surprising that a child called Gawain – or at any rate a child with parents who had the sort of attitudes that went with choosing the name Gawain – should turn out to be dreamy. Dyson saw that now. The intention had been romantic; to recall in the grey wastes of winter London those russet-autumn green-spring days when he and Jannie had been reading English together at Cambridge. 'Sir Gawain and the Green Knight' – fertility symbolism – Green Men peering slyly through the lush Middle English forest – Courtly Love – the red-brick maidentowers of Newnham embowered in green summer lawns and burnished prunus – days of longing and possibility. Dyson now made sporadic attempts to reform Gawain by calling him Garry, but it was futile. One look at Gawain and you knew his name couldn't possibly be Garry. Dyson was unable to suspend even his own disbelief.

He put the second apple back, and picked up a third.

'How about Damian?' he asked. 'How was he?'

Jannie sighed.

'Jack, Jack, Jack all day,' she said. 'Was it Jack who pulled the wallpaper off? Will Jack come and eat all our food up? After lunch Jack went away to stay with his Granny for a fortnight.'

'Perhaps we'll have a break while he's away.'

'No, he came back from his Granny's at teatime.'

The name Damian had turned out to have an entirely different effect from Gawain. It had made the younger boy rather earthy and coarse. 'Damian' had come to signify for Dyson bulging, polished red cheeks, and slow, hoarse laughter. Damian was an imaginative child; but what he imagined was extremely boring. More than anything except perhaps eating he enjoyed running jokes, which ran for weeks, until every possible permutation and application had been exhausted. From somewhere – perhaps from something that Gawain had said, or from hearing about Jack Frost, or Jack Sprat, or Jack the brother of Jill – he had evolved an all-purpose Jack, a formless, characterless, pointless personage to whom he attributed deeds and sayings of stupefying dullness, in a daily soap opera which often ran without respite from breakfast to bedtime. Jack's doughy presence had loomed over the family's conversations for months. Not that Damian was unresponsive to the views of the critics. 'Isn't it about time we packed Jack in now, Day?' Dyson had said once in exasperation, after listening all one Saturday afternoon to an account of what Jack had in his stomach. 'We're all sick and tired of him.'

'Jack's packing in now,' Damian had said thoughtfully at intervals since then. 'Jack's sick and tired. Jack's sick and tired all over the floor. Jack didn't have time to be sick and tired in the pot, so do you know, Mummy, Jack did be sick and tired all over the floor.' Already Dyson could see the name Damian Dyson on the spine of some thick volume embodying a lifetime's diligent pedantry, or an endless, worthy novel about feuds and forbidden passions through seven generations in a Norfolk rush-cutting community.

'We should have called Damian Gawain and Gawain Damian,' he said.

'Poor Damian,' said Jannie. 'I feel so sorry for him sometimes.'

'Do you remember when we used to meet for coffee in that seedy milk bar in Market Square? After your supervisions with that terrible man in Caius?'

Jannie smiled, looking at the cheese-board and tapping it softly with her knife.

'Ah, then,' she said.

Morning mist, thought Dyson, padlocks in bicycle baskets, cinemas showing old Marx Brothers films.

'I saw Dick Hemming today,' he said. 'At Bush House.'

'Dick Hemming?'

'Stand-up hair, bushy eyebrows. Perhaps you never met him. In Jesus.'

Jannie put down the knife and leaned her cheeks on her fists. She gazed at her husband intently.

'He went into the BBC,' said Dyson. 'I see him sometimes when I go to Bush House.'

'We've known each other almost half our lives,' said Jannie.

Dyson gazed back at her. It was odd to think that she was his wife. It seemed such a generalized, public category of being, dissolving her into wifeliness, allying her with goodwives, midwives, and fishwives, shutting her off in a dour sorority united in its complaints against the husband class. It was hard to think what she was like, she was so familiar. She was – well, she was Jan, she was Jannie.

Looking at her, Dyson felt free and yet secure, like a small ball-bearing which has been placed upon a very wide, shallow dish, wandered easily about for some while, approaching the edges but always turning back, and eventually found its way, as if by its own sure instinct rather than by external forces acting upon it, to settle in the very centre.

'I can outstare you,' she said. Dyson dropped his gaze for an instant.

'I thought I might get one of Mounce's people to take some pictures of me,' he said. 'Did I tell you the BBC had a letter from a girl in Conakry asking for a picture of me?'

Jannie said nothing, but after a while she began to laugh, still leaning on her fists and still gazing at him.

'Well, they did,' said Dyson.

'How's Bob?' said Jannie.

'Bob's well.'

'You'd better bring him back to dinner tomorrow night. He hasn't been this week.'

'I don't suppose he'll starve.'

'I'll get a joint.'

Rather thoughtfully, Jannie began to gather up the plates.

'Did it get dark here this morning about eleven o'clock?' asked Dyson suddenly.

'I suppose it did,' said Jannie, her mind on something else.

'It was as black as night in the City. There's a bit in the evening paper about it. I'll fetch it for you.'

'Poor Damian,' said Jannie. 'He even bores Gawain.'

'Very nice,' said Bob, finishing up the last spoonful of fruit salad. 'Very nice indeed.'

Mrs Mounce might have her shortcomings, he reflected, but she certainly knew how to open a tin of fruit salad. She sat at the table opposite him, watching him eat, with a whimsical smile on her sharp little face, from time to time turning her head, drawing down the corners of her mouth, and taking another pull at her cigarette.

'You enjoyed it, did you, darling?' she asked.

'Yes, very nice. Thank you.'

'The pleasure's mine, sweetest. There's nothing a woman enjoys more than cooking for a man. Especially if he really appreciates his food.'

'Yes. Well, thanks, anyway.'

She blew out smoke between her teeth.

'If I'd known what time you were coming in,' she said, 'I'd have cooked din-dins for both of us. I could have done something really nice. Do you like crispy noodles? And prawn balls in batter? And fried spare ribs? There – you didn't know I could do Chinese cooking, did you, sweets? Oh, yes – I've cooked Chinese food for experts. Do you know Mr Carlsson, who runs Carlsson Syndication Services? He's a *very* big man in Far East syndication. You should get to know people like that, darling, they could help you to get on. Anyway, I gave him chicken in almonds, sweet-and-sour prawns, crispy noodles, and bamboo shoots, and you know what he said? He said, "Glenda, darling" – because he's not a stuffy old stick-in-the-mud like you – he said, "Glenda, darling, I know the Far East intimately – Hong Kong, Singapore, the lot – and I have never, *never*, tasted such exquisite Chinese cooking." '

'Ah,' said Bob. He got up, put the dishes on the draining-board for the cleaning woman to do in the morning, and threw the various empty tins into the rubbish-bin. Mrs Mounce slid sinuously across to the armchair, and curled herself up to watch the television, where a girl with long blonde hair was busy shooting a solemn-faced man in a dark overcoat.

'I'd ask you downstairs,' she said, 'but my darling hubby would be livid if he found out I'd been having men friends in. He's jealousy incarnate, you'd never believe.'

She gazed at the screen, narrowing her eyes against the smoke she was blowing out. Bob lay down on the bed, and belched discreetly. He remembered that he had a letter from Tessa in his pocket, which he had picked up off the hall table on his way upstairs. He took it out and slit the envelope.

'What's that?' asked Mrs Mounce.

'A letter.'

'From anyone special?'

'No.'

He unfolded the thick wad of blue paper, each sheet densely covered with neat round handwriting. He turned to the last page. It was numbered twelve. He sighed, and turned back to page one. *The Rectory, Staple Tarland, Somerset,* it said. *Tel. Staple Tarland 17. Monday.*

'Bob my darling, Bob my dearest,' began the letter. 'I miss you most dreadfully, really dreadfully, much more than I ever thought possible. It's now three whole weeks since you were here, 21 days 19 hours and 12 minutes to be exact, and it seems like three centuries. There is really nothing else to say . . .'

'Do you like jealousy in a woman?' asked Mrs Mounce.

'No.'

'I think it's nice for someone to be jealous, within reason. You know where you stand.'

'. . . really nothing else to say,' said the letter, 'but I will recount the boring chronicle of my days so you can see just how much your silly T. does miss you. Honestly, I mope about the house like a sick cow. Mummy says I have become impossible to live with, and even Daddy has noticed. He says it must be love, so you can see he notices more than you give him credit for. I mean, he knows I'm having An Affair with you, but he's no idea exactly *quelle affaire* it is.'

Bob felt a familiar sensation, as if he were shrinking inside his clothes, or sinking slowly through the surface of the earth. He tried to fight it off, and skipped a couple of paragraphs.

'Mummy says I must go to the Rothensteins' on the 30th, if only out of common courtesy, and that I shall enjoy it once I get there. I say phooey to that, because I know I shall be unutterably bored without YOU there to Entertain and Delight me, but I suppose I shall have to go in the end, even though it means going back to college a couple of days late, and there are exams this term

(Social Dynamics, World Literature, and History of Ideas I – groan, groan!). Anyway, they (the Rothensteins, that is!) live near Taskerton, and have Pots and Pots of Money. Well, Daddy has thought of one of his Awful Romantic Ideas, that A and I should make up a party with the two Gillington boys and *ride* over! I ask you! Can you imagine A and I riding side-saddle in our ball-gowns?'

Not only could Bob not imagine it, but he couldn't remember which one A was. The Rectory was full of Tessa's sisters, all kindly and romantic and fond of animals, and all called A or V or G or B. It was like a department of the Secret Service.

'But Daddy says V could take our dresses over in the car, since her pony Jester is lame anyway, and anyway she despises riding as much as I feel I ought to in this day and age, though I must confess that as you know I do get a tiny guilty sneaking pleasure out of it.'

Bob laid the letter down. He couldn't conceal it from himself; he was embarrassed. All Tessa's letters made him sweat with embarrassment. She wasn't like that to talk to. But then she wasn't as articulate when she talked. Her handiness with the pen might mean that her letters tapped the real Tessa within. Could he in all honesty continue an affair with a girl who wrote letters like this?

'Bad news?' asked Mrs Mounce.

'No,' said Bob. 'Yes and no.'

He turned over a couple of sheets and took a sounding on page five.

'I think you must have made quite an impression on Daddy during your visit here. He didn't mention you at all until last Saturday, and I thought he must have forgotten about you altogether. Then suddenly out of the blue, while we were having tea, he asked which school you had been to. I had to say I didn't know, because strange to say you've never told me, and he said H'mph. And I said but you'd been to Cambridge, and he said Ha. Which coming from him is high praise, or at any rate a sign of some interest. You know how hard it is to get him interested in anything these days except the Liberal Party and German theology. No, I'm making him sound like some grouchy old eccentric, and he's really a very sweet and saintly man, and I *adore* him, second only to you. Incidentally, which school *did* you go to?'

He skimmed through a few more pages, trying to see if they contained anything he was supposed to do something about – an invitation, a question which needed to be answered, a rendezvous. Tessa's letters always made him anxious. Somewhere in that sea of words there might be some vital message bobbing about that he was failing to pick up. One evening she would arrive at the front door of his flat – he knew it. His face would fall in astonishment. 'Oh Bob!' – 'Oh God!' – 'Oh Bob, I *did* write!' He felt a flutter of indigestion at the thought.

'It's a funny thing about jealousy,' said Mrs Mounce. 'I'm quite broad-minded about Reg, but I *can* be as jealous as a cat, darling, believe me.'

Bob tracked backwards again through the text. Somewhere there should be an acknowledgment of his last letter. It had been rather an amusing one, he thought.

'. . . wonderful to get your letter. I carried it around unopened for at least an hour, inside my shirt, next to my heart. What a sloppy thing to do! Really I am a dreadfully sloppy person, not fit to know you. What does "sirjaspery" mean? I looked it up in the Shorter Oxford, but no sign. You wrote: "Oho then my proud beauty, he cried in sirjaspery tones." I think it must mean something like syrupy, with overtones of jasmine and raspberry. Am I right? And who is Captain Cosmo, master of the space-ship Staphylococcus? Is he a character I ought to know about? Or did you make him up? Oh, I feel such a fool reading your letters, and so unworthy of you. How can you bear to put up with me? I tried to read *Miss Lonelyhearts* as you suggested, but it was so miserable I gave up. I'm ploughing through *A Face in the Crowd,* which I must say is very interesting in its revelations about what goes on in "the communications industry". I've even got the library to get me *U.S.A.* by John dos Passos, but it's so enormous I can't imagine ever getting through it. It would take me all year just to read the books you mentioned when we happened to be talking about American literature. I shall *never* have read anything like as many books as you, however hard I try. Sometimes I despair. This is the *only* way I regret being nine years younger than you. You'll always be nine years ahead of me in reading and in knowledge of the world. Do you mind, dearest Bob? I *know* you mind. I *know* it irritates you when I don't understand, or don't recognize an allusion. Oh, I am a stupid child, and I'm sorry. Sometimes I'm almost sorry we met, I know I must irritate you so much . . .'

Bob put the letter down and stared at the ceiling, overcome with sadness and shame.

'What I'm going to do, sweetest,' said Mrs Mounce, 'is to get a spare key to this flat from Dotty.'

'Oh?' said Bob, thinking about his unworthiness.

'Then I can slip in before you get home from the office sometimes and have something ready for you.'

Bob went on thinking.

'A man needs someone to look after him a little, darling. Someone to spoil him occasionally.'

Bob sighed. Mrs Mounce jumped out of the armchair and dimpled across to the bed.

'You don't sound very grateful, sweety pie,' she said, making a reproachful moue. She sat down on the edge of the bed. Bob pulled his knees up to make room for her, and she leaned on them, her cigarette hand still aloft. Bob looked away, feeling low.

'I think he's a tiny bit scared of me, chaps,' she said. 'I think he thinks I've got wicked designs on him.'

Bob tried to smile. Mrs Mounce pushed her chin forward teasingly.

'Don't worry, darling – I shan't bite you,' she purred. She sucked in cigarette smoke, and let it out slowly, gazing at him through it with half-closed eyes.

'Or perhaps I will!' she said suddenly, and in the same moment leant forward and sank her teeth into Bob's leg, just above the knee.

'Arrrrrgh!' he shouted, springing up. The bite was

astonishingly painful.

Mrs Mounce had jumped up, too, and was streaking away to the door, laughing.

'I thought that might wake you up, sweetheart!' she said. 'Night night!'

Dyson lay in bed, glancing through the book reviews in the *Statesman*, waiting for Jannie to come to bed and turn the light out. 'Glyn's slow disintegration and inevitable breakdown are magnificently handled . . . Magda, abandoned by her lieutenant, goes to live with a senescent baron in his crumbling *schloss* in the Thüringer Wald; the atmosphere of decay and elderly lust is picturesquely conveyed . . . Riki's growing sense of isolation and despair is convincingly done, but her final breakdown seems a long time coming . . .' Dyson relished the reviews, the texture of the sheets and the softness and warmth of the bed. Outside 43 Spadina Road the world was senescent, disintegrating, despairing, and everyone was on his way to a breakdown. Inside, it was soft and warm and linen-sheeted, and everyone was in the pink of mental health. Jannie moved slowly about the room in her pyjamas, vaguely shifting heaps of clothes about. The whole room was full of heaps of clothes – his, Jannie's, the children's; some put out for cleaning, some for sending to the refugees, some to be decided about. We must get another chest of drawers, he thought luxuriously. It gave him great pleasure to see all the clothing about the room. Hundredweights of it – and all provided out of his earnings. Shirts, socks, dresses, stockings; silver dance shoes and thick winter overcoats – all quarried by his own labour. The bed itself; the butter downstairs in the refrigerator; the electricity they burned so casually; the telephone; the complex structure of beams and bricks and slates that housed it all; he, John Dyson, thought by some as a boy to be rather a fool, had got it all. Had got it by his sheer ability at maintaining the crossword stock, at checking points of theology and country lore, at explaining the intricacies of British politics to West Africans with lucidity and wit and some small measure of personal charm. Life was rich and satisfying.

Slowly Jannie got into bed, sighing at the clothes, and switched the light off. He put his head on her shoulder, and for a while she stroked his eyebrows. He wondered if he had Jannified her at all by calling her Jannie, as he had Gawained Gawain. As a girl she had been Janice, and no one had tried to shorten it. Janice Atterbury. He thought of her going off to school each day on a green double-decker bus, a Janice among Janices, a Janice Atterbury among Janice Leighs, Vivienne Williamses, Heather Marshalls, and Sandra Thompsons. Janice, you can share my crayons if you promise you won't let Heather have them. Janice Atterbury is a stuck-up pig. Atterbury, J. D., did useful work at left back, but must mark her man and tackle more aggressively. Janice Dorothy Atterbury has satisfied the Examiners in German (Written and Oral), Pianoforte (Grade V), Ballet (Intermediate), and Life Saving (Royal Humane Society Bronze Medal) . . .

He started to laugh, shaking the bed.

'What is it?' said Jannie, half asleep.

'You as a schoolgirl.'

'Oh.'

And then he had come on the scene to corrupt it, knocking on her door (J. D. Atterbury, it said on the card) in Newnham on those gusty spring afternoons. Jan, I just happened to be passing by, so I thought I'd look in. But don't you find Sir Gawain's predicament intensely *moving*, Jannie? Have you thought about what would *happen* if we ever have a Tory government again, Jan? Doesn't the name Bunk Johnson mean *anything* to you, Jannie?

John Dyson and Jan Atterbury – the names went together, as everyone in their circle quickly came to see. John Dyson and Jan Atterbury – John and Jan. The names went together like Huntley and Palmer, or Fortnum and Mason. It was difficult for everyone, in the summer term of their second year, to get used to saying Jan Atterbury and Lionel Marcus. It was like finding Fortnum and Mason had become Fortnum and Freebody. Nevertheless, people managed it, in time. Even Dyson grew accustomed to it. Lionel and Jan, or rather Jan and Lionel, since easy-going, amiable Lionel was always a pace behind . . . They haunted his last year, like the prospect of getting a third, and his failure to shine as a speaker in the Union.

Dyson thought he had been awake, until he turned over, when he realized he had been asleep. And then the arrangement of names had been Belinda Charles, Jan Atterbury, and Margaret LeRoy, next to the bellpush of a flat in West Kensington. And then, after a long time in which many things happened, some unhappy, some too embarrassing to recall, some meaningless, the names John and Jan Dyson had emerged. There was surely a chasm between Janice Atterbury and Jan Dyson. Those strong hands . . . those serious and sometimes sad brown eyes . . . Whereas he himself, he felt, had scarcely changed since the age of seventeen or eighteen . . .

His mind cruised slowly down into sleep, like a bubble drifting across the surface of an eye. A remote metallic clattering half-penetrated his consciousness, disguising itself in a suite of dreams. It was the noise of the Long Life beer cans being thrown back into the Dysons' garden.

Three

Dyson's awfully bad day was followed immediately by an awfully good one.

For a start, a producer in one of the commercial television companies rang him quite early on in the morning and asked him to appear in a programme. Dyson could scarcely contain himself. He walked up and down the office frowning furiously with pleasure.

'This is exactly what I've always wanted, Bob!' he said. 'Do you realize that? This is exactly what I've been waiting for!'

'I know,' said Bob. 'Congratulations, John.'

'Of course, it probably won't lead to anything. One obviously mustn't set too much store by it. I shall probably make a terrible cock of it.'

'I'm sure you won't, John.'

'I have a lot of experience in radio, of course. That must count for something. I have been consciously preparing myself for an opportunity like this, Bob. I haven't been waiting idly.'

He gazed out of the window, his hands behind his back, clapping the palms together.

'What sort of programme is it?' asked Bob. 'Something about Indonesia?'

'Indonesia?'

'Isn't that your great speciality?'

'Well, I know something about Indonesia. I know something about a lot of things. I'm a *journalist*, Bob.'

He sat down at his desk, very pleased with his calling, then almost immediately jumped up and began to walk about the room again.

'It's a discussion programme about race,' he said. 'Apparently they want someone with actual experience of living in a multiracial community.'

Bob stared at him.

'I didn't know you'd lived in a multiracial community, John.'

'Bob, you know we have West Indians living next door to us! We have four West Indian households in the road. You know that, Bob.'

'Oh, I see. How did the television people find out?'

'Well, the programme's being produced by a man called Jack de Sousa. Our wives were at Newnham together – we had the de Sousas out to tea one Sunday. As a matter of fact they almost decided to buy a house in the road, they liked it so much. Anyway, Jack wants me to take part in a discussion about the problems involved. Apparently the chairman's going to be Norman Ward Westerman. Have you seen him on television, Bob?'

'No.'

'He's *marvellous*, Bob. He's someone I really do feel the most tremendous respect for.'

It took some time before Dyson had simmered down enough for Bob to return to his work. He was writing a letter to Tessa.

'My darling Tessa,' he wrote, then remembered that very soon he was going to break the affair off. He tore the paper out of the typewriter and took a fresh sheet. 'Tessa darling,' he began, then remembered her letter, felt ashamed of himself, and took another sheet. 'My darling Tessa,' he began. He gazed out of the window for some minutes, wondering what on earth to say. Then he typed : 'How the Giant Dyson subdued the Tyrant Cox,' and underlined it.

'Now when Dyson returned from his labours in the City,' he wrote, 'where his education and literary accomplishments had been the wonder of the citizens, and his conversational stamina had severely taxed the strength of even his most loyal friends, he discovered that the seigneur of the estate adjoining his, the cruel and tyrannous *Cox,* had been laying waste the district, and terrorizing the inhabitants, with a fearful bombardment of old beer cans. Stopping only to refresh himself with a hurried snack, consisting of 47 packets of Smith's potato crisps, 3,287 stuffed cocktail olives, and four or five cartloads of broken cake and biscuits left over from the children's tea, Dyson hastened forth and challenged Cox.

' "Ha, Cox!" he cried in a terrible voice. "Come forth, Cox, or by St Eulalie I'll slap a writ on you! Where are you, you mother-fixated turdsmith, before I knock your grimy spectacles off and stuff an injunction down your shirt-front! Come out, you paraphrenic pissmain, you sub-anthropoid snotspray, or by St Archibald I'll tread on your heels and lay an information with the Sanitary Inspector about the state of your drains!"

'But the tyrant Cox, not recognizing the force of these arguments, remained where he was. Whereupon Dyson put his nose down Cox's chimney and sneezed with such panache and violence that the tyrant was blown out of the larder window, and fell to earth in Trinity Road, Balham. Dyson at once rushed after him, pelting him with the old beer cans and whatever else came to hand, which included: Tetley's tea-bags, ex-US Air Force sparking plugs, overdue library books, rubber reducing garments, and genuine reproductions of Old Masters. Without pause for breath Dyson chased him throughout the length and breadth of the land; *videlicet*, through Clapham North, Clapham South, and Clapham Common, Mitcham Lane, Mitcham Village, and Mitcham Junction, Collier's Wood, St Helier, Thornton Heath, and Norbury, paying no attention whatsoever to traffic lights or Belisha Beacons, and frequently going the wrong way up one-way streets . . .'

But by this time another nice thing had happened to Dyson.

'This is an awfully good day for me,' he said, putting the phone down and rubbing his hands together. 'You'll never guess who that was on the phone.'

'No?'

'Sir William Paice!'

'Oh.'

'You know, the unit trust man. You must have heard of him, Bob! He's a very well-known amateur ornithologist.

You remember, he married old Glenormond's daughter.'

'Someone I know?'

'Oh, *Bob*! Lord Glenormond, the shipping man. Oh God, Bob, don't you take any interest at all in the upper classes?'

'Well, you know . . .' said Bob, finding a soothing bag of peppermints in his pocket, and slipping one discreetly into his mouth.

'But Bob, they're *fascinating*! I should have thought a writer like yourself would have found them absolutely absorbing.'

Bob rattled the peppermint against his teeth with the tip of his tongue.

'I mean,' said Dyson, 'not for any snobbish reasons. But just as a sociological study I find them absolutely *fascinating*. Anyway, I've persuaded Sir William Paice to write us some "Country Day by Day". Rather a coup, I think.'

Bob returned to his letter.

'Now when they reached Sydenham,' he wrote, 'Cox snapped off the spire of St Wendy and All Angels, and turned, and fetched Dyson a terrific blow on the funny bone . . .'

'Sir William's initials are W.G.R.P.,' said Dyson thoughtfully, brooding over the *Who's Who* he kept on his desk. 'How do you think he'd like to be credited on the column, Bob? Just plain W.G.R.P.? Or Sir W.G.R.P.?'

'Search me,' said Bob. But Dyson wasn't listening, in any case.

'Oh God!' he cried, jumping up excitedly, and beginning to stride up and down the office all over again. 'This is such a good day for me!'

Old Eddy Moulton gazed thoughtfully at the piece he was copying out, roused by the sudden shriek of Dyson's chair being pushed back. He had been dreaming about someone he had not thought of for years and years – a character called Stanley Furle, who had fallen downstairs at the Press Club one night and blacked his eye on the silver knob of his cane!

'He was tight at the time, of course,' said old Eddy to Bob, shaking his head and smiling. 'He was as tight as a tick, poor fellow.'

Bob's own phone rang.

'Hello?' said Bob.

'This crap's from you, is it?' said a cross voice.

'What?'

'Don't give me that crap. This load of crap's your idea of a joke, I take it?'

'Is that Reg Mounce?'

'Don't give me that crap.'

'Reg, what are you talking about?'

'Bob, don't give me that crap.'

'I don't know what you're talking about, Reg.'

Mounce hesitated.

'It was you who sent me this crap, wasn't it, Bob?'

'What crap, Reg?'

'You know what crap, Bob.'

'Reg, I honestly don't know what on earth you're talking about.'

'You know all right.'

'No.'

Mounce hesitated again. Bob could hear him sucking in air through his teeth.

'Well, *some* bastard sent it,' he said.

'Not me, Reg.'

'Well, it was *some* bastard.'

'Yes, but not me, Reg.'

'The bastard.'

Bob waited.

'If I catch the bastard . . .' said Mounce.

There was another pause.

'The bastard,' said Mounce finally.

He rang off.

'What the devil was all that?' asked Dyson, as Bob slowly put his receiver back.

'Search me.'

Dyson's phone rang.

'Hello, Dyson . . .'

Dyson frowned as he listened to the voice at the other end, and raised his eyebrows at Bob.

'What crap?' he said. 'Look, is that you, Reg . . . ? Well, what crap, Reg . . . ? Yes, but *what* crap? . . . ? Look, for God's sake, Reg, *what* crap . . . ? Well, Reg, how do I know whether I sent you the crap if I don't know what crap it was . . . ? Yes, but what did the bastard do . . . ? Yes, yes – but what crap was it that the bastard sent you . . . ?'

Dyson put the phone back.

'Well?' said Bob.

'Search me,' said Dyson.

Dyson's awfully good day got better and better. Just before lunch one of de Sousa's assistants at the television company rang to say that Lord Boddy had agreed to take part in the programme.

'Who's Lord Boddy, John?' asked Bob, when Dyson reported this to him, walking up and down the office once again.

'Oh God, Bob, you're impossible! You must know who Lord Boddy is!'

'I'm sorry, John.'

'Eddy, Bob doesn't know who Lord Boddy is! Are you awake, Eddy? Eddy? Anyway, Bob, Lord Boddy's an extremely well-known man. He's the second baron, isn't he? Wasn't his father given the title by Ramsay MacDonald for something to do with the League of Nations?'

'I don't know, John.'

'I think he was. Anyway, the present Lord Boddy is tremendously interested in things like the colour problem – he sits on committees and Royal Commissions, and so on. Apparently there's also going to be a Mrs Somebody-or-other who's a social worker. And someone coloured, of course.'

'Anyway, congratulations, John.'

Dyson picked up the *Who's Who* and studied it in silence for some moments.

'His father was Edward Boddy, before he got the title,' he announced. 'The present Lord Boddy's Christian names are Frank Walter. Married, with two sons. Publications: *The Case for Disarmament* (1939); *Let Victory Be Ours* (1942); *The Russians – Our Comrades!* (1945); *World Communism: a Study in Tyranny* (1949); et cetera, et cetera . . . *Race: the Challenge Within* (1963) . . . oh, and (edited) *The Man in the Tweed Plus-Fours* (The Diaries and Letters of the First Lord Boddy).'

'I see,' said Bob. 'Why don't we go out and have some lunch before the phone rings again?'

'All right, Bob. Listen – this is interesting. His clubs are the National Liberal and the RAC.'

'What's interesting about that, John?'

Dyson snapped *Who's Who* shut and tossed it down on his desk.

'You're a shit, Bob,' he said, grinning. 'Eddy, we'll be in the Gates.'

There was the usual crowd in the Gates of Jerusalem – Bill Waddy, Mike Sparrow, Ralph Absalom, Andy Royle, Ted Hurwitz, Gareth Holmroyd, Lucy from the Library, Pat Selig – but today they had crystallized around Mounce. Mounce kept shifting about from foot to foot, restless with irritation.

'Well, *some* bastard sent it,' he kept saying.

People were passing round from hand to hand a grubby sheet of quarto copy paper with something typed on it.

'Seen this?' said Bill Waddy, handing it to Dyson and Bob as they joined the circle. 'Some joker sent it to Reg. He found it on his desk when he arrived this morning.'

It was a letter in the form of an office memorandum.

Editor to R. Mounce, *it said*, PRIVATE AND CONFIDENTIAL.

After giving the matter considerable thought, and taking advice, I have come to the conclusion that you would be wise to begin looking round with a view to making other arrangements. I do not feel that this office can give sufficient scope to your talents. Three months' notice is customary with us, as you know, but if you were particularly anxious to leave sooner I believe you would find us reasonably accommodating.

You have, I understand, a week's holiday entitlement outstanding. This would of course be paid in full. Or, if you preferred, you could take it as a holiday, and leave a week sooner than otherwise arranged.

'It was in a little brown envelope addressed "R. Mounce Esqre" just the way the Editor does it,' said Ted Hurwitz.

'I'd like to get my hands on the bastard,' said Mounce.

'One of your photographers, perhaps?' suggested Dyson.

'We thought of that, of course,' said Bill Waddy. 'But none of them can even spell, can they, Reg?'

'The bastards,' said Mounce.

'He's got the Editor's style exactly,' said Gareth Holmroyd.

'That's why we think it must be someone who does get communications from Room G,' said Bill Waddy.

'The bastard,' said Mounce.

'It could have been quite serious,' said Andy Royle, 'if this had been an office like the *Daily Express*, where people actually are sacked.'

They all sipped their beer thoughtfully.

'Hey, listen,' said Dyson, seizing the opportunity.

'Same again for everyone?' said Ralph Absalom, seizing it too.

'I'm going to be on television,' said Dyson.

'I think it's my round,' said Mike Sparrow.

'Tchah, tchah, tchah! Same again for you, Lucy? Pat?'

'I'm going to be on the box.'

'Have a pint this time, John.'

'With Norman Ward – No, just a half, please, Ralph – with Norman Ward Westerman – That's my glass by your elbow – and Lord Boddy.'

'Old Frank Boddy,' said Gareth Holmroyd. 'No, I won't, thank you, Ralph.'

'Go on.'

'No, I won't.'

'It's a sort of discussion programme.'

'Change your mind. Be a devil.'

'I said it's a sort of discussion programme, Gareth.'

'No, I really won't, thanks, Ralph. What was that about a discussion programme, John?'

'It's about the colour problem, with Lord Boddy.'

'Oh, I didn't see it.'

'The bastards,' said Mounce, looking into his beer and swaying slightly.

'Do you think one ought to join a club, Bob?' asked Dyson, leaning back in his chair and yawning. Things were very quiet in the office.

'What sort of club?' said Bob. 'You mean a night club?'

'Bob, you're a treasure.' Dyson yawned and laughed at the same time, then became thoughtful again. 'The point is, I could very easily get myself put up for the Garrick. Or the Savage. Or the Travellers', even. What do you think, Bob? One does need somewhere one can go. Somewhere one can take people. I mean, if one does a certain amount of work in television, as one is likely to do if one is in our position . . . Well, supposing I wanted to have a quiet talk with a producer, say, to outline an idea I had for a programme. Or supposing, just for the sake of example, Lord Boddy and I happened to get on rather well next Friday, and I wanted to invite him to have lunch with me somewhere. Where could one go?'

'Why not the Gates?'

'Oh, Bob, for heaven's sake!'

'Well, what's wrong with a restaurant?'

Dyson gazed at the window, wrinkling up his nose judiciously, and pursing his lips.

'I don't feel a restaurant would be right, somehow,' he said. 'It would be a little too *voulu*. Do you see what I mean? One's guest would know one was going out of one's way to entertain him, as if one wanted something out of him. Whereas at one's club one could sit in an armchair reading the paper while one was waiting for him to arrive. One could walk into the dining-room with him in a rather mundane sort of way, as if one did it every day. It would be more like asking him to drop in at one's home.'

'Why don't you ask him to drop in at your home, then, John?'

Dyson sighed.

'Well, you know, Bob. These days, when one doesn't have servants, with one's kids around, and broken toys, and this and that . . . Incidentally, I nearly forgot – Jannie told me to bring you home for supper tonight. Is that all right?'

'Yes, very nice. Thanks, John.'

Dyson looked back towards the window.

'Or perhaps the Oxford and Cambridge would be the right one,' he said. 'It is rather a nice place, you know.'

He drifted across to the window, clapping his hands together behind his back, and stood gazing down at the people crossing Hand and Ball Court. From time to time he yawned absent-mindedly.

'Do you think one should get one's suits made for one?' he said eventually. 'Perhaps one should take a little more trouble about these things if one's in the public eye.'

But Bob was absorbed in what he was writing. Dyson yawned again, became conscious of it, and tried to beat it out with his hand.

'God, I was going to have a blitz on "Thoughts" this afternoon, too,' he said. 'Somebody wouldn't like to give me a hand, would they? How are you placed, Bob?'

'Bit tied up just at the moment, John,' said Bob remotely, not looking up from his typewriter.

Dyson yawned again, uncontrollably.

'God oh God,' he said. 'I must knock off this beer at lunchtime. It's really wrecking me.'

'And when,' wrote Bob to Tessa, 'Dyson and his comrades sat down to carouse, the good ale wet their wits and loosened their larynxes, and they talked merrily and disputed learnedly far into the afternoon. What are you drinking, old alebladder? – No, it's my round, old weepbooze – By St Septimus, I'm in the chair! – My shout, by St Cynthia! – No, no, by St Yoland, I insist! – Well, a half, then, by St Uchtred. – By St Eusebius, have a pint! – Just a half, by St Sholtol! – By St Tib, I've come out without my money! – By St Almeric, that's three pints, two Guinnesses, one tomato juice, and five ham sandwiches! – No, by St Trixy, it's four ham sandwiches, three sausage rolls, four draught Guinnesses, and a bitter lemon! – And a packet of crisps, by St Ruby! – And two packets of crisps, by St Bogislaw! – That was half-a-crown I gave you, by St Lorinda! – By St Cecil it was a florin! – By St Hilarion, I wish I were lunching at the Oxford and Cambridge!'

Four

Jannie instinctively hid her cigarette behind her back when the kitchen door opened. John hated to see her smoking while she cooked. But it was not John – it was Bob. She brought the cigarette out again.

'Jannie,' said Bob, 'is there anything I can do?'

'Not really, Bob. You can stay and talk to me if you like, though.'

Bob drew one of the rush-bottomed chairs out from the great dining-table in the middle of the kitchen and sprawled in it. The room was full of the fat, brown smell of *gigot aux haricots*. It was a dish which Jannie often cooked for Bob. He was a glutton, and the rich heaviness which the golden-crusted beans absorbed from the exhalations of the mutton touched some deep chord in him. John hated the dish.

'Can't peel the potatoes or anything?' Bob asked.

'No. What's John up to?'

'He's reading the paper. Very good about him getting on the television. Are you pleased?'

Jannie leaned against the edge of the dresser, smoking and looking down at Bob. She bit her lower lip anxiously.

'I suppose so,' she said. 'I don't know.'

'He's as pleased as Punch about it. He's been bouncing about the office all day like a rubber ball.'

'You don't think he's going to make a terrible fool of himself, do you, Bob?'

'He'll be all right, Jannie.'

'I can't bear the thought of sitting here watching him. I don't know how I shall manage to look at the screen.'

Bob picked up one of the knives laid out for dinner and scored along the grain of the table with it.

'How are the boys, Jannie?' he asked.

The worried look on Jannie's face softened. She began to laugh.

'Poor old Bob!' she said.

'No,' said Bob, 'I'm very fond of them.'

Jannie smiled at him, wondering if he could even remember how old they were. When he came at weekends he played with them vigorously, until they screamed and wept with over-excitement. He was very good with them, as the phrase went. But Jannie was used to friends, particularly childless ones, who were good with the children to the point of dedication, and who a month later called Gawain Damian and Damian Adrian, or who sent the six-year-old Gawain a pull-along elephant for his birthday, and gave Damian a velvet party frock, in the belief that he was called Deborah, and was a girl.

'They're fine,' she said. 'How's Mrs Mounce?'

'Well,' said Bob, 'things aren't too good at the moment. She cooked me dinner last night. Just marched in and set to work. There was nothing I could do about it.'

'I think you ought to watch out for that woman, Bob.'

'I know. I know. But what can I do?'

'She'll land you in trouble.'

'You really think she's after me, Jannie?'

'What do you think, Bob?'

Bob sat back in his chair, playing with the pepper-mill, grinding a little pile of pepper into his left palm. He was like an old cushion in the chair, thought Jannie, a plump, shabby, comfortable old cushion. With his fisherman-knit Marks and Sparks sweaters, and his broad suède shoes, and his mild, sleepy eyes, he fitted into the background of 43 Spadina Road so well that you hardly noticed him.

'She bit me last night,' he said, dragging up his trouser-leg and showing her the line of tiny red marks. Jannie stared at them, trying to imagine the scene – Bob, retreating backwards round the room, and Mrs Mounce, on all fours, snarling and barking, snapping at his trousers.

'How on earth did it happen, Bob?'

Bob shrugged.

'She just suddenly bit me,' he said.

'But what led up to it? Something must have led up to it.'

Bob sighed.

'She said, "I won't bite you." Then I suppose she changed her mind.'

'Honestly, you are a bit wet sometimes, Bob.'

It occurred to her that she hadn't made the salad. She began to wash the lettuce, while Bob made the dressing, hunting luxuriously through her spice cupboard for the oil and vinegar.

'How's Tessa?' she asked.

'Fine. Do you think a little cinnamon would help?'

'No. Does she know about all this business?'

'All what business?'

'Mrs Mounce.'

'No, no. How about tarragon?'

Bob was always evasive about Tessa, which made Jannie suspect that he might be serious about her. It also made her want to find out more about the girl, and gave her a terrible desire to tease Bob about her.

'When she comes to London,' said Jannie, 'she can always have the spare room here, you know.'

'That's very kind of you, Jannie.'

But of course, thought Jannie, feeling foolish, Tessa would stay with Bob. Now Bob would think she disapproved.

'I mean,' she said, 'only if she wants to.'

'Yes, yes,' said Bob. He sounded embarrassed.

'I mean . . . Oh, you know what I mean.'

'Yes, Jannie. I'll put some sugar in the dressing, shall I?'

'I mean, there's a bed here if ever she wants it.'

'Sugar, Jannie?'

He was holding the sugar jar up questioningly. She gazed at it for some moments in silence, thinking about a flat in Manchester where she and John had spent a ghastly week one winter before they were married. It had belonged to a man called Flowers, and they had gone to Manchester just because he had offered them the flat. It had been bitterly cold. They had stayed in bed most of the time. In the afternoons they had walked around the cold, grimy streets. She had a picture of sooty red brick, quiet, empty streets with grey winter haze at the end of them, little corner shops with paper decorations left over from Christmas, gritty smoke blowing down from the chimneys. It had been just after Christmas; she had worn a new pair of fur mittens her sister had given her. She could remember standing by the window of the flat and crying, but not why she was crying, or indeed much else. Except that the mattress had smelt musty, and that as they lay in bed through those long cold mornings they could just see the spire of the Congregational church through the window.

'Half a teaspoonful, Bob,' she said.

'What were you thinking about?'

'Oh, things. It's funny how . . .'

She put the lettuce in a bowl and dried her hands, staring unseeingly at the loose tile above the sink. The grittiness of the coal smoke coming down on those gaunt January afternoons was still in her nostrils. She could hear the rising engine-note of the Corporation buses as they pulled away from the stop at the corner, coming from nowhere either of them had ever heard of, going on through the gathering winter dusk to destinations equally obscure.

'How what, Jannie?' asked Bob, taking a teaspoonful of sugar from the jar and slowly licking it up. Jannie pulled another of the chairs out from the table and sat down.

'How you suddenly remember something very vividly,' she said, 'and you think for a moment you've really got hold of it. But then . . .'

She hesitated again, dismayed by the difficulty of delineating such feelings, unshaped feelings in words.

'But then,' she said, 'when you try to think what it is you've got hold of, it's not very easy to say.'

Bob took another teaspoonful of sugar.

'What was it that you were remembering, Jannie?' he asked.

'Oh, a bleak time. A lot of things you remember like that are moments of desolation. Sometimes I wonder if one really knew they were so desolate at the time.'

She watched Bob as he took another spoonful of sugar. He followed her gaze, saw what he was doing, and quickly pushed the sugar jar away.

'Sorry,' he said. 'I didn't realize I was doing it.'

'You'll get fat, Bob.'

'I've got fat.'

She rested her chin in her cupped hand.

'Do you get on with women better than men, Bob?' she asked.

'I get on fairly well with everyone, to tell you the truth.'

She examined him curiously. He was definitely plump. When he turned his head to look at her the flesh folded underneath the jawbone into the beginnings of a double chin. He was so different from John in every way that it was amazing to think the human race could contain them both. She thought of her husband shaving in the morning, in trousers and vest. Dark, gaunt – almost emaciated – leaning forwards anxiously towards the mirror as if afraid his reflection might suddenly vanish altogether.

'What's Tessa like?' she asked.

'Oh, you know . . .' said Bob, a little uneasily.

'Dark or fair?'

'Dark.'

'What colour eyes?'

Bob frowned.

'I think they're brown,' he said, playing with the peppermill again.

'And she's attractive?'

'Oh, yes.'

'How old is she?'

'Oh, about twenty.'

Jannie felt she wanted to laugh.

'Why haven't we seen her here?' she asked.

'She hasn't been up to London yet. She's at a kind of college of citizenship in Bath.'

'You go down there?'

'Well, they're a bit tough about letting them out. It's a sort of finishing school, really.'

She couldn't prevent herself from bursting out laughing.
'Bob, Bob, Bob!' she said.
'What?'
'You. Carrying on with someone at a finishing school.'
'I know.'
John came into the kitchen, holding three half-full sherry glasses.
'I found a drop in a bottle at the back of the knitting cupboard,' he said. 'What are you two up to out here?'
'Oh, flirting,' said Bob, with a sigh.
'Charming,' said John.
'Got to earn my supper,' said Bob.

Bob and Jannie teased Dyson all the way through dinner, and he became more and more irritated.
'It's not just the money,' he said, stabbing at his beans and sending a scattering of them across the table. 'Though I may say that I shall be getting twenty-five guineas next Thursday for doing nothing but sit around in a television studio for half an hour, instead of beating my brains out all weekend to write a script for the BBC Overseas Service and getting ten guineas for it. That's of some passing interest to me, I must admit, even if it isn't to Jannie— though I dare say she'll help me spend the money.'
'I'll help you spend the money,' said Jannie, 'and you can use your free weekend to fix the leak in the wall.'
'I thought you told me you'd be getting a hundred guineas a time if you were a television personality, John?' said Bob.
'So I shall, Bob,' said Dyson irritably, 'if I make a success of this and begin to make a name for myself. And that's the real point. It's not just the money . . .'
'Though you don't despise the money,' said Jannie.
'Though I don't despise the money, certainly . . .'
'Because at your age you have to work all the hours God made, morning, noon, and night, seven days a week,' said Bob.
'Because indeed I have to work like a dog, and I'm mortgaged up to the hilt, and I live without any form of

luxury whatsoever except an occasional bottle of beer, and I sometimes *shake* with worry just to think about it all. Nevertheless, it's *not* just the money.'

He stopped suddenly and took another mouthful of lamb.

'What is it, then?' said Jannie.

'Well,' said Dyson, chewing hard, 'I must admit that I should like to make a name for myself, just for its own sake.'

'Oh, John!' said Jannie, laughing. Bob grinned silently.

'All right,' said Dyson. 'You may laugh if you like. But I'm thinking purely of the practical advantages.'

Bob and Jannie laughed again.

'Look, Jannie,' said Dyson seriously. 'Do you remember when we wanted to get Gawain into Almeira Road school, and we couldn't, because all the middle-class parents in s.w.23 were trying to get their kids into Almeira Road, and we lived just over the zoning boundary? Well, do you honestly think the answer would have been the same if I'd been Norman Ward Westerman or Lord Boddy?'

'You mean you'd have been able to pull strings?' said Bob.

'*I* shouldn't have pulled strings – other people would have pulled them for me! "If we had Lord Boddy in the Parent-Teacher Association," they'd think, "we might have a little influence at County Hall." Or they'd realize that it might be rather agreeable to say to visiting parents, "That's Noel Westerman – you know, Norman Ward Westerman's son. He's a scamp – aren't you, Noel?" Pat-pat on Noel's well-connected head.'

Bob and Jannie gazed at him.

'Listen, if I wasn't just John Dyson, but The John Dyson, people wouldn't even waste their time asking me to do ten-guinea talks for the Overseas Service – they'd know I'd be fully occupied doing pieces for *Playboy* and *Esquire* at a thousand dollars a time, and going on television at a hundred guineas an appearance. It's a matter of purely practical economics.'

'You sound very impassioned, John,' said Bob.

'Well, I *am*, Bob. I *am* very impassioned. Look, I don't

want to be so famous that I have to write autographs all over the place, and can't travel by bus in case I'm mobbed. Moderation in all things. But if I was The John Dyson, do you think crowded restaurants wouldn't be able to find a table for me? If I was The John Dyson, don't you think I'd have a better chance of getting theatre seats?'

'If a theatre's full, it's full,' said Jannie, 'even if John Dyson comes along.'

'But, Jannie, don't you understand, theatres *keep back* one or two seats each night in case someone like me comes along!'

'Anyway,' said Jannie, 'we never go to the theatre.'

'Well, perhaps we should go to the theatre if we were richer. I know you two think I'm a tit, going on like this. But I have a serious point here.'

'Eat up your meat, John,' said Jannie. 'You haven't put a mouthful in for the last ten minutes.'

'I have a serious point,' said Dyson, 'and that is that nowadays it's not excellence which leads to celebrity, but celebrity which leads to excellence. One makes one's reputation, and one's reputation enables one to achieve the conditions in which one can do good work.'

'You do talk a lot of shit sometimes, John,' said Bob mildly.

'It's not shit, Bob! Look, take me. Let's be honest with ourselves; I'm a small but vital link in the business of producing one of the most important daily newspapers in the world. But shouldn't I do better work if I weren't driven from pillar to post to supplement my salary? Well, *shouldn't I?*'

'You'd bring the crossword stock up to strength?'

'Among other things.'

'You'd find more financiers to write "The Country Day by Day"?'

'Well, why not? Are you beginning to see what I mean, Bob? I mean, if I were The John Dyson, the paper itself would pay me a bigger salary just for a start.'

'John, love,' said Jannie, 'do eat up. The rest of us have finished.'

'Or take you, Bob,' said Dyson. 'You're a writer.'

'*I*'m a writer?' said Bob.

'I didn't know you were a writer, Bob,' said Jannie.

'Bob is a *marvellous* writer!' said Dyson, his voice almost breaking with emotion at his own generosity. 'Perhaps a *great* writer.'

'I didn't know I was a writer,' said Bob.

'Bob, you're a *wonderful* writer!' cried Dyson.

'But I haven't written anything,' said Bob uneasily. 'Have I?'

'Exactly! *Exactly!*' Dyson leaned forward in great excitement. 'And why haven't you written anything? Because you're slaving away in that little office all day doing stupid, piddling little jobs for me! That's why!'

'Oh, I shouldn't say that . . .'

'I drive you hard, Bob. I realize that. I make you work like a dog. He writes like an angel, Jannie! And I make him work like a dog! I drive you hard because I drive myself hard, Bob . . .'

'Really, John, you're very reasonable . . .'

'No, no, I'm a slavedriver and I know it. But don't think I don't understand what it costs, because I do. You haven't written anything, Bob, because you haven't got the right conditions of life because you're not well-known.'

'But look, John . . .'

'I know you both think I'm an egotistical shit, going on about wanting to be famous. But it's not just for myself . . .'

'You want everyone to be famous?' asked Jannie.

'Everyone who has something to offer the world! I want to liberate myself from the tyranny of the BBC Overseas Service, certainly. But I also want Bob to become well-known, so that he can liberate himself from *me*.'

'What about me?' asked Jannie. 'Do you want me to become famous and liberate myself from you?'

Dyson put down his knife and fork, frowning, his exaltation all turned to dust.

'All right, pick holes,' he said sulkily. 'All right, I haven't got my ideas completely worked out and watertight. I know that.'

He pushed his plate away.

'Aren't you going to have any more?' asked Jannie.

'It's too rich for me – it always gives me indigestion. I don't know why you keep serving it.'

Jannie cleared the plates away, catching Bob's eye for a moment and pushing her bottom lip up in mock guilt. Bob looked quickly away, trying not to smile. Dyson sat pouting and rubbing his hands together, glaring down at various parts of the table.

'Shall we take our puddings into the next room and watch television?' suggested Jannie.

'Why don't we?' said Bob.

'Load of shit,' said Dyson.

'There might be a discussion about the colour problem,' said Jannie.

'Oh, very sarcastic.'

'It's the old movie tonight,' said Bob.

'Oh, go and switch it on then, Bob!' said Jannie.

'Condescending lowbrows,' said Dyson sourly. 'Highbrow lowbrows. No – not even genuine highbrow lowbrows. Middlebrow highbrow lowbrows.'

The old movie sent Dyson to sleep. Bob looked round to say something to him, and there he was, in the flickering bluish light from the screen, with his head back and his mouth open.

'We shouldn't have insisted,' said Bob.

'No, he must have been enjoying it,' said Jannie. 'He always goes to sleep when he's enjoying something. Open another bottle of beer, Bob.'

'Will you have some?'

Jannie was absorbed in the film again.

'I'll have a sip,' she said eventually. 'What's the name of the girl who's playing the reporter? I don't mean Myrna Loy, do I?'

'No, no,' said Bob, pouring the beer. 'I know who it is. I'll think of her name in a minute.'

He settled back in his armchair with his beer, full of mutton and beans and well-being. He felt as though there were a space for him in the universe, and he exactly filled it.

'I don't mean Carole Lombard, do I?' said Jannie.

'No, no. The name's on the tip of my tongue.'

White telephones were brought to night-club tables. Stars were surrounded by reporters as they emerged from stage doors. Tycoons snarled. Eyes sparkled mistily. There were skyscrapers and luxury suites.

Life was suspended . . .

Once Damian cried out in his sleep, and fell silent again. Once Dyson snorted, and Jannie leaned over and stroked his hair.

'It's not Jean Arthur, is it?' she said.

'No. I think the brother's the bloke who was in *The Philadelphia Story.*'

'Was that the one with Katherine Hepburn?'

'No – the one with Katherine Hepburn was the one with Cary Grant.'

From somewhere outside at one point there came a distant rumble and chinking, like old milk bottles clashing together.

'Is that the rubbish coming over the wall?' asked Bob.

'I suppose so.'

'Shouldn't we wake John up and tell him?'

'He'll find out soon enough.'

Bob opened another bottle of beer.

'Poor John,' said Jannie.

Dyson drove Bob home in the old Standard Vanguard, through the dank, dead streets of the inner suburbs, yellow under the sodium lights. Bob felt comforted by their calm and familiar variety. Yellow high streets, with yellow electrical shops, and in the windows of the multiple tailors blank-faced dummies leaning discreetly forward in eggily dark worsted. Yellow Victorian mansions, with their front gardens asphalted over to make yellow parking areas for the flatholders' yellow cars. Now it was mercury vapour country. Bluish second-hand car lots; sagging bluish fences; bluish Unitarian churches; small bluish factories, some

Odeon-fronted, some glassed and rectilinear, but set at odd bluish angles to their surroundings. Now they were back among the sodium, passing yellow pre-war flats – Keeps, Courts, and Mansionses, with yellow gables and yellow weatherboarding.

There were few people about, but many cars. As soon as they got within range of Dyson everyone seemed to drive badly. They overtook him when he wasn't expecting it; they pulled up at the side of the road and trapped him behind them; they got in front of him at traffic-lights and then decided to turn right. 'Oh, for God's *sake*!' snarled Dyson, snatching at the wheel, thumping the accelerator up and down uncertainly. He sat forward tensely in his seat, as if he found it difficult to see the road, and frequently wiped at the windscreen with his handkerchief. At one point something heavy fell off or out of the dashboard on to Bob's foot, and rolled away beneath the seat with a metallic ring. Dyson peered down into the darkness after it, driving the car steadily out across the white line in the middle of the road.

'Don't worry about that, Bob,' he said. 'That's always coming off. Incidentally, Bob, those brown patches on the wings aren't rust, you know.'

'Which brown patches, John?'

'I thought I saw you looking at them before we started. They look like rust – it fooled me at first. But it's rather interesting – it's brown undercoat. It's quite remarkable when you come to think about it. The car's fifteen years old, it stands out in all weathers, and the undercoat's still intact.'

'Remarkable.'

'Of course, it's not just the paintwork. Everything was built to a slightly higher specification then. They hadn't learned to cut quite so many corners. It's worth remembering, Bob, if you ever buy a car.'

Dyson swung left into a main road, looking over his shoulder to watch out for traffic from his right, and drove over the edge of the kerb. The thump of the back wheel coming back into the gutter brought Bob's window down.

'Jam it with that wedge of paper,' said Dyson. 'I suppose some damned fool left a brick lying in the gutter.'

In the middle of a yellow common the engine died, and the car rolled jerkily to a halt.

'That's funny,' said Dyson. He pressed the starter. He pressed it again. He went on pressing it until the starter-engine ground to a halt. Then they sat in silence for some moments.

'George God strikes again,' said Bob.

In a sudden access of enraged energy, Dyson jumped out of the car, slammed the door violently behind him, and wrenched the bonnet open. Bob followed him apprehensively. Dyson was glaring into the hot, oily darkness of the engine as if he was about to smash it to pieces with his bare hands.

'Perhaps it was that bump we went over,' said Bob hesitantly.

Dyson straightened up and transferred his glare to Bob.

'Do you know anything at all about cars?' he asked curtly.

'No, John.'

'Then be a good fellow, will you, and try not to make imbecile remarks.'

Dyson bent over the engine again.

'If you want to know,' he said, 'it's probably the points. Or something to do with the plugs.'

He put his hand into the engine, touched something hot, and sprang back a pace.

'*Christ!*' he hissed, sucking his knuckles.

'John,' said Bob, 'may I ask a very naïve question? Are you sure it hasn't just run out of petrol?'

'Oh, shut up, Bob,' said Dyson, peering into the engine and trying to see what it was he had touched.

'But would it perhaps just be worth looking at the petrol gauge?'

Dyson straightened up slowly.

'Look, Bob,' he said. 'I'm extremely tired. I'm extremely angry. I'm extremely likely to hit you. Every single thing without exception has gone wrong today. It's been the most awful day of my life. And now you pester me with idiot suggestions about something you know nothing whatsoever about.'

He plunged back into his contemplation of the engine. Bob did not like to remind him that up till then it had been an awfully good day for him, on which every single thing without exception had gone right.

He crept inconspicuously back to the dashboard, switched on the ignition, and looked at the gauge.

'The gauge doesn't work,' snapped Dyson. 'I know precisely how much petrol I've got because I know precisely how much I've put in and precisely how many miles I've been. I put in two gallons on Saturday, and I can tell you for a fact there's at least quarter of a gallon left. I hope that satisfies you.'

When Dyson was hidden beneath the bonnet again Bob tiptoed round to the boot and eased it open. Beneath a heap of old rags and newspapers and raincoats he found an empty petrol can. He put it under his overcoat, gently closed the boot, and tiptoed away along the yellow pavement in search of a yellow garage.

'I'm not waiting for you,' shouted Dyson when he was about fifty yards away. 'As soon as I've got the car going I'm off.'

Dyson undressed quietly in the dark, so as not to wake Jannie, sighing loudly in the hope that it would. As he got into bed she rolled over towards him and put her arms round him.

'What time is it?' she asked sleepily.

'Half past one,' said Dyson. 'I ran out of petrol.'

She ran her hand down over his chest and stomach, and seized him softly and irresistibly by the roots.

'No, Jannie,' he said. 'No, really . . . No, honestly, I'm terribly tired . . . No, honestly, Jannie, I shall be absolutely deadbeat tomorrow as it is . . . Now, Jannie . . . ! *Jannie* . . . ! Well, look, Jannie . . . Well, I suppose . . . Just . . . Oh, well . . .'

Five

Dyson made thorough preparations for his television appearance. All weekend he drove about the outer suburbs with Jannie and the boys, calling on relatives and letting fall the news in the course of conversation.

'The poor old souls like to know what one's doing,' he explained to Jannie, as they jerked along in the traffic stream between aunt and aunt.

At the office during the week he found circumstances made it necessary for him to ring most of his influential friends and acquaintances – Sims, the paper's tame QC; Sir William Paice; Brent-Williamson, the Literary Editor; Huysmanns at the French Embassy. 'I hope you'll be watching the box on Thursday night,' he said to each of them in a humorous voice. 'What? Well, *I'm* going to be on ... Yes! Isn't it preposterous? 10.45 on the commercial – some ghastly programme called *The Human Angle*.'

Bob's gaze disconcerted him. He would turn his back on him while he was talking, or look down smiling into the mouthpiece.

'It's naughty of me, I know,' he would say as he put the phone down. Or: 'I'm sorry, Bob. I'm behaving outrageously.'

And he would dial another number.

He also gave some serious thought to how he should look. Should he lean forward passionately and denounce things? Or should he sit back in his chair and smile calmly at the idiocies of mankind? He rehearsed a calm smile in front of the mirror at home; it looked like an apologetic grin. He tried an expression of passionate commitment; it came out indistinguishable from defensive surliness. Either way, his fingertips became moist with sweat at the thought of producing the expression in front of the television cameras.

There was also the question of what he was going to say. He began to note down suitable thoughts and epigrams on pieces of office copy-paper, not really with the intention of learning them off by heart, but with the idea that he might put them in his jacket pocket and touch them from time to time during the programme to give himself reassurance, knowing that if the worst really came to the worst he could take them out and refresh his memory.

'T prob of t multiracial soc,' he wrote, 'is in ess merely t mod versn of t time-hon prob of unitg tribes in nationhd.'

The real problem was to avoid the obvious. He was not being paid twenty-five guineas to tell people what they could manage to think out themselves for nothing.

'T troub is,' he tried, 'tt we aren't prej *enough*! Shd educ ourselves to be dply & bttrly prej – agnst prej!'

He tried it over uneasily in front of the mirror. If one of his deans or canons had written it in a Meditation he would have read it out to Bob in a mock-clerical voice, and deleted it, snarling. However, this was a television programme, not a newspaper article. Different criteria applied.

The trouble was that they would all agree with each other. They would all sit round deploring racial prejudice and suggesting how to avoid it. Perhaps he should try to play the devil's advocate? He noted down one or two cautiously controversial points. 'Mst try to undrstnd att of man whse hse val falls. – Ind ckng delightfl but hly fragrnt. – Mst admt I pers h diff in undrstndg next-dr neighbr's Eng.'

He would keep the liberal thoughts in his lefthand pocket, he decided, and the provocative ones in his right-hand pocket. Then he would be able to put his hand immediately on whatever he required. And jokes, of course – he'd need jokes. He could keep a list of jokes in his inside breast pocket. The idea of race opened up a few humorous possibilities. Something about the three-legged race, perhaps, or the egg-and-spoon race? Bn estab by scientists tt all races are of eql intell, except prhps egg-&-spn race. Something along those lines. Professionalism, that was what counted – thorough, serious preparation for even the most informal and evanescent of undertakings.

Whenever Dyson's phone rang that week it was the television company. Could he give them a few facts about himself for the company's press release? They hoped that he would be able to join the other participants for dinner at the studios beforehand. A car would be sent for him at seven-thirty. The final members of the team had now been settled – Miss Ruth Drax, a social worker, and Mr Lewis Williamson, a barrister from Trinidad. The car would be coming at eight. A list of likely topics of discussion was on its way to him by post. The car would now be calling for him at seven.

Every time the phone rang Dyson's fingers became moist with sweat. So did Bob's. Every time Dyson looked at himself in the kitchen mirror, trying to imagine it was a television screen, his stomach and Jannie's stomach turned over in unison. Jannie was beginning to doubt whether she actually would be able to bring herself to watch the programme.

'Would you like to go round and hold Jannie's hand on Thursday night, Bob?' said Dyson at the office one morning. 'I'd be awfully obliged if you would. She's in a terrible state about the whole thing, poor poppet.'

'I'm in rather a state about it myself, John,' said Bob.

'You can hold each other's hand, then. I'm in a frightful state about it, too, and there's no one to hold my hand. It's funny – I never get in a state about doing radio programmes. Do you, Bob?'

'I don't do radio programmes, John.'

'Of course you don't. I get a few qualms just before the green light comes on. Nothing to worry about, though. But I must admit, when I think about Thursday night I feel absolutely sick with nerves. Do you do any television, Bob? I can't remember.'

'You know I don't, John.'

'You're very sensible, Bob. Take my advice – stick to good old steam radio.'

Bob had troubles enough of his own.

'Bob my darling,' wrote Tessa. 'What a strange letter you wrote me! I know it's very stupid of me, but I couldn't understand what it was supposed to be about at all. Did John Dyson really have a fight with a man called Cox, or did you make all that up? It was all like something you read in a book. My private idea, which I hardly dare mention in case I've got it all wrong, is that you were copying the style of some book or other to see if I would recognize it. Darling Bob, don't be cross if I haven't got it right, but is it one of your beloved American writers? Is it supposed to be someone like John dos Passos or James Joyce?'

And Mrs Mounce was crowding him closer and closer. She had got a key to his room out of Dotty, as she had threatened. She came and went while he was out, tidying up, laying the table for his evening meal, and no doubt reading his letters and looking in his drawers to see if he had a rupture belt, or kept a stock of contraceptives. She left dishes she had cooked for him, with notes underneath them. 'Have a good nosh darling,' said the notes, or: 'Sorry Bob I broke the milk jug, I will get you another.' 'Have borrowed one of your Frank Chacksfield records, promise faithfully not to scratch it.' And, under not a dish but his pillow, folded into his pyjamas: 'How's the bite Bob, sorry but you did ask for it sweetie.'

Bob stayed away from home every evening, pursuing old Hitchcock films he had seen before to art cinemas in Kilburn, Tooting and Putney, and eating cheaply in Indian and Cypriot restaurants. But she usually heard him creep in, however late it was, and came scratching on the door just as he had got his trousers off, or just as he was scraping her uneaten steak-and-kidney pie into a polythene bag to throw away at the office next day. It embarrassed him to receive her in his dressing-gown. It embarrassed him still more when she arrived dressed for bed herself as well, a complex bundle of diaphanous nightwear from the midst of which her poised cigarette arm stuck out oddly, like an awkward projection emerging from some ill-wrapped Christmas parcel.

74

'I hope you're not shy, darling,' she said, kicking off her high-heeled slippers and snuggling sensuously down into his armchair. 'You've caught me in my frillies.'

'I'm sorry,' said Bob.

'Still, I'm sure you've seen girls in their frillies before. Haven't you, Bob?'

Bob made some small, non-committal noise. Mrs Mounce blew out cigarette smoke provocatively, narrowing her eyes against its sting.

'*And* without, I bet, sweety pie. Oh, you don't have to tell me. I know you're not one of these lily-white Mother's boys. I can tell a real man when I see one, believe me. I could tell you a thing or two, darling, I really could. I may look like a demure little wife who sits at home minding the house, but darling, I could tell you one or two things that would make your ears stand up on end.'

She was going to get him finally, he could see that. She was going to edge him into a situation where it would be openly discourteous to refuse her, and nothing in his education or his upbringing had prepared him to be discourteous to anyone, least of all a woman. He felt a terrible queasy emptiness in his stomach at the thought; it was as bad as the prospect of Dyson's going on television. Worse, Mr Mounce had begun to look at him oddly. Or so it seemed to him. When he met him in the office, or on the stairs, his habitually offensive glance seemed to have a new dimension of thoughtfulness. On the Saturday morning Bob came face to face with him as he emerged from the communal bathroom on the first half-landing. 'I want to have a little chat with you some time, Bob,' he said. Bob was numbed with fear. To be actually accused point blank by an outraged husband! He had never dreamed that it would happen to him.

He went out immediately, and stayed out for the rest of the weekend. He had an idea that he would find himself another flat, and he actually called at a number of agencies in the Bayswater area and asked for their lists. The prices were unbelievable. Small bachelor flats were offered at £500, £650, £1,000 a year; plus £1,600 – £2,000 – £2,500 for furniture and fittings. Where did the people who could pay such prices come from? What jobs could they possibly have? How could there be so many of them? Some advertisements asked for only 'a reasonable figure to cover F & F.' But how much was that? He could offer them – what? – not more than fifty or sixty pounds altogether. Was that a reasonable figure? He didn't have the nerve to ask.

He gave up flat-hunting and went to the cinema. After the cinema he had tea, walked the streets for an hour, had a couple of Guinnesses in a pub to keep out the sharp evening air, and ate a biriani. Then he went to a party. There was a party almost every Saturday night given by someone in his circle of friends. It was that sort of set. A motheaten sort of set, as he frankly recognized – indeed, as they all frankly recognized – left over from Cambridge, and outgrown and abandoned by all its more enterprising members. The remaining half-dozen or so clasped the last tattered shreds of the undergraduate life around them to keep out the cold winds of the world. The party that night was like all their parties. Old Dave Meadows put old Brubeck records on the gramophone. Old Mike Ramsden got out his guitar and sang old Tom Lehrer songs. Old Ian Strachan locked himself in the bedroom with old Caroline Pickthorn, and old Peter Staithes pissed out of the window and threw empty bottles down into the basement area. On Monday morning they would all disappear into the Shell Centre and Unilever House and various grim out-departments of the BBC, yawning rebelliously.

Bob sat up till three drinking red table wine from a bottle marked Red Table Wine, and talking to old Janet Moss about life and death and their relations with their respective parents. Then he dozed in an armchair for a few hours, until he was too cold and stiff to bear it any longer, when he got up and made tea for everyone, and discovered that there was nothing to eat for breakfast.

Sunday went by in a haze, long and grey and unreal. He sat over breakfast in a cafeteria for a long time, reading the Sunday papers. He walked round Kensington and Earl's Court and Chelsea until his feet were sore, met old Mike

Ramsden and old Caroline Pickthorn for drinks, had lunch on his own in a spaghetti house, walked again. Afterwards, he remembered that Lots Road power station had smoked whitely into a grey sky, and that along the Embankment a cold wind had been whipping off the river, driving spread-eagled pages from an old newspaper before it, and wrapping one of them round the legs of a tall, frail man in a tweed overcoat.

After tea he dozed through an old Peter Sellers film at the King's Road Classic, dined off a biriani, dozed through an old Tati film at the Baker Street Classic, and crept upstairs to his flat just in time to meet Mounce coming downstairs from his den.

'Ah,' said Mounce. 'The prodigal returns. I want to have a word with you, lad.'

'All right,' said Bob. He gave up. He had no fight left.

Mounce unlocked the flat which had been converted into a bar. He switched on the strip lights behind the bottles, and the electric fire, and poured out two large glasses of whisky. Bob perched on a bar stool, still wearing his overcoat. It was cold in the room, and the air smelt musty and unbreathed.

'The point is this, Bob,' said Mounce, leaning across the bar towards him and swilling the whisky round in his glass, 'I'm away a lot, as you know. I've got to be. I'm a married man – I've got responsibilities. You know what I mean, Bob?'

'Yes,' said Bob, remembering from his childhood just how much it hurt to be punched on the nose.

'The point being that while Dad's out earning the housekeeping, certain things could conceivably be occurring behind his back. I'm not saying they do. But you know what I'm driving at?'

'Yes,' said Bob. Or perhaps Mounce would punch him in the eye. A flash of light – then darkness – the sight perhaps permanently damaged.

'I mean,' said Mounce, 'I'm not going to give you a lot of crap about being pure as the driven snow myself. I'm not saying that. All the same, there are limits. There are some stinking limits. I don't know whether you'd agree with me on that?'

'Oh, yes,' said Bob. 'Yes. Yes, indeed.'

Mounce swilled his whisky round moodily for some time, as if trying to think what to do next. If he just suddenly hits me without warning, thought Bob, I shall almost certainly go straight over backwards with my feet still caught up in the bar-stool, and split my skull open on the floor.

'Do you see much of Glenda while I'm away?' asked Mounce.

'No,' said Bob eagerly. 'Oh no. Scarcely at all.'

'You never drop in on her?'

'Never!'

'You never ask her in for a drink?'

'No!'

Mounce frowned. Oh God, thought Bob. It's all just about to happen.

'You are a rotten sod, Bob,' said Mounce.

'Honestly, Reg . . .' began Bob, trying to get one foot down on the floor behind him.

'No, you're a rotten sod, Bob.'

'I assure you, Reg . . .'

'You're a rotten, stinking sod. You might just ask her in once in a while. You know, hold her hand and cheer her up a bit. Keep her out of trouble. Do you see what I mean?'

Bob took a long draught of whisky, spilling some of it down his chin.

'I never thought of it that way,' he said.

Dyson had expected to find the television studios a blaze of activity in the middle of the evening viewing hours, and humbly anticipated that he would himself be treated as a completely unimportant part of the machine – jostled indifferently in the corridors by actors, musicians, and cameramen, sighed at offensively in the studio by the technicians and professionals. But when he stepped out of the Hunter Snipe which had been sent to pick him up he found that the building was in darkness and apparently deserted. The only light he could see was in the lobby, and the only person in the lobby was an anxious girl with a clipboard who was waiting to greet him personally, and who seemed personally grateful for his skill in getting himself found and driven there by the company's chauffeur. She led him along deserted, echoing corridors; nothing was happening in the whole enormous building, he realized, but the tiny preparations for this one tiny programme. All the rest of the evening's television was pre-filmed, pre-taped, or provided by other companies.

The preparation for *The Human Angle,* Dyson discovered, were going forward in a room on the first floor furnished with a sea-blue fitted carpet, a number of discreetly abstract paintings, and a walnut sideboard. A dozen or so well-bred men in dark suits – some of them, noted Dyson with interest, wearing Brigade ties – were standing about drinking gin and smiling agreeably at each other's jokes. A selection of them pressed forward upon Dyson deferentially, introducing themselves, fetching him drinks and salted peanuts. Like the girl with the clipboard, they seemed consumed with gratitude and admiration for his skill in getting there. 'You got here all right, then?' they asked anxiously. 'The driver found you all right? You found your way upstairs without any difficulty?'

The only person in the room Dyson recognized was de Sousa, the producer, and he seemed to be the least important of them all. There was a woman – presumably Miss Drax, the social worker, and a man with rather dark skin – clearly Williamson, the Trinidadian barrister. Dyson never caught the names of any of the others, or found out what they did, apart from drinking the company's gin with a reassuring deftness. Dyson assumed they were the company's directors, bankers, and financial advisers; they all had an air of unassuming integrity and human dignity which in Dyson's experience was acquired only by daily contact with very large sums of other people's money. He liked them, he discovered. He liked their deference and he liked their gin, and within ten minutes he was explaining to them exactly how the daily supply of crosswords in a newspaper was maintained. They were fascinated. *'Really?'* they said. 'How extraordinarily interesting!' Dyson began to feel that everything was going to be all right. His pockets were full of remarks to make, and a bottle of bismuth in case he got nervous indigestion. He began to feel that he would not need either.

Lord Boddy arrived. He was a large, slow-moving man with bushy grey eyebrows and dandruff on his shoulders.

'I must tell you, Lord Boddy,' said Dyson deferentially, 'how very much I enjoyed that collection you did of your father's papers. Of course, I'm a great admirer of all your books.'

'Really?' said Lord Boddy, pushing up his eyebrows with no less deference in return. 'It's very good of you to say so. Most kind, most kind.'

Deference bred deference. Lord Boddy, grasping his gin-and-tonic in his right hand and talking about the greatness of Asquith, put his left hand in his trouser pocket. A moment later Dyson realized that all the men listening to Lord Boddy had their left hands in their trouser pockets, too. His own left hand, he discovered, was in his trouser pocket. He took it out hastily, lest Lord Boddy noticed it and jumped to the conclusion that Dyson was mimicking him, and transferred it to his jacket pocket. At once Lord Boddy did the same, and one by one, as they listened and nodded, everyone else followed suit. Embarrassed, now that he had noticed what was happening, Dyson removed his hand from his jacket pocket and slipped it inconspicuously behind his back. Boddy, describing very slowly and emphatically how Asquith had died just before he could meet him, put his own hand through the same manoeuvre, and one by one all the other spare left hands disappeared behind their owners' backs, too. Mutual deference could scarcely be carried further.

And yet, when Norman Ward Westerman arrived, it was. Dyson could imagine Lord Boddy and the executives gathered around him putting deference aside from time to time in order to get on with the gardening, or to discipline some delinquent guardsman. But Norman Ward Westerman was deference made flesh. When he bent that famous craggy face and strong jaw down from its natural elevation to the level of ordinary human beings it was not to advance any opinions or tell any anecdotes of his own. It was purely to bring his ear reverentially into line with the mouth of whomever was speaking. 'Exactly,' he murmured. '*Exactly*.' And Dyson knew from the depth of humility and reverence in his inflection that he was getting a larger fee than even Lord Boddy. Dyson felt awed by him. He felt awed by Lord Boddy, for that matter, and by the company in general. He felt awed by himself. They were all gods, gathered in godly discourse.

They moved into the next room, and sat down to dinner. White-jacketed waiters tiptoed reverently around them, pouring hock with the frozen scampi, a claret with a fruity, full-bodied label to go with the reheated roast lamb. 'Thank you,' murmured Dyson with heartfelt respect to a waiter at his elbow. 'Thank you, sir,' said the waiter. 'Thank you,' said Dyson.

'Or take Baldwin,' Norman Ward Westerman was saying to Lord Boddy. 'I find him . . . an enigmatic figure. Would you think that was a fair assessment, Frank?'

'Oh, indeed. Indeed, indeed, indeed. I think that's a very fair assessment of him. It's rather interesting you should mention Baldwin, as a matter of fact, because I never met him.'

'Didn't you? That's extraordinarily interesting.'

'No, I never met Baldwin.'

'You interest me, Frank, because I didn't know that at all.'

One of the financial figures was leaning deferentially across the table towards Williamson.

'You don't happen to know a man called Firmead, do you?' he said.

'Firmead?' said Williamson deferentially. 'Curiously enough I don't believe I do.'

'*David* Firmead, to be precise.'

'Curiously enough I don't believe I've ever met him.'

'He was in Trinidad for some time last year. Something to do with oil, I think.'

'*Really?* How very interesting.'

'I just thought you might have run across him. Awfully nice man. We were at school together.'

'Really? That is most interesting.'

The financial figure turned his head slightly to include Miss Drax in the conversation.

'You don't know him, do you, by any chance?' he asked. 'A man called Firmead, David Firmead?'

'As a matter of fact,' said Miss Drax, 'I don't think I can honestly say I do.'

'Awfully nice man,' said the financial figure.

Dyson felt he had grasped enough of the general principles of the conversation between Boddy and Williamson to risk joining in himself.

'I find *Halifax* a curiously intriguing figure,' he said when there was a pause. 'I don't know whether you'd agree?'

Westerman swung round in his chair to give Dyson his full attention.

'I think that is an awfully good point,' he said. 'Halifax is a figure who intrigues me, too. Do you find Halifax at all intriguing, Frank? Or do you feel that there's nothing really interesting about him?'

'No, I think as Mr Dyson says, Halifax is an extraordinarily intriguing figure. Most *extraordinarily* intriguing. But do you know, Norman, in all the years that Halifax held office I never met him once.'

'*Really?*' said Westerman. 'That is absolutely fascinating.'

'Not once.'

'That is most incredibly interesting,' said Dyson.

The meal went by like a dream. Dyson felt as though that small room, surrounded by the dark emptiness of the studios, was the one speck of warmth and life in an unpeopled universe. Of course, there were other subsidiary settlements if one stopped to think. Somewhere in the building was a room where a hired chef was unfreezing the scampi, reheating the meat, and opening the giant economy can of fruit salad. Somewhere there was a studio with five black leather armchairs waiting. But the real richness of life was concentrated here – brilliant conversation, warm mutual esteem, a man who had not known Baldwin or Halifax, and good claret warmed by discreet waiters on some radiator well out of sight. This, realized Dyson with a sense of homecoming, was where he belonged; this was the way of life for which his character and education had fitted him.

'Norman,' said de Sousa as the coffee and brandy were being poured, 'I wonder if we ought perhaps to have just a tiny natter about the programme.'

'I think that would be an awfully good idea, Jack,' said Westerman. He took some cyclostyled papers out of his pocket and looked at them. 'Well, as I understand it, Jack – tell me if I'm wrong – we open with the credits on telecine. Right?'

'Right,' said de Sousa, lighting a small cigar.

'Then we come up on me in the studio. I say, "Good evening. The film you're about to see is the record of a remarkable experiment in blah blah blah . . ." '

'All on Autocue.'

'All on Autocue. Then we have the film. Then we come back to me in the studio and I say, "The film you have just seen was an attempt to blah blah blah. Now we have here in the studio tonight four people who are vitally and personally concerned with the problems of living in a multiracial community. On my right is Lord Boddy, who was a member of the Royal Commission on blah blah blah . . ." '

'And you go right round the table.'

'And I go right round the table. Then I'll turn to you, Frank, and say, "Lord Boddy, what do you think of the experiment we have just seen? Do you think it holds out a ray of hope among the problems which perplex us all so sorely today?" '

'I say blah blah blah,' said Lord Boddy.

'You say blah blah blah. Then we all join in blah blah blah. Then when I get the sign from the studio manager I wind up and say, "Well, then, the conclusions we seem to have reached tonight are blah blah blah." '

'All on Autocue,' said de Sousa.

'All on Autocue. I think that's all fairly well tied up, isn't it, Jack?'

'I think so. Is everybody happy?'

'Indeed, indeed, indeed,' said Dyson. 'I don't think I've ever enjoyed myself so much in my life.'

They trooped down to the studio for the line-up, taking their glasses of brandy with them. A little of the festive warmth seemed to die out of the air as they took their places around the low coffee table in the corner of the great hangar. Williamson kept clearing his throat. Miss Drax smiled unhappily about her. Even Boddy, who had been telling Westerman as they came down the stairs how he had been at Bad Godesberg in 1938 just two days after Hitler and Chamberlain had left, trailed away into silence. Only Dyson lost none of his elation. When the studio manager asked him to say something to check the microphone levels, he recited the first few lines of 'The Wreck of the Deutschland' with appropriate gestures. It seemed to amuse the studio crew. Really, he thought, this was his evening.

By the time they had been to make-up, and tramped back up the stairs to have another drink, a definite uneasiness was beginning to settle over the whole company. The men with the Brigade ties and their friends were running out of potential mutual acquaintances to describe. Miss Drax seemed to have caught the frog Williamson had had in his throat. Williamson, coming back from his second trip to the lavatory, passed Boddy on the way out for his third. Westerman, shuffling the cyclostyled papers about in his hands, dropped his glass, and filled his shoes with brandy. Dyson watched them all with amazement. He himself was greatly excited, but not nervous in the least.

'The public just don't realize,' said Williamson to him gloomily, 'the terrific amount of work that goes into making one short half-hour of television.'

'Work?' said Dyson. 'It's pure pleasure. I've never enjoyed anything so much in all my life. I'm absolutely bubbling over. I simply can't wait to get on.'

'Good God,' said Williamson.

One of the financial figures, still smiling deferentially, poured them both more brandy.

'I wonder if you could try and keep the bottle away from Lord Boddy,' he said quietly. 'I think perhaps he's had almost enough.'

How interesting it was, thought Dyson, how extraordinarily intriguing, to find that out of the whole team the only one who was actually turning up trumps was himself.

'I think perhaps we might go down now,' said de Sousa.

'I shan't be able to watch,' said Jannie, as the film sequence in the first half of John's programme unreeled meaninglessly in front of her. 'Honestly, Bob, I shan't be able to watch. I know something awful will happen. Oh, Bob, supposing he's had too much to drink?'

'He'll be fine, Jannie,' said Bob. 'Stop fussing.'

Jannie gripped the arms of her chair, trying to stop herself jumping out of it.

'What on earth's this stuff they're showing us now?' she demanded irritably.

'It's the film they're going to discuss.'

'Oh God, I know he's going to make a fool of himself. I know it, I know it, I know it!'

When the film ended, and the face of the chairman appeared again, she put her hand over her eyes, unable to watch the screen. The chairman was introducing Lord Boddy. She had a vision of John sitting hunched up in his chair, as he did at home sometimes when things were going wrong, all dark and gaunt and unhappy. Oh, poor John! Poor John! But where was he? The chairman had been introducing people for an eternity, and still no sign of him. Perhaps he was ill. She imagined him standing in some white-tiled institutional lavatory, suffering from nervous nausea. Had he taken the bismuth with him? But better for him to be in a lavatory somewhere than for him to be sick on the programme! Of course, they would turn the cameras ...

'And on her left,' said the chairman, 'is Mr John Dyson, a journalist and broadcaster who lives . . .'

And there he was! Involuntarily she reached out and gripped Bob's hand. And what in the name of God was John up to? He was smiling and waving!

'What's he doing?' she cried, agonized, as the picture cut back to the chairman. 'It's not that sort of programme!'

'I don't know whether you noticed,' said Bob, 'but he was smoking.'

'Smoking?'

'Didn't you see? He had a cigarette between his fingers.'

'Don't be crazy, Bob. John hasn't smoked since he was an undergraduate.'

'Well, he's smoking now, Jannie.'

'Oh God!' said Jannie, holding Bob's hand very tight. 'I shan't be able to watch, Bob!'

'You're all right now, Jan. Lord Boddy's set for the night.'

But someone was saying something at the same time as Lord Boddy, making him falter and finally stop in mid-stride. The cameras hunted round the team, trying to locate the intruder. They were all smoking, observed Jannie, but John, as she saw when the camera finally settled on him, was smoking more than most. He was smoking and talking simultaneously, taking little melo-dramatic puffs between phrases.

'If I might butt in here,' he was saying (puff). 'If I might possibly butt in a moment . . . puff, puff) I should just like to say that I find what Lord Boddy is saying extraordinarily interesting. *Extraordinarily* interesting.'

He took another energetic puff, and blew out a dense cloud of smoke at the camera as Lord Boddy resumed his discourse.

'Oh God,' said Jannie.

'Sh!' said Bob. Dyson was back in the conversation again.

'That is fascinating,' he was saying. 'Most fascinating. I find that absolutely fascinating.'

Jannie squeezed Bob's hand so hard that he flinched.

'Poor John!' she said.

When Miss Drax's turn to speak came, Dyson was fascinated by her thesis, too.

'Indeed!' he kept murmuring. 'Indeed, indeed!'

'Why is he behaving like this!' cried Jannie. 'Why is he smoking, and waving his arms about in that awful way?'

'He waves his arms about at the office sometimes,' said Bob. 'I don't object to that.'

'But why does he keep saying things like "extraordinarily interesting" and "indeed, indeed"? I've never heard him say anything like that before.'

'I've never heard him say "indeed, indeed", I must admit.'

Williamson was talking. Dyson turned out to be extraordinarily interested in his views, as well.

'Indeed,' he murmured. 'Indeed . . . indeed . . . Oh God, indeed!'

Jannie sank down into her chair, trying to work out who would be watching the programme. All John's family, of course. All *her* family. Her parents had invited the neighbours in to see it, too. Her friend Belinda Charles – she'd rung up to say she'd seen John's name in an article about the programme in the paper. Out of nowhere the idea came to her that Lionel Marcus might be watching. Please God, not Lionel Marcus!

'John Dyson,' the chairman was saying, 'do you, as a journalist, agree with the suggestion that what we need is for the Press to take a firm moral lead and play down all news to do with race relations?'

Dyson did not answer at once. He frowned, then leaned forward and stubbed out his cigarette thoughtfully in the ashtray.

'He's got a sense of timing, anyway,' said Bob.

'I can't bear it,' said Jannie.

Dyson sat back and put his fingertips together, as if about to deliver his verdict. But at the last moment he changed his mind, and instead leaned forward again and took another cigarette out of the box on the table.

'Oh God, Bob!' said Jannie.

Dyson picked up the table-lighter, and with an absolutely

steady hand lit the cigarette. Then he snapped the top of the lighter down, drew in a mouthful of smoke, and let it out again slowly and meditatively.

'I think it's an extraordinarily interesting idea,' he said.

Jannie put her spare hand over her eyes as if shielding them from the sun, and closed out the sight of her husband.

'You're exaggerating, Jannie,' said Bob.

Later he said: 'People who don't know him wouldn't get the same impression at all.'

Later still he said: 'Honestly, Jannie, nobody watches this sort of programme apart from the relatives of the performers.'

It seemed to Jannie that the noise of John blowing cigarette smoke out almost drowned the conversation. She kept her hand over her eyes until at last Westerman halted the discussion and summed up. He paused before saying good night, and a voice from off-screen cut in at once.

'That is absolutely fascinating, Norman,' it said.

Jannie put her head on Bob's shoulder and wept.

Dyson walked up and down the bedroom in his overcoat, making large gestures, and trailing in his wake the cosy smell of digested alcohol. Jannie lay in bed, looking at him over the edge of the covers. It was after midnight.

'Honestly, Jannie,' said Dyson excitedly, 'I astonished myself! I simply didn't know I had it in me! How did it look?'

'Very good, John.'

'Really? You're not just saying that?'

'No, John.'

'I actually *enjoyed* it, Jannie, that was the thing. I was amazed! The others were all shaking with nerves! Even hardened television performers like Norman and Frank. But honestly, I could have gone on all night. I didn't use my notes at all.'

'I thought you didn't.'

'Didn't touch them – didn't even think about them. I was absolutely in my element! How did I come over, Jannie?'

'I told you — very well.'

'I didn't cut in and argue too much?'

'I don't think so.'

'I thought perhaps I was overdoing the controversy a bit?'

'No, no.'

Dyson stopped and gazed at Jannie seriously.

'I feel I've at last found what I really want to do in life, Jannie,' he said. 'It's so much more alive and vital than journalism. Honestly, Jannie, I'm so exhilarated . . . !'

He began to stride up and down the room again, smiling at himself. He glanced in the mirror as he passed it and straightened his glasses.

'What did Bob think?' he asked. 'Did he think I was all right?'

'He thought you were fine.'

Dyson stopped again, smiling reflectively.

'Frank Boddy is an absolute poppet,' he said warmly. 'He really is. Oh, Jannie, I adore television! I can't tell you . . . ! You really think I looked all right?'

Later, as he was crawling about the floor in his underclothes, looking under the bed for his slippers, Jannie asked :

'Why were you smoking, John?'

He straightened up and gazed anxiously over the end of the bed at her.

'You thought it looked odd?' he said.

'No, no.'

'You don't think it seemed rather mannered?'

'Of course not, John. I just wondered how you came to think of it.'

Dyson smiled with pleasure as he remembered.

'It was sheer inspiration on the spur of the moment,' he said. 'I just saw the box of cigarettes lying there on the table, and everybody else smoking, and I just knew inside me with absolute certainty that I should smoke, too. I think it absolutely *made* my performance.'

He fell asleep almost as soon as the light was out, and woke up again about an hour later, his mouth parching, his whole being troubled with a great sense of unease. What was occupying his mind, as vividly as if it was even now taking place, was the moment when he had said, 'That is absolutely fascinating, Norman,' and then realized it was supposed to be the end of the programme. Had he *really* done that? How terrible. How absolutely terrible.

He sat up and drank some water. Still, one little slip in an otherwise faultless performance . . . Then with great clarity and anguish he remembered the moment when Westerman had put his question about a moral lead from the Press, and instead of answering at once the idea had come to him of leaning forward and judiciously stubbing out his cigarette. It had been scarcely a quarter smoked! He lay down in bed again slowly and unhappily.

All the same, when he had finished stubbing the cigarette out he had given a very shrewd and pertinent answer . . . No, he hadn't! He'd taken another cigarette! In absolute silence, in full view of the whole population of Britain, he had stubbed out a quarter-smoked cigarette and lit a fresh one!

He turned on to his right side, then he turned on to his left, wracked with the shamefulness of the memory. It was strange; everything he had done on the programme had seemed at the time to be imbued with an exact sense of logic and purposiveness, but now that he looked back on it, all the logical connections had disappeared, like secret writing when the special lamp is taken away.

And what about the time he had interrupted Lord Boddy, and then realized that all he had wanted to say was that it was interesting? *Extraordinarily* interesting . . . Had he *really* said that? He himself? The occupant of the tense body now lying obscurely and privately in the dark bedroom of a crumbling Victorian house in Spadina Road, s.w.23? Was that slightly pooped gentleman with the waving arms who had (oh God!) told Lord Boddy that his views were absolutely fascinating, and (oh God oh God!) lit another of the television company's cigarettes with their silver butane table-lighter every time he had seen the red light come up on the camera pointing at him – was that exuberantly shameful figure really identical with the anguished mortal man who now lay here stretched as taut as a piano-string in the dark?

'Jannie,' he groaned. 'Are you awake, Jannie?'

There was no reply. He turned on to his right side. He turned back on to his left. He hurled himself on to his face. Still Westerman and Boddy and Williamson and Miss Drax sat around in conversation with him. He went through his whole performance second by second, from the moment Westerman had introduced him and he had *waved at the camera*, to the moment Westerman had summed up, and he had told him it was *absolutely fascinating*. He went through it again and again, trying to improve it slightly in his memory, in the face of an increasingly hostile reception from the other four. By the time morning came he was convinced he had been wide awake the whole night, though by that time he had remembered with the utmost clarity that the whole performance had taken place not in a television studio at all, but in an enormous public lavatory, with Sir William and Lady Paice among the large crowd around the coffee table, and that his final humiliation was to discover at the end of the programme that he had been sitting on one of the lavatory seats throughout, with his trousers down around his ankles.

Six

Raindrops trembled on the office windows, coalesced, and ran down, leaving paths like silver snail tracks against the lightness of the sky. Dyson watched them absently, grimacing as he bit each of the fingernails of his right hand trim in turn. Bob sat sucking toffees, and watching Dyson from behind his hand. Old Eddy Moulton, who was awake and in an unusually forthcoming mood, looked at Dyson and Bob alternatively as he talked.

'I knew Stanford Roberts,' he said. 'But then I knew most of them. Walter Belling, Stanley Furle, Sir Redvers Tilley – you name them, I knew them. Stanley Furle carried a cane with a solid gold knob – never went anywhere without it. The knob unscrewed and the inside of the cane was hollow. Stanley used to keep it filled with Scotch – three solid feet of Johnnie Walker. One night he was at the old Blackfriars Ring. At the end of every round off came the gold knob and up went the stick. He was with a man called Naylor – not Freddie Naylor of the *Mail*, but Allington Naylor, who worked for A. W. Simpson on the *Morning Post*. A. W. Simpson was one of the great ones. So was Allington Naylor. So was Stanford Roberts, for that matter. Real journalists. Real professionals. Stanford could turn you out an impeccable paragraph on any subject you liked to name at the drop of a hat. He'd have done a par about the lead in his pencil if you'd asked him – a stick and a half – a column – whatever you needed; and all of it full of wit and erudition.'

Dyson went on staring at the raindrops, saying nothing.

'Honestly, John,' said Bob, 'you were great. I don't know what you're worrying about.'

Dyson gave no sign that he had heard.

'Anyway,' said old Eddy Moulton, 'when Stanley Furle came out of the Ring at the end of the evening, he fell down the stairs and blacked his eye on the knob of his cane! I was in the Kings and Keys the night J. D. Maconochie told Bentham Miller that O. M. Pargetter's Tibetan Terror story was a hoax. Oswald hadn't been nearer Tibet than the end of Folkestone pier! I was in the Feathers the night Sandy MacAllister punched Laurence Uden on the nose for saying that Stanford Roberts had been drunk at poor old Sidney Cunningham's funeral.'

'Come on, John,' said Bob. 'Cheer up.'

'In fact,' said old Eddy Moulton, 'Stanford *was* drunk at Sidney Cunningham's funeral. I met R. D. Case afterwards – he was on the *Westminster Gazette* at that time – and he told me that Stanford was so drunk that he'd almost fallen into the grave! Apparently he'd just been caught in time by George Watson-Forbes, who later wrote a remarkable series of articles in the *Daily News* on the Home Rule question.'

Dyson stirred himself, and sighed.

'Would somebody ring Morley, Bob?' he said, scarcely opening his mouth to let the words out, 'and ask him where his copy is? I can't face talking to him today.'

'Now don't be silly, John,' said Bob. 'Jannie and I both thought you were tremendously good.'

'The last job I went on with Sidney Cunningham,' said old Eddy Moulton, 'was an explosion in a gas-main at Newark, which killed thirteen people. I travelled up from King's Cross with Sidney, Daryl Bligh of the *Graphic*, K. B. D. Clarke of *The Times*, "Tibby" Tisdale of the *News*, Stanford Roberts, of course, and I think we had Norton Malley with us, who would at that time I suppose have been on the *Morning Post*, though he later went back to the *Irish Times*. Anyway, the day after we all arrived in Newark, Tibby announced that it was his birthday, and Stanford had the idea of hiring a private dining-room at the Ram...'

Dyson suddenly turned on old Eddy Moulton, silencing him with the sourness of his expression.

'You never went on a gas-main explosion in Newark, Eddy,' he said irritably. 'You're getting mixed up with one of your "In Years Gone By" columns.'

Old Eddy Moulton stared at Dyson, his mouth slightly open.

'You did a fifty-years-ago about a gas-main explosion in Newark the week before last,' said Dyson. 'Don't you remember?'

'I went to Newark on the story, too,' said old Eddy Moulton.

'You're getting mixed up, Eddy.'

'That was my own story I put in the column,' said old Eddy Moulton stubbornly.

'Oh, for God's sake, Eddy!' snapped Dyson. He jumped to his feet and walked quickly out of the room, slamming the door behind him. Old Eddy Moulton looked at Bob, who looked away.

'I was only trying to cheer him up,' said old Eddy Moulton.

The rain had almost stopped, but various projections over the pavement in Fleet Street dripped on Dyson as he passed, wetting the lenses of his spectacles and making it difficult for him to see where he was going. He had decided to show himself to the crowd, and take the plunge into the humiliation that was awaiting him.

He walked with self-conscious haste up the south side of the street towards Temple Bar, staring into the face of everyone coming the opposite way, challenging them to give any sign of their pity and contempt. It was difficult to know whether they recognized him or not. Every time he removed his glasses to wipe the rain off them he could see that everyone was taking advantage of his shortsightedness to stare at him and grin and point. But as soon as he got his glasses back on again, they had all smoothed the hazy, unfocused grins off their faces and seemed intent on their own affairs. Several times he swung round suddenly to see if people were turning to stare at him from behind. They seemed not to be, but it was difficult to be sure that they had not simply managed to turn away again in time. Outside the Lord's Day Observance Society he caught the eye of a tall girl with a red face, who looked quickly away. He jerked his own head away almost as fast, galvanized by the shock of embarrassment. That had been recognition all right. That had been a pointed enough comment, by God! Or had she thought *he* was staring at *her*? He stopped, confused, by the bus stop opposite the Protestant Truth Society, and gazed unseeingly at the list of routes. Suddenly he realized that everyone in the queue was staring at him with frank interest and uninhibited hostility. This was it, then! They hated him! He had tried to rise above them, and had fallen back among them, there to be hated once for his attempt, and twice for his failure! He hurried away, his heart beating fast, shocked but obscurely satisfied by this revelation. He was across the road and halfway back down Fleet Street before it occurred to him that they had been staring at him like that because they thought he was trying to push in at the head of the queue.

He went into an Espresso bar and drank some coffee. No one turned round to look at him. He was a failure, certainly. Failure, it occurred to him, was the secular equivalent of sin. Modern secular man was born into a world whose moral framework was composed not of laws and duties, but of tests and comparisons. There were no absolute outside standards, so standards had to generate themselves from within, relativistically. One's natural sense of inadequacy could be kept at bay only by pious acts of repeated successfulness. And failure was more terrifying than sin. Sin could be repented of by an act of volition; failure could not be disposed of so easily. Sin could be avoided by everyone, if he chose, but failure could not. For there to be any who succeeded, there had to be some who failed; there was no better without worse. The worse had their function. Without himself, thought Dyson, or at any rate the possibility of himself, Norman Ward Westerman would be unadmired, unloved, and un-rewarded.

'Seen you somewhere before, haven't I, squire?' said a weary young man in a coffee-stained white jacket who was clearing the tables, without any great interest.

'Possibly,' said Dyson, feeling himself flushing at once with apprehension and pleasure. The young man sank slowly into the seat opposite him, and got out a cigarette.

'Yes, I seen you somewhere all right,' he said. 'Not in here.'

'No, I haven't been in here before.'

'Where was it, then, Captain? Up the Oasis, was it?'

'No, I don't think so.'

'Down the club, was it?'

Dyson discovered that he wanted the young man to know where it was more than he wanted him not to know.

'I do a certain amount of television,' he said offhandedly, with a slight disclaiming smile. The young man went on staring at him; the idea that he had seen Dyson on television seemed to be too far-fetched even to penetrate his consciousness.

'No, I seen you somewhere, Captain,' he said.

Dyson's slight disclaiming smile vanished.

'Yes,' he said rather irritably; '*On television.*'

The young man rose slowly to his feet, and took Dyson's empty coffee-cup back to the counter. He gazed mournfully out of the window into Fleet Street for some minutes.

'Up the Streatham ice-rink, was it?' he suggested.

Not to have achieved recognition as a failure, felt Dyson, was almost worse than the failing itself. It made him feel that he had failed even at failing.

When Dyson got back to the office old Eddy Moulton had subsided into sleep again.

'Thank God,' muttered Dyson to Bob intensely. 'I don't think I could have stood any more of *that* this morning.'

He sat down and plunged himself into his work. The item uppermost on his desk was a note in his own handwriting which said: 'Straker hol – chck Daw 1st 2 pts Pelling's chchiness.' What the hell was that supposed to mean? He looked up, frowning, and saw that Bob was gazing at him apprehensively.

'I've been walking up and down Fleet Street, if you

want to know,' he said, 'to see whether I could still show my face in public. Did somebody get some copy out of Morley?'

'It's promised for tomorrow,' said Bob.

'I'm sick of Morley. He's not a real professional.'

'He's a canon, John.'

'He's a stupid little prick. I'm not going to use him any more. That's final.'

He scrabbled angrily among the papers and galleys on his desk until he found the copy-pad, and wrote on it: 'Morley stpd lttle prck. Rmmbr n to use.'

Where had he been, when Bob had interrupted him? Oh, yes, looking at this note about Straker. 'Pelling's chchiness'? What in the name of God could that be? Well, he hadn't time to mess around unriddling Pelling's tomfooleries. He screwed the note up and threw it in the general direction of the waste-paper basket. Bob was still looking at him.

'How about a bite of lunch, John?' Bob asked anxiously.

'I don't want any bloody lunch,' said Dyson, thinking of the usual crowd standing round in the Gates. It didn't matter if you made a fool of yourself in front of strangers – he saw that now. It probably didn't matter much if you did it in front of your friends. The shameful thing was doing it in front of strangers, and being seen by your friends in the process.

He turned to the next item on his desk, a note on top of a copy-pad which said: 'Morley stpd lttle prck. Rmmbr n to use.' What drivel was this? He tore it off and threw it at the waste-paper basket. The next thing was a memorandum from Bill Waddy, the News Editor, which said: 'Your department's turn, I think.' Clipped to the back was a letter headed 'Magic Carpet Travel Limited. Specialist consultants in all forms of travel management.'

'Dear Sir,' said the letter. 'Magic Carpet Travel announce with pride the opening of an entirely new sunshine holiday area – the Trucial Riviera. The exotic shores of Trucial Oman, washed by the warm sparkling waters of the Persian Gulf, and rich in all the Arabian Nights romance of the

Middle East, offer something unique in holiday experience to the get-away-from-it-all holidaymaker ...

'To celebrate this remarkable new breakthrough in British holiday technology, we are inviting the Press to join us on a special round trip to Sharjah, the Pearl of the Trucial Riviera, next month ...'

Whose turn was it for a facilities trip? Bob had had the Bulgarian State Non-Ferrous Metals Trust jamboree the previous month, and he'd had the Cosmosair inaugural to Saarbrucken himself. It was old Eddy's turn.

'Eddy,' he said, 'would you like a little jaunt to Trucial Oman? Eddy?'

No reply. Well, to hell with him. If he chose to be asleep when the lollipops were handed round, that was his lookout. Dyson couldn't be expected to wetnurse his staff – he'd far too much on his hands already. In fact, he'd do the trip himself. He desperately needed a holiday. The Saarbrucken trip had been a disaster; it had rained continuously. In fact, it had just added to his burdens. He was ill with overwork. He really was. He was suffering from insomnia and hypertension. And now his tlvsn apprnce (his mind sheered off identifying it more fully even to himself) had finally set the seal on it all. His health was breaking down.

'I couldn't eat any lunch if you paid me,' he said.

'We could go to the Mucky Duck for a change,' said Bob.

Dyson sat hypertensely clenching and unclenching his fingers, trying to think of a headline with no more than ten characters for a piece about the dangers of the exaggeratedly indifferentist liturgical tendencies inherent in oecumenicalism. He could remember a time when he had fallen asleep as soon as his head touched the pillow, and when he had always had a healthy appetite. By half past twelve each day he had had a hunger pain. He had a pain in his stomach now, ironically enough, which felt almost exactly like a hunger pain. He knew what it was. It was the irritation of overstrained nerves. The stomach acid, with no food to work on, was quietly starting to digest and ulcerate the stomach lining.

'Perhaps I ought to try and eat something,' he said, 'to give the stomach acid something to work on.'

He jumped up hypertensely.

'The Mucky Duck?' said Bob, getting to his feet too.

Dyson shook his head impatiently.

'The Gates, the Gates, the Gates,' he said. 'Let's get it over with.'

'Aren't you on television tonight, John?' asked Gareth Holmroyd, as they all stood round gazing into their beer, trying to think of something to say.

'It was last night,' said Dyson.

Ralph Absalom looked interested.

'Did you say you were on television tonight, John?' he asked.

'Last night, last night,' said Dyson.

'Last night? Well, I wish you'd told me beforehand.'

'I did.'

'I'd have stayed in and watched if you'd told me. Did you see John on the box last night, Andy?'

'No,' said Andy Royle. 'I didn't know you were going on television, John?'

'*I* knew,' said Gareth Holmroyd. 'But I thought it was tonight.'

'I didn't know you were on, John,' said Pat Selig. 'I didn't know he was on. Did you, Lucy?'

'I knew he was on,' said Gareth Holmroyd. 'But I thought he said it was tonight.'

Everyone looked into his beer.

'Anyway,' said Gareth Holmroyd finally, 'how did it go, John?'

'Terrible,' said Dyson.

'He was very good,' said Bill Waddy, arriving with more drinks for people. 'He was very good indeed.'

'You saw him, did you, Bill?' said Andy Royle.

'No, I missed him, unfortunately,' said Bill Waddy. 'Old Harry Stearns told me.'

'John was very good,' said Bob, who had told old Harry

Stearns that he was very good in the first place.

'You saw him, did you, Bob?' said Ted Hurwitz.

'Yes. He was very good.'

'Yes,' said Bill Waddy, 'old Harry Stearns said he was very good.'

'Yes, he was,' said Bob. 'Very good.'

'I was terrible,' said Dyson.

'You were very good, John,' said Bill Waddy. 'Old Harry Stearns told me.'

'Good for you, John,' said Pat Selig.

'What was the programme about?' asked Gareth Holmroyd.

'The colour problem,' said Dyson.

'Well, anyway,' said Gareth Holmroyd, 'I'm glad you made a good job of it.'

It rained on and off most of the afternoon. Dyson sat back in his chair watching it, yawning, his hands behind his head. He was in a rather more agreeable mood. Jannie, Bob, old Harry Stearns, Bill Waddy, Gareth Holmroyd – they could scarcely *all* be wrong. In fact, if one tried to think about it objectively, they were likely to have been able to make a more accurate assessment of his performance than he could himself. One couldn't help being over-critical of one's own performance. One knew just how much labour and effort had gone into it. One knew exactly where there had been difficulties and compromises behind the scenes. But Jannie and Bob and old Harry Stearns and Bill Waddy and Gareth Holmroyd saw only what was put before them, which was in fact all that counted. And of course he had been extremely relaxed and natural, he could see that. He had been very fluent and articulate.

'Do you believe in success and failure, Bob?' he asked, yawning.

'I suppose so,' said Bob, not looking up from his work. He was subbing an article by a reader, rewriting it in the style laid down by the paper for reader's articles. 'There is a lack of good first-hand information about the opportunities for cruising in the Barents and Kara Seas,' began the original version. The paper didn't like that sort of opening in a reader's article; it gave a rather professional and businesslike air to what was after all really just another little essay on the pleasures of messing about in boats. 'Little did we realize,' wrote Bob, 'when we blithely set sail from Petsamo in *Lady Jane,* our trusty converted Carmarthen mussel boat, with plenty of paints and modelling clay to keep the children busy, and a supply of special seasick pills for Jason, the children's cairn terrier, exactly what fate had in store for us.'

'Do you think competitiveness is just an aspect of the society we live in, Bob?' said Dyson. 'Or do you think it's absolutely endemic in man?'

'I don't know, John.'

Dyson yawned.

'I think I'm really competitive by nature,' he said. 'I have a tremendous fundamental urge to get out and make my way in the world. Do you feel that, Bob?'

'No.'

'Well, of course, you're a writer. It's different for you. I'm merely an administrator, an organizer. It's natural for me to be more aggressive and pushing. I make no apology for it.'

He yawned again, uncontrollably.

'God, I'm really going to make a resolution about no beer for lunch,' he said. One fought and struggled, he thought. Sometimes one had terrible doubts about how one was doing. But one tried to put a good face on it and keep them to oneself. One could not afford to admit to weaknesses, the competition was so ruthless. Once one had slipped, no helping hands would be extended. Well, he liked it like that. He welcomed it.

And what happened if you failed to make the grade? You ended up like poor old Eddy Moulton, put out to pasture in some quiet department where nobody bothered to talk to you, doing small unworthy chores and dozing the day away. Dyson looked at old Eddy, head down behind the dusty newspaper files, nothing visible of him but his tousled white hair. Who knew now, or cared, what old Eddy had done in his prime? What stories he had beaten the great Stanford Roberts on, or even whether Stanford Roberts had been great after all? Well, thought Dyson suddenly, *he* cared. Old Eddy meant something to *him*. He would take him to the Gates that evening and get him talking. He would ask him about Stanford Roberts. About Walter Cunningham and Sidney Naylor. Just get him talking, and then listen, really listen, while old Eddy disinterred one man's life from the dust of time, and put it together again before his eyes.

There was something about old Eddy's appearance which had been worrying Dyson subconsciously for some minutes, and he suddenly realized what it was.

'Eddy,' he said sharply, leaning forward and bringing the front legs of his chair down on to the floor with a crash, so that Bob looked up startled.

'Eddy!' said Dyson, scrambling to his feet and going across to Eddy's desk. '*Eddy!*'

He hesitated, frightened of making an embarrassing mistake, then felt the wrinkled white hand lying on Eddy's desk top.

'Fetch someone, Bob!' said Dyson. 'I think Eddy's ill!'

From the scared tone of Dyson's voice, Bob knew that what he meant was that he thought Eddy was dead.

People kept phoning up, after the body had been removed, and Dyson and Bob were rushing to catch up and finish preparing the copy that had to be set overnight.

'I hear you were on the box last night,' said small, cheerful voices in Dyson's ear. 'I'm told you were rather good.'

'Very kind of you to say so,' Dyson would reply, not knowing what else to do, but turning his back for shame on Bob and poor old Eddy's empty desk. 'I'm glad your wife enjoyed it . . . Yes, I enjoyed doing it . . . Well, I thought it went off quite well, but one never knows with these things . . .'

Events were devoured by events, thought Dyson, states of affairs were overtaken by states of affairs . . . He cut five lines from 'The Country Day by Day' proof, then restored them, realizing that he had misread the layout sheet. He felt very shaky. How long had Eddy been dead before they noticed him? Already the phone was ringing again.

'Hello, David . . . Yes, I wanted to talk to you about your Country copy. You've written, "I saw a pair of golden plover . . ." What? Oh, it's very kind of you to say so . . . Well, I thought it didn't go off too badly . . .'

They went to the Gates afterwards to have a glass of whisky. It was late; they were both very tired and shaken. And Dyson felt that something ought to be said. But what? They sat in the private bar at the Gates looking down into their glasses, trying to think what it should be. Dyson tried over inside his head : 'It's funny to think that only this morning poor old Eddy was talking about Stanley Cunningham's funeral . . .' 'It's funny to think that only this morning we were trying to persuade poor old Eddy to go off and enjoy himself on a facilities trip to the Persian Gulf . . .' 'It's funny to think that just this afternoon I had the idea of getting poor old Eddy to come over to the Gates and tell me something about himself . . .' But the funniest thing of all, really, was that until just a few hours ago Eddy had been, and now he was not. That, thought Dyson, really was the funniest thing about death; that's what really took some getting used to.

He looked up and caught Bob's eye.

'God strikes again,' said Bob thoughtfully.

Seven

Tessa got out of the train at Paddington already painfully sensitive to the erotic implications of the city. Between Newbury and Reading a middle-aged man had pressed his knee against hers, and she had had to change compartments, doing her best to look unconcerned about it, as if she often heaved her suitcase down from the rack halfway between stations to try the view farther down the train. In the corridor she had passed compartments full of young men playing cards, who looked up and appraised her face and figure with impersonal interest, and when she found another seat it was in a compartment with three other women travelling up to London on their own, all with suitcases and trim suits and carefully made-up faces. The train hastened through the flat Thames Valley fields and flat western suburbs with single-minded impatience. Tessa felt that everyone aboard, like herself, must be on the way to some metropolitan sexual encounter.

And Paddington had changed. Whenever she had arrived before, with her mother, or on her way to stay with relatives and school friends, it had been full of innocent bustle presaging lunch at Marshall and Snelgrove's and tea at Fortnums. Now its innocence had vanished, and it was thronged with worldly-wise urban people intent upon sophisticated urban undertakings. It was half past four. Self-contained men in well-cut dark overcoats strode across the concourse with the air of being on their way from spending the afternoon in small Bayswater hotels with other men's wives. Girls with white faces and heavily kohled eyes hurried out towards Praed Street, as if hastening to appointments with abortionists in seedy consulting-rooms behind the Edgware Road. The taxi-drivers waiting on the rank looked knowingly at the racing pages of evening papers folded into quarters, ready to suggest to uncertain fares the addresses of drinking clubs and prostitutes.

Tessa did not take a taxi. She had been brought up to be thrifty and careful. She did not take taxis if she could walk. She did not throw clothes away if she could mend them, or alter them to make them more fashionable. She did not go up to London to see her lover without first drawing fifteen pounds out of her bank account, and thinking up a convincing story to tell her parents, and packing a good book to read on the train (it was *U.S.A.* by John dos Passos, and she had read four-and-a-half pages of it before she had been interrupted by her neighbour's knee), and looking up her lover's address in the A to Z.

She walked briskly out of the station, and set off in the direction of Bayswater, stopping every hundred yards or so to put down her dark blue Revelation suitcase (a Christmas present from her parents) and change hands. She did not like to stop and rest her arms for too long. She was afraid that one of the men who hung around the London termini waiting for girls arriving from the provinces would come up and offer to carry the case for her. She would not be taken in, of course; but it might be difficult to refuse politely.

She hated herself for being impressed and frightened by London, but she was impressed and frightened all the same. The long terraces of stucco'd houses – how self-sufficient and unattainable and urban they seemed! The traffic was somehow specially Londonlike, too. On and on it flowed past her, indifferent to her and her suitcase. Ford Cortinas, Minis, Volkswagen vans, Rovers – they all looked strange in these grey London streets, navigating with an inscrutable sense of their own direction and destiny. Even the grey, slightly misty afternoon light seemed impersonal and uniquely metropolitan. And the most impressive and frightening and metropolitan thing of all about London was that it was where Bob lived. At the thought of Bob, unpredictable and darkly smiling, her mouth went dry and her stomach felt liquid with impatience and nervousness.

She passed women with blonde hair and ski-caps, walking their dogs, and olive-skinned girls in belted raincoats, carrying portfolios or violin-cases. She knew they were more attractive than her. At every moment she caught sight of some light figure with twinkling knees, slim golden calves, and massed, luxuriant hair. She felt uneasy; she did not fit in here at all. Her raincoat was not belted – her skirt was too long – her brown hair hung down her back with a pale blue kerchief tied over the top of it to keep it clean on the train. It was all hopeless! She felt like a peasant. Well, of course, she could get her hair cut and buy new clothes. But she was the wrong shape altogether. She was tall and big-boned, with strong, thick legs, and big breasts that jounced up and down as she walked. She didn't know what to do about her breasts. If she strapped them up they stuck out like a shelf, and ached. If she strapped them down to make herself look boyish they just stuck out a foot farther down, and ached. And really her wrong shape was only a symptom. She was the wrong sort of person, that was the basic trouble. She was awkward, and naïve, and thrifty, and ill-read, and genteel. She had a great square face, with a large jaw, and cheeks that were permanently red. She had no right to Bob. She had no right to *anyone*, in a world so full of slight creatures with delicate bones and neat boyish faces. She wasn't a girl at all, in any sense that the fashion magazines would recognize. She was just a young female human being, fit only to be somebody's cousin or aunt.

It took her much longer to get to Leominster Gardens, where Bob lived, than she had expected. Streets which had looked short on the map seemed endless when one had to walk them with a suitcase. She lost her way; new flats had been built across roads marked in the A to Z, and it was difficult to find anyone who had heard of Leominster Gardens. The light became greyer and smokier. Small corner shops shut as she approached them.

But when she did find the street, it seemed curiously familiar. Bob had never described it to her; it just seemed right for him. The cream stucco on the houses – the imposing pillared porches with their black-and-white tiled steps; she felt as if she had seen it all before in a dream. Through the ground-floor window of one house she saw a room lined with dusty books. A man with his back to her bent over a large table covered with papers, his silver hair catching the light from an overhead lamp. She knew that if he turned round she would recognize his face. At other windows, she could see tables with folded paper napkins and nickel-plated cruets. They were small private hotels. She knew exactly how the dining-rooms smelt inside, and how they would look at seven o'clock, when the weak lights in their brown parchment shades were turned on, and large, ungainly old men with sticks stumped to their tables.

As she drew near to number 86, her mouth went dry again, and her heart beat painfully. She stopped and put her case down for a moment to try and collect herself; her hands were trembling uncontrollably from the weight. It was stupid to be like this. It was silly to have come at all if she was going to feel so shaky and helpless. Anyway, Bob probably wouldn't be home yet. Her plan was really just to find the place, then go away and have tea somewhere while she waited for him.

She tucked stray wisps of hair back under her kerchief, then picked up her case and walked up the steps on to the porch. 'Flat 4,' it said on the board, 'R. Bell.' His name! Somehow it was a terrible shock to see it. Her cheeks were blazing red, she knew. The bell-pushes on the board were all empty, so she tried the door and it opened. Inside was a hall with a dingy maroon carpet, and a massive veneered dining-table covered with old election pamphlets, soap coupons, and handbills from firms purchasing second-hand jewellery. She tiptoed up the stairs, wondering what she would say to anyone who saw her. One of the stairs cracked sharply beneath her foot; she heard the front door of one of the ground-floor flats open behind her, and as she turned the corner of the staircase she caught a glimpse of a single eye and a draggle of grey hair at the crack.

There were no windows on the first floor landing, and

in the dark it was difficult to make out the numbers on the doors. She crept about, grasping the suitcase, putting her eye very close to each of the two bell-pushes in turn. Absurd anxieties fled across her mind. Had she posted her letter telling Bob she was coming? Had she put a stamp on it? As she hesitated outside Bob's door she heard a muffled metallic thump from within, as of a saucepan being put down on a gas-stove, then the sound of a tap being turned on. He was in! She quickly rang the bell, not knowing what to think or feel. There was a silence, and then the sound of quick, light steps coming towards the door. He was running! Oh Bob, she thought. Oh *Bob*!

The door opened.

'Oh, Bob!' she said helplessly.

'Come on in, darling,' said the sharp little woman who was holding the door, screwing up her eyes shrewdly against the cigarette-smoke she was blowing out in order to speak. 'I'm just making the great man's supper. We can have a little heart-to-heart while we wait for him.'

'Throw all those bedclothes off the chair and sit down, darling,' said Mrs Mounce, peeling potatoes at the sink.

'I'm all right, thank you,' said Tessa, standing with her hands behind her back, pretending she was examining Bob's pictures.

'Lovey, he may not be back till eleven! Go on, sit down. I was airing his sheets, you see, darling. They never get aired properly if I don't do it myself. Go and pour yourself a drink, love – you look whacked. Do you know where it is? It's over on the bookcase.'

'No, thank you.'

'I'll make us some tea, then.'

Poor kid, thought Mrs Mounce, she really did look whacked. For a moment after she'd come in her face had gone all stiff, as if she was trying not to cry. Bob was a stinker. He could have been at home to meet her.

'He could have been here,' she said. 'It wouldn't have killed him to be here for once.'

'I expect he's busy.'

'I expect he's boozing.'

Tessa looked disapproving.

'Do you cook and clean for Mr Bell?' she asked.

'Oh, yes, darling!' said Mrs Mounce, turning her head upwards and sideways, so the smoke from the cigarette in the corner of her mouth missed her eyes. 'I'm just the skivvy round here! Cook the din-dins, put the cat out, clear up the junk on the great man's desk, and hope my lord throws me a kind word from time to time. That's me, sweetheart!'

And when he came in at eleven o'clock breathing beer and curry fumes, try to fight off his hot little hands. Oh, she knew what was going through his head all right, and how careful she had to be not to say or do anything he might misinterpret. And now she was expected to entertain his lady-friends until such time as he chose to remember they were there! Well, she knew who this lady-friend was, anyway. This was the famous Tessa, who wrote Bob twelve-page letters which he left lying around open on top of his desk. This was the famous lady-friend who went round wearing Bob's letters down her blouse. Frankly, she looked as if she'd got a few bundles of twelve-page letters stuffed up her woolly even now. Either that or she'd got two woollies on. Honestly, people talked about the kids today as though they were all Dior models, but they still had spots and puppy-fat just like kids always had, and always would have. Poor kid, she looked so pathetic sitting there on the edge of the chair, all stiff and upright like some tragedy queen, thinking Woe is me, my precious Bob has fallen into the hands of this designing woman. Well, making his room fit to live in was just possibly a better way to go about it than writing him twelve-page letters, as dearest Tessa might in time come to realize.

'The water's almost boiling,' she said. 'Incidentally, I know what you're thinking, and I'm not.'

Tessa's face went red all over, from neck to temples.

'I wasn't . . .' she said, 'I didn't . . .'

'I'm just a good fairy, darling. That's all. I live downstairs, you see. I just pop up from time to time to see if Bob's all right.'

'Well, of course . . . that's very kind of you.'

'Just keeping him in good condition for you, darling.'

'Thank you.'

Poor kid – she *was* out of her depth.

'Did you manage to get anything to eat on the way?'

'I had a sandwich at Taunton.'

'*Sweetest*! You must be *famished*! We'll get Bob's old birthday cake out! Though I must admit, I only have a bite at lunchtime myself. I have to think of my figure.'

'Your figure's very pretty,' said Tessa politely.

'Do you think so?' said Mrs Mounce. She swivelled round on her heel, and struck a pose with her left hip thrown sideways, and her cigarette hand extended in a rather classical way. She could have been a model, people always said so. She could have been a dancer if she'd taken lessons.

'Like a model,' said Tessa. 'Perhaps you are one?'

'I could have been. But you know how it is, with one thing and another. Of course, I have to keep slim for my hubby. He'd go mad if I started putting on weight. I put on five pounds at Torremolinos one year and he went on and on about it. Was I sure I wasn't pregnant? You know.'

'Well, I wish I looked like you.'

'You're absolutely lovely as you are, darling.'

And really, thought Mrs Mounce, she wasn't such a bad-looking kid. A little of the old black-coffee-and-orange-juice, and a good roll-on, and she really wouldn't look too awful.

'Are you an undergrad or something, darling?' she asked.

'I'm at a college of citizenship in Bath.'

'*Darling*! That sounds terribly brainy.'

'It's not, really.'

'Do you study economics and all that kind of thing?'

'A bit. We do History of Ideas.'

'Lovely.'

'And we have a course in World Literature. Last term it

was Russia. Next term it's India, China and Japan.'

'How super, darling.'

'Well, I'm not sure. One never seems to catch up.'

'I know, sweets – once you start swotting there's no end to it. That's what put me off studying, really. Do you do ordinary things like Domestic Science?'

'Well, we do Nutrition. And Contemporary Culture Appreciation, and Social Situation Training.'

'Super.'

'We all think it's terribly draggy. There's a terribly draggy lot of people teaching us.'

Mrs Mounce made the tea.

'I should be helping you,' said Tessa. 'How rude of me!'

'All right, sweets. Make the bed – then you can lie down and take the weight off your feet while we talk. But tuck it in properly, darling. Make proper hospital corners, or one of you will be falling out in the middle of the night.'

Tessa's face went red all over again. Mrs Mounce watched her with discreet curiosity. She'd never seen such a champion blusher. Kids weren't getting tougher these days at all – they were getting *soppier*. Well, she'd learn, she'd learn. She just needed someone to take an interest in her, someone to draw her out and tell her what time of day it was.

Mrs Mounce kicked off her beaded moccasins, curled up in the armchair with her cup of tea, and began to tell Tessa about her hubby and his job, about Dotty and the work they were having done in the house, and about their friends. Tessa first of all sat down on the edge of the bed, with her knees together, her feet crossed and slightly to one side, her back straight, and her cup and saucer at chest height, as she had learnt in Social Situation Training. By the time she had fetched her second cup of tea, Mrs Mounce was on to their relations with their bank manager, and Tessa kicked off her shoes and tucked her legs up beneath her to be companionable. Her third cup of tea she balanced on her stomach, lying full length on the bed and pointing her stockinged toes into the air, sighting various objects over them with one eye closed. 'How frightful,' she murmured from time to time, as Mrs Mounce catalogued another misfortune, another misunderstanding. 'How absolutely frightful.'

'Because there I was,' Mrs Mounce ran on, as the blue haze of cigarette smoke thickened in the dusk, 'honestly, darling, without a stitch on, and this lunatic hammering on the door and shouting he'd wake the whole hotel if I didn't open up . . . Anyway, I told Dotty, "Dotty darling," I said, "this terrible possessiveness of yours about the house is definitely something sick, something absolutely psychological." I mean, I had to be frank with her. "Dotty, precious," I said, "this is the sort of thing they lock people away in mental asylums for . . ." Well, I went to clinics, I went to specialists, they poked and they peered and they prodded, they took X-rays, they did tests, I don't know what they didn't do, and they all said the same thing. "Mrs Mounce," they said, "there's absolutely nothing wrong with you." Well, lovey, I knew there *was*, you see . . .'

It was half past eight when the key turned in the lock, and Bob came in. Tessa had turned on the little light on the bedside table, but otherwise the room was in darkness, and for some moments Bob stood by the door, twisting his head backwards and forwards, trying to take the situation in

'It's a pity you bothered to come home at all, darling,' said Mrs Mounce. 'We were having a very cosy little chat here.'

'Oh, it's you,' said Bob. He came over to the bed, holding up his hand to shade his eyes from the bedside light, and peering almost comically close, so that Tessa could smell the whisky on his breath.

'Who's this?' he said.

'It's me, Bob,' said Tessa in a small voice.

'Oh God,' said Bob. 'Tessa! What on earth are you doing here?'

'Didn't you get my letter, Bob?'

'Your letter? Oh, yes. Yes, yes, I did.'

'What did I tell you?' said Mrs Mounce. 'He'd clean

forgotten about it.'

'No, I got held up at the office.'

'You are a stinker, sweetie,' said Mrs Mounce. 'You really are. If I hadn't let her in she'd have had to sit on her suitcase in the hall for three hours.'

'I'm sorry, I got held up at the office.'

He went over and kissed Tessa, who was half sitting up, not knowing quite what to do with herself.

'Anyway,' he said, 'it's marvellous to see you.'

She hugged him roughly.

'You've been boozing,' she said.

'Of course he's been boozing,' said Mrs Mounce.

'I had to stop for a quick drink on the way home with John Dyson,' he said. 'I couldn't really get out of it.'

He straightened up. Tessa would have liked to hide her face in the covers and cry.

'Well, well,' said Bob. 'Where are you staying, Tessa?'

'Bob!' cried Mrs Mounce. 'You absolute skunk!'

'No, it's just slipped my mind for a moment . . .' said Bob.

'She's staying here, for heaven's sake. Where do you think she's staying?'

'Well, don't get excited – that's all I wanted to know.'

'I'm going to find a hotel,' said Tessa.

'You really *are* a stinker, you know, sweetie!'

'Look, she's perfectly welcome to stay here – I just didn't know exactly what her plans were.'

Mrs Mounce jumped out of the armchair and twinkled away to the door.

'Well,' she said, 'I'll leave you to it. There's din-dins for two in the uvvy. Tessa sweetie, be firm with him. And if you get depressed at all, come downstairs and have a chat.'

Tessa couldn't think of anything to say after Mrs Mounce had gone. She sat on the edge of the bed, looked down into her lap, and felt great tears run out of her eyes. They ran down her red cheeks, and splashed like huge summer raindrops on to her hands.

'Oh, *Tess*!' said Bob, sitting down on the bed and putting his arm round her shoulders. 'Don't cry, Tess. I'm terribly sorry everything got so buggered up. I must have misread your letter somehow.'

'I don't think you read it at all.'

'Yes, I did, Tess. Honestly I did. Only everything's been so buggered up today in general . . .'

'Anyway, it doesn't matter. I'm sorry to cry like this. It's just that everything's so different from how I imagined it. I kept imagining coming up to London to see you. And now I've come . . .'

She sobbed.

'And everything's just not quite how I expected it. I mean, arriving here and finding Mrs Mounce . . .'

'I'm terribly sorry you got stuck with her,' said Bob. 'She's a dreadful woman.'

'No, she was very sweet to me. I thought she was dreadful at first. I suppose she is rather dreadful. But, Bob, she's had such a sad life !'

She wept again.

'I just suddenly thought,' she said, 'everyone's life is very sad really.'

Bob got up and began to put the things on the table for dinner. Tessa stopped crying, and sighed a deep, uncontrollable sigh like a yawn. She got up, and seized Bob as he moved between table and oven, putting her face down on his shoulder and hugging him fiercely. She would have liked to dissolve into him and become part of him, so that she could never be subject to his indifference, or even be looked at by him in any objective way.

'Sometimes you're not at all good to me, Bob,' she said.

'I'm sorry, Tess,' said Bob. He kissed the top of her head, and moved on to get a saucepan out of the oven. She caught him again on the way back between oven and table, and sank herself into him once more, but after a moment became conscious that he was having to make a considerable effort to hold the hot saucepan away from her at arm's length.

When they sat down at table she couldn't manage to eat anything. She held Bob's left hand in both of hers under the corner of the table and gazed at him.

'Oh, Bob!' she said.

'Oh, Tessa!' said Bob, taking a forkful of stew with his disengaged hand.

The doorbell rang. It was Mrs Mounce.

'Sorry to disturb, darling,' she said to Bob, 'but I've brought you a bottle of Sauterne to wash the stew down with, so you can celebrate. I don't suppose you thought of bringing any booze home yourself.'

After Bob had closed the door he poured out two tumblers of the wine.

'To us, Tess,' he said. She took his hand again.

'To you, Bob. Whatever happens to us, I hope things always go right for you.'

Bob put his glass down.

'Tess,' he said, 'I'm honestly not worthy of you.'

'That's a silly thing to say, Bob.'

'It's true, Tess. You're generous and selfless in a way I could never be.'

He picked up his fork, prodded ineffectually at his stew for some minutes, and then withdrew his left hand from hers.

'I just want to cut up this piece of meat, Tess,' he said.

'I love you, Bob. I've never really loved anyone before.'

The doorbell rang again.

'Bob, sweetie,' said Mrs Mounce, 'I've just remembered you haven't got any salt. I thought I'd pop up with some. Don't worry, I'll leave you in peace after this. How's the stew?'

'Oh, Bob!' said Tessa, as Bob sat down again.

'Oh, Tess!' said Bob.

Bob lay in bed gazing vaguely up at the ceiling, which was glowing red in the light from the gas-fire, not entirely sure whether he was awake or asleep. There was a dull pain in his left bicep – Tessa's head was pillowed on it. He cautiously pulled his arm free. He couldn't think whether they had been in bed for an hour, or four hours.

'Poor Mrs Mounce,' said Tessa.

'Mm,' said Bob.

'I'm glad she's not your mistress, Bob.'

'What?'

'I didn't really think she was, of course. I thought she was the cleaning woman first of all.'

'I don't know what she is.'

'I think I'd understand if you wanted to sleep with other women, Bob. I know it's different for men. All the same, I suppose I'm glad it's not Mrs Mounce. She's so tied up with unhappiness. She'd pull you down into it.'

'Yes.'

'Poor Mrs Mounce.'

Bob dozed.

'. . . into Taunton yesterday,' he became conscious of Tessa saying some time later, 'to get some special new antibiotic for Jester. Did I write to tell you about Jester falling?'

'Mm.'

'Poor old Jester . . .'

Bob felt himself swooping down again into the great soft darkness of sleep. Somewhere down there he stubbed himself against an ill-defined but hard mass of fact, and brought it up to the surface to examine it.

'John Dyson was on television last night,' he said. 'Did you see him?'

'Is that the Giant Dyson?'

'What?'

'Who subdued the Tyrant Cox?'

'Search me,' said Bob, sinking slowly away into the depths again.

'. . . frightened when I arrived in London today,' he heard Tessa saying at some stage. Time was no longer sequential; it was mere isolated incidents unrelated by before and after. '. . . a stupid thing to feel, I know . . . on the train . . . cars in the streets . . . like a child . . .'

Tessa turned over, unwinding the bedclothes off him as she went. He turned over himself, to wind them back on. There was scarcely room enough to turn; it was surprising how obstinately single a single bed was.

'I'm right on the edge,' he said. 'Are you sure you

couldn't move over an inch or two?'

There was no reply; now that he was fully awake, she was fully asleep. He tried cautiously to shove her over by main force, but she was too heavy. He lay on his side, holding the covers over him by their edges, gazing at some of his copies of *Vogue*, which Tessa had been looking through and left lying on the carpet in front of the fire, where they glowed pink and red. He thought about models' bottoms, feeling Tessa's bulking large against the small of his back. Funny how he never seemed to meet girls . . . Just not attractive to women in some way . . . The copies of *Vogue* slipped slowly sideways and upwards, and disappeared into darkness . . .

'. . . told me,' said Tessa's voice hours or minutes later, 'that they've borrowed a lot of money from the bank to do some conversion work in their flat.'

'Um?' mumbled Bob. 'Whosiss?'

'Mrs Mounce and her husband. Her husband's impotent. Did you know that?'

'No.'

'But terribly jealous. She has affairs with other men and he finds out and flicks her.'

'Does what?'

'Flicks her. With the back of his fingers somehow. She says it hurts terribly.'

Bob felt suddenly wide awake. For some reason he had just remembered poor old Eddy Moulton.

'A man in the office died this afternoon,' he said, then immediately doubted his own words. Had it really been that afternoon? 'A man' – 'died' – could poor old Eddy, leaning drunkenly across the desk with his hand shading his eyes, really be fitted into those abstract, impersonal formulae? It seemed like some event described in a legend, remote and formal.

'Someone you knew well?' asked Tessa.

'He was a very old man who worked in the same room as John Dyson and myself.'

'Is that why you were late back this evening?'

Bob considered.

'I suppose it was,' he said.

'Why didn't you tell me?'

Bob tried to remember why he hadn't told her. It was probably because the blue fug of cigarette smoke in the flat when he had come in, and the light, and the voices, and the terrible feeling of guilt, and Mrs Mounce shouting, and Tessa weeping, had all swept poor old Eddy's death right out of his mind. But he couldn't really remember the reason. It was already lost – part of the jetsam of discarded immemorabilia which disappeared astern all the time. From hour to hour one's life slipped away from one into the haze, before one had really looked at any of it properly.

'I suppose I didn't think of it,' he said.

'You are a gink, Bob.'

Bob said nothing. The word gink seemed a good ten years too young to bear thinking about.

Tessa turned carefully over towards him, rolling the undersheet away from beneath his legs.

'I can stay for three weeks, if you'd like me to,' she said. 'Oh, Bob! Three weeks together – on our own!'

'Marvellous,' said Bob.

'Everything's always so much more complicated and awkward than one bargains for,' she said. She settled her head on his left biceps again and closed her eyes. 'I shall always love you, Bob, whatever happens to us.'

'I love you, too, Tessa.'

The doorbell rang.

'God in heaven!' said Bob, wide-awake, and casting about for his dressing-gown. 'God in holy heaven! Still at it, at this hour! This is the fifth time she's been up! I swear I'm going to throw her downstairs and break her neck!'

It was indeed Mrs Mounce yet again, and in her frilly nightwear, but Bob did not throw her downstairs and break her neck.

'Hello,' he said politely.

'Oh, you've gone to bed already,' she said, trying to peer past Bob into the room to see.

'Yes.'

'Oh, sweetie, I'm sorry! I just thought – Reg is away tonight, so why don't you and Tessa sleep in our double bed downstairs? There's a single bed in one of the upstairs flats I could sleep in. You'd be much more comfy – you don't have to tell me what it's like sleeping two in a single bed, darling.'

'We're very comfortable here, thanks.'

'Well, it was just a thought.'

'Yes. Thanks.'

Bob shut the door.

'Poor old Mrs Mounce,' said Tessa.

'But at four o'clock in the morning!' said Bob.

He looked at his watch in the firelight. It was quarter to twelve. Well, it felt like four. And four and a quarter hours later, when it actually was four, and the bedclothes both above and below were a mere conglomerate heap, and Tessa's strapping behind had pushed right the way across the bed, and Bob was cold and stiff from head to foot, and had been neither asleep nor awake for a moment, it felt as though the solar system had finally run down and stopped, and closed off the ever-renewing spring of pure, fresh time for good and all.

Eight

God knows I'm a failure, an insignificant speck of human nothingness trampled on indifferently by every casual passer-by, thought Dyson as he followed his wife out of the kitchen into the living-room, with his fists clenched in his trouser pockets, and his face set in an unyielding frown, but there is one thing in this world that I'm not going to stand for, and that's being nagged by my wife. I'm not reduced to *that*.

God knows, he thought, I shouldn't say anything about it if she nagged me in any halfway reasonable manner. I'm used to being treated like dirt – I'm not proud. It's this nagging by saying nothing that I can't stand. It's this terrible pseudo-rational nagging by just carrying on normally, as if she wasn't nagging me at all. It's this stupid leaving me to guess what I'm being nagged about. Well, I'm honestly not going to spend the whole of Saturday morning putting up with this sort of thing. I'll just go out of the house without a word, and stay at my club for a few days. Or I would if I had a club.

'Look, Jannie,' he said reasonably, following her back to the kitchen, 'just *tell* me what it is you're going on about. That's all I ask.'

'I'm not going on about anything, John,' said Jannie.

'Yes, you are, Jannie.'

'No, I'm not, John.'

'Look, we both know we're having an argument! Let's not have another argument about whether we're having an argument or not!'

Jannie gazed into the food cupboard, picking up cereal packets and shaking them to see if they needed replacing.

'There's some coffee in the pot, if you'd like to light the gas,' she said.

Dyson lit the gas absently. It was self-defeating, this sort of nagging, he thought. That's what I really object to. If I haven't the slightest idea what the hell I'm being nagged about, how the hell can I possibly do anything about it?

'Put some milk on, too, will you, John?'

He put some milk on, sighing. I mean, he thought, I know what's she's *up* to, all right. I'm not a complete fool. This was the classic method of brainwashing, after all, used by interrogators, priests, and psycho-analysts alike. 'I think you have something you want to tell me' – that's what their technique was. Then they simply waited for you to accuse yourself.

Jannie sat down at one corner of the great kitchen table and began to write a shopping list. Dyson stood by the stove, gazing down at her with serious ferocity.

'Jannie . . .' he began.

'Yes, John?'

Dyson stopped, frowning harder.

'Why do you call me John in that tone of voice?' he demanded.

'Don't you like me calling you John?' asked Jannie, not looking up from her shopping list.

'You don't normally go round calling me John all the time.'

She didn't answer. Good God, he thought, I should like to do something that would really make her jump out of her skin for once. He pictured himself smashing both fists down in the middle of the kitchen table, or taking a china jug off the shelf and hurling it across the room. It was absurd that Norman Ward Westerman and Lord Boddy should listen with real deference to his views on Halifax, while at home he couldn't even get a hearing from his own wife. Scribble, scribble, scribble, she went. Eggs, butter, tea, coffee – oh God, the *smallness* of things! The endless petty demands of life! They rained down like small coal from a sack, filling the air with choking dust which settled grimily over everything, and made the whole world smell grey.

'It's that patch of mould on the ceiling in the boys' room,

isn't it?' he said. 'That's what you're going on about, isn't it, Jannie?'

Rice Krispies, navy thread, tuna fish, wrote Jannie.

'Well, I can't do anything about it today,' he said. 'And that's final.'

One bottle Thawpit, wrote Jannie, cigs, birthday present for John's sister-in-law.

'Look, be reasonable, Jannie,' said Dyson. 'I'm going to be absolutely up to my eyebrows in work this weekend. I've got a piece to write for the Overseas Service. I've got an obit of poor old Eddy Moulton to do for *The Journalist*. How can I possibly make a career for myself when you keep on, nag, nag, nag, about patches of mould on the ceiling?'

Jannie looked out of the window, chewing the end of her pencil thoughtfully.

'The milk's boiled over,' she said.

'Oh, *God*!' cried Dyson, springing away from the stove, then springing back to turn the gas out. 'This is exclusively your responsibility! You realize that, don't you, Jannie?'

'The cloth's in the sink, John.'

'I don't see any reason on earth why *I* should clear this up. Where's the cloth? Why the hell is there never a cloth to hand when it's wanted?'

Oven-cleaner, wrote Jannie on her list.

'The phone's ringing,' she said.

Let it ring – what do I care? thought Dyson, as he hurled himself out into the hall to catch it before it stopped ringing. God really was seeping in this morning from every direction, and chiefly through the condition of marriage itself. That was what was holy about holy matrimony, he realized suddenly; it was just another divine instrument for increasing entropy, like damp and coronary thrombosis and woodworm.

'Hello; Dyson,' he snapped.

'Bob!' he said cheerfully a fraction of a second later, smiling warmly into the mouthpiece. 'How nice to hear from you . . . ! No, no – not an inconvenient moment at all . . . *Who*'s with you . . . ? Tessa? Is that your lady-friend from Somerset? Well, give her our regards, Bob . . . Can you do what . . . ? Oh, I see . . . Yes, by all means . . . By all means, Bob . . .'

Dyson walked back to the kitchen grinning. Ah, bachelorhood! The idea of being a bachelor, and having bachelor affairs, suddenly seemed almost unbearably sweet. A girl coming to stay in one's flat . . . He envisaged a slight girl with a tender face and dark, tumbling hair, wearing a pair of borrowed pyjamas which came down over her hands and feet . . .

'Bob's got his girl-friend staying with him,' he said to Jannie, still grinning, as he sat down at the kitchen table and sipped absently at the cup of coffee which had appeared there. 'She's called Tessa. Apparently her parents think she's staying with friends – Bob wanted to know if she could send them our phone number and say she was staying here. I said we'd be delighted. If anyone rings and asks for her, we're to say she's out, then pass the message on to Bob so that she can ring back.'

Dyson went on grinning to himself. The slight girl with the tumbling hair, he was thinking, would take a shower (bachelor flats had showers), putting her head back and letting the water cascade down between her breasts . . . In the afternoon they would make love, with the great windows open to the sky, and a hot, heavy summer rain falling, crushing the flowers and filling the air with the scent of roses . . .

'Did you invite them round?' asked Jannie.

'No. Should I have done? Wouldn't they rather just get on with it in peace?'

Jannie returned to her shopping-list in silence.

'Do you think we should?' said Dyson. 'If you'd like to, you go ahead.'

Leg of lamb for 6, wrote Jannie. Dyson remembered, at the sight of her silently writing, that she had been nagging him.

'Look, Jannie,' he said, his good humour abruptly vanishing, '*I*'m not going to ring them. It's the wife's job to send out invitations and manage a couple's social life, not the husband's.'

Paper napkins, flowers, wrote Jannie.

'Good God, Jannie,' said Dyson. 'It was your idea, not mine. If you want to satisfy your curiosity about Bob's girl-friend, you ring him yourself. I'm far too busy to mess about with this sort of thing today. And that really *is* final . . .'

'That was John Dyson again,' said Bob, as he put the phone down. 'He was inviting us for Sunday lunch to-morrow. I said yes – I hope that was all right. Their kids are quite sweet, as a matter of fact.'

Tessa watched him, completely absorbed in him, as he sat wearily down at the table again, located the brown sugar among the remains of the breakfast things, and dug a spoonful out to lick at. She was sitting curled up in the armchair like Mrs Mounce, nursing a final cup of cold Nescafé.

'You're very fond of the Dysons, aren't you?' she said.

'I suppose so,' he replied. He thought about the Dysons' solid, regular married life, and it filled him with nostalgia. The Dysons didn't have to exhaust themselves wondering if they loved each other, and what they should do about it if they didn't. They weren't overwhelmed by the sheer mechanics of daily life. Happily married couples, he thought, stood not face to face, absorbed in each other, but back to back, looking outwards upon the world. He gazed despairingly about the room. The breakfast things were still on the table; the bedclothes lay tangled on the floor; Tessa's clothes straggled across the carpet from her open suitcase. Tessa wasn't even dressed – she was wearing his old tweed overcoat over her pyjamas. By the time they had got the room cleared up and were ready to go out it would be getting on for twelve. By the time they had done the shopping and got back and Tessa had cooked the lunch (as she insisted on doing in her eagerness to keep house for him) it would almost certainly be something like three o'clock. A world of muddle seemed to enclose Bob like a jungle. He rubbed his eyes and yawned.

'Didn't you get to sleep at all?' asked Tessa.

'I think I must have dozed off about six.'

'Poor old Bob!'

He took another spoonful of sugar. It hadn't been a *night* they had lived through; it had been the Dark Ages — all seven centuries of them, with wars and oppressions, visions and turbulences. The worst moment of all, he thought, had been at a quarter to nine that morning, when he had been roused from the bottom depths of heavy, dream-tangled sleep by the doorbell, and when, having stumbled across the room, still not knowing where he was or what was happening, he had found Mrs Mounce at the door, asking if she could do any shopping for them.

Tessa came over and kissed him. He opened his eyes quickly, unaware until then that they had fallen shut.

'I'm going to have a bath,' said Tessa. 'Where's the bathroom?'

'Well, it's a bit awkward,' said Bob. 'There's only one in the house, on the landing halfway downstairs. Are you sure you want a bath?'

'Not if it would be embarrassing for you, Bob.'

'Oh, I don't mind. I was thinking about you, Tessa.'

'*I* don't mind. I've burned my boats now.'

'I suppose so.'

He took her down to the bathroom, and turned on the geyser for her.

'Are you going to come in the bath with me, Bob?' she asked, reddening.

'Well, I think I'd better wash up the breakfast things, if you don't mind. Otherwise we shan't be getting lunch till teatime.'

'Oh, yes. I'd forgotten about the breakfast things.'

Bob had almost finished the washing-up when the doorbell rang. He threw down the washing-up mop and stood stock-still for a moment, gripping the edge of the sink. He thought very carefully what he was going to say. 'Mrs Mounce,' he thought he might put it, in a calm, almost pleasant voice, 'if you ring this bell once more I will call the police and have you charged with causing a nuisance

. . .' No – '. . . will instruct my solicitor to proceed against you for trespass . . .' No, no. The bell rang again. He strode across to the door. The words '. . . unless I receive an assurance that you will seek immediate psychiatric advice . . .' flashed into his mind with horrible pleasingness.

But it was not Mrs Mounce – it was Mrs Hennessy, the cleaning woman. Bob stared at her with his mouth open.

'Forgotten I was coming, had you, love?' she said agreeably, rolling hugely past Bob into the room, from one swollen carpet-slippered foot to the other, trailing brooms, brushes and vacuum-cleaner behind her. She dumped all her equipment down, breathing heavily.

'You could leave it today, if you liked . . .' said Bob uneasily, stepping on Tessa's suspender-belt, and kicking one of her shoes backwards under the armchair.

'Don't worry about me, love,' said Mrs Hennessy. 'It'll only take me ten minutes . . . What have you been doing with your bed, love? Been having nightmares, have you?'

'Oh, yes,' said Bob. 'Yes, I did have rather a bad night.' Mrs Hennessy looked at the open suitcase.

'Going away for the weekend, are you, love?' she said.

'No,' said Bob, following the direction of her gaze only slowly. 'I mean, yes, I am.'

'Have a lovely time.'

'Yes, I will.'

Mrs Hennessy bent down and began to pick up the bedclothes. Bob bent down, too, and moved discreetly about picking up the more obviously feminine articles of clothing around the floor. He wished he didn't mind about it, but he did. He wished his first instinct had not been to conceal the traces of Tessa's existence, but it had been. It was not because *he* would be embarrassed if Mrs Hennessy knew he had a girl staying here, he told himself. It was not even because Tessa would be embarrassed. They were both a little too adult to care what other people thought. It was Mrs Hennessy he was trying to protect. It was she who would be embarrassed if she knew, or at any rate, if she knew that he knew that she knew.

'That's right, love,' shouted Mrs Hennessy over the

noise, as she switched on the vacuum cleaner. 'If you just clear your little bits and pieces off the floor I can get round with the vacuum.'

Bob pushed everything into the suitcase and crammed the lid shut, ignoring the various shoulder-straps and corners of translucent nylon which stuck out. He was just looking round for some quiet corner to put the case when faintly above the noise in the room he heard the doorbell ring. God, it was Tessa coming back from the bathroom! He hurried across to the door, still grasping the case.

'Bye bye, love,' shouted Mrs Hennessy. 'Have a lovely time.'

'Oh. Yes. Thanks,' shouted Bob.

He opened the door. It was not Tessa outside – it was Mrs Mounce.

'Bob, darling!' she whispered dramatically, taking his hand and leading him out on to the landing out of Mrs Hennessy's earshot. 'I meant to tell Mrs Hennessy not to disturb you. Shall I get rid of her for you?'

'No,' said Bob. 'That's fine.'

'I just thought I'd offer, sweetie.'

'Everything's fine. Don't worry about us.'

Mrs Mounce looked down at the suitcase.

'You off somewhere, darling?' she asked.

'No, no. Well, you know, we might go somewhere.'

'Well, don't forget I'm downstairs if you want me.'

'I shan't forget.'

He shut the door and carried the suitcase back into the room. Mrs Hennessy looked at him in surprise and switched the vacuum cleaner off.

'I thought you'd gone, love,' she said.

'Well, not quite.'

'What's the matter? Forgotten your pyjamas? Here they are, love – I was just going to put them under the pillow.'

'Oh, thanks,' said Bob. He opened the suitcase and crammed the pyjamas inside.

'Got everything else, have you?' asked Mrs Hennessy. 'Got your shaving kit? No, I can see it over by the sink.'

She rolled effortlessly across to the draining-board and

fetched it for him.

'Thanks,' said Bob, stuffing it into the case.

'You'll forget your own head one of these days,' said Mrs Hennessy. 'What else haven't you got? Slippers? Look, they're on the floor here all the time!'

'I don't really want slippers, thanks.'

'Course you want slippers! Catch your death on some of these cold floors. Come on, love, put them in. What about your dressing-gown? Your dressing-gown's hanging up behind the door! There you are, then. Now, are you sure you've got a change of socks?'

'Yes, yes.'

'And plenty of warm woollies?'

'Yes, yes, yes.'

Reluctantly, Mrs Hennessy bent down and switched on the vacuum cleaner again. Almost at once the doorbell rang. Bob hurried to answer it, trying to force the lid of the overloaded case shut as he went.

'You off then, love?' shouted Mrs Hennessy. 'Ta-ta. Have a lovely time.'

'Oh, thanks,' said Bob. 'Yes, I will.'

This time it was Tessa, holding her pyjamas in her hand and wearing nothing but the tweed overcoat pulled tightly around her.

'Oh, Tessa,' whispered Bob, pushing her back on to the landing and pulling the door to behind them. 'It's a bit awkward at the moment. Mrs Hennessy's here.'

Tessa gazed at Bob seriously.

'Who's Mrs Hennessy, Bob?' she asked.

'She's the cleaning woman, Tess.'

'*Another* woman who does your cleaning, Bob?'

'Oh, Mrs Hennessy's just, you know, the char. Look, I've put all your things in the suitcase. Take it back to the bathroom and get dressed there, Tess.'

Tessa gazed at Bob sadly in the half-darkness of the landing, and shivered slightly.

'I don't think you ought to be embarrassed about me now I'm here,' she said.

'I'm not embarrassed, Tess.'

'Well, *I'm* not, Bob.'

'I know. It's Mrs Hennessy I'm thinking of. I don't think we ought to embarrass her, you see. Look, all your clothes are in the case. I'll come and call you when things are a bit less hectic.'

He watched Tessa start reluctantly down the stairs, cradling the open suitcase in her arms, then went back into the flat, wishing it were the middle of the night once more.

'Back again?' said Mrs Hennessy, turning off the vacuum cleaner. 'What have you forgotten this time, love?'

'Oh, you know, I thought perhaps I'd just check through things and make sure.'

He began vaguely opening drawers and cupboards, trying to see out of the corner of his eye whether there were any more of Tessa's belongings lying about the floor. For a moment they caught each other's eye. Bob looked away hurriedly, and Mrs Hennessy bent down and switched on the vacuum cleaner.

The doorbell rang.

'Off again, are you?' said Mrs Hennessy, watching him run. 'Ta-ta, then.'

'Bob, I'll *have* to come in,' whispered Tessa. 'Mrs Mounce is in the bathroom.'

Bob pushed her back on to the landing once again, and again pulled the door to behind him.

'We can wait out here for a bit, can't we?' he asked. 'Mrs Hennessy won't be a moment, Tess. Let me carry the case for you, anyway.'

They stood, not looking at each other, with Bob holding the case. Tessa started to shiver.

'George God strikes again,' whispered Bob.

'What?'

'George God – he's getting at us.'

'Who's George God?' asked Tessa. Her teeth were chattering.

'I know,' whispered Bob suddenly. 'Mr Mounce is away,

so if Mrs Mounce is in the bath their flat must be empty, and she's probably left the door open. Go and dress down there.'

Bob watched her all the way down the stairs, agonized on her behalf; still more agonized when it occurred to him, just as she went out of sight, that he should have gone down with her and carried the case.

'Hello,' said Mrs Hennessy, turning off the vacuum cleaner once again as he came into the room. 'You remind me of radishes, the way you keep returning. I know what it is this time, though, love.'

'Oh?' said Bob. 'What is it?'

'You've left your money on the bedside table.'

'Oh, so I have.'

'Can't get far without money, you know.'

'No, you can't.'

Mrs Hennessy collected up her equipment.

'Well, I'll say ta-ta, love,' she said. 'Don't forget anything else, now, will you? Got your ticket?'

'Yes.'

'That's right. Have a lovely time, then.'

She rolled across to the door, trailing sticks and poles. Bob hastened across and then flung the door open for her. There on the threshold, barring her progress, stood Tessa, still wearing nothing but the tweed overcoat and still nursing the overstuffed open suitcase. She looked desperately from Bob to Mrs Hennessy and back again.

'I'm sorry, Bob,' she said wretchedly, 'but Mrs Mounce's husband's home now.'

'You get something on before you catch your death, love,' said Mrs Hennessy to Tessa reproachfully. 'If you're looking for your undies, I've folded them up and put them on top of the TV for you. Ta-ta, loves. Have a lovely time.'

It was Damian, the Dysons' younger son, who first brought up the subject of marriage.

He stood up on his chair all the way through lunch, with the gravy running down his great red face on to his bib, and flying off the spoon he was waving on to other people's clothes; and in his loud, pharyngitic voice he kept up a perpetual background noise of questions and comments. His brother Gawain ignored him, gazing at the salt cellar or the window for minutes at a time and stolidly chewing. So did Dyson, intent upon pushing a heavy agenda through committee – roast lamb, the state of the newspaper industry, the beauties of Tessa's native Somerset, second helpings of lamb, the shortcomings of primary education, the exact age of poor old Eddy Moulton, apple crumble, and how funny it was that only the morning that poor old Eddy had died, etc. He seemed unaware of the noise Damian was making. Bob's head ached and filled with fog at the effort of filtering the adult conversation out from it.

'Are Bob and Tessa married, Mummy?' he became aware that Damian was asking, over and over again. 'Are Bob and Tessa married, Daddy? Are Bob and Tessa married, Mummy?'

'No, we're not, Day,' he said, to halt the noise.

'Why aren't you married?' asked Damian.

'We're just not,' said Tessa. 'Not everyone's married.'

Damian thought about this, scratching his private parts thoughtfully with his spoon.

'Mummy and Daddy did be married,' he said.

'Sit down and eat up your lunch, Day,' said Jannie.

'Jack did be married,' said Damian.

'Oh, not Jack, *please*, Damian!' said Dyson.

'Who's Jack?' asked Tessa.

'That's impossible to explain,' said Bob. 'Who did Jack marry, Day?'

'Jack did marry his mummy,' said Damian. He looked surprised when everyone laughed, then joined in himself, with very hoarse, loud laughter which made everyone start laughing all over again.

'Jack did marry his mummy,' he said, as soon as the laughter had subsided, and laughed again himself, which made Bob and Tessa start again, too.

'For God's sake don't encourage him,' said Dyson

irritably. 'He'll go on for hours.'

'Jack did marry his mummy,' repeated Damian, beaming around the table with the confidence of a man who knows he has a fully pilot-surveyed and market-researched product to offer.

'That's enough, Day,' said Dyson sharply.

'Did you know,' said Damian to Bob in a specially humorous voice, and with a risqué expression on his great round face. 'Jack did marry his mummy?'

'Day!' said Jannie.

'Did you know . . . ?' began Damian to Tessa.

'*Damian!*' shouted Dyson.

'Did you know,' said Damian, leaning humorously across the table towards Gawain, who was gazing transfixed at the top button of Bob's coat, 'Jack did marry his mummy?'

Gawain roused himself from his daze.

'Don't repeat your jokes, Damian,' he said coldly.

Damian sat down slowly in his place, completely silenced by the rebuke, staring at Gawain as if he was trying to understand the thought-processes which had led up to it.

'Marriage is something which I must say I'm strongly in favour of,' said Dyson with comfortable good humour, cutting himself another sliver of meat off the joint. 'I think everybody should marry. Marry anybody. No nonsense about waiting for your one and only soul-mate to show up. It's the state of marriage that counts.'

'Not peating my jokes,' said Damian softly, gazing at his brother.

'That's a stupid thing to say to anyone, John,' said Jannie. 'A bad marriage is much worse than no marriage at all.'

'Not peating my jokes,' said Damian, slightly more loudly.

'Adaptation to the idea of marriage,' said Dyson; 'that's the only thing that counts.'

'Yes, you are,' said Gawain to Damian. 'You're repeating your jokes.'

'Not peating my jokes.'

'You've only got to look around you at the marriages of

people we know,' said Jannie, 'to see that's not true.'

'Damian's repeating his jokes again.'

'*Not* peating my jokes!'

'Good God, Jannie, think about it *statistically*! How many marriageable girls does a man meet? Or vice versa? Twenty? Fifty? A hundred? All right, say a hundred . . .'

'Damian *is* repeating his jokes, isn't he, Daddy?'

'. . . of whom we think in our romantic way that one and only one is the ideal mate. All right. Now the population of the world is 3,000 million. Divide by two for members of the opposite sex – 1,500 million . . .'

'You know this is preposterous, John. You're just being deliberately irritating.'

'Not peating my jokes, am I, Mummy?'

'. . . so *pro rata*, even by our own romantic criteria for singling out just one girl from the hundred we meet, there must be at least 15 million members of the opposite sex in the world who would make an ideal mate . . . ! What the *hell* is it, Gawain?'

'Damian's repeating his jokes, Daddy.'

'John, you're just trying to be shocking,' said Jannie. 'What do you think, Tessa?'

'I beg your pardon?'

'Day's repeating his jo-okes!'

'*Not* peating!'

'. . . about marriage . . . ?'

'Day's repeating his jo-okes!'

'Not peating! Not peating! Not peating!'

'. . . Oh . . . very much like to . . .'

'Like to what?' shouted Dyson. 'Shut up, Damian.'

'Daddy, Damian can't say "repeat", can he?'

'. . . get married . . .'

'Are you? Shut *up*, Damian – I mean, Gawain! Well, congratulations!'

'I CAN say peat!'

'. . . thoroughly recommend it . . .' shouted Dyson.

'Damian's going to cry-y!'

'. . . haven't had children . . . really lived . . . do you think, Bob?'

'Look, Daddy, Damian's crying!'

When everyone moved out of the kitchen into the living-room after lunch, leaving Jannie to put the coffee on, Bob lingered behind with her, savouring the sudden calm. He felt something like battle-fatigue – a great desire to lie down on the ground with his hands over his ears and take no further part in the war. He remembered now; he always felt the same by this stage of every visit he made to the Dysons' house in the daytime, while the children were about. Between visits nature obliterated the memory of them, in the same way that it expunged the dread of battle and the pain of childbirth, so that war and childbirth and social visits to the Dysons could continue.

'I like Tessa very much indeed, Bob,' said Jannie, lighting the gas and stacking plates.

'Do you?' said Bob, too worn down to think of any intelligent reply. 'Good, good.'

'You are serious about her, aren't you?'

'Oh, yes. Jannie, could I possibly borrow a couple of aspirins? I've got rather a headache coming on.'

'I think the aspirins are in the cupboard with the spice jars. She's very much in love with you, Bob. You know that, don't you?'

'Yes. Yes, I do. This cupboard?'

'That's right – at the back. It would be terrible to hurt her in any way. Wouldn't it, Bob?'

'I suppose it would.'

'You *suppose* it would?'

'I mean, of course it would. May I take four, Jannie?'

Tessa had subdued the two boys, Bob discovered with relief and admiration when he went out to the living-room. She was telling them a story, and they were sitting on either side of her on the sofa with their mouths hanging slightly open, Gawain meditatively fingering a lock of her long, dark hair, Damian staring at her and absently scratching his balls. Every now and then one of them would stand up on the sofa, and trample restlessly round like a dog resettling itself into its sleeping place. Bob sank into the scrunching springs of an old armchair, put a hand over his eyes, and watched them through his fingers. He was touched by the sight, and felt suddenly tender towards Tessa. If that feeling wasn't love, what was? He had felt sour ever since her arrival – he could admit it to himself now – but simply because it had all happened so unexpectedly and confusedly. He liked life to be predictable and orderly. He liked to have time to think what he was going to feel about something before it happened.

When Tessa went out of the room to see if she could help Jannie the boys turned to Bob at once with all their usual wildness, jumping up and down in his lap, punching him in the chest, and trying to pull off his shoes.

'Ouch! Ouf! You would, would you?' said Bob with as much avuncular bonhomie as he could force out of himself, feinting punches back at them, turning them upside down, and trying not to scream and double up when Damian trod on his genitals.

'Just chuck them off if they're a nuisance,' said Dyson, stretched out in the least broken armchair with the *Observer* and the *Sunday Times*.

'Oh, I don't mind them,' said Bob, wedging his head against the back of the chair, so that the colossal thumping going on inside his skull didn't shake it loose from its mountings. 'Do I, men?'

'Punch, punch, punch!' cried Damian, finding Bob's nose.

'Do you read Brooks, Bob?' asked Dyson.

'You mean the estate agent? No – should I?'

'I suppose you'll be reading him now. The thing is, Bob, if I may give you some advice based on long and hard experience, not to start off by renting somewhere, if you can possibly avoid it.'

'I suppose you're right.'

'Punch punch punch!' said Damian.

'You're just wasting valuable years, renting. Buy something, and get on the escalator. Then at least you're not slipping behind the field as prices go up.'

'I suppose not.'

'Bash bash!'

'And do be practical, Bob. So many people start off with some hazy idea of finding a little Georgian house in w. 1 for £5,000. The thing to do, Bob, is to face up to the fact right from the beginning that it's going to be something Victorian or Edwardian, and that it's going to be in some slightly less fashionable postal district.'

'I suppose so. Ugh! Gawain, that really hurt.'

'I don't know whether you know this area at all, Bob?'

'Well, you know . . .'

'Pinch pinch pinch!'

'It's got quite a lot to be said for it, Bob. For a start it's got a village atmosphere which I must say we find rather agreeable. Well, you know, there are little corner shops which still have some sense of individuality about them. There's a certain sense of community that you wouldn't find somewhere like Chelsea or South Kensington. You've met our neighbours, Ecosse and Princess St George?'

'Yes.'

'Then again, it's on the Tube, or almost on the Tube. And, Bob, it's an area that's bound to go up.'

'Bite bite.'

'Definitely no biting, Damian. Yes, I remember your saying, John.'

'Bound to. *Must* do, you see. Big, roomy houses – just right for expanding middle-class families. People have got to go somewhere. It absolutely *must* go up.'

'I suppose it must.'

'Snip snip – I'm a hairdresser!'

'Do fling them off if they're getting obstreperous, Bob. Anyway, I'll get Jannie to look in the local agents and keep her ears open.'

'Well – No, Gawain, let go! – thanks, John.'

Bob lit the gas-fire and sank down on his bed without even taking his overcoat off.

'You were very good with those children, Tess,' he said, with his hand over his eyes.

'It's just a matter of being sensible,' said Tessa, lighting the gas-stove and filling the kettle, without taking her overcoat off either. 'Will scrambled eggs be all right tonight, Bob? They're quite nice boys, but those silly people just let them run wild.'

'I don't think they really notice the noise themselves,' said Bob, slightly irritated that she should presume to call them silly when they were after all his friends. 'They're hardened to it.'

'I'm hardened to the noise that D and Baby make at home, but I don't let them get away with it while I'm around.'

'Perhaps it's a bit more difficult with children of your own.'

'Well, I shouldn't let them get away with it like that, all the same.'

Bob reflected in silence for some moments.

'Jannie likes you very much,' he said finally. 'She told me so.'

Tessa broke three eggs into a bowl, frowning.

'I'm not sure I like *her* all that much, Bob,' she said. 'I thought she was trying to marry you off.'

'Don't be silly, Tess. That was just some silly misunderstanding at lunch.'

'Was it?'

'Of course it was. Anyway, we've got wills of our own. There's no need to let ourselves be rushed into anything, just because other people think it would be a good thing. It's up to us, what we do, not anybody else. Isn't that right, Tess?'

Tessa said nothing. She beat up the eggs, splashed a drop or two on to the lapel of her overcoat and wiped it off carefully with her finger.

'Well,' she said finally, 'I thought your friend Mrs Dyson was a little bit in love with you, to tell you the truth.'

Bob sat up on the bed and gazed at her in astonishment.

'She wants to marry me off to you,' he said, 'and she's in love with me? What on earth are you talking about, Tess?'

Tessa banged saucepans about irritably.

'She thinks I wouldn't be too much competition for her,' she said, 'because she thinks you're not very much in love with me.'

'She told you this?'

'Of course not. It's just what I think.'

Bob picked up one of his bedside *Vogues* and withdrew into the world of the advertisements. One of them showed a pair of slim, naked legs, cut off a fraction of a millimetre below the groin, running through a meadow full of dewy grass and pale blue cornflowers. They advertised depilatory cream. He yearned for them, in all their innocence and simplicity, as if they were childhood.

'What was all this about a house?' asked Tessa.

'Search me,' said Bob.

He slipped a peppermint into his mouth and curled up, gazing at the legs. If only he were attractive to women!

Nine

Dyson was invited to appear on television again. He and Bob were rushing to get a whole day's work done before lunchtime, in order to get away for poor old Eddy's funeral in the afternoon, when a woman called Samantha Lightbody rang from the BBC. She said she was terribly sorry to disturb him. She wasn't disturbing him at all, said Dyson, swinging round in his chair and resting his elbow comfortably on the stacks of unsubbed copy and uncorrected proofs. She said she was sure she had rung at the worst possible moment – she always rang important people at the worst possible moment. The moment couldn't have been better, said Dyson, taking another armful of stuff from the messenger.

'The point is,' said Samantha Lightbody, 'I'm researching a programme about – well, it's about race relations, I'm afraid. I know – yet another. Groan, groan, and all the rest of it. I hardly dare tell anyone.'

'It sounds absolutely fascinating,' said Dyson.

'Well, we thought it could be quite fun if we got one or two really interesting new people like yourself to come along and take an entirely fresh look at the subject. I know you appear in programmes about race relations from time to time, but you're not one of the usual old gang of faces that everyone's sick of. Do you know what I mean? Anyway, could we *possibly* persuade you?'

'Well,' said Dyson luxuriantly, pressing the point of his pencil through the surface of a copy-pad, 'I am rather heavily committed, of course. When is it?'

'Friday the eighteenth, at seven o'clock, if that doesn't seem too hopeless. It's in a series called *New Perspectives*.'

Dyson slowly turned over the empty pages of his diary.

'I shall be away in the Persian Gulf that week,' he said. 'Oh dear . . .'

'It's a terrible bore, but something has cropped up out there. I don't think I can really get out of it.'

'So you can't possibly do the programme?'

'Oh, yes I think so. I mean, I shall be back from the Middle East on the seventeenth. It won't affect us at all for the eighteenth. I just thought I should mention it.'

'Oh, marvellous. That really is awfully kind of you. I know everyone here will be tremendously thrilled. I'll get our contracts department to ring you about a fee.'

Dyson sat back in his chair expansively.

'You know the man you ought to get for this sort of programme?' he suggested. 'Lord Boddy.'

'Oh, we have!'

'*Have* you?'

'He's one of the team. You know him, do you?'

'Oh, I know Frank Boddy very well. *Very* well.'

'I suppose it's another of these tight little worlds, is it, the racial experts?'

'Oh, pretty tight. Yes, pretty tight.'

There was one small question nagging him which he asked just as Samantha Lightbody was ringing off.

'Did you, as a matter of interest, happen to see me on *The Human Angle* last week?'

'It's an awful thing to have to admit,' replied Samantha Lightbody, 'but I'm afraid I missed it.'

'Did anyone there see it?'

'I'm not sure that they did. I'm terribly sorry.'

'That's all right,' said Dyson. 'That's quite all right.'

Dyson scarcely had time to stride up and down the office that morning, lecturing Bob on the importance of television, but he was in great form all the same. Bob was too busy to notice, but Tessa was in the office, trying to keep out of everyone's way and write a letter to her parents, and Dyson directed his surplus good humour at her. 'It is rather naughty, you know, my lord,' he would say into the phone; 'I shall be coming after you with a big stick if the copy's not here by tomorrow.' And he would catch Tessa's eye and make a humorous grimace, to show what he really thought about bishops. Tessa blushed at the sight.

Bob would catch her eye in his turn as he telephoned. But each time he looked quickly away. He was embarrassed, she knew, because she was sitting at old Eddy Moulton's desk, upon the top of which poor old Eddy had so recently laid down his head and died. She was sitting there because Dyson had invited her to, and Dyson had invited her to because there wasn't anywhere else to sit. But at the sight of Bob's expression she got up, blushing again, and walked about the room as if she were looking for something. She stood by the window for some minutes, looking down into Hand and Ball Court, where an old tramp was feeling his way round the walls and trying not to catch people's eye. She sympathized with his efforts. When she felt she could not naturally stand by the window any longer she went and inspected the gritty old review copies of books which had somehow collected over the years on the office shelves – *Take Your Car to North Africa! Think Your Way to Good Health and Dynamic Living! The ABC of Practical Woodworking. National Debt or National Death? – The Bankers' Plot Exposed.* She took one or two of them down and turned the pages over, trying to persuade herself she was reading them. But the meanings of the words seemed to dart away from her like a shoal of minnows as she advanced upon them, and she felt more uneasy still. She would never catch up with the enormous range of reading which seemed to be taken for granted by Bob and his friends, never.

'Tessa, Tessa, Tessa!' said Dyson cheerfully, pressing his receiver rest down and then dialling another number. 'Sit down and make yourself comfortable. I can't bear people who walk up and down the room all the time.'

'Sorry,' said Tessa. She blushed and went back to the chair in which old Eddy had died.

'Are you happy, Tess?' asked Bob, between calls.

'Yes,' said Tessa. 'I'm going in a moment, anyway.'

'Are you? Oh, all right.'

'I just want to know whether you want me to go to Mr Moulton's funeral with you.'

Bob's face went blank.

'Hello,' he said into the phone. 'Canon Morley . . . ? It's Mr Dyson's office here. Look, this copy you phoned in; when you say, "I know only that I have a deeply satisfying face which shines with a radiance beyond the brightness of this world . . ." – should that be "faith"? And what about ". . . justifying God's wheeze to man . . ."?'

'Bob,' said Tessa, when he had put the phone down again, 'do you want me to come to the funeral or not?'

'It's up to you, Tess,' said Bob. They were both speaking very quietly, so as not to disturb Dyson, who was still on the phone.

'I'll come if you want me to.'

'OK.'

'Do you think I'm dressed all right for it? This is the darkest outfit I've got with me.'

Bob ran a hand through his hair.

'You want to come, do you?' he said doubtfully.

'Only if you want me to. I didn't even know Mr Moulton.'

'I shouldn't come if you'd prefer not to.'

'But, Bob, what do *you* want me to do?'

Bob's phone rang, and while he was talking Dyson, who was sitting back in his chair and waiting for someone at the other end of the line, covered up the mouthpiece of his phone and said:

'Are you coming to the funeral, Tess?'

'I was just asking Bob if he thought I should.'

'Why don't you? Funerals are quite fun, you know. Well, perhaps "fun" isn't the right word. But the sheer language of the service is *marvellous*! "Man that is born of a woman has but a short time to live, and is full of misery . . ." Hello? Hello – Sir William?'

Bob put his phone down.

'The only thing is,' he said uncertainly, 'if everybody started turning up with their girl-friends . . .'

'I certainly don't want to embarrass you, Bob.'

'It's not that. But if everybody suddenly started turning up with their girl-friends . . .'

'All right, Bob, I won't come.'

'I mean, you're welcome to come as far as I'm concerned. But I somehow feel that it's not a sort of social occasion . . .'

Tessa folded up her half-written letter and put it in her handbag.

'If ever you don't want me to come with you somewhere, Bob, you've only got to say. I honestly don't mind. I wouldn't have come to the office in the first place if you hadn't asked me.'

'No, I was very pleased you came . . . You're not going now . . . ?'

'I thought I might go shopping, or visit St Paul's.'

'Well, if you want to . . . But don't feel in any way . . .'

Bob's phone rang. Dyson, putting his own down a moment later, as Tessa looked around for her gloves, said:

'*I* know what, Tessa. You look rather at a loose end over there. Would you like to become a journalist for an hour or so, and copy out one or two "In Years Gone By" columns for us from the files? It would help us out of a most tremendous hole if you would.'

Tessa was already turning the tatter-edged yellow pages over, trying to find the right date, when Bob put his phone down.

'I thought you said you were going?' he said.

'John asked me to do a job for him first.'

'I see.'

'Is that all right, Bob?'

'Of course it's all right. Why should I mind? It's nothing to do with me what you do.'

Dyson had brought his car into town specially, and everyone in the Gates at lunch wanted a lift to the funeral in it. With six large journalists aboard, all well filled with beer and sandwiches, there was scarcely room for Dyson to turn the wheel or change gear without jamming his elbow into Ted Hurwitz's stomach.

'Perhaps it's just as well Tessa didn't come, Bob,' said Bill Waddy.

'She could have sat in my lap,' said Gareth Holmroyd.

'Ay, ay!' said Ted Hurwitz.

'I thought she was a very nice girl, Bob,' said Gareth Holmroyd.

'Ay, ay, ay!' said Ted Hurwitz.

Laurence Evenden belched behind his hand.

'I *beg* your pardon,' he said.

'The point is,' said Dyson, thumping the car down into second to slow up at the traffic lights, 'a journalist ought to be specializing by the time he's forty. That's really why I'm rather pleased about this BBC thing. I do seem to be accepted as part of the regular television establishment. Do you know what I mean?'

'The light's green, John,' said Ted Hurwitz.

Dyson let the clutch in with a belated jerk, which brought some hard and heavy object tumbling down from the dashboard to hit Bill Waddy on the knee and roll away out of sight beneath the front seats.

'God Almighty,' said Bill Waddy, rubbing his knee. 'What was that?'

'The point is,' said Dyson, 'I don't feel one can go on just doing the general odds and sods indefinitely without more or less destroying himself. Do you see what I'm driving at?'

'It looks like the other side of the road to me,' murmured Bill Waddy.

Dyson swung the wheel to the left, then swung it sharply to the right again to avoid a lorry which was overtaking him on the inside.

'My God,' said Dyson, 'the lunatics you meet on the roads these days! I'm sorry to go on about this BBC thing, but it does seem important to me.'

Laurence Evenden belched.

'I *beg* your pardon,' he said.

It was like a holiday, driving out through the suburbs on a weekday afternoon. Every now and then the sun came out, lighting up women out walking with prams and push-chairs.

'There's the Royal Oak,' said Bill Waddy. 'Do you

remember the Siege of the Royal Oak in 1947, Gareth? When the old publican went off his head and shut himself up in the snug with an ex-War Department Very pistol, and shot distress signals through the serving hatch at anyone who came near?'

'That's right,' said Gareth Holmroyd. 'You were on the *Mail* then, weren't you, Bill? There was you and I there, and old Freddie Samuelson of the *Express*, and Walter Edgworth of the *Mirror* . . .'

'Old Walter's dead now, you know.'

'No! Is he? Poor old Walter!'

'He went out to a paper in East Africa. Got some disease out there.'

'What will you do now that poor old Eddy's gone, John?' asked Laurence Evenden. 'Will you get someone else, do you think?'

'I'll have to have someone, Laurence. I was absolutely run into the ground as it was. And now it looks as though I'm going to be tied up with television work pretty regularly.'

'You know Harry Stearns wants you to take over Lighting-Up Times and Phases of the Moon, John?' said Gareth Holmroyd.

'I know. I can't possibly do it. Not without more staff. I've told the Editor.'

'Charles Baker's trying to get rid of Shipping Movements,' said Ted Hurwitz. 'I bet he manages to land them on poor old John in the end.'

'He won't,' said Dyson. 'He can't. I can't do it.'

'He tried to unload it on me,' said Gareth Holmroyd. 'I told him I thought John Dyson was the man.'

'Well, I'm not,' said Dyson.

'Old John'll manage somehow,' said Bill Waddy. 'Why don't you change down, John? We've almost stopped.'

Bob, who had sat in silence from the beginning of the journey, crushed between Gareth Holmroyd and Laurence Evenden in the back, sighed meditatively.

'It's funny to think we're on our way to poor old Eddy's funeral,' he said.

'Look, Dancy Street,' said Bill Waddy. 'Wasn't that where some bakery foreman dressed himself up in a turban, said he was an Eastern potentate, and persuaded half a dozen women to move in with him as his harem? 1949, I think it was.'

'Nineteen fifty-one,' said Gareth Holmroyd. 'The old king died next day and killed the story stone dead. There's Holt's Depository—remember that? Where the kids shot the sky-rocket through the fan-light and set fire to all the furniture? You know who was on that story? Old Jimmy Mulholland of *The Guardian*. He's a PRO with the Coal Board now.'

'He's not, you know,' said Ted Hurwitz. 'He's dead.'

'No!'

'Died of lung cancer, last summer. I saw his brother in the Cock a couple of months ago.'

'Well, who'd have thought it! A great big, strapping man he was. Poor old Jimmy!'

'I can't help feeling, to revert for a moment,' said Dyson, 'that television is rather more my métier. I do think that one can put one's ideas over rather more forcefully and precisely when one's present in the flesh, with all one's conversational resources to hand.'

'Poor old Jimmy!' said Gareth Holmroyd.

'It's a funny thing,' said Bob, emerging from his silence again. 'I was just thinking about poor old Eddy. He'd have enjoyed being on this trip with us today, you know.'

'He wouldn't have enjoyed going to his own funeral, Bob,' said Laurence Evenden. 'He wasn't *morbid*.'

'I didn't mean that . . .'

'Do you remember Basil Merriman's funeral, Gareth?' said Bill Waddy. 'It was snowing a blizzard, and we got lost in the middle of nowhere out beyond Aylesbury?'

Dyson swerved to avoid a hole in the road, hit it dead in the middle, and brought Bill Waddy's window down with a crash.

'Don't worry,' said Dyson. 'That's always happening. Just jam it with that wedge of paper.'

Laurence Evenden belched.

'I *beg* your pardon,' he said.

Tessa sat at Bob's desk in the empty department all afternoon, newspaper files stacked in front of her, trying intermittently to finish the job that Dyson had given her. She didn't find it easy; she wasn't a great reader. Between whiles she got up and looked out of the window, watching the pale sunshine come and go on the elaborate mouldings and cornices of the offices on the opposite side of Hand and Ball Court, until she realized she was being watched from a window of the floor above by two young men in shirt-sleeves. They smiled and waved at her, and she hurried back to the desk, blushing.

It was quiet and calm in the empty room. From time to time one of the phones rang, and she stared at it and held her breath till it stopped. Now and then messengers would come in, look in the empty out-baskets, and go out again without a word; or put proofs on the desk beside her — rolled galleys, and damp, folded pages. 'Thank you,' she said, not daring to look them in the face. But most of the time the only reminders of the outside world were remote sounds which merely emphasized the quiet of the room itself — the murmur of traffic away in Fleet Street, a typewriter clicking somewhere, some girls giggling, milk bottles falling over, a boy whistling.

She looked through the drawers of Bob's desk, curious to explore even the most unconsidered corners of his life. She found a paper bag with two toffees in it; a book on Burma with a page of Bob's notes inside; yellowing, dusty copy paper, crumpled carbons, expired typewriter ribbons; a brier pipe, grey with age, left over perhaps from some previous occupant; a dusty brown shoe with a hole in it; three rusty razor-blades; an ancient copy of *Queen* magazine; a letter from herself . . .

She opened the letter and began to read it. 'My dearest, darlingest Bob,' it began. 'Masses of hugs and kisses from your silly adoring Tessa, because the sun's shining, and I *know* there'll be a letter from you tomorrow, and because anyway all I want to do is to send you masses of hugs and kisses . . .'

She put her hand over her eyes, too embarrassed to read on. How could she have written such stuff? How *could* she? It was like coming across an embarrassing old photograph of herself. The letter was dated four weeks before. It could have been four years. She felt that she had changed entirely since it was written; and chiefly during the three days since she had been in London.

How would she write to Bob now? She leaned on the files, making her sleeves grey with dust, looking up at the pale blue patches appearing and disappearing above the rooftops outside the window. 'Darling Bob,' she would start – nothing more elaborate, nothing more gushing. No, not even that. Just, 'Bob'. 'Bob, I understand now that nothing in life is as easy as it at first seems, and that being in love is a condition which can cause one a great deal of pain. Of course, I knew that before. But I supposed that it was only the sweet pain of yearning, the sweet uncertainty of what-may-perhaps-be. But now I see that the sweetness goes, and that the pain which remains is just the ordinary, unilluminating misery of humiliation, embarrassment, and inadequacy. You have hurt me a lot in the past three days, Bob, and I think you will hurt me a great deal more in the days to come. You don't love me very much. Perhaps you don't love me at all. But why should you? I can see how hopelessly unsuitable I am for you; all I ever do is misunderstand what you say, and weep. But you'll never have the strength to send me away – you're so *weak*, Bob, that it embarrasses me – and in the end the job will fall to me; I shall have to send myself away. What a miserable responsibility to be loaded with! I put it off from day to day out of pity for myself. For in spite of everything, you are present in all my waking thoughts. Whichever way I turn – you. I revolve about you, dazed and unhappy, with my eyes fixed on you hopelessly. Look how I write you this letter! I keep it inside my head, so that you'll never see it, or anything like it . . .'

Tears brimmed out of her eyes, and ran down her cheeks. She walked about the room, hating herself for pitying herself. She looked out of the window, carefully read the titles of all the books on the shelf, from *Take Your Car to North Africa!* to *National Debt or National Death? – The Bankers' Plot Exposed*, and stopped crying. She sat down and set to work on the files. The phone continued to ring from time to time; messengers continued to call. Once or twice people put their heads round the door and asked her if the Meditation proof was up yet, or whether she knew that she had four inches less than usual on page twelve. 'I'm sorry,' she told these heads, keeping her red eyes turned away from them, 'Mr Dyson and Mr Bell are at the funeral. I don't work here myself.' 'I see,' they said, not seeing, and withdrew uncertainly.

One of the callers came right into the room. He was a tall, wasted man with bushy grey hair, bushy grey eyebrows, and more bushy grey hair growing out of his nose and ears. He crept right across to her desk on tiptoe, as if to avoid obtruding too much on her consciousness, and smiled down at her with a wasted, ingratiating smile.

'Hello,' he whispered. 'You're the new girl, are you?'

'No,' said Tessa, blushing.

'Oh, I'm sorry. I hadn't seen you around before, so I thought . . .'

'I don't work here.'

'I see. I see. I just thought, seeing you working here . . .' He waved his hands uneasily, still smiling.

'Well, I'm working here now,' said Tessa, brushing nervously back at the hair hanging around her scarlet cheeks, 'but I don't actually *work* here.'

'I see. Anyway, I'm Mr Dancer, the Chief Sub-Editor. So now we know. Well, I'll say goodbye. I'm sorry to have . . .'

'No, no. I'm sorry I was . . .'

'It was nice to . . .'

'Yes . . .'

Still smiling his deathly smile, and nodding his head awkwardly, he tiptoed backwards to the door and disappeared.

Dyson fixed his gaze upon the east window of the crematorium chapel, screwing up his eyes, trying to fill his head with the radiating rods of light and a steady contemplation of death. Light; flowers; brass fittings; solemn intonation; and in that box the already decomposing remains of the man who had occupied the corner desk in Dyson's office each day since he had taken the department over. Then poor old Eddy had been a jungle of faint electric circuits connected to make thoughts and memories and aches and sleepiness, like a blackboard of chalk dust patterned to form the binomial theorem or the history of the Fourth Crusade. Now those slight differences of electrical potential had disappeared, like the chalk dust at the end of the lesson. Old Eddy had been wiped clean. Dyson tried to fix his mind upon the tiny grains of chalk fleeing before the duster, filling the air, and settling upon shiny surfaces, totally and eternally discharged of theorem and crusade, or any lingering imprint of them.

There were a dozen mourners from the family in the front pews – women with grey curls and mild glasses, an old man bent over a stick, his head projecting forwards from the unoccupied collar of his overcoat like a tortoise's; a school-boy in a neat navy-blue trenchcoat, holding a maroon cap. Women in tweed overcoats, men in dark melton overcoats – they seemed more overcoats than people; the sort of people whose personalities are not large enough to dominate their outdoor clothes. Two of the ladies' overcoats were sniffling, and with infinite discretion blowing their noses. I have a lump in my throat, thought Dyson. I definitely have a lump in my throat. I am pervaded by a deep and solemn sadness. Yes, yes, I am awed by a cognition of mortality. A *cognition*? Why not 'a sense'? God, one's thoughts need subbing at times! All the same, a cognition is what it feels like, set among these

flowers, these stabbing rods of light, these solemn sacer-
dotal periods, this indisputable lump in the throat. The
lesson was from Corinthians. 'If after the manner of men
I have fought with beasts at Ephesus, what advantageth
it me, if the dead rise not?' Such words! Such sonorous
words, breaking like a dark, silver-shot ocean upon this
unpromising overcoated shore!

'For this corruptible must put on incorruption, and this
mortal must put on immortality. So when this corruptible
shall have put on incorruption, and this mortal shall have
put on immortality, then shall be brought to pass the saying
that is written, Death is swallowed up in victory.' Yes.
thought Dyson, at that I can feel a prickling behind the
lids of my eyes! At that I am almost ready to break down
and weep! And yet . . . do I in any sense believe that poor
old Eddy shall put on immortality? Isn't it rather terrible
that what brings the prickling behind my eyelids is not old
Eddy's death, or even the thought of human mortality in
general, but certain strokes of rhetoric – certain allitera-
tions, repetitions, and verbal sonorities which don't hold
any literal meaning for me? I'm more moved by literature
than by what it describes!

The lump in the throat – where has it gone? Oh God,
have I forgotten how poor old Eddy sat at his desk in
Hand and Ball Court on the last day of his life, talking
about those past times which were most important to him,
and how nobody took any notice? Have I forgotten how
nobody really cared, how nobody really knew him? Doesn't
that bring the lump back to the throat, if one really dwells
on it? Well, doesn't it? And isn't it a little moving to think
of all these various people being moved by poor old
Eddy's death? Moved enough, anyway, to abandon their
day's work and come here to be told that the trumpet
would sound, and poor old Eddy be raised incorruptible?
There was anguish in thinking of the anguish felt within
the overcoats; and in the hearts of people from the office
with some substance and standing, like Gareth Holmroyd
and Laurence Evenden; and in the heart of one whose

face would be well-known to anyone in the front pews from their television screens, if they happened to turn round . . .

But I *did* feel something. In that horrible moment when I looked across the room and realized that poor old Eddy was dead I certainly felt something. I felt frightened, physically frightened. What else? I felt disbelief, and some sense of outrage that this should happen to me. Yes, I certainly felt *something*.

And when the priest came to commit poor old Eddy's body to the flames, Dyson felt something else. For slowly, propelled by some unseen force, the coffin began to jerk sideways, until it reached the wall of the chapel, when a trapdoor opened, and in a series of irregular jerks, man that was born of woman disappeared into the wings. Dyson was stunned by the vulgarity of it. That poor old Eddy should come to this! That he should last be seen being dragged jerkily offstage by theatrical machinery, like the cardboard ship in *Dick Whittington*! Dyson half expected him to come jerking back for a reprise of the First Collect. It would have been different if the trapdoor had been the actual door of the furnace; or if the coffin had been dragged by visible human operatives; or if it had gone smoothly, as by the hand of God or the power of irresistible mechanical principles. But as it was . . . As it was, Dyson had experienced a genuine spasm. And another, secondary spasm, when he thought about the first one, and realized that he was more appalled by vulgarity than he was by death.

With great discretion, the overcoats in the front pews blew their noses. With great discretion, Laurence Evenden released the excess gas pressure in his duodenum. With great discretion, Dyson yawned, straining his muscles to keep his mouth shut at the same time. He yawned again, uncontrollably, concealing it behind his service-card. God, he thought, I really must give the beer at lunch a miss.

Reg Mounce marched into Dyson's department, kicking the door open in front of him.

'Oh, it's you,' he said to Tessa, looking sourly round the room. 'Both at the wake, are they?'

He hesitated, frowning at a sheet of paper he was holding.

'It was one or the other of your bright boy-friends who sent me this, was it?' he demanded, tossing the paper down in front of her. She picked it up and read it.

Editor to R. Mounce. PRIVATE AND CONFIDENTIAL.

I cannot trace any acknowledgement from you of the memorandum I sent you on the twentieth of this month, regarding your talents and the scope for them in this office. Since the matter is important, I wonder if you would take the trouble to write to me again, indicating particularly whether such other arrangements as you will be making are likely to commence at an earlier date than one might otherwise suppose. Certain other arrangements which *I* must make naturally turn upon this.

I trust that your own other arrangements are proceeding satisfactorily.

'Some sort of joke, is it?' demanded Mounce bitterly.

'I'm afraid I don't know. It looks as if it's from the Editor.'

'Oh, it *looks* as if it's from the Editor,' said Mounce ironically.

'It says it's from the Editor.'

'Oh, it *says* it's from the Editor. The last one *said* it was from the Editor. But it wasn't. It was just a load of crap that some joker had sent. All this crap about "other arrangements"! It's just crap.'

'Is it?' said Tessa, wondering if perhaps it was. She tried to focus her mind on the words. 'Other arrangements' – well, other arrangements were alternative dispositions. And alternative dispositions were – well, they were other arrangements. But somehow, she felt, the words had passed right through her mind without leaving any deposit of meaning behind.

'Well, isn't it?' said Mounce. 'People aren't asked to make other arrangements on this paper, are they? Have you ever heard of anyone in this office being asked to make other arrangements?'

'Well, no . . .'

'So it's obviously a load of crap. Everyone saw that. This isn't the *Express*, after all.'

He took the note out of Tessa's hands and began to read it through again, rubbing his chin uneasily.

'I mean,' he said, 'you don't think this *is* from the Editor, do you?'

'I've honestly no idea.'

'I mean, this is just the sort of shit the Editor would write. "Other arrangements" – that's just the sort of stinking thing he'd say.'

'I thought,' said Tessa timidly, 'that you said people weren't asked to make other arrangements on this paper?'

'No, but what I mean is, if they *were* asked to make other arrangements, making other arrangements is just what the stinking Editor would call it.'

Mounce held the note up to the light, as if looking for a watermark.

'I wonder,' he said gloomily. 'Now you've put doubts in my mind.'

'I suppose you could ring the Editor's secretary and check . . .' suggested Tessa hesitantly.

Mounce stared at her absently, pushing his lower lip up.

'I suppose I could . . .' he said. He read through the note again, frowning. Then he went over to the window, and gazed down into Hand and Ball Court for several minutes, frowning and pushing his lower lip up alternately.

'I suppose that would be one way of tackling it,' he said. He took another look at the note, putting a finger into his mouth and trying to dislodge some irritating morsel of lunch from between his back teeth. Slowly, still rereading the note and still working on his teeth, he wandered out of the room.

'I'll bear it in mind,' he said gloomily, without turning

his head, as he went through the door.

'Hello,' said Bob, coming back into the office and holding out a bag of sweets to Tessa. 'Have a peppermint. How were things in the office, Tessa?'

'All right. How was the funeral?'

'Fine.'

He picked up the mail and messages on his desk, and at once sorted out a small brown envelope addressed 'R. Bell Esqre.'

'Oh God,' he said, 'something from the Editor.'

He ripped it open.

Editor to R. Bell, *it said.*

'PRIVATE AND CONFIDENTIAL.'

'Congratulations.'

'What does it say?' asked Dyson. 'You look as white as a sheet.'

Bob shook his head blankly.

'It just says "congratulations". But what on, for God's sake?'

Dyson thought for an instant, and then laughed.

'Bob!' he said reproachfully. 'On your *engagement*!'

Ten

Bob, arriving at the office before Dyson one morning, found a man he had never seen before working at old Eddy's desk. He appeared on the whole to be middle-aged. His face was middle-aged – unnaturally neat and pale, with spare flesh padding the line of the jaw, and lifeless sandy hair brushed inertly to the shape of the head. But his clothes were young men's clothes – a very dark jacket buttoned on four buttons, revealing a triangle of dark tan shirt with a strip of black suède tie, and an inch-and-a-half of tan cuff at each wrist. He looked up at Bob; his eyes were ageless and neutral.

'Hello,' he said, and returned to his work.

'Hello,' said Bob. He took off his overcoat and sat down at his desk, staring at the man. He felt he ought to query his presence – particularly his use of poor old Eddy's desk – but everything about him suggested that his right to be in the room was firmly established – perhaps more firmly even than Bob's. Besides, Bob felt diffident about challenging an older man. Without taking his eyes off him, he opened the drawer of his desk and felt about inside it until he had located a toffee. The man continued to work. He was writing something in longhand, the paper turned sideways, the pen flying along the lines away from him at great speed. His left hand rested on the desk, a silver ring set with a large brown stone on the little finger, and between the first and second fingers a cigarette with a thin blue tape of smoke rising steadily from it. The finger-ends were pale amber, the rest of the hand marble-white, and slightly fleshy. As Bob looked at it, the hand performed a sudden evolution like a conjuring-trick, turning over and producing from nowhere a pack of American cigarettes, with one of the cigarettes extended towards Bob. The right hand continued to write. The blue tape of smoke from the left hand snaggled for a moment, then the snaggle slid up the tape and disappeared, leaving the smoke rising as steadily as before from the underside of the hand.

'Cigarette?' said the man.

'No, thanks,' said Bob.

'My name's Erskine Morris,' said the man, vanishing the cigarettes as deftly as he had produced them, and continuing to write as he spoke. It looked like some sort of play he was writing, so far as Bob could see. There were names down the margin, each followed by a colon and a short sentence ending in a row of dots. 'I'm Moulton's replacement.'

'Oh, I see,' said Bob. 'Well, welcome to the department. My name's Bob Bell.'

'Hi, Bob,' said Morris expressionlessly. Bob wondered if he was an Englishman who affected American usages, or an American with an English accent. Was he a young American with middle-aged English characteristics? Or a middle-aged Englishman with middle-aged American mannerisms? Or . . . Another thought struck Bob.

'Does Dyson know you're joining us?'

'You tell me, Bob.'

'He hasn't said anything to me about it.'

Morris wrote on in silence.

'I don't think I've seen you round the office before,' said Bob finally.

'No,' said Morris.

'You've just joined the paper?'

'Sure.'

'Who were you with before?'

'I was at university before.'

Bob stared at Morris – mainly at the back of his head, since it was turned slightly away from him to follow the speeding journeys of his pen across the paper.

'You mean, you've just come down?' said Bob, trying out of politeness not to sound incredulous.

'Sure.'

'You mean, *straight down*?'

'Last year.'

'Forgive me asking, but how old are you?'

'Twenty-two.'

Morris's left hand stretched out from its one-and-a-half-inch cuff and stubbed out its half-smoked cigarette in the ashtray. Then, while the right hand wrote on, it conjured up the pack of cigarettes once again, conjured one out, and conjured a flame out of a butane lighter it suddenly turned out to be holding. Bob followed each movement with his eyes.

'Which university were you at?' he asked.

'Cambridge.'

'Cambridge? *I* was at Cambridge.'

'Sure.'

'John Dyson was at Cambridge.'

'Sure, sure.'

Morris administered his sures and sure sures in a soothing tone, like pats on the head for an importunate child. Bob felt rather like a child, talking to Morris. He went over to the window and gazed down into Hand and Ball Court. Reassuringly familiar, homely figures like Gareth Holmroyd and Pat Selig were arriving for work, pacing out the well-worn diagonal trail across the court from the end of Hand and Ball Passage to the main door of the office. They seemed almost embarrassingly innocent and unsophisticated, compared with Morris.

'Are you on the paper's graduate trainee scheme?' he asked.

'Sure.'

'I joined the paper as a graduate trainee.'

'Oh?'

Bob tried to imagine Morris completing the trainee scheme, joining the pensions fund, and going on to groove out the diagonal of Hand and Ball Court morning and night for twenty or thirty years. It was somehow not a very plausible picture.

Erskine Morris . . .

'That's a coincidence,' said Bob. 'You've got the same initials as poor old Eddy Moulton.'

'Sure.'

'I'll help you move poor old Eddy's junk out of the desk, if you like, so you can move your own stuff in.'

'Thank you, Bob – I've done it already.'

Going back to his desk, Bob looked discreetly over Morris's shoulder. The only page he could see of Morris's manuscript started off :

> BENNY : If Patrick says you're going to get done, you're going to get done, sunshine. Inne, Patrick?
> OLD MAN : No! No!
> PATRICK : You see, sunshine? You're going to get done. Patrick says so . . .
> [*The camera holds* OLD MAN *in M.C.U., tightens on his terrified eyes, then whip-pans to C.U. of knife in* PATRICK'S *hand.*]

'What did you do with poor old Eddy's stuff?' asked Bob.

'I put it in the waste-paper basket,' said Morris.

Dyson got off on the wrong foot with Morris from the very beginning, even though Morris politely stopped writing while Bob introduced them, and sat back in his chair to look at Dyson.

'Hi, John,' he said, with some slight suggestion of benevolence in his voice, as if he were taking Dyson on his staff in spite of a prison record.

'Erskine's just joined the paper as a graduate trainee, John,' said Bob. 'He's apparently coming to us as a replacement for poor old Eddy.'

Dyson was visibly irritated.

'I haven't heard anything about this,' he said. 'I think there must be some mistake here. Are you certain you were told to come to this office?'

'Sure,' said Morris.

'Well, I haven't heard anything about it. I'm certainly expecting *someone*. God knows, I *need* someone. But someone *experienced*! A trainee is no earthly use in here at all.'

Dyson took off his overcoat and went to his desk, frowning heavily. Morris said nothing. He put his cigarette to his lips, drew in smoke, sat silent and impassive for some moments, then blew the smoke out of his nose in two impassive grey plumes.

'You can sit here for the moment,' said Dyson, opening the mail from his in-tray, 'while we get this sorted out. You can watch us at work. I haven't got time to start showing you how to do anything. But you might pick up a thing or two just by looking. I suppose it's all experience. Has Morley produced yet, Bob?'

Bob shook his head.

'Oh, *God*!' said Dyson, clenching his fists. 'Oh God, oh God, oh *God*!' He looked across at Morris. 'It's a madhouse in here,' he said. 'Which university were you at?'

'Cambridge,' said Morris. When he was not writing or smoking, noticed Bob, he sat absolutely still, so still that the ribbon of smoke from his cigarette hung about almost undisturbed for two or three feet above his hand.

'Which college?'

'King's.'

Dyson was impressed.

'I was at Sidney,' he said in a different voice. 'Well, well. As a matter of fact, I started on this paper as a graduate trainee myself. It's not a bad office. Of course, it's not *typical*. But then I doubt whether such a thing as a typical newspaper office exists. It's a very funny business, the newspaper business.'

'Sure,' said Morris.

'You get quite a good general introduction to the industry as a graduate trainee, you know. You'll probably do six months in the news room first, then six months in the subs, then maybe six months in the commercial room . . .'

Dyson broke off in mid-explanation, frowning at a piece of copy paper he had taken out of a little brown envelope marked 'J. Dyson Esqre.'

'That's funny,' he said irritably. 'You *are* supposed to be here. The Editor's sent you.'

'Sure,' said Morris.

'I don't know why I wasn't told about this before,' complained Dyson. 'I think I should have been consulted. The Editor knew what the situation was in here.'

'Sure, sure,' said Morris soothingly, conjuring up the cigarette pack again. 'Have a cigarette, John, and tell me what I'm supposed to be doing.'

Dyson set Morris to work copying out the extracts for the 'In Years Gone By' column. But Dyson's opinion of him, which had risen noticeably on hearing that he had been at King's, had fallen back to zero again; his having been at King's was cancelled out by his having been right about his instructions to join Dyson's department.

A slight difficulty arose about whether he might type the extracts.

'Eddy always used to write them out in longhand,' said Dyson.

'I'd prefer to type them.'

'Yes . . . well . . . I suppose you could. There's only one typewriter in here, I'm afraid.'

'I'll use that for now. I'll get another one sent in later.'

'I'm afraid you won't be able to get another one,' said Dyson. 'We have to make do with one in here, sharing it. Poor old Eddy didn't type, you see.'

Morris typed throughout the morning, driving the carriage of the department's battered portable along with his two hammering fingers just about as fast as it would go. He worked with scarcely a break to search out a new passage in the files, or to pick up the half-smoked end of his last cigarette from the ashtray, stub it out, light a new one, and put it down in its place. The noise of the typewriter and the gathering haze of cigarette smoke in the room both seemed to disturb Dyson. He kept glancing across at either the typewriter or the cigarette in the ashtray, and frowning. Morris's presence also put him off his stroke on the phone. 'Good morning, Sir William, I hope I'm not intruding . . .' he would say, smiling self-deprecatingly at the distant Sir William. Then he would remember he was being watched by Morris, and he would frown, and stuff his finger into his left ear to keep out the noise of the typewriter. 'What was that, Sir William? You were just doing what, Sir William?' Then he would realize he was smiling again for Sir William's benefit, and swing round in his chair so that Morris couldn't see the smile.

But when Morris stopped typing, just before lunchtime, and sat back in his chair looking through his handiwork, the silence disturbed Dyson even more. He stared at Morris disapprovingly, as if Morris had spent the whole morning in idleness.

'How are you getting on?' he asked.

'I've done a week's supply, John.'

'Of hundreds or fifties?'

'The lot.'

'Twenty-fives and tens as well?'

'Sure, sure.'

'Let me have a look.'

Morris clipped the papers together and tossed them across on to Dyson's desk. Dyson had for some reason assumed that Morris would bring them over and stand beside him while he went through them. He went through them none the less, frowning. He had spent most of the morning frowning, except when he had been talking to Sir William Paice and others. Morris lit another cigarette.

'This is all right,' said Dyson, taking pains to ink in one or two faint characters and slipped capitals, in lieu of anything else to correct. 'This is quite good. Quite good work.'

'What next, John?' asked Morris.

Dyson gazed at the sheets of copy, shuffling them about in his hand, trying to think.

'You'd better do another week's supply,' he said.

Morris accompanied Bob and Dyson to the Gates for lunch. Bob invited him; Dyson frowned all the way there, and abandoned the other two as soon as they were inside.

'Every newspaper office has its own particular pub,' explained Bob. 'The Gates happens to be ours.'

'Sure,' said Morris, looking round the bar with his non-committal eyes.

'Well, some people go off to El Vino's or the Falstaff. But a certain set on the paper come here pretty regularly. You can usually count on finding old Bill Waddy sitting up at the bar here, and old Gareth Holmroyd hovering about somewhere.'

'Sure, sure,' said Morris. Bob introduced him to some of the usual crowd; and Morris asked Bill Waddy, who was buying, for a Pernod. They all stared at him over their halves of bitter. Morris appeared not to notice.

'Who's the joker up the end?' he asked Bob quietly. 'Is he one of your team?'

'The one leaning on the bar? That's Reg Mounce, the Pictures Editor.'

'He's high.'

'A bit, possibly. It's quite funny actually. You see that dog-eared piece of paper he's showing Gareth and Mike? That's a note he got from the Editor the other day, giving him the sack.'

'What's he flashing it around for, then?'

'Well, he's surprised by it, you see. The point is, people don't get the sack on this paper. It's that sort of paper. So he keeps going round asking everyone what they think he should do.'

Morris stared at Bob expressionlessly.

'And?' he said.

'Well, everyone thinks he should just ignore it. Pretend he never got it. People don't think the Editor would have the nerve to challenge him about it.'

'A popular man, is he, Reg?'

'Oh God no. Everyone thinks he's an absolute tit. It's just a matter of solidarity.'

'Oh. That.'

'It's that sort of office.'

'Sure.'

'It's really not at all a bad sort of office to be in.'

'Sure,' said Morris, conjuring another long cigarette out of the air. 'Oh, sure, sure.'

Relations between Dyson and Morris deteriorated still further after lunch. Morris left the Gates as soon as he had finished his Pernod. When Dyson and Bob got back to the office, he was at his desk already, typing. It was not the department's battered old machine he was typing on; it was a brand new electric portable. Dyson stopped in his tracks, gazing at it. He was almost too angry to speak.

'Look,' he said, 'I'm not standing for this. Year in, year out, Bob and I have had to make do with one rotten reconditioned typewriter between us. And the first day you arrive you contrive to get hold of this! Well, I'm not having it.'

Dyson wrenched off his overcoat, dragging the lining out of the right sleeve. He sat down at his desk, not looking at Morris, his face rigid with anger. Morris watched him expressionlessly.

'You can borrow it if you like,' he said.

'I can borrow it?' cried Dyson, flaring up at once. 'Did you say I can *borrow* it?'

'Sure. Whenever you like.'

Bob slipped a peppermint into his mouth, not daring to look at either of them until Dyson had found words to speak.

'That typewriter's going back at once,' he said inadequately.

Morris inhaled smoke, held it for some minutes, and then let it down his nose.

'John,' he said impassively, 'this isn't an office machine.'

'What?' snapped Dyson. 'What is it, then?'

'It's my own.'

'Yours? Where did you get it from?'

'I bought it.'

Bob averted his eyes again. It was as embarrassing to see a friend under the influence of adrenalin when one had not lost one's own temper as it was to see him under the influence of alcohol when one was sober.

'*Bought* it?' queried Dyson, as if the word were some rare form of Sanskrit preterite.

'Sure.'

'In a shop?'

'Sure.'

'In the lunchhour?'

'Sure.'

'An *electric typewriter*?'

'Sure, sure.'

Dyson continued to gaze at Morris for some minutes, his mouth very slightly open. Then, abruptly, without a word, he turned away, picked up a piece of copy, and began to correct it with short, violent strokes and swirls of his pen. Morris turned his head slightly and caught Bob's eye. Bob at once stopped moving the peppermint about in his mouth.

'If you pay Schedule D,' said Morris, 'it's tax-deductable.'

Bob made a point of taking a benevolent interest in Morris over the next few days, to balance out Dyson's hostility. He got him an office towel for the washroom. He told him to whom to apply for union membership. He showed him how to make out his expenses chits, filling in 'office duties, 5s. 6d.' for each day of the week, as laid down in the house agreement between union and management. Bob could remember his own loneliness and isolation when he had first come down and started work on the paper. Morris didn't *seem* lonely or isolated himself, but a hard shell was usually a sign of vulnerability underneath.

People were also taking a benevolent interest in Bob. Gareth Holmroyd, Ted Hurwitz, Mike Sparrow, Ralph Absalom – they were all keeping their eyes open for a house for him. Each day they brought him cyclostyled sheets from their local agents, and the telephone numbers of friends' relatives whose relatives' friends had seen a board up somewhere. Bob felt obliged to go and look at a certain number of these places out of politeness. He took mornings off from work to inspect houses of character in Ealing, imposing residences in Hendon, and important properties in select residential districts just 30 minutes from Waterloo. With unseeing eyes he gazed at usual offices, charming patios, 'Ideal' boilers, and mature fruit-trees. He asked the young men from the agents who showed him round if the pipes were lagged, and whether the soil was chalk or clay; he couldn't think of any other questions. Almost the only thing he could think of coherently as he peered at the Dutch tiles and crazy paving was that according to his last statement of account he had £67 12s. 9d. in the bank. He dwelt on the figure gratefully. Whatever happened, however far he was driven by forces outside his control, there was surely no way in which a man with only £67 12s. 9d. could find himself acquiring a delightful property or superior detached residence. In the last analysis the £67 12s. 9d. would stand revealed; the pen would be taken out of his fingers just before he signed across the excise stamp; gentle hands would conduct him back to the comfortable shabby gloom of Flat 4, 86 Leominster Gardens.

Jannie was taking a benevolent interest, too, inviting not Bob but Tessa out to look at houses she had found for them in s.w.23. The houses Jannie found did not have charming patios or mature rose-gardens. Most of them were noticeably short even on usual offices, and it did not occur even to the agents to describe them as imposing or delightful. Still, they had something; they had potentialities. And sitting tenants.

'It's just a matter of agreeing compensation with them,' said Jannie, leading Tessa in and out of rooms impregnated with such poverty and squalor as she had never dreamt existed. 'Everyone does it. The present owner would probably arrange it for you, if you feel awkward about it.'

'Yes,' said Tessa, trying not to breathe the sweet-sour air into her lungs.

'You could knock this wall down, and make one large room through from front to back.'

'Yes.'

'Or make the flat at the back into the kitchen, and rent

the basement out as a bed-sitter . . .'

For Bob and Tessa's house Jannie projected all the reconstruction and improvement which she and John had never found either money or energy enough to carry out in their own. As she took Tessa over a house, the West Indian family in the second-floor back dissolved in her mind into an *au pair* girl; the brass taps and greasy gasrings in the ground-floor scullery into a row of shining white domestic machinery. She had never had an *au pair* girl or a laundry room herself. Her visualization was as generous to Bob and Tessa as it was careless of the existing occupiers. All Tessa could do was blush. She felt she was blushing all the time on these trips, at the conditions of life they were intruding upon, at Jannie's plans to turn it to their advantage, at Jannie's evident affection for her. Jannie really seemed to like her, in her oblique, distracted way. Perhaps just because she was Bob's fiancée – but Tessa felt that it was for herself as well. She wished she could like Jannie more in return. She could see her qualities; she could see why Bob liked her. All the same, when Jannie spoke in that curious Oxford-and-Cambridge accent she had, she seemed to Tessa immeasurably remote and eccentric – a woman of some quite different generation. Then again, she was in love with Bob; and embarrassingly old to be. It was as if one's aunt were competing against one.

'It would be so nice if you did come and live near us when you're married,' said Jannie wistfully. 'One does feel a bit cut off out here.'

The whole business was ridiculous, of course. They would never get married – it should have been obvious to everyone. They *couldn't* get married. Bob wasn't in love with her. You didn't get married to people who weren't in love with you. But if Jannie couldn't see this for herself, how could she explain it to her – *now*, after they had trailed round looking at all those houses? How could Bob suddenly start explaining it to John, to Gareth Holmroyd, to the Editor . . . ? How could she and Bob even put it in words to each other?

'I mean,' said Jannie, 'it's very central here. It's just that one sometimes feels rather – oh, I don't know. You and Bob could get a mortgage all right, couldn't you?'

'Oh, I should think so,' said Tessa, blushing yet again. She didn't know whether they could get a mortgage or not. She had no clear idea of what a mortgage *was*. And she resisted finding out, in the way that other girls she had known kept themselves in deliberate ignorance of such things as impregnation, in the unarticulated hope that if they didn't know what it was it couldn't happen to them.

Mrs Mounce busied herself with being kind to Tessa, too. But this she found easier to bear, partly because Mrs Mounce had so many troubles herself that she was able to be kind back to her, and partly because Mrs Mounce's world and Mrs Mounce's advice seemed even more remote and unreal than Jannie's.

'Honestly, sweetest,' said Mrs Mounce, 'don't go lumbering yourselves with a house and a mortgage right at the beginning. Rent a nice little flat somewhere where you know exactly what your outgoings are – where you know you're not responsible for anything. You can always do a little bit here and a little bit there to brighten it up.'

Tessa liked her, in a dreary sort of way – the sort of way one liked picking one's nails or staying in bed all morning. They sat for hours drinking tea in Mrs Mounce's flat downstairs, while Mrs Mounce talked about her affairs with moustached men in export-import, and Tessa looked at the little bit here and the little bit there which Mrs Mounce had done herself to brighten her own place up. Most of the little bits seemed to be made of cream-painted hardboard and enamelled black wrought iron. She imagined showing her parents round a home of her own decorated in the same way. 'And this is the cocktail bar, Daddy. Bob and I made it out of hardboard and Formica . . . Do you like the individual wrought-iron bottle stands at the back? Bob screwed them on the mirror himself . . .'

The thought made her smile to herself, for what she recognized were basically snobbish reasons. She was pleased to find she was still able to smile, even snobbishly. She had the impression that she hadn't smiled for several months.

Steadily, quietly, electrically, Erskine Morris typed the 'In Years Gone By' column several weeks into the future. There had never been so much 'In Years Gone By' copy set, or so much waiting to be set. From day to day the dark shades of his shirts, ties, and high-buttoning suits subtly changed. But the pallid face above them remained impassive, and the waiting cigarette continued to smoke ritually in the ashtray, like a joss-stick before some inscrutable joss. And Morris's presence continued to cramp Dyson's style. He was if anything more irritated by the quiet drumming of the electric typewriter than by the clatter of the old mechanical one. It was harder to notice exactly when it stopped, and Dyson liked to know. Round about four o'clock in the afternoon he would sometimes forget Morris, and sprawl back in his chair with his hands behind his head, yawning and looking at the ceiling, just as he had before Morris's arrival. Then he would suddenly realize that the typing had ceased. Fearing that Morris had stopped to watch him yawning, he would at once return to his work, and try to conceal his yawns behind his hand. At other times, he would sit back in a thoughtful, philosophical mood, and ask Bob whether he felt one ought to have one's name printed at the head of one's private writing-paper. Morris's typewriter would stop at once. 'Oh, forget it, Bob,' Dyson would mutter. A great deal of work was done by all three of them.

Dyson became quite unlike himself in his dealings with Morris. Every time Morris got a telephone-call which sounded from his laconic replies as if it was private business, Dyson frowned at him warningly. He also prowled about the room from time to time, passing as if accidentally behind Morris's chair, and looking over Morris's shoulder out of the corner of his eye. It was in this way that he discovered that not all Morris's application with the typewriter was devoted to 'In Years Gone By'.

'What's this?' he demanded one day. ' "Terry had been on tea for four years before he first began using horse." What the hell's this?'

Morris helped himself to a couple of lungfuls of cigarette smoke.

'It's an article on junk,' he said.

'Junk?'

'Drugs. It's for the features department.'

'They asked you to do it?'

'Sure.'

Dyson walked round the room like a patrolling school-master.

'Have you written anything else for other departments?' he asked.

'Oh, a couple of leaders. Some diary pars.'

Dyson patrolled on.

'If you want to write anything for anyone else again,' he said roughly, 'do it in your own time, not in mine.'

'OK, John,' said Morris.

Dyson knew he was behaving stupidly, which made him more graceless still. Bob tried to talk him out of it when they were on their own, at the sandwich bar in the Gates.

'You'll have to find him something else to do, John,' he said. 'He's five weeks ahead on "Years Gone By" already.'

'But what else *can* I give him to do?' wailed Dyson. 'He's just a trainee – he doesn't know how to do anything.'

'He can learn, John, just like you and I did.'

'Bob, I can't let him sub, because I haven't got time to go through it all again and check it. And can you honestly imagine him ringing up Sir William Paice? Or the Bishop? Or even Canon Morley?'

'Well . . .'

'He's just not the type, is he, Bob? Anyway, poor old Eddy did "In Years Gone By" for over ten years; I don't see why Mr Morris shouldn't stick at it for a week or two.'

'Morris isn't the same sort of man as poor old Eddy, John . . .'

'Don't tell me! Honestly, Bob, that office was a happy

place until Morris came. To me he seems to cast a blight over the whole day.'

'You do overdramatize things a bit, you know, John. He's a bit shy, that's all.'

'Do you know what Bill Waddy calls him, Bob? Erskine Absinthe. Fancy coming in here and demanding a Pernod on his very first day at the office! And he didn't even buy a round himself! He just swilled down his Pernod and walked out!'

'He's a bit on the defensive, John . . .'

'He never bought a round! And all this classless business he tries to put across. Honestly, Bob, he went to Rugby! Did you know that? I asked the personnel director. You and I went to ordinary grammar schools, Bob – but we don't go round pretending to be classless. And he went to Rugby! Well, for God's sake, Bob! For God's sake!'

Remembering all the dinners he had eaten at the Dysons' when he had been living on his own, Bob invited Morris back to his flat one evening so that Tessa could cook dinner for him in his turn. Tessa was nervous about it; she had never entertained anyone in the flat before, apart from Mrs Mounce. She became worried about the appearance of the place, about her cooking, and about her anomalous position in the household. But Morris turned out to be completely uninterested in all three. When he arrived he put his cold, white hand in hers for a moment, and said 'Hello, Tessa' as if he had always been aware of her as part of the background furnishings. Then he ignored her for the rest of the evening. He produced a full bottle of whisky from his briefcase, poured out three tumblerfuls, and asked if he could have the television on.

'There's something coming up that I have an interest in,' he said, fiddling expertly with the controls of the set.

'Something you wrote?' asked Bob, remembering the dialogue he had seen on Morris's desk.

'Sure.'

'A play?'

'A song.'

'What sort of song, Erskine? A pop song?'

'Sure, sure. I'd just like to see how it goes.'

There was a whole programme of pop songs on. Morris sprawled back in the one armchair with his whisky, watching them all impassively. As each new number came up Bob looked at him and asked 'This one?' Morris shook his head without interest. Bob began to get nervous on his behalf.

'You're very casual about it, Erskine,' he said.

'What is there to get excited about?' said Morris easily, the flesh beneath his chin folding over the top of his collar as he leaned back into the cushions. 'It's just a song.'

'But to get it on television! Or have you done it before?'

'I've had a few numbers on.'

Bob stared at him.

'What a strange man you are, Erskine!' he said. The corner of Morris's mouth twitched up into his cheek and fell back. Bob became embarrassed at his own effusiveness, and turned back to the screen, tapping out the rhythm with his fingers on the side of his glass. 'What's this number of yours called?' he asked.

Morris blew smoke down his nose.

' "I Can't Stop Crying",' he said.

A girl with dark-rimmed eyes and long straight blonde hair appeared on the screen, picking her way through a number of abstract decorative shapes at the back of the studio.

'I can't stop crying,' she sang in a plaintive voice. 'All through the night, I can't stop crying. Know it's not right, but can't stop crying. I can't stop crying, 'cause I am crying for you.'

'Is this yours?' asked Bob.

'Sure.'

'I can't stop crying,' sang the girl. 'Though I'm a fool, I go on sighing. Know I'm a fool, not even trying. It can't be right to cry through the night. I can't stop crying for you.'

'Very good,' said Bob, when she had finished. 'I liked the tune.'

'I did the words,' said Morris. 'Someone else did the music.'

'The words were very good, too.'

Morris shrugged.

'It's what the children like,' he said. 'They don't like anything new or strange. Children are very conservative.'

They left the television on while they had dinner, because Morris wanted to watch a Western. Thinking that he wanted to watch it because he thought it was funny, Bob made a few humorous remarks at the expense of the characters on the screen. But Morris didn't smile. He watched silently and impassively, chewing his overdone steak, and retrieving his cigarette from the ashtray between courses. Bob took the point; Morris didn't think the Western was funny.

When the Western was finished they watched the hospital serial. And when the hospital serial finished they carried their coffee across to the set and watched the courtroom serial. Bob and Tessa sat on the floor, their arms round each other. Morris sprawled in the armchair, dispensing whisky. Mrs Mounce rang the bell, and was invited in. 'Hello, Glenda,' said Morris when Bob introduced them. She curled up on the floor and leaned against the arm of Morris's chair. He poured her a tumblerful of whisky.

'*Sweetest!*' she cried, flirtatiously. 'You're trying to get me tight!' 'Sure, sure,' said Morris absently, his attention on the screen.

And so they sat. The telephone rang three times; each time it was for Morris. 'Sure . . .' they heard him murmuring into the mouthpiece, between the noise of gunshot and the scream of tyres. 'I could be interested . . . I should want to use him in a completely different context, of course . . . Sure, sure . . .'

After the third call Morris said to Bob: 'I asked some people to step round.'

'Fine,' said Bob. 'They're welcome.'

But when they arrived, Morris didn't seem particularly interested in them; not, anyway, enough to stop watching the television. 'Lake, Brian, Andy,' he explained, scarcely looking up from the screen. 'Tessa, Glenda, Bob. Pour out the rest of the whisky, Brian.'

Brian and Andy lounged against the edge of the dining-table at the back of the group, half watching the television, half talking to each other. Lake perched on the arm of Morris's chair and stared at the screen. She was a girl; she was the girl who had sung 'I Can't Stop Crying'. Bob gazed at her, drinking her in. She shone in the half-darkness of the room. Her long bleached hair shone; her polished white raincoat shone; her white boots and her unstockinged knees shone.

'How did it look?' she asked Morris, not taking her eyes off the screen.

'Great,' said Morris, not taking his eyes off the screen either. He slipped a non-committal hand round her waist, so that the smoke from his cigarette rose past her left ear.

Bob couldn't stop staring at her, even though he had his arm round Tessa. He rubbed his chin absently on the top of Tessa's head, so that he could look over it at the girl. Tessa and Mrs Mounce, he knew, were watching her out of the corner of their eyes too, as silent and overawed as he was himself. He knew without even thinking about it consciously that she had no bottom worth worrying about. God Almighty! A girl in show business, with white boots and no bottom – in his flat!

'It looked all right, did it?' she asked Morris again, perhaps forgetting that she had asked him once already.

'Great, great. Have you eaten?'

'We're going to get something at Nick's. You coming?'

'OK,' said Morris. He stood up and put his cigarettes in his pocket. 'Thanks, Tessa. Thanks, Bob. I enjoyed that. Bye, Glenda. Bye!'

They had gone, all four of them, almost before Bob realized they were going.

'Darling!' said Mrs Mounce admiringly. 'I never knew you had such smart friends!'

Bob drew the curtain to one side and looked out of the

window. The four of them were just climbing into a long red two-seater sports car standing double-parked almost in the middle of the roadway. Its headlights came on full beam, and it accelerated away with a rising roar which brought heads to windows all along the street.

Silently, Tessa switched the television off and began to clear the table.

Eleven

Dyson wandered about the Final Departure Lounge at London Airport in a curious state of elation. The Magic Carpet Travel plane was late leaving; Dyson and the rest of the press party should have taken off for the Trucial Riviera ten minutes before. But he didn't mind at all. He loved airports. He would have liked to feel blasé about them, but he didn't have the opportunity to use them often enough. As soon as he got inside one he became elated. He seemed to have a heightened sense of reality. Moving staircases, rubber plants, low black leather armchairs; 'Flight BE 4029 for Copenhagen and Stockholm is departing now . . . This is the last call for passengers travelling on Flight LH 291 for Düsseldorf and Berlin . . .' He bought *Oggi* and *Neue Illustrierte* at the bookstall, even though he could scarcely read a word of either Italian or German, because being inside an airport made him feel that he could. The Final Departure Lounge, sealed off from gross particular Britain by passport and customs barriers, was a bright nowhere land, sterilized of nationality and all the other ties and limitations of everyday life. Here Dyson felt like International Airport Man — neat, sophisticated, compact; a wearer of lightweight suits and silky blue showercoats; moving over the surface of the earth like some free-floating spirit — from Karachi to Athens to Hong Kong, from Honolulu to Tangier to New York — unimpeded by the traffic problems of Karachi or the housing situation in Honolulu, not deflected from New York by any emotional attachment in Athens, or kept from Hong Kong by business entanglement in New York. Airports and television studios — this was the way of life Dyson felt he was intended for.

He could pick out some of the other journalists in the Magic Carpet group sitting about the lounge; they were all, like himself, carrying the folder of publicity material Magic Carpet had issued them with. There was a photographer who had checked in just ahead of him. He seemed to have brought a couple of models with him – badly-dressed girls with pained expressions and tragically thin legs. And the tall, cavernous man with the dark blazer and the ex-officer's moustache – wasn't he from the *Telegraph*? The red-faced young man with the thin hair falling all over the place was a humorous writer for somebody – Dyson had seen him on television. There was a man in a blue pinstripe suit, with elegantly grey curls, who freelanced food and wine, and an anxious young woman with dark eyes and three strings of beads to chew who did travel for one of the glossies; Dyson had seen them both on facilities trips before. Oh God, he thought, facilities trips! How awful they were! He could picture the holiday development at Sharjah already – new concrete hotels built too quickly, no amenities, the squalor of the local population beyond the new concrete reserves. It was only the travelling there and back which made them worthwhile at all. They could be hours late leaving for all he cared; he was quite happy to sit at London Airport all day and watch the aircraft coming and going.

Ah, the aircraft! He gazed at them through the windows of the lounge. They stood ranked on the apron, shimmering in the morning sunlight. The tangled confusion of ground equipment which surrounded them – the lorries, steps, and generators, the ordinary shoddy private cars in which the aircrew drove themselves out, the temporary sheds and stacks of building materials – only emphasized their remote and fragile perfection. They stood like swans standing – on unlikely legs, in tangled nests. Like swans they would fold their legs and beat up into the uncluttered, abstract sky. One of them moved off the stand as Dyson watched, its engines whining, the blast of air behind it crinkling the standing rainwater on the apron into a million fleeing furrows . . . And there, away across the grass a mile beyond it, one of the big jets was just starting its take-off run. Slowly, very slowly, the great bulk gathered speed, as if the Bank of England or the National Gallery had started to walk, and was trying to run. It drew level with the airport buildings, the colossal baggage of noise it trailed swelling at great speed now, but still heavy on the ground and never in a million years capable of leaving it – a great beast charging head down at central Middlesex. Then, suddenly, it lifted its head above the runway, looked round and sniffed the air for a moment – and went straight up into the sky like spring-heeled Jack; levelled off; and vanished against the shifting clouds. Four lines of brown exhaust, rounded off at the top, hung faintly in the air where it had leapt.

Dyson turned round, moved by the performance – and there behind him, about three feet away, picking absently at a morsel of food between his front teeth and twitching his nose from time to time to ease some hidden blockage in his nasal passage, was Reg Mounce. The supraterrestrial perfection of the Final Departure Lounge faded a little.

'Well, well, well!' said Mounce, taking his finger out of his mouth, as surprised as Dyson.

'Hello,' said Dyson unwelcomingly.

'What are you doing here?'

'I'm going out to the Persian Gulf,' said Dyson coldly. 'For the paper.'

'The Magic Carpet beano?'

'Yes.'

'Well, snap! Stinking snap!'

The Final Departure Lounge seemed to Dyson suddenly no more isolated from the imperfections of life than the saloon bar of the Gates of Jerusalem, and the great silver aircraft no rarer or lovelier than red London buses.

'I'm doing it for a load of crap called *Leisure and Pleasure* magazine,' said Mounce. 'They don't pay much, but what the hell? It's a week off from the stinking office, with nothing to do but collect a few pix from the firm, slap some sort of crap together from the handout, and get some serious drinking done.'

'I see,' said Dyson.

'Charge some exes up, of course. Charge a few more up

to the paper. It all adds up.'

'Yes.'

'To tell you the truth,' said Mounce confidentially, 'I can do with a few days in the sun just at the moment. All this business about Other Arrangements – it's been rather getting me down. I thought it might be clever to shove off for a few days and let it all blow over.'

Dyson said nothing. He was swearing a solemn oath to himself that he would be absolutely ruthless about Mounce on this trip. When they went aboard the plane he would firmly find himself a seat next to the wine-and-food man, or the girl with the beads, and ignore Mounce's existence until they were back in London.

'I think it'll all just simmer down, won't it?' said Mounce.

'What?'

'All this Other Arrangements business. It'll blow over. In a month's time we'll be laughing about it. Don't you think so?'

'For God's sake – *I* don't know.'

Mounce fell silent, thoughtfully trying to remove the last traces of breakfast from his teeth with his tongue. Dyson took the opportunity to move away and sit down on the other side of the lounge. He found that Mounce had followed him across the room, and had sat down in the seat beside him.

'We're twenty-five minutes late,' said Mounce.

'Yes.'

'These stinking trips are always late.'

A small man with an archaic toothbrush moustache and a wild tangle of stand-up hair above a domed forehead came hurrying across the lounge. About half his height seemed to be forehead. He had thick spectacles, behind which his eyes darted keenly about like goldfish searching for a way out from their bowls. He had introduced himself to the party earlier, at the air terminal, as Starfield, Magic Carpet's Air Transportation Director.

'Magic Carpet group!' he cried to the room, pressing his palms together as if about to sing a tenor aria. 'This is an announcement concerning the Magic Carpet party travelling to Sharjah. There is a slight delay, boys and girls, caused by the fact that the aircraft which will be taking us has burst a tyre on touchdown from Amsterdam, and there will be a slight delay on account of this cause while this fact is rectified. While we are waiting, I have arranged for drinks to be served at the bar, compliments of Magic Carpet Travel, and I would ask you to rest assured, believe me, that everything humanly possible is being done to facilitate our getting away at the earliest possible moment. Thank you.'

Mounce let his breath slowly out between his teeth.

'Here we go again,' he said. 'Bang on stinking form, as stinking usual.'

Morris's electric typewriter drummed steadily on. Bob sat with his chin in his hands, sucking a liquorice and watching him.

'I'm afraid John's taken against you for some reason,' he said.

Morris typed on, saying nothing.

'I don't know what's got into him,' said Bob. 'He's always been very good to me. You've rubbed him up the wrong way somehow.'

He leaned back in his chair and gazed at the people working in the offices on the other side of Hand and Ball Court. He felt disinclined for work. With Dyson away and the sun shining there was a certain sense of holiday in the air which made leaning forward over the desk somehow physically difficult. He swallowed the remains of his liquorice and took another one.

'It's not getting you down at all, is it, Erskine?' he asked.

'What's that, Bob?' said Morris, without looking up from his typewriter.

'John's attitude. It's not getting you down at all?'

Morris stopped typing, picked up his cigarette from the ashtray, and masticated smoke for some moments while he read through what he had typed.

'No,' he said. He started typing again. After a while

Bob picked up a piece of 'Country Day by Day' copy about stoats and weasels, and tossed it across on to Morris's desk. Morris glanced at it enquiringly as he worked.

'I thought you might like to have a go at subbing while John's away,' said Bob casually. 'Make a break for you.'

Expressionlessly, Morris picked the copy up and tossed it back.

'You do it, Bob,' he said. 'I'll look it over when you've finished it.'

Bob felt a little hurt. He had had a vague idea that he might try to teach Morris the rudiments of subbing and ordering copy while Dyson was away, so that Dyson would no longer have any excuse for refusing to let Morris do anything.

'Look, Erskine,' he said, 'you can take a rest from "Years Gone By" for the next day or two. I'll take full responsibility if John raises any question.'

Morris rested his pale, neutral eyes on Bob for an instant.

'This isn't "Years Gone By", Bob,' he said. 'This is a memo to the Editor about the new pre-teen page.'

Bob stared.

'What new pre-teen page, Erskine?' he said. 'I haven't heard anything about a pre-teen page.'

'You will, Bob, once the Editor's read this.'

Bob went on staring at him.

'There's a lot of advertising in pre-teen A/Bs,' said Morris.

Bob subbed all the copy that had come in by the morning post. Later, when Morris had finished his memo and put it in the out-basket, he came over to Bob's desk and helped himself to some of the subbed copy to study.

'There's nothing to it, really,' said Bob modestly. 'It's just a matter of checking the facts and the spelling, crossing out the first sentence, and removing any attempts at jokes.'

'Sure,' said Morris. He bent down and wrote something on one of the sheets.

'What are you doing?' asked Bob, rather sharply.

' "Exhilarating" with an "a", Bob.'

'Oh ... yes ...'

Morris looked through another page, and made another correction.

'Now what?' demanded Bob.

'The territory of the Canaanites was west of Samaria, not east.'

'Oh, was it?'

Morris began marking something on a number of pages.

'What's this, Erskine?'

'I've had an idea, Bob. I'm marking all next week's "Meditations" to be set in italic.'

'You're what?'

'I'm marking them for italic.'

'We can't do that, I'm afraid, Erskine, because ...'

'I think it'll look quite good, Bob. We'll put a heavy rule round it, set the head in 42-point Old English, and put a single flower from the print-books next to it.'

'I think it would look very pretty, Erskine, but it's not for us to ...'

'It'll look rather Giles Gilbert Scott – rather Guildford Cathedral. The G. G. Scott mood. It's the next one out from platform one, Bob.'

'Look, Erskine, this is Dyson's department. We can't make any decisions as major as this while he's away.'

'Sure, sure,' said Morris, putting the copy in one of the special envelopes with COMPOSING ROOM printed on them. 'Don't worry, Bob. I'll take responsibility if Dyson questions it. I see Morley's copy's not in yet, incidentally. Get on to him, will you, Bob, and find out where it is ... ?'

The Magic Carpet party got airborne eventually.

'Two hours late,' said Mounce bitterly, several times, as their secondhand turbo-prop climbed through ragged cloud into the world of shining snowfields above.

'For God's sake shut up, Reg,' said Dyson, gazing out of the window at the stark absolutes of white and blue.

'Yes, but two hours late! I could have mended the stinking puncture myself in that time.'

They were not flying to Sharjah direct. Dyson realized

he must have misread the invitation slightly. They were going to Paris first to pick up another party of journalists which had assembled there from the rest of Europe. The Continental contingent was waiting in the departure lounge at Le Bourget when the London party arrived, and had of course been waiting there for over two hours, consuming drinks supplied with the compliments of Magic Carpet. There were about thirty of them, some carrying complicated camera kits; some, as Dyson noted with approval, wearing silky blue overcoats; all of them carrying folders of Magic Carpet handout material. There were two models among the group, even worse dressed and more pained than the English pair; they looked as if they were already preparing themselves spiritually for posing in the middle of some Arab village or Bedouin encampment wearing nothing but see-through bathing costumes and gauze yashmaks. The Paris party stared coldly at the London party, associating them with the plane's puncture and its lateness. The London party stared back no less coldly, feeling that they would be halfway to Sharjah by now but for the selfish insistence of the Paris party on being fetched along too.

Mounce, however, began to cheer up slightly. He looked round the departure lounge with some interest, and sniffed the air.

'Ah, the smell of France,' he said. 'Smell it the moment you arrive. Have you ever noticed that, John?'

'Yes,' said Dyson. But the sight and smell of the departure lounge at Le Bourget had the opposite effect on him to Mounce. The pleasure he got from airports, it occurred to him sadly, was subject to the law of diminishing returns.

'Do you think the bar'll take sterling?' said Mounce. 'Let's have a quick one before they shove us back on that snotty little plane.'

'I don't think there's time. We'll be leaving again directly.'

But, it turned out, they were not leaving again directly. No announcement was made about rejoining the aircraft, and Starfield seemed to have disappeared. Gradually the

London party subsided into seats. A certain amount of muttering commenced within the various linguistic groups. Someone overheard, deduced, or invented the information that the Scandinavian party, which was flying down from Copenhagen to join the expedition, had landed at Orly instead of Le Bourget. Slowly the word crossed the various linguistic barriers, until even Dyson and Mounce had heard.

'Trust the Swedes,' said Mounce bitterly. 'Trust the Swedes to get the whole stinking thing screwed up.'

'But are they *still* at Orly?' cried Dyson to the wine-and-food man.

'I expect so,' said the wine-and-food man, sipping a lightly chilled Chambéry vermouth. 'I expect they're waiting for us.'

'*Où sont-ils?*' shouted Dyson boldly at one of the men in silky blue showercoats. The man shrugged his shoulders in a typically French way.

'Who knows?' he said, with a German accent.

'Trust the stinking Swedes,' said Mounce.

Starfield came hurrying anxiously into the lounge.

'Boys and girls!' he cried, pressing his palms together. 'I regret to have to inform you of the fact that we have a slight snag on our hands, owing to the fact that our Scandinavian friends are unfortunately not yet with us, the fact being that they were booked in error on to a flight arriving at Orly. As soon as they arrive we shall be departing as planned, though of course a little later than scheduled. In the meantime, there are drinks and a sandwich lunch available at the bar, compliments of Magic Carpet Travel. Thank you.'

But not much more than three-quarters of an hour later, just as everyone was moving on from the free apéritifs to the free champagne with the free sandwiches, Starfield came hurrying back.

'Sorry, folks!' he said, pressing his palms together once again. 'Sorry, boys and girls! There's been a bit of a misunderstanding over the plane. It seems that our Scandinavian friends are still at Orly, waiting for *us*, as a result of which I feel it would facilitate things best if we went on without them, leaving them to proceed independently by separate means of transportation and join us at the other end. Will you therefore proceed at once to the departure gate for immediate embarkation? Thank you.'

Grumbling, the party picked up its folders of publicity material and shuffled towards the gate, hastily draining glasses and gnawing at ham sandwiches as it went. The language barriers began to break down slightly under the common bond of mutual discontent. 'It is bad,' said a Dutch photographer to Dyson, shaking his head and pursing his lips. '*Ja*,' agreed Dyson emphatically. '*Ja, ja, ja.*'

As the plane rushed past the airport buildings on its take-off run, Dyson thought he could see a number of people jumping about and waving their arms in front of the departure gate. They looked to Dyson remarkably like Scandinavian journalists. Still, they had perhaps not missed very much, because as soon as the plane was airborne Starfield came hurrying up to the front of the cabin, pressing his palms together for yet another aria.

'Our next port of call, boys and girls,' he announced, 'is Amsterdam.'

A noise of multilingual outrage and complaint arose from the body of the plane.

'Amsterdam!' cried Dyson, unable to believe his ears. 'But that's in the opposite direction to the Middle East!'

'What do you expect, John,' said Mounce comfortably, from the middle of a benevolent haze of alcohol, 'with a load of crap like this?'

Starfield seemed astonished at the feelings his announcement had aroused. His eyebrows climbed out from behind the shelter of his glasses and attempted the ascent of his great forehead. Dislodged by the upward progress of the eyebrows, his glasses came landsliding down his nose. He pushed them back.

'Boys and girls!' he protested. 'If we want to get to Sharjah we have to go to Amsterdam first, owing to the simple fact that the plane which is taking us to Sharjah is waiting for us at Amsterdam!'

The noise of complaint continued.

'There'll be drinks at Amsterdam,' appealed Starfield. 'I'm radioing Schiphol Airport now to lay on full bar facilities, compliments of Magic Carpet Travel. Thank you.'

He disappeared hurriedly in the direction of the flight-deck.

'Oh, *God*!' said Dyson.

'Try and be philosophical about it, John,' said Mounce. 'Think of the drinks. The booze is always the only good part of these spotty jaunts. The rest's always just a lot of crap, one way or another.'

He was still looking on the bright side when they all filed into the transit lounge at Schiphol.

'I've always wanted to go to Amsterdam,' he said, looking round with interest. 'Do you know, John, the girls sit in shop-windows here, just waiting for you to go along and take your pick. How about that? They sit in stinking shop-windows, John – doing their stinking knitting!'

Schiphol, coming after Heathrow and Le Bourget, did not make Dyson feel like International Airport Man, free-floating in a medium entirely isolated from the world's troubles. It made him feel like a traveller on the District Line, forced by the tiresome vicissitudes of the Underground to change at Earl's Court as well as South Kensington.

The terrible claustrophobia of travel began to descend on him. He was trapped in the channels of communication, suffocating in the nothingness of neither-here-nor-there.

Bob had been going to take Tessa out that evening for a meal in some small Indian restaurant, so that they could tell each other their latest house-hunting experiences over the biriani and enjoy a quiet laugh together about the situation they'd got themselves into. At least they could still enjoy a joke together sometimes, thought Bob, or at any rate they could provided he avoided any literary allusions, and explained all references to the newspaper industry, well-known personalities, and politics. But Morris insisted that they both came out to dinner with him instead. Tessa wouldn't be pleased, Bob knew. She didn't like Morris — she didn't like any of Bob's friends very much, except Mrs Mounce and just possibly John Dyson. But there was nothing much she could do about it when Morris arrived with Bob at their rendezvous. 'Hello, Tessa,' said Morris, with no more and no less familiarity than he had at their first meeting. He didn't rest his hand in hers this time, however; but he put it round behind her back and laid it inertly on her farther hip for a moment or two, like a pound of Plasticine, in some notional representation of an embrace. After which he ignored her for the rest of the evening.

He took them first for a drink at the Ritz. He didn't much like the Ritz, he explained, as Bob and Tessa gazed covertly about at the furnishings, but they were meeting Lake, who was coming on from making a personal appearance at a convention of canning machinery manufacturers in the Westbury, just up the road. And when Lake arrived, her long silver hair breaking and spraying over her glossy black dress as she walked, like some unbelievable moonlit sea on wet rock, Morris laid his brief tribute of Plasticine on her hip, and took them all on to what appeared to be a private restaurant, in what looked like a private Georgian house just behind Park Lane.

Bob could not remember ever being inside a more visibly expensive eating-place. It had deep pile carpet and stripped pine panelling everywhere, as he imagined high-class gambling clubs had. And it had a great deal of space left between the tables. At current Mayfair land prices they would be paying about three-halfpence a mouthful for the surplus floor area alone. Looking at the distant tables round about, Bob thought he recognized some of the other diners who were shouldering a share of the rating assessment. He had seen them in films and plays, reading the eccentric will in Act One, or covering up for the hero as chairman of the Stalag Luft escape committee in reel six.

'Isn't this place rather expensive?' he whispered.

Morris looked round without interest.

'About the same as other places,' he said. 'It's handy to have it. I hate trying to think where to eat.'

The sight of the prices on the menu confirmed Bob's expectations, and brought on in him the symptoms of mild nervous indigestion. They ordered and ate their way through what might as well have been, from its cost and for all Bob could enjoy of it, portions of grilled, stewed, and marinated banknotes, and drank two bottles of a wine apparently fermented from the juice of sun-kissed golden sovereigns. When the dessert-trolley was brought round, and Lake asked for a helping of out-of-season wild strawberries, Morris commandeered the whole bowlful to share between them. Bob refused his portion queasily, too occupied with praying that he was right in assuming that Morris would insist on paying the bill. He slipped his hand into his back pocket and tried to feel how much money he had on him. It felt like four pounds, unless one of the notes had got folded over and counted twice.

Lake was the only one who talked much during the meal. 'Do you have trouble with your feet?' she asked Tessa. 'I've got rotten feet. They get so tender I can hardly walk on them. Sometimes I get a terrible sort of itch underneath the front part, just behind the toes. Know where I mean? Do you get that at all?'

'No,' said Tessa.

'Sometimes I get a sort of terrible tickle between the toes. I just want to kick my shoes off – doesn't matter where I am – and scratch, scratch, scratch. I've got really rotten feet.'

Morris seemed uninterested in conversation. But he was clearly well-known in the restaurant, and several people greeted him on their way in or out. A girl wearing what looked like backless striped pyjamas came over and held out her cheek to be kissed. Morris obliged without getting up. 'Hi,' he said, unenthusiastically. A couple of men came over to the table to talk business with Morris. One seemed to be arranging for him to organize an exhibition of somebody's paintings, the other for him to come in on a complex deal which involved selling share capital in a group of fashion photographers.

'You seem to have fingers in a number of pies,' said Bob admiringly, as Morris paid the bill.

'You've got ten fingers,' said Morris. 'Why not stick them in ten pies?'

Bob supposed that the evening's entertainment was over. But without a word Morris hailed a taxi and took them off to a pub in the Isle of Dogs to hear a new kid singing in whom he thought he might just possibly be interested. The taxi ride took over half an hour and cost twenty-five shillings; the extravagance of travelling to the East End by taxi made Bob almost as nervous as he had been in the restaurant. By the time they got to the pub the kid had sung her songs and departed. Bob tried to persuade Morris to stay and watch the female impersonator. 'Aren't they rather fashionable now?' he suggested, partly in order to justify the expense of time and money in getting there, and partly in the hope of making a business suggestion which Morris would find useful. But Morris shook his head without interest. 'They're finished,' he said. They took another taxi back to some sort of older children's night-club in the King's Road, at a similar outlay of time and money all over again. 'I thought night-clubs were finished?' said Bob, trying to get ahead of the game. Morris shook his head. 'Not yet,' he said.

It was far too noisy to talk in the night-club, which Bob found rather agreeable, since they had nothing to say to each other. He and Morris drank a lot of whisky, which made Morris more and more impassive, if that were possible, and himself more and more conscious of the girls' knees that came dancing by, and of Lake, with her moon-white bleached hair and her night-black artificial eyelashes. He invited her to dance, taking hold of her with the utmost precaution, like some rare and fragile artefact. But even this delicate touch seemed to surprise her. She backed away from him as if he had made an indecent assault upon her.

'What's all this?' she demanded suspiciously.

'What's what, Lake?'

'What you're up to.'

'It's the foxtrot, isn't it?' replied Bob uncertainly.

'The what?'

They moved about vaguely at arm's length, looking at each other with incomprehension.

'The foxtrot.'

'You're joking!'

He couldn't understand what point she was trying to make.

'Isn't it a foxtrot?' he said. 'Slow, slow, quick, quick, slow . . . No . . . Slow, slow, quick, slow . . . No, no . . .'

She stared at him.

'How old are you, anyway?' she demanded.

'Twenty-nine.'

'Oh. They used to do the foxtrot when you were young, did they?'

Poor Tessa's head kept sinking with boredom. Yet later they found themselves in Morris's flat, gazing impassively into space and sipping more whisky. It was a furnished flat in a pre-war block just off the King's Road. The furnishings suggested period, without tying themselves down to any one period rather than any other, and bore no imprint of Morris's inscrutable personality whatsoever. Lake kicked off her shoes, rolled down her stockings, and rubbed her feet. 'I had terrible corns, even as a child,' she said companionably to Tessa. 'Did you? I had a rotten childhood altogether. Spots and boils, the lot. I had ringworm once. Did you ever have ringworm . . . ?'

'What I can't for the life of me understand,' said Bob to Morris suddenly, 'is what made you become a graduate trainee on a newspaper at fifteen pounds a week, when you've obviously got so many other more profitable lines of business.'

Morris took in a mouthful of smoke and worked it over in his mouth for some time.

'I'm interested in newspapers, Bob. I think they still have a big future in front of them. I want to learn the business.'

'You really see yourself working on a paper for the rest

of your life, Erskine?'

'I see myself owning one, Bob.'

Bob, lying back in his armchair gazing up into the air, turned his head to stare at Morris.

'Sure,' said Morris. 'Why not? Someone's got to own them. Go into it through magazines. Buy up derelict properties like *Leisure and Pleasure* and tailor them for the right markets. Lot of markets still untapped, Bob. Take the fifties age-group. Maximum earning-power, children off their hands; ten years to go before retirement. Lot of money there, Bob. Sell them sports cars, jock-straps, buckskin boots – young men's kit. They've got the money to be young at that age.'

Hazed by the whisky, Bob felt himself becoming rather emotional.

'You could do it, too,' he said.

'Sure.'

'You could do it, Erskine.'

'Sure, sure.'

'All you'd need is the money.'

'The money's never any difficulty, Bob. All I need is a look at the industry from inside, and a nucleus of really smart young toreros. Interested?'

'Me, Erskine?'

'Sure, Bob.'

'I'm not a smart young torero, Erskine.'

'I could use you somewhere. One of the anchor-men. You're good with copy. You're slow and solid.'

'Yes, but . . .'

'You don't work too hard, Bob. That's what I like about you. Get some high-pressure team of kids working to build something up and they all work too hard. They work themselves dry – they start to make mistakes. I've seen it happen, Bob.'

'I don't know what to say, Erskine. I mean, in many ways I admire you more than anyone I've ever . . .'

'Sure. I just mention it to keep in mind. Nothing will be moving for a year or so yet.'

When Bob woke Tessa up to take her home he remembered that he had spent almost his last shilling in insisting on paying the bill at the night-club. He asked Morris if he could borrow some money for the cab fare. Morris, still leaning impassively back in his armchair, tossed him a fiver.

'An advance against salary, Bob,' he said.

There was one particular travel poster on the wall of the lounge at Schiphol Airport which became imprinted on Dyson's memory as the evening wore on. It was of a girl in a swimming-costume, frozen in the very moment of stepping off the side of a swimming-pool. It irritated Dyson. She had already stepped right out into unsupported space, and was looking down at the water beneath her with a slightly anxious smile of anticipation on her face. And there, in mid-air, she remained suspended. She was there at six, when it was still generally believed that the Scandinavian party they were all waiting for was somewhere *en route* between Paris and Amsterdam. She was there at seven, when the French journalists, who were beginning to emerge as the leaders of opinion in the expedition, put the story about that the Scandinavians had by an error been flown not to Amsterdam but back to Copenhagen. At eight o'clock, when the French announced that the Scandinavians' plane had crashed, the poor girl had still not got so much as a toe into the water. The anticipation in her anxious smile was as keen as ever at nine, when the French declared that the Scandinavians had landed at Brussels and were coming on by train. It had still not faded at ten, when all the various nationalities present abandoned interest in their Scandinavian colleagues, and instead rose and mobbed Starfield as he hurried anxiously between telephone and cable office, and threatened to petition their respective governments for the revocation of all Magic Carpet's licences and landing rights if he did not immediately arrange everyone hotels in Amsterdam for the night.

They took off soon after ten o'clock the following morning, without the Scandinavians, in another turbo-prop, larger and even more visibly secondhand than the first one. A small panel fell out of the internal trim in front of Mounce and Dyson just after take-off, and swung back and forth on the end of a piece of wire. Mounce, who had subsided into an early-morning liverish bitterness again, watched it sourly.

'This stinking plane's never going to get to the Middle East,' he snarled. 'It looks about a hundred years old.'

'Oh, for God's sake!' snarled Dyson, who was also a little hung-over. 'It's a jet!'

'It's got stinking straight wings, John!'

'All right – it's got straight wings! What's wrong with straight wings, for God's sake?'

'Because they mean it's just a cartload of old scrap-iron! It's obsolete!'

'Obsolete? How can it be obsolete when it's jet-propelled?'

'For God's sake, John – stinking jets have been around for a hundred stinking years. They were new when you were a kid – but that's a long stinking time ago now.'

Dyson was right though; the old plane did not break down. The loose panel swung and danced on the end of its wire, but the plane whined on across Europe unaffected.

'Anyway,' said Dyson. 'I don't know what you've got to worry about. I should be doing the worrying – I've got to be back in London on Friday for a television programme, on which I may say my whole future career depends.'

Mid-morning drinks were brought round; then pre-lunch drinks; then a sandwich lunch with lunch drinks, followed by after-lunch drinks. Everyone began to cheer up – even Starfield, who came working his way down the cabin, cheerfully saying a word here and a word there. 'All right, folks? Everyone happy, boys and girls?'

'We do still reckon on getting back to London by Thursday night, do we?' Dyson asked him.

'There's a lad here worried about getting back already!' cried Starfield jovially to everyone around. He turned back to Dyson and patted his shoulder reassuringly. 'Don't worry, boy,' he said. 'We'll get you back on time, never you fear.'

After the fifth lot of drinks Mounce began to take some sort of interest in the scenery. 'Rome,' he said, gazing vaguely earthwards out of the window. 'I'd like to take a look at Rome. Did you see *Dolce Vita*, John? Lot of crap, really. One or two quite juicy bits, though . . .'

Dyson tried to look out of the window over Mounce's shoulder, to see if they were in fact passing over Rome. But Mounce seemed to be reviewing the European scene at large. 'I wouldn't mind taking a gander at Hamburg, for that matter,' he said dreamily. 'See some of those old judies wrestling in mud . . . Or Beirut. Old Jimmy Knowles on the *Express* was telling me about Beirut. He said it was fantastic. "You lika leetle girl, sahib? I breenga you leetle seester for one half-dollar." All that kind of crap.'

There was a gap between after-lunch drinks and mid-afternoon drinks, however, during which Mounce began to subside a little into melancholy.

'I didn't know this stinking flight was going to take as long as this,' he complained. 'What time are we supposed to be getting there?'

'I don't know,' said Dyson.

'It's nearly half past two already! I thought we were supposed to be travelling in a proper plane, not some snotty old wreck out of the Science Museum with straight wings. Is that the Persian Gulf down there now?'

Dyson craned over and looked out of the window. They were flying over a deep blue sea studded with islands.

'I don't think there are that many islands in the Persian Gulf,' said Dyson doubtfully. 'I think that must be the Aegean.'

'The Aegean?' said Mounce indignantly. 'The one next to Greece? Don't talk crap, John! We've been flying for hours. This is a plane, not a horse-and-cart.'

More drinks were served, and more again. Just after four o'clock they began to descend. Starfield appeared at the front of the cabin, and pressed his palms together.

'In just ten minutes' time, boys and girls,' he began, 'we shall be landing to refuel at Beirut.'

He paused, as if expecting the same sort of reaction as

the announcement about Amsterdam had caused. None came; everyone took the news in silence. Dyson wondered if everyone but himself and Mounce had known already that they were only just over halfway, or whether, like himself, they were too stunned to speak, or whether, like Mounce, they were too boozed to take it in. Starfield himself seemed to be slightly taken aback by the lack of response. The glasses slipped down his nose disbelievingly.

'Anyway,' he said, pushing them back nervously, 'drinks will be served in the transit lounge, compliments of Magic Carpet. Thank you.'

Jannie hated it when John was away. He was away so rarely that she always forgot what it was like, and looked forward to it, thinking that she would be somehow free and able to get things done. She had a vague picture of herself, absolved from the necessity to cook proper dinners and to sit late over them talking about what Gareth Holmroyd had said to Harry Stearns and what latest outrage Reg Mounce or Erskine Morris had committed, reading good books instead, making clothes for the children, putting up the hems of her dresses, rearranging the living-room furniture, and thinking how she could earn some money to clear off their overdraft. But in fact she did none of these things. There was much less extra time created than she had imagined. And what there was she wasted. She couldn't settle to anything when she was alone in the house for the evening. She picked up a book; it bored her. She looked at the pile of mending, and thought, why do it now, when I've got an evening to myself for once? She tried to think about money-making jobs and activities, and her mind wandered immediately on to what she would do with the money once she had made it. In the end she turned on the television, to watch it for half an hour and settle her mind, and sat in front of it all evening with a growing sense of waste and guilt which seemed to make it not easier but more difficult from one moment to the next to get up and switch it off, until at last the BBC took the decision for her by closing down for the night.

She didn't even manage to get to bed early. After the television had stopped she sat about glancing at the daily papers, half-reading items which had already been made out-of-date by the news programme she had seen on television that evening. She trailed dismally to bed at a quarter to one, leaden tired, and hating herself for her feebleness. She had been going to wash her hair; she hadn't even done that! In bed she couldn't get to sleep. She kept turning towards the side on which John usually lay to put her arm round him for comfort. It was not only the bed that was empty. The whole room — the whole house — seemed filled with an unnatural quietness. In the morning she got up tired, shouted at the boys, and subsided before the television in the evening feeling even worse.

She felt somehow ashamed that having the boys about the house wasn't enough, and rather frightened to realize how dependent she had become on John's company. Living alone had seemed natural enough when she was single. But it wasn't natural — it was an acquired skill, and she had lost it. She thought with amazement about women whose husbands went away for weeks at a time on business trips — or for years at a time, on war service or to prison. How could the prospect of such separation be borne? The idea occurred to her while she was washing up, and came to her with such force that she stopped and gazed helplessly out of the window for some minutes, the mop and a plate trailing motionless in her hands. One forgot for years at a time, living in a round of only small anxieties and only small resentments, what ranges of human suffering there were — suffering beyond one's experience, beyond even one's imagination. She was appalled at the world of desolation she had stumbled on, and ashamed that she had thought about it only because she herself had been left on her own for four days. Four days! It was grotesque that on the basis of four days' separation she should presume to feel for the separated in general. And yet . . . Was this how her mother had felt when Father died? This frightening bleakness, as of unfamiliar country when the light began to go on a winter's afternoon? This grey filter coming down over one's senses, draining the colour and the savour out of things? This sudden awareness of oneself? When one was happy, one scarcely knew one was there. One was just a mathematical point at which rays of light from the rest of the universe converged. And then the balance of things was disturbed, and suddenly one became aware of the complex spiritual machinery which kept one going. It was like noticing one's heartbeats. The fragility of the whole mechanism became painfully apparent.

A grey, gritty smell crept into her nostrils, of smoke blowing down from chimneys along bleak terraced streets in some desolate city where she was a stranger.

She began to wash up again, tears brimming in her eyes – for herself, for others. She promised herself that she wouldn't forget how she had felt. She would do something about the world's miseries – about her mother, about everyone abandoned and separated. But even as she made the promise she knew that the moment John came home she would forget about her feelings entirely; would never mention them even to him. She would do nothing about her mother or anyone else – nothing, at any rate, without ungenerous reservations, nothing from a heart as open as for these few short moments it had been.

She remained in a curious mood all day, on a knife-edge between tears, and exaltation at her readiness for tears. When she fetched Damian from nursery-school she took him to the recreation-ground and played with him in a strange, wild way. She threw him up in the air and swung him round and kept laughing. Every time he stopped playing and became thoughtful, as if about to recount an incident from the life of Jack, she clapped her hands and chased him off on another game. The sudden intensity of all this fun unnerved him slightly. He became over-excited, then querulous, and finally so tearful that she had to take him home.

It occurred to her during the afternoon that the odd strand of excitement which was woven into her mood might have something to do with Bob. She at once felt guilty for even thinking such a ridiculous thought, which somehow seemed to discredit her feelings about John's absence, and about separation in general. She also felt more excited still. She immediately began to imagine getting a babysitter, and going out for dinner with Bob in some small restaurant in Soho. They would have wine – a whole bottle between them – and talk about this and that. Not about anything very deep or significant. They'd just gossip – but easily and intimately. They'd tell each other how they *felt* about things. She had feelings about everything today. She longed to tell them. She thought of Bob leaning on the table listening, looking at her with his mild, familiar eyes.

She had her hand on the phone to ring him at the office and suggest dinner when she remembered Tessa. How *awful* that she hadn't thought of her before! She bit her lip, shocked at herself. But after she had got used to the idea she began to think that it would be almost as good even with Tessa there. She would invite them both to dinner at the house. She saw herself being astonishingly kind to Tessa – astonishing Tessa, astonishing Bob, and even astonishing herself. They would all talk together with great ease and openness. Tessa, who was always so shy and unforthcoming with her, would start to feel secure in her friendship. All three of them could be friends, close friends. She wanted to be very close to Bob and Tessa. She wanted John to be close to them, too, of course.

She rang Bob, but even while she was waiting to get through her excitement ebbed, and she realized how awkward it might turn out to be, if Tessa didn't warm to her any more than she had on previous occasions. And when Bob answered he sounded preoccupied; he said Erskine was waiting for him to finish some job in hand. She talked about a house which she thought Tessa ought to see, then couldn't think of anything else to say, and in the end didn't invite him at all.

She watched the television again all evening, in fact, doing *The Times* crossword simultaneously to persuade herself that she was not being entirely supine. Once she thought she heard rubbish being thrown over the wall. Probably; the garden was full of rubbish now. She would make an effort and clear it all up. She'd do it tomorrow. No, she'd do it when John came home. She'd be able to start getting things done again when John came home.

At Beirut the Magic Carpet party's advance bogged down and stuck. The Scandinavians had got there ahead of them, and left again already. But the main party was unable to follow. According to Starfield there was a minor technical fault in the plane which would be rectified within the hour. But the hour passed and another hour followed it, and they were still in the transit lounge drinking down the compliments of Magic Carpet. They would be taking off very soon indeed, Starfield assured them. The warm Mediterranean dusk thickened outside the windows. The landing lights glowed brighter and brighter as the sky faded – red on the approaches, blue on the runways, green on the taxi-ways, like some dream vision of the jewelled Orient. It was the French who forced Starfield to get them all into hotels for the night; the rest were too reduced by alcohol and travel weariness to argue. It took a great deal of argument. Starfield threatened them that the plane would take off as soon as it was ready, and that anyone not aboard it would have to get himself repatriated at his own expense. He pleaded with them, begging them to consider that they had consumed some £5,000 worth of Magic Carpet's hospitality already. He swore he would report them all to their respective Press Councils for infamous professional conduct. He beseeched them to consider his own position. But the French were adamant, and in the end Starfield found hotels for everyone. Which was just as well, because when they got back to the airport next morning they found they were no nearer taking off than they had been the night before.

It turned out that the fault the aircraft had developed was not a technical one; it was financial. At some time in the past the aircraft's operators had failed to pay a bill for landing dues at Beirut, and now the Lebanese authorities had distrained upon the aircraft, and impounded it until the bill was settled. At first Starfield denied this. But as the day grew hotter, and the drinks at the bar, compliments of Magic Carpet, flowed more and more like water, he shifted his ground slightly, and denied only that the debt was in any way the responsibility of Magic Carpet. It had been incurred, he said, by Nederlandse Zonnenvaart Luchtbedrijs, of Amsterdam, the company from which the plane was chartered, and he implored them to be patient, because they would be taking off just as soon as N.Z.L. had paid the necessary sum into the Lebanese Government's account. He spent the morning hurrying from telephone to cable office to police headquarters, and just before lunchtime was able to report that N.Z.L. disclaimed all knowledge of the debt. Apparently they didn't even own the aircraft. They were operating it on long-term charter from another company, Overland en Overzee N.V. of Rotterdam. It had become uncomfortably hot in the lounge; Starfield mopped his brow, and pressed his palms together, and then had to mop the palms, explaining all this to the journalists. But he had already cabled O & O, he assured them hoarsely, and he expected the matter to be settled within minutes.

It was only halfway through his seventh lager that Dyson realized he was sitting exactly opposite a poster with the girl from Schiphol on it. She was still just stepping out from the side of the swimming-pool into empty air; she still had the same anxious smile on her face; and she had still not got her toes wet. He got up and moved to another seat, so that he had his back to her. It brought him face to face with Mounce instead.

'I mean,' said Mounce, chinking the ice about in a large glass of whisky, 'it'll all have simmered down by the time this lot's finished, won't it?'

There were drops of sweat running down Mounce's temples. He looked tired; the strain of fetching drinks and keeping an eye on his publicity folder seemed to be telling on him. Whenever he asked Dyson yet again if he thought things would have simmered down or blown over by the time he got back, Dyson realized how much he preferred it when Mounce explained to him about intending to have it away with one of the model girls as soon as they got to Sharjah; though as soon as he started to explain about having it away with the model, Dyson immediately realized that it had been the topic of simmering down and blowing over which he had really preferred all the time.

'I mean,' said Mounce, 'what do you think personally?' Dyson rested his head against the back of the chair, gazing up at the ceiling.

'Even if we take off for Sharjah immediately,' he said, 'I don't see how I'm going to be back in London in time for my television programme on Friday night. I just don't see it.'

He fanned himself meditatively with his publicity folder.

'I mean,' said Mounce, 'have you taken a look at the one they call Daisy-Claude? Haughty and naughty—that's how I like them. You wait till we get to Sharjah. First night in a proper hotel and I'll be away.'

Dyson watched the shadow of Mounce's chair creep millimetre by millimetre nearer the toe-cap of his right shoe.

'If I miss that television programme,' he said, 'I swear to God I will take Starfield and his crapulous company to court and sue them for every penny they've got.'

Mounce swirled the bits of ice round at the bottom of his empty glass, until they shot out over the side and fell on the floor.

'I wish you'd stop crapping on about your spotty television programme,' he said. 'You're getting a real bore about it.'

Starfield did not reappear until teatime. Apparently Overland en Overzee knew nothing about any bill for landing dues at Beirut. At the time of the alleged tort they had been chartering the plane to Lineas Aereas Pan-Balearicas of Palma, a company whose affairs now seemed to be in the hands of the receiver. The French were very firm with Starfield when he had explained all this. Magic Carpet, they insisted, would simply have to settle the debt itself, and sort everything out later. The Belgians agreed. So did the Germans and the Dutch, and indeed everyone who was not too drunk to express an opinion, except Starfield. Magic Carpet couldn't settle the debt, he explained, until it had received the subsidy it was getting towards the cost of the press trip from the Joint Tourism Committee of the Trucial Sheikhdoms. And when would that be? demanded the French, with the full support of the Dutch, the British, and everyone else. When it had delivered its cargo of journalists into the Committee's hands in Sharjah.

Slowly the sun settled towards the west, and the airfield was covered once again in red, blue, and green jewels. Starfield hurried desperately in and out telephoning his directors in London and trying to placate the French. 'Listen, boys . . . !' Dyson could hear him pleading haggardly. 'Gentlemen, I beseech you . . . ! We shall be taking off any moment . . . ! Friends, I beg of you to facilitate proceedings by remaining calm . . . ! I implore you . . . ! I give you my solemn oath . . . ! For God's sake talk English – I can't understand a word you're saying . . . ! Oh, go and jump in the sea, you stupid ignorant Frogs, I'm sick of the sight of you . . . !'

Another night in a Beirut hotel, with windows open once again on the soft Levantine air, and the noise of Beirut's traffic. Dyson liked the noise of the traffic. It soothed him as he lay on top of his bed, unable to sleep, because it was tangible evidence of the real and romantic world which existed outside the confines of international airports. He hoped he would never see another airport in his life again after this trip. Every time he closed his eyes the blank waiting faces of the passengers came back to him, and the roaring and whining of jets and turbojets, and the characterless international voice of the loudspeaker system announcing the departure of Flight ME 731 to Baghdad and Tehran, the further delay in the arrival of Flight ME 491 from Istanbul and Ankara . . . Oh God, how he hated airports!

And in the morning – back to the airport. But there was a surprise awaiting them. Starfield – unshaven, exhausted, and triumphant after sitting up all night telephoning and negotiating—had found them a fresh and unencumbered plane. It was older and even more visibly secondhand than the one they had arrived on; it had piston engines, which caused Mounce to start predicting a stinking sticky end for it even before they were aboard. Prudently, Starfield waited until they were airborne before he pressed his palms together and announced where they were going. The stewardesses would be coming round immediately with drinks, he said, compliments of Magic Carpet, and they were on their way back home to Amsterdam. Having said which he at once helped himself to a bottle of whisky from the galley and locked himself in one of the lavatories with it, while the French beat on the door in vain. For Starfield the war was at last over.

Mounce made a few indignant noises about Starfield's stinking cheek. But they sounded mechanical; Dyson had the impression that even Mounce was privately relieved. Everyone was relieved, except the French, who had a great sense of responsibility. The trip had been one long series of disasters. God clearly did not want them in Trucial Oman, and there was nothing for it but to retire to Amsterdam in good order, drinking to keep their spirits up as they went.

Dyson felt a deep content. He would be back in Amsterdam by evening, and on his way to London first thing Friday morning, in plenty of time for his programme. He felt the sort of happiness he had always expected to feel when he had been a homesick Boy Scout at interminable summer camps in waterlogged meadows, if only he could have found an excuse for getting himself sent home early.

The feeling persisted until teatime, when in front of his incredulous eyes the starboard outer propeller came spinning to a halt, and they landed in some haste, with fire-engines and ambulances standing by, at Ljubljana.

Twelve

Everyone thought that Bob ought to do the programme if Dyson wasn't back in time. They kept ringing him at the office all through Friday morning to urge him.

'It's not just my idea, Bob,' said Jannie. 'John wants you to do it, too, if he's not back. He made a great point of it when he rang from Ljubljana this morning.'

'How did he sound?' asked Bob. 'Was he in a great state?'

'No, he was surprisingly calm.'

'Poor old John.'

'He'll almost certainly be back in time, Bob. You'd just be standing by in case. It's really simply that this Samantha Lightbody woman at the BBC has got in a great tizzy about it. She keeps ringing up to ask if I've got any more news.'

'She keeps ringing me up, too.'

'What did you tell her?'

'I said I didn't know anything about race relations.'

'Oh, Bob! Don't be so feeble. You know as much about them as John does.'

'I can't think why you're so keen for me to do it, Jannie.'

'I'd just like to see you on television, Bob. I just think you'd be terribly good.'

Bob sighed.

'Yes, well,' he said, 'I've got some work here that Erskine's waiting for.'

Ten minutes later Samantha Lightbody rang again to say that she gathered Bob *did* know something about race relations – she understood he'd shared rooms in college with a Siamese. Bob gazed longingly at some layouts for the new pre-teen page which Erskine had asked him to look through. There was nothing he wanted more in life, he realized now, than the chance to get on with a little quiet work.

'Who told you about the Siamese?' he asked.

'Mrs Dyson,' said Samantha Lightbody. 'She's just very kindly phoned about it. Honestly, we're absolutely scraping the barrel. Every expert on race relations in London seems to be sick, or away at some conference.'

'I'm very sorry . . .'

'We'd only use you in the very last possible resort.'

'All the same . . .'

'Can we leave it that you'll think about it?'

'Well . . . all right, I'll think about it.'

As soon as Samantha Lightbody rang off, Tessa was on the line.

'Your friend Mrs Dyson's been ringing me,' she said. 'She told me to try and persuade you to appear on this television programme.'

Bob slipped a peppermint into his mouth, and rubbed a galley between finger and thumb. He liked the coarse, soft texture of newsprint.

'Go on, then,' he said.

'How do you mean, go on?'

'Go on and persuade me.'

'Well, do you want to do it, Bob?'

'I don't know. Do you think I ought to do it?'

'Bob, I don't want you to do anything you don't want to do. You know that.'

'Yes.'

'I only want you to do what you want to do. *I* only think you ought to do it if *you* think you ought to do it.'

Bob felt suddenly exasperated.

'Tess, you never have any opinions of your own! There's never anything you actually want yourself!'

'Bob, that's not true! I want you to be happy and do what you want. I don't want to stand in your way. Bob, you're the *man*! You've got to run your life and decide things for yourself.'

It embarrassed Bob to argue on the phone in Morris's presence. Morris gave no sign of hearing. He typed on behind the wavering blue tape of cigarette smoke, then wrote odd sentences in longhand, clipped bundles of paper together and tossed them on to Bob's desk.

'Erskine, do you think I ought to do this damned programme?' Bob asked him.

'Sure,' said Morris soothingly, without breaking off his work.

'I knew you'd say that,' said Bob gloomily. 'You really think I should?'

'Sure.'

Mrs Mounce rang.

'Darling, I just had to ring. Tess has told me. Sweetest, you're not going to turn a chance like this down, are you?'

'I'm thinking about it.'

'I mean, it's nothing to do with me, sweets. But, Bob, do be *serious* about it, darling. Opportunity doesn't knock twice, you know, and you are going to have a family to support. I know what it's like, I can tell you, trying to live on the money that paper pays.'

'I'm thinking . . .'

'You've got to start making a career for yourself, darling. You've got to get *on* – you've got to try and make a teeny weeny bit of progress. Think of Tess, Bob . . .'

'Well, I am thinking of her . . .'

'Now, sweetest, will you promise me you'll ring the television people at once and say yes?'

'I honestly am thinking about it . . .'

'Well, will you promise me you'll think about it very very very very seriously . . . ?'

At one point in the morning he had Samantha Lightbody back on one line, asking if he had made up his mind yet, and Tessa on the other, worrying if she had said the right thing earlier.

'Perhaps I ought to push you more, Bob,' she said miserably. 'I suppose you're someone who needs rather a lot of pushing. Mrs Mounce thinks I should push you. I'll certainly push you if you think that's what you need to get the best out of yourself, Bob. But I don't want to push you into being pushed. Do you see what I mean, Bob?'

Jannie rang back, too.

'Bob, you'd be terribly *good* on television,' she said. 'I only want you to go on because I'm sure you'd do it well. You remember how I hated it when John went on – I knew he'd overdo it and just be embarrassing. But you'd be a natural, Bob!'

Bob gazed out of the window at the great whiteness of the sky.

'I honestly don't feel I'd be much good, Jannie,' he said.

'Bob, you make me so *mad* sometimes, the way you underestimate yourself! It's not proper modesty – it's something really horrible and pathological.'

Bob felt hounded.

'I *am* thinking about it,' he said. 'I've agreed to do that. I wish everybody would let me get on and think about it in peace.'

'But, Bob, it might be your chance!'

'My chance? What chance?'

'Well, for heaven's sake, Bob – your chance to break out of that office, for a start. You don't intend to stick there for the rest of your life, do you, just being John's dogsbody?'

'I don't know. I suppose I'll move on eventually . . .'

'*Eventually*? It'll be too late, *eventually*! You'll be there when you're forty, Bob, you really will. You and John – you're both getting stuck in the rut. But at least John makes an effort to get out. You won't do anything! You just plod along taking everything for granted, waiting for people to come and bring you your life on a plate.'

Bob doodled on the edge of a galley – a little bald egg-headed man putting his tongue out.

'You're in a funny mood today, Jannie.'

'I'm always in a funny mood when John's away.'

'It's not like you, going on about things like this.'

'Well, I *am* going on about this particular thing, Bob.'

'You're mothering me, Jannie.'

'Somebody's got to mother you, you poor orphan boy.'

She sounded both cross and tender – perhaps cross at her own tenderness, thought Bob, rather like a mother might be.

'I'm sure your mother would say just the same if she were alive. She'd push you on and make you do something with your life.'

Bob sighed, watching the endless blue smoke rising from Morris's cigarette.

'Perhaps you're right,' he said. 'Anyway, I'll think about it.'

Jannie *was* in a funny mood, she knew it herself – an even funnier mood than the one she had been in earlier in the week. Her tense anxiety for John to return and her excited longing to help Bob and Tessa had both turned to irritation now that they were frustrated. She was irritated with John for so typically getting himself aboard a plane which had a defective oil-feed system in the starboard outer engine. She was irritated with Bob for being so wet and unhelpable; it was like trying to mould milk-pudding. Above all she was irritated with herself, for allowing herself to be so pointlessly and inappropriately irritated.

Because she was irritated, of course, everything around her conspired to irritate her further. The phone kept ringing. Each time she heard it she literally ran to it, thinking it might be John in Ljubljana, or Bob ringing to say that he would do the programme after all. But each time it was someone banal, with some entirely banal message. It was the BBC wanting to know if she'd heard anything more from her husband (she'd told the stupid woman she'd let her know as soon as anything happened), or John's brainless sister-in-law chattering about children's illnesses, or the bank manager pestering on about their overdraft. Most irritating of all, because so entirely meaningless and irrelevant, was some stupid old woman with a condescending voice who kept calling long-distance and asking to speak to a Miss Pennycuick. Nothing Jannie could say seemed to convince her that she didn't have a Miss Pennycuick concealed about the house. Apparently poor old Miss Pennycuick had gone off to stay with friends in London, and had written back to say that their number was VINcent 4763. Jannie could imagine the poor old soul peering with maddening short-sightedness at VINcent 4673 on her hostess's telephone, or seeing it correctly and transcribing it with infuriatingly slow, methodical wrongness, never guessing that what she was doing would cause some innocent stranger to be pestered almost out of her mind.

'For the last time,' Jannie snapped, when that terrible condescending voice came back on the line yet again, 'you have the wrong number. The name of the people in this house is Dyson. There is no Miss Pennycuick here. There is no maiden lady of any sort living or staying here, and there never has been. Now will you *please stop ringing me*?'

Oh, thought Jannie, the chaos and fragmentation of life! On a day like this nothing fitted. Nothing made any continuous sense or pattern. John should have been home and wasn't – not for any reason which arose out of his character, or which had any significance outside itself, but because a small part had failed in one engine of a plane he shouldn't have been on in the first place. Bob should have agreed to take John's place on the programme if necessary, but wouldn't – for a reason which undoubtedly arose out of his character, but which was so tangled and obscure and unsatisfactory that even a broken oil-feed would have been better.

And even if you fitted all this lot together to make some sort of sense, what about the wrong numbers, and the garbage collecting in the garden, and the slates falling off the roof? She roamed through the house doing nothing, waiting for the telephone to ring, waiting to collect Damian from school. Life was all thumbs, she thought, a long series of wrong numbers.

'I suppose perhaps I ought to, oughtn't I?' Bob asked Morris, unable to concentrate on the pre-teen page for indecision.

'Sure,' said Morris, typing.

'I mean, I don't want to do it, Erskine. I'm honestly just not interested in this sort of thing. But I suppose it's an opportunity I ought to take, isn't it? What do you think? I suppose one ought to try and make some effort to get ahead in life and so on, oughtn't one?'

'Sure.'

'Of course, I know you think that. But would *you* do it? Would *you* appear in this programme?'

'Surely. Like a shot.'

Bob opened a new tube of chocolate caramels and slipped one into his mouth.

'I suppose you would,' he said.

It was not in the first place the condition of the starboard outer engine which detained the Magic Carpet party at Ljubljana; it was the condition of Starfield. Starfield had to be got into normal negotiating condition before work on the engine could even start.

He had not envisaged a stop at Ljubljana, of course, when he had retired to the lavatory with a bottle of whisky after take-off from Beirut, and the first difficulty was to get him out of the lavatory again, since he was sitting on the floor inside with his back against the door, and seemed unresponsive to all entreaties to move himself. When they had extracted him from the lavatory they had difficulty getting him down the steps, and when they had got him down the steps it was the ground that proved too much for him. He was propelled slowly across the tarmac with Dyson holding him up on one side and the man from the *Telegraph* holding him up on the other; there was a general feeling among the party that as a British citizen he was a British responsibility. 'Beseech you, boys and girls . . .' he said vaguely as they went. 'Implore you, folks . . .'

A group of Yugoslav officials had appeared on the apron, and the Magic Carpet party advanced to meet them from the direction of the plane, parading Starfield in front of them like some sacred relic or regimental mascot. The two parties halted face to face. Silently the Western Press held Starfield up for inspection, so used by now to his authority that they somehow assumed it would be self-evident. Silently, the Yugoslavs inspected him, giving little sign that any impression of authority was registering.

Dyson and the man from the *Telegraph* hurriedly conferred together.

'Know any Serbo-Croat?' asked the man from the *Telegraph*.

Dyson shook his head.

'I'll try them in German then,' said the man from the *Telegraph*, and turned to the silently gazing Yugoslavs.

'*Dies ist unser Führer*,' he said, pushing Starfield a little farther forward.

The officials examined him even more curiously.

'*Euer Führer?*' they repeated musingly. '*Ah, so.*'

'Be taking off in a few minutes, folks,' said Starfield, his eyebrows going up, his glasses coming down, and his eyes focusing on a spot some five feet through the other side of the Yugoslavs' heads. 'Give you my solemn oath.'

'*Er ist wenig*, oh, what's the word?' said Dyson. 'Well, *malade*.'

'*Ah, wirklich?*' said the Yugoslavs, inspecting Starfield again.

'*Nein, nein*,' said the man from the *Telegraph* frankly. '*Die Fakt ist, unser Führer ist ein wenig getrunken* — no, *getrinken . . . getranken . . .*'

'*Detronken*,' said Dyson.

'*Betrunken*,' suggested some of the German journalists helpfully.

'*So, so*,' mused the Yugoslav officials.

'Drinks will be served in the bar,' said Starfield. 'Compliments of Magic Carpet . . .'

But for once drinks were not served in the bar. The Yugoslavs insisted on examining all their passports, and then took a representative selection of the party, including Starfield and his supporters, and the captain of the plane, who was Lebanese and spoke neither Serbo-Croat nor

German, into the airport offices to discuss the situation. Starfield, the only one with any powers or experience to negotiate on their behalf, sat in the position of honour in the middle with his head dangling very slightly to one side.

'If this is Amsterdam,' he said indistinctly, 'I'm a Dutchman.'

The Yugoslavs displayed a clear sense of priorities. 'Nun,' they began. '*Wer zahlt?*'

'Who pays?' translated the Germans.

'Him,' said everyone at once, pointing to Starfield. '*Er, lui.*'

'*Jauohl,*' said the officials. '*Seine Papiere, bitte. Seine Ermächtigung, seinen Kreditbrief.*'

'His authorization and letter of credit,' translated the Germans.

Someone went back to the plane and fetched Starfield's briefcase. The officials opened it and spread the contents out over the desk. Very slowly and patiently, with the assistance of everyone present, they went through them all document by document.

'Per-son-al Assid-ent In-shoor-ance,' they would read slowly aloud.

'*Personalunfallversicherung,*' the Germans would translate, and slowly, regretfully, the officials would lay the document aside and take up another one.

When a collection of documents had at last been assembled which satisfied the authorities, a number of Yugoslav forms were run to earth in distant offices and laboriously completed by the officials. Dyson and the man from the *Telegraph* had to wake Starfield up to sign them, because he had fallen uncomfortably asleep with his head on his chest. It was difficult to wake him; it was more difficult still to get him to write. His eyes were bleary, and his hand moved waveringly over the paper. The officials compared the marks he had produced with his signature on the documents from his briefcase, and shook their heads regretfully.

'*Nein, nein,*' they said. '*Nicht gut.*'

They tried again with the man from the *Telegraph*

steering Starfield's hand, but the result was worse. Dyson asked if they would let him forge a signature. '*Ja, ja!*' they said, quite eagerly. But when they had seen the result they shook their heads again. '*Nein, nein,*' they said sadly.

'*Er kann in die Morgen unterschreiben,*' said the man from the *Telegraph* hopefully. '*Er wird in die Morgen ganz OK sein.*'

'*Nein, nein,*' said the Yugoslavs dogmatically.

Dyson and the man from the *Telegraph* took Starfield outside and poured cold water over his head. The British party took turns at walking him up and down the car-park, trying to exercise the alcohol through his system faster.

'Honestly,' said Mounce, as he and Dyson sat resting in some grass at the edge of the car-park, 'it's a bit stinking much when the stinking organizer of the expedition gets stinking himself.'

'Bang goes my television programme,' said Dyson bitterly. 'Bang goes most of my life, in fact.'

'It's stealing the booze out of *our* mouths, for a start,' said Mounce. 'It's just downright selfishness.'

From time to time Starfield was taken back to the office to try another signature. Most of the officials had gone home for the evening by this time, but the ones that remained shook their heads politely. Dyson and the young British humorist with the hair all over the place held Starfield up while he was sick next to the taxi-rank. 'Now he'll be all right,' said the humorist. But he wasn't; he was worse. He groaned and rolled his eyes and was sick again in the middle of a flower-bed. After that he refused to be walked any more. He lay down in a quiet corner behind some oil-drums and went to sleep. They covered him with his own silky blue showercoat, and he slept for several hours. When he woke up it was dark. Dyson, who was keeping watch at a discreet distance, heard him sit up, and groan, and blow despairingly through his teeth several times. He got up, and a moment later there was the noise of a thin but powerful jet booming against the side of an empty oil-drum and trickling away across the tarmacadam.

Starfield emerged into the moonlight and washed himself under a tap sticking out of a wall. Then he lifted his head and gazed thoughtfully upwards for a long time. Dyson supposed for a moment that he was staring at the moon, then followed the direction of his gaze more carefully and realized that he was studying the sign on the side of the control-tower which said LJUBLJANA.

Starfield hurried into the departure lounge, where the rest of the Magic Carpet party was scattered, lying on benches and propped up in armchairs, trying to snatch a few hours of cramped and fitful sleep.

'Boys and girls!' he cried, pressing his palms together as anxiously and operatically as ever, and waiting till everyone had woken up. 'We regret this delay, folks, which is due to unavoidable causes beyond our control. I do assure you that we are doing everything in our power to facilitate our speedy departure, just as soon as it can be arranged. Meanwhile, drinks will be served at the bar, compliments of Magic Carpet. Thank you.'

They heard him in silence, perhaps because they were half asleep, or perhaps because, like Dyson, they were all lost in astonishment and admiration. The bar, of course, was closed, and remained closed. There was no possibility of starting work on the plane that night, and there was no one left in the Putnik office to arrange accommodation. So eventually everyone settled back to spend the night on the seats in the departure lounge – too beaten down by fate now even to curse, too weary in mind and body even to mutter to themselves.

Just before dawn Dyson got up to stretch his aching legs. He walked outside into the road in front of the airport. It was cold, and he shivered violently. Slowly his eyes got used to the grey pre-dawn light; he made out the shapes of cars parked by the roadside, covered by a thick white dew, and soft banks of mist lying motionless in the fields all round. Beyond the mist the dark grey of the surrounding hills was just detaching itself from the lighter grey of the sky. Everything was quiet, and completely still.

He turned up his lapels, and cringed along the road with his hands in his pockets, feeling cold and miserable. The banks of mist in the fields showed whiter as he looked at them, and odd little hills loomed between them. A whiff of manure lingered on the air – human manure, taken brown and liquid and disconcertingly acrid from farmyard tanks. Gradually he began to warm up and feel more alive. He stopped and pissed into the ditch with a great sense of satisfaction, shivering pleasingly as he did up his trousers. Then he ran along the road as fast as he could, until his heart was pounding, and getting his breath was like dragging rocks into his lungs, and his eyes were streaming from the effort in the cold air.

He slowed down and let his pulse return to normal. On and on he walked through the grey light, thinking about Jannie and the boys, and whether he would be able to get any breakfast at the airport, and about his boyhood, and night exercises in the army, and poor old Eddy Moulton, and how he had once walked all night, when he had been an undergraduate, from Murat to Salers, over the Peyrol pass. That was fifteen years ago now. Fifteen years! Perhaps a quarter of his life.

There was a section of drystone walling to the left of the road. He hoisted himself up on to it and sat down. On the other side was a field full of weeds and erratic patches of mist, with a small windowless brick building in the middle of it, surrounded by barbed wire and warning notices, which presumably housed either a transformer or some outlying piece of airport radar equipment.

What had he done with that last quarter of his life? He had married; had fathered two sons. He had made some progress in an honourable career; had considerable prospects of success in various fields; was happy. He was having a good life, undoubtedly. And yet . . . Half of it had gone – gone like a dream, slipped through his fingers. He couldn't give any account of it. He had spent his youth as one might spend an inheritance, and he had no idea what he had bought with it.

Except himself, as he was now. He hunched up, and

pursed his lips, and gazed at the little brick building without any windows. He was rather a silly man, he could see that. Vain and splenetic – passionately devoted to futile objectives. He remembered the television programme he was so anxious to get back for, and couldn't help grinning to himself at the thought. Here he was, at daybreak, sitting on a wall in the grey morning light, looking at a field full of weeds and a meaningless brick structure of unknown function somewhere in the middle of rural Slovenia – and that evening he was supposed to be in a television studio in London, sitting in a pool of unnaturally brilliant light and greasing up to the second Baron Boddy, who was if anything a sillier tit than he was himself. He could not see himself managing such a sudden and total transformation, whatever happened to the plane. They were in two different worlds, and there was some much vaster gap between them than could ever be bridged by a battered old DC6, even with all four engines working. About these weeds, this wall, and this ugly box in the middle of Slovenia nowhere there was something indissolubly solid and smelly and tangible. The second Baron Boddy, and the views which he might or might not exchange with the second Baron Boddy, and the gin-and-tonic and smoked salmon sandwiches which he might or might not share with the second Baron Boddy beforehand, were as factitious and insubstantial as fairyland. He could not help laughing aloud to himself at the optimistic presumption of the universe in thinking that it could contain both Dyson-here and Dyson-there. He remembered with rueful amusement that there had been earlier states of Dyson-here – such as Dyson-yesterday and Dyson-the-day-before – which had worried themselves raw in their anxiety to become Dyson-there. For a few short minutes, at any rate, Dyson-here occupied him completely.

Somewhere behind the mist and the grey hummocky landscape there was a noise of aircraft engines starting up. It was a long way away, but in the still, quiet air it carried clearly. Dyson sat up rigid. It couldn't possibly be the Magic Carpet plane, of course. It needed only a moment's reflection to realize that it couldn't conceivably have been repaired yet.

The noise grew faint, then boomed out loud again through the mist, and died away almost to nothing. The plane was taxi-ing. Dyson strained his ears. It couldn't possibly be . . . The engineers couldn't possibly be at work yet . . . There was not the slightest need to worry . . . Dyson held his breath, trying to work out what was happening on the airfield. Once again the engines were run up, then died away, then roared out again, and grew steadily louder and louder. A moment later the plane passed almost over Dyson's head – a twin-engined Dakota climbing into the opalescent sky, its navigation lights winking with reassuring calm.

But Dyson was still sitting rigid with anxiety, even after it had cleared the hills to the east and disappeared in the direction of Zagreb. Dyson-here was once again no longer enough. He jumped down from the wall and began to walk quickly back towards the airport, and the possibility of smoked salmon sandwiches with the second Baron Boddy.

None of the usual crowd in the Gates realized that Dyson was overdue. They had scarcely realized he was away in the first place. 'Where's John, then, Bob?' they had asked vaguely earlier in the week. 'In the Persian Gulf,' Bob had explained at least a dozen times. Now that he proved not to have been in the Persian Gulf at all, but at Beirut, and was now no longer at Beirut but at Ljubljana, and should not even have been at Ljubljana, but here sinking half-pints of bitter in the Gates, people had at last got used to the idea that he was in the Persian Gulf. 'John still in the Persian Gulf, then, Bob?' they asked today. Dyson had disappeared from their lives almost as completely as poor old Eddy Moulton. They were like a self-sealing petrol tank; when sections were shot away they closed up automatically and filled the gap, spilling not a drop of the precious communal spirit. But then no one – not even Bob – had noticed Mounce's absence at all.

Still, they were amused by Bob's account of Dyson's slow progress to nowhere, with bits dropping off the plane every time it got into the air. 'Trust old John,' chuckled Bill Waddy, 'to get himself on a plane which falls to bits in the middle of Yugoslavia!' 'Poor old John!' said Gareth Holmroyd. 'He'll never live this down.'

And everyone, when Bob asked them, assured him that he ought to do Dyson's programme.

'Oh, definitely,' said Ted Hurwitz. 'I don't think there's anything wrong with – incidentally, Bob, what are you drinking? – I don't think there's anything wrong with doing a spot of television on the side.'

'It might be sensible when you come to think about it, Bob,' said Mike Sparrow. 'You've got to reckon on getting out of this job – bitter, please, Ted – by the time you're forty.'

'Hey, steady on, Mike,' said Bill Waddy. 'I'm thirty-eight, you know. Thanks, Ted. I'm thirty-eight, Mike.'

'I'm forty-six,' said Gareth Holmroyd.

'I didn't mean . . . Well, I mean, you're both specialists,' said Mike Sparrow. 'What I really meant was, you've got to either get out or specialize by the time you're forty. Is this my bitter, Ted?'

'What about Laurence Evenden?' said Gareth Holmroyd. 'He doesn't really specialize, and he's in his fifties.'

'Well, Laurence is an exception,' said Mike Sparrow.

'Old Laurence is all right,' said Bill Waddy.

'Laurence is different,' said Andy Royle.

'What about old Harry Stearns?' said Gareth Holmroyd. 'He's not really what you'd call a specialist.'

'Old Harry's rather an unusual case, of course,' said Ted Hurwitz.

They all sipped their beer in reflective silence.

'I mean,' said Mike Sparrow, 'I'm thirty-two myself, for heaven's sake.'

'I'm thirty-four,' said Ted Hurwitz. 'How old are you, Bob?'

'Twenty-nine,' said Bob. 'I'll be thirty next month.'

They relapsed into silence again, some looking into their

beer, some at the floor, and some over everyone's heads at the advertisements round the walls. The last time they had had this discussion, about a month ago, thought Bob, Bill Waddy had been thirty-seven. And Bob could remember a similar occasion in the past when it had been Bill Waddy himself who had talked about the need to get out of journalism by the time one was forty. He had been thirty-five then, Bob seemed to recall. Bob was still thinking about this when he realized that he had definitely decided to do the programme.

Hammersmith was solid with evening rush-hour traffic. The taxi edged along yard by yard, and Dyson craned haggardly forward in his seat trying to spot some break in the jam ahead.

'Oh God, oh God, oh *God*!' he cried. 'We've only got thirty-five minutes before the programme actually starts! Suppose it takes us ten minutes to get through this lot, then say five minutes to get up to Shepherd's Bush . . . Shepherd's Bush will be solid, of course . . .'

'You spent the whole stinking morning,' said Mounce, 'telling me that you didn't care about this snotty programme any more.'

'Oh, for God's sake!' snapped Dyson. 'That was in Ljubljana!'

The traffic in the lanes on either side of them began to flow forward without obstruction.

'Oh *God*!' shouted Dyson. 'If we don't start moving within the next minute I swear I'll smash this taxi to pieces with my bare hands.'

'You went on and on,' said Mounce, 'about how you'd seen through the whole spotty business.'

Dyson wriggled his fingers, tapped his feet, and drummed his clenched fists up and down on his knees.

'If only we'd been twenty minutes later leaving Ljubljana!' he groaned. 'We'd have missed the connection from Amsterdam and everything would have settled itself!'

'I don't know,' said Mounce. 'For stinking consistency you just about take the stinking biscuit.'

They reached the Television Centre in Wood Lane some ten minutes or so before the programme was due to go on the air. The sight of the place brought on a new spasm of anxiety in Dyson.

'Oh God!' he cried. 'I haven't even thought what I'm going to say! I haven't got anything prepared at all!'

He sprang out of the taxi as it drew level with the entrance and rushed up to one of the girls at the desk inside as if he were going to strangle her.

'*New Perspective*!' he shouted. 'Which studio? Which studio?'

The girl examined a list. Very slowly she ran a finger down one page, then turned over and ran it down another.

'Oh, for God's *sake*!' cried Dyson. 'It's starting in ten minutes!'

'Here we are,' said the girl. '*New Perspective*. They don't do that one at the Centre – it's Lime Grove. Out the back gate – down Frithville Gardens. It'll only take you five minutes, if you run all the way.'

It was in effect a race between Bob and Dyson, though neither of them was aware of it as such, which perhaps didn't matter greatly in the event, since it was won by Erskine Morris.

Morris was actually on the screen when Samantha Lightbody showed Dyson and Mounce into Hospitality Room Number 8 at Lime Grove. They were both panting hard.

'My God!' gasped Dyson. 'Not *him*!'

The room was full of people sipping gin-and-tonic and nibbling smoked salmon sandwiches. 'John!' cried several of them, turning at the sound of his voice. Bob was the only one Dyson took in at first.

'Bob!' he cried. 'You mean to say you let them put that unspeakable little tit on my programme?'

'John,' said Bob quickly, 'do you know Erskine's friend Lake?'

Dyson turned round in surprise.

'Honestly, Bob,' he said, 'couldn't you have stood in for me yourself? You are a rotten swine. You really are.'

'John, I can't explain now,' said Bob. 'Why don't you say hello to Jannie?'

Dyson turned round in surprise.

'Jan!' he said. 'What are you doing here?'

'Sh!' hissed a number of people sitting in one corner of the room – the friends and relations of the other performers, perhaps – who were gazing at the monitor screen as if they actually wanted to see what was going on.

'I came to watch Bob on the programme,' whispered Jannie. 'He was supposed to be on it.'

'We all came to watch him!' cried Mrs Mounce. 'Didn't we, Tessa?'

'Well, well,' said her husband. 'I didn't expect to see *you* here.'

'Reg, darling! Where have you sprung from?'

'Bei-bloody-rut and Ljub-stinking-ljana, if you're interested.'

'Darling! How super!'

'Sh!' hissed the viewing faction.

'Let me get you both drinks,' whispered Samantha Lightbody to Dyson and Mounce.

'If Bob was supposed to be on the programme,' said Dyson, trying to keep his voice down too, 'why isn't he on it?'

'That's a long story,' said Bob.

'I'm afraid there was a slight misunderstanding,' said Samantha Lightbody. 'Let me get everyone drinks.'

'Bob just let himself get shoved out of the way like a booby, as usual,' said Jannie.

'Sh!'

'Jannie, that's not really fair,' said Bob. 'Erskine must have thought I was inviting him to do the programme instead of me. I couldn't really insist on his standing down again after he'd gone to all the trouble of coming out here.'

'You were shoved out of the way, Bob,' said Jannie.

'Sh! Sh!'

'It was just one of those balls-ups,' whispered Samantha Lightbody. 'Let's all have stiff drinks and forget about it.'

Dyson sank down into the chair next to Jannie's with his

glass of whisky, and put a hand over hers.

'Jan,' he whispered, squeezing her.

'John,' she said, putting her other hand on top of his.

They gazed at the screen. Morris appeared on it again, talking about certain social developments he had noticed in the Western Region of Nigeria when he had been out there earlier in the year. His voice flowed on like the smoke rising from his cigarette, steady and unemphatic, but definitely hypnotic.

'There goes my future,' said Dyson sadly.

Jannie rubbed his hand.

'Bob's future, too,' he said. 'We're both washouts, Jan.'

Morris cut Lord Boddy off in mid-reminiscence with a deftly-placed Sure sure, and put the chairman right on a couple of points of fact.

'He's good,' whispered Bob.

'He's a nasty little prick,' said Dyson.

Mounce leaned across to Bob.

'How are things at the office these days, Bob?' he asked in a low voice. 'Has all that Other Arrangements business blown over yet?'

'Haven't you been in this week, then?' asked Bob.

Mounce thoughtfully eased some shreds of Yugoslav ham sandwich from between his teeth.

'Perhaps I'll stay away permanently and see if anyone notices,' he said. 'Really give it a month or two to sort itself out.'

Lake was talking to Mrs Mounce.

'My feet feel as if they've been put in a vice,' she whispered. 'Do you suffer with your feet at all?'

'With me it's my glands,' whispered Mrs Mounce. 'Honestly, darling, you'd never believe the amount of time I've spent seeing specialists ...'

The door opened, and a commissionaire ushered a tall, gaunt woman in a hat into the room.

'Miss Pennycuick?' called the commissionaire. 'Is there a Miss Pennycuick in here?'

'Mummy!' said Tessa, jumping to her feet and going bright red.

'Hello, Mrs Pennycuick,' said Bob, getting up too.

'Mrs Pennycuick . . . ?' said Jannie, in an appalled whisper.

'What are you doing here, Mummy?' asked Tessa.

'I've come up to town to look for you, Tessa. We'll talk about it afterwards, outside.'

'Oh, my God!' said Jannie. 'This is entirely my fault! I simply didn't know that Tessa's name was . . . I mean, I didn't realize . . . It didn't occur to me that . . .'

'Shush!' hissed the enthusiasts.

'I'll talk about it privately with my daughter afterwards, if I may,' whispered Mrs Pennycuick.

'Yes, but for heaven's sake don't think . . .' said Jannie. 'I mean, don't imagine that . . . I mean, after all, they are *engaged*.'

Mrs Pennycuick stared at the television screen, as if unwilling to commit herself to looking at any of the people in the room. Tessa gazed at it, too, to hide her confusion, and after a few seconds Bob and Jannie turned their heads towards it as well. Everyone in the room found it a convenient place to rest the eyes, except Lake, who had drawn her right foot up into her lap to examine the condition of her toes, and Dyson, who had his head back and his mouth open, and was falling asleep. In silent conciliation, Bob held out his tube of peppermints to Mrs Pennycuick, half turning his head towards her, so that he could see Lake with her slim white knee drawn up to her ear, and the long bleached hair tumbling around it.

Morris gazed impassively out at them all, the flesh bagging judicially along the line of the jawbone.

'Sure,' he said, with the suggestion of a cryptic smile. 'Oh, sure, sure.'

Fontana Books

Fontana is a leading paperback publisher of fiction and non-fiction, with authors ranging from Alistair MacLean, Agatha Christie and Desmond Bagley to Solzhenitsyn and Pasternak, from Gerald Durrell and Joy Adamson to the famous Modern Masters series.

In addition to a wide-ranging collection of internationally popular writers of fiction, Fontana also has an outstanding reputation for history, natural history, military history, psychology, psychiatry, politics, economics, religion and the social sciences.

All Fontana books are available at your bookshop or newsagent; or can be ordered direct. Just fill in the form and list the titles you want.